I0822617

THE ANCIENT TALES OF SORIA

THE ANCIENT TALES OF SORIA

J. ERIC FRAZE

Section I
THE SETTLING OF SORIA

Section II
TALES FROM THE AGE OF DIVISION

Section III
THE CYCLE OF CHRONO AND AHTEN

The Ancient Tales of Soria

Including The Cycle of
Chrono and Ahten, and Other Stories

J. Eric Fraze

SECOND PRINTING
First Edition
Printed in the U.S.A.

ISBN 979-8-9919232-0-0

Cover art "Ologéo and Dynis" by Jon Fraze

© 2025 Jon Fraze
All rights reserved.
No portion of this work may be reproduced or copied by any method without the express written permission of the publisher.

No generative artificial intelligence (AI) was used in the writing of this work. The author expressly prohibits any entity from using this publication to train AI technologies to generate text.

CONTENTS

THE ANCIENT TALES OF SORIA

THE LAND OF SORIA DURING THE AGE OF LEGEND
TOË
MOUNTAINS OF DIVISION
GRIËS PASS
Mt. Ethel
Mt. Depharmen
GENESËR R.
C'HETAR R.
THE SURMONT
Lucré
Riteól
Liaibíri
Teletirë
Tryndom
Timotéa
The Table
The Lamp
NIYARC
C'HUNA R.
VORDÓT
Lapaz
GALDAN R.
Denedhros
GULF OF VINTEREN
BATTACK
TÜREM MTS.
Homadal
THE SCARP
THE INTERIOR
SOUTHERN TABLE
VINTEREN
Chiccir
Derideth
PROTUS
THE SOUTHREALM
CYLOS PLAIN
Grotto of Sonoros
Këuca
GULF OF IDÛN
THE PINTUS
EGANO
Fords of Dunar
Garadenthi
NÆUS R.
THE HIRNA
AQALI RE.
No'Cerës
BARRIA
Toreth Gandauin
THE INVIANT
Omaë
Battle of Ahten and the Cerites
Eisoros
STRAIT OF ENDREV
Ravine of Pirin
LODB
STEGGAN
Mizgad
Battle of Chrono and the Sea Monster
THERESIA
THE SEA

FOREWORD

This volume consists of a compilation of tales from the ancient days of Soria, a period known to Sorian scholars as the "Age of Legend." It was assembled during the reign of Manoto as Emperor of Homadal, and published by an unknown author or editors. It was said to have been begun under an edict simply to collect and edit the traditional tales of the earliest days of Sorian myth, from "creation" to the lives of Sorios and Cynodias; but it soon grew into a complete compendium of origin tales of the various Sorian Tribes and Kindreds, representing virtually all the popular folklore handed down among the Sorians of Homadal.

The work is divided into three sections: "The Settling of Soria," the "Tales of the Age of Division," and the "Cycle of Chrono and Ahten." Part I forms a more-or-less continuous narrative of the earliest ages of Soria, pertaining to the origins of Soria's three Kindreds: the god-like Terumani, and the mortal Sorites and Pleïstians. The tales of Part II are centered around the mortal Kindreds, and include origin stories of several Tribes and their Heroes. In the original it included the Chrono tales, but I have separated these as they form a narrative of their own. The tales are largely self-contained: one could be forgiven for reading them out of order. The Sorians would have done so.

The scope of the material here gathered is the pre-historical era of Sorian legend. Before the publication of this collection, many works regarding that period were already in existence, of varying degrees of reliability. Until this publication, however, none had attempted to compile the traditions and legends of prehistory into anything like a single authoritative volume. The Homadalan work, originally published under the title of *Tales from the Age of Legend,* was soon recognized by the best historical and linguistic scholars of the Homadalan Academy as the definitive source for this material.

These legends are recorded mostly from oral tradition. While some of the tales were circulated in written form prior to publication of this compendium, these differ in many significant ways from the forms found here, and were strongly influenced by the cultural conventions of the times in which they were published. Different versions of the origins of the Kindreds and Tribes circulated in Homadal at different periods, some being clearly the product of the respective religious and cultural movements of their day.

The versions recorded by this writer (or writers), while appearing later, seem to reflect earlier, and more pure, forms. They do not contain lengthy introductions by the collector or editor which might have explained their origin, but it seems certain they predate in basic form and pattern most of the written historical matter of the Homadalan literature.

The spirit and tone of the tales as recorded here are decisively more true to that of the earliest records of the Homadalans than are many intervening works. And while in those earliest documents little was said of the terumani or the Ádolthi who dominate these tales, the Homadalans were clearly familiar with the hierarchy of these ancient and venerable Sorian beings.

While the original sources for this information are left obscure, it seems from evidence that in the Age of Legend the Terumani were considerably more approachable in their relationships with the denizens of Soria than in the later historical period. While direct interaction with the mortal Kindreds was later frowned upon by the Terumani, the practice was never strictly forbidden, and occasional contraventions to the rule occur even in the historical record.[1] It's not impossible that oral traditions were passed down from actual encounters with Terumani themselves, even assuming such encounters were uncommon.

By the time of this written record, interchange with the terumani had become rare: a fact made clear by the very existence of the intervening Sarist and Havuist religious sects, in which the presence of the Guardians was assumed to be remote and mystical. Thus for the greater part these versions are most likely passed down through generations from their original sources, whatever those sources may have been.

The period represented in these pages was of great antiquity, and for the most part the mortal Sorians remained in something of an advanced stone-age technology. Among the Sorians there would have been little or no metallurgy, and the use of the wheel was unknown. No form of writing had been devised anywhere in the land, excluding whatever symbolic marks were used on the journey-staffs mentioned in the stories. Architecture, as such, was unknown among the Sorians: most buildings would have been serviceable structures on the order of homes and storehouses. Many of the tribes and clans mentioned, in fact, would have lived a nomadic or itinerant lifestyle.

In spite of a somewhat primitive technology, however, it is clear that the culture of the Sorians had obtained a high level of sophistication. Commerce over broad areas was common. Arts and elaborate oral traditions were disseminated. They possessed a proficient pharmacology. Weaving, woodworking, leather-craft, and the use of ceramics were well-developed, as well as the occasional use of beaten copper or gold. A few examples of large, megalithic structures are known to have been built. Thus the subjects of these tales are not to be mistaken in any way for mere troglodytes.

1 Most notably the physical aid Jeïnaric is recorded to have provided the Homadalans in their return to Homadal in 1358 S.C.

As for the Terumani, the extent of their technology and culture is left without detailed description, although it was certainly much further advanced than that of their Sorian charges.

Some Notes on Translation

Regarding the terumani: this word has frequently been left untranslated, there being no English parallel. At times the terms "nymph," "sprite," and "gnome" have seemed appropriate for the lesser terumani, but these are something of a compromise. While "nymph" is a close approximation for the female terumani, the term "sprite' bears rather frolicsome and fanciful connotations which do not adequately describe their male counterparts. I've therefore used the rather archaic alternate spelling of "spright" throughout this work.

The lesser terumani, or nature terumani, were sometimes referred to by more specific terms describing their habitat or role in the Sorian cosmos: Specifically, these were the *suraterumani*, or woodland nymphs and sprights; the *huraterumani*, or water nymphs and sprights (including the Seafolk); and the *lamaterumani*: the earth sprights, or gnomes. In these cases the terms "naead," "dryad," and "oread" would have seemed appropriate, as the roles of these lesser terumani were similar to those of their Greco-Roman counterparts. But in Western mythologies such beings are always female in form. In the Sorian cosmology they are described as being of either gender. For this reason I've chosen to creatively re-spell these terms as "næad," "dræad," and "oræad," to provide alternatives lacking gender specificity.

At times the terumani may appear in these tales to be something akin to minor gods or demigods, shaping many of the events of Sorian history. But they would not have been regarded as such among the Sorians. They were held by the Sorian Kindreds to be flesh-and-blood co-denizens of the land: mysterious, yes, with powers, technologies, and cultures surpassing their own, but otherwise as natural as the rocks and trees of the land itself. They were not as a rule worshiped or held as divine.

It may be noticed that throughout this work the term "terumani" frequently appears capitalized as "Terumani." This is intentional. When capitalized, it is being used as a proper noun, usually referring specifically to the Ádolthi and Ídolthi, the highest of the terumani. Elsewhere the word is left as a common noun referring, in a more generalized sense, to the race of the terumani, or individuals of that race. (A similar situation exists regarding the various uses of the word "sea," which at times is capitalized as the proper name used for the Great Sea which surrounded Soria.)

Ádolthi and Ídolthi are also untranslatable. These were the highest and most powerful of the terumani, recognized by all as the shapers of the land

and cultures of Soria. "Ádolthi" is generally used to denote all of this group, whereas the Ídolthi are considered a subset of the Ádolthi: But usage in these tales is not consistent.

Despite their elevated rank, as with the other terumani, these were not generally held to be divine or even supernatural beings.

A final note regarding these matters is that occasionally the non-terumani Kindreds are referred to in this translation as "mortal." This is something of a poetic compromise. The word used in these instances is better translated as "mutable," or "insubstantial." The same word is used by the Sorians to describe toys and playthings. The terumani, in fact, were never described as "immortal" in the sense of undying, but like the other Kindreds of Soria had their own distant and unknown fate; indeterminate and separate from that of the "mortal Kindreds," perhaps, but no less "mortal" in our sense.

This term "Kindred," especially when capitalized, has a specific meaning in the Sorian context. It refers almost always to the major divisions between the different "races" which inhabited the land, and most specifically, to the two non-teruman populations. The physiological distinctions between these two major groups went beyond that of mere race, and quite likely reflected that of an entirely different species or even genus. The term "race" thus seemed inadequate to its purpose. In addition, that term currently carries with it specifically modern (and primarily negative) baggage which would not only be inaccurate in the Sorian context, but misleading and inappropriate in an English context.

The term "Tribe," when capitalized, has a similar function. This term refers to the various Sorian ethnic sub-populations. During the period described in these tales, these were for the most part cultural groupings or lineages; but by the time of the Homadalans who recorded this volume, tens of thousands of years of evolution, and the creative actions of the Terumani, had brought about such drastic physiological distinctions between the Tribes that they may perhaps be considered as separate species. The Cylosites, for instance, were *stymphoi*, that is, one of the short races which might even be described as pygmies: they averaged under four feet in height, were wide-bodied, broad-shouldered, and heavy-boned; while their Sorite relatives the Lophusites on the other hand were typically over six feet tall, thin, long-necked and lightly built. Both were Soritic, and had the feathery hair and other distinctions of that Kindred, but the Tribal differences were vast and unmistakeable.

Care should be taken to distinguish between the very similar words "Sorian" and "Sorite." The terms are not interchangeable. "Sorios" is the name given to the first mortal creature to receive the ability to speak. All the descendants of Sorios, therefore, were the Sorites, and these were one of the two mortal speaking Kindreds of the Land, as distinguished from the Pleïstians.

"Soria," on the other hand, is the name of the Land itself, that is, all the country south of the Mountains of Division, and the setting for all these tales.

"Sorian" therefore, in its broadest sense, covers everything pertaining to the land of Soria, whether animate or inanimate. When dealing with the inhabitants of the Land it can describe any or all of the speaking Kindreds, both Sorite and Pleïstian, whether as individuals or as a group. It's often used as a catch-all term to describe any integrated group of individuals or clans where a number of Tribes or Kindreds might be represented, such as the "Sorians" of Homadal.

One additional curious point arises regarding this matter: The Pleïstians and Sorites are always clearly distinguished, and no collective "humanness" was assumed, thus the Sorians had no common word for "man" or "woman." That is, no umbrella terms existed which referred generically to both Sorites and Pleïstians. The word *hacoron/hacorë* was used to denote an adult male or female, but its usage was strictly limited to questions of maturity or "adultness." The terumani, in fact, seem to regard both groups as something akin to speaking animals. At times this results in some lexical peculiarities, as this translation lacks such terms as people, man, woman, or any similar nomenclature.

I have cleaned up the speech of the Giants throughout this work. As is made clear in many points, the speech of the Giants is crude and vile, and the original text sometimes included various crass and even obscene expletives. These have been softened, or deleted from this translation. It is enough to imagine the crudity of their conversation.

At places it may be noted that the translation resorts to the use of quasi-archaic language, particularly in the use of "thee" and "thou" in the discourse of the Seafolk and other terumani. This vaguely reflects an archaic structure found in the original text, occasionally resorted to when certain of the terumani are conversing with the mortal Kindreds. Its use in this translation is intentionally inconsistent, to avoid abstruse text; but it should be pointed out that while "thee/thou" is often used for the second person singular pronoun, "you" (but rarely "ye') has been retained for plural instances. This is not to be considered an oversight. Similarly, use of the archaic *-eth* form of third person singular verbs follows a somewhat Shakespearian inconsistency, for the sake of clarity or fluidity.

Overall, the tone of this translation is deliberately formal and admittedly at times old-fashioned. This, again, is in accord with the somewhat formal style of the original texts.

Readers interested in the proper pronunciation of the various names of persons and places in this volume are referred to Appendix D in the closing pages, which describes the method used for transliterating names from the Sorian texts into English equivalents. A table is also included on the following page listing the major teruman characters mentioned in the tales.

TABLE OF THE TERUMANI

Names in italics denote those regarded as Ídolthi. Couples/consorts are linked with daggers (ǂ). Progeny of these pairs are inset below them in the listings. Other familial connections are linked by brackets. No consort is listed for a number of individuals, either because they had none, or their identity is unknown. (There were many more Terumani dwelling in Soria than are mentioned by name in this volume.)

THE ÁDOLTHI — THE HIGH ONES

	Name	Epithet	Attributes & Influence
ǂ	VÉLOPAR	The Maker	Shaper of the land and nature to its uses.
ǂ	*WÉODAR**	The Mistress of Air	Mistress of the airs and skies. Sister of Cosimë.
ǂ	PHACTORIAS	The Provider	Bestower of gifts/inspires artifice. Former caretaker of the Kindreds. Brother of Bël.
ǂ	MARCET		
[progeny]	*DEÏNI*		Discoverer and caretaker of the deïnings
[progeny]	*HIREN*		Guardian of the Hirnan Cerites
	BËL	The Messenger	Messenger of the Terumani. Sister of Phactorias.
ǂ	*OLOGÉO*	The Proud	Keeper of knowledge and reason.
ǂ	*COSIMË*		Caretaker of living things. Sister of Wéodar.
ǂ	PHREÏS	The Builder	Builder/caretaker of Lands and Gardens. Inspires craftsmanship and construction.
ǂ	PHREÏA/BENË	The Gardener	Caretaker of Lands and Gardens. Inspires cultivation.
[progeny]	JEÏNARIC	The Guide	Caretaker of the Sorian Kindreds/Sitedal
[progeny]	MAREC		Caretaker of the Sorian Kindreds/Lon Homa
[progeny]	SIZHEIA		Sister of Jeïnaric and Marec
	STOREIA		Inspires Heart and Imagination
[progeny]	*WENDA*	The Speech-Giver	Giver of Speech and Reason to Sorites
[progeny]	*DÔNI*	The Deliverer	Giver of Speech and Reason to Pleïstians
	TRYMA	The Wise	Inspires wisdom/Emissary between the Terumani and the Kindreds

OTHER ÁDOLTHI MENTIONED IN THE *TALES*

	Name	Epithet	Attributes & Influence
	REINODAS		
[progeny]	ERESCAL	The Lost	Progenitor of the Giants
	PARINTËS		
[progeny]	SESTREL		Co-progenitor of Giants/Companion of Erescal
	DURAN*	The Watchman	Sentry of the Ádolthi
	CATOS*	The Willful	Guardian of Carnochites and Predorians
	ANEON*		Caretaker of lands near Egano
	LEGEN		Caretaker of lands of the Hirna

THE NATURE TERUMANI (NÆADS, DRÆADS)

	Name	Epithet	Attributes & Influence
	DREITON	The Great	Lord of the Sea and the Seafolk
	GRËNAS		Lord of the dræads (woodlands and country)
	NILON		Lord of the næads (stream, lake or pond)

MINOR TERUMANI MENTIONED IN THE *TALES*

	Name	Epithet	Attributes & Influence
ǂ	MERTEN		King of the Seafolk of the south
ǂ	AVIAH		Queen of the Seafolk of the south
[progeny]	AHTEN		Consort of Chrono the Sorite/Founder of Chronosites
ǂ	ONTARIËN		Ruler of the Seafolk of the north
ǂ	SENECA		Matron of the Seafolk of the north
ǂ	CORNÆOS		Caretaker of Egano
ǂ	ANNÆ		Caretaker of Egano
	DYNIS		Caretaker of northern Batack. Companion of Ologéo. Foster-Mother of Terris and Pyterris
	VERIAS	The Ambitious	Guardian of Menothians

Other minor nature terumani are mentioned, sometimes at length, in the *Tales*, having only less-significant, local influence. These would include the dræads Garadenië, Piriën, and Sëluria; the næads Esperiénië and Sonoros; the Tritynoi Ériven and Miriën; and the Gauphrin Lorumack, Thrittin, Neborrick Tur, and Agrar Denn.

* The status of those so marked is conjectural, whether Ádolthi, Ídolthi, or exalted nature-terumani, though they are treated here as Ádolthi.

PART I

THE SETTLING OF SORIA

THE GILL
TOË
MASTOZIANS
EXTENT OF THE ICE
THE SURMONT
PYTERRIANS
FRINGES OF BATACK
GAULIANS
THE RODE
MOUNTAINS OF DIVISION
Mt. Ëthel +
DIATRIANS
C'HETA R.
GRIËS PASS
GENESË R.
Box Canyon
Tryndom
Mt. Toë +
The Stair
+ Mt. Depharmen
The Shelf
RHOTIËSTIR
Riteól
Liaibíri
Lucré
Teletirë
MENETHERIANS
THERESIANS
Muskrat Lake
V O R D Ó T
N I Y A R C
THE YARD
Melórdir
Timotéa
The Pillows
Table Mountain
TRACHIANS
DONITES
FAIR FIELD
CARPET PLAIN
Lamp of Durán
Moason
Lake Deception
Plesion
Highgrove
C'HUNA R.
CYLOSITES
GLYPTIANS
Lapaz
GNATHOSIANS
GALDAN R.
Denedhros
EXTENT OF THE ICE
GNATHOSIANS
BATACK
Dapplëwood
METERRIANS
GULF OF VINTEREN

PART I

THE SETTLING OF SORIA

THE GILL
TOË
MASTOZIANS
MOUNTAINS OF DIVISION
Mt. Ëthel
DIATRIANS
EXTENT OF THE ICE
THE SURMONT
GRIES PASS
C'HETA R.
Mt. Toë
Mt. Depharmen
Lucré
The Stair
The Shelf
RHOTIESTIR
Liaibiri
Box Canyon
Tryndom
Ritéol
Teletirē
PYTERRIANS
GENESË R.
MENETHERIANS
Muskrat Lake
VORNDYÓTARC
THERESIANS
The Pillows
Melórdir
Timotéa
THE YARD
Table Mountain
TRACHIANS
DONITES
FAIR FIELD
CARPET PLAIN
Lamp of Durán
Moason
FRINGES OF BATACK
GAULIANS
Highgrove
C'HUNA R.
THE RODE
Lake Deception
Plesion
CYLOSITES
GLYPTIANS
Lapaz
GNATHOSIANS
GALDAN R.
Denedhros
EXTENT OF THE ICE
GNATHOSIANS
BATACK
Dapplewood
METERRIANS
GULF OF VINTEREN

DEÏNI AND THE GIFT OF WENDA

1. The Mission of Tryma

There are all sorts of terumani in the world. Some, it must be admitted, are quite aimless, and are practically useless. They see as their only purpose the building of the nicest Halls, or the tending of the choicest gardens, and they go about their business as if no one and nothing in Soria really matters but themselves. But there are also the High Ones, those who have made it their business to keep order in the land, and to oversee the country entrusted to them.

Among these was Teruman Tryma the Wise. Tryma is of the Ídolthi, whom many hold to be the highest order of the Ádolthi, and he was among the highest, and the eldest, of that Order: all the terumani revered his wisdom and foresight. At that time Tryma lived with a few attendants in a remote Hall which he named Phortúen, on the Sorian side of the Barria Heceïca, the Mountains of Division. Phortúen was not a grand Hall, but it was a quiet and pleasant place. Tryma loved the mountains, and loves them still. The stars are brighter in those elevations, the air is crisp and clear, and the silence is deep and magnificent, which is most conducive to reflection and study. It is true there were dangers in the mountains, even in those times before the Giants came. Great bears wandered the ranges, large as a house, and it is said that wyverns[1] lived in that range as well. But the terumani had little to fear from that avenue, for all creatures high and low could be made to bend to the will of that Kindred. So it had always been.

But that was about to change.

Now the terumani had dwelt in Soria for quite some number of years, cultivating and propagating the country according to their own designs, when it came to pass one year that Teruman Phreïs called on Tryma in Phortúen. In spite of its remoteness, many of the terumani, both high and low, would come at times to Phortúen for advice or counsel, and many also came simply to enjoy Tryma's company, for he was known as a witty and entertaining host. Phreïs, it can be guessed, came for both those reasons, since he had known Tryma since his early youth.

Phreïs had two sons, still young by the account of the long lives of the terumani—Jeïnaric and Marec—who had come into Soria with the terumani, and it occurred to Phreïs that he might seek advice from Tryma on

1 This was a large, reptilian, winged carnivore, but there is no evidence that it breathed fire.

their behalf. "They were very young when we came into this land," Phreïs said, "but they are of an age now when they ought to have a calling and purpose of their own. Have you any advice I might pass on to them when I return to Timotéa?"[2]

Tryma nodded at the request. "If you wish, I might submit you to interrogation and ponder this question. Perhaps some worthwhile insight might come to me." He paused. "Or perhaps not," he shrugged. "One never can be sure."

Phreïs agreed to this, so he sat for a while with Tryma as Tryma questioned him deeply about his sons. Tryma's skills depended on knowledge: Tryma was wise, and could discern much and guess much that other minds would miss, yet he was no magician—he required information to pursue his inquiries. When he had finished questioning Phreïs, he went into his private study to consider the matter, while Phreïs awaited him in the vestibule.

Tryma had the discernment at times even to auger events that were yet to come, a gift belonging to no others of the Terumani. Sometimes he merely puzzled these things out in the capacity of his own wisdom and insight. But at times visions would overcome him, beyond his control. Whether these were sent to him from Havui, or were the unbidden apparitions of his own ruminations, it cannot be guessed, but these visions were overmastering and inerrant. It was one of these visions that overwhelmed him as he pondered Phreïs' question.

Phreïs rose to his feet when Tryma at last reappeared from his study. "Have you received any insight?" he asked eagerly.

Tryma's face was contorted into a troubled frown. "I am afraid so," he said.

"What is wrong?" Phreïs asked, suddenly concerned.

Tryma looked up at Phreïs as if just becoming aware of his surroundings. "Oh, nothing concerning your sons. They will be fine."

Phreïs calmed himself slightly. "Thank you for the fright," he quipped irritably. "But you look shaken. What has happened?"

Tryma relaxed. "I'm afraid I have little to say of your sons. I see a part for them, possibly a very important role, but it is far in the future. They are yet young, do not worry on their behalf. But in pondering this question, I received, well, glimpses of a strange future for us all." Phreïs encouraged him to go on, and he said, "The vision was vague and shadowy, as if many possibilities and many paths might diverge or converge, and nothing concrete could be guessed at. But one thing seemed clear. I glimpsed a future where the terumani seem to share the land with others: mortal creatures, but creatures with many of the same masteries as the terumani themselves. Creatures that would not submit, unquestioning, to our influences and com-

2 Timotéa was the Hall of Phreïs in Niyarc.

mands. I could make no sense of it. And frankly, I am not certain whether to fear this world or welcome it."

Phreïs was intrigued, and it must be admitted, a bit worried. "What sort of mortal creatures?" he asked.

"I cannot say," Tryma shrugged. "A vision is not always like clear sight."

"Is there anything we can do to stop this?"

Tryma smiled indulgently. "I do not think it can be resisted. We can only prepare."

"Then we must go to see Ologéo. He will know what to do."

Tryma smiled wryly. "He will certainly have an opinion, at any rate," he said. "But you are correct. We should call the High Ones to come together in Liaibíri. This will, I think, effect us all." The Hall of Liaibíri was founded by Ologéo as a place of learning and knowledge where all could come to receive inspiration and instruction. He had other Halls, but Liaibíri was, even in those earlier days, the greatest. It lay in the gentle hills in the east of Niyarc, in a district known as Rhotiéstir where many of the terumani had Halls or homes.

"Then let us call for Bël," said Phreïs, "and have the council meet us at Liaibíri. We shall have to make our own way there as soon possible."

This of course was obvious. All the terumani have powers which exceed those of the mortal Kindreds, and among these, they are able to travel more swiftly than the mortal kinds. But Bël is the messenger of the terumani. Her powers far exceed all others, and no one knows the mystery of how she proceeds. Moreover she has this additional gift: that she is able to hear the calls of the terumani from wherever they hail. All depend on her to deliver tidings throughout the lands.

"Then the sooner we leave, the better for all," Tryma said. "There are no speedy paths for us."

"Well do I know it," Phreïs said, who had walked the whole way to Phortúen from Timotéa, his own Hall. "But this vision you foresaw..." he added nervously, "When will this come to pass?"

"That, also, is unclear," Tryma said. Phreïs looked at him blankly. Tryma grinned. "I am not of much use, am I?" he added.

Phreïs sighed. "So we don't know what this creature might be, nor do we know when it might appear? Perhaps it would be wise to be wary along the way? The trails in the mountains are untamed."

"I think that would be advisable!" Tryma admitted.

Then he and Phreïs prepared for their journey, and set out on the trails from the mountains toward Niyarc.

Liaibíri lay far to the east, below the Barria Heceïca, the ranges of the Mountains of Division, across the plains and hills of green Niyarc. While the terumani have their own means of conveying themselves across great distances quickly, unknown to the other Kindreds, they do not use these courses lightly, and they do not serve all points equally, so Tryma and Phreïs tramped the distance by foot despite their apprehensions. There were no easy trails out of the wildness of the mountain country in those days, so the road was slow and difficult, by narrow paths through districts rocky and choked with tangled woods of pine and fir, and it consumed not a few days of travel. They had scant rest in all that time, camping nervously along the trails, and were ever watchful and on alert. Even when they had exited the wilderness of the mountains and marched across the less tangled northern reaches of Niyarc they would not let down their guard.

When they had been traveling for some days in this country they came to a crossroads, where Phreïs said, "If we go south from here we shall come swiftly to my Hall Timotéa. There we might breathe more easily and take our ease for a spell. From thence an easy trail will carry us directly to Liaibíri."

Tryma agreed to this course, and they soon found themselves in the comforts of Phreïs' Hall.

Teruman Benë, the spouse of Teruman Phreïs, greeted them, and they were quickly refreshed from their journey. Tryma was given a room of his own for his repose. For the first time since they had departed from Phortúen he could pause alone with his thoughts, and when they had supped and washed he retired to reflect and ponder their further course.

This was, perhaps, an indiscretion on Tryma's part, though as it turned out a fortuitous one, for the talents and calling of Tryma made him at times subject to unsolicited visions. So his thoughts as he meditated alone were disturbed that evening by another premonition, in this case one which was quite clear and lucid, and easy to interpret. When his mind cleared once more he sighed, shook his head, and went out at once to find Phreïs.

"I am afraid you will need to complete your journey to Liaibíri on your own from here," he said. "I have had another vision of sorts, and I must make a side trip. I will leave in the morning."

"Your visions of late seem to be all inconveniences and disturbances," Phreïs said. "But I shall go along with you, if you wish," he offered.

Tryma shook his head. "That will not be necessary. I must take the road to Teletirë, the Hall of Phactorias, and it will be out of your way."

"Phactorias has surely been informed by now," Phreïs said. "He must have been among the first to receive the call, or do you think Bël would overlook her own brother?"

"I am not going to see Phactorias," Tryma declared. "It is someone else... I am uncertain of who exactly, but I am very clear on where and how to find her. She is young, but she must be called to the council. This charge falls upon me alone."

"Very well," Phreïs said. "We will assemble as planned, and await your arrival."

While these events were transpiring in the north, Bël had been making her own more-swift journeys about the land carrying Tryma's message, for this is her own special talent and calling. As Phreïs had assumed, Teruman Phactorias had been among the first to receive the message, and he quickly made plans to go to Liaibíri along with his spouse Teruman Marcet.

His son Hiren by this time had a small house of his own, but his daughter Deïni in those days still made her home at Teletirë. With her in Teletirë was her friend Wenda, who often visited that Hall for days at a stretch. As they were to be left alone in the place, Deïni and Wenda decided that they also would make a journey, and began to pack and make their plans for an excursion to the shore.

Deïni and Wenda were the closest of friends. They had grown up together, for Wenda dwelt with her mother, Teruman Storeia, and her sister Dôni, in a house which Storeia used to keep nearby, a few hours jaunt to the east of Teletirë. They were young by the accounting of the Terumani, having been born in the land of Soria, daughters of the Ádolthi. These two were found together more often than they could be found apart: Since their early childhood they had shared in all their play, and as they grew they shared in all their industry.

Deïni and Wenda were born of the highest order of the Ádolthi, although neither had yet discovered their peculiar talents or vocation among the High Ones. Wenda was a daughter of Teruman Storeia, who was called by some the Mother of Imagination, and was among the most renowned of the Ídolthi. Deïni, of course, was the daughter of Teruman Phactorias and Teruman Marcet, and few among the Ádolthi had higher prestige than they. Phactorias, in fact, was known as Phactorias the Provider, who equipped the Halls of the Terumani, and he was held on par with Teruman Vélopar who had shaped the land, and Teruman Ologéo the champion of knowledge and reason.

As they readied themselves for their excursion, Wenda was preparing her pack, when a blue-gray cat entered the room and announced itself with a plaintive mew. Deïni started at the sound and drew back. "Your animal is here," she said sourly, frowning at the creature.

Wenda laughed and stooped to pick her up. "Why do you hate Shadow?" she asked.

Deïni sighed. "I suppose I do not hate the thing. But you know I have no rapport with animals, and the creature reminds me of my defect."

"It is no defect," Wenda said, trying to reassure her friend for perhaps the thousandth time.

"You have always had a way with the mortal creatures," Deïni complained. "They do whatever you wish. Me, they despise."

"The gifts of all the terumani are unique. You will discover yours in time."

"But do you know of any other teruman, high or low, who has no influence at all on the creatures? I cannot get into their minds as do the others. They are not interested in me, and I have no interest in them. To be honest, they bore me."

This, indeed, had always been the one contention between Deïni and Wenda. Wenda took after her mother: she was warm and passionate, creative and imaginative. Wenda was in love with all creatures that moved upon the land. Big or little, whether feathered or furred, Wenda loved them all, and they seemed to love her as well. But Deïni took after her father. Sensible and sober, she saw little use in such creatures. Even as children this contention had arisen: as much as Wenda tried to share her love of the creatures of Soria, so much the more did Deïni disregard them. She had tried to do her duty and care for many creatures in her domain, but she found the effort troublesome and disheartening.

"Well," Wenda said reprovingly, "Shadow will come with us to the shore. She follows me everywhere and I can hardly stop her from coming, even if I wanted to."

"As you wish," said Deïni. "But I know of no other teruman who would be followed by a cat. Those creatures are the worst."

They finished their preparations casually, not expecting Phactorias or Marcet to return for a stretch of days, and at length they took to the trail southward. The day started off sunny and warm, and they made good time on their trek through pleasant countryside. They marched for several hours, enjoying the hike, and working up a hearty appetite, until they came at last to a pleasing overlook they knew of: a high embankment with a view of a marshy lake surrounded by grassy lawns and bowing woods. An ancient, shady willow draped its arms around them on the knoll. They stopped here to rest and take their noon meal while Shadow took a nap.

Deïni at last stood up and hoisted her pack, looking at the sun. "We should be moving on. Ahead of us is a cabin where we can rest for the night, but we should try to reach it before sundown, and it is still quite some distance away."

Wenda agreed, and woke her cat from its nap. Taking up her own pack she said, "Come, Shadow: we must keep moving if you wish to keep up with us."

As they had enjoyed their rest, and now as they continued toward the coast, the weather had begun to change. A breeze was now blowing steadily inland, cool with the moisture of the sea on its breath. Deïni shivered and hugged herself.

"Are you cold?" Wenda asked, concerned.

"I was not expecting this breeze," Deïni complained. "I have a cloak, but it's packed away in the bottom of my pack," she snarled.

"Take my cloak," Wenda said. "I am not cold." She removed her pack from her back and quickly slipped off her cloak. She shook it out and handed it to Deïni.

Deïni thanked her and pulled it over her shoulders, drawing the hood over her head. "When we come to our next rest stop I'll dig my own out of my pack. There's a crossroads not far ahead, with benches under an arbor, and a fountain where we can refill our water bottles. We'll stop there."

Wenda halted suddenly and with a panicked look slapped at her belt and checked her pack. "My water bottle!" she said, looking back in the direction from which they'd come. "I must have left it at the lookout!"

Deïni rolled her eyes. "Well, we can't go on without your water. We still have a long walk, and not many more founts along the way."

Wenda growled at herself. "It is not far," she sighed. "You go on ahead. I'll run back and retrieve it. You can wait for me at the fountain, I suppose."

She turned to go back, but Shadow began to follow her. Wenda paused and commanded the cat to go with Deïni, but it would not stop following her.

She sighed. "You must take Shadow with you," she said to Deïni. "I cannot make her run the whole way back to the lookout with me."

Deïni scowled. "The creature will not follow me."

"You will have to carry her." She picked up the cat and held it out to Deïni. Deïni looked at it unpleasantly, but took it in her hands and tried to hold it on her shoulder. The cat made an unpleasant mewing sound like a low growl and clutched at her cloak with angry claws.

"It does not like me," Deïni said flatly.

Wenda scolded the animal. "Shadow, be good!" The cat settled tensely onto Deïni's shoulder. "You must go with Deïni. I will not be long." She turned and rushed back up the trail and was soon out of sight.

Deïni frowned at the overstrung animal on her shoulder. "Well, come on then," she muttered. "Let's get to the crossroads where I can put you down."

It was another hour's walk before she spotted the trail ahead which crossed paths with her own. A small arbor of birch trees marked the crossing, with four curved, stone benches encircling a stone fountain in the middle. As she approached she realized that one of the benches was occupied by a figure in a gray cloak, white-haired, and looking rather pleased with himself.

"Teruman Tryma!" she declared when she recognized him. "You are far from your Hall! What brings you to this lonely spot?" She set down the cat from her shoulder and withdrew a small cup from her pack. She dipped it into the water of the fount as she spoke and gave it to the cat to drink. "If you are on the way to Liaibíri you are far off course!"

"I believe," said Tryma, "I am here to find you. It's Deïni, if I'm not mistaken? You are Phactorias' daughter, are you not?"

"Phactorias and Marcet, yes."

Tryma nodded. "You have grown since last I saw you. I did not recognize you in the vision."

Deïni looked at him doubtfully. "Vision?"

"Yes, yes. There was a vision. I am here to find its fulfillment."

"Then perhaps I should be off and leave you to your task," Deïni said. She looked up the road anxiously, wondering suddenly if she should head back in the direction she'd come, to meet up with Wenda. "I wish you luck, then, Tryma. I'm sure it must be very important to bring you here all the way from the mountains."

"It is undoubtedly important. And I have already met with all the luck I require. You have arrived, just as foreseen."

Deïni was taken aback. "Me? What have I to do with anything?"

"It seems you are the one. You are the key to the mortal creature which will begin a new age in Soria."

Deïni laughed out loud at this. "You have the wrong person. I have no bond with the mortal creatures at all. You have no idea! They have no interest in me, and I have less in them. You must have been meant to find my friend Wenda. She shall be along shortly." She looked over her shoulder back at the trail, expecting to see Wenda catching up at any moment.

"But you are the one that I've found at the crossroads. I'm afraid the vision was clear on this point."

"The vision was wrong. I cannot be the one."

"The visions are never wrong. I may not always understand them correctly, but they are not wrong. You are the child of the Ádolthi who was found at the crossroads, wearing a blue cloak."

Deïni looked in surprise at the cloak over her shoulders, and quickly pulled the hood from her face. "It is not my cloak!" she protested.

"In the vision you would be found drawing water for a small, gray cat."

Deïni gasped. "It is not my cat!" She nudged the creature away, expecting it to run off into the brush, but it sat down near her feet and began to groom itself contentedly. "Both the cat and the cloak belong to Wenda!"

"But you are the one bearing them." Tryma smiled knowingly. "I'm afraid there is no mistake."

"What is it you expect of me?"

"I expect nothing of you. That is, I expect you only to do what you will do."

Deïni scowled. "I have no idea what you mean by that."

"I mean the vision does not command, it only shows what will be." Tryma laughed. "Pay no heed to my nonsense. As it happens, I am on my way to a council of the Ádolthi. I have had a vision regarding the mortal creatures, and a change which is coming upon us all. It appears you will have an important role in this matter. In any event, you must come."

"To a council of the Ádolthi?" Deïni was incredulous. "I am too young to stand among that crowd. They will question how I dare show my face among them!"

"Ah, but I think not. It would appear that you are more important than you realize."

"This is all a mistake. This must be meant for Wenda."

Tryma's face became grave and he said, "Deïni, do not doubt this. You have a power within you that none other of us has. I do not know what it is. Nor, I think, do you as yet. But it will come to you when the time is right."

"When the time is right? When might that be?"

"That part of the vision, I fear, is dark." Tryma shrugged. "That is the way of visions. Many things are left to us to muddle out on our own. If we did not, there would be no point in showing us the vision at all, I suppose. At any rate, you must come with me to Liaibíri."

Tryma was venerable, respected by all, and seemed very sure of himself. Deïni sighed her acquiescence. "What will I tell my father?"

"You may tell him when you arrive. He will be there, too, of course."

Deïni looked back up the trail. "We should wait for Wenda. She will wonder where I have gone. And," she glanced distastefully at the cat preening itself at her feet, "she did leave her animal in my charge."

Tryma paused. "She should come, also. I suspect she will have her own part to play in this matter before all is over."

2. The Quest of Deïni

Tryma led the way to Liaibíri, and in a few more days Deïni and Wenda had arrived at Ologéo's great Hall.

Liaibíri is the Great House of Lore, which Teruman Ologéo had built in Vordót, eastward in Niyarc. It was an imposing place, designed to daunt and impress: it was framed in obsidian, glistening like glass; and many were its chambers. It commanded a hilltop where a green sward swept down from a colonnaded portico, guarded by columns carven in the image of nymphs. A whispering grove of alder trees was planted around it, and a tall hedge framed the precinct.

This Hall was open to all the Terumani: all were welcome there, and many came to study and to contemplate in the chambers of Liaibíri, for Ologéo was the master of learning, and he was a mentor to many. In his chambers many found clarity and knowledge. Liaibíri was a resort to all the Ádolthi, and to the lesser terumani as well.

Here Ologéo had made a great Lyceum as a meeting place for the Ádolthi. This chamber could accommodate many souls, and it was intended as a congress of sorts, where the important matters of governing the land might be discussed and decided. Although no formalities forbade the entrance of any, neither Deïni nor Wenda had at that time even yet earned the title of Teruman, though both of them were born into high families of the Ádolthi. Nevertheless at Tryma's word both Deïni and Wenda were accepted into the Lyceum when the council was called to order.

Ologéo as the master of that Hall took charge. "Teruman Tryma, whom we all know, has evidently had a vision which, while perplexing, is... well... on the unnerving side. I will leave it to Tryma to explain."

Tryma then took the dais and related once again the vision which he had revealed to Phreïs at Phortúen, as well as he could make it out, of how a mortal creature would arise which might in some ways rival the authority of the terumani themselves. "It may be a creature already dwelling among us," Tryma said. "Or something we have not yet discovered. It may be a creature that does not yet even exist. But it will overturn the world we know. We will need to decide how we will act."

When he had finished Ologéo wagged his head disparagingly. "How can we make such a decision now, when we possess such scant information? You've told us nothing of use, Tryma. Only shadowy ghost-stories of a mysterious being which we cannot control." He waved a hand dramatically.

"We must know more," Teruman Reinodas agreed. "What did the vision reveal? Will this thing resist us? Will it oppose us? Will it seek to overthrow us? What exactly did you see?"

"You may misunderstand the nature of this vision," Tryma said. "Perhaps 'vision' is entirely the wrong word in this case. It is a certain foreknowledge, but I have no clear picture to give you. I foresee conflicts, but nothing concrete is manifest. Will it have the power to do all those things? I think so. But whether or not it will, I cannot now predict. That is why we must decide how to respond to it. It is our whole duty to keep the world orderly and at peace."

Teruman Phactorias, the father of Deïni, then spoke. "Let us all keep in mind that we ourselves have the power to do all those things Reinodas has described. But we have managed to live together in peace. A creature which is independent of our will may just as likely live peaceably alongside us as otherwise."

"This is very true," Tryma said. "And this is precisely why I have thought it necessary to reveal this to us all, before we are surprised, and we react in fear or anger, and ruin our chance for peace and order."

"It is not a question of fear or anger," Ologéo countered. "It is simply a matter of preserving order in the world. We must act to assert our authority, whatever this thing might turn out to be."

Many questions were asked, and many concerns raised, but Tryma could provide little more information than what he had already given. Many opinions were offered, and many theories advanced, but all was guesswork and supposition.

The debate went on thus for quite some time. Deïni had sat listening impatiently throughout all this, and had begun to wonder why so much fuss was being made over the matter. This was nothing more than a mortal creature which was not subject to the will of the terumani, and the whole of the assembly seemed inordinately terrified of the very idea.

At last she could bear the wrangling and turmoil no longer, and she stood up to challenge the assembly. "Are you all claiming that the whole purpose of things is for the terumani to rule all, and the mortal creatures to submit without choice?" There was an audible gasp from the floor, from all but Tryma.

"You are young, Deïni," Ologéo said condescendingly. "Allow me to explain. You and I are of the Ádolthi. Ours are the greatest powers, but also the greatest responsibilities. It is upon us to plan and order the world. To make sense of it and keep things from running amok.

"Below us are the lesser terumani, the sprights and nymphs of the natural realms. We do not rule over them, but they have, let's say, a more limited scope. They keep the trees green, the animals in their proper spheres, the springs and rivers in their proper courses, and so on.

"Below them are the living, mortal creatures of the world. They are the lowest of all. They are subject to us. They obey and are governed by us and the lesser terumani. This is how it has always been. This is how order is kept."

"Then what purpose are they?"

Ologéo paused. "The mortal creatures? They have no 'purpose.' They are... the world. They are what we are here to govern."

"We can't know every creature that exists in this land. Might there be some hidden mortal creature that also has the power to govern?"

"Of course not," Ologéo sneered. "How can we govern a creature that is also trying to govern? That would be... absurd."

"Why must we always command? We might be partners with it."

Ologéo shook his head. "That is a strange thought, Deïni. But it is no matter. No such creature exists." He shuddered at the idea. "Nor should it."

"But maybe it will, and maybe soon," Phreïs suggested. "Unless I'm mistaken, preparing for that inevitability was the whole point of this assembly, was it not?"

"As I see it, at issue here is only the question of how to maintain order by remaining in authority, even over a creature that may be immune to our natural influence. If we lose that authority, we lose our whole purpose for being here."

"Our whole and only purpose?" Deïni asked indignantly. "A teruman who has no influence over the mortal creatures has no purpose?"

"This is what we were sent to do," Ologéo said. "It has always been this way. Why, I will not venture to explain. The purposes of Havui we can only guess."

Deïni smiled at the irony. "If we can only guess at the designs of Havui, how can we be sure of all the purposes Havui has prepared for us?" She pressed on with her question. "It seems as if some new creature, with a new relationship to us, is yet to be discovered. And if that is true," she looked squarely at Ologéo as if in challenge, "perhaps we Terumani have not even yet discerned our own true purpose in this land. Perhaps it is not our purpose to only rule, but to guide, to aid, or to protect."

At this statement Tryma paused and raised an eyebrow, and perhaps a vision even came to him at that moment, but if so, he mentioned it to no one. Nevertheless he said, "That is a wise speculation, Deïni! There may indeed be mysteries and purposes yet to discover. Who could deny such a suggestion?"

Phactorias nodded approval. "My daughter may be contentious, but she is astute," he said, and a wave of pride swept over Deïni.

"This is nothing but speculation," Ologéo complained.

Reinodas groused. "Nothing will be certain until the being is revealed."

Deïni did not hesitate. "I will find it, then."

A silence fell over the whole of the assembly, as if no one else had even thought of this obvious idea. At last Phactorias said, "There may be some risk, Deïni. It will not obey you or respond to your influences."

Deïni laughed. "None of the mortal creatures obey or respond to me! I will hardly notice the difference. I will simply look for a creature that is willing to work alongside me even without the so-called powers of the terumani. That should not be hard to spot!"

"I will go with you, if you will have me," Wenda declared. "How marvelous it would be to find such a creature!"

"Your talents would be useful," Deïni said. She scowled wryly at the cat which sat, inexplicably contented, at her friend's feet. "If the creature will not obey you, it will obey no one."

So it came about that Deïni's proposal was accepted in the end, and she and Wenda returned to Teletirë to consider their plans.

There between them they devised many clever tests whereby they might discern the nature of the mortal creatures, to see whether any there were which would obey and do the will of Deïni who had no powers of control, or would defy Wenda who excelled at the art. Then they would know it to be different from all the other creatures of Soria.

When after much labor they were confident of their designs Wenda asked, "How shall we begin? We don't know how this creature might even appear, whether large or small, with fur or feathers or even scales. Will it go on four feet or two? Will it walk, or fly, or creep?"

"We cannot know," Deïni shrugged. "We must try them all, I suppose. But there are many we can dismiss from the start, for they and their ways are well-known to us all."

"Perhaps we might survey the terumani, to see if anyone might give us a clue, or guide us to any strange or unknown creature we might put to the test."

"We might begin with those which show signs of intelligence." Deïni added, smirking, "Few as those are."

So they set off to begin their quest in earnest. Now although they did not have the powers of Bël, Deïni and Wenda were terumani yet, and were able to travel to many distant parts of Soria, to inquire of the Terumani who dwelt there about the creatures of their domains. But for all this labor they learned nothing new, and no creature to which they were led showed any sign of independence. Not even Teruman Cosimë,[1] the custodian of living creatures in Soria, could direct them to such a thing. All the creatures seemed foolish to Deïni. "They are nothing but animals," she complained. "No different from all the animals. We have found nothing of importance. But I am not surprised."

"Shall we return home, then?" Wenda asked. "Perhaps the creature cannot yet be found?"

"Return home? We know only that no one else has yet discovered it!" Deïni said. "There are many creatures the terumani have not yet found or cultivated."

So Deïni and Wenda trekked into many dark and hidden places of the land to discover whatever unknown creature they might find. The sprights and nymphs of the country aided them in this search, helping them to discover many things which no eyes had yet beheld. They found secrets which not even Ologéo had yet discovered.

Many creatures they tried, from the spotted beetles to the mighty mammoth. Some were more reciprocal than others. Many showed no response to their tests at all, but scuttled or slithered about their business without any concern or acknowledgement. Others became devoted to their presence, nuzzling and following them about like Wenda's cat, craving attention and desiring praise. But none showed any sign of independence.

This work delighted Wenda, but Deïni was still disgusted "They are all stupid," She at last grumbled. "They are hardly even aware that they themselves exist."

---

1 She is the spouse of Teruman Ologéo.

Wenda said, "We have tamed or tried every creature we know, and still you are not satisfied."

"Not one of them is the being of Tryma's vision."

"Perhaps for all our effort, our tests are unsatisfactory?"

"Perhaps," Deïni mused. "We have treated them as pets and captives. How can we recognize independence when we treat them as subjects? Shall we go out into Soria, and meet them in their own realms?"

So Wenda agreed, and they set out together to explore the far reaches of the land. Wherever they could do so safely, they met with the creatures of Soria in their own habitats, on their own terms. They tried in every way to live among them as if of their own nature,[2] performing their tests stealthily and surreptitiously. But still nothing new was discovered, and no creature they met satisfied their tests.

How many days or years they spent on this quest none can say, nor does any tale recall. But years it must have been, and Deïni grew weary and aggrieved by her continual failure. Every creature disappointed her, she declared every creature a failure, and came to carp on the matter continuously.

One day at last Wenda moaned at yet another failure. "I am tired, Deïni. I wish to go home to my family, and to Shadowcat. Let us return and admit our failure."

"We cannot fail," she said. "What will the Terumani say if we return in humiliation? They will call us frivolous, and regard us as silly children."

"We have worked long and hard at this quest. They cannot disparage us for that. It is no shame to try and fail."

Deïni was aghast. "A want of success is not the same thing as failure. Success may yet come, today or tomorrow. But if we go home, we have failed."

"But what more can we do? Would you start from the very beginning, and try every creature of Soria over again?"

Deïni became stern and very serious. She spoke quietly, as if afraid to speak the words on her mind. "There is yet one country which we have not tried, of whose creatures we know nothing. Let us go to the Stair of Depharmen, and seek to enter the lands beyond. If Soria has failed me, perhaps Toë shall restore my hope at last."

Deïni of course had seen nothing of the lost lands on the far side of the Mountains of Division, for she had been born in Soria and was a child of that country. The terumani called those lost lands Toë, and even the elders could say little of them, for in the days since they had arrived all the country beyond the Mountains of Division had been given over to Boros, turbulent with storm, wind, and freezing cold, and none could venture there any longer.

---

2 This was perhaps not so outlandish as it sounds, as this was the usual the practice of the dræads and næads, who lived as one with the natural realm.

Wenda's eyes grew wide. "Are you mad?" she asked. "No one has ever returned across the Barria Heceïca. It is thought to be impossible. Why, even the Stair itself is said to be a perilous challenge which as likely as not would end us. If we were to fall into the long sleep in that lost country, we might never be found, and never return to this world till the end of days." Now although the souls of the terumani do not flee this realm, if their bodily frame is gravely injured it must be recovered and restored until the soul can return to its form.

"The two of us together can do this," Deïni asserted. "If one of us should fall, the other might aid her, or return to fetch aid. It is the last place to look, Wenda. We must try it."

Storeia, Wenda's mother, had a Hall on the Shelf, the plateau which sat at the lap of Mount Depharmen, and Wenda had from there often seen the terrifying heights of that great mountain, and she knew the awful reality of the Stair which climbed its westward shoulder. "It is not a place for living creatures," she insisted.

"We cannot be certain until we have tried it. Come, Wenda! We have, I feel, exhausted our hopes in the settled lands. But I am not defeated. I cannot rest until every chance has been tried."

But Wenda was afraid. "I cannot go," she said meekly. "And you should not either."

"Will you run home then, rather than do all in our power to complete our mission?"

"I cannot dare the pass of the Stair or enter Toë."

Deïni was appalled. "Then go!" she spat. "I do not need you. Run home and forget me!"

"I will go," Wenda said, "but not forget you. Please return with me, now."

But Deïni was wroth. She gathered Wenda's pack and her gear, and threw them from her out of the camp.

So Wenda gathered up her belongings, and she left Deïni, and returned quietly to her home in Niyarc, to Storeia her mother and Dôni her sister.

Then Deïni sank into a black mood. For days she sat alone in the wilderness and brooded. "Have I then failed?" she said to herself, "I will look the fool to all the Terumani after all my efforts. I have made a mockery of myself in promising to bring back this creature. How can I return and face my kindred? Tryma will scoff. My father will be ashamed. Even Wenda my companion has abandoned me."

In the darkness of her humor Deïni frowned bitterly and said, "If I must go alone, then alone I shall go, come what may."

So Deïni made the long journey back to Niyarc. She did not turn aside along the way, and she spoke to no teruman, neither friend nor kin. She could not bear to be seen or discovered, so she took secret paths through the country, that she might meet with no one. She skirted the settled places of Vordót and Niyarc, and came at length to the very feet of the Mountains of Division.

Gray and forbidding, they rose before her into the sky, like the vast, jagged walls of a fortress bounding the edge of the world. Clouds swirled above the sky-distant peaks: Wisps of mist and blowing snow ripped from the mountaintops: tattered banners whipping in the fierce winds far overhead. The threatening rumble of thunder could be heard from the unseen heights beyond, like the deep-throated voice of Boros raging. A cold fear gripped Deïni, but her heart was resolute, and she was stubborn.

She squared her shoulders and continued. The only known pass through that range was the Pass of Toë: a deep gap between the great height of Mount Toë to the west, and the over-towering massif of Mount Depharmen itself to the east. The pass, however, could only be reached from the south by the Stair of Depharmen, and it was no easy way. The pathway, if it could be called that at all, scrambled up a series of steep and perilous cliffs.

Up she went, and were she not Teruman herself, and born of the Great Ones at that, she might have perished in the climb. A full day it took her, putting forth all the strength of her exalted kind, and she spent herself in the effort. The sun was low in the sky to the southwest when she reached the pass.

There she found she could go no further. It was deathly cold in the screaming winds of the pass. Before her and below her she could see no lands at all: only the roiling clouds of Storm, flashing with lightning, and icy winds so bitter the cold seemed to chill her blood. Beyond the clouds were more mountains, and beyond them still more. The place was as remote as the very edge of the world. Havui was just as silent there as he had always been in the lands at her back, and she learned nothing.

"There is nothing in Toë," she said hopelessly, staring into the impregnable country beyond the pass, "and nothing beyond the mountains. Surely no creature can live in that fearsome desolation, and my quest is at an end."

The pass at this point was a narrow gap between the two mountains of the Gleaming Gateway, Mount Toë to the west, and Mount Depharmen to the east. Here she stood on the shoulder of those peaks, her legs trembling from her long exertion, and the massifs rose away beyond vision above her. The freezing winds assaulted her, and she knew she was in great peril there.

"I cannot return down the Stair by night," she said to herself. "I must find shelter and hope to live until morning."

She huddled from the freezing winds against the wall of Mount Toë. She worked her way around the rock face until she had come into a slight hollow, somewhat out of the force of the gale, and there as she stood and cowered from the blast she noticed something very peculiar:

Bones of stone, preserved in the very rock of that pass.

A great jumble of bones, as of long-forgotten, mortal creatures, were embedded into the very rock face, and to all appearance formed of stone themselves. She had no explanation for such a phenomenon, and it sent queer shivers up her spine that had nothing to do with the freezing winds.

The world had been made of Storm in ages past. But how many years or ages had passed since Havui had built those mountains none could say. These bones seemed to Deïni to be from an age long past, before the coming of the terumani, before Teruman Vélopar the Maker had shaped and graded Soria into its many realms and habitations.[3] It was a long forgotten realm of which none knew. Not even Ologéo in all his knowledge, or Tryma in all his wisdom, had guessed of its existence. But Deïni now saw clearly what they had never imagined.

Perhaps if the creature cannot be found, it is only because it has passed from the world, Deïni thought. *I must restore it to life.*

What happened next Deïni could never clearly say as to whether it happened before her eyes in the actual world, or whether it was a vision of her delirium. The air on the mountain grew dim and red, as red as living blood. It seemed to her that the bones in the mountainside were moving. Just a waver at first, then a visible shock, and then the rock in which they were embedded seemed to fall away around them in a great cloud of swirling dust. Out of the mass an assemblage of the bones seemed to arrange itself before her into the shape of living things, and the dust and vapor of the disintegrating rock condensed around the boney forms, wrapping them in sinew, and flesh, and skin. From the jumble of bones four figures arose and took shape before her eyes. They stood before her like terumani, with arms and legs, and heads mimicking her own, yet strangely distinct. Two of them seemed delicate and birdlike, and two seemed robust and wolfish, but all seemed to her familiar and affecting.

But the eyes which formed in their heads were dead and without light, looking past her without seeing. For a moment she was terrified of them, and she backed off as if to run, but on the crest of that pass at the setting of the sun there was nowhere to go but back to the impossible descent of the Stair. She stopped to face the creatures. And for a moment a spark of compassion warmed her soul. For the first time that she could recall, she felt a connection with a mortal thing, long-departed and unremembered though it was, and words came to her nearly unbidden:

3 For a deeper account of these matters the reader might refer to Appendix C of this volume: The Works of Vélopar.

Bone of stone, and blood of rust,
Instead of breath a choking dust.
A naked skull where was an ear.
A finger cold, and black, and sere,
A hollow where an eye should be.
You cannot touch, you cannot see.

Imprisoned in a stony wall
From distant ages past recall.

Were you like us when your were whole,
With light to guide your mortal soul?
What empty worries filled your years?
What joys? What hopes? What shivery fears?
Did you know pain? Did you know mirth?
When once you padded on this earth.

How many years? How long an age,
To be entombed in pitiless cage!

She knew nothing of their history, or how their bones had come to this forsaken place from distant ages long past. But she knew, somehow, that they belonged here, now, in her world.

At that moment the words of Tryma came full into her mind. *You have a power within you that none other of us has. I do not know what it is. Nor, I think, do you, as yet. But it will come to you when the time is right.* She knew suddenly what that power was, and that this was the moment Tryma had foretold.

She closed her eyes, gritted her teeth, and shouted out a single word.

"Live!"

She felt all her energy concentrated and flowing through her in a great and overwhelming rush. It seemed to spark in the atmosphere, chasing away for a moment the red gloom, and reached out in her vision to the lifeless creatures standing before her. Then her legs quivered and gave way, blackness crept into her vision, and she lost all consciousness. She fell to the earth as if her soul had fled.

Many days passed, and no one knew where Deïni the daughter of Phactorias had gone. Wenda at last became concerned, and she went to the Hall of Phactorias, and asked if perchance Deïni had come home in secret. "Many days ago I returned from our quest," she said, "and I had hoped Deïni would soon follow. But she has not come, and no one knows where she might be."

"Bring me to the place where you last saw her," Phactorias said.

They arose together and Wenda guided Phactorias to the site of their camp, as swiftly as they could travel. But Deïni had long ago departed, and there was no trace left of their presence. Nor was there any hint of where Deïni may have gone from thence, nor even in which direction she may have turned. Even the creatures they had been dwelling with in the place had disappeared and gone on their way.

"We left each other in ire," Wenda said tearfully. "I worry that she may not return at all. Something terrible may have happened to her, alone and in the wild, with only beasts for company."

"I'm sure all is well," Phactorias said, but in his heart he had begun to worry.

"I'm afraid there is more you should know," Wenda said. "Before we parted, she had proposed we go to the Pass of Toë and ascend the Stair. She thought the things we seek may live still in the lands beyond. I fear she may have followed through on that venture."

Phactorias frowned. "These are indeed grave tidings," he said. "None has ever returned to that country, and it is thought none ever shall to the end of the days of Soria. Even the pass is perilous. Would she truly risk so much for this quest?"

"All are depending on her, and she was ashamed of her failure."

"She is no failure who has tried her utmost. I must go and seek her there. If I can find her I shall bring her back down myself, even though she may have fallen into the long sleep of the terumani, from which her awakening will be laborious and slow."

Wenda raised her head and said, "I will go with you!"

"It is a long and dangerous journey," Phactorias warned.

"I abandoned her once out of fear," Wenda said. "I cannot take that back, but I must now do whatever I can to save her."

"Very well," said Phactorias. "I only hope I do not end up with two souls to rescue from the mountain."

So the two of them, Phactorias the father of Deïni, and Wenda her devoted friend, set out for the Mountains of Division to seek her. Wenda refused to complain or to flag on the trail, difficult though it was, and together they made the toilsome ascent of the Stair of Depharmen after her. When they reached the crest they saw her some distance beyond, near the far edge of the crest whence the winds from Toë blew, but she lay on the frozen ground, her back against an icy boulder, insensate and unmoving. Then Phactorias' shoulders slumped, and he said, "We are too late."

"But look!" Wenda said. She took his arm and pointed.

With Deïni were two creatures such as neither of them had seen before, a male and a female, that walked like the terumani. They were like the mortal creatures of Soria in nature, yet in a new and unfamiliar form, with smooth skin much like that of the terumani, and feathery hair the color of the earth. In many ways they mimicked the terumani themselves, but with arms more slender, and walking on long, muscular legs. Most remarkable of all were their deep and expressive eyes, unlike the eyes of any other mortal creature in Soria.

"Do you know these beings?" Wenda asked. "They are caring for Deïni. Would they do so if she had entered the long sleep?"

They paused for a moment to watch in wonder. Deïni clearly was unconscious, and even had she been awake she had no power to control or influence the mortal beings on her own, yet they were laboring independently and of their own will to aid her. They struggled to keep Deïni warm. They were bringing her food. They brought water and made her drink. By their care they had been seeking diligently to hold back her soul from sinking into the long sleep.

"I do not know them," Phactorias declared. "Let us only hope their vigil has not failed." So he and Wenda crossed over the crest to join them.

The new creatures spotted Phactorias and Wenda, and at once they approached them without fear, seeking their aid. They took them both by the hands and brought them to Deïni. Phactorias went to his daughter and examined her. "She has only swooned," he said gratefully. "She will recover quickly, if we can bring her safely down from the mountains."

As he tended to her the creatures stood aside and watched, with concern flashing in their expressive green eyes.

From their vantage at the crest of the pass they could look into the realm of storm that lay beyond them to the north, and a spark of insight chilled Wenda's spine. "These creatures have come from the lands beyond the mountains, from the lost countries of Toë, to aid her!" Wenda declared. "They must have been sent by Havui into our land to fulfill her quest at last!"

"On that I have no opinion," Phactorias said, "but we must certainly be thankful for their appearance here!"

Teruman Phactorias then lifted Deïni his daughter in his arms, and carried her down from the Stair. Few there are, even of the Terumani, who would have had the strength or skill to perform such a labor in that trying pass. With him went Wenda, fretting for her friend the whole way and helping in the descent as she was able. Following them both came the creatures of Toë which had cared for her on the mountain, cleaving to them as if aware that their futures were bound together.

When they had made their way down as far as the plateau below Depharmen which was called the Shelf, Phactorias paused to restore his daughter, and she awoke from her swoon. Wenda sat beside her, holding her hand as her eyes fluttered and she awoke, but Deïni looked past her without a word or sign of recognition. Instead she raised her head and asked her father, "What has happened to the creatures of Toë, which came to rescue me? I owe them my life."

The two creatures rushed to her side, and they rejoiced to see her well. "Where are the others?" Deïni asked.

Phactorias frowned. "There were only these two creatures when we arrived. Do you know them?"

Deïni smiled mysteriously. "That is strange. They were four when I was on the mountain."

"We saw only two," Phactorias assured her.

Deïni sighed. "Two of them looked longingly away to the north, while only these two looked southward. I suppose the others must have gone down the far side of the pass, into Toë and the cold lands beyond. I could not have held them back. Perhaps they belong in that treacherous country: They were the hardier and more robust. Or, I wonder... perhaps their time has not yet come."

Deïni began to speak to the two who remained, kindly, as to a favored pet, and they doted on her in return. "These two shall be enough. These will have mastery over the things of this land, same as we, though they are mortal." She turned to her father and said, "You may tell Tryma that the day he foresaw has come. I have found the creature of his vision, and my long quest is over." She glanced coldly at Wenda. "I have found them myself: I alone."

Wenda bowed her head. "It was wrong of me to abandon our quest when we had been through so many things together."

Deïni looked at her in stoney-faced silence. "Did I not tell you to forget me?" she muttered. She turned her back and returned to the creatures from Toë.

Wenda turned to Phactorias and said sadly, "I am not wanted. And now I must earn her love all over again."

"She has come through a great trial," Phactorias said. "She may think more softly when she has fully recovered."

Deïni however spoke but few words to Wenda, and would not let her approach or minister to her in her convalescence. She remained for a time on the Shelf of Depharmen while she regained her strength. The creatures of Toë were with her continually every day, bringing her whatever food, drink or other comforts she might require, and being careful of her every need. She called them after herself, and named them the deïnings.

Wenda at last gave up her hopes. So she went on her way and returned to her mother Storeia and her sister Dôni, and to Shadow her cat.

There at the knee of the mountain Deïni built a place for the deïnings. Phactorias then called for Vélopar, and together the two of them built there a Hall for Deïni his daughter, and filled it with furnishings fit for Teruman, nigh to the camp Deïni had made for the beings. There she kept them and nurtured them, and they returned her care in kind, working alongside her in her labors, and playing alongside her in her leisure. So the deïnings grew, and bore young, and prospered in that place.

But the deïnings could not speak, and it entered the mind of no one that it should be otherwise.

3. The Gift of Wenda

So it was that the vision of Tryma was said to have been fulfilled. Phactorias called the Terumani to council and informed the assembly that the creature which governed itself, uninfluenced by the terumani, had entered the land of Soria, and could be found in Deïni's care on the Shelf of Depharmen. Many came to see them there, and were reassured that the deïnings seemed to pose no danger to their world.

Years uncounted passed, and their home on the Shelf soon became too restricted to accommodate the new generations of that race. They spread out from thence, and wandered throughout Vordót, and into Batack, and into many distant places of Soria. This new folk came to be loved by many of the terumani, and the deïnings found pleasure in the company of the terumani in kind. Many became companions, forming bonds nearly as warm as friendship.

Even Wenda found pleasure in the deïnings, though it hurt her heart that she had lost her friend Deïni by their coming. Generations of that Kindred grew up in the land, and Wenda watched their success with both joy and melancholy. Then a strange thing came into the heart of Teruman Wenda.

She and Deïni had seen many things on their long quest together, and had learned of many wonderful creatures. She knew the bright birds of the forests, the singing birds and the perching birds, and the luminous birds that walk upon the earth: and they gave her delight. She knew the creatures of the earth, the fox and the squirrel, the deer and the lamb, and all things downy and soft: and these creatures also charmed her. She knew the buzzing insects, the lustrous scarab, the spotted beetles; the industrious bees and bright butterflies, and these things enchanted her.

But she saw now the deïnings, the companion creatures of Deïni her friend of old, and it seemed to her that of all those that moved upon the land, the deïnings were the most intriguing. They were not soft and warm, nor were they bright and beautiful, but an air mystery and dignity clung about them which could not be ignored: some hidden secret or undiscovered capacity which begged to be unveiled.

More than this, they were precious to Deïni.

Wenda grieved that she had failed Deïni in the end, and had abandoned her before the deïnings were discovered after all, when all hope seemed to have failed. Their friendship had waned after that. Deïni spoke with her at times out of necessity or propriety, but without affection. She would reluctantly do her favors now and again, and when it was noted that she had the gift of granting life, Wenda had even persuaded her to preserve the life of Shadow. But Deïni no longer came to visit at Storeia's Hall, and when Wenda went to see her at Teletirë it seemed that somehow Deïni was always busy or distracted. She remained cold and unmovable, and never had they rekindled the bond they had formerly shared.

Wenda yearned to accomplish some great thing which might restore her into favor with her friend whom she loved, to atone for her own failure. So it seemed good to her that she might grant gifts to the deïnings, to set them above all the other creatures of Soria. And a thing came into her mind which, had she but known it, would come to change the nature of all things.

Teruman Storeia was once sojourning with Teruman Phreïs, and she and her daughters were residing for a season in the Hall Timotéa, the Hall of Phreïs in Niyarc: a fine and handsome place of lumber and bright red brick. That Hall was not far distant from the vale known as Ëthiri, the Pillows. This was a valley nestled among the hills which groped southward from the Mountains of Division, with a broad floor bedecked with a blanket of blooming clover. The white chalk walls of that valley were rounded and softly billowing like the pillows of the Terumani: in those walls were many caves, bright and airy and dry. Here a colony of the deïnings had established themselves, and their chief, Sorios the Deïning,[4] would visit the place often, journeying from his home on the Shelf near to the Hall of Deïni. Sorios was of the deïnings which Deïni herself had given life: He was advanced in years, but having been given life by Deïni he was still in his vigor, and showed no signs of the mortality of the rest of his kind.

Wenda went out from Timotéa, and she found Sorios there: She smiled on him confidingly, and taking him by the hand she said, "Come with me into the house of the Terumani." Then she led him to the chamber of her lodgings at Timotéa in Niyarc.

There were many unremarked rooms in Timotéa, and no one noted his presence there. Wenda brought Sorios into the place secretly: Whether for good or ill, she did not counsel with Storeia her mother, or with Phreïs her host, or with any other Teruman. It cannot now be guessed whether much discord may have been avoided had she done so, or whether measureless blessings may have been forever missed. Be that as it may, she told no one of her design, for she hoped to astonish all with the marvel of her accomplish-

4 The name "Sorios" is first used here, and it may be a name given to him by Deïni herself. It is implied at times that the land of Soria was named for him, but the converse may also be true.

ment should she succeed, but most of all to bless her friend with an illustrious surprise.

All terumani have the power to influence the minds and hearts of their subjects. But it must be understood that Storeia and her daughters were gifted in this realm beyond all others. This is indeed the special gift of Storeia: Her daughters have proven no less skilled in such matters. Teruman Wenda was like her mother, skilled in the arts of the imaginings and inspirations of the soul.

"I see something in you, and in your kind," she said to him, gazing into his deep and sensitive eyes. "Let us see if I can fan it to life."

She sat down with Sorios, and touching her forehead to his own, she probed with her spirit, and entered deeply into the mind of that soul. She explored, and learned, and brought light into the dark corners of his awareness. There was a skill in her probing, a gentleness and intuition which glowed like a welcoming light in a dark valley. Then she began her work, crafting and striving in secret, weaving intricate designs into the spirit of Sorios. She poured much of her own perception and light into the empty pathways she found, and she urged the workings of his mind to her will. Sorios, for his part, received her joyfully, and eagerly came to her each day to pursue this exercise.

For many days she hid away with Sorios in her chamber working at this craft. At last she exhausted her labor. Then she sighed wearily, and said, "I have done all I can. I may have succeeded, or I may have failed. But in any event, now I must go to rest."

As she turned to leave the chamber Sorios opened his own eyes, and in a voice of his own he stammered uncertainly, "Then... are we... finished?"

Wenda gasped. She rushed back and grasped him by the shoulders. "Can you speak as I speak?" she said to him.

Sorios laughed. His voice was at first halting and uncertain, but his words were plain and without confusion."I cannot claim to speak as you yourself. But my mind is filled with words and thoughts, and my tongue cannot help but to speak them aloud."

Wenda felt flushed and steadied herself against the wall. "I have done it!" she whispered. Never before had any of the terumani, not even from among the High Ones themselves, accomplished so great an act or given so great a gift. "This is astonishing beyond measure!" she said to Sorios. "But you must keep quiet for now, and not reveal your gift openly. When the time is right we will go to Deïni your mistress and surprise her."

Wenda imagined in her mind's eye the wonder and elation which Deïni would display at the revelation. "Now at last I might restore our friendship!" she thought to herself. "But I must wait, to see for certain whether this gift turns out to the good."

Wenda then sent him back to be among his own folk, when he had promised not to reveal his secret to the terumani. She returned to the house of Phreïs to rest and recover from her exertions. She remained in her own chamber, away from the eyes of Storeia or of Phreïs, pretending to be deep in study so that they would not question her absence. When at last she had fully regained her strength she rose from her bed, and rushed out to the Pillows to learn how Sorios was getting on with his new gift.

Sorios greeted her sadly. "I possess a gift beyond reckoning. But with my own kindred I cannot commune: they are as yet dumb as are the animals of the land. They have no more understanding than the fox or the raven. Please, then, give this gift of speech to all my kindred, that we might share our minds and thoughts one with another."

Wenda sighed at this request. "I wish that I could," she said. "But such work is too great even for me. There are a great many of your kind in Soria, and I have exhausted myself with this labor for you alone."

Sorios cast his eyes down. "It will be lonely having none with whom to share my mind, and speech will be more torment to me than gift."

"You will have me," Wenda said. "And there will be others. You will soon have many others of my kind wishing to speak with you."

"But I will be estranged from my own kind," Sorios pleaded.

Wenda frowned thoughtfully. At last she said, "Bring me your mate, and your children. If my strength and skills fail me not, I shall give this gift of speech to them, also. After that, if I have guessed correctly, it shall pass to their descendants, and all who are born of that lineage shall have the gift of speech."

Sorios had many descendants. He had always been a leader of the deïnings, a master over many: having now the gift of speech, he seemed as a god to them, like the Terumani themselves. So he went out from the house of Phreïs and chose from among them six young ones whom he deemed of great worth, eager to learn, and with talents and cunning above the commonplace. These he brought back with him to the Ëthiri, the Valley of the Pillows, along with Archea his mate.[5]

When he had assembled all these, Wenda brought them secretly into her private chambers in Timotéa: as yet she had told no one of her work. She feared the Terumani might discover her designs before she had brought everything to fruition, and spoil her surprise.

She set herself to her labor once again, delving deep into the minds and spirits of the children of Sorios and of Archea. That effort taxed her unto her utter strength. After many days she lay down once again, exhausted: but

5 Archea, also, is said to have been one of the two deïnings whom Deïni had given life in the Pass of Toë.

the tongues of the Sorites were loosed and their souls filled with the light of language. Sorios and Archea and the children they had gathered became as terumani in that house.

So she sent them out from her, and they returned to the Pillows. There they mingled with the deïnings, and brought forth new families after the design of Wenda. It soon became clear that their children also received the gift of speech.

Wenda watched with pride and wonder as their tribe grew. But still she had not revealed her work to the Terumani, or to Deïni her friend. She was patient, and wished to mark whether this gift truly proved a blessing to that Kindred.

Such a marvelous thing, however, could not easily be hidden.

It so happened that one day Teruman Ologéo was walking in the north country accompanying his spouse, Teruman Cosimë, the custodian of living creatures, as she went about her own business observing the creatures of her domain and tending to them. As they approached the valley called the Pillows Ologéo saw a column of smoke rising into the sky.

"What teruman dwells in Ëthiri?" Ologéo asked.

"To my knowledge there is none," Cosimë replied. "It is the home of the deïnings, who inhabit the caves of that valley."

"Then why is there fire?" Ologéo asked.

Cosimë was alarmed. "We must check this matter out at once. If some stray spark or combustion has started a wildfire it must be stopped before it spreads."

"Perhaps it is no more than the camp of some wandering teruman on a pleasure jaunt."

"But if it is a wildfire the deïnings may be in grave danger."

Ologéo shrugged. "It is nature. If they are meant to perish then it is nothing more than their natural fate."

Cosimë squinted disapprovingly. "They are my charges, nonetheless, and we should help them if we might."

"If you must," Ologéo balked. "I will return to our place and await your word." So Ologéo turned back to return to the house they kept in that vicinity, while Cosimë made her way to the valley of the Pillows.

The column of smoke did not seem to be spreading or growing, and it took her some while to discover its source. At last as she made her way through a stand of bamboo she spied several of the children of Sorios sitting together in a clearing, warming their hands at a fire, and speaking to one another in the language of the terumani. Disbelieving her own eyes and ears, she approached the party, but when they discovered her they were afraid and fled. She called out and tried to follow, but she could not track them through the thick growth, and no one returned her calls.

Cosimë returned to her place, to Ologéo, and he said to her indifferently, "Did you find the source of the smoke that worried you?"

"I did," Cosimë replied, "But you will not believe me." He urged her then to continue and she said, "I found a company of the deïnings sitting unafraid by fire as if they had kindled it themselves, and they were dressed in garments. But more surprising than all, they seemed to be speaking to one another in language such as the terumani use, not the coarse and hollow grunting of the deïnings."

Ologéo frowned. "You heard wrong," he insisted.

"I know what I heard. It was no apparition or illusion. I would hardly have credited it myself but for the fire which still burned when they had fled."

Ologéo had no cause to doubt Cosimë's report, and he said, "Can you lead me to this strange sight?"

So Cosimë brought him to the Pillows, and they searched together, until they found the tracks of a company of the Sorites foraging in the brush. This track they followed, but both Cosimë and Ologéo hid themselves by the craft of the terumani, so the Sorites would not perceive their presence.[6]

In this manner they succeeded in coming upon the company as they walked through the countryside. Thus they heard the children of Sorios talking and singing together, as if they were terumani themselves.

Now Ologéo was astonished at this, for no such thing could he have imagined. They returned at once to their place, and Ologéo sent word out among the Terumani, saying, "Come at once to my Hall Liaibíri, and let us all take counsel together. Something singular and aberrant has been found in the valley of the Pillows. The mortal creatures of the deïnings have been discovered using speech and living as terumani. I have no explanation for such an event, and we must determine together what do about this."

Wenda also received the call, and saw that her work had been discovered. So she came to Liaibíri herself, and when Ologéo had called their council to order, she stood up before them all and said, "There is no mystery. I have given the gift of speech to Sorios the Deïning and his family."

A murmur of amazement and awe passed through the room at this revelation.

All of the High Ones had arrived. Even Teruman Vélopar himself was astonished at that accomplishment. "Your council must be adjourned," he said to Ologéo. "We must go out and see this thing ourselves!"

Ologéo frowned, but he could hardly defy the word of Vélopar. The Terumani rose up from the Lyceum of Liaibíri, and followed Vélopar together to Ëthiri where Wenda's clan was dwelling.

6 It is one of the special abilities of all the terumani, that they are able to conceal themselves and their works from the eyes of the mortal kinds, and walk unseen in their midst.

When they came to the Valley of the Pillows they found the Sorites just as they had been described, speaking among themselves as if they themselves were terumani, and laughing, and singing. They found them already working together to fabricate their own needs and arts. The Terumani observed these changes with amazement, then entered the valley to address them face to face.

The speaking deïnings were at first afraid, for in all the time they had been flourishing in Ëthiri they had never met with any teruman, high or low, besides Wenda herself. So Wenda went among them and reassured them. When they had calmed themselves somewhat, she brought in the Terumani and introduced the two races. Those who had come with Vélopar went out among them, and sat with them, and met with their families and groups. They found that they were fully able to converse with them, soul to soul and spirit to spirit. Their astonishment at this miracle was beyond measure.

Then many were praising Wenda mightily. No such thing had been done, or even conceived, since the terumani had come into Soria. Teruman Phactorias was overawed, saying, "This is a magnanimous work! This child[7] has proven herself equal at least to the greatest of us."

Wenda was flushed with gratification, and exultant in the attention and applause. Since first she had devised this scheme she had pictured in her imagination the look of rapture which would light Deïni's eyes at this surprise, and she looked now hopefully to find her friend. But Deïni was frowning more bitterly than ever, standing apart at the edge of the valley. A wave of doubt passed over Wenda.

She approached Deïni cautiously and clasped her hands, and said to her pleadingly, "Come down and see what a miracle you have brought into this land! Your deïnings are as kindred with our kind!"

But Deïni sneered at Wenda reproachfully and said, "What have you done?" Then she pulled away her hands, and turned her back upon her friend, and went away to sit in a quiet place alone to sulk.

4. The Debate of the Terumani

The Ádolthi camped in the Valley of the Pillows for weeks, to watch and study the Sorites and discover the depth of this change in the creatures. Some remained in concealment by the art of the terumani, so they could not be perceived, and could observe in secret. Some also went openly among them and conversed with them. Their admiration of the Sorites, and of the greatness of Wenda's gift, continued to grow.

---

7 The Sorian word means a young female lacking status, not quite an adult. But she was "young" by the counting of the terumani only: clearly she has lived for ages of "mortal" years.

But when Teruman Ologéo had studied the scene for some time, his disquiet grew ever greater. He returned at last to Liaibíri in a dark mood. Many began to gather with him there, and form a party in opposition to Wenda, for there were many with him who felt that this gift had been both rash and dangerous, and their party was growing.

When Deïni heard of it she came to him at Liaibíri and met with him in private. "Wenda is ruining my deïnings," she complained. "How can we stop her?"

Cosimë was also present, and she consoled Deïni, saying, "At least you can take comfort in this: The deïnings do not live long in this land, as do we ourselves. This generation, at least, shall soon pass. This foolishness cannot last long."

But Ologéo had been observing and making his deductions concerning the new clan, and he said, "I fear that is not true. There are a great many individuals with this infection, surely already more than a single generation. And there are very many children among those. Wenda cannot have spread this thing to so many on her own, no matter how great her powers."

Deïni was aghast. "But if not Wenda, than who? Are you saying she is not acting alone?"

"I am saying this gift may be even more insidious than I had feared. Wenda must be called to Liaibíri to give an account of herself."

So he sent word to Teruman Vélopar and Teruman Tryma, and insisted Wenda be brought to Liaibíri to face questioning about this act, hoping when they saw the full import of the matter he could win them to his own side. Word was sent to Wenda that the High Ones had convened at Liaibíri to demand her defense.

Wenda had been disheartened by the rebuff of Wenda, but she had remained at the Valley of the Pillows where her supporters surrounded her. When word of the summons arrived she became afraid. "Have I done something wrong?" she asked.

Storeia her mother stood by her and complained, "Teruman Ologéo is being presumptuous. But we must go and face him. I will go with you to defend you."

Phactorias also was present. "I shall go as well. Ologéo cannot exclude me simply because I've praised you. If he has something to say he will say it to all of us." Then together they departed for Liaibíri.

"What is the meaning of this?" Phactorias asked when all had gathered in Ologéo's private chambers. Wenda sat with downcast eyes, backed by Storeia and Phactorias. Teruman Ologéo sat before them with Cosimë and with Deïni as accusers. Vélopar and Tryma looked on passively. Phactorias continued. "You do not have the authority to censure any one of us."

"I merely want facts," Ologéo purred. "If Wenda has transgressed in this matter we must call for a full council."

"Agreed," Vélopar said. "But I do not see her transgression. She has given a gift to these creatures. Is that not our right as caretakers of the land?"

"I do not say this gift was not a work of exceeding powers. But I question: Is it fit for these deïnings to have speech like the terumani, in empty mockery of ourselves? The nature of this gift is, shall we say, exceptional."

"Whatever anyone else may think of it," Teruman Tryma declared, "it must be admitted that it is astonishingly great, and we should accord it the esteem it deserves."

"Were the deïnites not fitting enough as they were brought into the land?" Deïni objected. She scowled at Wenda. "Does this so-called gift of speech improve them or ruin them?"

Ologéo continued. "This gift was unwelcome and unsolicited. It has taken something of dignity and made it absurd."

Storeia spoke up in defense of her daughter. "You, perhaps, do not see the charm which this gift imparts. But to many of us it is as wondrous as magic."

"That is not the point," Ologéo carped. "It is unnatural."

"It is not merely absurd and unnatural, but dangerous," said Teruman Cosimë, appealing to Vélopar. "We were given the land of Soria to be its caretakers. Suddenly we have competitors, and we are asked to share the land with a strange and ignorant race. This scourge of speech can only confuse and confound all our designs," she added.

"I will grant that it changes our role here," Storeia said. "But I don't see them as competitors. Wenda's gift has made them our compatriots. Now they have powers to help us shape the land, and even to shape their own destinies within this land."

"Perhaps," said Ologéo, "this 'gift' would not be so odious, were it not spreading as if it were a disease. Would it change your opinions to learn that this gift of speech does not end with those unto whom Wenda has given it? It passes on to their generations without lessening. Indeed, if anything, the progeny seem yet more infected than the parents."

There was a moment of silence. Phactorias turned to Wenda. "Is this true?" he asked.

Wenda frowned and stood up to defend herself. "The deïnings are mortals," she said. "Their kind pass from our world after but few of our years, like a wisp of down on the breeze. Would it be fair to gift but one generation, only to see the gift disappear from the world at their passing? This gift was given to all generations, that it would not fail in the land until that day in which the great Storm is pacified."

"Then it is as I feared," said Ologéo. "And you confess that this was your design?"

"It was my hope," Wenda admitted. "The nature of the deïnings as Havui made them is perhaps more to be credited than my own efforts."

"Then you are saying you have no power to, well, 'take back' this gift?" Ologéo demanded.

"I would not, even if I knew a way!"

"Nor does it seem appropriate, or moral, to take it back, even if there were a means," said Tryma. "They are now moral souls with rights of their own. And the deïnites seem to welcome this 'scourge.'"

Deïni cast a scathing glance at Wenda. "Look now," she complained, "if we do nothing to stop this, in some few generations all the deïnings shall be supplanted, and your Sorites shall take their place."

"Perhaps," Phactorias suggested, "the Sorites will grow to despise their unspeaking kin. If so, they will no longer take mates from among them, and the unspeaking deïnings would endure as you wish."

Wenda pleaded with Deïni. "But would it not be better if all your Kindred shared the gift of speech? My hope was to enrich them, not to steal away and supplant them. I thought," she cast her gaze to the ground, "I thought I might at last make some amends for failing you in your quest. It was meant as a gift not to the deïnings alone, but to you!"

Deïni then said, "Then should I have not been consulted? They are my special charges, and they bear my name."

Teruman Storeia shook her head. "Come, Deïni, you are not the only one who bears interest in this race. The deïnings have spread among us all, and all of us have been stirred to help and to guide them. All the Terumani feel this kinship. You have no peculiar claim on them to choose their fate alone."

"But by whose permission was this decision made?" Ologéo demanded. "Who was consulted before such an evolution was imposed onto them?"

Teruman Vélopar quipped, "Can we assume, Ologéo, that you have consulted us all for every decision you have made? I seem to have missed those meetings. Was I overlooked?"

Phactorias agreed. "Perhaps all the forms of propriety were not kept," he admitted, "but none of us have consulted the whole council of our order before every choice we make, regarding either the deïnings, or any other creatures of the land. We often act alone and without guidance or counsel."

"But this choice effects not only the creatures themselves, but all of us. And there is no end in sight."

Phactorias called things to order. "Let us get to heart of the matter. I do not see what can be done. The gift is given. It cannot be taken back."

"This is why I say we must call for a council of all. We must decide our course, before this spreads yet further. There may be options we can pursue."

"Very well," said Vélopar. "As you wish. But to me it seems a small matter. We can aid them or ignore them as we choose. I for one have had little to do with the deïnings up to this point, and I see no reason to change my habit."

So Teruman Ologéo called once more for the council of the Terumani to re-convene at the Lyceum of Liaibíri. Even Phactorias agreed that the matter was of concern to all.

Many of Wenda's supporters had followed her to Liaibíri, and others soon began to arrive when the call went out. Ologéo's camp was eager to come and make their complaints. So the Hall began to fill once again. When the assembly had returned Teruman Ologéo called them to the Lyceum.

Ologéo explained the situation to all, revealing that the gift of Wenda threatened to fill all of Soria with these new Sorites, supplanting the deïnites they had known. A commotion passed over the assembly at this revelation. Many eyes turned to Wenda accusingly, and even her supporters gazed at her, stunned. "We are the caretakers of the land," Ologéo declared. "It falls upon us to decide what to do with them, before it is too late."

At this news many of the terumani began to fear once again the prophecy of Tryma, that these deïnings might become their rivals for the governance of Soria, and might threaten to resist or even rise up to oppose them. But others saw the promise of this new opportunity, desiring nothing more than to continue to do as they'd always done: to strive to improve the lot of their charges as wisely as possible.

The debate could not be settled. Many proposals were made on both sides, and all were shouted down. Some there were who insisted that the tribe of speaking Sorites should be contained in the Valley of the Pillows, never to leave its confines. Others wished to destroy them all and cleanse the land of the abomination. Still others were in awe of what had been done, and vowed to protect the tribe against their detractors, and even to encourage them to thrive and spread. The only matter upon which all agreed was that they should not be taught to live as do the Terumani, in their great Halls, with the luxuries and comforts of that race.

Arguments continued to fly about the Lyceum for many hours. Indeed, the contention went on into the evening, and continued when the council reconvened the following day. Another day passed, and yet another, and no progress was made. Few changed their positions, and each side became if anything yet more emotional as the days of debate compounded.

Now Teruman Vélopar was recognized as the mightiest of that company, who had shaped and graded the land of Soria and given them all their homes. Though none considered him a lord or a leader, yet all respected and venerated him. Teruman Vélopar at last arose before them all and said, "This debate tires me, and I have no interest in its outcome. I am returning to my own

Hall. You may all remain here in Liaibíri and debate until you have worn yourselves to the bone, for all I care."

So Vélopar abandoned the council and returned to his great Hall Lucré.

Those who remained were abashed, and others soon began to depart quietly on their own. Even the supporters of Ologéo grew weary of the debate and began to leave. At last Phactorias came to Ologéo and said, "It appears this council has disbanded, and we have agreed on nothing."

Ologéo declared, "There is little to be accomplished when so many folk will not listen to reason and good counsel. But this is not over. We shall see which side shall prevail."

As for Wenda, she left the Hall of Liaibíri sad and disheartened, most of all for the loss of Deïni's trust. She returned to the Hall of Storeia her mother and confined herself alone in her chamber, with no company but her cat. But Storeia at last went in to her and said, "Do not languish here. You have done a great thing, Wenda. Go out to the Valley of the Pillows, and tend to your charges there. The joys of guiding the growth of children will outweigh the missing pleasures of soured friendships."

So she did as her mother had advised, and went out and met with Sorios and his kin in their home at the Pillows. In that place she was held in reverence, for all the Sorites knew what a surpassing work she had done on their behalf. They spoke with her daily, and communed with her, like children with a mother whom they loved. So she built for herself a house in that valley: her heart took comfort, and she became resolute that the gift she had wrought was to the benefit of this new mortal Kindred.

The supporters of Wenda joined her, and watched over them carefully and cautiously as they multiplied and prospered, and they proved to be clever. Although the Terumani had decided to withhold from them the trappings and luxuries of their own culture, the Sorites invented and discovered new ways to live from the land on their own.

As they flourished, Ëthiri became too strait for their clan, and they began to move out into the countries of the north. They learned to build houses of clay and stones, or of sticks and branches and limbs, or of straw and turf. They fashioned weapons for themselves to aid in their hunting, and indeed became equal to the wolf or the great cats in the skills of the hunt. Others learned to weave, and to make fine crafts of all kinds: of wood, of leather, of ivory and bone, clay and stone. They also soon learned the uses of fire.

Whatever they put their hands to, they excelled thereat, and whatever material they found about them, they learned to put it to use, as no other creatures of Soria had done. It became clear to many that there was a new Kindred in the land, with purposes and privileges of their own, equal to those of the terumani themselves.

Ologéo, however, called his supporters to meet with him privately. "Perhaps," he proposed, "our party can work together to thwart these misguided efforts." So Deïni and Ologéo conspired, and enlisted others of the Terumani to follow their lead. Together this party sought to curtail the spread of the speech of Wenda, shunning the Sorites, neither communing with them nor aiding them in any way, and shaming those who did so, and doing all in their power to prevent them from mingling with the deïnings as they came out of Ëthiri.

"If we prevail," said Teruman Cosimë, "then perhaps the Sorites might pass from this land in a few generations, and the land shall be cleansed of this taint once more."

So things were to stand for many years: some of the Terumani aiding, and others hoping to thwart the children of Sorios. In the end the Terumani themselves could not agree, and the fate of the Sorites was left hanging in the balance.

5. The Solution of Tryma

The children of Sorios and Archea had heard nothing of this debate, and Wenda thought it wisest to say nothing to them on the matter. So their race continued to thrive in innocence. They mastered many things, learning to build, to create, and to share their knowledge. They made houses, and tools, and art of many kinds. In many ways they had become so like terumani themselves, that they seemed clearly to be a kindred race, the co-inheritors of the land of Soria together with the terumani. So the Terumani called them a Kindred, and named them the Sorites after their patriarch Sorios. Great care and affection the Terumani then lavished upon this new race, thinking to guide and train them to be masters of nature.

Teruman Tryma the Wise had observed all these things, though he had said little in the debate. He considered the matter deeply as was his wont, judging for himself whether this gift of speech and reason redounded to the good or to the ill of the land and the Sorites themselves, and whether this development was the fulfillment of his foretelling. He found he had mercy on the Sorites, for now that they had speech and their minds were no longer as the dumb beasts, he felt akin to them, and felt obligation towards them as unto the Terumani themselves.

"The Terumani have debated the fate of this Kindred endlessly," Tryma mused. "But no one has invited them to speak for themselves."

Therefore he went to the Valley of the Pillows, and he found there Diatron, a Sorite, a son of Plateos. Diatron was peaceable and thoughtful, and well respected among his kindred, even by Sorios himself. Being certain that he was away from the eyes of Ologéo, Tryma said to Diatron, "If you would, come with me to a secret place in the mountains, and we shall build there a Hall. I shall teach you what I can of wisdom and foreknowledge, that you might be a guide for your own Kindred. Then we shall see of what you Sorites are capable. If truly you deserve the right to determine your own fates, we shall prove it before the eyes of Ologéo and the rest."

Diatron agreed, for he was humble and willing to learn. Thus he became the disciple of Tryma: and Tryma himself, together with Diatron his disciple, established the Oracle of Diatron on Mount Éthel in the foothills of the Barria Heceïca. Now this was the first Oracle of Diatron, but this Hall was destined to be abandoned after the tragedies of the Year of Sorrows, when the Oracle would move to the Inviant, following the uprooted Diatrians. But at this time, and for an age of the world, the Oracle remained in Vordót of the north.

Diatron devoted himself to learning all the lore which Tryma could teach him. They sat together daily for hours as Tryma expounded on the means of discerning truth from falsehood. They went out into the country together to learn the lessons of nature and the wisdom of the beasts. Diatron learned to read the messages and meanings of the stars, and the seasons, and the winds and the airs. His mind became full and his insights keen, as keen as if he were teruman himself. Though Tryma himself had no rival for wisdom and foresight, yet he was pleased with his disciple, and gave him his full approval.

Then Tryma thought it wise to settle this matter of the Sorites. So he sent emissaries, calling both Teruman Deïni and Teruman Wenda to Mount Éthel. As it was an honor to be called to Tryma's own Hall, both Deïni and Wenda agreed to come, although the purpose of this audience was a mystery to them both. Likewise, neither knew that the other had also been called.

According to the design of Tryma, they did not chance to meet upon the trail to the Hall: Wenda was welcomed first, and Deïni was escorted to the place several hours later. When Deïni was brought in her eyes fell upon Wenda, and she frowned, and turned to go, saying, "Why have you brought me here to see this faithless wench?"

Tryma held her back, and said, "You must not leave. It would be an insult to your host to turn your back before you have enjoyed his hospitality. Besides, there is something I want you both to see, and it is best you see it together."

So Deïni reluctantly returned into the Hall, and greeted Wenda coldly.

"Come with me," Tryma said. "We will sit down together to eat and to talk. There is another party who shall join us, as well, and I think you shall find his company most intriguing."

So they came in, and entering the banquet hall of that house they found there awaiting their arrival a Sorite, dressed incongruously in an embroidered robe like Tryma's own. For a moment they were both taken aback by the oddity of this sight, but the Sorite seemed comfortable in their presence, well-prepared to greet them, bowing politely and addressing them with all the formalities of their own kind. "I must apologize for the shock," he said wryly, "but this was Tryma's idea of a surprise. You'll have to forgive us." He introduced himself as Diatron, the disciple of Tryma, and he spoke with them civilly and fluently, so that his manners could hardly be discerned from those of the Terumani themselves.

They sat down together and shared their meal. At Tryma's urging they discussed many things, and sat for hours together at table. Both Deïni and Wenda could not help but to observe how articulately this Sorite expressed himself and his sentiments, nor could they miss noting his depth of knowledge and wisdom. Their astonishment at this growth and refinement went beyond measure.

At last Diatron stood up from the table and bowed. "I believe it is time for me to excuse myself," he said with a courteous nod. "Tryma, I think, would like to be permitted a few words alone with his guests."

When he had departed Wenda spoke first, saying, "What you have done here is extraordinary! Ologéo, and all the Terumani, should be made to know of this accomplishment."

Even Deïni admitted in a flush, "You have indeed done a marvel."

Tryma shook his head, "Not I, but you. Both of you together have brought this about. I have been little more than the catalyst."

Deïni and Wenda glanced at one another quickly, and Deïni said, "I do not understand."

Tryma sighed. "I have merely demonstrated, through the person of Diatron, what you have already brought about."

When they still indicated that they did not grasp his meaning he sat them down once more and expounded to them, saying, "I began this thing many years ago, for it was my vision which sent the two of you off together on your quest. Perhaps it is only meet that I should hope to bring it to a fitting end.

"Now look." He waved a hand in the direction of Diatron's chamber. Addressing Deïni he said, "It is true that the deïnings were your own special gift to Soria. We have all been enriched by their presence. But I see clearly now that they were brought into this land not only as a blessing to us, but that their kind might receive a gift themselves. It is by your hand, Deïni, that they were restored to this world, where they might gain the gift they were owed, the gift that Wenda has bestowed on them.

"More than this, I see now that you were more than prescient, Deïni. As I recall, you once questioned whether our own kind might have an as yet undiscovered purpose. Now a new and greater purpose is given to all the terumani. We are no longer merely caretakers of lands and properties, but we are the guardians and guides of souls equal to our own. I think no greater purpose could we have achieved! And we owe it to the two of you, and the gifts you have brought. Both of you played your parts. Neither of you could have achieved this purpose on your own."

When Tryma had finished his speech, Deïni turned to Wenda and squinted. "I don't suppose there's any chance you could forgive me for my coldness?"

Wenda held back a sob. "Of course! If you can forgive me for acting rashly without first considering your feelings?"

Deïni shrugged. "I suppose so."

Wenda ran to her and threw her arms around her neck. "We must always be friends, Deïni!" she said.

Deïni rolled her eyes but smiled. "Yes, I suppose we must, at that." Thus were Deïni and Wenda reconciled at last.

Tryma then charged them to return to Rhotiéstir, and to make this matter known to Phactorias, and to Storeia, and to the rest of the Terumani.

As for Diatron the Sorite, his wisdom would become famous throughout the north, both among the terumani and among the Sorites themselves. It would come to pass that the Sorites would make pilgrimage to Mount Éthel for guidance in difficult times, and for enlightenment of their questions, and for foretellings when the paths of the future were clear to be read.

Ologéo wagged his head when he learned of it, thinking it foolishness to impute wisdom and foresight to the Sorites, as it were to simple beasts. But the abilities and capacities of the Sorites could no longer be denied, and many began to fall away from his party at that time, and to take on the tasks of inspiring and aiding the Sorites.

So despite Ologéo's complaints the Sorites continued to expand in discernment and knowledge. The line of the Sorites prospered and flourished, and the vale of the Pillow soon grew too strait for them. They spread out from thence, and generations passed, and they filled all the country of Niyarc and Vordót. Wherever they went in the land, their children had the gift of speech, and they proved themselves clever beyond all other mortal creatures.

THE TRAGEDY OF ERESCAL

Among the Terumani who inhabited Niyarc in those days was one Teruman Reinodas, a neighbor of Teruman Phreïs. Teruman Reinodas was of the camp of Ologéo, and was cold towards Phreïs and Storeia. He lived reclusively in his own Hall, not desiring the company of his neighbors in the land. This Teruman Reinodas had a son, by the name of Erescal. Erescal was young in the land, of the generation of Wenda and Dôni.

Erescal was an admirer of Ologéo and of Deïni, and had taken their side in the division over the speech of the Sorites. For though he had no great love for the deïnings, he burned with jealousy concerning Wenda, for many of the Ádolthi praised her and her work mightily. Erescal was ambitious, desirous of adulation, and it goaded him that Wenda, who had spoiled the deïnings and imposed lunacy into Soria, should have such praise while he himself remained obscure. He grew to despise the Sorites, wishing them nothing but trouble, and he followed the leading of Ologéo not only in avoiding them at all costs, but in harassing them when they could not be avoided. For some of the Sorites had begun to build homes in the vicinity of the Terumani, living alongside them and even communing with them as neighbors and peers.

More than many others of the Ádolthi, Erescal was insubordinate and emotional, and at length it came into his heart to devise an act greater even than that of Wenda, and so to put her in her place.

Erescal had his own Hall in the highlands of Batack overlooking the vale of the River Galdan: this Hall he had built with his own hands and craft, distant from the Hall of his father in Niyarc. He had named it Lapaz, which means the Playground, for there he had first gone to escape the watching eyes of his father Reinodas, when in his earlier youth he desired freedom to follow his own pursuits. It was a pleasant place of mud-brown brick and stone, built along the north face of a gentle slope, with several large courtyards, and open fields where he would practice at various sports with his friends: for he often received visitors there from among his cohorts. He spent many days away from his father Reinodas in this hall, sharing it often with Sestrel the daughter of Teruman Parintës, who was his intimate and partner. His friend and cohort Buleos also came to Lapaz often, and had his own chambers within that Hall.

After the debate concerning the Sorites had died down, Erescal fretted that no decision had been made, and that the Sorites continued to thrive and spread. So he had taken himself off to Lapaz, and hidden himself away. He sequestered himself there in an inner chamber of Lapaz, deep in study. For many weeks he brooded alone.

Sestrel and Buleos were residing in their own homes in Vordót, and Erescal had sent them no word or message for many days. So Sestrel went to the house of Buleos and said to him, "I have seen nothing of Erescal for all this time, and do not know what has become of him."

"He is indignant over the state of the Sorites, and broods in anger concerning Wenda," Buleos said. "But he cannot hide himself away forever. Let us go down to the Playground to see if perhaps he is lurking there."

Sestrel agreed to this, and together they traveled down to Batack, and arrived at length at Lapaz.

Erescal received them into the Hall, and he welcomed them cooly. He gave them chambers in which to reside. But he did not explain himself, and remained aloof, deep in private thought and conniving in his study. At last Sestrel conspired together with Buleos and said, "We must go together and confront him. He is moody and troubled, and I am concerned he may act against his own benefit."

So the two of them sought him out in one of his inner chambers, and Buleos said, "What is it that consumes your thoughts? It seems we have hardly spoken with you since we arrived here, for many days now, and you worry us."

Now Erescal had been considering his course for all this time, and he decided at last to reveal his plans to them. So he said, "You are my closest cohorts. Can you be trusted to keep a confidence?"

"We can," Sestrel insisted. "Only tell us what possesses your mind."

So Erescal confided, "I have in mind to do a work more illustrious than that of that wench Wenda. If I can accomplish my goal, we shall have honor exceeding hers, and cut down her pride. Even Ologéo himself shall extol my work."

Sestrel also shared his jealousy of Wenda, and she continuously inflamed his mind with thoughts of rivalry. So she said eagerly, "Tell me what this is you have devised! If what you plan is possible, I shall happily follow you in this endeavor!" Buleos also agreed at once, for he revered Erescal and was ever anxious to please him.

Erescal said, "I will explain it all when the time is right, but first I shall need the cooperation of others. What I have in mind to do cannot be done alone. It will take more than the three of us. The more we shall include, the greater will be my victory."

So Buleos said, "Then let us go out to our cohorts and companions, and recruit allies. I can assure you, there are many who would happily knock Wenda off her pedestal over what she has done to the deïnings."

Erescal replied, "We must be cautious. I would not boast openly before I have succeeded, lest we look the fool and Wenda's glory shine greater than ever. We must act in secret. Only when I have succeeded can we speak openly on the matter."

"Well enough," said Sestrel. "Then we shall choose our allies discreetly. But allies we shall have!""

To this Erescal agreed.

So the three of them, Erescal along with Buleos and Sestrel, went out from Lapaz, the Hall of Erescal, and returned into Vordót. They went about the country visiting the houses and Halls of the Terumani, speaking privately with their companions—the Terumani of their own generation, those of the Terumani who had been born within the land of Soria. Above all they sought out those who disliked Wenda for what she had done with the deïnings, engaging their displeasure to entice them into Erescal's confidence. Erescal whispered to them, "Come to me, to my Hall hidden in Batack, away from the eyes of our elders, who have blithely permitted the disgrace of Wenda. Together we shall do a work so great that Wenda shall seem a mere novice in comparison."

Thus they secretly recruited a party of supporters. Erescal was prominent among his peers, handsome, charming, and popular, and he spoke with a smooth voice of authority: Many were thus enticed to join him in his secret work.

Among these was also Jeïnaric the son of Phreïs. In those days Jeïnaric was yet young, and had not yet received any authority or notoriety in Soria, but he was well-liked by the Ádolthi. Jeïnaric was no friend of Erescal, yet they had sat together under the tutelage of Ologéo in Liaibíri. When Sestrel approached him, both Erescal and Buleos demurred, saying, "Can this one be trusted? He is a son of Phreïs, and wishes to ingratiate himself with the elders of our Kindred."

Sestrel defended him, saying, "Jeïnaric is an admirer of Ologéo, and he prized the deïnings greatly before Wenda gave them speech. Although he has not spoken openly against Wenda or her accomplishment, he has not spoken in her defense, and it is well known that he hungers for the praise of Ologéo." Erescal and Buleos therefore gave in and took him as an ally. Others, also, from among their companions, Sestrel defended against their prejudices.

When Erescal had called them all together, and they had come to him in his Hall in Batack, Erescal said to them, "Join me in this work I am devising, and we shall obtain glory unrivaled. Should we succeed we shall earn the praise of Ologéo, and of Deïni,[1] and of my father Reinodas: as well as the praise of all those who did not esteem the abomination of the Sorites. Even the faction of Storeia will have to respect our cunning and great skills."

1 It is possible this tale fits into the chronology before Tryma had reconciled Deïni to the Sorites.

So his assembly asked, "What is this work you intend, and how can we be of help in it?"

Erescal said to them, "I shall tell you all. But first you must swear to secrecy until we have finished, come success or failure." So they swore to him.

Then Erescal said, "I shall enter the minds of each of us, and bind us all together into a common mind, as the mind of a single individual. We shall perceive one another's thoughts without words, that we all might think as one in full accord. So my mind might be in you all, and you all shall be in me. So much greater than speech will this accomplishment be, that there will be nothing too hard for us to accomplish; for we shall share our knowledge not with the imperfect instrument of mere words, but we might think and act as one entity. So unparalleled will this work be that all the Terumani will honor us and jealously desire this new gift we devise."

Thus his companions were beguiled, for Erescal spoke cunningly. Few perceived that in this plan he sought only glory for himself.

Some of his companions, however, became afraid at these words, and among these was Jeïnaric the son of Phreïs, but when they had announced their misgivings Erescal constrained them to remain, saying, "You have sworn yourselves to secrecy. Only abide here until the work is done, lest any go home and reveal this plan before the project is completed." So Jeïnaric and the others who would not submit to the plan agreed to this request out of respect. Erescal gave them a room in his Hall, that they might remain in the house at Lapaz while he and his remaining confederates attempted his work.

But Buleos said to Erescal in private, "Did I not say they could not be trusted? These cowards may flee to their homes, and your plans shall be revealed before the time."

Erescal agreed, saying, "Your shrewdness is clear. We must lock the doors of their chamber that they may not leave. But my own powers of binding are not so great as those of Sestrel, and it is at her word that many of these spineless toads are here at all. Let us compel her to place charms of binding on the chamber, that they might not depart."

So the two of them, Erescal and Buleos, went to Sestrel and demanded her attention to the matter. Sestrel's devotion to Erescal was great, so she agreed. When the dissenters had settled into their chamber, therefore, she put forth the strength of her craft, and barred the door that none might exit. Nevertheless she became suspicious at this request, and worried that they were carrying matters too far.

It was not long before Erescal's friends discovered that they were confined, and they were wroth "Why have you put restraints on us that we might not leave," they complained. "We have treated you only with respect and courtesy!"

Erescal spoke softly to them, saying, "Be patient yet a short while, and do not be angry with me for my precautions: for even well-intentioned words may let secrets slip, should you return to your homes before the time. Rest assured, that when I am through you shall surely be sent forth speedily as witnesses of my success."

Sestrel was ashamed of her part in this matter, but she could not bring herself to defy Erescal. So she saw to it that the dissenters in his Hall were provided with every comfort, and were treated generously: nevertheless they became as captives in Lapaz.

There remained twelve of the youth of the Terumani in his cadre, male and female, who had been born in the land of Soria. To these remaining confederates Erescal then said, "Let us swear oath now to one another, to complete this task together." So all swore their fealty to Erescal. They went with him, ready to open their minds to his delving.

Now the Terumani have influence over the mortal creatures of Soria, but entering deeply into the minds of their fellows, of the Terumani themselves, had never been attempted. So Erescal said to them, "Let us go out from this house, and find deïnings in the country, and bring them here to serve as our guides. Thus we can practice and perfect our work in their minds. In this way we might map the paths of understanding which we must follow."

So they all went into the country round about Lapaz, and each of them found their own subject, whom they carried by deceit or by force into the Hall of Erescal, to serve as subjects for his experiment.

Then Erescal set to work. Erescal expended himself zealously in his endeavor; probing, testing, weaving and re-weaving into the simple mind of his deïning. He found his patterns, and planned his course, and the mind of the deïning was subjected to the control of Erescal.

When he had searched and practiced long and diligently, Erescal felt he knew the path to chart, so he instructed each of his companions how they might also enter into the minds of their own deïnings and uncover the course and pathways of sharing and control. Thus together Erescal and all of his companions practiced and learned for many days together, until all agreed they knew his design; but the deïnings, their subjects, were fearful and bewildered by this probing, and whined whenever their masters came near.

Much time passed in this way, and the companions who had refused Erescal began to chafe at their confinement. Sestrel herself said to Erescal, "The friends and parents of these dissenters will surely soon come seeking them, for they have been absent now for many weeks. Should we not give them leave to return home, before we are discovered?"

Buleos, however, said, "This will not do. Our peril is greater if we release them than if we hold them here."

Erescal considered the question, and at last he said, "We have practiced and learned enough. The time is come, and I think we are all ready to complete our design."

Sestrel replied, "I can speak only for myself, but I am as yet uncertain of the way. Though I see the paths and patterns of your designs, I do not feel strong enough to control my course." Others of his troop agreed as well, asking for yet more time and practice.

But Erescal had grown impatient. "You have sworn oath to follow this path to the end, and you cannot break an oath. If any among you is yet fearful to proceed, let him join with the others of my guests until we have finished." Saying this he waved dismissively toward the locked chamber where the dissenters waited.

All of his companions then agreed, saying, "We are ready. Only tell us now what to do, if you know."

"Do not give in to fear," Erescal said. "Your minds shall touch my own, and I shall lead us in the way."

Erescal then brought them into an inner chamber of Lapaz. He darkened the room, and lit a fragrant incense which conditioned their minds to open to his influence, as they had all done as well with their deïnings. "You have all practiced alone with your own subjects," Erescal said. "Now however we shall all join together. As you have probed the minds of your deïnings, so now probe the minds of one another, and seek my presence in your own minds." He bade them all to sit together in a circle, covering their eyes with their hands that they might shut out all distractions.

Erescal said, "If you will now open your minds to my probing, I shall guide us all. You shall perceive my own will encroaching on yours, but do not be afraid. When I have finished we will all think as one, and know one another more completely than any yet has imagined." So he induced the twelve companions to submit to his designs. Now he secretly hoped not merely to commune, but to command: In his pride Erescal held that he alone had the strength of mind to bind them all together under his own will.

Thus he wrested his way into the minds of his friends, and of Buleos his cohort, and Sestrel his partner, and he set his plans into action.

At first the going seemed clear. With a sense of elation Erescal began to perceive the thoughts and emotions of his companions. He set to work, trying to tie the paths of their speech and understanding into his own. As for his companions, each of them found themselves giving in to his will, yielding their minds over to his control.

The deeper Erescal delved, however, the more manifest it became that his tests and his probing had led him astray, and his impatience had deceived him. For they had all practiced on the unreasoning deïnings, and the paths of the mind they had learned did not lead to reason or communication. So the very paths of understanding at length began to forsake them: Rather than creating a new and wordless connection from mind to mind as he had dreamed, Erescal discovered a fog that grew and consumed, and could not be thwarted. The fog swelled, and he and his companions began to lose the capacity of their own speech, and no surpassing work of Erescal's replaced it.

Sestrel and the others began to moan in fear, unable to withdraw from the experiment or from Erescal's control, and Erescal dimly realized that he had lost his way. Seeing this, he exerted himself yet more to rein in the fog. Yet the more he tried to control it, the greater the blackness and emptiness that spread throughout the souls of his companions. He gazed upon Sestrel, and saw nothing but blankness and fear in her unseeing eyes.

His misgivings then gave way to panic. Turning back from his path, he tried now to extract himself. But he had nothing to replace what he had taken from the minds of his friends but the deepest of his own motives: his selfish pride, his bitterness and jealousy, and his ignorant ambitions. His own mind, as well, he felt slipping into blackness as he melded with the ruined minds of his companions. He broke free at last, and all fell to the ground in exhaustion. They rose slowly to their feet, their self-will their own once more. But now they stared about the chamber with feral eyes, and could not know where they were, or what they had been. Erescal had gone too far, and his craft had failed him in the end: so he destroyed the minds of his friends and much of his own mind.

Thus it came to pass that Erescal and his subjects lost their own power of speech, becoming as unreasoning beasts, with feeble minds barely above those of the deïnings whom they had trained upon, yet brutish and self-seeking. Little was left to them but the corruptions of the heart of Erescal: a hatred of the Sorites and distrust of the Ádolthi, and of all things orderly and beautiful.

So Erescal and his cohorts became mad, having no longer the reason of the Terumani nor any love of beauty or craft: and in their madness they began to tear down Lapaz, the Hall of Erescal, the Playground, leaving it in ruin. Erescal himself was the first to fall into delirium, in his rage and confusion casting down the brazier in which the incense burned. Then others of the confederacy began to stir as well, tearing the hangings from the walls, and the doors from their hinges, breaking and beating them into scrap and rubble. Hammers and clubs they wrested from the broken furnishings of that Hall, and turned at last upon the very walls themselves.

From within the chamber of their confinement, Jeïnaric and those with him heard the howling of the Terumani whom Erescal had debased, and they became afraid. Jeïnaric then said, "It is clear that something has gone terribly wrong with the designs of Erescal. Perhaps our friends need our aid, but whatever this disaster, we surely must now escape this chamber on our own." So they exerted their powers together upon the seals of the chamber, and at last their efforts broke the bindings of Sestrel, and they freed themselves. Perhaps even then they would have failed were it not for the ravings of Erescal and his companions, who themselves were tearing at the very substance of the Hall.

That which the companions of Jeïnaric beheld when they came forth turned their hearts cold with terror and revulsion. Erescal and all his confederates lurched about as maddened beasts, with no light of recognition in their eyes. Jeïnaric and his cohorts tried to calm them and quiet their minds, but their speech and craft were of no avail. Try what they might, the followers of Erescal could not be brought back from their madness. With what rude speech remained to them, they mocked Jeïnaric and his companions, treating them as cowards, and they provoked them into brawling. Then the companions of Erescal took up arms, raising them against their own kind, and their own friends, and falling upon them in mindless fury. These then feared for their lives, and escaped, fleeing into the forests of Batack to hide from their pursuers.

In shame and horror at what had happened, many feared to return to their homes. Jeïnaric, however, returned north to Niyarc, to the Hall Timotéa, the house of his father Phreïs. There he bowed his head in chagrin and reported all that had happened.

"You have sworn yourself foolishly," Phreïs scolded. "Great harm could have been prevented had you behaved with honor. It would have been better to stand and oppose wrong, even without victory, than to run from a fight." But he shook his head and did not punish him, for Jeïnaric had at least preserved himself from the horror which had transpired.

Then Phreïs called upon Reinodas, and told him the news he had learned. Reinodas denied it coldly and would not believe, saying "Your son is lying."

"Perhaps he has been misled," Phreïs said, "but I think we should go together out to Batack, to the hall of Erescal, to see for ourselves. I fear something abominable has transpired in this land."

"I have heard nothing from my son for many days," Reinodas agreed grudgingly. "Perhaps it is time to pay him a visit at the Playground, if only to prove you wrong."

So they followed the pathways into Batack and took the way to Lapaz. When they arrived at the site they were appalled at what their eyes beheld. The hall of Erescal lay in ruin: even the walls were riven and the roof itself demolished, and everything of craft and beauty had been defiled and broken. They found Erescal and his subjects roaming about, without recognition of their elders, eating whatever vile thing they could catch in the wild. Then

Reinodas saw the corruption of his son, and the terrible thing he had done. He became very silent, and sat down upon the earth, and stared unseeing at the ruins of the Hall.

Phreïs then called for Bël, and he sent word to the Terumani, the elders, and the parents of the companions of Erescal, saying, "A hideous evil has befallen the land of Soria, and our own folk. We must gather these corrupted youth back to our custody by force, to see whether we might repair the damage done."

So gathering together in strength, the elders of the Terumani subdued them. They brought them back together into Niyarc, to the house of Vélopar. Vélopar then scraped from the mountains a stone-walled ward, very strong, and bound with powerful charms of binding: there they kept the ruined children of the Terumani until they could discern what might be done with them.

Great was the consternation of the Terumani at this time, for no such thing had been done among them since they had come into the land. Many lamented the ruin of these youthful terumani, wondering what might be done, and whether they might be saved.

The parents of the ruined companions of Erescal then called the Ádolthi together, gathering to the house of Vélopar all who could be compelled to come. Putting aside all differences, they called also for Storeia and Wenda, for even those who had opposed Wenda had to recognize that she had proven herself great in the crafts of speech and thought. Even Ologéo would not disapprove of this course. For many days they strove together in their work, deftly weaving their compassionate craft into the minds of Erescal and his companions. But even these mighty ones exhausted their strength at last, and could do no more. No one of them, nor all their strength together, was able to heal the minds of the allies of Erescal. They could accomplish little more than to restore a smattering of speech, rude and vile though it had become.

When many months had passed and all hope had failed, Vélopar called the Terumani to pass judgment, saying, "These children of our race are broken beyond repair. They are mad and wild, having become as beasts. What then shall we do with them? I do not want them here on my estate, but they are no longer fit to live among us in our Halls. They violently attack all who come near, having no fealty to any but themselves."

Some had said they should be cared for in their own Halls, in the Halls of their parentage, as befitting those who are ill. Others had thought to create for them a special hall of their own, where they might be attended to. But Reinodas had watched his son carefully and strictly, along with his companions. "Alas!" he said, "We have cared for these children for many days here in the house of Vélopar. They languish here, like animals in a cage."

Parintës the father of Sestrel then said, "Reinodas speaks the truth. They know us no longer, and they want nothing of us but to be let alone and wander the wilds like the deïnings. With what clumsy speech she possesses, she who was once my daughter begs daily for her freedom, to return to the forest where we found them. So say they all."

Now although the tribe of Erescal had lost their former estate, they retained at least the capacity of beasts. They were therefore able to hunt on their own, to forage, to form packs, and to fend for themselves in the wild places of the land.

So it seemed to all that this was perhaps the proper and fitting environment for them: a place where their burning brains might cool and be at rest. All those of the Terumani whose children had fallen into corruption agreed with this plan, for it seemed the merciful and kind thing to do for their ruined children. But it broke their hearts to do so. Reinodas gave Erescal his freedom, and Erescal with his allies betook themselves to Batack, far from the Halls of the Terumani.

This perhaps was a mistake on the part of the Terumani, for no good has come of this debased and wicked folk in all the long ages of the world.

So it was that Erescal and his twelve companions became corrupted, and went out into the world. There they mingled with the deïnings, for they were now much alike. The children of that race were tall and ponderous: greater than the deïnings, though lesser than the mightiest apparitions of the Terumani.[2] These also passed on their corruption in mind and form: in appearance they are as imitations of Terumani, but lumbering and vile in their manners, and hideous to behold.

From Batack this folk spread abroad into all of Soria, though as the years progressed their progeny diverged: some lines regained some small portion of their senses, while others grew yet more corrupt: The lineage of Batack is always violent and murderous, while in other places they are often merely stupid and foul. But in all places they are to be avoided, for they are selfish, and scorn the speaking Kindreds and terumani alike.

Yet this one mercy results from their mingling with the deïnings, that their lives in this world are shortened, so their corruption would not last the ages of the Terumani: their years became few, as the years of the other creatures and Kindreds of the land. And who knows, but perhaps when they pass from this world, they are freed from their corruption in that realm.

These are the Erescali, the Giants, who have plagued the speaking Kindreds of Soria ever since, living as if half Teruman and half beast. From the wardhouse of Vélopar they spread out into the world, crossing Vordót into

---

2 The Terumani were evidently able to alter their dimensions as needed, though their normal appearance in Soria approximated that of the Sorites.

Batack, and thence into the distant mountains, and wherever such dark creatures might hide and conceive mischief in their darkened minds. They have been a plague to the children of Sorios for all the long ages of their endurance.

OLOGÉO AND DYNIS

Teruman Ologéo the Proud often walks throughout Soria, investigating the realm; in ancient days there was much to learn, and to this day he is forever eager to unveil anything new and undiscovered, for he values knowledge and reason above all things. No mystery is beyond his pursuit and his probing, and though he does not know all, he always strives to learn more. His breadth of knowledge therefore is great: because of this he is the most proud of the Terumani, and he loves to be admired.

Ologéo had a great Hall in Vordót in the north, which he named Liaibíri, and he dwelt there together with his mate, Teruman Cosimë. It was not his only Hall, but Liaibíri was his favorite, and he lavished attention upon it; it was the greatest of the Halls of the Terumani. But he often departed for many days at a time, leaving his home and departing from Cosimë, to seek out new mysteries, to stimulate the cravings of his mind.

Now it came into his heart to make a study of Batack, the great forest which filled the plateau south of Vordót. The region was dark, and full of secrets, and there was much to learn and discover in that place. Discovery and the solving of mysteries was the passion of Ologéo, and he determined to know all that could be learned of the great forest. So he left Liaibíri and journeyed down to that country, bringing with him those devices and trappings that he always used to investigate and to record his discoveries, and he began to walk about the paths and hidden places of the forest.

One day while exploring the deepness of the wooded valleys he spied Dynis the nymph walking in the dappled light of the woods. Now Dynis was comely, more radiant than many of the Ádolthi themselves, and her motion was like the swaying of delicate branches in the breeze, and lovely to behold. She was tall and lithe, and strong in the manner of the nymphs, with shining hair of rich green like the leaves of the cypress, tinged with silver, which she bound with a circlet of ivy; she wore a diaphanous gown as of woven moss which flowed around her limbs like gossamer as she walked.

Now it was the practice of Ologéo to go about his business always in secret, hidden by the special arts of the terumani, lest he disturb the very things he was attempting to observe and study; Ologéo's skills of concealment are great, even among the terumani. So when he came upon the nymph she was unaware of his presence. He thought it best to ignore her and continue with his own studies, but her presence nearby distracted him, and he was drawn to stop and watch her. He did not wish to disturb her in her rounds, so he did not reveal himself.

When the afternoon was spent, Dynis moved on from that place, and he looked after her in wonder. But he restrained himself and continued on his own way, for Ologéo told himself, "She is but a nymph, and there is nothing new to learn here."

But the next day also, as Ologéo went about the woods of Batack in secret, once again he came upon Dynis as she walked in the coolness of the morning. Although again he tried to go about his own business, he found he could not ignore her. It entered his mind to speak with her, but he was proud and would not have her mistake him for a common swain, so he continued to remain hidden. At length he went away again, and she went on her way, not knowing of his presence.

Among the nymphs Dynis has a great domain, and she watches and cares for trees and the woods along all the borders of Niyarc from the Sea to the Rode. She walked throughout that country, always about her business. So it came to pass that now many times Ologéo happened upon her in the woods and forest. Her form and her grace captivated him, so that whenever he came upon her, he found he could not turn away his eyes from following her. But likewise he was too abashed to reveal himself, for the longer this went on, the more unseemly it felt to do so.

When at last he returned to Liaibíri, he found that the nymph was still on his mind. So after a spell he decided to return to Batack, for it was true, after all, that there was still much to learn in that country, and he had every reason to go and continue his investigations. It was little accident that while in that country again, he often came upon Dynis on her rounds.

So it was that months went by. Ologéo would return home to Liaibíri, then would return again alone to continue his studies in Batack. At length he found that he would come down to Batack intentionally to seek out the nymph, and to find her on her walks. Finding her he would pause to watch her, always with reverence and delight, but never revealing himself, and always dismissing his motives, for, he thought, he did her no harm thereby. Each time he went on his way, telling himself he would not return again.

Yet again and again he did return, as if under a spell. Months passed in this manner.

At last he could bear the preoccupation no longer. "What harm would it be to make her acquaintance?" he thought to himself; so he began to ponder how he might now reveal himself without appearing foolish before her. He said to himself, "Surely the nymph shall disdain me for my effrontery and boldness. I have played a fool in pursuing her these many months without her knowledge."

So he thought, "I shall leave gifts for the nymph, such things as she loves and delights in. Perhaps one day she shall welcome her devotee, but even if not, at least she might be pleased, and that is enough."

He had by then discovered many of her likes and fancies, and knew as well many of her paths and resting places. So he went go back to Liaibíri, and in his own chambers he made beautiful gifts to please her. Then he began to travel to the woods of Batack, and seek out her whereabouts, and he would go privately to the place he guessed she would rest in the evening: for Dynis had many redoubts throughout Batack. There at the threshold he would leave a single gift each time: beautiful flowers and orchids from his own gardens at Liaibíri; a silver pitcher for her watering; a living broach of holly for her gown; sandals of finest poplar fitted with straps of living vines. He did this for many days, and departed, and did not appear before her.

Each of these things Dynis discovered in the evenings, for coming in to settle from her labors and to rest, she would arrive at her wonted camps. Ologéo at times remained to watch in secret, long enough to discern whether she might be pleased with his offerings. As for Dynis, puzzled though she was, the nymph smiled at each gift, and whenever Ologéo saw it, the brightness of her countenance gladdened his heart. But Dynis wondered who in all of Soria might be fawning thus upon her.

Matters went on in this way for some months, Dynis always smiling with pleasure at the mysterious gifts of Ologéo: In those days the terumani were always honorable and without offense, so although she was perplexed, she had no cause to fear. Beyond this, the attentions of her admirer were flattering, however mystifying.

But at last a day came when Dynis found a gift at her threshold, and she did not accept it. Rather, she stood resolutely before her place, and stomped a foot and said, "It is clear that one among the terumani is striving to win my favor. Whether it be spright or nymph I know not, and what might be the purpose I cannot say. But this game has played its course, and I shall not accept another gift unless it be given me face to face."

Ologéo had remained nearby that evening to see how she might accept the gift, and this reaction now disheartened him. So at last he decided he must come forth and reveal himself. Appearing in her presence, he said to her, "My pardons, your grace. I have no purpose, unless it be to delight one so comely and precious as Dynis the nymph. If my gifts have given her joy and placed a smile upon her lips, then the world has been brightened thereby. Is that not purpose enough?"

Dynis did not know who he was, but she knew at once that he was of the Ádolthi, among the greatest of the Terumani that dwelt in Soria. She drew back afraid, and said, "What have I to do with the great ones of the Ádolthi, for I am but a nymph, who cares for little but the verdure of my domain: I have no great powers to merit the courtesies of the high ones."

But Ologéo said, "Yet mighty are the powers of your charm, for you have subdued the heart of Ologéo himself. Do you not know that I am Ologéo, among the greatest of the Ídolthi?"

Ologéo's reputation was well-known among all of the terumani, and all in Soria knew of him. But he is known among the terumani as cold and proud, and Dynis feared him. For she is warm and humble, always seeking ways to serve the lesser nymphs and næads in her domain, and the cool heart of Ologéo is not of like kind with her own. So she said, "Forgive me, my lord, but I shall go on my way. Surely my humble company shall be a disappointment to one such as you."

So he pleaded her pardon, but she would not be swayed, and he left at last, dispirited and disappointed. "It is as I feared," he said to himself, "and I am unwelcome. Nevertheless, one so altogether lovely cannot be so easily dismissed."

So she remained on his mind. It was not long, therefore, before he returned to her country, and he was moved to seek her out. When he had found her, he produced for her a small gift, merely a cluster of gladiolas which the nymph loved. Laying this before her he said, "You need not commune with me, but you cannot prevent me from leaving you gifts as I see fit." Then he bowed and left her, and she smiled inwardly.

So Ologéo continued to bring tokens for her: small gifts merely to please her passing fancies. At times he came to her openly, and always showed himself courteous and ingratiating in her presence. At other times he would leave tokens for her in secret, as in the past. But always he demonstrated respect and blameless propriety. Thus her heart began to warm to him.

Among the many redoubts of Dynis was a certain grove of birch trees, in the hill country near the seashore on the east of Batack. This grove was of exceptional beauty, with ancient and venerable trees, smooth of trunk and limb, and dappled with golden light. In its midst was a moss-covered hollow, surrounded by fern, and by bright, thornless holly. This grove she called Dapplewood for the beauty of its dancing lights, and it was among the favorites of all her abodes. In it were many trees which she loved as if they were family, and many of them had names of their own, for Dynis was a wood-nymph, of course, and the trees are like children to such folk.

It came to pass one day that Dynis returned to this abode to discover an ailment in Dapplewood: The leaves of many of her birches had turned white as with a frost. She tried to care for them to restore their health, but soon the leaves began to shrivel and fall, and the trees would die or grow sickly. This malady spread from one tree to another, so that her grove lost the beauty of its light, and the magic of the grove was ruined.

Try as she might, the powers of Dynis were unable to undo the damage of this blight, and many good trees began to fade. She feared for them, and her heart became forlorn, for she was unable to aid them.

Now Ologéo one day coming to call upon her beheld the darkness of her countenance, and perceived that she was dispirited. So he said to her, "What can be the concern which so troubles the heart of the lovely Dynis? One so gracious should not be tormented thus without solace."

Dynis said to him, "Behold, the birch trees of Dapplewood my abode are stricken by a wasting blight, and I am unable to aid them. I have failed in my charge as a dræad of the forest, and am unworthy of my calling. And the worst of it is that the trees which I love shall perish, and there is naught I can do to save them."

In saying this a tear fell from her eye, and Ologéo was so stricken with compassion that he swore at once to aid her. He said, "The occupation of the dræads is to love and care for the growth in their domain: This have you done in overabundant measure. You have not at all failed your charge. We may labor and strive, but chance may determine the end of our labors. Nevertheless, I myself have great powers to solve many mysteries of the land wherein we dwell, and I shall surely do all in my power to restore your subjects to their fulness of strength if I might."

Thus Dynis took the hand of Ologéo for the first time, and looked him pleading in the eyes, and the cold heart of Ologéo the Proud was softened.

So Ologéo applied his diligent arts, and for many days he dwelt in that country, looking deeply into the blighted wood and uncovering every secret of the malady. Dynis stayed by his side in all that time, working with him as she might, and meeting his needs as he worked. Now the powers of Ologéo to penetrate the secrets of living things far exceed those of any others of the Terumani, and no one better could Dynis have discovered to seek the causes of this blight. Moreover Ologéo, perhaps alone among the Terumani, is able to manipulate the inner workings of life, to alter and change their nature to his designs. Thus at last he uncovered a cause of the withering death, and he himself devised a cure to destroy this wasting frost. So Ologéo set to work for many days, treating the blighted woods, until the grove had recovered and grew healthy and green once more, while Dynis aided him and attended to him.

Then was Dynis truly grateful, and with a wistful smile she said, "Ologéo the Discoverer of Secrets has indeed worked wonders, as if a dræad himself, and brought health and aid where I alone could not."

Thereafter Ologéo spent many days in the woodland of Batack, communing with Dynis and doting on her. For her part, Dynis also grew in her devotion to Ologéo, for the wonder of the work he had done on her behalf. So the two, Ídoleth and dræad, found companionship and warmth in those days.

But Ologéo revealed to none where he went, or with whom he spent his days.

Now in Vordót Ologéo maintained his great Hall of Liaibíri, and there in that Hall he was wont to receive all of the other terumani, high and low, for he had made Liaibíri a place of congress for all. He often received sojourners there, for he loved to dispense knowledge, and to receive the praise of others for the depth and breadth of his studies. Many came to him seeking to learn of the mysteries they encountered in their own domains. There were many rooms in that capacious Hall, for many of the Ádolthi were wont to sojourn there at times, and even to receive visitors of their own. Even Teruman Storeia had chambers in his Hall, which he had given to her: for though Ologéo and Storeia are opposed to one another, she is one of the Ídolthi, equal in stature to Ologéo himself, and they have respect for the status even of their opponents. Liaibíri was open to all, and Ologéo received all who came.

Yet Dynis he would not invite to Liaibíri, for he was embarrassed, and feared the judgements of the other Terumani. Moreover, his heart was kindled with the flush of secrecy.

Therefore Ologéo went into the deepness of Batack, and he found there a green valley of that country, with bones of granite; fern-banked and cloaked in the flowers of spring. There the sun shone like liquid fire on the verdure of the place, and the air was ever sweet with the scent of growing things. He built a Hall of sparkling granite, which he named Denedhros, which means the Enclave. But though he named it as if it were a meeting place, this Hall he revealed to none of the other Terumani, and none were invited to visit there, as they are invited to visit Liaibíri. In this Hall he made a dwelling for himself, that he might live comfortably in Batack, and be near to Dynis in her own domain.

To Dynis alone he revealed the Hall of Denedhros, and when it was finished and he had filled it with light, and had made it a place of beauty, he found Dynis in the forest, and he brought her to his Hall. So she came, and he received her warmly, and he communed with her there.

"This Hall," he said, "I will give to you as your own possession. You may dwell in this place as you wish, and have been granted the power to enter even when I am not here to open the portal for you."

But Dynis was unhappy, and said, "A hall of stone is not fit for a child of the forest. You forget that I am a nymph, and not one of the high ones of the Terumani. The wilds of the land are my home and my domain. I shall sleep in the fern and the fragrant mould of the forest floor, and find rest beneath the leaves of the sycamore."[1]

So she left the hall, and wandered again in the woods and glades of Batack.

Then Ologéo built at Denedhros a garden room, and filled it with all the secret tools of cultivation such as the craft of the dræads required. He made in the room a great window open to the airs of the forest, that the scent of wood and forest floor would fill the airs of that room, and the song of bird and bee would gladden the heart. Around the hall he planted a bright garden. Then he went out again, and he found Dynis walking in the forest, and he brought her back

1 The Sorian sycamore referred to was known for its enormous leaves, which were large enough to use as a blanket. It was one of the most common trees of northwestern Batack, and its leaves were sometimes dried and used as thatch.

again to Denedhros. The garden room he gifted to her, and said, "This shall be your own place, that you might remain here peaceably, and be near."

But after some days Dynis again grew restless, and she said, "Such a place is not fit for a wanderer of wood and meadow. For all this beauty, it is yet enclosed in stone and iron. The coldness of stone chills my soul."

So Dynis left again, and wandered the woods of Batack.

Now Ologéo longed for Dynis, and desired above all to have her near. So he tore down the walls of stone, and he built Denedhros again with walls of living wood, branching and green with foliage. He roofed it over with the breathing branches and boughs of the trees. Dangling orchids he grew there to decorate the halls, and ivy twisted around the pillars of that hall. A font of water sparkled in the atrium into a pool of alabaster.

Then Ologéo went out once again, and found Dynis wandering in the woods and caring for her charges. He brought her back once again home with him to Denedhros, and she came willingly. He showed her the Hall that he had built, and he gave it to Dynis to be her own. So Dynis smiled.

But days passed and Dynis grew restless, for Ologéo wished to spend all his days with her in the Hall of Denedhros and its garden. So Dynis said to him, "It has pleased me to be the object of your devotion, and you have been courteous far beyond your reputation. But I did not ask for a Hall in which to dwell. And in all the days wherein you returned to your home in Liaibíri, did I ever complain that you had not invited me to sojourn with you there? I do not require a home or a hall. I am a dræad, a nymph of the woods, and I am happy when my home is the woods themselves."

Ologéo then said, "Is there more that I might do to make this Hall a home fit for the comeliest of the nymphs? Shall I expand the gardens, or open more windows, or bring in the bees and birds to share your rooms? Whatever you wish, I shall accomplish if the power be in me."

But Dynis said, "You cannot keep me as a trophy in a house, however lovely. Yet you may come and visit me in the woods, if you will, for that will always be my home. And if you ask me to sojourn in your Hall, I may come for a spell. But my home is the wild wood, and that you must accept."

So it came about that for years Ologéo would repair at times to his home in Liaibíri, but his soul was bound to Batack, and he returned there ever and anon. Thus he would spend months at a time in his secret Hall of Denedhros, and Dynis would come to him at times, and gladden his heart. At other times he would go about the woods, watching and admiring her, and giving her aid in her labors. This he accepted at the behest of Dynis, and was content. While Dynis also was pleased with his admiration, and was content.

Yet she could not fully comprehend the mind of Ologéo, for he was ever prideful, and ever curious, delving deep into the minutiae of all that he examined. But Dynis was content to appreciate the broad wonder of the world, and would not spoil the joy and rapture of mystery. So there was ever a barrier between their souls.

Now the comings and goings of Ologéo he hid from the others of the Terumani, and none knew where he went, nor why he spent so much time far from his home in Liaibíri. The Terumani wondered at this mystery, and talked privately among themselves.

So the day came at last when Ologéo returned from his Hall in Denedhros, and Cosimë his spouse confronted him. Stewing in bitterness she said to him, "Once again for many days you have been gone from your home in Liaibíri, and no one knows where you go. What is this mystery and this secret you keep?" For Cosimë had become jealous and suspicious.

Ologéo replied, "I walk in the land, and I walk in the woods of Batack, seeking to learn all that there is to learn of that place. For Batack is the border of Vordót, and it behooves us to know all that we can of the place and its secrets, lest some unknown marvel come from the wood and take us unawares, and disturb our peace."

"Yet never do you reveal the secrets you learn there to the company of the Terumani. It seems to me the only secret in Batack is the one you hide within your own breast."

Thus Ologéo and Cosimë contended one with another. Cosimë would not give up her suspicions. So Ologéo grew morose, and said, "Is it not my calling and my duty to wander, to walk about Soria, and to learn? Would you forbid me from my duty, woman?"

But Cosimë demanded, "But you shall certainly not go again into Batack alone! If these sojourns were of your vocation you could perform them in the open for all to see. But this betrayal shall surely not continue."

So Ologéo brooded in his rooms at Liaibíri, and his thoughts were dark and morose. He refused to receive visitors, and shut himself away from company. Even for Ologéo this seemed out of sorts, so all who frequented that Hall began to wonder at his dispirited mood. He immersed himself in private studies, hoping to keep his mind occupied, but his efforts accomplished little.

At last he could bear his private musings no longer, and he forced himself to a decision. Conferring with no one, he gathered his wits about him, and rose up from his place by night. He departed his house in stealth, and in secret he rushed to Batack.

There he diligently scouted the woods and groves, until he had found Dynis once more, for a plan had come into his heart. So he took her by the hand, and said to the nymph, "Come back with me to the highlands of Niyarc, and I shall build for you there a secret Hall of magnificent grace, like unto our hall Denedhros. I shall outdo it in beauty and tranquility and wealth, and it shall be surrounded by woods. There you can be comfortable, and your soul filled to overflowing. I can provide all things to make you happy. I have the power to conceal it from the eyes of the Terumani, but you will always be close by. In this way none shall miss me when I leave, or have cause for suspicion, and I might see you at our ease."

But Dynis complained, "Would you then imprison me, and hold me as a pretty jewel for your enjoyment? For this is the life into which you ask me to submit. I should surely pine and pass from this world if it were so."

"It is not for myself alone, but for you as well. I may no longer come to see you in Batack, and this fate we must allay. Is not our bond worth saving?"

"But Ologéo, I cannot depart from my domain. I am made for wood and weald, as surely as the Seafolk are made for the sea. Batack is my domain. If I were separated from such country I could not live."

"Then I will risk my honor, and abandon Liaibíri, and come to live at Denedhros."

But Dynis shook her head sadly and touched his arm. "But that must not be," she said, "and this you know as well. You are of the mighty ones of the Ídolthi, and many depend upon your powers, your skills, and your insights. You must not abandon your own realm."

"Then how shall we go on?"

"We must each face our fate and our obligations. The time has come, I think, for us to part ways. Though it is a good thing that Ologéo the Proud has learned a love of beauty and warmth, yet our worlds have no common ground." Gesturing to the forest about them she said, "The world of Dynis is to revel in the dark and secret places of nature, and to enjoy the beauties of their mysteries in simplicity. The world of Ologéo is to unravel all beauty and uncover all secrets, and reveal all to his compatriots among the Ádolthi. But you may never uncover all the secrets of the heart of Dynis, and never should. Moreover, it is not meet that the revealer of secrets should himself walk in secrecy."

So they departed from one another. Ologéo returned in sadness and melancholy to the Hall of Liaibíri in the country of Niyarc. There he nurtured his bitterness for many days, but he left off his dalliance at last.

But Ologéo ever after carried in his heart a warmth for Dynis and for the wooded country of Batack. At times in later years he would sneak away to sit in his Hall Denedhros and pine, until in after ages the Terumani abandoned their Halls, and Denedhros also returned to the woods, and could no longer be distinguished from the forest itself.

THE TRIALS OF SORIOS

1. The Estrangement of Archea

It turned out that the Sorites were not unequivocally benefited by the gift of speech. Even the unspeaking animals will spit and slash at one another betimes, but to have really true and fiery contention, one must have speech.

Speech brings knowledge, accord, and harmony; but disagreement and argument are nourished by it as well. The Terumani who watched over the Sorites were disheartened to discover that rivalries and jealousies, quarrels and clashing, arose among the Sorites. So the great blessing of Wenda was mingled also with burden and trouble.

Not even Sorios was spared this scourge.

After Deïni had become reconciled to Wenda, she returned also to Sorios and Archea, and began to commune with them genially and familiarly. It had soon become clear that both Sorios and Archea, who had received life at the command of Deïni, were not aging as were their children and descendants. They knew their children, and their children's children, and their children also, for many generations. Though they showed outward signs of aging, they retained much of the vigor of their youth.

So Deïni and Wenda together had built them a house of stone on the Shelf, nearly equal to the Halls of the Terumani in comfort, although such trappings and luxuries were denied to the rest of the Sorites. This house was near to the ledge of that plateau, so it commanded a view of the verdant lands of Niyarc below, stretching into the blue haze of the horizon. It was a pleasant place in those days, surrounded by groves of shady trees and scented gardens.

But at last Archea could stand the place no longer. "Let us rise up from this home," she said to Sorios, "and go forth from this country, and see what else might lie beyond the light of our eyes."

"There is nothing to see beyond our country that might please me better than what we have here in our own home." Sorios replied with a satisfied smile. Sorios was content at the Shelf, and loved his home, which they had filled with all manner of comforts. Many children had they raised in that house, and sent on their way: Every corner of the place, and every patch of their gardens, held memories dear and poignant. There he had his family and kindred, and generations of relations dwelt in the vicinity. Also the Terumani were near: Deïni his first guardian and Wenda his benefactor especially, whom he loved, were but a short walk from his own door, down dappled flagstone paths enclosed by tall hedges. They often visited and communed with him there. So he leaned back and said to Archea, "Why should we seek novelties abroad when comforts surround us at hand?"

But Archea sighed in disgust. "The sun rises and sets over the same scenes each day, and the deeds of each day vary little, for year after year. I have grown weary of the days. Many of our children have moved on from our presence, and many have even passed out of the world. The little ones who were our joy in their youth we have seen grow aged and depart this world from before our eyes. The joy of life has wilted in my breast." Thus they argued with one another for many days, and the contention became great between them.

At last Sorios could bear the quarreling no longer, and he submitted to Archea's desire. So he went to Deïni to complain. "Archea will not give me rest while we remain at home in this land," he said. "Soon we must leave this comfortable place and face the hardships of the trail."

Deïni smiled at him patiently. "You must be willing to take on adventures, Sorios," she said, "and not cower away behind walls of familiarity."

"Can you not come with us to be our guide?" he asked. "You have filled her head with tales of the sunny and bright countries of the south. You should guide us there. It is Archea's intent to journey beyond Batack."

Deïni gasped. "You must certainly not travel alone through Batack!" she warned. "There are dangers in that dark wood. The Giants, the ruined children of Erescal, have infested that country, and they hate all your kind. Not to mention the many wild beasts and other dangers of the road. If you go, you must go with a large party for safety."

"Then go with us, and be our guide and protectress," Sorios asked.

Deïni shook her head. "Let me ask my brother Hiren if he would go. He loves adventure, and has never traveled so far from home. He would relish the excursion. I think Archea will not be happy if I attend you, for she hopes to escape all things safe and familiar."

Sorios pouted and looked at the ground unhappily. "I am too old to trust the unfamiliar," he grumbled.

So Deïni called upon Hiren her brother, the son of Teruman Phactorias, and she enlisted him to attend them on their journey, both as guide and guardian. Hiren accepted the call enthusiastically, for he, too, wished to be fêted by new sights, and he and Archea sat together and eagerly made their plans.

Meanwhile Sorios and Archea assembled those of their own kin as would be most useful on a long journey, and as many as desired to go with them, as their intent was to travel far and long. They each brought together a company of their own, gathering the favorites of their own households. In their company went Ceras, a daughter of Archea, and sundry of her family; and Steggan, a son of Sorios, with his kin.[1] Altogether Sorios and Archea

1 Their exact descent from their "parents" cannot be determined, but they are clearly not brother and sister.

and the rest of their company made sixty souls, and Teruman Hiren as well.

In this company they set their paths to southward; crossing out of the country of Niyarc they passed the borders of the forest of Batack. Now the Sorites, and the deïnings before them, had long feared the darkness of Batack, and seldom ventured there, so it was but little inhabited. Only few and scattered tribes of deïnings might be found there: and the Erescali, the Giants, were in that country.

They braved the forest, but they rested little, pressing ever southwards at the urging of Hiren. Although Hiren had never been so far south himself, it was well known among the Terumani that the forest did not go on forever, and that the airs grew warmer in the south. After many days of difficult travel the forest at length began to change; the trees as they progressed southward became more graceful, the canopy more airy, and the gallery brighter with sparkling beams of sunlight, until at last the deepness of the wood opened up into a pleasing country of grove and copse and scattered woodlands. The air was scented with grass and clover and sundry blossoms, for the springtime was in full bloom. There the travelers relaxed at last, and set their minds to sojourn for a space in that land.

In that country was the Hall of Teruman Aneon, of the Ádolthi. So Hiren sought out his Hall to beseech his hospitality. Now Bël the messenger of the Terumani had sent word to Aneon beforehand of their travels, so Teruman Aneon received Hiren graciously, and asked immediately to see Sorios and Archea, for these two progenitors of the speaking Sorites were by this time well-known throughout the land of Soria. There before the Hall of Teruman Aneon the whole party camped for some months, as the fresh dews of spring burned into the bright glory of summer. Sorios and Archea he brought into his house, his own Hall.

Now the summers of Niyarc are not to be compared with the summers of the south, for warmth and for the splendor of sunlight in its fullness. Even the skies of this domain seemed more richly blue than the skies of Niyarc. The Sorites were delighted to remain in that country. Moreover Aneon rained showers of hospitality upon Sorios and Archea and their party, and they were grateful and charmed by all that he offered them.

Teruman Aneon dwelt in the open country near the shores of the great lake Egano. He showed them all his country. Aneon had worked for many years on his domain, and he was proud of his land: of the airy beauties of his leaf-carpeted woods, his fragrant grasslands, and the lucent silver sheen of Lake Egano, brimming with fish and graced by the wistful cries of his gulls. There was much to see, and he escorted his visitors on many pleasant jaunts and outings about his lands.

Archea, and indeed all of that party, were greatly enchanted by all that they saw. But the more his company enjoyed themselves, the more Sorios hunkered into a cloud of envy and doubts, for he felt their allegiance fading away. And he truly could not deny that this country was in many ways more delightful than the home awaiting them in faraway Niyarc. He fretted over what more might happen to draw his folk from his side.

There were deïnings also in that country.

While Sorios' party sojourned in the Hall of Teruman Aneon, it so happened that Steggan the son of Plateos the son of Sorios went out among them, and while there a female of that race found him and began to cherish him: beautiful, steadfast, and kind-hearted. Now in those days the Sorites and the deïnings were not so far estranged. Though the deïnings had no gift of speech as did the children of Sorios and Archea, nor did they have the use of fire, yet they built shelters not much different from the homes of the Sorites, and many of them even made crude tools, and otherwise lived much like their speaking kindred. So it was not unusual that the two kindreds still mingled anon. Steggan therefore was happy to take her to be his mate, and she was pleased with the match. She was a deïning, and had no name of her own, so Steggan gave her the name Enodië, which means Inspiration.

This was pleasing to Archea, and she doted on the newcomer among them. But when Sorios heard of it he became angry, and he called Steggan to come before him. "Why have you taken this deïning into our camp?" he insisted. "What will you do when it is time to return to our own country?"

"She will be my mate and my wife, according the customs of our folk," Steggan said. "I love her, and will not send her away shamefully."

"Are you binding yourself to this country, when we shall so soon depart for our own homes and halls?" Sorios said.

"She will come with us into the north when we return," Steggan said. Now he said this to pacify Sorios, for he did not wish to anger his patriarch whom he loved and respected. Nevertheless his heart was saddened by the thought of taking his bride out of her homeland.

With this promise Sorios grudgingly agreed to allow the pairing, but his worries increased.

After this Sorios could not set his anxieties aside. The southlands had woven spells upon his folk, and the northern country he loved seemed distant and forgotten by many in his party. He began to argue that they should soon make their plans to return, but Archea said, "We have only begun to see the world! Return to Niyarc? We should rather move onward, and see yet more distant lands!" This contention also became a bur between them, and they argued over it for days.

At last Archea won her way once again, for Hiren counseled that autumn was drawing nigh. "It is too late in the year," he warned. "Travel may become impossible in the high country of Batack if winter storms should arrive during our journey. Let us tour eastward to see what we might see. To the east lies the Hall of Teruman Legen, where we might hope to receive a welcome. The winters are mild in his realm, if the reports of Deïni and my father are true."

"Is it truly the winter you fear? Or do you to merely hunger for more diversions?" Sorios grumbled.

In spite of Sorios' objections and fears the company accepted the word of Hiren, and they at last broke camp and bade their farewells to Aneon.

For some weeks they traveled, taking a leisurely pace, following the valley of the broad River Næus eastward, and when they had rounded the terminus of the Mountains of Lodbarria they headed south, and did not stop until they had come to the coast where lay the Hall of Legen. There they were received by the servants of Legen, for some of the næads and dræads of the area had placed themselves into his service, as Legen was an attentive master of the natural lands.

Legen was not so convivial as Aneon. He had little interest in the Sorites, nor the deïnings, nor any of the Kindreds or creatures of the land. His interest was in the country and the plantings of his domain. Nevertheless, he provided them a place to camp at some distance from his Hall, and Hiren he received into his house.

The land about his Hall overlooked the sea from a high bluff. This was a magnificent cliff like a sable wall sixty feet high, capped with gnarled and wind-blown tousles of cypress and pine. The country there was warm in the bath of the sun, with a radiance that drenched them. The hillsides behind them were golden with the crown of summer's end, with rippling stands of wild oats, and barley, and wheat. Even the nights were warm, so that many slept under the gleaming stars without cover.

The gulls piped and wheeled over Legen's house, and the greater seabirds dove into the waves for their catch. Below them the endless sighing of the tolling waves drummed upon the rocks. Off the shore, as far as the eye could see, the Great Sea shimmered azure, and gold, and green-gray: ever in motion and bewitching to behold. Dolphins and whales could be seen from afar, dancing and sporting in the glimmering waters as is their wont. More beautiful to the eyes of Archea and the Sorites was this Sea, by far, than were the cold, gray and fog-shrouded seas of Niyarc and Vordót.

The country of Legen dazzled the Sorites, as no place they had seen before in all the long days of their existence.

When some weeks had gone by Ceras the daughter of Archea said to her own folk, "Why do we remain in tents and hutches out in the open in this camp? The winter rains will soon be upon us. There is good clay here, and timber and sod in abundance." So she and her household began to build houses of clay and sod for themselves there in their camp, in the neighborhood of Legen's Hall.

When Sorios saw it, he objected strenuously, and stormed to Teruman Hiren to complain. "My daughter Ceras, the daughter of Archea my mate, has settled in this country, establishing a house of clay and sod on Legen's land. Does Legen know of this intrusion? Or does Legen approve of it?"

Hiren sighed and rolled his eyes, but he approached Legen, and informed him what had been done. Legen shrugged and gave it no thought. "What is it to me if these Sorites should settle round about me?" he said. "I have no concern what any of the creatures of this country might do: They build their nests and dens and burrows as they please. They are of little interest to me at all, save as they amuse me at times to watch them at sport. Let the creatures settle where they might, only let them not bother me in my own Hall."

When Hiren reported this to Sorios, he was dismayed, and determined at once to return to Niyarc, lest this desertion spread throughout his kin. But Hiren would not allow it, for the journey through Batack would be long, and winter was nigh.

Archea also dissembled, saying, "This land is pleasant, and an excellent place to winter over. Ceras has done the proper thing, for when the rains of winter arrive we should all have snug shelters in which to remain warm and dry."

All of that party hearkened to her, and they began to make for themselves houses such as those they had left behind them in Niyarc, or to delve dens out of the hillsides.

So the Sorites of Sorios' camp made a settlement in the neighborhood of the Legen's Hall. They lived off the land, learning to hunt the game and gather the fruits of that country. They made for themselves implements, and tools, and furnishings, and filled their homes with comforts. The winter rains fell, but they kept themselves dry and warm in the houses and dens they had made. They built also a common-house, a long hall where cheery fires were kept burning, where they gathered to celebrate together, and feast in good days, and sing songs of the new country which their bards crafted. They remained there for months, until the season of rains waned, and the weather grew warmer, and Hiren at last agreed that a journey through Batack would be safe.

But when the time came to begin preparations for their journey, Ceras the daughter of Sorios said to her father, "This land is good, and everything we need to live comfortably can be found here in abundance. Indeed, our comfort and ease is greater here than ever it was in Niyarc whence we came. My family and myself wish to remain here in this country. We are young, and have all whom we love with us: there is no need for any of us to return to Niyarc. Join us, and let us all remain in this country together."

Sorios was greatly saddened by this, and attempted to persuade his daughter to change her mind. For days they argued on this point, but Ceras would not recant.

Now Archea loved Ceras more than any of her other children who remained in Soria, and she was loth to part with her. So Archea also grumbled to Sorios, "Why indeed should any of us return to that cold country of the north? For Vélopar has truly fitted a land for Sorites here, more to our liking than the gray lands of Niyarc. Let us remain here, and make new homes for ourselves in this place."

But Sorios was sad and embittered, and he said, "We have yet many descendants in Niyarc whom we have left behind, kindred whom we love. And our hearts are bound to Wenda and Deïni, and those others of the Terumani who have benefited us. Shall we abandon them all without a word, to whom we owe so much?"

Archea protested, "Is this your true reason to return? To go back to Wenda that Teruman? Is your devotion to Deïni greater than your devotion to me? Why else would you defy the desires of your own mate, to return to that unlovely country?"

Sorios said, "My attachment to the Terumani is the love of a child for a parent, who has lavished both of us with all good and necessary things. Do you not also feel it? Shall we be ungrateful for such devotion?"

But Archea would not be placated. Going yet further in her complaint, she said, "When we took each other as mates, we had neither of us the gift of speech. Our choice was made in the dimness of our former darkened minds. Perhaps we chose not wisely, having yet no speech nor wisdom of our own."

This jab pricked sorely at the heart of Sorios. "Has this land stolen so much from us?" he said.

At last Archea said, "I will remain behind in this country, come what may. You may return to cold Niyarc alone if you so desire."

At these words Sorios knew in his heart that she would not be moved, and that her heart had left him for sake of this country and for the sake of her daughter Ceras. So after having led the Kindred of the Sorites for many generations, Sorios and Archea parted ways at last. Sorios went to Hiren and to his party, and made preparations to leave for the journey homeward.

But many others of the Sorites also wished to remain in the south, so the party which had left Niyarc was greatly reduced, and but fourteen were left to return with Sorios to the north. Even Hiren said, "I shall go with you to guide you and guard you on the journey, but when you are safely brought home to the Shelf, I also shall return hither, to the country of Legen. My heart also is taken by this good land, and the Sorites whom we leave in this place will need a guardian to watch over them. Legen has little interest in the Kindreds and creatures of his country, but cares only for his own comfort and amusement: he cannot be trusted to be a guardian for your Kindred there. I shall return again and be a guardian for Ceras' tribe."

Sorios surveyed the small party which had gathered for the return, and sighed. "It seems I never cease to lose my children, and now I have lost my spouse as well."

So with a heavy heart, Sorios prepared to return to the Shelf of Depharmen in Niyarc. Hiren led the band across the highlands of Batack, keeping them safe, for their numbers were lessened, and the travel difficult. When they had returned to the Shelf Deïni could not but notice the reduction of his company, and the sorrow of Sorios, and she feared the worst. "What has happened along the way?" she asked anxiously. Sorios would not answer, but slunk to his house with his head hung low, and would not come out for days.

Hiren answered on his behalf. "No one has been lost. He is merely aggrieved that many of our party have chosen to remain in the south. And I also intend to return at once to Archea and Ceras."

"What of Archea?" Deïni asked, for she had noted her absence.

"She also has remained, and forsaken him," Hiren admitted. "She will not return."

So Deïni was sorrowful on Sorios' account, but he would not allow himself to be comforted.

Word spread quickly of the goodness of that country, and others also requested to accompany Hiren when he returned. When at last he departed, therefore, a great company went with him: several hundred descendants of Sorios: Sorios mourned the loss of each of them. Hiren brought them all safe into Legen's country. There Hiren raised a Hall of his own, from which he attended Archea and Ceras: for Archea had appointed Ceras the matriarch and leader of her tribe, as Sorios had been their leader in the north, in Niyarc.

All of the Kindred of the Sorites who came into that country, and all who were born of them, swore allegiance to Ceras. Hiren requested of Deïni that she might grant Ceras life, as she had given life to Sorios and Archea, that Ceras might govern her clan for many years. So Ceras became a ruler there, and the Tribe which descended from her company became known as the Cerites. (From that stock also came the Raccosites and Protosites in later days.) They named their country for Hiren, calling all of the land of their possessions the Hirna. Thus the Cerites came to be the first Tribe to part from the Sorites, and they have been a Kindred apart ever since.

As for Archea, she at last grew weary of the world. It is said by some that she returned to Niyarc by long paths before the end, and went to her rest in Ritéol the Mansion of the Heroes when her days in this world had ended. Whether she was reconciled with Sorios at last, or with her other children, none can say. But the Hirnans deny this, for they say that she sleeps in a secret Hall veiled from the eyes of all in the very heart of the Hirna, and they have named a mountain after her, Mount Arq'heatha in their own tongue, where they say this Hall lies hidden.

2. The Desertion of Steggan

For some years after the return from the Southrealm, Steggan and the others of Sorios' party remained satisfied at home in Niyarc, and were a comfort to Sorios. Steggan repined over the lands of the south they had left behind, and often wistfully dreamed of that warm and pleasant country. He would recount its beauties and pleasures to any who would listen. But he was faithful to Sorios, and respectful above all else.

Sorios came often to give him counsel and advice, and it must be admitted, to assuage his own loneliness in the company of his most faithful son. At the request of Sorios, Steggan was granted length of days by Deïni, for she wished to ease him over the loss of Archea. Sorios doted first on Steggan's children, then on his grandchildren, and still the clan grew and expanded. Other households allied themselves with Steggan as well, and became his attendants and lieges.

The house of Steggan was in the plain called Feldreth, which means the Carpet, for it was fertile and blanketed deep in shaggy grass. This house and this community were far from the Shelf where Sorios his father dwelt, yet Sorios often came to call on him, for Steggan was his favorite.

Now it happened that in those days, while the clan of Steggan was increasing in the Carpet Plain, the weather in Niyarc and Vordót was growing cooler. For an age the Kindreds of Toë had survived the winters of the north with little discomfort. They dwelt mostly in snug shelters walled and roofed over with turf, and from the Terumani they had learned the value of fire, and had discovered how to make fire themselves long ago.

But a year came when the winter fell upon them frigid and terrible. So cold was it, and the squalls so bitter, that the houses of the Sorites were but scant shelter for them. They huddled beneath their furs throughout that cold season, putting their hopes in the coming of spring and the return of warmth. But the springtime came cold and damp, and the sun hid his face behind a shroud of gray. Even the summer brought little comfort, for rarely did the sun burn through the mist and cloud, while the days were gray and dreary, and the nights a sodden cloak of fog. Winter returned, and another bitter spring and summer, and in such manner this spell of cold weather spanned years, until all the Sorites began to complain of their constant misery.

As the weather in Niyarc worsened, Steggan began to watch his wife Enodië with worry in his heart. She had dwelt contentedly among his household for many years,[2] and had enjoyed the blessings of a large family. But she had

2 It would seem that Deïni had prolonged her life as well for Steggan's sake, though she was a deïning and did not have the gift of speech.

been born and spent her youth in the Southrealm, where the days were warmer and the summers longer. The colder the weather grew in Niyarc, the more miserable and forlorn Enodië became. She could not complain, having no speech and no words to utter, but Steggan understood her nonetheless, and it was clear to him that she suffered, and that she pined for the lost country of her youth. So he brooded over the wrong he had done to her.

It came about then one winter, when this had gone on unabated for years, that Steggan's deputy Hesperan came to counsel with him, along with his son Qentero, both of whom were elders and leaders in his clan. They came to the house of Steggan, and sealed the door,[3] while the wind blew chill without, and flakes of snow whistled in through the gaps.

"The cold of this winter is, if anything, worse than all before it," Hesperan complained. "The snow is thick upon the ground, the rivers are frozen solid, and there is no game to ease our hunger. How shall our clan survive another winter in this country?"

Steggan said sadly, "Perhaps the time has come for our clan to disperse, that we might find enough forage from the land to last us through the winter months."

But Qentero said, "You say to disperse, but I wonder, why do we endure this misery, and this bitter country, at all? You yourself have told us tales of the Southrealm, where the clan of Ceras dwells. Does the sun truly shine there as in the tales?"

Steggan grew momentarily pensive, and a smile touched the corners of his lips. "Yes, and more gloriously than I can describe. It is like liquid gold on the hills and woodlands there, and it sparkles on the waters and the seas. Even when the years here were good, the climate could in no wise compare with the warmth and pleasure of those distant fields."

"Why then do you remain here in these damp and miserable lands?"

Steggan was flustered for a moment. "It is our home," he stammered. "It has always been our home, since the day that Sorios entered this realm."

Qentero looked past the fluttering door and shuddered at the cold wind which piped in around its edges. "Might we not seek a new home?" he brooded.

Steggan gazed pityingly at Enodië, who huddled in a corner of the hut, wrapped in furs, her breath steaming in the cold, and looking utterly miserable, and he suddenly wondered why he had allowed this to go on for so long. "Would you be willing to take on such an undertaking," he asked Hesperan and Qentero, "along with all our children and elders? The Southrealm is very far from here. It is a long and dangerous journey, and we have none to guide us or defend us on the way."

3 The "door" described would have been a pelt or hide stretched over the opening of the hut.

"We might ask Deïni to send along an escort," Hesperan suggested, "as she did for you on your journey."

"I could not," Steggan said. "Such a journey would be a defiance of Sorios, and she would surely tell him."

"Then let us go to Sorios ourselves," Qentero suggested, "and ask him to go with us to the Southrealm. There we might all live together in comfort, away from this endless misery."

Steggan pursed his lips thoughtfully. "He is stubborn. He would refuse to go with us. Many years past, when we enjoyed the warmth and sunlight of the Southrealm together, he wanted nothing more than to return to his dreary home here in the north. The passing years have only hardened him and his ways. He is ancient by the count of our folk, and I fear he has grown intractable and inflexible."

"Then would you dare to go without him?" asked Hesperan.

"I see no other way."

Qentero proposed, "He will come to visit with us here in a few months, when the less miserable days of summer arrive. We might ask his blessing and wisdom on this matter."

"No, but it would break him," Steggan said charily. "You did not see the heartbreak I witnessed when he lost Archea his spouse and Ceras his daughter to that land. He mourns their loss to this day. I cannot bear to tell him we would be leaving him for that same distant country. I have neither the heart nor the courage to do so."

"Would you then go without his advice and counsel?"

Steggan sighed. "It is for the best. The alternative would be to defy him to his face. That I must not do."

"We shall go alone, then," said Hesperan.

Steggan nodded reluctantly. "But let us first seek the judgement of all our clan," he said. "If we are all agreed on this, then we shall dare the forest trails, and find our sister Ceras in the Southrealm, and Archea our matriarch. They shall welcome us, and we shall have a new home where our children shall know the blessing of warmth. But Sorios must not be told."

Steggan therefore conspired with the elders of his kinsmen. Quietly he and his companions sent out word of their intent, wishing to include as many of their relations as might be willing to journey with them. It was no secret or surprise that many had grown hopelessly weary of their never-ending misery, so the word of Steggan's plan was received as a dream of hope. Few of his household and his relations refused, and none brought word back to Sorios or to the Terumani.

As the winter proceeded, all the folk of Steggan's clan began to secretly pack up their belongings and their supplies, telling none of the neighboring clans of their intent.

The snows at last subsided, and the yellow grass had begun to green, and Steggan sent word to all the leaders of his clan, declaring, "It is time. Pick up your things and let us slip silently from this land."

So he and all his company gathered on Feldreth, the Carpet Plain, under the damp and drizzly skies of springtime. A great host they were, and the neighboring clans could not help but notice their gathering. Their astonishment was without measure when the whole of that host raised up camp, and headed southward, crossing the foaming fords of the River Genesë, and traveling onward through the mud and mist even to the borders of Batack.

Many curious followers and onlookers tailed them along the way. Some of them approached, saying "What does this mean? Where are you going, and what is your intent?" But Steggan gave no answer, nor did his kindred, for they feared the displeasure of Sorios and the Terumani.

Then one morning they broke camp, and the whole host entered under the dripping, mossy boughs of the Forest of Batack, out of sight and out of knowledge, leaving behind the lands of Niyarc.

The followers who had trailed them thus far would not enter dark Batack, but waited for their return the whole day, and the following day as well. At last they gave them up for lost. So those who had followed turned back, and returned to their own homes, bearing news to their families of the departure of Steggan: thus the word spread throughout Niyarc that Steggan had abandoned the north country, and the land of his fathers, and Sorios himself, and had vanished into the forest of Batack. What became of him and his host after that none could say.

Word of this exodus came at last to the Hall of Deïni. Deïni refused at first to believe the rumor, for Steggan had always been among the most loyal of Sorios' kin and followers. So she told Sorios nothing of the matter, and she sent emissaries secretly to the Carpet, to discover whether the tidings were true. They found the houses and homes of Steggan and all his folk abandoned, emptied of their furnishings and goods. Then Deïni could doubt it no longer. She stole apprehensively to the house of Sorios.

"Steggan your son has abandoned the country of the north," she told him sadly. "He and all his clan. They were seen entering into the forest of the Batack, and have not returned. Their houses and property lie empty and forsaken."

Sorios was silent for a long minute at this news. At last he dabbed at his eye and said, "Then he is returning to the Southrealm, to seek out his sister Ceras."

"So I had thought, as well," said Deïni.

"Has none, then, gone with him on the way, to see that he is safe?"

"He sought no aid from any, but went away in utter secrecy."

"Then we must send someone out to find him, and succor him along the way. There are many dangers in Batack."

"Batack is vast and dark," Deïni said. "How might any hope to find them?"

"Can you not send Bël? She sees much that is hidden to others."

"Bël is of the terumani: she sees and hears the terumani; I do not think she will be of much help seeking folk of your kind in the shadowed vastness of Batack. But at least she can send word to any terumani who might be of aid. Perhaps word might reach Archea and Ceras, that they might at least expect them and welcome them."

So Bël was called, and at the urging of Deïni and Sorios she went out to Batack, and made her rounds in her own mysterious way, seeking any news of the company of Steggan. Now in those days there were no roads or trails in all that vast and unsettled country, so the paths which Steggan may have taken were entirely a mystery, and no one knew where to seek them. There were few Terumani in that country at all, and even the sprights and nymphs of the realm were sparse; none she encountered knew anything of their passing. Only one dræad had report of a great company which had passed through his country, but their route was uncertain and circuitous, and they had again been lost to all knowledge in the darkness of the wood.

Bël at last chose to go to the Hall of Hiren, where she might hope to find Archea and Ceras, to seek their aid on Steggan's behalf.

Now Archea and Steggan had had no communication with Sorios, nor with any of the Terumani, for many long years. Even Hiren had sent but few and vague reports of their progress in their new home. They were far from Niyarc, and isolated completely from their former kindred, and no one knew anything of the state of their affairs.

When Bël therefore arrived with her message, Archea refused to admit her. "I have nothing to say to Sorios, nor do I desire any word from him or from any of the insolent folk of the north. Let us be, as they have let us be, forgotten for all these years."

So Bël returned to Deïni disappointed, and reported to her all that she had done, and all that she had heard.

When Sorios learned that Bël had returned from her mission, he went to Deïni to ask what she had learned. "It is no good," Deïni told him. "They have disappeared into the shadows of Batack, as it were, and are lost to the world."

"Will no one then go after them?"

"If Bël could not find their party, they cannot be found. We can only hope they come out safe on the far side of Batack when their journey is through. Then perhaps we might receive news."

Though aged in appearance, Sorios was yet hale enough to travel far. When it had become clear to him that neither Deïni, nor any others of the Terumani, would pursue this matter any further, he donned his traveling cloak and his hat, and he went out on his own to follow Steggan and his company.

So it was that he left his home on the Shelf, and crossed the plains of Niyarc, to the country of the Cylosites on the borders of Batack. Two weeks he spent on the way, but he stopped to speak to no one until he had found Cardach the patriarch of the Cylosites, and he asked him, "Can you show me the spot where Steggan and his clan entered the forest?"

"I can," Cardach replied. He brought him to the threshold of the forest, the very spot where the tribe of Steggan had disappeared. Sorios thanked him, and he made as if to enter the wood himself.

"You must not go into the forest alone," Cardach declared. "You are unprepared. You have no guide. You would surely go astray and perish, lord."

"But I have found none to attend me," Sorios said dourly.

"Then I shall go," Cardach said. So Cardach hurried home to gather supplies for a journey, and returned to Sorios. Then they followed the trail of the company of Steggan into Batack.

The forest grew ever thicker, and ever darker, the further south they progressed. Cardach took his ax, and he began to cut saplings along the trail as they went, and to cut notches into the bark of the trees as they passed. "What is the meaning of this?" Sorios asked, for he was impatient to follow the trail of Steggan.

"I mark the way of our going," Cardach said. "I will return alive. We will not disappear into the forest as did Steggan, to be seen no more."

"Well enough," Sorios allowed. "But we must not delay, for it is now many weeks since they left the trail."

"You must trust me, lord," said Cardach, and he continued to mark the trail as they proceeded.

It had indeed been many weeks since the departure of Steggan, and little sign of their passing remained. Sorios would have walked blindly into the desolation, trusting to his luck to find the way of his quarry; Cardach, however, would not allow it. He caused him to stop many times, and consider their way, and choose the more likely paths into the depths of the woods.

In this way they passed yet two more weeks wandering the tangled understory of the forest. Sorios traveled as one obsessed, taking no thought for his safety. Cardach, however, would allow no such incaution. When the lumbering footsteps of some massive beast were heard to approach, Cardach took Sorios to the safety of the trees, and made him hide until danger had passed. When wolves howled in the night, Cardach built a great fire, and kept watch with a firebrand in his hand in case they were set upon. When they stumbled upon the foul nest of a Giant, one of the kindred of Erescal, Cardach made them take a long detour around the place that they might be far from discovery.

In all this time, the forest grew darker, the paths more wild and unkempt, and no sign of the passing of a company of travelers was to be found.

At last Cardach said to Sorios, "We must return, lord. We have no path to follow. Our dangers here are great."

"But Steggan. My son," Sorios lamented, and his voice broke in sorrow.

"Steggan has chosen his path. We cannot follow. Let us return."

So he took Sorios by the hand; Sorios bowed his head and did not resist. Thus they returned the way they had come, following the signs and marks Cardach had left along the trail.

When they were at last returning from the darkness of the wood into the open country of Cylos' folk, they found Deïni and Wenda on the trail coming toward them. "Where have you gone?" Deïni said sternly. "You left your home without a word, and none knew where you were."

"I have been following Steggan into Batack, in hopes of catching up to him. Since none would go to succor him, I hoped to convince him to return. Or if that were not possible, only to see my son once more. But I have failed. And Steggan my son is gone from me now forever."

"It was a foolish thing to do," Deïni scolded. "It is well that Cardach left word of his departure with his own clan."

But Wenda said, "It was a noble and good-hearted thing, Sorios. But I am glad Cardach has returned you to us alive."

So they returned to the Shelf. But Sorios was in mourning for Steggan, as if he had perished; he shut himself up in his house, and he would not receive any company for many weeks in his sorrow.

3. The Aspirations of Steggan

Steggan knew nothing of this, nor could he guess at any of the acts of Sorios or Deïni. Yet he worried daily, and his heart misgave him, doubting whether he had behaved properly towards his patriarch, or whether he had done well in departing Niyarc at all. But the journey was difficult, and none knew whether they might come safely through the forest in the end: all his clan were looking to him for guidance. So he said nothing of his misgivings, but led his clan on their way in silence.

For many days the company of Steggan struggled through the highlands of Batack, having little leisure to give thought to Sorios, or really to any of those they had left behind. The snows of winter had not yet receded on the upper reaches of the plateau, so they donned boots and fur-lined cloaks and slogged into the slush. The travel was slow, for the company was very large, and included the young and the frail. Moreover Steggan had no guide, and they had no clear path or trail, wherefore their scouts often returned with little option but to reverse course and find alternate routes to proceed. Thus their course through Batack meandered, and a journey that had taken but a few weeks with Hiren as guide, became a journey of months.

As they traveled, Steggan alone pondered the welfare of Sorios, and the folk they had left behind. A thought at last came to Steggan, and it came about in this wise:

Throughout the journey Steggan assigned recorders from his party to detail the route through the forest, that as their paths rambled and wandered they might be prevented from repeating the worst routes, wasting days in retracing their missteps. He placed his son Qentero in charge of this task, and Qentero's scouts and recorders devised marks and pictographs to identify the landmarks along the way, making note of the unmanageable paths and impossible passages. They marked, as well, the easiest paths among the valleys, ridges, brambles and obstructions, and the fords of the rivers and streams, that the scouts might bring them confidently by way of the best passages. So they avoided the danger of becoming hopelessly lost in the wilderness.

So also was kept a complete record of their journey as they went, and it came into the heart of Steggan that he might make use of such a record. But he had no leisure to pursue this plan, for his constant concern was the safety of his clan.

Despite the length of the journey, and the many dangers that all knew existed, they were fortunate to meet with little trouble, their company being so large and formidable that the dark or dangerous creatures of the deep woods feared them, letting them pass without assault. The distant wail of wolves they heard by night, and the great footpaths of drakes[4] they crossed, but they were not challenged. It may have been mere fortune that they came across none of the Giants, for that folk is as likely to charge a great mob as a lone traveler, and Steggan's clan had no Teruman to defy them. No other child of the Sorites did they meet in all those days, and if any spright or nymph watched or wondered at their passing, they knew it not.

As they went south, the rains of the north grew less frequent, and though the air in the highlands was cool, the sun could be seen sparkling through the budding canopy overhead. The snow and slush melted away, and as spring faded into the long days of summer the company of Steggan at last came to the thinning of the forest, and they left Batack behind.

Here Steggan found a shade-mellowed hilltop grove to his liking, and he said, "We shall remain here while we explore the country." So he established a camp for his folk, setting up their tents and canopies, and building huts and hutches for a long stay. He constructed a stockade to defend his folk from any dangers which might come out of the forest, and set watchmen to guard the site.

When all this was done, Hesperan the deputy of Steggan said, "This place is good; there is good forage to be had, and game to be taken in the woods. Shall we settle here, and make this our new home?"

But Steggan was not satisfied. "This is not the place," he said. "It has been

4 The identity of this creature is uncertain, but it appears to have been a large, reptilian carnivore.

our goal from the start to find again Ceras my sister, and Archea our matriarch, and heal the rift of our kindred, that we might all dwell together in this realm. Only so shall this journey justify its purpose, and perhaps we might honor Sorios whom we have abandoned in Niyarc." He sent scouts therefore into the country round about, to see if they could find any who remained of the clan of Archea and Ceras whom they had left behind so many years before.

The scouts traveled far, in all directions, seeking signs of habitation, while Steggan and his company waited. After many days word came back at last of a settlement of Sorites in the hill country beyond the great rivers. But the scout had not approached, for their aspect was dark and they were armed, as if expecting enemies.

Steggan, however, rejoiced, and said, "These are surely our kindred, the tribe of Ceras our sister. They shall receive us without fail, and if they are armed against dangers in this land, we shall swell their numbers against those foes." Steggan, of course, knew nothing of the tidings of Bël, and he had no reason to suspect anything from Ceras but welcome.

So the whole company decamped once more, and all that folk followed Steggan on the path found out by the scout. At last they came upon a settlement of the Cerites, and Steggan went forth cheerily to meet them.

The Cerites, however, had spotted the approach of a great host such as none had ever before seen traveling together. So they had gathered an armed company against them: a large force of warriors, armed with spear, mace and sword,[5] and arrayed in helm, breastplate, and jerkins of leather. This company set a line before the host of Steggan's folk, blocking their way, and set their shields in place as a wall.

An emissary strutted forward from their ranks. He raised a spear bedecked with fluttering pennants as warning, and he called from a distance, "What company is this that assaults the settlements of Ceras in our own country? Are you come from the north to mock us? Or are you in league with the Giants who assault us?"

Steggan was of a simple and ingenuous nature, and did not perceive their mood. Nevertheless he halted his company out of caution, and he went forward alone, unarmed, to speak with the emissary; his own folk took up their spears and axes warily behind his back.

"We are Sorites from Niyarc, your brethren," Steggan said. "We are not in league with any, neither have we encountered any enemies in our trek. And I myself am Steggan, a brother to Ceras, who traveled with her to this far country in our youth. Surely she shall receive me and my company with gladness."

But the emissary said, "Then it is as we were warned: Ceras alerted us that

---

5 A "sword" in this age would most likely have been a dagger-like flint or obsidian blade attached to a bone or wood handle, as metallurgy was unknown at this period, even among the Cerites.

invaders were coming from the north. I tell you what we were instructed to say: that you must return the way you came and leave our country."

At this rebuff Steggan was startled, and hardly knew what to believe. "We come only in friendship," he said, "hoping to join you in settling this land."

"We need no aid in settling these lands." The emissary waved a hand across the obviously uninhabited hills and bluffs around them. "All the country you see about you belongs to Ceras and her tribe: even to us, and to our children, and to our own subjects. We have no wish to divide it with foreigners. You yourself, even now, trample private holdings, and break our laws. We ask only to be left alone and in peace, or we shall defend our property by force."

Steggan was chagrined by this reception, and said to the emissary, "I shall send my folk away, to camp wherever you might allow. Only let me speak to Ceras, for I have longed to see her once again since first I conceived to journey back to these parts."

The emissary conferred with his cohorts, and at last he said, "Only you, alone, if what you say is true. But I do not think Ceras shall salute you." According to Steggan's promise, Hesperan then removed the company a day's journey to the north, to a barren field below a ridge: The armed force of the Cerites kept a watch over them, standing guard on the ridgeline. Steggan meanwhile was ushered into the settlement of the Cerites under guard, and brought to the house of Ceras.

Ceras had become a ruler of many, and she had grown proud and haughty, such that Steggan hardly knew her. She compelled him to bend a knee before her, and she said, "You say you are Steggan, who journeyed with me when we first arrived with Sorios when we were both young? Yet even if so, you returned with Sorios, and your allegiance was to him. What business have you in the Hirna, our country, we who have made a new and better home for our Tribe?"

Steggan then said, "I do indeed honor Sorios our father, the first of our Kindred, who dwells yet in Niyarc. Yet we who have come this far bear allegiance to none; we speak for ourselves alone. We come seeking new country to settle, in better clime than that from which we all came, and to restore faith between those of Sorios' domain and our sundered kindred of the south. The land is wide and open, and there is plenty of room here for all to prosper."

Ceras said in reply, "The lands of the Hirna are divided among our elders and thanes. None shall willingly give you their lands."

"Though I see that you have indeed become a numerous and prosperous folk, yet surely these lands of Soria are greater than your numbers can settle alone."

"Be that as it may, all that you see is part of the Hirna, the country of the Cerites, my kindred, for many day's journey hereabouts: it is all under our dominion. If you desire lands of your own, you will swear allegiance to our country, and swear fealty to my rule, and pay us the land-taxes we demand. Yet know this: we desire no commerce with outsiders, who have abandoned us here for these many decades without a clement word, nor any display of concern for our welfare, and have left us unaided in our fight against the Giants who attack our settlements." Ceras spoke harshly, for Ceras, and Archea her mother, had over the long years grown embittered against Sorios and the Sorites of Niyarc. Sorios, after all, had indeed abandoned them in ire when he left.

So Steggan left the house of Steggan dispirited and bitter, for never had he foreseen such malice possessing his former companion Ceras. He returned to his company with this news and with these demands. Much discussion arose among his captains and cohorts, but none were willing to submit to Ceras in her overarching pride. Then Steggan was aggrieved, and he said, "Then we have failed, and we have dishonored Sorios our father for nought."

Hesperan his deputy said, "What would you have us do? We have been rejected by Ceras. But we will not return to gloomy Niyarc! Shall we return to our camp on the edge of Batack?"

"No," said Steggan. "It is too near the dangers of that forest." Steggan had explored the country many years ago with Hiren as guide, and he looked now westward. "We have failed in our purpose," he sighed, "But there are many open lands in this realm. We shall go west, far from the influence of Ceras and her froward folk."

At Steggan's signal they broke camp early in the morning, the whole company together, and they moved out of that country, marching resolutely westward through the hill-country. The company of the Cerites dogged them from the hills, keeping watch, that Steggan's tribe might attempt no aggression or defiance, nor make any show of seizing what was not theirs.

So the folk of Steggan departed from the Hirna, the country of the Cerites, turning their backs upon them happily, and shaking off the dust of their feet against them. The guards of the Cerites returned to Ceras with the news that Steggan's company had departed. Only then was Ceras satisfied, but she dispatched sentries nevertheless, to watch the borders of the Hirna, to assure that they would not return.

As for Steggan and his company, they continued westward, crossing over the Lindian Mountains which came down to the Sea at the west of Qesed, until they were many day's journeying distant from the Cerites. There along the coastlands they found country to their liking, with a pleasant clime and fields abundant with game and forage. The shore lands also were rich with sea-life, and the settlers found there precious, pearlescent shells, more lustrous than any they had known in the north.

Above all, Enodië the spouse of Steggan became buoyant and joyful in that place, and Steggan rejoiced to see her well again at last. So putting all thought of the Cerites behind them, they settled there, and made houses and homes for themselves.

Here the tale might have ended, for the folk of Steggan were pleased with their new settlement, and the climate cheered them; they had as well many resources in this new realm to make them prosperous and comfortable. But Steggan did not forget Sorios; he was plagued by remorse over his departure, and his aspirations did not cease.

So when their colony was established and their folk were prospering, he called Qentero his son to him, the master of the recorders he had assigned to log the details of their journey, and he said to him, "Your recorders kept many notes on our journey from the lands of Sorios, whom we have assuredly angered by our parting. Would it be possible to gather the notations you have made, and to build from them a plan that would guide one quickly and safely through the forest?"

"Of what use would such a plan be?" Qentero asked. "Surely it is not your intent to have us all return to bleak Niyarc, when we have accomplished so much in this new place?"

"I have asked only if such a thing is possible."

So Qentero shrugged, and went away to confer with his recorders. When they had discussed the matter among themselves at length he returned to Steggan and said, "It would take tremendous effort. We would have to conform all our many markings into a single scheme that all would agree upon. Then whoever might wish to use the scheme would need to be trained in its meanings and uses. A great effort. But yes. It could be done."

"Then let this be our objective," Steggan said. "Report back to me when you have finished the task."

So the recorders of Steggan's clan set themselves to this work, and they contrived to place their markings onto staffs that could be carried on a journey, marked with carven devices and knotted cords to instruct the bearer along the way. Qentero at last returned to Steggan his father timidly and showed him the staffs. When he had explained their use, and the meaning of the markings, he said, "We have only to train trail-masters in their reading and their making."

"Then begin to do so at once," Steggan said, "for we shall have need of them soon enough."

Qentero said, "If you wish. Only do not ask us to return to cold Niyarc, for we will not go."

"I have not asked you to do so. Only train your trail-masters."

So Qentero shrugged again, and went away to find and train his scouts in the use of the journey-staffs. Thus the folk of Steggan first devised the journey-staffs which were used for many an age, before the contrivance of map or letter, whereby the learned might read the details and landmarks of his route.

Meanwhile Steggan gave further instructions to Qentero, saying, "Send out your scouts to investigate the country around us, and discover the best paths to the borders of Batack from here. And when you have done so, mark these paths also on journey-staffs according to the scheme your recorders have devised."

So Qentero sighed, and said, "We will do so, only do not leave us and return to that dismal land, for you have guided us wisely up until now, and we would be lost without you." So he sent out his scouts to explore the realm.

After this Steggan called to him Hesperan his deputy, and said to him, "Do the folk of our clan have all that they need in this place?"

Hesperan said, "They have all that they need, and yet more. Their houses overflow with the surplus of this country."

"Yet is there nothing lacking, which we had in plenty in Niyarc?"

So Hesperan went among the folk of their clan, and canvassed them, and reported back to Steggan. "The folk of our clan complain that their tools become dull, for the stone of this country is not to be compared with the fine obsidian we had in the north. Likewise we have little wool, and none of our folk are skilled in the weaving and dying of what we do have, as were the kindred of Plateos. Some also complain that the pottery they have brought with them has broken, and they miss the fine craftsmanship and white stoneware of the clan of Cylos. Only all beg of you: do not make us return to wretched Niyarc, for we would rather live in rags here than return to that cold and miserable country."

"I have only asked what they lack. So now I ask that we gather up of the surplus of what we have gained here, all that can be spared. And if any might produce yet more from the fruit of this land, let them do so. Then we shall pack them snugly into bundles and onto sledges for transport."[6]

So the agents of Hesperan groaned, but they went about the country and gathered a great stock of pearlescent shells, and pearls and beads, and skillfully wrought embroidery such as the folk of Steggan were famous for. A source of alabaster had also been found, and the craftsmen of the Stegganese made of it finely fashioned vessels, lanterns and ornaments. All this surplus and more Steggan gathered and stocked in storehouses and silos in the center of their settlement. And all the folk of his clan wondered at the meaning of this.

At last the folk of Steggan's clan could bear their agitation no longer, for one and all had begun to fear the intentions of their leader. They called to them Qentero and Hesperan and demanded of them, "What is this that Steggan is planning? For we do not wish to return to Niyarc: not one of us!"

---

6 The sledges of the period were lightly built carts with large, curved runners of cane, designed to slide along a dry trail and over most obstructions with relative ease, in a culture that had not developed the wheel. It could typically be pulled by one or two handlers, and had a rail at the back to aid in pushing over steep uphill climbs.

Qentero and Hesperan sighed, and said, "We can dismiss this no longer. We must compel an answer from Steggan."

So they went to Steggan in private, and said, "You must not keep secrets from us any longer. Your tribe is restless and worried, and must be informed. What have you been planning covertly against the wishes of your own clan?"

Steggan said, "I have been unsure of myself, and did not wish to declare my intent until I knew that all I had in mind could be done, and all was in readiness. Perhaps the time is now ripe. Call the folk together, and I shall explain."

They called the folk of his clan to counsel, and all gathered to him in the central plaza of their settlement. Steggan said, "We are established in this country, and our settlement is at peace and prospering. It is my desire now to open a trail between north and south, to open commerce between our kindred and those we have left behind, that we might come and go as ever we wish. In this way the parting from Sorios and the northern tribes might not be absolute."

A great murmur of relief passed over the whole of the assembly. But Hesperan asked, "Will you then go the north to see Sorios, and leave us here without a leader?"

Steggan replied, "Alas that I cannot go, for I have many duties in this place. Nor could I bear to face Sorios my father, whom I have dishonored and abused by my actions. But you will go to Niyarc as my emissary. It has been my heart's desire, since the day we arrived safely in this land, to send news back to Niyarc of our achievement, and to send salutations to Sorios, and ask his forgiveness."

So he gave his deputy Hesperan authority to assemble a company of merchants, and he said, "Let us load our packs and sledges with goods for trade, and send a company of our folk to pass through Batack to Niyarc of the north."

When the folk of Steggan's kindred heard this plan they were eager to see it through. They rushed to produce yet more wares, so that the storehouses of Steggan were overflowing. Many also came to the merchants whom Hesperan had chosen, ordering from them such items and goods as they lacked or desired, if they could be found in Niyarc. Heralds also were to be sent, to bring messages to those they had left behind (for in those days there was no writing).

When all had been prepared, Steggan dismissed his caravan onto the trail with a blessing—a large company of merchants, traders, and porters—and Hesperan went with them. All the folk of that clan cheered to see them off, and to wish them well.

The journey between Niyarc and the Southrealm was long and perilous, so Steggan armed his merchants and porters, with javelins for hunting that they might gather food on their way, and with spears and maces for defense against the dangers.

The journey was arduous, and dangers were faced and overcome, but not so prolonged as when they had found their way across the forest on their own: for now they had the guidance of the journey-staffs to lead them by the better paths.

So it was that within three weeks they arrived at Niyarc, and were welcomed with astonishment by those who met them, for Steggan and all his party had been given up for lost long ago. Word went quickly throughout the country that heralds from Steggan had arrived from the south, bearing messages and goods for trade.

When the rumor reached Deïni, and she had assured herself that it was true, she went at once to the house of Sorios. "Are you able to make a journey again, out to the country of the Cylosites near the borders of Batack? There is news afoot which may be of interest to you, my friend." She smiled, but she would not reveal what she knew.

So Sorios accompanied her, and she brought him into the lands of the Cylosites. There she found the camp of the Stegganese merchants. The place bustled with activity, for many had come to trade with them from throughout Niyarc and Vordót. Sorios surveyed the scene in astonishment. Then among the crowds he recognized Hesperan the deputy of Steggan, and he rushed to greet him.

Hesperan embraced him warmly, and said, "We are well met, Sorios, for I had need to deliver you greetings, and the journey from here to the Shelf is yet far. You saved me a great detour!"

"Well met, indeed, and I rejoice to see you again alive in this world. But what of Steggan, my son? Why is he missing from your company?"

"Steggan is lord of a prosperous folk now, and has much to keep him busy at home in our new land. But he sent me to deliver you a message in his name, assuring you that he is safe, and that his admiration and respect for you live on undiminished by the distance. And he begs your forgiveness, Sorios, for he has wronged you by leaving without a word." So Hesperan brought Sorios into his tent, and there he delivered to him the fulness of the words which Steggan had sent.

Sorios finally said, "There is no affront to my honor. Steggan has perhaps chosen the wiser course. Many grow discontented with this damp and dreary land. Indeed, were I not so old I would perhaps follow him."

So Sorios gave Hesperan a message to return to Steggan, assuring him that he was forgiven. Many things in addition they discussed, for Hesperan had many tidings to tell of their folk and of their new country.

When days had passed, and all the trading had been finished, Hesperan and his merchants loaded up their packs and their sledges with goods from Niyarc, and prepared to return to the Southrealm. Then Sorios and Hesperan bid one another farewell. They embraced many times, and Sorios gave him greetings to send to Steggan. "Let there be commerce forever between north and south," he said, "and no longer let the miles, and the darkness of the forest, divide our kindred."

4. The Dilemma of Cardach

So it came to pass. There was commerce thereafter between Niyarc and Steggan for many years as Sorios had wished it. Trails were marked and paths were cleared between the two regions, although few settled in the forest itself for fear of the Giants. Every summer the caravans of Steggan would arrive, and folk would flock from throughout the Northrealm to their markets.

But the trials of Sorios were not to end.

The fame of Steggan's settlement continued to grow in the north. The folk of Steggan's clan prospered, and as had the Cerites before them, their settlers spread into the regions about them, into the lush valleys of the country. They called their country Steggan, and their Tribe the Stegganese, and this land became their homeland for all generations. To this very day the Stegganese dwell in that land and defend it.

The climate of Niyarc meanwhile continued to fester in muddy misery. Yet further ills soon befell the country, for at this time evil things began to make raids into Niyarc from out of Batack: great prowling drakes; and roving packs of wolves; and even troops of Giants.

The descendants and households of Cylos' Tribe lived nearest to this region, and in all of Vordót, their tribe bore the greatest burden of these new trials. Though they patrolled the borders of the forest, the incursions could hardly be contained; the fringe of Batack was vast and remote, and many dangers slipped past their watch. So a mood of heaviness settled onto the folk of Cylos, as gray and heavy as the mists that plagued their country.

Rumor of this came to Steggan in the Southrealm, by way of the caravans which returned from Niyarc. So he sent word to Cardach, the patriarch of that tribe, saying, "Why do you remain in that accursed land, when new and better lands await in the south? There is endless open country, and we would be glad of the neighbors. Come to the Southrealm, then, and join your kindred."

When the elders and chiefs of Cylos' tribe heard of it, they agreed, and said to Cardach, "Steggan has done well in moving out of this country and prospering in a new and better place. Why should we not follow suit? The paths are open to the south. Let us join the caravans from Steggan when they return through Batack, and find a place of our own."

Cardach was the liege of Sorios, and this matter seemed harsh, for he himself had witnessed the pain of Sorios at the loss of Steggan and his kindred. So he said to them, "I will not sneak away under cover of night, like a miscreant in the dark. Steggan did so, and regretted it. We must seek the blessing of Sorios."

"But Sorios will never allow it," the elders grumbled.

"Only Sorios can say what Sorios will allow," Cardach replied.

Now it so happened that Sorios was in the country of the Cylosites even at that hour, for he often came down to the camp of the Stegganese when they came to trade, that he might share the company of his relations, or exchange messages with Steggan through their heralds and pages. So Cardach found Sorios in the camp, and said, "My Tribe is envious of the Tribe of Steggan. They have asked to depart for the south."

Sorios became crestfallen at once, for he felt sure he already knew the import of this statement, so he said warily, "And what have you told them, my friend?"

"I have said nothing, my lord. I came to ask your will in the matter."

Sorios said, "It is not for me to decide. You must do as you see fit."

"But what is best?" Cardach said. "I am not wise."

"And I am very old," said Sorios, "and bone-weary. My wisdom is not to be trusted."

"Then where shall I find an answer? My folk will demand it of me."

Sorios replied, "Let us go together to the Oracle of Tryma in Mount Éthel. Many have found answers in that place."

Since the earliest days of the Sorites, when Sorios' own son Diatron had first been trained under the charge of Tryma, there had always been an oracle in the Hall of Tryma on Mount Éthel. Many folk had sought wisdom and guidance in that Hall, and none had ever complained that they were led astray. Moreover Tryma and his oracle had often displayed the gift of foresight, beyond any others of the Terumani, even sage Ologéo. But the oracle, and the Hall in which the oracle made proclamation, were far away in the Mountains of Division, a long and difficult journey. Few were the visitors to that Hall, but those who returned seldom bemoaned the hardships of that trail.

"It is far from here," Cardach warned. "It is a formidable pilgrimage."

"But the words of the oracle are unfailing."

So Cardach said, "I will go. And I will do as the oracle says, no more and no less."

"As for me," said Sorios, "I shall accept the judgement of that sage, whether to my boon or to my bane."

Thus Sorios and Cardach together set out on the road[7] to Mount Éthel.

---

7 The term "road" is probably an anachronism, as only the Terumani maintained anything like paved roads in this distant era. But as the oracle on Mount Éthel was a Hall of Teruman Tryma, it is not impossible that Tryma himself kept a highway from that country into Rhotiéstir where many of the other Terumani kept their Halls.

Few paths led to that country, and still fewer travelers could be found along the way. The paths went through severe country, barren in many places, rocky and steep. Any sojourner might easily have gotten lost in those lonesome lands, but white stones along the way marked the pathways towards the country of the oracle at every crossroads, and stone lodges with snug roofs were kept along the road to shelter travelers from the weather, a day's journey each one from the other. These were empty for most of the year, and musty in their loneliness. But firewood could be found there, along with flints and kindling, and furs and raised beds for repose.

Sorios and Cardach trudged from lodge to lodge along the trail, resting for each new day's trek, while the country grew steeper, and the white wall of the Division Range drew nearer. If they met any other traveler along the way the tales do not tell of it. Not until they had entered the country of the Diatrians did they have any to guide them on the way.

The Hall of Tryma was built on the peak of a small but rocky mountain, in the far north of the country of Vordót. The valleys and hill country below that peak were the domain of Diatron's descendants, a sober and priestly folk that kept the ancient customs of their father; a hardy stock they were, who did not mind the often bitter cold of that region. A long age had they dwelt there, and a much longer age would they dwell there yet.

But the peak of Mount Éthel itself was remote even to them, lost in the clouds overhead, a cold and isolated redoubt which could only be reached by a narrow, gravelly pathway which switchbacked up the dizzying slopes of the massif.

It was to this path that they were guided when they came to the country of the oracle. "But do not attempt the path late in the day," their hosts warned. "You must start with the dawn if you hope to attain the Hall of the oracle before nightfall. And you must attain the Hall before nightfall: there are no lodges on the mountainside, and the nights on the mountain are cold, and windy, and not to be born, even for the young and hale." Saying this they glared at Sorios, who showed all the appearance of great age, but they did not know that he was Sorios himself, their ancient patriarch.

Cardach and Sorios therefore camped that night in a lodge at the foot of the pathway, and slept deeply in preparation for the morning's trek.

The dawn broke dim and gray, as it always did in Vordót in those days. A heavy layer of dark clouds hid the top of the mountain from view as they broke fast, so Sorios asked their host if it would be safer to wait for better weather before attempting the ascent.

"There is no better weather. Even in the days of our fathers, when the years of sunlight formerly blessed Vordót, the weather on the mountain was seldom clement. If it were, I suppose Tryma would devise some other trial to beset the traveler."

"Then we had best depart at once," Cardach said. "Let us pack lightly, food and water for the ascent only. We must travel quickly."

Sorios agreed, and leaving their heavy packs and gear in the lodge where they had slept, they set out onto the path in a cold, early morning drizzle.

The path began pleasantly enough from the western approach to the mountain, going upward steadily, but not too steeply, through rocky country punctuated with windswept pines and wide-spreading, black-mantled firs. It did not rain, but the constant drizzle dampened and chilled them, and depressed their spirits. Soon the nature of the trail changed, and as the climb steepened they found themselves on the very mountainside, trudging over gravel that slid beneath their soles, on a narrow lip of a path that often dropped off to the side into sheer, vertical depths. They spoke little, but pressed on, even Sorios complaining nothing of the strain of the climb.

But by noon things had grown still worse. The clouds had lowered, or they themselves had climbed higher than they had imagined, and they found themselves lost in a deep mist of blinding gray. The trail could hardly be picked out from the naked mountainside, and it was wet and slick. More than once either Sorios or Cardach slipped, and only by good fortune, or kind fate, caught themselves, or caught one another: the depths beyond the trail could not be seen in the blank emptiness of the fog, but they had little reason to doubt that any fall from the trail would be the end of them.

They stopped to take a brief rest and nourishment from their packs, both of them by now breathing heavily from the exertion, their legs trembling from exhaustion. Cardach said to Sorios, "Shall we turn back?" He peered unseeing into the mists above them. "We do not know how far we have come. We do not know how much further above us the mountaintop yet lies. But if we turn back now we shall at least be sure of reaching safe ground below before nightfall."

"We shall be safe, perhaps, but we shall be no wiser."

Cardach kicked a stone off the trail and listened as it clattered down, down, and further down the unseen mountainside below them. "It would be foolish to lose our lives for the sake of a bit of wisdom which we might gain on our own by careful consideration."

Sorios shrugged. "It is a trial," he said. "Tryma will not give his word lightly. But he rewards with words of like value as the trial."

"Then we have already earned weighty words," Cardach said. "Let us press on and earn words weightier still."

So on they climbed, while the afternoon waned. The air grew ever more chill. Gusts of icy wind began to churn the swirling mists around them, and threatened to push them from the narrow trail. They could not help but to slow their pace, bending low to duck the blasts, and keeping a hand on the wall of the mountain beside them whenever possible.

At last the trail disappeared completely, and nothing rose before them but what appeared to be a steep stair of natural blocks of stone. The mists seemed lighter, but the sky seemed darker, and Cardach feared that night would soon entrap them.

"It is a dismal and treacherous path! It was foolish for me to take Sorios my lord here," Cardach lamented.

Sorios smiled wearily, "It was I who brought you," he reminded him. "Let us have no regrets about it. We have no choice by now but to press on." He took a last bite of food and a last sip of his water, and began to clamber up the rocky way. Cardach followed.

So weary had they become that they could climb only a few steps at a time before stopping again to catch their breath. But so steep was the ascent that they quickly left the trail far below them. Both of them stopped at last, doubled over in fatigue, their hearts pounding. Doubt swirled in their minds like the mists swirling in the winds about them.

But all at once a gust of wind enveloped them, and they shielded their eyes and braced themselves against it. When they looked up, the mists which had shrouded their way a moment earlier had blown away, and they found themselves above the clouds: a vast blanket of white like an endless sea of fleece lay at their feet, gently seething away to the horizon. Mountaintops rose above it here and there like snow-mantled islands. And the sun shone, low in the sky to the southwest, but brighter than they remembered it had ever been.

Above them, the trail appeared to graduate into a level area no more than twenty feet above their heads. "We are here," Sorios declared, and began the final scramble to the top.

There they were astounded at the sight of the compound of the oracle rising before them. The whole crown of the mountain was a great, shallow dome, like a plate turned over, swathed in a surprising garden of lush green: mosses, grasses, and wildflowers carpeted the rocky soil; spreading fir trees, and bright holly punctuated the vista; a number of Tryma's disciples were seen coming in for the evening from a field of rich soil planted with crops which commanded the far side of the dome. Other disciples sat together in conversation on benches in a formal garden. A dense forest appeared to descend from the peak down the southern slopes on the far side of the mountain. It was all just about the last thing either of them had expected to find at the top of that barren peak.

The Hall of Tryma itself rose from the highest point of the crown, built of local stone perfectly fitted without mortar, so that it seemed nearly to grow from the landscape as if of living rock. It was not ornate, but it commanded an air of great dignity in its many square corners, windows, and portals. A towering roof of shining slate crowned the structure, steep-pitched to fend off the heavy winter snows. Cardach paused in awe when he beheld it, having never seen a Hall of the Terumani.

A path of white cobblestones led from where they stood, up a slope in a gently curved line to the entryway of the Hall. At the portico stood a pair of sentries: beautiful næads of the wood: one a spright, the other a nymph. Both of them bowed to the travelers as they approached, as if they were the ones honored by the visit.

"Tryma welcomes you to his Hall," said the nymph. "Come in and rest, and restore yourselves from the hardships of your journey."

The spright added, "You may partake of our table, and rest here for the coming night. It is presumed you have a question for the oracle. He shall receive you on the morrow."

The morning came bright and sunny on the mountaintop, and a rap on the door of their chamber brought Cardach and Sorios to breakfast in a sunlit room overlooking the eastern mountains. The sea of clouds still swept from horizon to horizon below the peak of Mount Éthel. They ate alone, a breakfast of cold meats and warm, rich bread which had been left for them, with no other guest and none to serve them.

At last one of the disciples of Tryma entered the room and bowed his head. "If you are rested and refreshed, Diatron is ready now to hear your entreaty."

Diatron had been the name of many oracles: some claim to this day that these are not merely the descendants of Diatron the disciple, but in many cases Diatron himself is reborn in the person of his progeny. Whether this be true or not, all the oracles of that line have had the wisdom of Diatron, for they are trained in the rites of truthfinding by their elders, and by Tryma himself: only those who display the deepest perception and greatest mastery might advance to the highest office.

The disciple led the way into the recesses of the Hall. Great as it had appeared from the edge of the mountaintop, it seemed still deeper and greater from within. Sorios and Cardach were brought down a long and dimly lit corridor which seemed to descend into the mountain itself, and the room they entered at its end had the appearance of a natural cave. Lanterns were set into the walls, shedding light of an unknown source: warm, golden and unwavering. A single stone seat was set up at the far side of the chamber, and on it sat an intensely frowning Diatrian, with a thick ruffle of fuzzy hair falling over his shoulders, and a nose like a hawk's beak. He rose when they entered, and gestured to a plush blanket spread on the floor before his own seat as the disciple bowed out of the room.

"Be comfortable," he said flatly. "Your journey has earned you the right." He looked hard at Sorios, and said, "You have overcome much. I think we have never known anyone of such venerable age to have conquered the journey to the apex of this mount."

"This is not any mere elder," Cardach declared. "You are speaking with

Sorios, our father and your own. He has been granted vigor beyond his years by the Terumani."

At this word Diatron paused uncertainly and his eyes widened. "Can this be true?" he asked.

"It is true," Sorios said plainly.

"Then I should be humbling myself before you," the oracle stated. "You should not sit at my feet."

"I come to you as any petitioner with a hard question, seeking the wisdom of the oracle."

"Nevertheless, this is not fit, and I feel the fool," the oracle said. He stepped forward from his seat as if to join them on the rug, but Sorios stopped him.

"There is no need," he smiled. "If you do not treat me as all others, how shall I perceive the gravity of your words?"

Diatron took his seat once more, but he had lost much of his solemnity. "Tell me then," he said, "What great need or question brings Sorios our father to the oracle of Diatron?"

"The question is that of Cardach, the elder and leader of Cylos' tribe." He nodded in the direction of his companion. "I have come because he has first asked me, and I cannot give him an answer myself. The verdict, moreover, will affect me deeply as well."

"Then ask," he said, turning to Cardach. "Together we three shall summon the guidance you seek, if indeed you do not already know the answer within yourself."

So Cardach asked the oracle what he had first asked of Sorios: whether he should lead his folk out of Vordót, and through Batack the great forest, to uproot them forever from their homes, and to seek a new country in the Southrealm.

"I cannot tell him yea or nay," Sorios said. "I have seen too many good and pleasant things fade, or depart from my side, or leave the confines of the world itself. I know this is as it must be, yet my spirit is wounded on account of such losses. How can I advise in such a case?"

"Would it be good, or ill, for the folk of Cylos to dwell in a pleasant homeland?" the oracle asked. "The answer to that, if you know it, would bear great weight."

Sorios parried. "Is it good or ill to deprive a father of his children, and many times over? I cannot proclaim that a life here in our ancient home will be better than a life in sunnier climes. Yet I cannot say such a choice would be ill! And how can I know whether the clime might turn again tomorrow, and days of sunshine and warmth return to Vordót and Niyarc?"

"My folk hang upon my own choice," Cardach said. "I might lead falsely. Or," he glanced at Sorios, "cause pain for no purpose. We might even depart one adversity merely to face new adversities in a new place. I might lead my clan to poverty and ruin. I would be to blame."

The oracle nodded. "Such matters are difficult to see. They require not only wisdom but foreknowledge. And foreknowledge is the daughter of knowledge. Will you stay with me a while, and accept my questioning and probing? I must ask many questions, and receive many answers, before I can hope to make such a judgement. And even then the light of foreknowledge may fail. It is an uncertain thing."

So they sat in the presence of the oracle for many hours, and discussed many matters. Many things he asked which seemed to Sorios and Cardach to be of no point, meaningless to the question at hand: yet Diatron had been trained for many years by Tryma himself, and his means of questioning provided many answers to unasked questions, teaching him much that Sorios and Cardach did not realize they revealed at all. Deep in the darkened chamber of that Hall they could not perceive the passage of time, and the words and conversation of the oracle possessed them such that they were unaware of anything else around them.

At last the oracle stood up suddenly from his seat and declared, "It is enough. Now I must go and meditate on these matters, and perform the rites of discernment, and seek the guiding light that shines within. I shall call for you when I have an answer." He disappeared into a narrow passage behind the stone seat.

Sorios and Cardach rose, and bowed out of the chamber. The disciple who had guided them earlier met them outside the entrance as if expecting them, and led them back up from the depths. "You will want food," he said unceremoniously. "The day is spent, and you have not eaten." Only then did they notice the pangs of hunger that beset them. "When you have had repast, you may return to your rooms to await the judgement of the oracle."

Diatron, for his part, descended into secret chambers deeper within the mountain where the rites and lore were to be practiced which he had learned from his elders, and from Teruman Tryma himself. Those secrets none know but a few among the Diatrians, and even the nymphs and sprights who ministered in that Hall knew nothing of them.

Yet he could find no sure answer. He pondered the question for many hours, deep into the night, and after he had rested, he pondered it further. And no answer came to him: none at least that satisfied his conscience.

Now Teruman Tryma dwelt in this Hall on Mount Éthel at times, but he possessed other Halls throughout Soria where he might sojourn. So it was that he had been absent when Sorios and Cardach had arrived. But when the oracle had been pondering the matter of Cardach's question for some while, Tryma returned to the place, and Diatron received news of his arrival.

So he set aside his probings, and departed from the Chamber of the Rites, and went up to greet him. When they had exchanged formalities as was their wont, Diatron explained to Tryma the question of Cardach. "And what path have you foreseen?" Tryma asked.

"I have seen many paths. All lead to benefits, but all also lead to woes."

"Then what path have you given him?"

"Sorios himself, the father of us all, is with him. I do not know how to answer him."

"You will answer him with the truth, as you always have done."

"But my eyes may be blind to the truth in this matter, fogged over by the severity of the burden. How can I see past the stature of the one who asks?"

"The truth cares nothing for stature or prominence," Tryma replied. "Only examine the facts: discard the pathways of wishes, hopes, and fears; and look for the light of sooth. Nevertheless it is a difficult question which bears on many things for all our folk. And it is a question which was bound to arise among us eventually. Come to me when you have your answer, and I will judge your wisdom myself."

The oracle bowed to Tryma his master, and he returned to the deep chambers of the Hall to continue his probings. He freed his mind, then, of his presuppositions and misgivings, and there he began to foresee great changes coming upon the lands of the north, and indeed all of Soria, and all its inhabitants from the lowest Sorite to the highest of the Terumani. When he felt confident of the issue, he brought his answer to Tryma.

Tryma examined the questions and Diatron's conclusions, and when he had satisfied himself of his own judgement, he said to Diatron, "I have analyzed your method and your answers, and the signs of nature and the heavens. Your words are true. But you have left out one matter."

Diatron hesitated. "There was one more thing. But it seemed... extraneous."

"Nothing is extraneous which is part of the truth."

"It does not bear on their question."

"I may not seem so to you, or to me. But these words will go out into all the world. They will find those for whom they hold meaning."

Diatron sighed. "Then I shall add words of the new folk to come. I do not understand the meaning, and I fear many changes shall come on the land because of that one small detail. But I am blind to them all."

"I once foresaw the coming of the deïnings, but it seems my vision was incomplete. And I think perhaps Deïni did not reveal to us all that she saw in the Pass of Toë." He shrugged. "It does not matter. For now, go to Sorios and Cardach and give them your answer."

"I fear they will not be pleased."

"But they have asked for the truth. I have myself had forebodings of these changes. It has been many years in coming, and many things have led us here. But the dam shall break, and the flood shall come, and your word in this matter is true."

So the oracle returned to the chamber of questing, and called Cardach and Sorios to return to him.

Sorios and Cardach had been waiting patiently in the chamber which had been assigned to them, with little to do but wait and wonder. The Halls of the Terumani were wondrous to Cardach, and endowed with many comforts, but so long had their patience been tried that Cardach at last said, "Can it be that even the oracle of Diatron cannot answer us? Have we suffered the trials of this journey to no end?"

But at last the disciple who had served as their guide returned to the door of their chamber. "The oracle is ready for you," he said. "And your question has been honored: Tryma himself has judged this matter, as well."

So they arose and followed once more into the depths of that Hall, and to the chamber of questing where Diatron sat on the stone seat of judgement. There they sat down in his presence as before, and the oracle spoke solemnly to Cardach, saying, "Are you willing to receive the word of the oracle, and the judgement of Tryma on this matter?"

Cardach replied, "I am."

He then approached Sorios, and placing a hand on his shoulder he said, "And you, father?"

"I will receive the word of Tryma, though I fear I know the answer before I hear it."

"Well enough," said the oracle. "Hear then the wisdom of truth, which has been given me to deliver to you."

Then turning again to Cardach he said:

"This land has been our lasting home,
A birthplace and a bosom warm,
Where we were born, and brought to be.
Here were we weaned on Wenda's knee,
And woke unto the wealth of words,
Our cradle when we came aware.

But bedsteads break, and blankets fray,
Timeworn trifles tossed away.

"So too this land of childhood cheer
Now blinks forever bleak and blear.
The days are dank, the drafts are chill;
The drought of daylight drains our will.
Winter gives us gales of grief,
And summer seldom sends relief.

. . .

This was the berth where were we born,
It granted gifts; but we are grown.

"Vordót shall drain its droves away,
To be reborn abroad one day.
The splendors of the Southrealm call,
The scions of Sorios seize it all.
Our folk shall flee their lands of birth;
Deserted dwellings fill the north.

The lilt of laughter they shall lack;
Their fragrant beds shall moulder black.

"No clink of tool, no clattering loom;
And darkness dreary as a tomb.
Nor song nor speech shall sate the ear
While house and hearth lie fallow here,
Till new folk come to claim these lands,
Surrendered into strangers' hands.

Cast off your qualms and quit this place.
This realm must raise a rival race."

When he had finished proclaiming this prophecy he added, "These are words of truth, and they are sure. Go in peace."

So Cardach and Sorios arose, and they departed from the Hall of Tryma in silence, with their heads bowed. When they had come some way down the mountain Sorios at last said, "You must, of course, do as the oracle has said. A new realm awaits you and your folk."

"And all of your kindred, to your own greater glory. All are your children, father."

Sorios sighed sadly. "The glory of a father is to be surrounded by his children."

"Then come with us, lord. Nothing the oracle has said prevents you from joining us."

"I think I shall not," Sorios said. "I shall return to the Shelf, where I might commune with Deïni and Wenda, with Phactorias, and Phreïs, who have cared for me these very many years. I think my days of walking openly among my children in the land are growing short. I must soon withdraw, and perhaps rest. It is the way of things."

"It is not a good way," Cardach lamented.

"But it is the right way."

So it was that Cardach and Sorios returned down from Mount Éthel.

There in the cold mists at the crossroads by the feet of the mountains they parted ways with many tears: Sorios went east, to return to his home on the Shelf below Mount Depharmen; but Cardach went south, returning to his own folk, and he saw Sorios no more in this realm.

Cardach sent word to all the households of his folk, and all the households agreed as one. When therefore the next of the summer caravans arrived from the Southrealm the whole house of the Cylosites arose from their settlements in Niyarc; they presented themselves to the Stegganese as companions for the road. When the caravan of Steggan had finished trading, and prepared for the return journey, then Cardach and the Cylosites assembled in a great company, and took the trail southward along with the Stegganese, away from Niyarc and Vordót, the country of their origin: so their land became devoid of any folk.

When Deïni heard of it, she approached Sorios cautiously, and said, "Have you heard that the folk of Cylos have risen up and gone into Batack, abandoning their homes for the Southrealm?"

Sorios merely nodded. "The matter is known to me," he said. "They have gone with my blessing."

5. Epilogue

As for the Cylosites, when they had at last exited the Forest, the Stegganese said, "We proceed now southward towards our own land. Will you follow us to that country? For there is much open land yet to settle, and we would welcome the confederates."

But Cardach said, "We shall camp here, for this country is pleasant. We shall send scouts to spy out the land, and find a place fit for ourselves. But we shall always welcome the folk of Steggan, and keep the roads open along with you."

The Cylosites went to the west, and there they found, near the great lake of that country called Egano, a land of rolling green hills, and copse, and hillock, which reminded them of their former homes in the north. There Cardach came upon a country which pleased him well, so he and his tribe founded there a settlement. The Cylosites claimed all this country for their own, from the edge of the Great Forest all the way down to the shores of the Pindus on the west, and began to establish dwellings there.

The word of the Oracle of Diatron came to be told and retold throughout Vordót. Few there were that doubted the foretelling of the Oracle, for Mount Éthel had been established since the first days of speech as the mouthpiece of Tryma himself. The word went out, also, that even Sorios himself had accepted the foretelling as truth. From household to household it spread; from village to hamlet; from family to clan. Soon all were saying openly that the days of the north were numbered, and that the future of the Sorites lay beyond Batack. And for many hope rose in their hearts at the promise of a better homeland.

The departure of Cardach and the Cylosites could not be hidden. When rumors of their successes in their new settlement trickled back to their neighbors, all in the north knew that the warm lands of the Southrealm beckoned to them. Then the exodus came upon the north like a storm, for the tribes and clans of the north questioned whether there was land enough in the Southrealm for all, and a rush to stake their own claims possessed them.

Thus it came about that the Sorites began to migrate to the south with the caravans from Steggan and Cylos. Some asked for leave from Sorios their patriarch, but many went away with nary a word even to their own neighbors. Sorios sighed at every loss, for these were to him as his own children.

Some migrated in companies with kin and clan; others migrated by themselves, or by families, in company with the Stegganese caravans. Some there were that even ventured to trek unattended (for the trail was now well-trodden and not difficult to follow) braving the dangers and troubles which abounded in the darkness of that forest. Though none knows what became of these, certainly not a few completed their journey safely, but some also were lost.

There in the Southrealm new settlements were founded, and new homelands claimed, and many new Tribes and clans were born. They spread throughout the countries south of Batack, from the forest to the sea, and all around the shores of the Circumpintus. The Sorites filled all those lands in those days, and the commerce among them was without bound.

The Cerites, however, rebuffed all who approached, so no caravan or traveler dared enter the country of the Hirna. Thus the Cerites were forgotten, and they became ever more estranged from the other Tribes.

So it was that the northlands, the country of Vordót and Niyarc, began to empty. Neighbors grew scarce and distant, and many homes and hamlets of the north lay empty and abandoned in the diaspora of those days. The remnant who remained gathered in enclaves of their own: in the heart of Niyarc near to the mesa known as the Table, in the country called Trachia; and in the vicinity of Mount Éthel where the Tribe of the Diatrians kept watch. Few other communities remained, only small clans and lonesome mavericks, scattered from one another and isolated from their kind.

In spite of all this, Sorios chose to remain in the north, in his house on the Shelf below Mount Depharmen near to the Hall of Deïni.

So it was that the foresight of Tryma and Diatron proved true, when the Tribes of the Sorites began the settlement of the south, dispersing throughout the regions of Egano and the Circumpintus. But few among the Sorites had noted the final words of the oracle. And the Northrealm lay forsaken and empty, silently awaiting the new folk of the prophecy, and whatever strange and unforeseeable changes that event might bring.

THE CHILDREN OF CYNODIAS AND PLEÏSTË

1. The Conspiracy of Dôni and Jeïnaric

Years passed in this way, and the north was emptied of the Kindreds of Toë as Tryma had foretold, leaving only a remnant who fretted but little over the dampness and cold. They were of a hardier stock, perhaps, or more resourceful in their provisions, and found the country yet to their liking, even in the cold and dank years. The Terumani of Vordót watched sadly as the land emptied, and waited for the new folk of Tryma's prophecy to arrive, but no one came, and the land sat empty.

Now the plateau called the Shelf, where Sorios still dwelt with a few of his closest kin, had in earlier days been a pleasant place of green grass and pine woods, boasting an expansive view to the south. So it was that several of the Terumani had built retreats in that place. But the Shelf was now frigid in the winters, more so even than the lower lands to the south, and few remained through that season. Even in the summers the Shelf was now shrouded in clinging fog. Only Deïni and a few others would visit to commune with Sorios and his kin.

Among these was Teruman Storeia: there she kept a Hall where she was dwelling with her daughters Wenda and Dôni. But it so happened one year that Teruman Phreïs was visiting along with his family when the snows of winter began to descend early upon the Shelf.

Phreïs frowned when he observed the black skies lowering over that country, and he said to Storeia, "The winter will soon be here. The other Terumani have already departed for the season. Come and sojourn at Timotéa for a while, where the weather is, well, at least less disagreeable, until winter has passed."

Storeia looked about the plateau as wind-whipped specs of icy snow pricked at her cheeks, and she sighed. "This place has become miserable," she said, "and the winters are a torture. I am ready to abandon it forever. We shall come: and perhaps we shall build a new Hall in Niyarc, in a more hospitable site." So she prepared to vacate the place.

But Teruman Dôni, the sister of Teruman Wenda, objected, saying, "Then who will keep watch over the country and its few inhabitants? The winters are harsh, and they will have need of the care of the Terumani."

Storeia smiled, for she knew the soft heart of her daughter, but also knew her to be impetuous and incautious. "You might stay, if you see fit. But it is a difficult season, and you would be alone. There are still strange words of Tryma and Diatron waiting to be fulfilled. You must promise to call for us if you need help. Bël will hear. Or come to us at Timotéa, the Hall of Phreïs."

Jeïnaric the son of Phreïs said, "I will stay as well. There's no need for Dôni to be left here alone without aid." Now Dôni and Jeïnaric were fast friends, and had been since their early childhood.

"As you wish," Phreïs shrugged. "You may have your fill of the pleasant weather of the Shelf in our absence. But come to us in Timotéa when you can bear it no longer." Then he promised to return with the Ádolthi at winter's end to check on them both.

So it came about that Storeia abandoned her Hall on the Shelf, and she went to sojourn with Phreïs, and Wenda went with her. Phreïs also left with his family. But as they went Storeia said to Phreïs, "Are we doing the wise thing, leaving our children alone in that bleak place? There is much that can go wrong."

Phreïs said, "They are grown now, and are Terumani of their own right. They can handle whatever troubles might come their way."

"You are right, of course," Storeia said. "Nevertheless a mother can worry, can she not?"

So they shrugged off their doubts, and they left the plateau of the Shelf for the less cruel clime of Timotéa. Then that place was empty but for Sorios and a vestige of his kin. Only Dôni and Jeïnaric remained behind in the abandoned Hall of Storeia.

It had been Dôni's habit to go among the Sorites along with Wenda, openly at times, but often concealed as many of the terumani are wont to do. Even when hidden from the vision of the mortal kinds, the Terumani have the power to touch their spirits and inspire them, or to warn them through prescience of imminent dangers when necessary. So have the High Ones always given aid and inspiration to our kind.

As winter was already setting in, Dôni said to Jeïnaric, "Let us tour the country, watching for dangers and opportunities, that we might be of secret aid to the Sorites." So they took themselves off into the high country of Niyarc, nigh unto the Mountain Wall[8] which divides the land.

As they patrolled, Dôni spied beneath the clouds over the mountains a wheeling of vultures, their black wings like dark fingers stretching forth, high above the ravines. The vultures were omens of death and corruption, and they discomfited her. She pointed them out to Jeïnaric, and said, "This is curious: what living soul might they have found in that barren terrain in this season?"

"Whatever it might be," said Jeïnaric, "it would appear it will not live long."

But Dôni said, "But the vultures remain in the air, circling, waiting for death to come. Whatever is there yet lives."

---

8 This is an alternate name for the range known as the Division Mountains, or the Barria Heceïca.

Jeïnaric scowled up at the rocky heights. A flash of alarm swept over him as he realized what Dôni was contemplating. "They are far away, and remote," he said. "There is little to be done."

"What if it is one of the Sorites, lost and far from home? Or it may forebode some danger of which the Sorites must be warned. Whatever creature is there, I cannot let it die alone. We must go up into the mountains and investigate."

"It is a perilous climb," Jeïnaric warned. "We should call for Storeia, or my father Phreïs, or any of the Ádolthi, and get their aid."

"Help is far off: our kin are far away in the Hall Timotéa. No others of the Terumani remain nearby. But we must hurry, while there is still hope to save whatever living thing has wandered into that place."

"What of Sorios, and his kin? Surely they will help?"

"Sorios is aged and does not often roam far from his home, and I could not impose such danger onto him, or any of that mortal kind. You may go and seek help if you wish. I will not delay."

Jeïnaric sighed and said, "You certainly cannot go alone into that range. Deïni once tried it alone, and even she nearly fell into the long sleep. I shall have to come with you." Dôni smiled, but Jeïnaric shook his head slowly at the foolishness of this plan.

With that they made off toward the circling vultures. The sun was low and brown in the sky even in the brightness of noon, and long shadows groped across the crags and peaks. The airs had grown bitter, and winds rushed down from the north, howling into the valleys and ravines which scoured the sides of that range. All lay bleak, as the northern borders of Soria are at their bleakest.

As they came over an unfamiliar ridge a cascade of cliffs rose before their eyes, one after another, up to the heights where the snow ever falls and the ice never melts, and the peak of Mount Depharmen loomed beyond. There Jeïnaric paused. "We have come to Conviniën S'tarotho, the Gleaming Gateway, and this is the foot of the Depharmen Stair!"

Though the peak of Depharmen loomed over the Shelf, the ravine which hid the pass of the Stair was unseen from that plateau, wrapping around the northwest face of the mountain, and few even of the terumani ventured that valley, for they were in awe of it.

"This pass is a strange place, and full of mysteries," Jeïnaric cautioned. "Deeds done here have changed the course of many events."

"It cannot be helped," Dôni said. "The vultures circle over this very ravine. What we seek is above on the mountainside."

Jeïnaric hesitated, but he said, "It is against my better judgement, but I will not abandon you."

The pass before them ascended into the heights in cliff after sheer cliff of bare rock, enclosing a river of slowly cascading ice, in form appearing as a monumental stair down from the fogs of Toë. That pass thunders eternally like the voice of the Storm, as the river of ice creeps ponderously from the heights. It is the only pass known through the Mountain Wall, but it is not an easy way.

Dôni gazed up apprehensively into the pass. She shivered and said, "We may find nothing but some abhorrence hidden there, beyond hope of aid or life. But if something yet lives, they have no one else to help."

Jeïnaric placed a hand on her shoulder and stood beside her. "Then let us trust to Havui who has led us here, and begin our ascent."

So the two exhausted themselves for hours climbing over steep slopes of loose rock and talus. They left the level ground, and made their way beyond the plateau of the Shelf, further up and into the ravine than any had dared in a long age. Had Dôni tried the pass alone she would surely have failed, but the two together were able to help one another over the perilous crags, until at last, no more than halfway to the top of the pass, they came to a broad slope overlooking the great blocks of ice. There they spied a party of souls at rest, gaunt and wan, huddled upon the bare and unforgiving rock as if stricken down by an enemy; while the vultures of death circled overhead, awaiting their demise.

"They are Sorites!" Dôni declared, rejoicing that she had dared the climb, if only she might still be in time to rescue them.

"How might that be?" Jeïnaric questioned. "How can any party of Sorites have strayed so far into the passes of the Mountain Wall? And why?"

Dôni ignored him, and called out to them in the speech of the Sorites. But they gave no answer, nor any sign of recognition. They did not even look her way at the sound of her voice.

"It is too late," Jeïnaric lamented. Something about the look of the party made him nervous. "We should leave."

"No, but the vultures have not descended," Dôni said resolutely.

So she left Jeïnaric behind, and scrambled across the slope quickly to give aid. But when she came near she drew back aghast. Her skin crawled like one who reaches for a stick, but discovers a serpent. For these were not children of Sorios at all. Never before had such a folk or Kindred been seen in Soria, and Dôni was afraid.

These folk which were hunched at Dôni's feet were both like the children of Sorios, and yet queerly unlike them. In form they were similar, yet these were coarser, their motions unfamiliar and eldritch to her eyes. In visage they were uncanny, hard to read, for their countenance was shrouded with thick hair, unlike the feathery pate of the Sorites: beards grew upon the faces of the males, and even the females had down upon their cheeks. Nor were they smooth even upon their limbs or their backs, as were the deïnings. They seemed to Dôni outlandish, as if from some other world or some other age of the world.

Yet looking upon them Dôni was moved to pity. So she gathered herself and tiptoed cautiously across to meet them. There she found the elders who appeared to be their leaders, a male and a female, and issued them water, reviving them in the hope that perchance they might tell her whence their party had come. But the strangers looked at her blankly, not comprehending her words, for they had no speech, and were in their minds as unknowing as the beasts.

Jeïnaric finally went across to join her. He was as confounded as she at the strange appearance of the party. A chill ran down his spine. "Who, or what, are these creatures?" he asked. "And why are they in this land at all?"

For a moment the strange prophecy of Tryma flashed through her mind, but she said nothing. "It does not matter," she said, kneeling beside them. "They are lost and destitute, near to their own deaths, and yet see how they huddle together in their want, as if in protection of one another." In this harmony she saw them as like the deïnings, whom Havui had gifted with empathy beyond that of the other creatures in the land even before they had received the gift of speech. "And I see the light of understanding in their eyes," she added.

"Your imagination may be carrying you away," Jeïnaric said. "But I suppose we must help them."

Dôni and Jeïnaric then gave water and food to each, as much as they could spare from their own provisions, reviving them somewhat. But they had not carried enough sustenance to restore to them all their strength. Their elder got to his feet, and stumbled a few steps, then sat down again on the cold rock, hugging his knees and shivering.

"They will never be able to make the climb down from here in this state," Dôni said desperately.

"Then we must return down the mountain now and get aid," Jeïnaric said. "We must find someone to bring them food and water, and furs to keep them warm in this blistering cold, until they revive fully."

"There is no time," Dôni said. "Their situation is urgent, and they will certainly perish if we delay."

"Then let me go down the mountain myself, and get food and water."

"It is no good," Dôni said. "I do not think either of us can manage the pass alone. I must go with you."

"Then we must leave them here alone." He gazed up at the vultures, which continued to circle overhead. "Do you think it wise?"

"I cannot lose you on the mountainside, or remain here trapped alone. We shall do what we can to protect them, and return as quickly as we are able. If only they could speak like the Sorites, so we could make them to understand."

So Dôni and Jeïnaric worked together, gathering stones to build a rough shelter against the wind and the blowing snow. Though there was little growth upon the slopes of the mountain, they scraped together enough wood that they were able to build a fire, and they showed the elders how to fuel it with sticks and branches in the hopes it might be made to last through the night. Then with many gestures, they tried to make it understood that they would return with more supplies, but they could not tell if the creatures comprehended them at all. At last they were forced to abandon the site, and they scrabbled their way back down the mountain.

It was dark before they reached safe ground, and neither of them would dare the pass at night. So they made all haste to the Hall of Storeia, and when the following dawn broke they gazed upward doubtfully. But the vultures still circled lazily overhead. So they gathered their provisions, and repeated their climb to the shelter.

The beings they had left behind rejoiced to see them. The fire had gone out long ago, but Jeïnaric had brought furs, into which they wrapped themselves gratefully, several gathering under each. There were not enough mantles to cover them all, but they selflessly shared the boon: some stood aside to allow the weakest or most miserable to recover, then those would make way for others. When Dôni and Jeïnaric gave them food, they distributed it fairly, that none might go hungry, giving more to the weakest among them.

"See how they care for one another," Dôni remarked. "Surely these are not mere beasts."

Jeïnaric stood apart and eyed them warily. "But what are they?" he said.

Dôni had no answer. "Whatever they are, we cannot abandon them to the vultures."

"I suppose you are right," Jeïnaric sighed. "Annoying, as usual, but right."

For eight days, then, they made their way down the mountain, and returned laboriously each day to the shelter they had made, bringing food, and firewood, and more furs. The creatures revived and grew stronger, yet they made no attempt to remove themselves from that camp, waiting each day for their deliverers to arrive.

"We cannot do this forever," Jeïnaric said at last. "They are well enough to travel, I deem, yet they depend on us. What are we to do with them?"

"I think they have become our responsibility," Dôni said. "We must take them down from here ourselves."

He looked down wide-eyed at the precipitous trail they had ascended. "Down to where? You cannot think to bring them to your Hall on the Shelf. The house of Sorios and his kin is not distant from that place, and we know as yet little of this kindred, and don't even know whether they might be a danger to the Sorites." He gazed at them nervously. They were large and broad shouldered, with thick and muscular necks, unlike the Sorites, and even Dôni found their aspect disquieting.

Dôni considered the problem. "At the foot of the Stair is a secluded hollow, hemmed in by the walls of the canyon and the glacier. We can hold them there until we know what to do with them, and whether they can be trusted."

So they brought packs for each member of the party, supplying them with food and water for the climb; taking their leaders by the hands they made them understand that they were all to descend the mountain together. So they led them cautiously down from the perilous mountainside. The length of a whole day the journey required, with Deïni and Jeïnaric guiding and aiding their charges over each difficult passage. At last, as the sky faded to gloaming, they descended the final cliff, and reached the safety of the grounds below.

The last of the vultures finally gave up their frigid vigil, and one by one circled away to their place beyond the mountains.

Dôni and Jeïnaric made a camp for the creatures there, delving caves into the sides of the ravine, and building for them a house for protection from the cold of the season, that they might recover their full strength. This place they built craftily that it might not be seen from the highlands above. But the walls of the valley they reinforced that it might be unscalable without aid. The waters issue in a torrent from the skirt of the glacier, sealing off the egress of that valley as if by a frigid moat. So they arranged it that the strange new folk might not wander far nor invade the lands beyond.

When this work was complete, Jeïnaric said at last, "Now I'm sure you will agree that we must send for help. Certainly the Ádolthi must be made aware of this new creature. I shall go to my father Phreïs at Timotéa and ask for his aid."

"I think we should not," Dôni said uneasily.

Jeïnaric gaped at her incredulously. He sighed and rolled his eyes. "I thought you might say so. But why?"

"We know Ologéo and his ilk. If they discover this folk they will treat them as invaders infesting the land. Who knows what they might do to them?"

"Perhaps they would be right, Dôni."

"I cannot say, but I cannot allow them to be persecuted or perish when Havui has clearly sent me to be their deliverance."

"Then what will you do with them?"

"For now, it is my duty to provide for them," she said. "I agree with you: We cannot allow them to run free in this country until we are certain they are not a danger. But why should I have rescued them from the mountainside only to let them perish now in the winter snows? They may even be the new folk which Tryma prophesied would replenish the north."

Jeïnaric raised an eyebrow. "That is a curious suggestion!"

Dôni ignored him. She regarded her tribe with a sense of obligation, for she had after all been their savior and deliverer.

Jeïnaric shook his head slowly and sighed. "I suppose we might keep them hidden here until springtime when the Terumani will return," he conceded, "just to observe them, to learn what manner of creature they might be. But whatever we do, eventually the Ádolthi will discover them. You know that."

"Then I must devise a plan to that eventuality. If it cannot be prevented, it must be managed."

Thus Dôni began to minister to them and watch over them, while Jeïnaric observed them silently and distrustingly. She brought them what supplies she could manage, and taught them to forage food for themselves such as that valley provided. She also made raiment for them fit to protect them from the winter's chill. It soon came to pass, then, that the creatures ran to greet her and flocked to her whenever she appeared among them. They fawned upon her, and tried to serve her and bring her gifts of the forage they gathered. They proved to be gentle and sociable with her, and they clung to her as a savior and deliverer.

For many days they dwelt in that place in secret. Dôni began to fret every day, and worry every night, that they might be found out, and she considered what she might say of this new kindred if they were discovered.

When the less frigid days of spring began to arrive, and the snows were beginning to melt from the mountainsides, a day came when Dôni was ministering to the tribe by a campfire she had built in the hidden enclave, and Jeïnaric stood behind her watching uneasily. Sitting down beside Dôni he said, "What are your plans? We still know little about this folk, if 'folk' they can be called. I cannot guess whether they are a danger to the land or not."

Dôni scowled at him impatiently. One of the creatures came and bowed at her feet, accepting a gift of flatbread she had cooked for them over the fire. It took the offering and divided it with a crude wooden blade it had fashioned on its own, to share with its cohorts. "How can you watch them and not see how enlightened they are? They behave just like the deinings."

"You may be right. But we are guessing. We should seek help, Dôni. This group has made it through the winter. All are hale and fully recovered from their mysterious ordeal. The summer season is not far off, when the Terumani will return. We must soon decide what to do with them."

Little by little an idea had come to Dôni which she could not set aside. She answered timorously. "What if this new kindred, too, was meant to have the gift of speech, as do the Sorites? Having that gift, they might be able to explain themselves and answer all questions. Then they would be held as kindred with the Sorites, and even with the terumani."

Jeïnaric was incredulous. "How will that help your cause? Even if they are the new creature Tryma foretold, Tryma said nothing of speech! You have seen how Ologéo and the others treat the Sorites. They are already jealous over that folk. Will they willingly share the land with yet another speaking Kindred? Would you have this folk, too, be despised in the same way?"

"Despised by the camp of Ologéo, perhaps. But consider this: though many have objected to the Sorites, none has dared lay a hand upon them to this day. Many of them have even come to support the Sorites. I could assure their security in this land. At least they could not be driven out or destroyed."

"Do not underestimate Ologéo. His influence is great. Such a disruption may well push him beyond endurance. And many will fall in with him."

"They will come to accept the new folk as well. You will see. But it may be to no end. I may not succeed at all."

"What is your plan? Would you call Wenda, and ask her to do this thing?"

Dôni frowned. "Perhaps I, too, can grant such a gift. Have they not been given into my care, to grant them boons as I see fit?" Now it was no secret that Dôni was envious of her sister. Though Ologéo and his camp had reprehended Wenda for giving the gift of speech to the Sorites, there were many in the land who lauded her above all, and even Storeia her mother was ardent in the plaudits of her sister. Dôni had come to feel small and insignificant in the presence of Wenda.

"But only Wenda has ever succeeded in such an endeavor," Jeïnaric said. "It would be wise to seek her help."

"The risk would be too great," Dôni said. "Even if she would help, could she be trusted not to inform Deïni and the rest of Ádolthi?"

"Would that be so wrong?"

"They would put an end to it before I began."

"You cannot attempt this alone!" Jeïnaric said, and a new fear crawled into his mind. "Do not forget, Dôni, that I was there in the house of Erescal when he entered the senses of his companions, and he destroyed their minds, and all of them went mad. I saw their madness with my own eyes. Their progeny are ruined beasts to this day. I cannot allow you to take such a chance. No one knows the mistakes of Erescal."

"But I will not make those mistakes," Dôni said confidently. "And don't you see that I must do this alone for that very reason? If I am wrong, and I fail at this endeavor, no one else must be harmed in the doing."

"But what would I say if things went wrong?"

Dôni smiled, "You will tell them that I was willful and impetuous, and I did this thing secretly without your consent."

Jeïnaric shook his head slowly. "I think this plan will bring us trouble. More than you imagine, Dôni. But if I cannot stop you, I must be at your side. Perhaps I might rescue you from the brink."

"Then you also would be held responsible. You would take such a chance?"

Jeïnaric rolled his eyes and made a growling sound. "I have kept your secret thus far. I will continue in this plot. I am already in it too deep to save myself. But whether you succeed or fail, I assure you that this is going to work to our detriment! The Ádolthi will be no more pleased than they were with the gift of Wenda."

"Pleased or not, they will not harm my charges."

So it was that Dôni carried out her plans alone and in secret, as her sister Wenda had done. Only Jeïnaric remained with her, watching over her to assure himself that she did nothing foolishly or rashly.

The next day they went down together to the valley, and they brought eight of the creatures covertly into the old Hall of Teruman Storeia her mother: the two eldest who appeared to be their leaders, and six of the youthful creatures of breeding age. When she had made them comfortable, Dôni sat with them, and began to apply herself strenuously to the skills which were unique to the daughters of Storeia.

Though none could say what was the error of Erescal, yet Dôni by the directions of her own kind nature did her work slowly and cautiously, never seeking to control or dominate as had Erescal. She brought into her work no unkind motives, and no deception or pride. Only a cool elation pervaded her mood as she saw the work progressing. Jeïnaric stood by and watched, in private awe at the skills and confidence his friend displayed.

Dôni made a language for the new creatures, fit for their own tongues, and different from the language of the Sorites, that it might stand as her own creation. This tongue she wove into the minds and hearts of that Kindred. At Jeïnaric's request, she also was able to teach it to him, using her skills of inspiration to impress it into his mind.

It was no surprise to him that after many days Dôni's labors succeeded. Her guests gained the boon of speech: their minds were enlightened, and they received understanding like the Sorites and Terumani. Then Dôni was flush with her success.

Yet Jeïnaric could not help but worry that the outcome would bring strife into the land.

The eldest of that clan she gave the name of Cynodias, he who seemed to be their leader, and his mate she gave the name of Pleïstë, for she had received the gift of speech.[9] Their Kindred came to call themselves the Pleïstians, as it has always been the custom among that folk to name themselves after the line of their mothers.[10] The Pleïstians they are called to this day.[11]

She gave names and speech to six others of that company also, and these

9 Cynodias means "the elder." Pleïstë translates roughly into "One who speaks" in Sorian, but others derive the name from the Dônish "Phulêgis," which means "a pathfinder."

10 This is a generalization. Although it was common among the Pleïstians to use the mother's name as a surname, in fact there were many Tribes and families of the Pleïstians who were named after their fathers, as well.

11 Not mentioned are two other lines known as Cynodians: the Mas'chians and the Gnathosians. It is thought by some that they descended from Cynodias at a later time, and through another line, not through the line of Pleïstë.

became the progenitors of the six lines of the Pleïstians: These six were Gnathos, a father; then came Menoth, and Aucheni the twin sister of Menoth; Glyptas, a mother; Predorës; and Therës, fathers. These are the Sorian forms of their names: In Donish their names are Agñeth, Maghot, Aukhêni, Glyphthad, Pferdan, and Theirarh.[12]

When the work was complete and Dôni had rested from her labor, Jeïnaric said to Dôni, "At last we may learn of them who and what they might be, and whence they have come, that we might have an answer if they are discovered."

So she agreed, and she called the company of the creatures to her chamber. "You have arrived in this world as strangers, unknown to us who hold the guardianship of these lands," she said firmly. "We have seen no other creature like yourselves. Many shall question why you have come. I am not the highest of my order, and I shall need to give answer to all who question me. So tell us now: Whence have you come? And what is your purpose in these parts?"

But Cynodias was ignorant of his history, and he could not give an answer. "We remember nothing of a former home."

Pleïstë said, "Until the hour that we gained speech and understanding in this Hall, we had no words by which to preserve our thoughts."

"Come with us then," Dôni said, "to the place where you entered this land, to see whether the sight of it brings back your recollection."

She and Jeïnaric got up from the Hall, and they took Cynodias and Pleïstë, together with the six others, and brought them out of her Hall. They led them back to the Stair, and showed them Mount Depharmen and the Gleaming Gateway where they had been found. The winds were chill out of the icy pass that day, and the scent of wet stone was heavy in the air, as it had been on their journey down from the pass. Cynodias and Pleïstë breathed deeply of that atmosphere, and closed their eyes, and shivered.

"I can tell you nothing of the land of our origin," Cynodias said. "I remember only that all turned to ice, and we fled. I have only visions of great hardship: perils and troubles along our way. Before this disaster I have no memory at all, for my mind was as yet dark and without understanding."

"I, too," said Pleïstë, "recall little beyond images and sensations of biting ice, miserable cold, and unrelenting hunger... and travel for many days beyond counting, ever seeking escape from bleak and bitter places. I feel, but I cannot say why, that we have been long in an icy realm, and have seen many generations of our own children come and go, and these souls with us are all who remain."[13]

Dôni and Jeïnaric questioned Cynodias and his clan as well as they could.

---

12 The names as given here belonged to more distant descendants of Cynodias and Pleïstë who would not actually have been present at this time. The names of these original progenitors are not known.

13 It is implied here and elsewhere that these forebears were not immediate children of Cynodias and Pleïstë, and probably had spouses of their own when they entered the country.

But there was little to glean, for they had nothing but scattered, wordless memories like the dim memories of childhood.

From the fragments of their recollections Dôni learned of vast fields of ice, where the tribe of Cynodias could find little food, but for an occasional bird which had become lost and perished in the storms. There were images of dismal swamps and marshlands: a wide-spreading country of mire, where travel would have been impossible had the land and the waters not frozen solid. At last they remembered the vultures, the omens of death, which had gathered overhead to haunt them day by day.

In the end they had spied the peak of Depharmen and the pass beneath its shoulder, and hope rose in their breasts at the sight of that mountain, glowing amber in the sun of the south, for it appeared to be a gateway into a better and brighter country. But the pass below the peak led them to the Stair of Depharmen, and they had looked down with dismay at the cascade of cliffs descending before them. With no choice left, and being near the end of their strength, they began their descent: but their strength had given out at last. Lacking sustenance, they had looked for nothing further but death on the mountainside, had Dôni and Jeïnaric not arrived to deliver them.

"As to our purpose," Pleïstë said, "we have none, nor ever had any, but to escape our ruined homes to a place of warmth and comfort. If indeed you keep the gates of this country, we ask only relief for ourselves and our household, that we might find a place to rest at last."

Jeïnaric turned aside with Dôni and said, "The land they describe is unlike any we know in Soria. Clearly they have fled from beyond the Mountain Wall, from lands we have never seen."

Dôni said, "Can anyone deny that they have been rescued by Havui, and guided into the land of Soria, just as the Sorites were sent from beyond those mountains, and our own folk before them?"

"From Toë, or further still," Jeïnaric suggested.

Dôni's heart had gone out to them. "I am no gatekeeper," she said to the couple, "nor do I have any status among my Kindred, yet I promise you shall have a home in this land. It is clear to us you have been guided to this land, just as our own kind were sent. None can now deny you an equal place."

Jeïnaric also agreed with her, saying, "I will stand by them, as well." He lowered his voice, however, and looked furtively over his shoulder, as if expecting they were being watched. "But we must consider now what we will do with this Kindred. What you have done is astonishing, Dôni, and far beyond my own skills. But there is now a new speaking Kindred in Soria, and it cannot be hidden or taken back."

"I do not repent of this gift. But..." she sighed, "now that it is done, I feel certain it will be scorned. Ologéo and the others of his mind will certainly be wroth."

Jeïnaric smiled. "Indeed they will! How shall we explain ourselves?"

"Can we not keep the matter a secret? Let us find this clan a refuge of their own, far from the Sorites, and far from the Halls of the Ádolthi. There they can thrive, and become established. Perhaps by the time they are discovered their presence will require no further explanation."

"They have the gift of speech. I have my doubts that Ologéo will be so easily fooled!"

"Have you any better plan?"

He shook his head slowly and resigned himself to the scheme. "Finding such a place will be no easy task."

"Soria is vast, and there are many lands that have not been settled."

Jeïnaric, however, knew more concerning the lands of Soria than did Dôni, for the study of that lore was a favorite of his. "There are many unsettled countries, but how many of those places are congenial to such a tribe as ours? There are deserts, and swamps, and mires in abundance. There are forbidding mountain realms in the south. There is cold taiga in the north, where the ground is frozen for much of the year. Would it be kind to send them to any such place?"

"I think they would be happy in any place where they might find food and warmth, after the trials they have suffered on their journey here."

"We must be careful to confirm the prospects of any land before we consign them to it. What resources will they have? What dangers will they face? Will there be game or forage fit for their palates and abilities? Will there be poisonous plants, or venomous creatures to beware of? We must learn all we can of the country before we send them there on their own. If we intend to keep them secret, they cannot simply leave if the country displeases them. They must be prevented from migrating to some other country where they might be more easily discovered."

"They should name you Jeïnaric the Cynic," Dôni complained. Her shoulders slumped. "Such a search will take years."

"If we wish to succeed we must be prudent."

"But what can we do with them in the mean time? The Ádolthi will be returning here to the Shelf soon enough. The secret enclave we have made for them at the foot of Depharmen has gotten them through the winter, but it is far too small," Dôni said.

"And too near to Sorios," Jeïnaric agreed. "We will need to avoid the error of Wenda. We must find a better place to hide them, where we can care for them ourselves until we are ready to move them."

"Their clan is not yet numerous," Dôni said. "Surely we can find some hidden valley out of sight of the Terumani to secure them for a time."

"There are lost and hidden valleys enough here in the north," Jeïnaric mused. "But if their clan grows and leaves their enclave, they will quickly be discovered."

"We will have to make do, and hope that luck is with us," Dôni said. "We shall begin our search in the morning."

But their plans were to be interrupted. As they prepared to leave the Hall of Storeia the following day, they were surprised by a knock on the door, and found Phreïs, the father of Jeïnaric, entering the place.

"I apologize for the surprise," Phreïs said cheerfully. "I thought after the long and lonely winter you might appreciate a little company. And I'll admit, I was a bit worried for your welfare."

Dôni and Jeïnaric exchanged nervous glances. "We have been fine, here," Jeïnaric said reassuringly. "There have been many things to keep us busy."

"That is good to hear," Phreïs said. He paused and seemed to be waiting for something. "After my long journey here on foot, I expected you might offer me a bit of hospitality."

"Of course!" Dôni said, clearly flustered. "Please come in and make yourself comfortable." She ushered him into the Hall and welcomed him to the guest chamber where he usually stayed. As he settled in to the place, Dôni and Jeïnaric met together quickly in the corridor and spoke in hushed voices.

"What will we do?" Dôni whispered. "We must move the Pleïstians before Deïni returns for the summer, and we have yet to find a suitable place for them. How shall we search with your father here?"

Jeïnaric threw up his hands in frustration. "We must take turns searching. One of us will stay here with my father to keep him occupied. The other will go out and search for a redoubt. Perhaps he will leave before long. In the meantime we must be cautious if we visit the Pleïstians in their enclave."

"True. We must not give him reason to follow us or search the area."

Jeïnaric smiled wryly. "It would be best if we could manage to keep him inside the whole time."

So they set about to place this plot in motion. But the more they tried to cover up their activities, the more curious Phreïs became. The more they tried to keep him indoors, the more interested he became in wandering outside. Phreïs did not show any sign of hurrying to go, and seemed to be enjoying his stay all the more. As a matter of fact, Dôni and Jeïnaric were not particularly good at stealth, and Phreïs seemed to be amused by their obvious discomfort.

Meanwhile they took turns searching that country and reporting back, traveling many hidden paths by foot. Mostly they remained in the foothills of the Division Range, in the most remote glens and canyons they could recall. But the days ticked by, then a week, then two, and still they had no luck in finding a spot remote enough, yet large and verdant enough, to meet their needs. And still Phreïs remained at the Hall as their inconvenient guest.

Phreïs meanwhile could hardly help but to notice their mysterious behavior. It was clear something was being plotted behind appearances, and though he questioned them they revealed nothing of their secret. Nevertheless Phreïs was no fool, and was able to read many signs in their furtive behavior and their deceptive talk, and he was able to guess much. At last one evening when both of them happened to be at home he decided to confront them on the matter.

"It's clear something has been going on behind my back," he said affably over dinner. "I've hardly seen the two of you together the whole time I've been here. Where have you been going on these frequent disappearances?"

Deïni answered confidently. "We've been out exploring the remote canyons and glens of the countryside. Searching for any remaining Sorites who may need our help." This seemed a credible excuse, at any rate.

"Well, you won't find any Sorites in this country," Phreïs said. "Other than Sorios and his small company here on the Shelf."

"So it seems," Jeïnaric said, playing along with Dôni's story. "Things have changed much since the Sorites left."

"Indeed they have," Phreïs said. "The northern lands are sad and lonely now. Even many of the Terumani have followed the Sorites into the Southrealm." Phreïs paused as if making a decision, then he leaned forward and spoke intensely to Jeïnaric. "Have you been back to Box Canyon? We used to camp there when you were young, but that was long ago. I would hate to see it now, lonely and forsaken as it is. That canyon had everything one would need for sustenance: game, fish in the stream, abundant forage... yet the last of the Sorites left that place decades ago. Why, I don't think anyone has even been to that valley since. Not even the sprights or nymphs go to that out-of-the-way place now."

Dôni and Jeïnaric glanced at one another.

"In fact if one were looking to keep something secret, hidden from the terumani, they could not trust in a better place." He seemed to wink meaningfully at Jeïnaric. "If one needed a secret stronghold, that is."

He quickly changed the subject, as if nothing on the matter had been said at all. But after they had finished their meal he stood up resolutely and said, "I should probably be leaving soon. Perhaps I will go in the morning." He became serious again for a moment. "Keep in mind, though, that Deïni, and some of the others, will probably be arriving before long. The weather is..." he smirked at the gloomy gray sky lowering overhead, "well... improving. For the season."

True to his word, he packed up his effects the following morning, bade his farewells to Dôni and Jeïnaric, and took to the trails back to Timotéa.

When he had gone Dôni said to Jeïnaric. "What do you think? Was he advising us to go to Box Canyon?"

"I have no doubt of it," Jeïnaric said. "How he discovered our secret, or why he chose to help us, I cannot guess."

"Perhaps he merely trusts that our motives are good. He knows you well." She smiled. "You are perhaps the most cautious and judicious soul I know!"

"Then let's trust his word, and check out the glen. I remember it fondly. It does seem a suitable place, if it is now as forsaken as my father describes."

So Dôni and Jeïnaric went to the site together: a secluded gap in the foothills of the Mountain Wall, which was known as Shuë Vidril, the Box Canyon. A narrow and long-forgotten path led into the canyon through a forest of pine. Dôni and Jeïnaric pushed their way through, over root and rock, until the pathway opened up into a broad valley. Its verdant floor snaked into the highlands, walled in by tall cliffs of silver-shining granite. Beneath the lip of the canyon were airy caves for shelter, and stone houses[14] where clans of Sorites had once dwelt.

Dôni gasped when she saw it. "This will be our place," she said.

The valley within was wide, and was carpeted thick and deep with grass, with tubers, and with berries; fish filled the stream which wound through, and leaped in its pools: birds and game abounded in the pines, the firs, and birches which dappled the valley floor, and willows tickled the waters with delicate fingers: all things the Pleïstians might need to thrive were found there. It had once been a place of beauty, and even in those gloomy and dank days a ghost of its appeal remained.

"It is too near the Halls of the Ádolthi," Jeïnaric fretted, "and will become too small if their clan flourishes."

Dôni rolled her eyes. "But it has all they need to thrive until we can find them a permanent place in the land," Dôni said. "Trust me. We will make it work!"

Dôni and Jeïnaric labored together to weave spells of concealment about that valley, to hinder its discovery, strong enough, they hoped, even to confuse the terumani.

When all was in readiness, they went out to Depharmen, and gathered the clan of Cynodias, and brought them secretly to Box Canyon. Dôni herself stayed with them to teach the clan all they would need to flourish in that land: They had come into Soria knowing nothing of the country, of the nature of its produce, or its game, or how to seek sustenance from the country at all. Dôni also taught them how to make use of the available remedies and healing plants, and taught them which plants were harmful and to be shunned.

When she and Jeïnaric were confident the Pleïstians could survive on their own they took Cynodias and Pleïstë aside, and strictly ordered them not to allow any of their clan to wander beyond its borders. Then Dôni said to them, "We must go now, to search out a lasting home for your tribe. There

14 The "stone houses" of the mortal Kindreds of Soria for many millennia were bare structures roofed by great slabs of rock propped upon boulders, or set into slopes over crude excavations. These were often sealed further against the elements with mud walls, and leather or fabric hangings as doors.

are many places in Soria of fairer clime than here in the bleak and bitter north. This land of Soria is vast, and surely a secure and genial home can be found, where you may establish yourselves without fear of discovery or conflict. Remain in this place until we return."

"We are content to wait," said Cynodias, "for our situation here is as a holiday after the trials of our escape."

"Rest then, and grow strong," Jeïnaric told them. "Until we come to collect you, remember that you must not leave this valley. There are others in this land, like yourselves, who have a gift of speech and reason. They may fear your kind and oppose you. Who can say what troubles will arise if you are discovered before the time is right?"

"We shall do as you say, and follow where you lead," said Cynodias. "You have been our deliverers, and our friends."

So Cynodias and Pleïstë agreed. Then they turned to Dôni, for she had shown herself to be their mightiest ally. "We shall ever be thankful to you, our protectress," Pleïstë said. Then they bowed to her, and bade their farewells, and Dôni and Jeïnaric departed.

2. The Indiscretion of the Pleïstians

After this Dôni and Jeïnaric began to go about the land searching for a homeland for their Pleïstians, carefully and in secret, that they might not reveal their intentions to any. They went out by turns, that the Hall of Storeia might never be wholly abandoned, and their absences might not be noted. None among the Terumani discovered their secret or became suspicious of their many departures.

Jeïnaric knew much about the distant realms of Soria, but his knowledge was neither deep nor exhaustive. So it was necessary to visit many countries, and explore the lands themselves, and study them deeply. They wished to know each land in all seasons, and learn its secrets, both favorable and perilous. Many places they tried, and in many they were disappointed. The best places were too near a Hall of the Terumani, the home of some overseer of the country who would be keeping watch over their lands. Some were too near the settled lands of the Sorites. Some lacked resources the Pleïstians might need; some were infested with dangers they wished the Pleïstians to avoid. Others were prone to long droughts in the summers, or floods in the winter rains or springtime melts. Some were simply too exposed, and difficult to conceal, and they feared their Pleïstians would be discovered by mere chance.

It must be said, moreover, that both Dôni and Jeïnaric grew perhaps too cautious, or too demanding. No place they found satisfied them fully. In addition, the secret enclave of Box Canyon had proved safe, and they grew perhaps too confident in the security of the site, and too complacent of their situation. As time passed the dangers of discovery seemed remote.

The ageless Terumani do not regard time as do our own folk. Years passed in their endeavor, more years than either of them noted or realized. By the reckoning of the Pleïstians their sense of urgency seemed to have waned in a distant past, and their promises seemed forgotten.

The Pleïstians, meanwhile, were prospering and multiplying in their secret home. Their numbers grew, and the time came when Box Canyon seemed too strait for their clan. A new generations of the children of Cynodias arose which had not known the warnings of Dôni or the promise of the their parents, and the dangers of discovery were forgotten. These were not content to remain in the safety of their hidden camp, but desired to move out and claim country for themselves and their families.

So it came to pass one year that the patriarchs Menoth and Therës spoke to their clans and said, "Our homes are filled, and our folk need room to grow. We shall go out ourselves and explore the country. Then we will bring back word, and we shall claim new homes in new lands." So they took up their spears and javelins for the hunt, and loaded packs for a journey, and ventured forth from Box Canyon. This plan seemed only just and reasonable to them, and they saw no need to reveal their intent to their elders Cynodias and Pleïstë. As for Dôni and Jeïnaric, these guardians of their folk had been off on another long absence, and Menoth and Therës had no idea when they might return, if at all.

But they had forgotten the spells of concealment that had been woven about their redoubt.

For some days they explored the woodlands south of Box Canyon, intending to find some nearby hollow or meadow where new homes might be raised, and new hunting grounds might be exploited. But when they tried to return home to the canyon, neither Menoth nor Therës could find any trace of the entrance, nor did they even recall where to look.

"How could we have we gone so far astray?" Menoth asked. "We see the mountains from whence we came, yet the entrance to our home is nowhere to be found."

"It is a spell of confusion," Therës said sourly. "Our carelessness has doomed us. Now we must wander the lands without home or family, unless all our tribe should chance to follow us out of the valley."

Menoth sighed. "We shall certainly not find it ourselves. Let us scour the country, seeking the Terumani. Only one of that Kindred might open our eyes once again to the valley of our home."

"But where might we find the Terumani?" asked Therës.

"If I remember rightly the lore we had received from our elders, the north country is remote and unvisited. Let us head to the south and see what is there."

So southward they went. For a length of days they followed the rushing torrent of the C'heta River, its rocky gorge spilling through wild pinewoods. They met no one and crossed few paths. When they exited the woods at last they found a country long abandoned by the Sorites, an empty wilderness where the silence was broken only by the wind and the mournful calls of hidden birds. Tall weeds and brush had overrun the lands. A mere shadow of trails and tracks remained, so overgrown they could scarcely be distinguished. A few ruined cottages they spied, empty and lonely places now, with roofs caved in and abandoned furnishings rotting in the weedy yards, as the words of the oracle had predicted. Any folk who remained in the country were scattered far and wide, and Menoth and Therës came across no other soul.

Their path took them far to the south, and heading eastward they passed near to the mesa known as the Table.

Now that country held an enclave of Sorites who had remained in Niyarc, a tribe who called themselves Trachians. They had banded together when many of their kinsmen had departed for the Southrealm, in a fertile region of Niyarc far from the perils of Batack. Seldom did any caravan arrive from the Stegganese in those days, and that tribe was remote and alone in the land, and nearly forgotten even by their kin.

A community of this tribe had settled the Table itself, for it commanded a clear view of the country for many miles round about. From thence they could watch for any sign of rare traders or travelers from the Southrealm, or any sign of Giants or wolves, or other dangers which might from time to time beset their country. If ever some surprise was spotted, whether good or ill, horns would be sounded, calling the folk of those parts either to take shelter or to greet their visitors.

Teruman Deïni also had a Hall on that mesa, which she visited from time to time as the mood struck her.

As Menoth and Therës reached the country, therefore, they were spied by watchmen of that settlement. At the sight of them, a commotion arose at once, and the watchmen called for their captain, a commander named Hadero. "Shall we sound an alarm, or the horns of welcome?" they asked. For they could not make out from a distance whether these newcomers were friends or dangers. They walked in the manner of Sorites or terumani, and were dressed in raiment similar to their own, but even from that distance they appeared strange and unfamiliar. It was clear that the party was armed, and they were large and formidable in aspect.

Hadero observed them from above, but he could not decide which call to make. "Whether friend or foe, we must not allow this party to go by unmolested. We do not know who or what they might be, nor do we know their intent. Perhaps they are some aberration of the Giants, or a new and unknown danger from beyond our ken." So he quickly assembled a company of his clan, who took up weapons themselves, and they went down to confront them.

Menoth and Therës knew none of this, and had proceeded on their way unconcerned. But as they came over a rise the company of the Trachians suddenly appeared before them, rattling weapons above their heads and shouting for them to halt.

Menoth and Therës paused and stared at the strange creatures curiously, wondering what this apparition might mean. All the Pleïstians are brawny, more sinewy than any but the greatest of the Sorites, and Menoth and Therës were more tall and powerful than any of their kin. The Trachians on the other hand were among the most slight of the Sorites: hardy of constitution, perhaps, but neither powerful in sinew nor in strength. Though outnumbered, Menoth and Therës merely smiled at their attackers.

The Trachians, for their part, grew yet more agitated at the sight of them, and at their apparent serenity in the face of their warning cries, so at a command from Hadero they made a charge at the intruders, hoping to frighten them off. Menoth and Therës raised their own spears and prepared to defend themselves from attack.

Now Dôni had warned her charges that the lands abroad were populated with others like them, having a speech of their own, and understanding like their own. The Trachians were also clothed, and armed with weapons fashioned by hand. So Menoth said, "Let us stay our hands! These are creatures with understanding, like us and the Terumani, and are not dumb beasts." So they stood down and lowered their weapons; they called out to the Trachians, begging them to halt and to do no violence. Hearing the voice of speech, Hadero called a halt to their advance in amazement; both parties then set aside their weapons, and approached each other cautiously.

They stood then face to face, examining one another, bewildered and astonished. Bloodshed was averted, and the two Kindreds were spared woe. In this way the Pleïstians and the children of Sorios first met. Violence and injury were avoided: but the two Kindreds could not understand one another, and they wondered at one another.

Teruman Deïni happened to be dwelling at that time among the Trachians of Niyarc in a house which she kept on the Table, so Hadero said to his company, "Let us send to our Teruman: she will know what to do with this strange folk."

So one of the company was dispatched to call upon Deïni and seek her audience, while Hadero and the rest of the company sat down in the field together with Menoth and Therës, examining the newcomers and their equipment, and attempting to make themselves understood.

When the herald arrived at the Hall of Deïni and tried to explain the matter, Deïni could make no sense of the thing at all. Until that very day no news of the Pleïstians had reached the Terumani, for Dôni and Jeïnaric had kept them well hidden. "I am as confounded as yourselves," she said. "If these creatures are as you describe, and their babblings are truly a language of their own, we know nothing of them."

"I saw the beings myself," said the messenger. "I assure you they are just as I have related: neither Giant, nor Sorite. Nor are they teruman, unless there be terumani we have not known."

"Then this is strange beyond measure," said Deïni. "I must go down with you and see this thing."

So she went with the messenger out of her Hall, and down from the Table, and allowed herself to be led to the place in the field where Hadero and his company sat with Menoth and Therës.

When Deïni saw them she was taken aback for a moment, for something about their form seemed familiar, as from a long-forgotten memory, yet at the same time she was certain beyond doubt that she had never seen these two beings, or heard their strange speech, in all her days.

The two Pleïstians rose to their feet when they saw her, for they knew at once that she was Teruman, and of the same order as their protectress Dôni. They bowed their heads repeatedly in deference, and tried to explain themselves, but Deïni was unable to comprehend their speech, and could not unravel their tale. Even the name of Dôni she could not recognize, for their accents were harsh and strange to her ears.

So with signs she urged them to follow to her house on the Table. For a moment they hesitated, but Menoth said to Therës, "Let us go with this one willingly, for she is Teruman and will surely treat us honorably."

"It seems we have little choice," Therës grumbled. "The Terumani are more powerful than we, and would compel us to go if we resist." His spear he had laid aside as a gesture of goodwill, and he now wished it were in his hand.

The troop went off together then, and climbed the ascent up to the Table, and Deïni brought them into her house. There she examined them carefully, as well as her skills allowed, but she was able to learn nothing of them. "I am at a loss," she finally said to Hadero. "I will send to my father, Teruman Phactorias, for help. Perhaps he knows something of these creatures." So she sent to Phactorias, inquiring whether he had been enlisted to furnish these creatures a home. But Phactorias also knew nothing of them; coming to the Table himself to investigate, and seeing them, and hearing their speech, he, too, was confounded.

In all this time Menoth and Therës were detained in the house of Deïni, unable to make their petition heard, and they were distressed.

"It can be delayed no longer," Phactorias sighed. "For good or for ill, we must call Ologéo to us here. The investigation of new and strange things is entirely his domain."

"We will have no rest once that one is involved," Deïni complained.

"Nevertheless, I do not think there is another who might unravel this mystery."

So Bël was called, and she sent word to Teruman Ologéo at Liaibíri, asking him to come at once to Deïni's house on the Table in Trachia.

Ologéo came quickly, being stupefied himself regarding the matter. He shut himself into the chamber where the Pleïstians were being kept and examined them deeply, even probing their minds with his own, but he could make nothing of this investigation, for their language was strange beyond his experience. He examined and studied their artifacts: their clothing, their tools, and their weapons. He went out to the place where they had been discovered, and studied their trail as far as it could be followed. Other probings he was able to make, into the very substance of their nature, things which are beyond the ken of all the other Terumani. Yet for all this, he learned nothing to explain their sudden appearance in the land.

When he had finished his scrutiny Ologéo went out to Phactorias and said, "These are a new thing in the land, of another kind than all before them. They hail from another country, we know not whence, and they are ill-fitted for Soria. They do not belong here among us."

More than this, he regarded them with suspicion, for they had the gift of speech, and it was unlike that of the Sorites and the Terumani.

"What then is to be done with them?" Phactorias said.

"We must first find out their homeland to learn how many they are," Ologéo said. "Where there are two, there must be more of their kind. Yet until we can discover their speech, we can learn nothing of them."

"Then it would be my thought to call the house of Teruman Storeia for her aid in this matter," said Phactorias. "Both she and her daughters are mighty in the powers of language and understanding. She may shed light on the matter, and may even be able to learn their speech."

Ologéo agreed to this, though he had no great love of Storeia or her daughters, and Bël was enlisted to call them to the Table.

Meanwhile Menoth and Therës were still constrained at the Hall of Deïni on the Table, and complained of their condition: but none could understand them, nor did any consider their plight.

Now Storeia had built herself a new Hall of her own, not far from Timotéa. To this Hall Bël hurried, and delivered the message of Ologéo and Phactorias. "You are wanted in Deïni's house on the Table in Trachia," she explained. "A strange new kindred has been discovered there, speaking in a language which none can unravel. Two of their kind are being kept even now in that house. It is hoped that you or Wenda might question them, and might be able to bring their speech to light."

Dôni was also by chance visiting with her mother at the time, and this message reached her as well. With a sudden shock she realized that her Pleïstians had dared to venture from the valley of the Box Caves. She caught her breath and said, "I must go also." Storeia agreed, not questioning this request, and the three of them departed for the Table.

When they arrived Storeia first was ushered in to see the Pleïstians, but even after much probing and questioning she was able to discern little. Wenda, who had given speech to the Sorites, was brought in next, but neither was she able to make any headway with this strange folk.

Dôni waited and worried in the hall outside the door of the chamber as her mother and sister tried to interview the newcomers, but she had no doubt what folk were hidden within, even without having seen them. At last she decided the thing could be delayed no longer, and she spoke up, enjoining Deïni to allow her to see the strangers. So she was ushered into the chamber.

At the sight of their protectress and deliverer, Menoth and Therës both cried out together and ran to her side, explaining their plight, how they had become lost from Box Canyon, and how they had been held in this place against their will for many days, and pleading with her to help them regain their freedom. Then Dôni replied to them in their own tongue, "Aghra neh ighri," which is to say, "Trust in me."

She turned stoically to Deïni and demanded their release, saying, "These are my own folk, whom I have discovered myself and saved from death in the pass out of Toë, and they are under my care. Release them, that they might return to their kindred in peace."

When the others beheld the Pleïstians conversing with her familiarly, and heard her speak to them in their own tongue, they were astonished. "Who are these folk?" Storeia asked. "And where have you kept them?"

"Give these two their freedom, and we shall show you," Dôni said.

So Menoth and Therës were given into the hand of Dôni, and she dissolved the spell of concealment, and brought them back to their home in Box Canyon. The others followed her, that they might observe this new tribe in their place. There they found a community of the Pleïstians, dwelling together and filling up all the habitable nooks of that valley. They built houses like the Sorites, and dressed themselves in garments of fur and fabric and leather. They made tools and vessels similar to those of the Sorites, and some among them even cultivated small plots of favored crops.

But most disquieting of all, all of them conversed in the strange and unfamiliar language of Dôni. At this revelation Ologéo was greatly disturbed.

Ologéo demanded, "These are mortals. How came this mortal Kindred to have speech?" Saying this he cast an accusing glance at Wenda.

But Wenda denied it, saying, "I know nothing of this Kindred, still less of their speech. Both are entirely foreign to me, both to eye and ear: and I am as confounded as you all as to their origin."

Dôni did not hesitate. "It was I," she admitted. "I acted alone in this matter."

Both Storeia and Wenda were ready to congratulate her on this accomplishment, but Ologéo cut them short. "On whose authority did you commit this act?"

"On the demands of nature and fairness," Dôni said. "They entered the land like the Sorites, and I could not deny them the chance to share the fate of the Sorites."

"But the fate of the Sorites was also granted without conscience," Ologéo objected. "You have done a great wrong to this land."

Phactorias also was among the party, and he said calmly, "The work of both the daughters of Storeia is great, and they have proven themselves equal to the greatest of us in powers. They deserve honor more than accusations. But I will admit this gift has raised a concern among us once again, which we must now settle among ourselves."

"Indeed," grumbled Teruman Ologéo, "If we cannot retract these ill-conceived errors, we must contain their effects. This foolishness has gone too far. It shall take a council of all the Terumani to decide this case."

3. The Ire of Ologéo

Rumor of this new kindred quickly spread, and a stream of the Terumani soon made the journey to Box Canyon to see the colony for themselves. Phreïs also heard the rumor, and he sent word to Jeïnaric his son, who was at the abandoned Hall of Storeia on the Shelf at the time. Jeïnaric realized at once what had happened, and he rushed to Box Canyon to find Dôni.

"I have told no one of your part in this matter," Dôni said when they were alone. "Things have not gone as we had planned. Perhaps it would be best to remain quiet."

"What is the mood of the Ádolthi?" Jeïnaric asked.

"It is hard to judge," Dôni said.

Among the observers who had flocked to Box Canyon were many who were fascinated by the new creatures, for nothing new had appeared in the land for a long age. Though their tongue was strange and incomprehensible, it was clear that these were creatures on par with the Sorites, whom many had already come to accept as fellow-tenants of the land along with the terumani themselves.

Many, however, quickly made up their mind to oppose this strange new Kindred, and felt their intrusion was a pollution to Soria on par with the profanity of the speaking Sorites. Even some who were partial to the Sorites protested: these feared the daunting Pleïstians. Still others worried that the gift of speech was now given too freely, and wondered how it might be contained. So discord spread among the Terumani, and they were uncertain what to do.

"Are the folk we discovered in danger?" Jeïnaric asked.

"I cannot be sure. There is talk of destroying them, or banishing them from Soria, as there was with the speaking Sorites. I do not think they will prevail, but Ologéo is angrier than I have ever seen him."

"Did we go too far in this deception?"

"We can only wait and see. We will have defenders, I think. At any rate, you must not implicate yourself. I am to blame."

"If there is blame, I shall accept it along with you," Jeïnaric said. "I have been complicit in this matter from the start."

"The matter of speech, however, was my own decision. And I think this will be the hub of the contention."

Indeed, this proved to be the case almost at once. Wherever the Terumani gathered, new discord arose over the Pleïstians. Ologéo did not wait long to put his antipathy into action. Bël was once again called into service, and Teruman Ologéo sent word to all the Terumani to come to council in Liaibíri.

By this era many of the terumani, high and low, had come to accept the company of the Sorites, and conferred with them on many small matters. But Ologéo strictly warned all to come to council secretly, unknown to the Sorites and the Pleïstians. "We must discuss this matter among ourselves, privately, away from the ears of these folk which the daughters of Storeia have corrupted. Let no Sorite or Pleïstian know of our assembly, for there are weighty matters upon which we must confer. We ourselves—apart from the consultation or opinion of these... others."

So began the greatest council of that age: All parties saw the fate of Soria hanging in the balance. The elders of the Terumani congregated at Liaibíri: the Ádolthi and the Ídolthi, along with many of the lesser of the terumani... Phactorias, along with Deïni his daughter, protectress of all the deïnings, and Hiren his son, who watched over the Cerites; Teruman Tryma the Wise who watched the Diatronites; Dreiton of the Seas, and Nilon of the Waters, together with Grënas her consort, the lord of the dræads; and many others from about the land of Soria. Even sundry of the dræads and næads made their appearance, for some of them were now confederate with the Sorites in the woods and pools and streams of Soria, and considered them friends or compatriots. Only Teruman Vélopar would not come, not even at the behest of Ologéo and Phactorias.

Dôni and Jeïnaric found the place swarming with activity when they arrived. Jeïnaric went to join his father and brother in Phreïs' small chamber, leaving Dôni to make her way to the chambers of Storeia her mother. Every chamber and room of Liaibíri was full, and many who came to council were forced to camp on the great lawn before the portal.

Storeia, as the Mother of Imagination, had her own wing in Liaibíri, and it teemed with visitors and supporters. Many dark glances were cast at Dôni as she passed, even there, among the supporters of Wenda. So Dôni abandoned the place and went out into the gardens to sit by herself and brood.

She sat there alone for some while, wishing that Jeïnaric might come out and find her, but afraid to go back into the Hall to seek his company. When she heard steps approaching on the pathway behind her she turned her head hopefully. Instead of her friend she was surprised to see Teruman Phactorias. "Storeia told me I might find you here," he said. "Come with me to my own chamber, if you will. There is something I wish to discuss with you."

Dôni was puzzled, but agreed to brave the scowls of the crowds and follow him. When they arrived at his room she was surprised to find Deïni present, and her sister Wenda waiting for her, as well. Phactorias shut the door.

"Pardon the secrecy, but I feel we need to speak with you both, away from the crowds," Phactorias said. "You should be warned: The mood here is against you and your folk. You must be careful what you say when the council is called."

"That is certainly no news," Wenda quipped. She glanced at Dôni. "To either of us, I presume."

"Certainly not!" Dôni pouted.

"It may be more serious than you realize," Deïni said. "I know the moods of Ologéo, and the influence he has over many. I was once in his camp, you may recall. I think he will seek to have you both censured in some way. He will certainly call again for the destruction of the speaking Kindreds."

"The Sorites are established in the land!" Wenda objected. "Many of them have friends among the Terumani by now."

"And I will not abandon the folk of Cynodias," Dôni said. "I also have allies."

"This is exactly my fear," Phactorias said. He turned to Dôni. "I understand what you have done for the folk you discovered. But I am afraid you may not have fully grasped the import of your actions. Not only have you opened old wounds, but new indignations have sprung up, as well. The situation is becoming precarious."

"Would you have us abandon the Kindreds we have taken under our care?" Dôni asked indignantly.

"Certainly not!" Phactorias said. "But you must be cautious how you present yourselves. My counsel would be to show yourselves humble and compliant. If compromises are offered, give them consideration."

""Humble and compliant'?" Wenda said sourly. "Have you given this same speech to Ologéo?"

Deïni laughed. "Well, you must show yourselves to be better than Ologéo. You might gain allies and make plain his petulance."

"Thank you for your advice," Wenda said. "Can we hope you will defend us in the firestorm?"

"We still hope to avoid the firestorm," Phactorias said.

"This is why we called you both here," said Deïni. She glanced at Phactorias her father for permission to proceed. "We have a plan to end this debate, but it will impact you as the guardians of your Kindreds. We cannot attempt it without your assent."

"Tell us, then," said Wenda.

"It may be moot," Phactorias warned. "I have some influence, but my voice alone may not hold much sway in this debate. It will require the aid of one greater than myself. Of course we cannot count on help from Ologéo."

"Then there is only one other," said Wenda. "We must acquire the aid of Vélopar."

"But Vélopar will not come," said Deïni.

"So it has proven," Phactorias said. He shook his head. "The Ádolthi have pressed him continually for his opinion. Both Ologéo and myself have urged him repeatedly to come to council. But he stays at home enjoying his ease and bothering little with anyone else."

"Then tell us what you intend," said Dôni.

So Phactorias and Deïni explained their thoughts. They described at great length a vision they had formed to bring matters to a conclusion. "It will change many things in Soria," Phactorias said. "But I think it will heal many wounds, as well."

Wenda at last said, "If you can bring this about it would be good for us all. I agree to this plan."

"As do I," said Dôni. "But how shall we get Vélopar to agree?"

"There's the rub," Phactorias shrugged. "Well, let us see how the debates go. It may be unnecessary. On the other hand, developments may yet force him to come to council."

When the halls and chambers of Liaibíri were filled to overflowing, Ologéo called the council to order. The Lyceum was packed to the walls; many stood around the peripheries or crowded the doorways.

The crowds parted for Dôni as she entered, many scowling at her, and she made her way to join her mother Storeia and her sister Wenda near the front of the room. Phreïs was seated alongside Storeia together with his sons, and Dôni took her place at the side of Jeïnaric. They exchanged a silent, conspiratorial glance.

Teruman Phactorias stood before them all on the platform, and spoke first, saying, "We all know why you have called us here, Ologéo. But before we debate your question, many here are curious about the coming of this new kind among us. Remove yourself from the dais, that we may allow Dôni to explain their story to us all."

Ologéo shot Dôni a cold glare, but he submitted to this call, and stood aside for her. Dôni whispered to Jeïnaric, cautioning him to keep silent, then she took her place shyly before the entire assembly of the Ádolthi.

There she explained how she had found the clan of Cynodias and Pleïstë as refugees in the Pass of the Stair, and had rescued them, and given them a place to hide until such time as she could find them a homeland of their own. She confessed that they had flourished there beyond her expectations, and had come out of their redoubt before their time. "They want nothing more than a place of their own," she said, "where they can live in comfort far from the deprivations of the frigid regions they have left behind." The Ádolthi were hushed as she told this tale, and all seemed to feel sympathy for Dôni and her charges.

But when she had finished Ologéo clapped his hands slowly and ironically. "That is a charming tale," he said, "but you have passed over the one detail which brings us here today. You not only gave them shelter and retreat, Dôni. You also gave them the gift of speech, just as your sister gave speech to her Sorites without sanction. Once again we are brought to contention over this matter of speech."

"I found these creatures helpless and near death on the very borders of Soria," Dôni protested, "in the storied pass that enters our land from out of Toë itself. It seemed clear to me, if not to you, that Havui had sent them here just as he had sent us, and just as he had sent the Sorites. It was therefore only fitting that they should be equal to the Sorites in all regards."

Then Ologéo suggested, "Why Havui has chosen to send them into this country we cannot say, but many creatures have been given to the kindreds of Soria both as prey and as livestock."

Now Deïni had begun to have suspicions of her own as to how this Kindred had arrived in the land, and how they may have first appeared. At Ologéo's declaration she was aghast. "Who can deny that Havui brought them to this land just as he brought the deïnings? They were discovered at the very portal of our land, the Gleaming Gateway at the Pass of Toë itself. If you deride these Pleïstians, you deride the deïnings also."

"More than this," Dôni objected, "It cannot be coincidence that I discovered them on the very brink of their demise, in just the right moment: such fortunes must have been destined. Surely they were brought into this place for one reason: that they may dwell among the Kindred of Sorios as equals. And if equals, they, too, should have the gift of speech."

Now Storeia their mother was proud of her daughters for reason of the surpassing skills they had shown. Nevertheless she scolded, saying, "This work was great and your passion was great; but Dôni, surely the elders of the Ádolthi should have been consulted before such a choice was made?"

Teruman Phreïs japed. "Had she done so, she would still be waiting for her answer. It seems we can do nothing without endless debate."

Dôni scowled at Ologéo and said, "Do we not know the mind of the elders, who would have unfairly derided such intent? And the gift due this kindred by Havui would have been denied."

Teruman Tryma himself suggested, "It indeed does seem cogent that this kindred came to the land in the right place and the right time to be rescued by the one individual among us who was both capable and willing to grant this gift. I for one am unable to dismiss this evidence."

Ologéo grumbled at this retort, but went on with his case, saying, "For long years have we born these Sorites among us, and against my own judgement many have even come to accept that speaking Kindred as rightful sharers of the land of Soria with us. But it does not even end there! Now these Pleïstians also have been given speech as well. The daughters of Storeia spread speech to whomever they like, and there is no end to be seen of this unchecked absurdity."

"We know your sentiments on this matter, Ologéo," said Teruman Phactorias. "But what would you have us to do?"

Ologéo purred, "It is not for me to decide, but I may offer my advice openly. Let us consider, all of us, whether the land we received is more harmonious as it was made, or as the daughters of Storeia have transformed it from under our feet. If it is in our power to return the country to its pristine state, should we not perchance choose that path? We have seen that the gift of speech can be removed, even from our own kind," and saying this he frowned at Reinodas the father of Erescal: Reinodas bowed his head in shame and sorrow. Ologéo continued, "If you will not allow us to purge the land, let us then seek to restore these speaking folk to the proper state in which their race was conceived. Then we may all enjoy the land of Soria and its gifts as we ever did, and nothing shall be lost."

At this suggestion a cloud of dread descended on the room, and an uproar was raised. For the act of Erescal was considered a horror and an abomination by all.

But continuing in this speech Ologéo went on, "Moreover, I suggest—and yet," he added, bowing his head in mock humility, "this is only my opinion, a matter for us all to consider, and I myself do not judge—that the daughters of Storeia have committed a crime against the land, and against our purposes here. If this be so, and if we so convict—and as there seems to be no stopping them in their designs upon the creatures of this land—they should perhaps be exiled from this realm, and banished to that estate from whence we first came."

The tumult was great at this saying. Storeia shouted to silence Ologéo; but others of the Terumani immediately took his side, saying that the daughters of

Storeia were arrogant and ungovernable, and could not be trusted. Many dark and angry accusations were cast at Wenda and Dôni. Jeïnaric squirmed, looking to Dôni for permission to speak, but she shook her head.

Tryma then spoke rationally, "Now Ologéo, we may discuss these matters as you have suggested, but consider yet these two things. First, that none of us has ever returned to that estate from whence we came. Those paths are behind us, and we do not know if such a path is even possible. Our natures are conformed to this land, and here we must remain. I should suggest that no such punishment, untried and uncertain as it would be, should be considered. Secondly, that the methods of Erescal to erase the gift of speech are unknown to us, and indeed would seem to have been a great error on his part. That which transformed the followers of Erescal was a monstrous thing, and we should fear that path, not seek it."

Cosimë the spouse of Ologéo then said, "But are our hands entirely tied in these matters? Why should we not restore the land to its former state, if we so choose? And should there not be some consequence meted out to the daughters of Storeia for their audacity?"

Teruman Storeia spoke then, saying sternly, "You call it audacity, but have we not, all of us, done nothing but alter and shape the land? Vélopar has taken the land into which we came and graded it, moved it, and shaped it into the myriad wondrous forms which are a joy to us all. Each of us, in turn, has taken our own inheritance and planted, cultivated and shaped it to our own pleasure. Some of our works are lesser, and some are greater: but all of us have placed our mark on this country. The works of my daughters I count among the greatest. Punish, you say? I say they should rather be celebrated and rewarded for the wondrous things they have accomplished."

"But where does it end?" Cosimë demanded. "Shall we give speech also to the dog? Or the horse? Or the lizard that scutters under the rocks?"

Marec the son of Phreïs smiled at this and said, "You jest, but would such a world be so terrible? For many it would be a delight."

Teruman Phreïs said gravely, "Two Kindreds seem enough for us to worry over. I am also in awe of the skills of the daughters of Storeia, but," he looked in their direction, "perhaps we might agree to set a limit to such endeavors?"

"The limit was set by Havui himself," said Dôni. "No other creature of the land has a claim upon such a gift; but these two Kindreds came to us, appearing as if sent by Havui at the very Pass of the Stair, like we ourselves, and for this cause their lot is above that of all the other creatures of Soria."

Teruman Ologéo dissembled, mumbling, "Perhaps not to receive the gift of speech were they sent."

But Teruman Phreïs said, "Yet unless my ears have deceived me, somehow they do speak. They cannot now be treated as mere beasts."

Ologéo then complained, saying, "So once again the ambitious daughters of Storeia have tied our hands and forced us to a brink? There are options open to us. We might provoke war or pestilence, that these Pleïstians be removed from the land. Indeed, why stop even with this? It is not too late to cleanse the land of all these ridiculous speaking creatures! The land given to us was a beautiful and sensible thing as we received it, and now all has become grotesque and absurd."

Others were appalled at this suggestion, for there were among the Terumani those who, like Hiren, cared for their own favorites as if they were children; many had followed the path of Tryma and Deïni, and now considered the care of the Sorites the highest purpose of their kind. But there were also among the Terumani a party who agreed with Ologéo's judgment.

So the debate raged. Arguments were made on all sides, and for all causes. One clamor after another rose and rippled through the room in waves. For the rest of that day the strife continued. Wenda and Dôni sat quietly while the tumult swirled about them, as others sought to determine their fates, and the fates of the Kindreds under their care.

Ologéo at last called to adjourn. "We may continue this debate tomorrow. We are clearly coming to no consensus today. Perhaps wisdom will prevail after we have eaten and rested for the night, and a decision will be made in the morning."

But the morning brought no wisdom, and no decision. The debate went on for days. The Terumani argued among themselves in the council chamber. They argued at table, and they argued on the grounds when they went out to rest. Many who had been friends and cohorts found themselves bitterly at odds. Tempers grew hot, and many grumbled against one another in barbed whispers. But this is the very nature of heated argument: rather than convincing their opponents of their position, each camp became ever more entrenched as the arguments continued, and more radical in their intentions. In this the terumani are no wiser or better than the mortal Kindreds.

Ologéo at last grew tired of the debate. When the council next met for discussion he said to all, "We can stay in my Hall and debate this matter among ourselves for an age without conclusion, and my kitchens are being stretched thin. We cannot disperse without a decision this time. I propose to end this. As of now we have four paths to choose from: we might put an end to the speaking Kindreds and restore the land; we might attempt to remove the gift of speech from the speaking Kindreds; or we might banish them from Soria, sending them back across the Pass of the Stair and into Toë. Or… we might allow things to continue as they are, and leave the daughters of Storeia victorious: unpunished and unrestrained. We must choose one of these paths, or the final option becomes our choice."

"How are we to make this choice?" Phreïs asked. "Or have you failed to notice our obvious skills at compromise and consensus? You are not a ruler or lord over us, Ologéo, to decide this matter yourself; and even Vélopar, if he came, could not decide for us all."

"I propose that we take a referendum among ourselves. Is that not fair? Rather than arguing each day to convince one another, let us each take our stand and make our own choice. All of the Ádolthi are here, with the exception of Vélopar. Even a multitude of the minor terumani throng the place. Surely we have enough voices here to compound a decision that would bind us all."

"Your optimism on this may be unfounded," Phactorias grumbled.

"But it is my prerogative to call for a vote."

Deïni spoke up. "That you may, Ologéo. But you must give us time. All of us must be allowed to canvas our own supporters and prepare our final arguments."

"Well enough," Ologéo sighed. "I am nothing if not fair to all. Let us come together again in one week, and make our final decision."

So the council was adjourned, and all the parties went their separate ways to make their plans.

Wenda and Dôni made their way to the chamber of Phactorias. Phactorias opened to them and said, "I expected you to come to me, but I'm afraid there's little I can do."

"We cannot allow this vote," Doni said. "The Kindreds have no one to speak for them, and no one to listen to them. They have not even been allowed here to defend themselves. There are many among us now who speak of destroying them, or trying to remove their gift of speech."

"It is true," said Wenda. "The number of their enemies has grown, and Ologéo trumpets their cause. His influence among the Terumani is weighty. If any of his plans is chosen I fear the consequences."

Phactorias frowned at the suggestion. "Ologéo is the incalculable risk in this debate," he admitted. "Any such verdict would raise unprecedented resistance among those who support the Sorites, and I do not like to consider the crisis which would follow."

"The Sorites would defend themselves," Wenda said. "They will not submit to such an injustice."

"I fear that will amount to little against the Terumani," Phactorias said. "The greater concern is how their teruman defenders will react."

"I, for one, would defend my Sorites at any cost," Wenda said. "Even against Ologéo."

"We will have many allies," Dôni declared.

"This is precisely my fear," said Phactorias. "If Ologéo prevails, this matter will go beyond mere bickering. No one will sit idly by to watch his party destroy the Sorites, and the Pleïstians will be forced into that alliance as well. Hostilities will flare into fighting, and fighting into actual warfare. I have already heard whisperings. Such a disaster among our kind is unthinkable."

"Then what of the plan you described to us?" Wenda said. "You have not even proposed it to the council."

Phactorias threw up his hands in defeat. "What could I say? Without the support of Vélopar it would be empty words with no weight."

"Then go to Vélopar again," Dôni begged, "and implore him to come."

"I have sent word to him through Bël every day. He ignores us. But I cannot leave this place now. There is much to be done before Ologéo forces a vote. There are many reasonable minds I still hope to bring over to our side. If I am not here to persuade them, I promise you Ologéo will not be idle."

So they left the chamber of Phactorias discouraged and dark in mood. Wenda spoke angrily to her sister, "This has gone too far. I should go now to the Sorites and warn them. They must begin to prepare for warfare."

Dôni shook her head. "I think we should wait. It would create a rift between the Sorites and the Terumani forever, and we do not yet even know how the vote will turn out. We should not destroy their composure for nothing. It would be better, I think, to first shore up your defenders among the Terumani. Then if war should come, your tribe can be assured who their friends are."

"What of you and your tribe?"

Dôni sighed. "I have few supporters, I fear. I can only hope your camp will defend my cause as well, in the end." She glanced down the corridor towards the chamber of Phreïs, where Jeïnaric undoubtedly waited in silence. "There is one I can count on," she said. "Perhaps it's time to ask his aid. He may help bring others to our side."

The chamber which Teruman Phreïs occupied at Liaibíri was small and obscure compared to the suite which Dôni's mother Storeia commanded: a single room along one of Liaibíri's many corridors and aisles. The corridors were not empty. As she passed, a few sympathizers stopped to assure her in whispers that she and Wenda would have their support in the coming vote. More, however, scowled as she passed, or looked away in bitterness or embarrassment.

She knocked uncertainly on the door to the chamber she hoped was his, and was relieved when Phreïs opened to her. Jeïnaric asked if he might speak with her alone, and Phreïs obliged.

Jeïnaric read her mood at once, and tried to reassure her. "I will not abandon you, or the Pleïstians," he said.

"You do not need to admit to your part in this, if you fear the crowds that are against me."

"Now is the time to take my place alongside you. If we do not show our own courage, no one will have the courage to support us. If the vote does not go our way, we will stand together to prevent their demise."

"It will take more than the two of us alone," Dôni said. "How many do you think you might bring to our side?"

"Not many," Jeïnaric admitted. "My brother Marec, certainly. My father perhaps: he will not be happy over the secrets we withheld, but I think he will understand our need. My mother and my sister, I think, will abstain from voting at all. Among our friends we shall certainly find a few. Our best hope is to find allies among Wenda's supporters."

"Many of them fear the Pleïstians."

"So I have seen in the debates. But they may yet see that the fates of the speaking Kindreds are intertwined. Are any of the Ádolthi prepared to stand with us?"

"I could not guess. Phactorias has expressed his concern, but I'm not sure he would join us if it came to an actual fight. He fears the contention will lead to violence or war." She then explained to Jeïnaric the outline of the plan Phactorias had related to her and Wenda, hoping to end all fighting.

"Why has this not been brought to the council?" Jeïnaric asked.

"We would need Vélopar to agree to it, and Vélopar will not even hear it."

"Then he must be made to hear it!"

"How? He will not leave Lucré to come to council, and he will not receive the messages of Bël. The debate has wearied him."

"He may not know the danger we now face. A war among the terumani? That would be an irreparable disaster for all! If we could end this debate before Ologéo forces a vote, we might prevent many schisms and restore many broken bonds. Someone must go to him and make him listen."

"Phactorias cannot leave now. Too much depends on his persuasion here."

"Then you must go yourself!"

Dôni gaped at him. "I?" When she was certain he was serious she stammered, "Why would Vélopar speak with me? I am nothing in the eyes of that great one!"

"I think you do not know your own fame," Jeïnaric said. "He will certainly receive you. He may not agree to your plan, but he will not turn you away if you make the journey to Lucré to engage him."

"But what of our work here? We must campaign to shore up our allies."

"Leave that to me," Jeïnaric said. "Marec shall certainly join me. We shall find others. Go! While there is still time."

Dôni did not hesitate, but immediately packed for a journey, and took the eastward roads into the mountains. The terumani do not tire easily, but even at her fastest, the journey to Lucré encompassed two days of hard travel on Niyarc's damp and muddy trails. There at last the road brought her to a shining turquoise lake sheltered in a pleasant green valley. From the shores of that lake spread the grassy lawns and formal gardens of Vélopar's estate of Lucré.

The great Hall itself was enclosed behind stone walls and an iron gate. A bell was hung there: she rang it, and waited anxiously for a response.

Teruman Vélopar was highly regarded by the terumani of that country, and he had attendants from among them who served him there. One of these came to the gate to enquire after her. Her stomach fluttered and she flushed self-consciously, wishing that Vélopar had come to the gate himself: demanding to be seen of him was more intimidating than facing him.

"Who will I say is come to call?" The attendant asked. It was rare for strangers to show up at Lucré uninvited.

"I am Dôni, Storeia's daughter. My business is urgent, if you please."

The attendant raised an eyebrow. "I can guess your business," he said. "I cannot guarantee Vélopar will choose to see you."

"He must," Dôni pleaded. "I have come a long way, and the matter is urgent."

The spright nodded courteously and departed for the main Hall.

It was not long before Teruman Vélopar himself appeared at the portal, striding briskly to the gate. He was larger than she recalled: an imposing figure with broad shoulders, strong arms, and a visage like a storm cloud. He wore rings of black iron on his arms, wrought with images of charging aurochs. An aura seemed to surround his person, invisible to the eyes, but unmistakeable to the senses. He was dressed in gold and scarlet robes.

"My gate is not locked to the Terumani," he said. He swung it open and ushered her in. "Please accept my hospitality. The daughters of Storeia are welcome in my Hall."

She thanked him, bowing graciously in the manner of the terumani, and followed him up the pathway to his Hall.

Dôni was invited to sit with him at table, together with Wéodar his spouse, allowing them to provide refection after her long journey. She had sense enough to delay getting to her point, knowing Vélopar's aversion to the discussion of the speaking Kindreds; in any case this was the polite behavior of the Terumani between host and traveler. The purpose of her visit was left unmentioned, and for a good while they made small talk, discussing whatever bits of news or opinion they were sure would be pleasing to all parties.

At last a lull came in the conversation, and Dôni felt she could delay no longer. She shuddered within, but steeled herself and said to Vélopar, "I suppose you must have guessed that there is a reason which compelled my visit?"

Vélopar frowned for the first time, but he spoke politely. "I have been avoiding the question, but I suppose you must be out with it. You are a charming girl, and I will forgive you."

Dôni tipped her head. "I have come from the council with a message from Phactorias. We would ask a favor of you, if you will hear me out."

Vélopar growled. "Just do not ask me to go to Liaibíri to listen to Ologéo and the others blather on about the speaking Kindreds! They shall weary themselves to the tomb as they go on about this."

"It has gone beyond talk and blather," Dôni said. "I understand that the speaking Kindreds are of little concern to you, and the debate tires you. But Phactorias, and others, fear there will soon be outright warfare among the terumani. Does that perhaps concern you more?"

"Warfare?" Vélopar harrumphed. "Surely that is a stretch."

"Phactorias fears not. Ologéo wishes to force a vote, and if things go as Ologéo expects, there are many who will take up arms to defend the speaking Kindreds. Whatever is decided, it will pitch one side against the other, and violence will follow. Already alliances and stratagems are being formed."

"Can those fools truly have taken things so far? Such an end would be catastrophic. Still, I do not see how I can help. My opinion, if I even had one, could only inflame the factions more."

"We don't ask for your opinion," Dôni said. "Phactorias has devised a scheme which he hopes will silence the entire debate once and for all. Then," she smiled, "we all might leave you in peace at last! But we would need your aid. You alone have the craft and authority to carry this off."

Vélopar sighed deeply. "Speak, then, and I shall hear your proposal. But do not hold out any great hope!"

Dôni related the secret plan of Phactorias, with as much detail as she could recall. "It is a good plan," she finished. "Wenda and I have already agreed to it."

"And Phactorias? He is truly willing to take on such a burden? Hmph! It seems unlike him."

"It is Phactorias' plan in its entirety."

Vélopar shrugged. "Fine!" he declared. "If it is Phactorias' plan, it must be a practical and profitable plan. I shall follow you back to Liaibíri, and speak with Phactorias myself. If he truly wishes to propose this to the whole council, I will back him."

"Thank you!" Dôni sobbed. This was the first glimmer of real hope she had seen in days, and a tear came to her eye.

Vélopar placed a gentle hand on her shoulder and smiled. "Come. I have means of travel which will outpace your own. We must hurry, for if Ologéo forces this vote, the die will be cast, and the battle lines will be drawn. There will be no peace trust or among us once that is done."

So it was that Teruman Vélopar and Dôni rushed to Liaibíri. His arrival could not be hidden, and rumors began to fly about the corridors and meeting rooms of that Hall. "You should return to your own rooms," Vélopar said quietly to Dôni. "Let them all talk and wonder for now. I must find Phactorias."

"Phactorias will be busy, trying to win folk over to his side. I cannot guess where he might be at the moment."

"Then I will wait for him in his chambers. I have no desire to wander the halls like a beggar."

Dôni thanked him again, and departed. Vélopar then went straight to the chamber of Phactorias, without turning aside to speak with any other.

Phactorias was, as Dôni had surmised, busy about the halls of Liaibíri, but at last he returned to his place for a brief rest. There he was astonished to find Vélopar waiting for him, leaning against the wall in a chair, with his feet propped on Phactorias' desk. "At last!" Vélopar huffed. "I was beginning to imagine you had abandoned your responsibilities altogether and left for Teletirë."

"Teruman Vélopar himself!" Phactorias exclaimed. He greeted him heartily. "I cannot tell you how welcome is your appearance here! What could have compelled the great Vélopar to come to the debate after all?"

"I have not come for the debate," Vélopar said gravely. "I am told you have in mind a scheme to end the debate. But it hardly sounds like you, as it would require a fair degree of altruistic commitment on your part. Can it be true?"

"I have an idea, if I can get you to agree to it. Is it altruism? I cannot say, but it could bring these debates to a close. And it would take Ologéo down a notch, if that might be incentive enough."

Vélopar laughed. "Well, enough. Let us hear it from your own lips, then."

Phactorias and Vélopar then sat down together in secret meeting in the chamber of Phactorias, and discussed the matter far into the evening.

The guests lodging in Liaibíri meanwhile milled about, spreading rumors, and wondering what the arrival of Vélopar might portend.

It came as little surprise, then, that Ologéo called the council to order the following morning. The assembly gathered at the great hall of Liaibíri amid a babble of speculation, but as they entered the Lyceum they beheld Phactorias sitting at the head of the hall: behind him sat Vélopar, his arms folded and with a cloud about his head. All were astonished at his presence there, their curiosity for the moment overcoming their discord and plotting.

Ologéo said, "Teruman Phactorias, it would appear, has something new to say to us all, and even Vélopar has at last deigned to join us. Out with it then, for I am certain we would all like to get back to the business of arguing among ourselves in private."

Phactorias said, "This strife must end! Let us come to an agreement that will end the debate before we all resort to infamies we cannot recall. You, Ologéo, have given us four paths from which to choose. I propose a fifth.

"Here is our offer. There will be no vote. There will be no plan to eradicate the speaking Kindreds, or to meddle with their souls in an effort to remove their speech. These options must be removed from the table. Ologéo may not see it, but any of those paths will lead us all to violence."

"That leaves us only the fourth option, then," Ologéo complained.

"No," Phactorias said. "Your fourth option was to do nothing and allow things to continue as they have been. That is too dangerous. The speaking Kindreds have had no status, no voice, and no protection. That must change."

"Dare I ask what you're suggesting?" Ologéo said.

"I'm suggesting that we regard them as beings with the same rights as we ourselves have. You will not allow them into Liaibíri. So they must have their own council with equal authority to our own."

Ologéo scoffed at this suggestion. "They are little more than ignorant brutes! And you would give them power to overrule us? Most of them will go through their entire short lives without having an idea more profound than how best to make a pointed stick. You are asking infants to command the parents!"

"You cannot deny, Ologéo, that there are among them individuals who stand above the rest, and show themselves worthy even of your respect. You have seen Diatron, the disciple of Tryma; not to mention Sorios who is called the friend of the Terumani, and Archea of the Hirnans, who are respected by all their own kind. There are others, and we can find more." He waved a hand at his daughter Deïni and offered her the floor.

Deïni stood before all and said, "I have the gift of life within my hands. It is within my power to extend the lives of the Guardians, as I have done with Sorios and Archea, so they may serve as an enduring congress for the mortal Kindreds as long as our own lives in this land continue, and defend the rights of their own kinds. The mortal Kindreds will be in charge of their own affairs."

Teruman Reinodas said with disdain, "And you would bring those folk here among us, into our own congress, as our equals?"

"I think not even Vélopar could persuade Ologéo of that," Phactorias mused. "I myself will act as intermediary between our kinds."

"What is in this for you, Phactorias?" Ologéo said incredulously. "You set yourself up for endless labor and worry for such a small end."

"The end is peace. Is that not enough?"

Ologéo wagged his head. "I do not see how this heals the land or ends our strife. You have simply declared victory. Are we all merely to submit to you without complaint?"

"It is not victory," said Phactorias. "Maybe you were not listening. Neither Wenda, nor Dôni, nor any of the terumani, will be responsible for these Kindreds any longer. Although many of us find fulfillment in guiding and aiding these folk, we must from now on do so only under the authority of their own heroes and guardians."

"Your proposal is merely an administrative change. The land is to continue in absurdity. I cannot agree to that, and many are with me."

"We have considered your party, as well, Ologéo. Hear us out: We cannot return the land to its former state. You will have to accept that. But this much we cede: there are now two speaking Kindreds in Soria beside ourselves. It is enough! This must end, and in this we are in agreement with you." He peered at Wenda and Dôni, and they nodded their assent. "Yet more than this: we terumani have many other unique powers and assets. Who knows what further discord or dangers might arise if we share our powers and technologies with these Kindreds, or with any other creatures? We terumani can no longer act alone, without council or guidance. Henceforth any who might think to give any new powers to the creatures of Soria must plead their case before the whole council of the terumani, and the council of the Heroes of the Sorians."

"That is a fine ideal," Ologéo conceded, "and one I wish we had all respected long ago." He scowled at Wenda and Dôni. "But it is an ideal without claws or teeth. No one has respected this rule in the past, and I fear your lofty words will have no more weight than my own."

"But I come to you with more than lofty words," Phactorias declared. "Do you think I've brought Vélopar here merely to play jackstraws while we prattle?"

Vélopar's presence had been overlooked as Phactorias explained his proposal, but now all eyes turned to him. He stood up to speak, and all in that Hall hushed themselves to hear him: even Ologéo was silent.

"You all know," Vélopar rumbled, "that it was I who cultivated and established the settled places of Soria wherein we have made our Halls. I myself built many of your dwellings by my own craft and strength. Havui himself has given me mastery over all the settled country of the Ádolthi. Perhaps you have all forgotten that I have the power to take back what I have wrought, and return it to its raw state, and to undo all that we have done. Our Halls I may plow to dust at a word, and our gardens turn to brambles.

"This then shall be the law: None of our kind may lay plans against the Kindreds of Phactorias to do them harm. But likewise, none of our kind shall seek to spread their strange gifts further." Dôni and Wenda blushed. "Henceforth, whoever shall defy either of these edicts will be banned from their halls and gardens. They shall live uprooted in the land, as exiles in Soria."

"I have not the strength of Vélopar," Phactorias added, "but I have filled many of your Halls with goods and conveniences of my own device. I have some small power to recall many things of my own making, as well, and I will add this penalty also to the bans."

Ologéo narrowed his eyes. "Are you declaring law, or requesting a vote?"

Phactorias shrugged confidently. "You may vote on this or not as you wish. Vélopar is prepared to enforce the decree whether you agree or not. But it would be best if we swear ourselves with the unwavering oath of the terumani, lest any act on their own to destroy the peace."

"It seems you give us little choice," Ologéo sighed. "It does not fix the damage already done to our realm. Nevertheless it will contain it, and strip the daughters of Storeia of their powers. I will swear to keep these terms, if all will agree to be bound by this law."

Many of the camp of Ologéo grumbled, but as it would accomplish little to defy Vélopar, they could see no way out of the ultimatum. They swore, one and all, to abide by the law of Phactorias and Vélopar.

Then Vélopar said, "And may it so come to pass that none ever bother me to fulfill this sentence. I am sick of hearing of these things, and I would be done with this matter once and for all!"

Then Vélopar went to Depharmen, to the Shelf of the Toëites. There in the neighborhood of the house of Sorios he began work upon the great Hall of the Kindreds.

Phactorias joined him in this endeavor, and said to him, "How shall we make a Hall fit for the Kindreds of Toë? Shall we build it like their own houses and dwellings, of mud and turf? Or hollow out a great cave for them like the caves of the Pillows or Box Canyon?"

Vélopar frowned at this, however. "Pah! This shall be the great congress hall for the Heroes of that folk, who have been given a gift of life like our own. We shall build it after the manner of our own folk, full of the wonders and advantages of all we can provide, that it may compete with Liaibíri for glory."

"Do we risk defying our own law if we do so?"

"I think not. It is to be a Hall of their exalted Heroes alone, not for mortals. Should any mortal of their kind arrive at its corridors and chambers, they shall consider the Hall and its furnishings the trappings of the exalted, and shall not regard such things as their own. And their culture is yet very young: Who knows but what in times to come, they may even outdo us in such things?"

So they built the place into the very edge of the Shelf, on a cliff thirty mecaths[15] above the country, with a grand facade of silvery stone facing Mount Depharmen, and descending from the Shelf on the other side a vertical cascade of shining balconies and gardens. This Hall they named Ritéol, meaning, the End of Strife. For that was their hope, that in that place the speaking Kindreds would have representatives to defend their cause, so that no longer would any be permitted to speak of destroying them or altering their nature.

When it was built, Sorios himself entered in to examine it. Now Sorios was very ancient by the counting of his own Kindred, and was weary of many things. But he was astonished by the beauty of this Hall, and he explored it with the joy and wonder of youth. It was filled with light, with many chambers and corridors. Its floors were of smooth and shining stone, its ceilings high and graced with stately ornamentation. Windows and porticos over-

15 That is, about 200 feet, or 60 meters.

looked quiet gardens, and the balconies which hung out over the edge of the cliff watched over the distant vistas of Niyarc below. Moreover, Phactorias had filled it with the finest works of his craft, so every comfort and advantage of the Ádolthi could be found there.

"The Heroes of your Kindred shall come to this place, and meet with you here," Phactorias said. "It shall be a place of rest as well as of work. I shall come often to confer with you as well. Let us hope that we can do good on behalf of your kind."

Word came at last to Dôni and Jeïnaric in Box Canyon that the place was finished. So they came before Cynodias and Pleïstë and told them, "A new Hall is built for the Heroes of the mortal Kindreds. Your own time has come. Let us make a journey to the place, and see Sorios the first father." So they rose up and took to the roads together, and led them back to the Shelf where they had first gained the gift of speech, and brought them to Ritéol.

Cynodias and Pleïstë looked about the halls and gardens in wonder, for no such marvelous creation had they ever seen or dreamed of. Even the house of Storeia was humble in comparison.

At last Cynodias stopped and gazed slowly about, reverently fingering one of the golden lamps of the terumani which lit the space. "Is this now to be our home?" he asked with awe.

"If you choose," Dôni said. "You are to be Heroes of your Kindred, exalted and honored, and may enjoy all the trappings of my own kind."

"And our Tribe?" asked Pleïstë.

"Such things are not for mortals," Jeïnaric warned. "Your mortal kindred must make their own way in this land."

"Then have you found us a place at last?"

"The secret of your presence is revealed," Dôni said, "so you and your folk may leave Box Canyon at will. All the abandoned lands of the north lie open before you, if you will have them. Only live at peace with the Sorites, and all shall go well."

Pleïstë then excused herself to explore the chambers and halls, but Cynodias remained and said, "I should like to meet with the father of that race, if he will agree. Perhaps together we can forge peace among our Kindreds forever."

"Forever is a very long time," Jeïnaric said. "But we can hope, can't we?"

"Sorios is near at hand," Dôni said. "Let us go to him."

Sorios was found with several relations on one of the balcony-gardens on the cliffside, gazing out across the misty blue hills below. Little whispers of drizzling rain fingered their way among the rills and valleys, lit up here and there like flares by breaks in the gray ceiling. Even in those days, when the weather was always dreary and gray in Vordót, the view beyond the edge of the Shelf was often breathtaking.

Dôni bowed. "We have brought you a visitor," she said, and presented Cynodias to him. Then she bowed out, and the relations of Sorios followed her, leaving the two patriarchs alone.

"I expected you would come soon," Sorios said.[16] He looked his visitor up and down curiously. "Your kind is strange to my eyes," he said with a smile. He shrugged. "Don't be offended. Anything strange and new is good. It can be weary—and lonely—to go on and on like this." He sighed. "You will learn, soon enough."

"Pleïstë and I will have much to learn of you," Cynodias said. "You were the first of the speaking Kindreds in this country, and have been here for many years."

"Many years, indeed," Sorios laughed. "It's good to have someone new to speak with! Come and sit with me, and tell me all your story."

Cynodias hesitated, bowing to him, "Sit with you? To you and your descendants was given the land of Soria in an age past. Who are we to sit in your presence?"

"Come now. You also have been granted speech and understanding by the Terumani. You shall be as brother to me. We shall have much to do together in this Hall to watch over our children, I imagine."

"Not as a brother," Cynodias said. "You are the elder, by a long age. I am but a child before you! Will you accept me as a son?"

"As a son, then," Sorios said. "But a son and a co-regent. By adoption you and your kind shall also be called children of Sorios, then." He winked. "Outlandish and strange as you are!"

This then is the manner by which Sorios came to be called the father of the speaking Kindreds. Now it is said that this Hall of Ritéol stands to this day on the plateau of the Shelf, overlooking the lands of Niyarc in the north. But like all the great works of the Terumani it cannot now be found. For after the Year of Sorrows when the Terumani were forced to conceal themselves from the Kindreds, it, too, was concealed by their peculiar craft, and is hid from our eyes. So say those who know these things, and who shall doubt their word?

16 No explanation is given as to how they were able to speak with one another. One must assume, perhaps, that the Heroes of Soria were also given the ability to understand one another's speech.

THE LOST COLONY OF MAHOTO

It had come about after the Compromise of Phactorias and the founding of Ritéol that the Pleïstians began to move out of their secret home in Box Canyon, and to disperse into the countries of the north. The canyon, after all, had become too strait for them and all their clans, and Phactorias had allowed them freedom to mingle among the tribes of the north.

Coming out into open lands they found many abandoned hamlets and homesteads, the late haunts of those Sorites who had departed gray Niyarc and Vordót for the brighter lands of the south: they moved into these places and restored them, and they prospered and multiplied. The Pleïstians had never known a more clement country, and the damp and misty lands of Vordót did not depress them. Indeed to this day many tribes of Pleïstians prefer days of mist, fog and rain over days of burning sun.

Among these folk was Menoth, a son of Cynodias.[1] Menoth had lived long in the land, and all that Tribe knew him as father. He was among the tallest and strongest of that Kindred, regal in stature and in visage. It was even rumored that he had once defeated a rampaging Giant in single combat. Moreover, he was decisive and circumspect in all that he undertook, so his folk looked up to him as their leader and counselor.

When Menoth came out of Box Canyon he found a pleasant woodland to the east at the foot of a certain hillock: a round dome of granite called the Dome of Verias, for it was the dwelling place of a spright by the name of Verias who watched over that country. He settled there with Peneca his spouse and his many children, and the whole Tribe of his descendants soon followed him. They became established in that country, and grew.

There, for good or ill, it became the fate of Menoth to meet with Verias, the dræad of the Dome, and the two became close companions, for they were much alike in heart and spirit. Verias, thereafter, was always very familiar with the Pleïstians who had moved into his domain. Menoth and Verias would sit together long hours and talk, dreaming of fame and distinction, and encouraging one another to deeds of enterprise and renown.

Menoth, of course, had learned of the Compromise of Phactorias and the council of the Kindreds at Ritéol. After some years had passed he thought to himself, "My own Tribe is growing great among the clans of the Pleïstians, and we have no voice in the council at Ritéol. We have no heroes of our own but myself, and I am busy here among my folk."

1 If Menoth is to be taken as the same Menoth of the prior tales, he had evidently been granted extended life by Deïni: A considerable amount of time would seem to have passed.

So he went to Verias the Dræad, and said to him, "You have been our friend since we came into this country. Will you go to Ritéol on our behalf, and ask to be made our guardian? You might aid us in our affairs as a vassal of Cynodias our father, and even represent our interests before the councils of the Terumani at Liaibíri."

This appealed to Verias at once, for though he was but a dræad of the woods, he aspired to distinction. What greater distinction might he dream of, than to be known to the Ádolthi, and to be accepted among those Great Ones as one of their own? So he readily agreed to this plan, and went to Ritéol, and asked to be seen of Cynodias.

Now if there was a flaw in the scheme of Phactorias, it was this: that the mortal Kindreds had none of the powers of the Terumani to travel or receive news quickly from throughout the lands of their folk. Nor did they have the power to inspire minds as did many of the Terumani. Thus Sorios and Cynodias, and all of that council, depended still upon the Teruman guardians of their Kindreds.

So Cynodias consulted on the question with Pleïstë his spouse, and with Dôni his guide. "The clan of Menoth is growing great," said Cynodias, "and will surely continue to grow yet greater. It is too much for us alone to watch over all the folk of our Kindred. This was the very plan of Phactorias, after all: that we would have Guardians and Heroes to aid us in our work."

Verias was merely a dræad, and was counted neither among the Ádolthi nor the Ídolthi, yet he was teruman after all. So after some discussion it was decided to allow him this distinction. Dôni herself placed her trust in Verias, and sent him on his way.

If all the terumani had proved to be responsible guardians, things may have gone very well.

Verias returned to his home on the Dome of Verias. He became both counsellor and inspiration to Menoth, and he walked in secret among the Menothians, as the Terumani are wont to do, inspiring them at times to watchfulness, that they might have a helper on their side. He took great pride in his new role, and in those days he was diligent about the work.

It came to pass that Verias began to counsel Menoth, saying, "Is it enough that you are regarded as a leader by your own clan? How much greater would be our glory if all the clans of Cynodias looked to you as leader! And why even rest upon that? For you might be renowned even among the Sorites who dwell in this country!"

It did not take much persuasion to convince Menoth of this. So Menoth began to frequent all the lands of the north. He went out among the dwellings of all the Pleïstians, his own Kindred, and all came to know him. He also began to mingle freely among those clans of the Sorites which still dwelt in the north, making himself known to them as well. He learned the speech of the Sorites—the Sorian tongue of the terumani—and he studied the craft and lore which that elder Kindred had developed in their long age in Soria. Thus Menoth became a friend of the Sorites.

Among Menoth's sons was Mahoto, who was his youngest, and near to the heart and mind of his father. From the day Mahoto was old enough to travel, he would go with his father on his sojourns. He also became known among the Sorites, and he learned the Sorite tongue as fluently as his own, so none could tell his speech from that of the Sorites. The Sorites of Niyarc, the remnant who had not gone south, all knew Menoth and Mahoto, and as Mahoto grew to maturity they respected him as if one of their own.

In those days, before the days of the Ice, the caravans of the Stegganese would arrive at times from the south: There were still Sorites enough left in Niyarc with whom to trade, though their numbers were dwindling. One summer, as Mahoto traveled with his father in Niyarc, they arrived at Fair Field, which was a broad tract overlooking the western banks of the C'heta River, at the crossing of a ford.[2] There the caravans of the Stegganese would set up their camps, and the Sorites would come from across the river to trade their own wares for the goods of the Southrealm.

When Menoth and Mahoto arrived the plain was filled with the booths of the Stegganese, hawking pearls, and fabulous bead work; jade and alabaster stoneware; and many other things finely wrought and beautiful. Some of them carried colorful birds which could mimic speech, while others sold strange little chattering animals on leashes which were taught clever tricks. In addition they brought fruits and spices and aromatic delicacies unheard of in the north.

Mahoto was astonished at this, for the goods they had brought to trade, and the aromas of their foodstuff, were exotic and wondrous to him. "Who are these folk?!" he asked his father. "And whence have they come?"

So Menoth said to him, "Have you then never heard of the Stegganese, and the countries of the Southrealm?"

Mahoto replied, "No word of this folk or their country has ever reached us until this day!"

Menoth smiled. "Perhaps I have been remiss in your education," he said, "The lands of the Southrealm are open to all. If you wish, we might journey there ourselves."

"We must go!" Mahoto said, for the spirit of adventure at once overwhelmed him.

"Let us first seek the counsel of Verias, who is our guardian," Menoth said. "It is a long journey, and our folk have never gone so far. Perhaps the Terumani would not approve."

---

2 In later years a stone bridge was built here which became known as Fairbridge, though the market fairs of the Stegganese had long-since ceased.

So they went first to the Dome of Verias, and found Verias there in his usual place. When they had been welcomed and made comfortable, Menoth explained their purpose. "Mahoto and I have traveled throughout the countries of the north, and have become familiar with all this land. Now the lands of the Southrealm beckon, where the Stegganese live."

Verias placed his fingertips together and nodded theatrically, making a show of great deliberation. Now the Southrealm was far way indeed, and Verias himself had little desire to go so far from the Dome or to keep watch over such distant parts on his own, so he asked, "What is it you wish to accomplish in that far country?"

"Only to see new curiosities and taste new wonders," Mahoto ventured.

"And to return to the north when you have done?"

"Of course," Menoth said. "Our homes are here in Vordót."

"Mm hmm," Verias said slowly. "But you will of course contact the folk of those distant realms, that they may be enlightened concerning your own fame in the north?"

The prospect of renown and reputation had always been a goad and encouragement to Menoth, so he at once agreed. "How could we do otherwise?"

Verias nodded approvingly. "So those in the Southrealm will also learn of Teruman Verias." For so he now styled himself, though he was but a spright of the woods.

"I shall certainly drop your name among those whom we meet on the way," Menoth said, "if that is your desire."

"My desire? No, no!" Verias corrected. "Do as you wish on your journeys!" Yet as he said this he could not help but to instill a bit of inspiration to spread his name abroad. "Go forth on your trek, and be magnanimous, earn respect. And when you have seen all there is to see, bring back report to me when you return. We shall have many new tidings and tales to share."

So he sent them off with his own blessing. Now perhaps Verias should have reported such a matter to Cynodias and Pleïstë, or to any of the Terumani, who may have considered the matter with greater caution. The journey of Sorios and Archea to the Southrealm, after all, had changed the world they knew forever. But Verias did not think so deeply on the matter, and Ritéol seemed far off, so Verias said to himself, "I am their guardian, and it is my business to inspire and lead, that Cynodias and Pleïstë need not bother themselves with such matters at all."

So it was that Menoth and Mahoto returned to Fair Field, and when the Stegganese gathered up their goods to depart, they joined their caravan on the journey through Batack to the countries of the south. When they had emerged from the gloom and the dangers of the forest, Mahoto was enchanted with the lands they passed through.

Everything about the realm was new and exotic. It was not merely the lack of rain, mist, and cloud, for Mahoto had been raised in the gray weather of Niyarc, and the dank climate of that age seemed comfortable and homely to him. But the new landscapes and vistas of the Southrealm stirred his soul. The trees were new and unfamiliar; the grass, the grains, and the shrubbery which covered the hills were unique; there were strange new folk living in curiously built villages and houses. The very quality of the air exhilarated him. All in the Southrealm was adventure and quest to Mahoto.

The Stegganese traders of course pressed them to continue on their march homeward to Steggan's realm, and had no interest in any such silly diversions as turning aside merely to see sights or enjoy the scenery. When they came to the borders of the Stegganese country, therefore, Mahoto said to Menoth his father, "Let us turn aside from the trail and explore this country on our own. There are many curious and wondrous sights here for us to discover." So they departed from the caravan and roamed about the countryside on their own.

Now as it happened, few of the Sorites who dwelt in that region had heard of the Pleïstians, for most had been born in that southern land, and had dwelt there their entire lives. So wherever they went in that country the folk they encountered were fearful and suspicious: Menoth and his son were taller and more brawny than all whom they met, and their woolly hair and beards appeared queer and frightening to the Sorites. Even the hair of their arms appeared to these folk as if it were the fur of an animal. Although they spoke to the Sorites in their own tongue and treated them with respect, they were received coldly.

Nevertheless Mahoto was inspired by a sense of adventure, not to mention a desire for greatness equal at least to that of his father. Suddenly no adventure seemed greater to him in his youthful humor than to relocate to a distant and exotic land.

At last they came to the valley of a gently flowing river which went down to the lake Egano: In the midst of the river was a large and fertile island which could be reached by several fords. It was verdant and luxuriant, forested with fruit and nut trees in abundance, interwoven with sunny meadows and clearings. Mahoto was charmed by the place, and he called the valley Omaë, which in the Donish speech means "our place."[3] There Mahoto halted and said, "Where else in all of Soria might one hope to live better? Let me bring a company of our folk back to this place, and plant a colony of our clan here!"[4]

But Menoth would have nothing of this plan: Though the valley of Omaë had few inhabitants, all the Sorites they had met in that region were suspicious

3 The word appears to be akin to the Homadalan Sorian "Lon Homa," which was the name of one of the Two Kingdoms of Homadal, and carried the same meaning.

4 This island was reputed by the Menothians to be the site of the city of Omaë which was to be founded many hundreds of years later.

and hostile. "The Southrealm is the land of the Sorites," he said, "and we are not welcome here. Let us return to Niyarc, to the northern lands which Dôni has bequeathed to our Kindred."

Mahoto submitted to his father's will, and they went on their way. So at last Mahoto and Menoth his father found a caravan heading back to Niyarc, and they returned together to their home. But Mahoto had not forgotten his idea.

When they had returned, Verias called upon Menoth, and Menoth went to the Dome to be his guest as was their habit. There they sat down together cordially, and Menoth described the journey and all which they had seen on the way. Then Menoth laughed and said, "So taken was Mahoto with the adventure that he wished to establish a colony of our folk in that place."

At this statement Verias raised an eyebrow and said, "What did you tell him?"

"Of course I told him we would remain in the north where we belong."

"It would be a shame to quell the enthusiasm of youth!" Verias said. "Mahoto's proposal is not without merit. Think of it. We have already spread our renown throughout the north, and even among the Sorites we are well-regarded and honored. Why should we not go even further, as far as the Southrealm, and earn the regard of the folk in that place as well?"

Menoth frowned at this suggestion. "Mahoto is grown to maturity, but he is yet young by the measure of our folk. His mother and I would be loth to lose him to so far a country!"

"Yes, yes, you are right of course," said Verias obligingly. "Perhaps it would be an absurd plan." But secretly he did not relinquish the idea.

Verias cannot be blamed in whole for all that was to come to pass, but it must be admitted that he was not wholly without fault. After this discussion, he followed Menoth secretly back to his house, and found Mahoto. Of course he could place no specific command into Mahoto's mind—not even the highest of the Ádolthi dared to so tempt the fate of Erescal—yet he was able to encourage Mahoto's desire for adventure and excitement: even a spright of the woodrealm is able to do so much.

Furthermore, it was his habit at times to go about the country of Menoth's folk stealthily, concealing himself after the manner of the terumani, acting as a secret aid among them. But now he looked for opportunities to touch and inspire the minds of Mahoto's friends and kin into the same passion. Thus the allure of adventure spread through the folk of Menoth like a vine which overwhelms a house by degrees.

It was not long, then, before Mahoto began to broadcast his fervor for the Omaë Valley, and his desire to colonize the island there. Perhaps this was inevitable, whether Verias had encouraged them or not. Whatever the case, Mahoto's words inflamed many to curiosity, and many began to call for Mahoto to be their leader, to bring them to that fruitful land.

Before long, fully three score of his folk had joined him in this design. Among these were not a few of his brothers and sisters, and other relatives close to Menoth and Peneca the wife of Menoth.

When Peneca learned of this, she said to Menoth, "What have you done? Now we shall be bereaved of our children, as Sorios has been bereaved of his." Menoth also was concerned, for the design did not seem shrewd.

Calling Mahoto to him, Menoth reasoned with him: "Why would you leave the land of your own kindred, Mahoto? You shall be surrounded by none but those froward Sorites, who distrust and dislike our Kindred."

To Mahoto this was not a dissuasion at all, but inflamed even more his sense of adventure. But he reassured his father, saying, "We shall make our place there. I know the speech and customs of the folk who will live around us, so we shall be at peace with them, as you and I have had peace with the Sorites of Niyarc."

"Yet Mahoto, you go to a place so far from home it will be as if you had passed the very gates of life itself, and your mother and I shall see you no more."

This also appealed to Mahoto, for so much the greater would be the adventure and the allure stirred up into the deed. But he said, "We shall not be gone, Father, for the caravans of the Stegganese come every year to Niyarc. We may pass messages through the heralds[5] of the Stegganese, and I myself will return at times. You also may visit at will, and yet return to your home here in Niyarc."

So they conversed, but all the pleadings of Menoth his father, and of Peneca his mother, could not dissuade Mahoto from this venture. At last Menoth and Peneca yielded, and Menoth took upon himself the task of preparing his children for their journey and their new home.

When all preparations had been completed, Menoth went once more to the Dome to speak with Verias. "In spite of all my good advice," Menoth said wearily, "Mahoto my son has chosen to go into the Southrealm to find again this valley of Omaë, and settle it on behalf of the Pleïstians. He will take with him a company of our dearest folk. It will be as his mother and I had feared."

"It is a shame," Verias bluffed, "but it is difficult indeed to curb the zeal of youth."

"The traders of the Stegganese will arrive soon. When they depart, Mahoto will depart with them and travel through Batack. I shall go with them, as well, to see my children settled in their new place. But Cynodias should be informed. Will you take word of this development to Ritéol?"

"Of course," Verias agreed. But he had doubts whether Cynodias and the others would approve of such a venture. Furthermore, the passage to Ritéol was long and troublesome, so he thought to wait until Mahoto and Menoth had indeed left for the Southrealm before making the journey.

5 There was no written language at this time: "heralds" of the day would memorize messages, often in verse form, and deliver them in person to the recipient.

The spring weather returned to the north, and Mahoto found the first caravan of the Stegganese. When that caravan had finished its trading and made ready to return to the south, Mahoto brought all his company to them and asked to join their traverse.

Now the Pleïstians and the Sorites had lived peaceably in the northern realms, but the Stegganese of the Southrealm were suspicious of the large and outlandish Pleïstians. The Stegganese, therefore, were alarmed by so large a group of hulking Pleïstians, and feared to take them with them. Nevertheless they said, "You may follow along a day's journey behind us in your own company. The trail will be well-marked and you shall not get lost. Only do not come with us into our own country, lest our folk assume we have brought an invasion into their midst."

So all this group followed after the Stegganese when they broke camp at last and returned to their homelands beyond Batack.

Before they entered the trail, however, Menoth dispatched a messenger to Verias to inform him that he and Mahoto's company had departed for the Southrealm. Verias gave it little thought, however. "I shall wait for word of the venture to return to me, whether they have been successful or not, before going to Ritéol with this report." So he put it out of mind, and busied himself with other affairs, and it wasn't long before the matter was forgotten.

When Mahoto's company had crossed the Fords of Dunar which traversed the River Næus, they turned aside from the trail and found once again the Omaë Valley which Mahoto had determined for his new settlement. Throughout the months of the summer Mahoto and his clan built their dwellings and compounds, and three sturdy, log bridges across the fords to the island. They went out from the island of Omaë and explored the country round about to establish their foraging grounds.

Though Mahoto had discovered few other inhabitants in the regions, those whom they met greeted them with suspicion and fear: Not only was the appearance of the Pleïstians alarming, but except for Menoth and Mahoto, the newcomers spoke a queer language, unintelligible and coarse to their ears. Their very clothing and adornments were strange and frightening, for they wore heavy garments of leather, and fur-trimmed jerkins, unlike the linen tunics and embroidered robes of their own kind.

So passed the months of summer as they completed their dwellings, until it came to pass that a party of Lophusites and Plateosites came down to them from the highlands, bearing weapons and demanding to speak with the leaders of the settlement. Mahoto and Menoth came out to them, and Mahoto spoke to them in the Sorian tongue, saying, "Why do you come to us in such a manner, armed and fierce in expression? We have done nothing to harm you or any of your folk."

"We do not know you: neither who you are, nor what manner of being you might be. Whence have you come into our land, and how have you usurped the gift of speech, which was given only to us of the tribes of Sorios?"

Mahoto answered, "We are children of Cynodias, Pleïstians from the north where our folk have dwelt for generations. Dôni the daughter of Storeia has herself given our folk the gift of speech, like as yourselves, and Sorios has adopted our folk as his own. We come from the countries of the north to share the broad lands of Soria, just as our folk share the northlands with those Sorites who yet remain there."

The Sorites scowled. "We do not know this Cynodias, nor do we know Dôni. We know only that you have barred us from our island camps, and built for yourselves houses in our foraging grounds, and you and your queer folk take from the land what belongs to us. This we cannot allow!"

Mahoto said, "The country round about is wide and bounteous, with forage enough for all. We have no need to fight over anything."

The captain of the party however said, "Go back whence you came, and then we shall have no need to fight."

But Mahoto did not have the even temperament of his father Menoth, so he became adamant; and said to them, "Do not choose the path of conflict, for our folk will not be daunted. Go back to your own homes, and leave us in peace. You yourselves shall choose whether to find us amicable neighbors, or adversaries."

So the emissaries of the Sorites returned to their place without satisfaction, and plotted among themselves how to bedevil the Pleïstians. Thereafter whenever the Mahotians went about foraging, if any Sorites came upon them they would harass them, shouting out to thwart their stalking, destroying their traps, and raiding their stockpiles when they found them. Thus Mahoto and his own folk grew wary, and began to erect stockades about their settlements, and to carry their weapons with them when they went out into the countryside.

In this state of affairs the summer drew toward its close, and Menoth prepared to return to Niyarc. But he appealed once more to Mahoto and his other children, saying, "You see you are not welcome in this country, for the Sorites here are froward and restive. It would be better to return to our own country, where we all live at peace."

But Mahoto would not be turned from his purpose. At last Menoth returned alone to his home in the north. There he reported all that he had seen to Peneca his mate. Together they fretted for the security of Mahoto's clan.

When Verias heard that Menoth had returned, he called him to the Dome to learn more of the colony. Menoth arrived in a foul mood. "The Sorites of that country are insolent, and my son intractable," he complained.

Verias shrugged off the concern. "Mahoto will win their respect, I'm sure."

"If Havui be with him. Until then he is surrounded by enemies, and his mother and I will worry for his safety every day."

"Perhaps I shall go and see the settlement myself," Verias mused, "and see how they get on in their new country." He tapped his forehead knowingly. "I may have some influence over the Sorites. I'm certain we can smooth this over."

"Then go," Menoth groused. "See if you do not agree. Then convince our children to return to us here in Niyarc where they are at peace."

In spite of these ill tidings, Verias still saw no reason to travel to Ritéol to report on the matter. "I will give them a full report when I have seen things for myself," he said.

But the journey to the Southrealm was long and troublesome, even for a spright of the woods, so Verias put off the venture. "Next week I shall go," he told himself. Then it became "Next month will be better, and I shall go then." Then it was "I shall surely go in the spring, when the travel is easy." One excuse led to another. So a year passed, and the next as well. Verias became busy with improving his hall in the Dome, for he wanted a home fit for a Guardian, like the Halls of the Ádolthi. Eventually the whole matter was forgotten among the personal projects and matters closer at hand which absorbed his attention.

In the meantime Menoth and Peneca awaited the arrival of the caravans from the south each summer, for Mahoto and his brethren would send messages by the couriers of that folk. Each summer the couriers of the Stegganese brought messages from the colony, encouraging their hearts. From time to time some one of that clan would join the caravan, coming from the south to visit their relations in Niyarc. But never did they come bearing news of peace with the Sorites. Seldom did any report arrive without tidings of conflict and troubles.

Years passed, and the caravans of the Stegganese came less often, for there were ever fewer Sorites left in Niyarc with whom to trade. (The Stegganese had few customers among the Pleïstians, for that folk did not speak their tongue.) Nevertheless each summer a message would come from the tribe of Mahoto, brimming with boasts of success, and exuberant avowals of the adventure of the thing.

Until one year the first caravan of the summer arrived, and there was no message from Mahoto, nor from any of that tribe. Moreover the Stegganese reported that they had met with none of that folk at the crossroads from Omaë, where they were wont to meet at the start of the season. The season passed, and another caravan arrived, and likewise there was no word from Mahoto, nor from any of that tribe.

At last Menoth could no longer bear his uncertainties, and he determined to return to the south to see for himself what might be the state of the settlement and the folk he had left behind.

Now it had so happened that the Sorites of Omaë had at last joined together in force, and they had stormed the bridges of Omaë, and stricken the households and settlements of the Pleïstians grievously. Mahoto and his clan had defended their homes with might of arms, but the numbers of the Sorites were too great for them. The stockades had been breached, the settlement demolished and burned to the ground, and all their goods plundered: all their work, and all they had gained in their years of labor in that place, came to nothing. Moreover blood had been shed, so that now the enmity between those Kindreds was firmly established. As for Mahoto himself, and the remnant of his clan, they found refuge in the woods and caves of the valley, where they determined to make their stand and survive, and vowed to take vengeance on their oppressors.

But of these survivors no word came to any in the north, and their fate was to remain unknown for many generations.

So it was that when Menoth arrived in the south and went to the place of Mahoto's settlement, he found it in ruins. The bridges had been burned, every home and barn razed, and none of that folk could be found. Moreover the site still bore the signs of violence and bloodshed. Menoth did not know that Mahoto yet lived, nor did he know the fate of any of those relatives who had gone south with him, so Menoth rent his garment and cried out, saying, "Surely I shall have vengeance on this wicked folk, these Sorites: they have robbed me of my children!"

So Menoth returned to the north in fury, not waiting for any caravan to make safe the way, but facing the dangers of Batack alone. He fought his way north in short time, and bearing news of the destruction of Mahoto and his clan, he began to go about the villages of the Pleïstians, raising their ire. Thus he began to assemble an army of his Kindred, for it was his intent to return to the Southrealm to mete punishment on the Sorites there.

As for Verias his Guardian, Menoth did not go to him, either to inform him of the tragedy, or to ask counsel, or to seek aid. For in all this time Verias had done nothing to aid Mahoto or his clan, and in fact, all his advice had led only to disaster in the end. Menoth in his wrath rejected Verias and all the Terumani.

VÉLOPAR DIVIDES THE KINDREDS

Now Menoth was blinded by his fury and his sorrow, so it did not enter his burning heart to take counsel: either with Verias who had failed him, or with Phactorias, or with any other of the Terumani. Nor did he trouble himself to make the detour to Ritéol to seek the wisdom of Cynodias and Pleïstë, though he knew his elders yet to be living in that place.

Rather he went immediately to Therës,[1] his companion of old, and said, "The Sorites of the Southrealm have killed my son and all his clan. They have broken faith with our Kindred and demanded violence for violence. Let us go out together among our own Kindred and raise a force of armed troops: we shall cross Batack and obtain vengeance on this wicked folk."

Therës answered, "These Sorites have been hostile to us from the start." So he agreed to go with him, and to help him go to war. The two of them traversed the countries of the north, wherever the Pleïstians had settled. Everywhere they went they told the tale of Mahoto and the destruction of his settlement, and they preached violence against the Sorites of the Southrealm.

Thus were the Pleïstians outraged and inflamed. A large force attached themselves to Menoth and Therës their leaders, many thousand warriors in strength, assembled from all the clans and families of the Pleïstians. They armed themselves with spears, and with pikes; with hammers and clubs and axes. Whatever they could find that might be used as a weapon, they took up and brandished in their zeal. Therës also began to gather provisions to support journey through Batack, and assigned porters to aid them on the march, for they would need to support a large party of armed folk for the long trek. All these raging warriors, and all these weapons, and all these provisions, they began to muster on Feldreth, the Plain of the Carpet in Vordót.

Menoth nurtured his anger and fed it daily with sorrows and loss. Peneca his spouse also fed his malice, for she lamented the loss of her son continuously, blaming Menoth for bringing him to the Southrealm where he met his demise.

But there were among the Menothians and the Theresians certain ones who doubted this course, for it seemed rash and unconsidered. These met in private, away from their leaders, or from their husbands and spouses who had departed for the ranks of war, and they said to one another, "Menoth is

1 Therës would also evidently seem to have been granted an extended lifespan.

mad with grief. He cannot annihilate the whole of the Sorite Kindred. This will only usher in a profusion of woes upon us all."

So it was quickly decided to send emissaries to Ritéol, to Cynodias and Pleïstë, that they might be warned of this maneuver, in the hopes that their wisdom and council might devise a better plan. They hastened to Ritéol, taking little rest on way, and coming to the portals of that Hall, they begged to see their elders at once.

So it was that both Cynodias and Sorios were at last informed of this matter, and Pleïstë attended them as well. When the whole history had been explained to them, Pleïstë said to Cynodias, "How is it that we have heard nothing of this up to this hour? Have we given no attention to the folk of Menoth's clan in all this time?"

"This is the venue of Verias, who petitioned to be a guardian on their behalf," Cynodias said. He asked the emissaries who had come to Ritéol, "Why is it that Verias has not brought us this news himself?"

The emissaries looked at one another blankly. "You mean that Verias, who is building himself a grand house on the Dome? We know nothing of this one, but that he has been the friend of Menoth, and walks among our folk from time to time."

"We must call Verias here to give an account of this affair," Cynodias said.

"First we must attend to the matter of Mahoto," Pleïstë said. "Time is already short to prevent this disaster from redoubling."

So they dismissed the emissaries that they might take council together.

Then Sorios the father of the Kindreds shook his head sadly and said, "Are we so soon come to this pass? Have our two Kindreds so quickly resorted to violence to settle their differences?"

"Menoth is of our Kindred, and the Sorites are of yours," Cynodias said. "Might we go to our folk and find a way to prevent this evil from spreading among them?"

Pleïstë said, "We do not know for certain what has happened in the Southrealm, for none of us has been there to investigate. I cannot doubt there was violence, but if Mahoto might yet be found alive, perhaps Menoth might be allayed of his wrath, and the matter brought to a just conclusion."

"We have not the powers of the Terumani," Cynodias bemoaned. "We cannot hope to arrive in the Southrealm before Menoth himself arrives with his host. How might we manage to investigate, let alone learn anything which might turn aside his wrath?"

"Nor do we have the powers of mind of the Terumani," said Sorios, "to examine the truth, or to influence the hearts of our kin. We must send for Phactorias our caretaker at once. He alone can aid us in this extremity."

Now Teruman Bël is always able to hear the calls of her own Kindred when tidings must be sent, for that is her special gift among the Terumani: Phactorias had instructed her as well to be attentive to the calls of the Heroes of the Toëites. So Sorios put out the call for Bël, and she came swiftly to receive his message. When all had been explained to her in full, she rushed to Phactorias, to call him to Ritéol.

Phactorias deferred. "I must first go to investigate the matter," he said, "Our urgency is great. Return to Ritéol at once, and I shall speed to the Southrealm. If they are able, let Cynodias and Pleïstë go to Menoth, to dissuade him from this foolish course. I shall meet them on the Plain of the Carpet."

So Phactorias made all haste to reach the Southrealm, and he found the ruined colony of the clan of Mahoto, just as he had been warned. Though he searched diligently for the truth, he could learn nothing of their whereabouts, but neither could he find proof of their demise. He found in that region only certain of the Plateosites whom he questioned: He would not reveal himself there as Teruman, but he secretly and silently touched their minds, and found them angry and dark within. No fact could he glean from them.

At last he said to himself, "I am gaining nothing by this search, and the hope of preventing violence grows less with each passing moment. I shall first return to Cynodias and Pleïstë, to see how they have fared with Menoth. If things are as I fear, I must then go to Ologéo for help, much as I deplore that option."

So he sped his way to the Carpet Plain, and found there Cynodias and Pleïstë alone, and the camp of Menoth empty and abandoned.

"We are too late," Pleïstë bemoaned. "Already the muster has departed for Batack, and they shall soon reach the edges of that wood. They are on the march, and we have no hope of catching them."

"Perhaps it is for the best," Cynodias said. "Who is to say but what Menoth is justified in this matter? The Sorites surely deserve punishment for what they have done."

"The guilty deserve punishment," Phactorias said earnestly. "But war does not discriminate between the guilty and the innocent. No one deserves war."

"What would you have him do?" Cynodias questioned.

"I have no answer to that," Phactorias admitted. "But if war can be prevented, it must be prevented. No war has stained this land since first we came to inhabit the country. Woe to us all if we trip blithely down that path."

"What then? Will you place Menoth, and all his army, into chains? I think it will take so much to stop them by now."

Phactorias sighed. “It is too much for me to decide alone. I must go to Liaibíri to counsel with Ologéo. We must call again for a council of the Terumani. And Ologéo will certainly not be pleased.”

So Phactorias departed for Liaibíri, and once again Bël was sent out with the report of this crisis, calling the terumani, great and small, to come to council: any discord dividing and enflaming the Kindreds of Toë against each other would effect all in the land. A confusion and alarm among went up among them, and many terumani began to appear at the portal of Liaibíri. But many were far away, and even the powers of the terumani could not bring them there on such short notice. And once again, Vélopar ignored the summons, for he had little interest in matters beyond the confines of Lucré his own Hall.

Phactorias and the other terumani began to assemble at Liaibíri, and Ologéo was called from his studies to meet them. Phactorias explained the situation, and Ologéo frowned. “Why have you come here squabbling in my halls?” he said testily to the growing crowd. “Are these Kindreds not the responsibility of Phactorias? Let him do as he wishes with them.”

Phactorias grumbled and said, “Do not patronize me, Ologéo. My design was to act as intermediary, not lord.”

Ologéo sneered. “Your liberality has proven vain. Behold how quickly this folk resorts to violence and warfare. I thought they had a council of their own? Does their own council have no power to stop this?”

“Their council has asked for our help. But in this much you speak the truth, Ologéo: I have been remiss, and have trusted too much to chance.”

Ologéo shrugged and said, “This then is the end result of giving speech to these baser Kindreds. Now do we all see the evil it has perpetrated on these pitiful creatures?”

“I have not called us here to revive this pointless debate,” he said. “What is done is done. We must decide now what action to take regarding the Menothians. And we must decide soon!”

“Good enough,” Ologéo said. “I am proven right, at any rate. Let us all repair to the lyceum to discuss how to amend your errors.”

At the urging of Phactorias the assembly gathered as quickly as possible, and when all had settled in Phactorias gave a full account of all he had learned. “We do not have time to await a full council of our order,” he said. “Time is short to repair this situation before peace between the Kindreds is destroyed. We shall have to choose a course quickly, and soon.”

Teruman Tryma the Wise stood before them, and said, “No course comes without liability. We must choose between perils. And consider that what we decide concerning Menoth we decide for all. This will not be the last conflict to arise among these Kindreds. Whether Menoth is thwarted or not, the Pleïstians and the Sorites cannot be kept apart forever.”

"Why must we do anything?" shrugged Ologéo. "Whether dumb creatures or moral souls, if bloodshed and division is their intent, it is their own business."

Verias the guardian of Menoth had at last arisen from his Hall to come to council: it gratified him to include himself among the Terumani, and to be looked upon as the guardian of the Menothians. He stood now to defend their cause, saying, "If there is now bloodshed and division, it is not the fault of the Menothians! It was the Sorites who were first to raise an army and shed blood. Would we leave Menoth without justice for his children?"

"War is not justice," Phactorias scolded. "Injustice is enlarged beyond its capacities by war, and it gathers hatred and misery like a landslide. Surely we can agree that war is to be avoided!"

Many spoke out at once consenting to this conviction. But Ologéo laughed at them and said, "And just how will you hope to accomplish this? Will you enter into the minds of these Sorians like Erescal, and overrule their thoughts with your thoughts?"

"It was for freedom that the Sorians were granted speech," Teruman Wenda admitted sadly, "that they might determine their own courses, and be neither ruled nor controlled by any of us."

Teruman Tryma concurred, saying, "Indeed it seems our hands are tied in this matter, for having speech are they not our moral peers? Now each shall bear the consequence of his own choices, even as we ourselves. We cannot make such choices on their behalf."

Teruman Storeia shook her head and said, "Why this talk of compulsion? We have influence over the spirit of these folk. Might we not inspire them without resort to compulsion?"

Verias said, "The heart of Menoth is impassioned, and we have seen the hearts of the Sorites are stiff in this matter. Persuading them from this course will be no simple feat."

Teruman Dôni said, "The heart of Menoth is inflamed by the disappearance of his son and his kindred, whom he believes are dead. Shall we not merely find out the truth of the matter and hope to settle his mind?"

"The truth is not so easy to learn," Phactorias said. "I have been to the Southrealm. The Sorites there revealed nothing to me, but it is clear that they did indeed intend to eradicate that clan, whether or not they succeeded. Even should Mahoto yet be found alive, I do not think the enmity between Menoth and the Sorites will be lightly set aside."

Ologéo derided them, saying, "For this one time I find myself in agreement with Wenda. Why not let these Kindreds settle their own disputes in their own manner? If they would kill and commit war, let them kill. Perhaps we might even be rid of both of these ridiculous tribes for good."

Teruman Phreïs objected, "So then, you ask us to sit by and watch the unchecked spilling of blood! I'm sure this will be a thrilling spectacle!"

At last Teruman Deïni stood and silenced the forum. "Time is growing short. If we cannot compel them, and we cannot persuade them, we must simply stop them," she declared. "Menoth and his army must be prevented from going into the south."

Ologéo shook his head in derision. "You are not thinking! Would you raise an army of the terumani, and stand before them on the road, to prevent their campaign from departing Niyarc?"

"Surely they would be overawed by a show of our strength?" said Marec.

"Perhaps," Phactorias ventured, "but perhaps they would resist us and raise weapons against us. Would we prevent war by going to war? Ologéo is correct. Such an outcome would be worse than what we are trying to prevent!"

"There must be other ways," Deïni suggested. "Can we obscure the paths through Batack? Someone among us must have strength to set up barriers and prevent this march."

At this all eyes turned to Ologéo, but Ologéo said, "Even were I willing to engage in such a labor, it would do no good. I might cause the paths to overgrow and become embroiled in confusion, but even I would need time to bring such growth about, and time is what you do not have. Nor can I hope to block every byway they might discover: Batack is vast."

"A wall then?" said Deïni. She looked to Phactorias and Phreïs. "There are great builders among us. Might a wall be built to block the roads?"

Phactorias shook his head. "I will concur with Ologéo. Such a project would take months, if not years, to complete. And walls can be scaled."

"The rivers might flood and overwhelm the fords. Fog and darkness might blind them on the way."

"I have no such power," Ologéo grumbled.

"Nor has any of us assembled here," Phactorias admitted.

The room grew silent. At last Phreïs quipped, "Behold the powerful Terumani! We've gathered our highest and greatest, and all of us together can do nothing."

"There is yet one," Phactorias said. "Not all of our Order have come to council."

Ologéo smiled. "Ah! If only Vélopar were here to save you once again!"

Teruman Phreïs said, "It seems summoning Vélopar to council is like asking a tree to uproot itself. Perhaps if Vélopar will not come to council, the council should go to Vélopar."

A chuckle passed over the room, but Phactorias said, "You may jest, Phreïs, but you may have provided us a solution. I propose we adjourn our meeting here and re-convene on the doorstep of Lucré. He cannot avoid this question when we bring it to his own house! There may yet be time to stop this violence if he will intervene."

"You would risk raising the ire of Vélopar against you?" Ologéo asked.

"Perhaps the ire of Vélopar is precisely what we need."

"This I should enjoy seeing!" said Ologéo. "I, for one, would be happy to accede to this plan."

With little further debate the thing was decided. At the urging of Phactorias the whole of that council rose up from Liaibíri to march to the gates of Lucré. At the head of the march went resolute Phactorias, and Ologéo marched alongside him in wry good humor.

A great company it was, and they filled the road for miles. Such a company could not be hidden, and the dræads of the valley of Lucré who were beholden to Vélopar could not fail to notice their approach. So they rushed to Vélopar and warned him, saying, "A great host of the terumani is on the road, coming to this place. We cannot guess what might be their purpose!"

Vélopar growled, "They have surely come to quibble once more about the Kindreds of Toë. They will not leave me in peace!"

So he stormed out of his Hall, and stomped down to the gate before his premises to await them.

The council was not long in arriving. When they began to gather before his walls Vélopar called out, "What is the meaning of this intrusion? Can a soul not find peace from debate within the walls of his own house?"

"Peace is exactly what we hope to gain by this debate!" Phactorias said. "Our hope is that the strong arm of Vélopar might open to us solutions we haven't yet considered. We have exhausted our own options, and you have not come to council."

"Have I not made it clear that I do not wish to be bothered with these trivialities?"

"It is clear to me," Ologéo said. "And had my word been regarded we would have been done with this matter long ago, without need for your attention."

Vélopar raised his head and shouted to the gathering crowd. "Then take the advice of Ologéo and be gone from here!"

"I'm afraid you cannot retire from the matter so easily," Phactorias said.

"I might easily go into the house, and leave you all out here without the gates to prattle among yourselves."

"Then we will need to break down your gates and claw at your doors and windows." Phactorias smiled waggishly and waved at the throng which continued swarming into the place. "These folk have come a long way, and are restive from the journey. They will be heard."

The road approaching Lucré was indeed still teeming with the terumani who continued to arrive from the council at Liaibíri. There was a bit of open lawn before the gates of the precinct, which was soon trampled and overrun, while more thronged in from the road behind them. Even the woods surrounding the place were soon packed with those hoping to get close enough to hear and be heard.

"It is your calling to shape the land," Storeia said calmly. "But Vélopar, it is ours to care for it, and it is your duty to aid us."

Vélopar rumbled and his face clouded with discontent. "Then be quick and be gone."

So the whole of the matter was explained once again, but it was not quick. On and on it went, as explanations, questions, and interruptions continued, seemingly without end. Each of the Terumani wished to state their case before Vélopar, hoping he would take their side. Both great and small shouted their opinion, hoping for their voice to be heard among the din of voices. It was not long before Vélopar began to lose patience with the mob.

At last Vélopar shouted, "It is enough!" He turned his back to the crowd and stormed fuming into his house.

For a long moment silence fell. Ologéo and Phactorias looked at each other doubtfully. The rest of the assembled Terumani, and the dræads and næads as well, said nothing and waited, wondering what to do next.

There was a rumble like a storm from within Lucré, and a cloud suddenly issued from the place. Vélopar could be seen in the cloud, furious and bearing his staff of iron, rushing away to the north.

So he sailed into the north to the Mountain Wall, and there he unleashed the bonds of Boros from their straits. Only Vélopar, of all the terumani and Ádolthi, had such authority and power. Then the icy breath of Boros escaped, and it began to blow southward into Soria from that hour: Blast and storm unprecedented rose up behind the Mountain Wall like mammoth towers piling upward into the heavens, and soon the Storm overflowed the Wall and began streaming into the land. Over the spine of the range it poured, and down through the passes and valleys. The trees bent and trembled before it. Dark clouds spread over the skies. Great and sudden was that tempest, and snow and frigid gales began to overwhelm all the corners of Niyarc and Vordót.

Vélopar's own Hall of Lucré was not spared. Blowing drifts of icy snow pummeled the place, and the crowd of the terumani who had camped there shivered and huddled beneath their cloaks.

Phactorias frowned. "It would appear we have been evicted," he sulked. There was little to be done: all were forced to flee that place to find refuge in their own Halls, houses, and redoubts.

...

As this debate continued to rage on the doorstep of Vélopar, the troops of Menoth's army assembled at the fringes of Batack, at the trailhead of the fastest route through that forest. A settlement of the Cylosites had once guarded that portal, but it had been abandoned long ago, and the houses and compounds now lay empty and decaying about the site. Menoth himself took over the largest of these structures, and he and Therës plotted together as the troops settled in and the provisions were organized.

"I have never made the journey to the Southrealm," Therës said. He gazed out the doorless opening of the hut at the shadowy woods beyond them. "How shall we defend against the dangers of the forest?"

"We are a large company, and the Giants and drakes will seldom attack so large a force," Menoth assured him. "Nevertheless we must taken caution. There are camps where we may gather, but the path through the densest parts of the forest is narrow: Only two or three abreast might navigate it, and we shall be spread thin. Our strongest and best shall take the fore, but we cannot leave the mass of our troops and our porters undefended."

"I shall divide our forces into companies, and assign to each a commander, that they will not be without leadership if any part of the caravan is molested along the way."

Menoth looked at the skies, which were, as usual in Niyarc, cloudy and gray, but he detected a change in the atmosphere. "That is wise, but we must do so quickly. It is already late in the autumn, and we must be across the high plateau of Batack before the winter snows set in."

"We can depart in the morning," Therës said. "When we gather to camp after the first day's march, we can review our situation and make adjustments along the way."

"Well enough," Menoth said grimly. "We should be beyond the depths of the wood in three weeks. There we can muster and regain our strength. I shall take only a few spies southward from there to find out the Sorites. Then we shall bring down all our force together: We shall attack them in their homes, and their camps, and in the field, and make them pay in blood for what they have done."

So it was that early in the morning Menoth called his troops to order, and the march into Batack began. So great was the force that an hour had passed before the whole column had entered the trail. But as the hours passed and the troops marched, the day became darker rather than brighter. A new wind came from the north, which whistled and howled through the treetops like the wailing of wraiths, icy and chill. A tremor of cold and disquiet shivered along the whole length of Menoth's army.

Before noon the first snowflakes had begun to spin down through the trees. Menoth looked upward uneasily. All that could be seen was the waving and shuddering of the branches above, as the wind tore the leaves from the boughs, and the black sky lowered overhead. And beneath it the swirling eddies of snow. Flurries of icy blue twisted down from above like living things, and began to gather on the trail and the forest floor about them. Snow, snow, and ever more snow. It drifted and piled, and soon dragged at their boots.

Therës huddled into his cloak and looked back at the line of troops trudging behind them. "Such a storm I have never seen!" he declared. "If we go on, we shall all be trapped in the forest, and perish here."

Menoth growled. "It cannot last. The brunt shall soon pass and we shall be on our way."

But it did not end. By the time they camped at the end of the day's march, the clouds had become blacker and lower, and the blanketing drifts of snow had grown ever deeper and thicker. Their tents and lean-tos blew to the ground as soon as they were erected. Fires could scarcely be kindled in the gusty wind, and when kindled were soon blown out and drowned in snowfall. Their supplies of water began to freeze, and even the running creeks nearby were quickly beginning to ice over. The army shivered through the long night in misery, cowering under their woolen coats.

Morning came slowly and dimly. The camp was blanketed, with drifts in places as high their shoulders. And yet the storm did not abate. Still more snow came down from the skies, and still more it blustered around them.

Menoth hugged himself and scowled at the sky. "It is no good," he admitted at last. "We must return to our own houses and live. We shall pursue this again when the better days of spring arrive."

So they suffered and struggled through the wet, the cold, and the masses of heavy snow which blocked their return: back through Batack, back to the edge of the forest. Fully four days it took to return on a path that had taken them merely a day as they entered. The misery of that march could not be measured. Those who saw it through to the end would shudder and grow silent at the recollection of those terrible days.

They found shelter at last in the abandoned village of the Cylosites, but the ever-piling snow was to give them scant rest. Some eventually forced their way to their own homes to wait out the winter. Menoth and his most fervent followers took up camp there in the abandoned settlement, and hoped their provisions would see them through the worst of the winter, to the better days of spring.

But spring did not come. Through the season of spring, and on into the summer, the cold did not relent, and storms brought nothing but snow or hail: never the looked-for rain. Menoth and his army at last conceded that their campaign could not be carried through, and returned home in disgust.

So went also the following winter, and the winter after that. Menoth grumbled and stewed at home, fretting over his lost children and the vengeance he was powerless to exact.

The Terumani were astonished, for the snows piled one upon another. It is said that Wéodar the spouse of Vélopar had come forth, and sailed to the east, and meddled with the sea currents and airs, so that the warm rains from the east ceased to fall upon Batack in season. Tree and grove failed, and many dræads and næads were unhoused. The Giants, as well, and other great creatures which haunted the forest, shivered in their caves and hollows, and sought better country on the fringes of the icelands.

Year by year the snows remained upon the ground across the vastness of the northlands, covering the Batack and the Rode, from the coast to the furthest fringe of the land, until the northlands had become a great plain of ice ten thousand feet deep[2] at the command of Vélopar: barren, frozen, and impassible. The Sorites of the Southrealm could no longer leave their domains, nor in any wise northward cross the great plains of ice. So ended at last the caravans of the Stegganese.

As for the northlands, the years passed without a spring. Yet through all this Vélopar had mercy on the lands of Niyarc and Vordót, and Wéodar provided a warm breath of wind from the southeastern seas to blow in upon Niyarc: so the springs and summers would come to that country, an island of green amid the sea of ice, and though the seasons of frost and snow were longer and more bitter, yet the ice did not gather there as on Batack. Thus the Ádolthi and their Halls were spared, and the Kindreds of the Sorians that dwelt there survived, an enclave surrounded by an impassible waste.

In this manner the Pleïstians were cut off from the children of Sorios. Then Vélopar was satisfied, and left off his work.

The Terumani saw the wisdom of the plan of Vélopar in these events. The plans of Menoth were thwarted, yet the freedoms of the speaking Kindreds were not removed. No longer would any of the Pleïstians go into the Southrealm where the Sorites had made their homes.

Dôni also became reconciled to this turn of fate, together with her supporters. Her Kindred was allowed to prosper in its own place, shielded from fear of the Kindred of the Sorites or the ill-will of their Guardians. So the Pleïstians spread through the remaining countries of the north: through Niyarc and Vordót and those areas of the Rode and the Surmont which remained free of ice and glacier.

There were also left in Niyarc a remnant of the Sorites who had never gone south. Some also who had dwelt in the forest of Batack fled northward

2 Literally, a thousand mecaths, or approximately 6,500 feet. The term is an expressive idiom denoting a particularly large measurement, and probably an underestimate.

as well, to escape the encroaching snows and ice from the breath of Boros. Dôni took these under her care also, together with the Pleïstians. Thereafter these descendants of Sorios became known as the Donites, and they learned the Donish speech which Dôni had gifted to the Pleïstians, and dwelt together in the north at peace with the Pleïstians.[3]

Thus came the Years of Ice, and the Age of Sundering, into the land of Soria. For a long age it would last, for many generations of the children of Sorios and of Cynodias.[4]

3 The Diatrians, another Sorite Tribe who remained in the north, are not mentioned here, either because they are inaccurately included as "Donites" in this context, or because in later ages some had considered them to be related to the Pleïstians.

4 This is the end of what in the original text was designated as Rede II. The stories which follow are of a different nature, and are collected from many ancient tales of the origins of the Tribes.

PART II

TALES OF THE AGE OF DIVISION

THE TALE OF TERRIS AND PYTERRIS

1. Dynis and the Orphans

Terris and Pyterris were brothers. They lived in the days of the Sundering, when the Ice covered the plateau of Batack, dividing the Pleïstians in the north from the Sorites of the south. They were descended by long lineage from Gnathos the son of Cynodias.

In those days the Pleïstians and the Donites had prospered, and the lands of Niyarc and Vordót had grown crowded with those kin; many clans of Niyarc became restless. Many had already begun to spread outward from the grassy fields and hills of Niyarc, seeking new homes in the mountains and open lands of the north. The northern reaches of the Great Forest of Batack had been spared from the Ice, but it was the haunt of Giants, and wolves, and other beasts.

The children of Gnathos dwelt on the plains of the west, near to the eaves of the forest; Giants and wolves would at times come out from the forest itself and raid their homesteads, doing damage and spreading terror. So the Gnathosians had said, "Why should we have fear of the forest when we are under attack even at home? For in the forest we might find refuge among the trees, but here we sit in the open, awaiting destruction like lambs awaiting the slaughter."[1]

So that Tribe had departed from Niyarc to roam those forests, learning to avoid the dangers of the wood. There they remained, a small and secretive Tribe, which had little to do with the other folk of Soria. They wandered in Batack in the shadows beneath the boughs, making safe nests high in the limbs and branches of the forest canopy, or delving burrows among the roots and brambles like the Gauphrin;[2] hunting and living off the wilderness as they might.

The family of Scaphis and Asha'id was among these, and they wandered with their clan in the forests of Batack. They had two sons, Terris and Pyterris.

Both Terris and Pyterris were small children, still clinging to their mother. One day the tribe of Scaphis was out on the hunt, when a party of Giants surprised them and attacked them. This came about in this manner.

The company came upon an open glade in the midst of the forest, where

1 The idiom in the original text was "like *nêvusi* waiting for the pot." *Nêvusi* were the giant edible snails of Batack, which could be effortlessly plucked from the forest.

2 "Gauphrin" was the proper name for the Kindred of the gnomes, and the name most often used by the gnomes themselves.

the grass grew thick and tall, and the sun glistened brightly. Here they heard the warbling of quail in the grass, and looking down into the glade they beheld a flock of quail, roosting among the tussocks.

The hunters of the tribe lowered their voices to a whisper, and their chief said, "Here is food enough to supply us with feasting for days. Let us all approach the flock as one, that on my signal each of us may take a bird or two before the flock might flee."

So Scaphis turned to the children, for they were too small to hunt, and said to them, "Lie here quietly in the grass. Keep yourselves hidden, so that you cannot be seen. Make no noise and no motion until we come to retrieve you."

Then all the tribe stooped and crept low to the ground, hiding themselves in the tall grass. Brandishing javelins and darts, they approached in utter quiet the glade where the quail roosted, as Terris and Pyterris hid silently in the tufts at the ridge of the slope, peering down into the glade.

But as they crept forward, a dim and threatening shadow stirred in the forest beyond. With a noise like the crash of a sudden waterfall the flock of quail burst up in unison and flew off in a panic, leaving the hunters thwarted and confused. As for Terris and Pyterris, they had seen the motion in the shadow of the woods which the company below had missed, and the hair on their necks rose up. They froze and dared not move.

The hunters, however, thinking that they had flushed the quail by their own incaution, grumbled, "Our commotion has sounded the alarm, or perhaps some one of us has been seen. Now we have lost our quarry, and will not feast tonight." So standing up and leaving the cover of the grass, they cursed their misfortune.

But as the company turned to retreat, a party of Giants broke without warning from the brush and attacked, howling in the madness of their darkened minds, and swinging clubs as thick as tree trunks about them, at all that they could reach. A foul and fetid monster led the pack, with a twisted face grimacing in delight at their sport. Then Terris and Pyterris cried out in terror, but Asha'id the mother of Terris and Pyterris called up the grassy slope, saying "Hide and be silent! Let no one find you!"

In the horror of that assault some of the company raised spears to fight, while others tried to flee, and all was mayhem and terror in the glade below. But the spears of the Gnathosians were mere annoyances to the Giants, and the party had been taken utterly unprepared, so in the end none remained standing, and no one returned for the children. The Giants, laughing, stole all that they could carry and, retreating into the shadows of the forest, they disappeared. They had not discovered the children in the grass above the glade. Terris and Pyterris saw them no more.

The children remained hiding in the grass for a very long while, unable to avert their eyes from the silence of the scene below. But none below them stirred in all that time, and none came to their aid. At last, not knowing what to do, the youngest of the brothers, Pyterris, began to cry; but Terris stood up and steeled himself. With tears still moist on his cheeks, he went down into the field of the quail, into the midst of the carnage, and recovered the spear of Scaphis his father. He then collected whatever food and supplies had been missed by the Giants, and brought them back to his brother.

He said, "Our parents have bought our lives for us, at the greatest cost. Now we must wander alone. But one day I shall have my revenge on these beasts." So the children disappeared into the forest.

They slept in dark thickets and scrapes as they had been taught, always fearful that the Giants might return and find them. Terris took his father's spear, and tried to hunt, but his hands were untrained, and his arm had no strength, so he was unable to gather more than the most meager of provisions. They could find no meat, nor forage from the forest, for they were young, and had not yet been trained in the lore of the forest.

The children wandered in this manner for several weeks, growing ever weaker. At last they returned unwittingly to the field of the quail. The grass and vines had grown quickly, and had shrouded the signs of the battle, but Terris and Pyterris knew the place. Then Terris despaired of existence, his mind in a fever. He said to Pyterris his brother, "Here is the very spot where we lost our parents. Let us sit down here and die, for what better place to go to meet those whom we have lost than here at that same glade where we were parted."

Here the children collapsed, and lay near the point of death, sensing nothing more.

But it so happened that Dynis, a dræad of the forest of Batack, was surveying her own country, for in those days the terumani went forth and walked openly among the realms of Soria. Now Dynis was a guardian of tree and woodland within the remnant of Batack, along the fringes of the great forest in the north. All this country had been spared during the Age of Ice, and the borders of the forest had even expanded to the north during that long era. Thus she dwelt in the forest, walking all that country on her rounds, and caring for all the verdure of Batack north of the wall of the Ice. Beautiful in form was Dynis, like all the terumani, with a cascade of hair the hue of the holly tree, and clothed in a veil of green light, as a gown of radiance.

Now Dynis passing by that way came to the meadow of the quail, for she had many retreats in Batack whereto she came for restoration, and this meadow was one of these. But passing into the meadow the stench of death and the odor of Giants lingered there, so that she recoiled. She looked about, and discovered the signs of the battle and death which had occurred there. Dynis lifted up her voice and wept, saying,

"This ghastly grave was once a glade of gladness,
Where sunbeam slept on silver-shining sward.
A refuge and retreat remade in malice,
Mirth and merriment by murders marred.
Ruined now by raiders rank and ravenous,
Victim of a vile and vicious horde.
This hollow, once my hallowed home,
A slough of sorrows has become.

But as the dræad mourned over the suffering which had ruined that place, her sensitive ears discovered the quiet moan of fleeting breath, and she realized there was yet life to be found in the place. She searched the grass, and in the thickness of the tussocks she found the two children lying: Terris and Pyterris, insensate, with the breath of life but light upon their lips.

Dynis could see that the children had been orphaned by the destruction of the Giants: her heart bled for them, and she had pity on them. So she took them, and nursed them to life. When Terris and Pyterris awoke to their senses, they wept, and clung to Dynis as a savior, and would not be parted from her.

Dynis' heart was moved, and her soul bonded with the children. But she thought, "These are surely children of the Tribe of Gnathos, the mortal folk who wander these woods. Their own clan is slain and they have no home. But surely others of this Tribe will receive them. It would be best to leave them in the care of their own kind."

So bringing the children with her, she searched the hidden groves of Batack until she discovered a clan of the Gnathosians. There she commanded the children to reveal themselves to the folk of that clan, that they might take them in. But Terris and Pyterris clung to Dynis, and would not depart from her by any persuasion. So the heart of Dynis was moved to love them.

Dynis said to herself, "It is not customary that there should be union between the Children of Toë and the terumani. Yet these are but children, and they have already received more than their life's share of suffering. Surely it would be a good thing to take them into my care, to shield them in this life from further anguish?"

So Dynis took the children, and raised them as her own. But she did so in secret, revealing this confidence to none but her most trusted allies among the dræads: for she feared that should Teruman Grënas the lord of the dræads discover them, the children might be commanded from her care: and she had come to love them dearly.

Years passed, and Dynis conveyed Terris and Pyterris with her wherever she wandered throughout the remnant of Batack. The boys grew strong and healthy. Dynis became a devoted foster-mother, caring for them diligently, so that they knew no want. Slowly the wounds in their hearts healed, and as they grew older their memories of fear and horror faded. They came to love Dynis as their own mother, until at last they had forgotten the sorrows of their infancy. They knew only the woodlands of Batack, and the love of their foster-mother: and no memory of former days haunted them.

In all this time, Dynis had not introduced the children to any other soul but her own. So as they grew up the memory of their own kind left them, and they did not remember that there were others in the woods beside themselves. In time they forgot even their own clan and their own parents.

But the brothers developed a firm bond with one another, and loved their foster-mother with the greatest devotion.

Thus they grew up as the terumani, learning all the lore and the secrets of woodland and tree. Dynis spoke the Sorian tongue with them, the language of the terumani, so they forgot even their own tongue.

The brothers grew into youths, and gained both strength and wisdom. Terris, the older, became stocky and strong, an athletic youth who took joy in exertion and activity. He ran swiftly, his arms became strong, and his eyes were keen. The suffering of his childhood was buried deeply, and only Dynis could discern the pain and hardness hidden in the shadows of his soul. He was a solemn youth, always intent on his purpose, stern and headstrong.

Pyterris grew into a hardy youth, thinner and smaller than his brother, but wiry and strong. He had great endurance, so that he could run for miles and not grow weary. His was a quiet soul, thoughtful and meditative. He was intelligent, and crafty, and skilled with his hands. He was able to fashion many artful things from wood, from bone, from stone and leather: all that the forest supplied he could work skillfully.

As they grew older, Dynis began to allow the boys to wander on their own, for she had taught them the lore of the woods, and given them whatever gifts she might, so she felt confident that they would be safe on their own. She gave them but one command, saying, "If you come upon any other folk in the wood, do not speak to them or reveal yourselves to them. But conceal yourselves as I have taught you, and leave them alone."

So Terris and Pyterris agreed, for they had always trusted the word of their mother to keep them from harm. They wandered the woods freely, and Dynis had little fear for their well-being.

Now as the boys grew in stature, they came to realize that they were unlike their mother in form. Dynis was tall and lithe in the form of the terumani, and they were short of limb, and coarse in features.[3] So they thought, "Perhaps it is because of our misshapen form that our mother hides us, that we might not be

3 The Gnathosians were one of the *stymphoi,* or small-statured Tribes of Soria. By the historical era they were commonly short enough that they might be considered a pygmy race.

persecuted by others who would find us terrible to behold, like creatures misborn." So they themselves became ashamed of their appearance, and were afraid to be seen by any but their mother.

Pyterris used to go out into Batack and explore the high country. In that country there were great rocks, ridges, and fells, which were open to the sky. There Pyterris would sit for many hours and contemplate. He used to watch the birds as they soared overhead. In the spring, he watched the geese and the shorebirds flying northward, into the countries of Niyarc and Vordót from their haunts in the far south; in the fall, he would watch the flocks as they returned southward in their long journey beyond the Ice.

It came to pass one day that as Pyterris sat on an expanse of rock in the fells of Batack, he heard a sound of commotion, the cacophony of a flock of ravens in distress, and the snarl of an animal on the hunt. He got up and followed the sound, and beheld the flock thronging the trees of a rocky hollow, above the cover of a windblown juniper bush.

There he discovered a fox snapping at a raven which was taking refuge among the branches, leaping and clawing to defend itself. But it could not fly. Now all about the stricken raven the body of the flock called out, harassing the fox and defending their companion, but the fox would not flee.

So Pyterris took pity on the raven, and picking up a stone, he threw it at the fox. His aim was sure, and he struck the fox squarely on the snout. The beast yelped in pain, and seeing Pyterris it fled, for the foxes fear all the Children of Toë.

Then the flock of ravens calmed themselves, and cleared the way for Pyterris: but the stricken bird tried to hide among the branches, and said, "'Auris is no good for meat or for pelt. Leave me to perish in peace."[4]

Pyterris had been given many gifts by Dynis, and among these was the ability to understand the voice of many animals. So he said, "I have not come to finish what the fox has begun, but to save your life, if possible."

The raven was suspicious, and said, "The children of Sorios are not friends with the birds. If I come forth you will break my neck."

Pyterris answered, "I know not what the children of Sorios might do. But I am the son of Dynis the dræad."

The raven said, "Yet your look and your scent is like that of the children of Sorios. I should take no chance with you."

---

4 It is doubtful this conversation is intended to be taken as factual. Elsewhere it's explicit that only the Kindreds of Toë had the gift of speech. Another more fabulous version of this tale exists in which the animal companions of the brothers play major speaking roles. It is likely this version retained only the introductory speeches of the animal figures, either out of sentiment or for narrative clarity. In any event, the dræads likely had a rapport with the animal world which bordered on communication.

Pyterris said, "Your wing is broken. This fox may be gone for now, but it may return when I have gone. And even if not, surely other beasts shall come. Allow me to splint your wing, so that it heals. Then you may abide with me until you can fly again, and I shall protect you from harm."

The raven replied, "The ravens of the wood are faithful to those who do them well, and vengeful to those who do them ill. 'Auris shall ever be the friend of the son of Dynis if he plays him no trick and does him no harm: much benefit can come to you earthbound folk by the sight of the ravens. But should you deceive me, my flock will haunt and harass you to the end of your days."

Pyterris continued coaxing, and the raven at last came out of the juniper. Pyterris set the bone, and fashioned a pliant splint of juniper wood, and bound the wing of the raven. Then the raven willingly perched upon the shoulder of Pyterris, and Pyterris returned to his foster-mother.

Then Dynis said, "What is this bird? What business do you have together?"

Pyterris replied, "The raven was in danger of its life, and I have granted it safety in my keeping until its wing shall heal. In return, I shall have the freedom of flight. The eyes of 'Auris can see what I cannot from beneath the boughs of the forest, and the bird will warn me of danger and lead me to safety. And to whatever place I cannot reach, the cries of 'Auris shall bring word on my behalf."

Then Dynis said to Pyterris, "Learn from the raven cleverness, and liberty, and loyalty to one's own; but do not learn foolishness, trickery or spite."

Pyterris said, "Who should be foolish, with so wise a mother as I have had?"

Dynis said, "I fear sorrows will result from this pursuit. But your heart is strong, and I shall not lose faith in you, my son."

So it was that Pyterris became a friend of the raven. He began to go out with 'Auris upon his shoulder, and when the raven was able to fly once again, it learned to retrieve items at his request, so nothing in the woods was out of his reach. The raven was able as well to spy out the country as Pyterris wandered, so that if there were any danger it would cry out a warning. All the ravens of that country came to accept Pyterris as one of their own.

Terris also explored the hills and hollows of the country. One day as he was walking beneath the canopy of the forest he heard the clamor of baying, and the snapping of jaws: and he felt on the air the energy of the hunt. He came upon a rocky hollow below the trees, where a pack of wolves had cornered an aurochs of great size, with curved horns massive and formidable. As Terris watched, the beast drove toward the largest of the wolves, and lunged as if it would force the wolf into the rocks and impale it.

Terris' heart went out to the wolf, for it seemed a brave and cunning animal to him. Now Terris still carried the spear of his father, though he no longer remembered the hand that had made it. Dynis had taught him how to use it to defend against the dangers of the woods, so taking up his weapon, he cast it at the aurochs. So great had the strength of Terris become, and so skillful his hand, that with one cast he struck the breast of the beast and brought it down.

The wolves had not yet seen Terris, for he knew much of the craft of the dræads for concealing himself in wood and foliage: nor had they spotted his spear. Seeing the aurochs go down they fell upon it, thinking they had taken it by their own strength.

But the largest wolf, that which the aurochs had wounded, saw the spear of Terris, and he growled in the speech of the wolves, "What creature of the Children of Toë dares to hunt the prey of Diris?"

But Terris knew some of the language of the wolves. So he came forth from his concealment and said, "I intended not to hunt, but to save the life of an ungrateful dog."

The wolf was amazed, and asked, "How do you come to speak the language of wolf?" Never had any of the kindreds spoken to him in his own tongue.

"I am the son of Dynis the dræad, she who cares for this wood. I know many tongues. But if you have no grace to thank a benefactor, I shall take my spear and depart in regret for an unthanked deed."

The wolf said, "Your look and your scent is like the children of Sorios, and never have I given thanks to a child of Sorios. But if you are indeed a friend of wolf, I shall admit my debt."

Terris said, "I am a friend of none, but Pyterris my brother. Nevertheless, I should gladly accept the friendship of Diris."

The wolf said, "Then friend shall you be. Since you have shared in the hunt, you may partake of the kill."

So Terris joined the wolves, but he said, "I have never eaten anything but the fruit of the forest which has been provided by Dynis my mother. Regardless, I shall gladly accept the fellowship of Diris and his pack." When the wolves had satisfied their hunger they disappeared into the wood.

So Terris went home to his foster-mother, and said, "Today I have learned to hunt with the wolves. I shall take my spear, and be a hunter with them."

Dynis said, "It is a hardness of this world, that one soul must perish that others may live: for such is the way of the Storm that undergirds the world. But so has it always been, and it is fitting that you learn even this lesson."

Terris replied, "The hunt is a noble skill, and has much reward in itself."

Dynis said, "Your heart is good, Terris. But you have no need to hunt for flesh, for I shall provide as I always have, and you shall never know want."

But Terris said, "The wolves need flesh, or they shall not live. I shall share in the hunt as their companion, only."

Dynis said, "There is much to learn from the tribe of the wolves. You might learn from the wolf of nobility and faithfulness; of family and companionship. Yet do not learn savagery, for that will be the way of undoing."

But Terris said, "How can one become savage, who has learned mildness from you, my mother?"

"Nevertheless," said Dynis, "I foresee further sorrows from this passion. Only keep your heart pure, my son, and I shall not despair for you."

So it was that Terris became a friend of wolves. He went about venturing with Diris and the wolves, and he learned to stalk, to pursue, to chase, and to hunt. He ran swiftly like the wolves, and was strong and courageous. Then the wolves were glad of his company, for he became a skilled and stealthy hunter.

2. The Secret of the Gnathosians

One day as the summer was drawing to a close, Pyterris was out walking in the woods with 'Auris flying on ahead, when the raven became nervous and squawked its alarm. The bird took rest high in a tree beyond the crest of the ridge before them and crowed its displeasure. Pyterris crept to the top of the ridge, and listened. There he heard the sounds of hunters stalking, walking quietly among the underbrush, and speaking to one another in whispers. Something deep in his soul was moved, and he felt a longing unlike any he could remember. He wished to see this folk, and commune with them. But the warning of his mother rang in his memory, that he should make no contact either with any child of Toë, nor with any teruman. So he turned aside.

When he returned to the place of his mother and his brother, he was afraid to report to Dynis. But Terris he took aside, and said to him secretly, "Today while wandering in the forest we came upon a band of the Children of Toë. They softly spoke in a language I could not understand, and stalked prey in secret among the glens. My soul stirred at the sound of it. But the word of our mother stayed me, and I dared not reveal myself. Yet I would like to learn more of this folk: who they might be, and what manner of being."

Terris also was curious, and asked, "Might you find these hunters again?"

Pyterris answered, "'Auris can fly far overhead and spot anyone in the woods below. Diris and your wolves are master trackers, as well, who can find the trail of hart or rabbit, and follow it by nose to its place. Surely our companions could track these folk to their camp. But to what end? We are forbidden to meet with them."

Terris considered this, and after a while he said, "I would not disobey the word of our mother. Yet we both would like to learn more of this folk. Let us go in hiding to watch them. Thus may we obey the word of our mother and yet satisfy our longing. When we have filled our curiosity to the brim, then we may leave them in peace, and no harm shall have been done."

This seemed good to Pyterris.

So the next day Terris and Pyterris went together into the wood, where

Terris called to Diris and his pack, and they returned to the glen where the raven had discovered the hunters. Diris went down into the glen, and he picked up the trail of the hunters, and followed it into the wood, with the brothers following.

When some hours had passed, and miles had been trodden, the wolves stopped at last, and would proceed no further. So Pyterris sent the raven ahead, and when 'Auris had found the camp he took up roost on the branch of a tree and began to call loudly in the voice of the ravens. Terris and Pyterris then crept forward carefully through the brush and foliage of the understory, until they spotted the camp of the hunters. Their skills of stealth were great, so there they lay in hiding, and were unseen and undiscovered. They watched these Gnathosians in awe, for they saw now that the form of the Gnathosians was like their own.

The brothers were filled with wonder, for never had they met another soul, neither dræad nor Sorian, in all their days with Dynis. Their souls were stirred, but they did not understand the cause, for neither Pyterris nor Terris yet remembered their own past nor the folk of their clan.

There they stayed and watched the camp of the Children of Toë. Many of that folk milled about in the glade below, twenty or more, both male and female. They had dug homes from among the roots of the trees, and in a glade before their burrows they burned fires in pits. There were pelts drying, and meat was cooking. They spoke among themselves in the strange language of the forest folk which neither Pyterris nor Terris could remember. Children were there as well, playing together in the camp, like the young of all animals, in untroubled joy.

As the day grew long, Terris and Pyterris knew that they should return to their foster-mother. Then Terris said to Pyterris, "We have followed and watched this strange folk all the day, yet my curiosity grows no less. Rather, my heart burns within me more than ever."

Pyterris answered, saying, "My soul also hungers, and tells me that there is much we should learn from them. Let us now return to our abode. But we should come to this place again tomorrow, and learn more, that perhaps our curiosity would be satisfied."

Terris agreed, saying, "Yet I feel that our mother would be grieved to learn where we have been. I think we should not tell her what we have done this day, nor where we go tomorrow, for I would not cause pain to our mother's heart."

So the brothers went home to Dynis. But this secret they held close to their breast.

Terris and Pyterris returned to the camp of the Children of Toë the next day, and for many days following. From Dynis their foster-mother the youths had learned great skill in hiding, nearly as masterful as that of the dræads, to blend into the forest as if they themselves were bark and tree: and Dynis had moreover charmed them herself with a gift of concealment. The sounds of their motion were as natural as the sounds of leaf and bird. None ever heard them approach, and no one in the camp discovered their watching.

In this manner they haunted the clan, coming secretly to observe them throughout the long winter of the north. When the hunters went out to hunt, the brothers followed. When the foragers went into the woods to forage, the brothers followed. So noiseless and crafty was their stalking that none of the Gnathosians knew they were trailed, and the brothers were not discovered. They learned the Gnathosians' manner of stalking prey; and how they fashioned spears and knives of stone, and bone, and wood; how they dressed their quarry in the field, and how they carried the meat back to camp. They learned the making of leather, and how to fashion cords and clothing and belts and vessels. They learned their methods of cooking, and what the Gnathosians gathered for food and medicine. They learned their songs, and their dances, and their celebrations and their lamentations.

They listened also, and absorbed the words of the tribe. They learned the language of the Gnathosians, for they had forgotten the Donish of their childhood; and they began to speak secretly between themselves in the Donish tongue.

Each soul of that clan they came to know: father and mother, brother and sister, grandmother and grandfather—each one they came to know by name. Even the children they learned to recognize.

As they became familiar with this clan, they came to feel a kinship with them, as if something in their past had awakened. But they soon discovered that something else had awakened: a darkness began to haunt them, a fear and rage which smoldered in the lost regions of their minds like a smokeless coal glowing deep within a cold firebed. They could not remember what suffering they had borne, but they felt there was some forgotten secret locked away in the cavern of their memories.

They bore this secret in their hearts, hidden from their foster-mother. Yet Dynis discerned a brooding in her sons: and her soul became troubled, for she feared that they might grow distant from her.

At last the day came when Terris and Pyterris could bear their secret no longer, and Pyterris laid his heart before his brother, saying, "For many weeks now we have come to know this clan of the Children of Toë, and the more we follow them, the greater grows the anxiety in our hearts. It does not abate, but waxes stronger. Shall we go to our mother at last, and reveal what we have been doing, that perhaps she might help us to learn the cause? She may know what secret haunts us, and it is certain that she shall do whatever she can to steal away our fears and anxieties."

But Terris said, "Our mother has for all these years cared for us, to keep us from harm and suffering. Now we are grown, so is it perhaps not proper that we should follow her example? My counsel would be that we preserve her from pain on our account."

"How then shall we uncover the secret lurking hidden in our hearts?"

Terris said, "I have been considering this question, and I feel that the time may have come for us to go to these Gnathosians at last, and reveal ourselves to them. The darkness within our own hearts is clearly linked to this clan, and it may be that they can reveal secrets we do not understand."

Pyterris was astonished at his brother's words, and he said, "Shall we disobey our mother, who has strictly warned us against such a meeting?"

Terris said, "I fear that we are bound now for sorrows, come what may, whichever course we choose. To learn the truth may bring unforeseen sorrows, from which our mother would shield us if she could. Yet to know nothing will only prolong our turmoil."

Pyterris replied, "I have never hesitated to follow your lead. What does your heart tell you to do?"

Terris reasoned, and said, "The command of our mother is given us from the love of her own heart, to spare us pain. If we can ourselves find the cause of our fears and so bring our pains to an end, we shall have fulfilled her desire for us. And we shall spare her trouble and worry thereby."

So Pyterris assented. "You are correct, of course," he said. "Perhaps indeed it might even bring her joy. Is not the wish of any mother that her children grow to maturity, and learn to govern their own lives?"

Terris and Pyterris made their decision, and one morning they bid their mother farewell, saying, "We are going into the forest, and mean to travel and explore for days."

So Dynis said, "You are wise in the ways of the forest. Only be cautious as I have always taught you, and I shall not fear for you." And kissing them sent them on their way.

So they set their course for the camp of the Gnathosians.

Now Dynis, also, had finally been overwhelmed by her concerns for her sons. She determined to follow them on their venture, to see for herself where it was they went, and see if she might discover the cause of their darkness. Dynis was teruman, though but a nymph, and her natural powers of concealment were beyond even those of her sons; for the terumani are able to watch over the Children of Toë undetected, and might be seen only if they choose to reveal themselves.[5] So it was that she followed her children in secret, and Terris and Pyterris were unaware that she watched and followed as they went on their way.

5 Elsewhere it's made clear that there are exceptions to this: those who have been accustomed to the signs of the terumani could occasionally spot a nymph or spright on their own, and under certain conditions even the Ádolthi or their hidden Mansions could be discovered.

When they had traveled the pathways, hidden but familiar, which took them to the Gnathosian camp, Pyterris said, "How shall we proceed? Will this folk not be astonished by our appearance here, and fear us?"

Terris answered, "My counsel would be to pretend to be Gnathosians such as they, for clearly they are in appearance such as we are. It is best if we do not reveal our true parentage to these Gnathosians. Nor shall we speak our own tongue among them. We shall say that we have been lost in the forest since our youth, and tell them nothing further of our upbringing."

"Then perhaps also we should not reveal that we have followed them these many days, and know them and their families by name."

Terris agreed to this also, and said, "I also shall lay aside my spear, and you should lay aside your knife[6] as well, that we demonstrate no threat to them."

So they agreed. Then they stepped openly into the camp of the Gnathosians, and hailed them in their own tongue, and greeted them.

As Pyterris had foreseen, the Gnathosians were startled by their emergence; they instantly took up their arms, and sent their children to cover. But Terris and Pyterris greeted them peaceably, and spread their arms wide to show that they had come unarmed and amicably into their midst. The elder of the clan came forward cautiously and asked, "Who are you, and whence have you come to us unseen and unheard?"

Terris bowed to the elder, and said, "Our names our Terris and Pyterris, and we dwell alone in the forest. We discovered your camp by fortune some time past, but have feared to reveal ourselves to you. Thus have we traveled in stealth and secrecy. But we dare come to you now openly, seeking answers to our own riddles. For we carry secret fears within our souls, which we cannot unravel alone. By your grace, we would like to speak with you and your clan, to learn what you might teach us. Your very appearance, and the ring of your voices, fill both of us with a dismay that we do not understand."

Then the elder welcomed them into the camp, and they went in with him by hidden entrances among the roots of a great tree into the meeting-house of the camp, where they sat down with many of the elder folk of the clan. This was a large den roofed by the roots of the forest, with a hard clay floor and a smokey fire in the center of the space. The elders sat on wooden benches around the edges of the room, while Terris and Pyterris sat on blankets on the floor in the middle of the space.

There they questioned one another to see if any answers could be found. Terris and Pyterris learned of the history of the Gnathosians, and the history of the clan; they were told the lore of that folk, and what things they feared in the forest, and the fears of the night which betimes haunted their children. There were no secret fears of that folk which the elders failed to reveal. But

6 Presumably a stone blade wrapped with a handle of leather, as the use of metal was unknown at this time.

nothing they spoke of settled the misgivings of Terris and Pyterris, nor spoke to their hearts.

One of the elders by the name of Griën spoke, saying, "Your mystery may be best solved if we knew something of your past: who you are, and whence you have come? For we have never come across a trace of you in our years of wandering here, nor do we know of any others who wander the woods alone as you do."

On this point Terris and Pyterris were reticent, but Terris revealed, "We are children of the Forest, and cannot say what our lineage might be, for we have wandered our years alone together." In this answer he did not lie, for the brothers had spent much time alone together as wanderers in Batack, nor had they ever questioned who their father might be.

Then Griën said, "I perceive then that you are orphans. It so happens that at times our folk are taken unawares in the forest by Giants or drakes, or some other disaster. Now I know this: that some years ago in our wanderings we came upon an open field, many days north of this camp, in which lay the clear signs of a massacre, wherein the folk of that clan had been killed by Giants. We mourned them and set up a memorial cairn on their behalf. It is place of loathing and fear to us, and we do not go there. But if any small child had escaped that place, they might now be of such an age as the two of you."

But Pyterris said, "No, this cannot be. We know our mother, and have seen her but scant days ago." They did not say, however, that she was no Gnathosian such as the clan which had been taken in the woods. Dynis their mother was unlike that Tribe, and they suspected the Gnathosians would fear them on that account.

Griën merely shrugged and said, "That may be, but perhaps she also escaped and has traveled alone, in fear or shame that she alone survived of her clan. Has she no answer to your riddles?"

"We know only that we have always lived and traveled with her alone," said Terris. "No other history has she divulged, and never have we questioned beyond this fact."

"She may, then, bear secrets in her heart that would answer your questions. My counsel would be to question her directly on these matters."

At the end of the day the brothers left that camp, and retreated together into the forest. Then they sat down together and confided. Terris spoke his doubts, saying, "This thing cannot be, for we know our mother, and she is no Gnathosian."

But at the words of Griën the brothers' hearts had given way within them, and they felt sick with fear. For visions came to them unbidden, of a figure whom they did not know. In their mind's eye they saw her, and saw her perish at the hand of a Giant.

Pyterris lamented, "It is clear to me now that we are not the sons of Dynis, as we have long believed; but we are Gnathosians, like these folk whom we have been observing. So who then was our mother, and what is our origin?"

"If we would learn the answers to all these questions, we must ask our mother Dynis to tell us all that she knows. She alone knows what happened, and whence we came, and what our true heritage must be."

"But to demand such a thing from her would grieve her beyond measure. How can we think to hurt her so, who has worked so hard to bring us nothing but peace and contentment in this world?"

So the brothers returned to their foster-mother, heavy of heart, and sorrowing, and fearing to know the truth. But they said nothing of what they had learned.

Now Dynis also, who had followed her children in secret, mourned this discovery, for it was clear that she would need to reveal to them all the truth of their past, and so bring heartbreak and sorrow into their lives, which she had long labored to keep from them.

When they had returned to their place, Dynis steeled her heart, and did not reveal what she had learned. But she said to the brothers, "Come. Let us set forth on a journey through the forest together, as we did in days past when you were but children."

So Dynis and her foster-children set out together through the woods. They were on the trail for days, comforted in one another's company. But when they had traveled for many miles from their home, she brought them to an open field with a cairn of stones mounted in the center. She then bowed her head and said, "You are now grown, and I deem the time has come for you to learn of your origins. Behold the place of our meeting."

Then Terris and Pyterris looked upon the field of the quail, and their memories returned to them in full. Trembling with rage they remembered the horror of that day, and the flight of the quail, and the evil ferocity of the Giants. Then weeping they remembered their mother and father, and the clan with whom they had wandered. And they remembered the day that Dynis discovered them at point of death, and rescued them.

There they learned the truth: that they themselves were Gnathosians, and not the sons of Dynis as they had thought.

Terris said, "Now we must know: who then was our mother? And how did we come to be the sons of Dynis?"

So Dynis wept, saying, "Long years have I feared this day, and tried to prevent it from arriving. For I thought that if you discovered nothing of your past, your sorrows would remain far from your souls, and you would be comforted always in the love your foster-mother.

"For indeed, as you have discerned, I am not your mother, but your foster-mother, who has raised you as her own children from the day she found you weeping and forlorn here in the field of death."

Then Dynis explained to them how she came upon them that day, lying at the point of death near the bones of their clan; she told them how she loved them now as her own children, and had hoped that if they knew not the truth, they might live with her all their days.

"Yet always have I known that one day we would part ways," said Dynis. "For it is unheard of that there be such familiarity between the terumani and the Children of Toë, and I have given you knowledge and gifts which are forbidden for your kind. I knew that if ever the truth were known, you would no longer remain in my care. Moreover, your length of days is that of the Children of Toë, while the life of the terumani in this land endures for ages beyond the lives of your Kindred. One day, no matter how well I guarded my secret, you yourselves would depart beyond the halls of this world, and I would remain behind here in the forest of my domain. So should we have been parted forever, until perhaps the Storm at last is pacified and Havui restores all things."

Then Dynis told her children, "The days are now short wherein we may find joy in one another's company. Come now: let us go out and see the wide world. We must make one last journey together as mother and sons."

3. The Gifts of Ologéo

It was now the beginning of springtime in the Northrealm, and the bitter north winds of winter gave way to the warm airs of Wéodar blowing into Vordót from the southeast seas. Dynis then led the brothers on northward trails: Before long they passed the ragged fringe of the woodlands and entered the open skies and the green carpet of the hill country of the Glyptians. It was the season of wildflowers: all they saw was beauty such as the forest had never opened to them.

From that point Dynis had them travel in secret from grove to grove, and from grotto to hollow: for the terumani prefer to travel unseen by the eyes of the Children of Toë, and she wished to keep her sons from the scrutiny of the inhabitants of that land. So they took long paths through the foothills of the Surmont, then crossing the wide valley of the Griës Pass they came to the range of the Barria Heceïca and turned eastward. For many more days they traveled in secret among the mountains: and they relished these fleeting days together.

At last as the days of summer were growing short, Dynis brought her sons one day on an eastward trek: their paths led them over rocky and windblown ridges, and before their eyes rose the glowing peak of Depharmen in the distance, its golden crown lifted above the shoulders of its jagged neighbors.

They continued from thence through difficult country of stoney mountain and deep-riven valleys, until after days of hard travel Dynis brought them to the foot of the Depharmen Stair. There they stopped and looked up in wonder. In a valley between the ridges of Mount Depharmen and its sister Mount Toë the land rose beyond them and beyond the very mountains in a series of great cliffs: a vast, broken river of ice and snow descended from the ridgeline as if from the very sky. The untrodden cliffs of the Stair rose up far beyond their path, on into the frightful, everlasting ice and winds of that pass, across which few had come, and none returned. At the knees of the great mountain to the east loomed the plateau known as the Shelf.

Then Dynis said, "Here at the Depharmen Stair, below the peak of Depharmen, is the pass whereby your ancestors first entered into the land of Soria. That great mountain overlooks all this range, and is ever in the light of the sun, even in the midst of the long winter days. Down from that Stair came the ancestors of all who dwell in Soria, and there upon the Shelf lies the Hall of Deïni herself, the Lifegiver of the new Kindreds; nigh unto that is the great Hall of Ritéol where Sorios the father, and the Guardians of the Kindreds, hold council. Beyond that pass lies a history long forgotten by any, and lands to which none shall return in the ages foreseen. But our paths shall take us by open roads southward, into the land of Niyarc where the Halls of the Terumani can be found."

So they turned to the south, and followed openly the trail which led from that pass southward. Here they came into Rhotiéstir, the ancient country of the Terumani: in this realm many of that race had built homes and Halls for themselves for many generations of the Children of Toë, and in those days they lived openly among those Kindreds. The trail became gradually wider and more well-trodden, until eventually it had become a pleasant road with houses of teruman and Sorian side by side along its progress. Then they began to encounter others along the way, who nodded politely as they passed, but showed no other concern or curiosity.

At last Dynis turned from the highway, and followed a paved way westward towards a great sloping hillside. As they approached they spied a large compound framed by majestic rows of ancient alder, and at the crown of the hill the great Hall of Liaibíri, the congress of the Terumani.

"This is our destination," Dynis said. They followed the path to its end, and ascended the steps which led to the threshold of that Hall.

"Remain here for the moment, my sons. I must enter into this place and request permission for your admittance, for this is a great Hall of the Ídolthi, and even I may not enter lightly."

So Dynis opened the door and entered the corridor of Liaibíri.

Several of the Ádolthi were visiting at the time, for in those days the Terumani traveled freely about Soria, and many came to commune together, or to find inspiration at Liaibíri. When Dynis entered, all eyes turned to behold her; for though she was only a nymph of the forest, she was lovelier and more stately than many of the High Ones. Thus she was quickly attended to, and she asked at once to see Ologéo, the master of that Hall.

Now Dynis had formerly been familiarly acquainted with Ologéo, but they had grown apart after many years, and neither had seen the other in an age of days.[7] Of this affair none of the Terumani had been privy, so a great deal of curiosity was roused when she spoke her request, and murmurings passed quickly through the many chambers of the Hall.

When word arrived to Ologéo that Dynis the nymph awaited him in the great corridor, he was astonished, and he caught his breath, and his face flushed. But regaining his dignity at once he spoke briefly to the messenger, saying, "She is a friend I have not seen in many a long year. I shall go out to her myself and see her in."

So Ologéo went out to the corridor, and quickly ushered her away from the eyes of the Ádolthi who had congregated in the hall, and unseen by Cosimë his spouse. He brought her into his own chamber and shut the door.

When they were in private he greeted her warmly, but being embarrassed by her presence there he said, "Why did you not go to Denedhros and call me from thence? For surely hearing your call I would have quickly come to meet you there." Denedhros was the Hall Ologéo had built for Dynis in Batack, but which now lay empty.

"It would have been unfair to you, for you would have misunderstood my purpose."

Ologéo replied, "Your purpose matters not to me. I would a relish a moment or two in your presence, whatever your purpose might be."

Then Dynis smiled and touched his arm, saying, "Do not think me cold, Ologéo, for I do not regret the days we spent together. But I come to you now merely to make a request, which I think only you might have the power to grant. I feared you would deny my petition had I not come to you openly in the presence of all the Terumani. For I know you, and I know your distaste for the speaking Kindreds of the land!"

"Although you have understood my sentiments well, yet out of fondness for you there is little I would deny you."

"You know not my request!" said Dynis wryly.

"Speak then. What boon would you have of me? If it is within my power I shall grant it in honor of days we shared in the past, even though I may not hope for such times to be again."

Dynis now was embarrassed in her own turn, but she steeled herself and said, "See before the gate of Liaibíri two Children of Toë. They are Gnathosians, descendants of Cynodias: against the custom of our folk I have raised

---

7 See the tale Ologéo and Dynis, page 51 above.

them as my own. I knew this was improper and wrong. But their own true parents were killed by the wayward children of Erescal,[8] and when I found them in the forest they clung to me as their savior and would not part. Now they are to me as my own children, and I love them as my own.

"Yet the time is coming when they must leave my care and live among their own folk. Their days in this world shall be short, as are the days of all their Kindred. So before they depart from me to join with their own kind, I seek a boon for each of my sons, that they not forget the mother who loved them."

"What boon do they ask?"

"If you promise to help, I shall put the question before them. Then they shall consider the matter themselves, and ask what they will."

"Then perhaps you should have brought them to Tryma, instead. He at least might have imparted wisdom into those youthful brains. I fear that they shall seek nought but foolishness from me. Nevertheless I have given you my word, and I shall not deny you your wish." This he promised, without the knowledge or consent of the Ádolthi, and it is likely that none besides Dynis the nymph could have exacted such a promise from Ologéo.

With this pledge, Dynis went out to her sons, and said to them, "I have received a promise from Ologéo, that each of you may receive a gift from him on my behalf. Do not ask for mere trinkets: By these gifts you shall know throughout your lives in this world that you have been sons of the terumani. Ologéo is a great master of the craft of the Terumani. There are few who surpass him in skill, and there is little he might not accomplish if he sets himself to the task, whatever your hearts might conceive, for he is one of the High Ones of the Ídolthi, who built this very Hall.

"So now, consider for yourselves: One boon each I have been promised for you. One surpassing gift that you might remember Dynis your mother, and the love with which she cared for you all the days of your childhood. Consider now, and take wise counsel within your own hearts, that you may ask wisely."

So chambers were prepared for them within the Hall of Liaibíri, and Dynis and her sons entered.

That night the brothers slept little, but pondered what gift they should request. Terris at last spoke to Pyterris in private, and said, "I know not what to ask. For years I have run with the wolves, and the exhilaration of the hunt is all I have known. I have desired little else of life."

So Pyterris replied, "Then it seems to me that your heart has already told you what you desire, and you have your answer. But likewise I know not what gift would suit me. For I too have enjoyed my life in the forest, and lacked nothing. I have envied no one, save perhaps the birds of the air."

Terris said to him, "Follow then the leading of your own heart."

---

8 I.e., the Giants. See "The Tragedy of Erescal," page 40 above.

When morning came, Dynis called them, and said to them, "We go now to see Ologéo, and I shall ask for you whatsoever you wish. Choose now gifts fit for yourselves. By these gifts you shall remember your heritage. So you shall know that I have given all that any mother could give. Have you considered well? Speak, and tell me your desires."

Terris was a friend of wolves. His heart loved the hunt. He remembered now the death of his natural mother and father, and of his clan, and he was haunted by the laughter of the Giants: It filled his soul with rage. So Terris said, "I have but one wish, and if Dynis my foster-mother shall grant it to me I will know forever that her kindness and mercy are upon me. I have no need of anything in this world, but this one thing to give rest to my soul. I ask you to grant me vengeance upon the Giants who slew our family. If I but had the gifts to do so, then like the wolf I would track them down, and find them, and see them pay with their own lives for the cruel suffering they have caused."

Dynis considered this, and she nodded solemnly. "I pity you the pain in your heart, Terris, and understand the longing which plagues you. I have already given to you the power of the forest, to hide and to travel unseen, and always to be secure among the trees. Ologéo may increase your strength and skills as a hunter. But know this, my son: vengeance is a blade which may wound the hand that wields it. In the end it will not bring rest to your soul."

Then Pyterris asked for his gift. Now Pyterris was a friend of the birds of the air. His heart loved freedom. He also remembered the day of the death of his tribe, but he remembered the quail, that they had flown to safety while the folk of his clan had perished. He had long watched the migrations of the flocks, and had envied them their liberty. So Pyterris said, "I possess all that a youth might wish, and am in need of nothing. But this one thing I have wished from my childhood to this very day: that I might have the skills of the birds, to fly among the trees to safety, and travel above the forests to far off places. If Ologéo shall grant me this skill, then I and my children shall have safety from enemies which my parents did not have, and none may do them harm. Then I shall know that Dynis my foster-mother has had mercy on me."

Dynis shook her head. "You ask much, Pyterris, and I fear that such a gift will bring you sorrow as well as joy. Bear in mind that you would possess what others can only envy. And envy is the twin brother of jealousy and malice."

So the brothers came before Ologéo. There at the urging of Dynis they ventured to make their requests, audacious though they seemed. When they had spoken their full hearts on the matter, Dynis said to Ologéo, "Such are the desires of my children, whom I love as my own. Have you the craft to grant them these boons?"

Ologéo shook his head. "I do. But I shall surely regret this in days to come. Yet my fondness for you makes it impossible for me to deny your wish."

So he took the youths into his inner chamber. There he examined and delved, until he had reached the uttermost depth of their being, and he made his plans and constructed his mechanisms.

First to Terris he came, and he said, "Your boon is the easier of the two, yet the end of it is beyond my powers. I can give you the gift of the huntsman, the envy of wolf and every hunter from among the Kindreds of Toë, that you might track truly, and never lose your quarry. Your senses I might heighten, that you might see in light or dark, might be guided by the slightest motion, might track by scent like the wolf. I might give you the memory and recall of the mammoth, who never loses her way nor forgets her paths. You shall become more fleet than the roe. I can quicken your reactions and strengthen your limbs, and endow you with such skills that your stroke may never miss its mark. With these gifts vengeance shall be within your grasp. But vengeance is a matter of the heart, and that I will not tamper with. If you choose this path, the responsibility and the consequences are your own."

To Pyterris he said, "The gift you ask is a great one, and I shall need to dig deeply into the makings of your nature, and change your form down to the most elemental particle. You may grow wings as the wyvern[9] and your frame must be changed to support and manage such wings. Such things cannot easily be hidden from the others of your folk. The gift you have chosen is strange indeed, and if I do as you ask, this form shall be passed to your children as well, to all generations. It may well be that they shall see it as a curse, and not as a gift, for they shall be unlike the rest of the Children of Toë, and shall surely be outcast and feared by all."

The brothers however were not swayed, and both persisted in their desires. So Ologéo, when he had satisfied himself that they understood the import of their choices, began his work.

Now the craft of the terumani is not through magic or sorcery, but is slow, deep, and intricate. The changes of Ologéo would alter the nature of their being, evolving as days and weeks passed. Many days were spent there in the Hall of Liaibíri under the care of Ologéo and Dynis. As the weeks progressed, the sons of Dynis began to note changes in their nature and form.

Terris, the elder, discerned that his senses grew more keen. His eyesight grew sharper, his sense of smell more acute. He found that he could not lose his sense of direction, however confounding his paths, but was always aware of his surroundings. He developed precise mastery over every motion of his body, so that both hand and arm became sure and true in every action. Even

9 The precise identity of this creature is uncertain, but was a large, two-legged, reptilian beast, a winged creature neither bird nor bat.

the form of his body became altered: his shoulders more broad, his legs more splayed, his back stronger, and his arms longer. He found that when he wished he could run on all fours like the wolf, more swiftly than the hart.

But with these changes he found the pangs of memory had also grown more keen: he could not forget the sorrows of his childhood, nor the mockery of the Giants, and these memories inflamed him.

Pyterris, the younger, was still more astounded by the changes which engulfed him. His legs grew shorter, and his bones grew lighter and more flexible. His chest grew deeper, and his arms and shoulders grew stronger. From his wrists new joints formed and extended from his arms, and wings began to grow from these new limbs to his ribs, supple and leathery like those of the wyvern: They spread wide when he stretched them out, but were so jointed as to fold in close to his arms when he chose.

Along with these changes he began to see that all regarded him strangely, from the terumani sojourning at Liaibíri even to his own brother Terris. So he became discomfited and wished to hide from the eyes of others.

Then at last Ologéo said to Dynis, "My work with these sons of the Pleïstians is done, and they shall become what they have desired. It is perhaps time for you and your sons to leave, for your presence here pricks my very soul, having you so near, yet ever having to avoid you. But consider my gifts a pledge of my continuing devotion, and remember me fondly."

Dynis replied softly, "I shall not forget."

Then Dynis went out to her sons, and when they had prepared for their journey they departed from the Hall of Liaibíri.

They traveled together southward towards Batack, now taking open trails across the plains of Niyarc, for the time had come to take swift paths: The summer had long since passed, and the months of autumn had fully run their course. The first of the winter snows had begun to flurry in the hills of the north, and the mountains frowning over the country were already blanketed in white. The bitter storms of winter had begun to gather their might, and travel would soon be all but impossible.

So they made fleet progress along the southward trails. Many there were who wondered at their passing: a nymph from the Great Forest; a Sorian who could run like the wolf; and another with wings like the wyvern.

By the time they reached the forest of Batack the snows had set in, so Dynis brought them home to one of her enclaves in the wood, where her own powers had sway. There they sat down together for a few final days of rest and comfort.

At last Dynis said, "Now is the time come when we must part ways. For now you have grown to your full stature, and moreover, you know that you are children of the Pleïstians. You shall go your way, and I shall go mine, and seldom shall our paths cross again. From I am dræad, and my paths are hidden from the eyes of the Children of Toë.

"Remember always the care you have received from Dynis, and carry with you all your life the skills and wisdom which I have imparted, for you know the ways of the forest better than all the folk of Batack, either Gnathosian or Mas'chian.[10] Use the gifts you have been given by Ologéo only for just and honorable ends! These gifts place you above your fellows in many ways, and you must never abuse your privilege. Should I learn of such behavior I shall be ashamed and sorely disheartened."

Terris then said, "But you are the only kin we have known! Where shall we go? And what shall we do?"

Dynis answered, "Your place is with your own Kindred and Tribe. Seek them out and dwell with them, and you shall be great among them. This is as it should be, and perhaps it was so destined by Havui from the beginning of your troubles."

Then the brothers dissembled, and Pyterris said, "But we are different from our fellows! Surely we shall be outcasts from their clans."

"You must take the stew from your own pots! You have chosen your gifts, and you must make the best of them," Dynis said. "Nevertheless, I shall see what can be done to ease your transition. Leave me for three days, and when you return I shall give you my gifts."

Dynis then hid herself away within her enclave, and when she had given thought to her plans, she set to work. When Terris and Pyterris returned she sat them down before her and said, "These two final gifts I may grant, to ease your ways in the world. Take them, and use them wisely: and think well of me your mother."

To Terris she presented a great cloak like a blanket: soft and light, infused with secret herbs and crafted by her own charms. She said to him, "Take this blanket, and keep it with you wherever you may wander. It is well crafted by my own hand so that it will neither wear out nor age. Whenever your mind is too fraught with turmoil, with anger, or confusion, you may lie down wrapped in this cloak, and it shall give you the gift of restful and dreamless sleep. In this way you may find relief from your tortured mind, and be refreshed for awhile."

To Pyterris then she presented a flowing robe with great sleeves, bound at the wrist with cuffs so that only his hands were visible. She said, "This robe also is similarly woven, and shall not wear thin. Wear it always, wherever you wish to keep your secret. It is so colored and charmed that shadows obscure the forms over which it falls, so the shape of your wings beneath shall be hid-

10 The Mas'chians were another mysterious forest folk who have been previously unmentioned in the text, but would have been familiar to Sorian readers.

den from the eyes of others. Although the strangers among whom you shall live may wonder at your garment, they shall not perceive your wings."

So the brothers thanked her with grateful hearts.

Dynis finally said, "I have given you all that a mother can give, and have instilled in you the virtues of good character and valor. Now it is time for us to part. You shall go from hence and find your own folk, and dwell among them. I shall mourn your loss, for nothing in my long existence has given me more joy than caring for you. When you return to this place, or to any of my haunts, they shall be hidden from you, as they are to the rest of the Pleïstians that roam this wood."

Terris and Pyterris knew that this was proper, and desired now to be among their own kind. Nevertheless they did not wish to leave their foster mother whom they loved. They fell upon Dynis and begged her not to send them away, but she could not be persuaded. Yet her eyes were moist with tears as she said, "Be strong, my sons. Do not despair. I shall still keep watch over you from time to time, and perhaps betimes we may chance to see each other. For you have the eyes of the terumani, and are more attuned to seeing the hidden things of the wood than others of your Kindred."

So at last they went out from her enclave, and when they turned again, they could not find her place among the woods and thickets.

At last Terris said, "Now I understand in full the warnings we were given. For our foster-mother, whom we loved as our own mother, is now taken away from us, as if carried off. And we can do nothing to prevent this loss."

"What shall become of us?" Pyterris asked. "Now we have learned why our mother desired us to have no communion with the Children of Toë: that we should not learn the truth, and lose our beloved mother herself thereby."

Terris sighed deeply and said, "Our place now is with the Tribe of the Gnathosians. Let us return now to the camp of Griën, and see if they will allow us to join them."

Then Terris and Pyterris set their paths toward the clan of the Gnathosians whom they had followed for many days. At last they came into the dell where the Gnathosians camped, and they revealed themselves once again to the clan of Griën. There they were tested and purified according to the customs of the Gnathosians, and were received among them.

4. The Gift of Terris

When Terris and Pyterris had established themselves in the clan of Griën, Terris found again Diris the wolf, and they traveled and hunted together.

Terris was skilled in the hunt, and he had the help of the wolves when he went tracking. When he stalked his quarry, he could become as if invisible among the trees: and he knew how to cover his scent and his sounds, so that his approach was unmarked. The skill of his arm was true, so that he never missed his kill. He became a mighty hunter and a hero among the Gnathosians. He was greatly honored and admired by the other hunters, and his skill provided more than they needed. His bounty made them rich in all the products of the hunt: in leather and sinew, bone and ivory, meat and tallow. They traded with other tribes, and with the Mas'chians: thus they became wealthy and influential among the clans of Batack.

Yet in all this time, the anger of Terris did not abate, nor did the sorrow of his heart lessen. But ever when he remembered the death of his mother, and the loss of his foster-mother, his rage burned within, so that he could not rest were it not for the cloak of Dynis to comfort his sleep. He became bitter and dark of visage. So the folk of his clan wondered what would become of him, and whispered among themselves, saying, "There is some dark secret in his heart. Surely there is something fell about him that means to do him harm."

One day Terris went aside with his brother Pyterris, and said to him, "My anger burns within me, so that ever before my eyes is the picture of the mother of our birth being struck down by these Giants. Their evil faces are now burned into my memory, and I cannot forget. For many months I have born this burden, but out of fear of displeasing our foster-mother I have tried to suppress it. Now I think that despite her warning, I can no longer live without seeking and finding these Giants who have done us harm. If the brutes still live, I will not return until I have slain them all."

Pyterris said, "It is many years since the crime was done. In all our days among the Gnathosians, we have met none who had any news of these Giants, or saw the attack of that day. The Giants who did this great evil have gone their way unscathed, and who can hope to find them again?"

"Our clan would know nothing, for the field where our folk were waylaid is far from here. Perhaps if I return there, some hint of the crime may still remain. I may find a clue that will lead to the murderers."

Pyterris said, "Then I shall go with you, and die by your side if this is my fate."

But Terris said, "Indeed you shall not! Vengeance is my burden, and my burden alone. When we asked gifts from our foster-mother, it was I who asked for this, and upon me these double-edged gifts were bestowed. I will endanger none but myself. I shall take with me none but Diris, if even he is willing to run with me. I vow, however, that I shall return, bearing the trophies of these Giants. Then perhaps my soul shall rest."

So it was that after much debate, Pyterris at last yielded, and allowed his brother to depart alone. Yet Pyterris feared for him.

Terris disappeared into the wood, and sought out Diris the wolf. "Long is the trail cold, and the scents have long since faded," he said. "Yet I must somehow find these Giants and slay them, for the honor of my family and all that clan. Come if you will! We shall find a trail together."

So Terris journeyed northward, seeking the paths he had taken with Dynis his foster mother the prior year. And Diris and his pack followed.

He searched for many days, until at last he found again the field of the quail, and the cairn which had been erected to honor the lost clan. In that place his mood became black. Here he burned incense to the memory of his parents, and slept at the foot of the cairn: He would not wrap himself in the cloak of Dynis, so his dreams in that place were filled with dread, and sorrow, and anger. The wolves kept watch.

When daylight came again, Terris searched throughout that open glade, dismal though it was to his heart. He weeded through every clump of grass, and under every shrub. He searched in the woods surrounding the glade for any remaining hint, or scent, or fragment to guide him. The wolves of Diris' pack searched as well. But nothing could be found.

At last Terris called Diris to himself, and spoke his thoughts, saying, "It is no use. Every hint of the crime is gone. But perhaps someone yet lives who remembers the day. Let us go out and seek the folk and clans that may pass through this wood, and see what we can learn."

So he took Diris, and they went into the wood, to see whether there might be Gnathosians or even Mas'chians living in that region. Using all the senses that Ologéo had granted him, he searched all around the glade, going further each day, but returning each night to the cairn.

At last one afternoon, far from the field of the massacre, Diris picked up a trail. He barked his excitement, and Terris rushed to his side. Then he himself picked up the scent, for his nose was as keen as that of the wolves.

So at last Terris and his whole pack bounded off, in the manner of wolves on the hunt, growling and howling as they went.

They pursued the scent into the evening, and on into the following day. At last Diris halted, and would go no further.

Then Terris' own hearing and smell determined that a camp of Gnathosians lie just ahead. Leaving Diris behind, he stepped forth into the camp.

The Gnathosians had retreated to their platforms in the trees when they had heard the approach of the wolves, but seeing Terris enter their clearing, they came down and greeted him.

Terris explained his quest, saying, "Some years back, when I was but a child, my clan was waylaid by a troop of Giants, who slew them all and left me and my brother as orphans. Now I come to seek vengeance. The attack took place not far from here, in an open field where a cairn of stones now serves as the only memorial of my kin. If you know anything of this attack, and can guide me to those who perpetrated it, I shall be in your debt."

So the folk of that clan conferred together, and their elder said, "We know the field you speak of, and we know the cairn; but the clan who died there we did not know.

"Nevertheless this we can tell you: About a day's run distant—among the ridges between the rivers, in the rocky combes where the morning fogs lie thick—there is a cave where Giants have dwelt for as long as we know. Long have they plagued this land, so that all creatures fear them and must be on watch against them. They dwelt there in the times of our parentage, and so would have been there at the time of your childhood."

Terris said, "Could you take me to that cave? Though many years have passed since that day, I will know them if I see them."

But the Gnathosians balked, saying, "We will not go near the place, lest we bring the attention of those brutes upon our own clan. We would counsel you to forget your quest, and live. No one attacks a troop of Giants and lives another day!"

Terris would not tell them of the gifts of Ologéo, but he said, "Perhaps not, but my pain and rage overwhelm my caution. Only give me directions and point me to the trail, and I shall do what I can, or die."

So the clan gave him directions, as clearly as they could explain the route. But they said, "Promise just this one thing: that you do not lead the Giants back to this place! Your blood be on your own head. This is all we can offer you on your quest."

Terris said, "It is enough. We shall seek out these Giants, and see what we shall find."

When he had passed from their presence the Gnathosians shook their heads and said, "He is fell, and goes out seeking his own doom."

Terris and Diris with the wolves set off to the east, following the crest of the highlands between the rivers. Late in the morning of the second day, the wolves began to grow nervous, and they became cautious. Then Terris sniffed the air, and he said, "The odor of Giants is upon us. It cannot be far now."

So they went down from the ridge, into the valley from whence came the scent. As the dark of the woods grew more dense, the wolves began to sniff the ground and scatter about, until at last one of the pack found a scent trail, and called out to the rest. Then Terris and the wolves bounded forward at full run to follow it to its source.

They came at last to a cave, a dark hole in the rocks, from which the stench of Giants emanated. At the threshold to this cave the wolves stopped, snarling eagerly, but they would not go forward into the dark.

Terris then hefted his spear and withdrew his knife. Standing before the yawning hole, he shouted in a loud voice, "Show your faces, you who cower there in the dark! I must see if you are the vile brutes whom I seek."

Grumbling was heard from the shadows within, and presently at the mouth of the cave five great Giants appeared. They towered over Terris like trees: brawny, and awful of visage. They scowled down upon him.

In spite of the many years which had passed, and the remoteness of the memory, Terris recognized their faces at once, for the keenness of recall bestowed by Ologéo proved true. The rage burned hotly within him, as he recalled the day of his parents' demise, and the scoffing and laughter of these Giants. But one above all he hated the most: their leader, the most foul and twisted of the pack, who had gleefully given the command on that day, and had cheered and howled with every blow his company had dealt.

Terris called out, "Many years ago you struck down a band of my folk; a clan of Gnathosians who were hunting quail in an open glade, and were doing you no harm. You came among them and battered them into the earth, one and all, for wanton pleasure, and left none to return to their homes. Or so you thought. Yet I and my brother lived, unseen of you. I have returned now to exact requital upon you for your bloodshed."

The Giants derided him, and laughing they said, "A field of quail we remember, and a band of Gnathosians. We enjoyed the sport that day, and we feasted well that night. The bastards of Sorios[11] were careless, and deserved to perish."

"Yet it is the custom of my kind to requite bloodshed for bloodshed. Even so shall your blood be spilt this day."

Again the Giants laughed, and said, "No imp of Sorios has ever been a threat to us in all our days. We kill when we will, and destroy when we please. Shall you then stop us, a single whelp of that folk, with no tribe to defend him?"

But Terris merely smiled. "I shall. If you do not believe me, then come out and slay me yourselves! Or you may go back into your cave and cower in the dark. But when you come out to hunt, I shall slay you all, one at a time if need be." With this word he withdrew into the shadow of the trees, and he hid himself among the branches, and disappeared to their eyes.

This challenge enflamed the Giants, so they went out snarling to follow him into the woods, brandishing their clubs. But Terris remained hidden in the dark of the forest, as only one could do who had learned his skills from Dynis his foster-mother. He called out to the Giants repeatedly from hiding, taunting them, until in their rage they lost all caution and plunged heedlessly into the thickets.

At this Terris gave a signal, and Diris and the wolves of his pack laid in, rushing among the Giants, baying and snarling, snapping and biting at them viciously. The Giants forgot Terris for the moment to defend themselves

11 The Gnathosians were descendants of Cynodias, not Sorios. The Giants would likely have been unaware of this fact, but it is also possible this tale took its form at a period when the Gnathosians were thought to be an offshoot Tribe of the Sorites.

against the wolves, taking up their clubs and swinging wildly to fend off the pack. While they were so distracted, Terris made his way into the trees above them, climbing as skillfully as the wildcat, and he targeted one of the great brutes. From there in the branches he cast his spear, and his mark was true as only one with the gift of Ologéo might cast true, and the creature fell. Then dropping silently from the tree Terris retrieved his weapon before any knew what he had done, and he disappeared again into the shadows.

It was not long before the Giants realized what had happened, and only four of their company remained to battle their assailant: Then they ceased all laughter.

Giants have little love for their companions, but now in their selfish hearts they became fearful and angry. In the manner of Giants they began to bellow their contempt, swinging their clubs, and thrashing about in increasing fury. But Terris could not be found. Rather he followed them secretly from the tree tops, and when the moment was right he chose another target, and removed that Giant from the fray in like manner as the first.

The remaining Giants discovered the act, and now they truly began to fear. Never before had an assailant so skilled been able to defy them or remain hidden from their fury. So with the wolves still at their heels they rushed for the safety of their cave. But Terris following from the forest canopy above picked off yet another of the brutes, and the two remaining Giants howled their defiance.

"Come in and get us, if you dare!" the twisted Giant shouted from the dark. "When you do we shall break your bones and crush you!"

At this Terris dropped from the trees, and stepping into the clearing he laughed, and replied, "I am pleased to wait until you come out to play! I can wait long, for my wolves shall keep watch should I need rest, and wake me for the party when you arrive. Should you choose to sleep at night, I will hear your rasping snores, and I might dispatch you in the dark. You cannot hide within for long!"

At this taunt, one of the two ran out of the cave roaring, and hurled its club at him. Terris, however, easily dodged the weapon, and disappeared once again into the forest. The Giant, thinking he had fled, guffawed at his cowardice, and stooped into the brush among the trees to retrieve its club. But Terris had once again ascended into the trees, and from above he disposed of that enemy, also.

Now only the one Giant remained to defy him: the most twisted and cruel of the lot. Terris could hear its ragged breath from within the cave, as it sat and nursed its wounds. The jaws of the wolves had punished it already. Terris' heart raced, and the rage within him continued to burn. "Stay inside as long as you wish, and hide in the dark," he called to brute. "But I shall be waiting, and you do not know when I shall strike."

That standoff proved long and tiresome. For two days the Giant defied

Terris from within its hole, but neither Terris nor his wolves would leave. Each time the Giant tried to leave the cave, the wolves would take up their howling, and the Giant would hurry back inside for fear of the unerring spear of Terris. Nor could the Giant close its eyes to sleep for fear.

At last Terris could wait no longer, so he stood in the open before the mouth of the cave and shouted into the blackness, "The days are passing, and you cannot stay awake much longer. It would not be fair to slay you in your sleep. Come out, and face me in the open sunlight."

But the Giant said, "If you are the hero you claim, come and meet me in the dark. I shall find you and crush you."

Terris laughed, "The dark means nothing to me, for I have been given the eyes of the cat, and I see in darkness as well as in light. The disadvantage would be yours. Come out, where you have room to swing your weapon, and we can battle as equals. Though you gave no such advantage to my parents or my clan, yet I shall treat you with fairness."

So at last the twisted creature appeared at the mouth of the cave, and seeing Terris standing before him in the broad daylight it roared its challenge.

So began the final struggle of Terris to fulfill his destiny. For a long while the battle continued, and great was the din of it. The Giant was massive and powerful, and more careful than most of its kind. It had learned the lesson of its companions, and it would not enter into the forest where Terris might strike from hidden darkness. It swung its club fiercely, shattering rocks and trees; but Terris was quick, and adept in all the skills of battle, and did not tire easily. He was able to dodge every blow, and did not lose his weapon, but waited for each opportunity to strike and withdraw to safety, losing himself among the brush and the rocks of that clearing.

But the end of that fight was inescapable, and the Giant at last made its mistake. Diris watching from the shadows gave a yelp of encouragement, and the Giant swung about thinking the sound had come Terris himself, hiding in the forest. In that moment it turned its back upon Terris, who appeared suddenly to take his advantage. He struck his final blow, and at last the Giant who had destroyed his clan joined the others of its mob.

Then Terris was silent. For he knew that his work was done, and his long rage was finished. Yet he felt no joy nor satisfaction in finishing the deed, but only rued the ferocity within his own heart that had brought him to this place. So Terris said, "From this day on I shall be known as Meterris, for my unrest is unabated."[12]

He then looked about to assess the battle.

Two of his wolves lay broken in the forest, brought down by the clubs of the

---

12 Mehterh in the Donish speech means "restless" or "troubled."

Giants. Several others were injured, and sat now licking their wounds. He patted Diris on the head consolingly, and said, "It is my fault that these good wolves have given their lives. Such a loss should not have been yours to suffer."

Then the pack howled, giving honor to their departed companions, while Terris built a cairn to honor them after the manner of his own folk.

As for Terris, he felt hollow and empty, and his fevered mind could find neither rest nor peace. At last he wrapped himself in the cloak of Dynis, and gained strength to continue.

So Terris and Pyterris were avenged in the end for of the loss of their parents. Terris thus received the fulness of the boon of Dynis, along with its bane.

After this Terris returned to the Gnathosians. This great deed was lauded by all, and Pyterris his brother rejoiced to see him yet alive, and bearing trophies of his victory. The reputation of Meterris grew and spread throughout that country. He was well-respected by all, and no Giant ever dared to assault that clan in all the days that he lived among them. But he was bitter and dark all the days of his sojourn.

He took to wife Vinterë, the daughter of Griën the elder of the clan. His progeny were numerous, and became a great clan among that folk. The line of Terris prospered, and his surname Meterris was magnified. He was held in high honor throughout all that region. When Griën the elder at last passed from Soria, Terris was chosen to lead the clan. The clan of Terris became a Tribe, and he called his clan Meterrians after the name he had given himself, and so is his Tribe called to this day.

It is said that in the end Terris could bear his unrest no longer. So he sought out Dynis his foster-mother in the secret places of Batack, and she allowed herself to be found once more. There he begged for rest from his anger and emptiness, so Dynis brought him before the Terumani once again. It is said by the Tribe of the Meterrians that he was granted rest, and sleeps yet in a secret place in the forest of Batack, in a hidden redoubt of Dynis his foster-mother, awaiting a time of return. Others claim that he became a Hero of his folk, and that to this day he appears at times in hidden forms among his Tribe, unknown, giving counsel, strength, and guidance to those in need. Whether this is true I cannot say.

5. The Gift of Pyterris

Pyterris also returned to the Gnathosians, and 'Auris the raven returned to his shoulder.

Pyterris was wise, and crafty, and skilled with his hands. His mind was clever and creative. His craftsmanship was beyond compare. The Gnathosians were in awe of him, and respected him greatly. He devised many tools and made the life of the clan of Griën easier. Many of the Gnathosians came to him to repair their goods, and to create new tools for them.

Despite the great skill and craftsmanship he displayed, the folk of his clan pitied him, for they thought he must have some injury or deformity which he kept hidden. They did not know of his wings, for they were always kept folded out of sight, but his arms moved stiffly and strangely to their eyes. Moreover he was never seen without the robe of Dynis, which she had given him to conceal his gift. So it was that many said of him, "He has a deformity, and for this reason he is never seen without his robe."

The fact was that Pyterris would never allow his wings to be seen, for Terris had counseled him, saying, "The folk among whom we live will fear your form. You would be wise to keep your gift hidden, lest they cast us from their presence out of revulsion or superstition."

So taking the raven with him, Pyterris would at times go away in secret, to camp alone in the forest for days at a time, and none would know where he went. There he communed with 'Auris and watched the flight of the birds. He built for himself a treehouse after the style of the Gnathosians among whom he dwelt, high on a hilltop in the forest, where he could see clearly for miles. Even Terris his brother did not know the whereabouts of this retreat. There in secret he would open the sleeves of his robe, and extend his arms. Great wings would he then stretch forth: nearly two mecaths[13] they spanned from tip to tip.

But Pyterris did not know how to use his wings to fly.

One day he heard the cry of geese, and looking up he beheld the flocks flying northward towards their summer homes in Niyarc and Vordót. A longing entered his heart like pain, and he thought to himself, "The birds fly freely where they will, even into Vordót where the Terumani dwell, and there is none to hinder them. Why was I given these wings, and yet I have not the gift of flight?"

He said to 'Auris, "Teach me the secret of flight, as the birds fly. Reveal to me the feeling of the air beneath the wings, the means of lifting oneself from the earth, and of turning in flight, and diving, and of alighting safely again." So he turned loose the raven, and studied him as he flew. He examined every move and motion, the stroke of the wings, the spreading of the pinions, the pitch of the body and its twists and turns. He watched as 'Auris glided, and how the wind caught, and swelled, and lifted; how the bird adjusted to each current and surge of the air.

He made drawings, and diagrams, and plans. He studied also the falling of leaves, and the fluttering seed pods of ash and maple. He built models, and dropped them from the tree, and studied how they glided to the earth; when

13 That is, about 13 feet, or four meters

the winds blew he suspended these contrivances from his platform to feel how the air lifted them, and tested their handling. Many weeks he spent in this study, for he was patient and cautious.

Finally he began to close his eyes, and unfold his own wings in the tree top from the platform of his redoubt. He felt the force of the air as if it were something alive, and in his fancy he imagined himself flying as he had seen it and studied it. He found he could feel the sense of air and flight as if in a vision.

At last he called 'Auris to him, and said to the bird, "Tomorrow I will fly."

That evening he returned to the village of Griën, and went to the den of Terris his brother. Speaking quietly so that no one else might hear, he said to him, "I have now possessed these wings for many months, which Dynis our mother gifted me through Teruman Ologéo. I have studied all the secrets of flight. Tomorrow I intend to fly on my own, come what may."

Terris, it must be said, had never approved of his brother's gift, and he feared for his safety, so he complained, "This is not wise. The Children of Toë were meant to go upon the earth, not in the air as do the birds. Do not place yourself in such danger."

Pyterris replied, "I have little fear, for I have absorbed all that can be learned from 'Auris and the birds of the air. Nevertheless, it is for this reason that I reveal this to you now: I need you to come with me tomorrow, to watch my trial. For if perhaps you are right, and I have deceived myself, I do not want to lie alone and broken in the forest, far from aid. I would need you to carry me back to the village."

Terris shook his head and said, "No! I could not bear to see you injured, or worse. Do nothing so foolish as this!"

Pyterris however said, "But tomorrow I do intend to fly, whether you are there to aid me or not. You may worry yourself over me here at home, or you may worry yourself at my side. But if at my side, you may lessen the very danger you fear."

So Terris agreed to go with him, though unwillingly. He found his brother's gift unnerving, and though he did not wish to see his brother fail, he likewise had little desire to see him succeed.

Pyterris brought him the next day to his secret house on the hilltop. There they climbed together to the platform high on the tree, where the breeze blew freely. Below them was a space clear of obstructions: a small open glade where no other trees grew.

Terris looked down from the platform. The Gnathosians of Batack have little fear of heights, for they often dwell high in the trees above the reach of Giant or drake. But as Terris looked down that day he grew faint, and he said to Pyterris, "From this great height you must make no mistake, for if you fail, you will die."

Pyterris answered, "I think not: I have built and tested and made many trials, and though I may not fly as I hope, I think I shall not die." So taking a deep breath, he spread his winged arms and stepped from the platform.

At once as he dropped he felt the substance of the air fill his wings, and he pressed against it to ease his fall. With a brief stroke or two he rose slightly, then sailed on the breeze. He tilted his wings and circled back into the clearing, and let himself spiral to the earth like a leaf falling from the tree. He flapped into the breeze as he approached the ground, as he had seen 'Auris do many times, and stretching forth his legs he lit upon the earth. Stumbling forward he folded in his arms swiftly and regained his balance. 'Auris the raven flew down beside him, crowing excitedly.

From the heights of the tree above he heard a whoop of excitement, and looking up he saw that even Terris was cheering this success.

Terris quickly clambered down the rope and ran to congratulate his brother. "Never did I expect to see a child of our Kindred sail in the air like a bird! Yet you have done so!"

"It is but a first step," Pyterris declared, "but even the baby birds must drop from the nest before they may rise into the sky. I must learn to remain longer in the air, and to rise fearless to heights above the treetops, and to maneuver down among the trees in the heart of the forest. Stay with me for a while this day, and watch with me as I practice."

Terris said, "I shall worry myself half to death this day, but I will stay and watch. Only promise me you will attempt nothing beyond your limits."

Pyterris laughed and replied, "I do not yet know my limits. But I shall do nothing until I am confident."

So they remained together at Pyterris' redoubt all that day as Pyterris practiced, repeatedly climbing to the platform, and dropping from the height as Terris kept watch. The next day also, and the day after that, Terris remained while Pyterris' skills grew greater, and his confidence increased continuously.

After this Pyterris came often to the platform, sometimes with his brother, and sometimes without. For many weeks he practiced, and learned, and increased his skills, until he was able to leap into the air from the earth, and flit among the trees of the forest, and soar high above the canopy: flight became as natural as walking or running to those of us who are earth-bound. At last even Terris said, "You fly as easily as 'Auris your raven. I have no more fear for you."

However, he continued to counsel him to keep his gift a secret, for the Gnathosians among whom they dwelt were superstitious.

The day came, however, when Pyterris wished to take a wife, as Terris his brother had done. Pyterris had for many days cherished Ramphië, the youngest daughter of Griën, and Ramphië for her part admired and honored Terris for his cleverness, his wisdom and his skills. The match seemed good to them both: But Pyterris would not take action to secure the matter, for he greatly feared the sight of his wings would repulse her or frighten her, and her father would refuse the match.

At last Ramphiё confronted him, saying, "We have spent many days enjoying one another's company, and I'm confident my father would approve a match between us. Will you not seek my hand, that we might fulfill that which we both desire?"

Pyterris deferred, however, saying, "I am afraid to do so, for Terris my brother has counseled me against such things. He is older than I, and wise, and I have always trusted his counsel."

Ramphië grumbled, "Do you wish to wed your brother, or me? If you want me, you must choose me and ask for me. Or must I seek another match, a thing which neither of us desires?"

So Pyterris begged for one more week to decide, and he went to Terris in private to discuss the matter.

When they were alone he said, "I think the time is come to reveal my secret to all. I cannot hide myself and my gift away forever. It is too much to bear."

But Terris continued to be skeptical. "That you can fly is a marvelous thing, and I have come to admire it. But I fear that the Gnathosians will not accept this matter. They are a primitive folk—unlike Dynis our mother—and they are afraid of that which they do not understand. You have wisely kept this secret these years. Why should you ruin yourself now?"

Pyterris said, "I should be allowed to live in the open, and have a wife, and raise sons and daughters for myself. I cannot keep my secret and do these things. It may go well, or it may go ill, but I must reveal the truth, and be ashamed no longer."

"I fear that sorrows will come of this, as Dynis our mother predicted."

Pyterris however answered, "Have I striven so hard and for so long for my own pleasure only?"

Terris at last conceded, saying, "I shall not stand in your way: do as you see fit. Yet I think that your lofty hopes will come to nothing in regards to this folk."

The next day Pyterris found a quiet spot in the forest, and when he had roused his courage, he spread his arms, leapt into the air, and took flight. He rose above the treetops, and flew to the camp of the Gnathosians. For some while he circled in the sky above, unseen by any of his clan, until at last he said to himself, "The time has come. I must do this thing, or live in shame." Then he flew down into the midst of the clearing.

The Gnathosians in the camp had been about their business, heedless of the skies, when suddenly a figure like one of their own, but with great wings like the wyvern, dropped into their midst from the treetops like a terror from a nightmare. A shock of dread struck through every heart at the sight. The children ran screaming into huts and dens, or into the forest. All drew back in fear, while the guards and watchmen of the camp took up spears and prepared to attack. Others hastily fit arrows to their bows.[14]

But Pyterris said, "Do not be afraid. It is Pyterris, your brother!"

So the Gnathosians lowered their weapons, and they approached him cautiously. He showed them his wings and said, "I am who I have always been among you, and have never given you cause for suspicion or fear. This form is a gift from the Terumani, from Ologéo himself."

Terris his brother also came forward and said, "It is true. Years ago we journeyed to Liaibíri in Vordót, and there we were granted boons from the Terumani. He has hidden his form from you all this time, that he might prove his character through long association. If you have admired him in the past, do not fear him now."

Thus were the Gnathosians pacified. After this Pyterris began to fly openly, leaving his place in the camp of the Gnathosians and soaring over the forests. The folk of that clan began to fear him, and they grumbled against him, but Terris spoke to them, saying, "Allow him this passion, for he is doing no one harm thereby."

Now it so happened that Ramphië, when she beheld the wings of Pyterris, rejoiced to learn that he was not maimed or deformed as many had thought. More than this, she was intrigued by his wings and his skills. Even more exotic and desirable did he seem to her after that, and it gratified her that her suitor was so singular among the youths of that clan; the other maidens of the clan came to be daunted by her. So the fears of Pyterris regarding her were allayed, and he soon came to Griën to ask her hand in marriage.

Griën, however, was disturbed by this turn, and feared Pyterris, so he refused the match. Pyterris was inclined to accept this judgement, however unhappily, for he had already resigned himself to being an outcast when his wings were discovered. But Ramphië would have none of it. It pleased her to be the center of so much contention, so she defied her father before the maidens of the clan, and in private she pleaded with him, and pouted, and continually aggrieved him. At last Griën said to her, "Your mother and I will receive no rest until you have your way. Let it be on your own head, for I fear you will come to regret your choice."

So Ramphië and Pyterris came together and were espoused. For some years they had peace, and although many of that clan feared him, they had respect for his wisdom and cleverness. Pyterris and Ramphië had four children: two sons and two daughters. The sons they named Geneterris, and Scaphis. The daughters were named Qedzetalë and Calwë.

---

14 This is the first mention of the use of the bow and arrow. Other sources claim that Pyterris himself was the inventor of the hunting bow.

All of his children were born with the gift of Ologéo: wings as plain as those of their father. They did not learn to fly, for they were still very young. But Pyterris would hold them on his shoulders, or lift them above his head, and allow the wind to fill their wings. He continually told them, "When you are older, you shall fly above the treetops like birds!"

As is often the case in such matters, the children of the clan were less frightened of Pyterris than were the adults, and those that had grown up with his own children least frightened of all. Many, in fact, were envious of the wings of their playmates.

When the time came for Geneterris the son of Pyterris to learn flight, Pyterris promised to train him privately, but he warned him, "Tell no one, for the folk of this clan are superstitious and may fear you."

Geneterris, however, boasted to his friends, and provoked them thereby.

A certain of Geneterris' companions, a youth by the name of Caris, became jealous of the wings of his friend. So on the day when Geneterris was to begin training, Caris followed him stealthily into the forest, to the secret hilltop redoubt that Pyterris had built for himself when he had taught himself to fly years earlier. From a hiding place in the foliage he watched as Pyterris held his son above his head, and allowed him to spread his wings, and let the breeze lift him gently from his hands. Then a fire burned within the heart of Caris. He watched until Pyterris had finished with his lesson, and had gone away to bring Geneterris back to the camp of his clan.

When Caris was certain he was alone in the place, curiosity and desire overcame him, and he thought to himself, "I shall climb into the treehouse of Pyterris, and see what secrets lie there." So he made his way up the tree, and entered the redoubt.

Now before Pyterris had dared his own leap into the air, he had spent many months studying the secrets of flight. He had watched 'Auris the raven, and studied the flight of the geese and the eagles. He had built models of various wings, and studied how they flew or fell. Among these models was a large replica he had contrived of bamboo and leather, half the size of his own wings, in the form of a kite which could be folded and unfolded like his own. This model he had been wont to attach to various cords, weights and contrivances to study how it handled in the wind, and how it would glide or fall, and how best to maneuver it to cause it to turn, or dive, or brake against the wind.

When Caris saw this model his eyes grew wide, and a foolish idea came into his head. When he assured himself that he was indeed alone, he folded the model, and bundled it up, and removed it from the redoubt of Pyterris. Then he secretly brought it home to his own place, and hid it away.

The next day when Geneterris and Pyterris had gone into the woods for their lesson, Caris thought to himself, "Surely my theft shall be discovered today, and my plans will be ruined." So he went into his place at once and brought out the model of Pyterris' wings. These he strapped onto his back, and he climbed into a tree at the edge of the camp where his friends were gathered. He unfolded the wings, and locked them into position, and turned into the breeze so he could feel the lift of the air. Then he shouted out so all would look, "Behold! I, too, have the secret of flight. I shall sail in the air like Pyterris and the birds."

His friends looked up, and seeing him they taunted him, saying he had no courage to dare a flight. Caris however, was young and impetuous, and had no wisdom. So he stepped from the tree.

But Caris had no skill nor strength to control his flight.

Had the wings of Pyterris not been strapped to his shoulders he may have perished in that drop, but even so he plunged to the earth out of control and crashed hard upon the ground. His legs were broken, and he lay unable to move, crying out in great pain. The children all ran away, and the adults of the clan rushed to see what had happened. Finding Caris in this state they carried him home, and set the bones as well as they could, and treated him with herbs and extracts for pain and healing. Nevertheless it would be many months before he had healed; his legs thereafter grew stunted and bent, so that he became lame, and could not walk again without aid for the rest of his days.

When the parents of Caris saw what had happened, and discovered the wings of Pyterris on his back, they were enraged. They came to Griën and the elders of the tribe, and demanded that Pyterris be sent away. All the folk of the tribe were in an outrage, agreeing that Pyterris' gift was a danger to them all.

Ramphië the mate of Pyterris then became afraid and ashamed of the wings of her mate. So she was also ashamed on behalf of her children, and she made robes for them after the pattern of Pyterris' robe, which he had received as a gift from his foster-mother, although she could not reproduce the shadowy fabric of Dynis which disguised his form. She strictly forbade Pyterris thereafter from teaching the children to fly.

So Terris came to Pyterris in private, and said to his brother, "It is as I had feared. Now all are against you, and all the good you have done for this tribe has come to nothing. Many wish to send you away, and I think that Griën himself will agree."

Pyterris said, "If this is the will of the clan, then I shall go away and dwell by myself in the forest. For my own mate is against me, and the children have been sequestered from me."

Terris said, "If you choose to leave, I will not let you go alone, but I would join you in exile. We who have lost both our mother and our step-mother should not abandon one another."

Pyterris said, "I would not ask you give up all that you have gained among this folk. You also have a wife and children among them."

Terris answered, "I hope that we may yet avert the worst. If you promise to give up the use of your wings, and fly no more, I imagine the clan will accept you again. The folk respect me and my word. Griën, also. I think we can win them to this compromise."

Pyterris complained, "In all my days, this one thing have I longed for more than life itself. This gift of flight is the one boon granted to me by our foster-mother, to remember her care. Shall I then give up that which alone has given meaning to my days?"

Then Terris relented and said, "I cannot counsel you to sacrifice the gift of our foster-mother. But do not use it in the open. Go covertly into the forest, as you did when you first learned your skill, and do what you must in secret. But among the folk of Toë do not be so bold. Hide your gift, covering your wings with the robes of Dynis our mother."

To this Pyterris agreed.

So Pyterris returned again to the camp, and did as Terris had advised. He devised an artful crutch for Caris, that the youth might get around with it, so his parents would not need to carry him about on a pallet. So the Gnathosians accepted Pyterris' presence, but they were ever after afraid of him, and thought him unnatural.

Years passed, while Pyterris kept his gift a secret from all. He would disappear for many hours at a time, and none knew where he would go; yet as none ever saw him fly, the clan was placated. But Pyterris' spirit grew heavy within him.

The little ones of Pyterris and Ramphië meanwhile had grown into youngsters. It came about that one day Pyterris was walking in Batack with his children, gathering provender, when a great crashing noise was heard in the forest. Suddenly a drake[15] was spotted crashing among the trees. The children of Pyterris were terrified, and knew not what to do, for the creature had come upon them suddenly in an unfamiliar place, and there was no opportunity to climb into the trees.

Now Pyterris might have easily escaped, for his wings were hidden but ready beneath his cloak, yet he could not abandon his children. Therefore he hid the children among the roots of the trees as quickly as he could, concealing them among the foliage. "Be still," he said to them in a whisper. "And I shall watch over you from the treetops." Then he rolled back his sleeves, and extended his wings from beneath his cloak, and ascended into the trees above to keep his eye upon the drake.

---

15 This was a large, two-legged, predatory reptile. It's exact identity or description is uncertain.

The drake had heard the stirrings of motion, and turned aside from its path to investigate, cocking its monstrous head and sniffing the air. It came upon the scent of Pyterris and the children, and it began to sniff the ground round about. Pyterris worried lest the terror of his children get the best of them, and they give away their position. The drake also grew ever nearer, and Pyterris knew that the power of the drakes to scent their prey is nearly as strong as that of the wolves.

Pyterris therefore flew down from among the trees, and shouted aloud to draw the creature's attention. The beast saw him, and stomped after him, its jaws yawning wide for the catch. But Pyterris was too nimble: he flew out of reach of its gnashing teeth, and landed again a short distance away. The drake was startled, and stood aghast for a moment in confusion, whipping its great tail about in agitation. But spying its prey once more on the earth it lunged for Pyterris. Once again Pyterris leapt into the air, flying a short distance further.

So he continued to do, always staying just clear of the jaws of the beast, until he had drawn it far away from the children. Then at last Pyterris leapt into the air, and flew above the treetops, and made his escape. He returned as quickly as he could to his children. When he had called them from their hiding places he brought them hurriedly to the safety of their camp, where all could ascend quickly into their familiar treetop redoubts, or take cover in their dens among the roots and rocks, should the beast return.

After this Pyterris became indignant. The next day he called his children to him in private, and said to them, "It is not right that my own flesh and blood should be helpless in the face of death, when you have the power to save your own lives. From this day I shall teach you to fly like myself, that you need never fear enemies again. Only speak no word of this to your mother, nor to anyone of the tribe of the Gnathosians, lest they fear us and cast us from their midst."

So Pyterris taught each of them to fly. They were willing students, glad to learn this skill, for they trusted their father, and they took after him in their temperament. The children learned quickly, and soon all could fly as skillfully as the father.

But when Terris his brother discovered this he called Pyterris aside and rebuked him harshly, saying, "What you are doing is unwise! Is it wise to teach the children flight, when it has been expressly forbidden by the tribe and your own mate?"

But Pyterris would not relent, and said, "Is it wise to leave my children helpless when they have the power to escape their foes?"

Terris answered darkly, "I can teach them the arts of the hunt. To fight is better than to flee."

Pyterris replied, "He that fights may live or die. He that escapes with his life both confounds his attacker, and keeps his life. Is it cowardice to wear armor into battle?[16] Or is it timidity to ascend into the safety of the trees? To defeat the purposes of your enemy is to prove the victor."

Terris shook his head sorrowfully. "What you have done cannot be taken back. Whether it ends in good or ill, only Havui might know."

Years passed, and the children were careful to disclose their secret to none. They often went out with their father in secret, and took flight above the forest. At times they would take journeys far from their camp, even flying at times so far as the edges of the Ice itself. In all that time, none discovered their secret but for Meterris their uncle.

But when all the children had grown to adulthood, the time came to seek out mates and raise families. Then they were distressed, and they came to their father, saying, "How shall we find mates for ourselves? For we have the gift of flight, and our children shall have the gift of flight. Surely such a gift cannot be hidden from our mates?"

Pyterris said to his children, "Do not speak openly of flight among the families of the Gnathosians. If there be any you wish to court, take them aside privately, and in secret find out their own mind on the matter. If they are pleased to raise up children with such a secret, only then may you accept them as your mate."

But the children questioned their father, saying, "Why should we hide this skill? The ability to fly like the birds is a great power, which should be held in honor of all."

Pyterris cautioned them, saying, "I learned in my youth, many years ago, that it is not wise to flaunt one's strengths. They shall fear your skills, and despise your persons."

Pyterris' children said, "We are not afraid of the opinions of this clan, for we are as strong as they. If they fear us, or despise us, we do not need them."

Pyterris said, "Think then of your own children. One day they also will need to wed, and you will need to find wives and husbands for them. We must not abandon the clan, or our line shall die out."

Pyterris' children countered, "We are not bound to this clan or tribe. We, of all the Gnathosians, have the ability to seek mates from even the most distant of clans. We can fly swiftly wherever we wish, and seek the best for ourselves, and for our children also: those who regard our gift and are stirred by the wonder of flight. Then we shall become a Tribe ourselves, and none shall despise us."

So the children of Pyterris did not take their father's counsel, but they

16 It is unlikely the Gnathosians wore full armor in the age. In later years, at least, the Meterrians were known for their distinctive cuirasses, which sported a peculiar ridged crest along the spine.

openly declared their skills before all. The folk of Griën's clan once again did as Pyterris had predicted. They grumbled against them, and feared them, and demanded they cease their unnatural practices. Nevertheless, the children of Pyterris sought diligently among all the folk of those parts, and beyond. In due time each of them found mates of like mind as themselves, who took pride that their children would fly in the heavens. So they all married, with the blessing of their father.

But Ramphië their mother was fearful of her clan.

When the children of Pyterris began to have children of their own, the clan of Griën grew ever more disturbed. At last a party of that folk gathered together, and went to Griën, and demanded of him, "Do not let these aberrations dwell in our midst! Their families increase, and they multiply, so that before long all the clans of Batack shall fear us and shun us: and our own children will be unable to find mates."

Griën however would not agree to cast out the family of Pyterris. He was elderly, and Meterris the brother of Pyterris was close to him, and had great influence with him. Moreover his own daughters were married to the brothers, and he would not send them away. But he said to the party of his clan privately, "Do what you must. Only do no violence to my daughter or her children."

The folk of Griën's clan then began to persecute the clan of Pyterris. They spoke harshly to them, and would not accompany them or aid them in any endeavor, whether in foraging, or hunting, or building, or mending: all were induced to shun them. Some went so far as to vandalize their homes, and spoil their property, even casting stones at them as they went about their business, or spitting upon the ground when they passed by.

The children of Pyterris could bear it no longer, and they gathered, and said to their father in great ire, "These folk are as small-minded as you feared. Why then should we stay here among them? We are a clan as strong as they. Come with us, and be our elder. You are the wisest of all the Gnathosians, and more crafty than any Child of Toë who has ever walked upon the face of the Soria."

Then Pyterris remembered the words of his foster-mother Dynis, that his gift would bring isolation and loneliness for himself and his descendants. Sorrow filled his heart, for he had lost the clan among whom he had dwelt for 30 years. So he went one last time to ask counsel of Terris his brother.

Terris then said, "It comes to pass now as all had foretold. I cannot change the hearts of this folk. Let us then go into exile together, as I had promised to do in years past."

"No, but your place is here," Pyterris insisted. "You and your wife, and all your children, are highly respected by all in this clan. They will not come with you, and your proper place is with them."

"But I see no way to resolve this matter here," Terris said. Then tears welled in his eyes. "Must we then part at last, who have been through so much together from the days of our earliest childhood?"

"If exile from this clan is the only way to bring peace to my children, then I shall depart with them. We shall find a place of our own where there are none to persecute us."

Then Terris fell upon the neck of his brother and wept. "Do what you must for your family. But know this: that you yourself shall always be welcome in my own house."

Pyterris also wept, and said, "I have the gift of flight. Though we settle far from this place, or far from Batack itself, I shall always return, that we might visit one another in secret."

So at last Pyterris accepted the plan of his children, and they departed from the tribe of the Gnathosians. He took his sons and his daughters, and their families, and they departed far away, into the hill country of the Surmont to dwell by themselves. But Ramphië his mate would not go with them, and remained in Batack with her clan. Thus the tribe of Pyterris has ever after been solitary, and secretive, and they have few dealings with the Children of Toë.

The Pyterrians passed on their gift from each generation to the next. The Gnathosians and the Mas'chians fear them and shun them to this day. So the Pyterrians dispersed, and hid themselves in secret retreats. Some returned to the Batack, and found hidden enclaves in that forest. In a later age when the Ice at last retreated, some moved to the cliffs of the Scarp along the North Plain, and near the Southern Table, where the updrafts were strong, and flight was glorious and easy. And some, it is said, even went over sea and found distant islands in the north, far from the suspicious folk of Soria, where their descendants prospered.[17]

But Pyterris, as he grew older, grew ever lonelier in his exile. Although at times he returned to Batack to commune with his brother, the day came at last when Terris himself had grown weary of the world, and he went to find Dynis, to gain rest for his burning mind. Then the visits of Pyterris ceased. He and his tribe had no more dealings with the clans of Batack, except when his folk went out to seek mates among that Tribe.

It came to pass that one year, when autumn arrived, and the flocks were migrating into the south, that Pyterris heard the call of the geese. His heart drifted southward, back to the forests of Batack whence he had come. He remembered Dynis his foster-mother who yet roamed that domain, and the

17 This is most likely a reference to the Drëconi, who appeared in Soria from distant islands in historical times.

tender care with which he had been raised in those woodlands. He said in his heart, “My mother is a wood nymph, one of the terumani, who do not die or grow old. Surely she lives yet. Perhaps it would be my fate to see her once more before I pass.”

So Pyterris said to his children, “I am going into the highlands, to observe the flocks that fly south. Wait for me until I return.”

Then Pyterris went to the highlands, and listened for the call of the geese. His children and their children waited for him, but he did not return. None ever saw him again in the Land of Soria.

But some months later, merchants of the Glyptians were met upon the trails, and the children of Pyterris were trading with them. One of them who had been in the south weeks earlier, trading on the fringes of Batack, reported a strange sight, and an omen: for he said, “I have seen a Child of Toë flying like a bird, heading south with the geese.”

So Pyterris’ children were comforted, but they awaited his return to the end of their days in Soria, and did not lose hope. To this day, also, all the Pyterrians await his return still.

As for Pyterris, it is said that he, too, was reunited with Dynis his foster-mother, and there he found again his brother Terris who is called Meterris. Whether they rest at last, or labor and watch as guardians of their Tribes, none can say.

THE SORROWS OF ARENDILAS AND PARINTËS

The snows of Vélopar continued to fall for year after year, and the Ice built up on the highlands of Batack. So all the terumani who dwelt in that place were forced to find refuge in warmer countries.[1] There they remained for a long age.

The Giants, however, were not of the terumani, but were ignorant, and had no defense from the cold. So they wandered about, following the terumani. Thus many of them made their way into the fringes of the forest on the north and the south. From this event that violent folk was brought near to the Kindreds of Toë.

Now the Giants, the descendants of Erescal and his cohorts, have no love for any of the speaking Kindreds. They are jealous of them, and a burning bitterness rages in their veins against all who share the gift of speech, for in some dark corner of their mind they know what they have lost. But the Ádolthi they fear, and will seldom bother them.

The lesser terumani, however, the Giants will persecute. These must avoid the Giants, for even when they are not violent, they are foul and coarse.

But when the Giants came across the settlements of the Kindreds of Toë, a new hatred arose unlike any they had known. Perhaps some dim ancestral memory reminded them that Erescal their forefather's jealousy over the gift of the Sorites was responsible for their debased state. Or perhaps the fact that the Kindreds of Toë were mere mortal creatures who dared to use the gifts of speech spurred them to deeper realms of spite. Perhaps it was merely that the Kindreds of Toë lacked the gifts of the terumani to defend themselves, and so the power of the Giants to torment them was so much the greater.

Whatever the cause, when the Giants first came out of Batack and encountered the Kindreds of Toë, violence arose at once.

As the great desolation of the Ice was growing in Batack, the Pleïstians were prospering in the northern countries, in the lands known as Niyarc and Vordót. That Kindred had spread southward and westward, into lands that had long lain empty, ever since the Sorites had departed for the Southrealm. They built homes and settlements in the grasslands of the Carpet, and beyond, to the very fringes of the Great Forest.

The Giants had spread far and wide through Batack, roaming alone, or in

1 In this case the terumani referred to are most likely the many dræads, næads and oræads of that region.

small companies of two or three, always hiding in the darkness under the trees of Batack. Few Giants had wandered far across the open plains in all that long age. In the emptiness of the Great Forest their darkened minds had little to trouble them. They persecuted the gnomes, the nymphs, and the sprights when they found them, but these were too tricky for them, and easily escaped their violence. Moreover the homes of the dræads and næads were secret and hidden, and the Giants could not find them.

But when the Ice sent groups of Giants at last to the fringes of the forest, they looked out into the sunny hills and plains, and they saw the homes of the Glyptians: cozy dwellings of stone and turf rising like grassy hillocks from the earth, with sweet-smelling smoke curling from their chimneys. Then Giants began to come out of the woods to see what manner of dwelling these were.[2]

The Giants, of course, were monstrous and fearsome to behold: so the Pleïstians when they saw them were afraid, and they ran and hid. The Giants would laugh and revel in this sport. Moreover they soon discovered that the homes of the Pleïstians were filled with food, and tools, and other good things: so they began to smash the homes of the settlers, and rob their larders and storehouses.

When they came upon any of the Pleïstians in the open, they would chase them down, scoffing and laughing at their impotence. If they caught them they would bash at them with their clubs, or bare hands, or stomp upon them with their heavy feet. It was even held among the Pleïstians that the Giants hunted them for food, as any other prey, though whether this abomination be true we cannot say.

This onslaught was greater than in all the ages before the Ice. It soon came about that all that country lay in fear. Some fled to caves and caverns if they could find them, while others fled to the mountains of the Division Range, for there were no Giants in that cold and forbidding region. But all lived in fear.

The Giants found the settlements of the Pleïstians easy prey, so they moved ever further into Vordót, striking from hiding places in the woods and hollows.

These tribulations increased and spread throughout the northern realms. All the Pleïstians complained and were fraught with worry over this threat. But the Tribe of the Glyptians had settled nearest to the forests of Batack, far in the south and the west of Vordót. So they bore the harshest persecution from the Giants.

---

2 This account would seem to conflict with the details of the origins of the Gnathosians as recounted in the Tale of Terris and Pyterris above. It is likely that a great number of years are assumed to have passed from the days when the Gnathosians dwelt on the fringes of Batack, as the Glyptians in this tale appear to have been settled in that same country for many generations. At any rate, the occasional forays of the Giants out of Batack in the days of Terris and Pyterris are not to be compared with the onslaught recounted in this tale.

There dwelt in that country a certain descendant of Glyptas, Arendilas by name, whose name is Arghendâl in the Donish speech. The family of Arendilas had dwelt in that country for generations, near to the fringes of Batack. His homestead was expansive, comprising many snug and homely dwellings, storehouses, and barns built in the manner of the Glyptians, so that the dale he inhabited housed not only his own family, but the families of his relations and a number of workers who served him.

Among his relations that dwelt with him in this grange Arendilas had a sister, younger than himself, whom he had doted on since his youth. This sister's name was Ilurië, and she dwelt with Arendilas in his own house, along with his wife and his own children. Ilurië was bright and merry, always laughing and bringing joy to all around her. She used to follow Arendilas wherever he went.

As for Arendilas himself, he was well-liked in the region. He was comely of visage and noble of aspect: always cheerful and helpful to his neighbors, and to all among whom he dwelt.

It happened one day that Arendilas said to his family, "Our larders are getting bare. I must go out and find provender to sustain us."

Ilurië then said, "I shall go with you! I can carry much and help you bring home your goods."

But Arendilas said, "No, you are yet young, and I shall be hunting. Stay here, safe at home. I shall return in several days." Now he said this only because she was as yet too young to join him on a hunt, not having learned how to handle a weapon or silently stalk prey: among the Glyptians the females and the males would go out together hunting in the fields and woods.

So Ilurië pouted at home, while Arendilas and a few companions from his homestead were out in the countryside, hunting and foraging, leaving the household in the hands of his relations and servants.

As they roamed the country, the glance of one of their number caught a motion on the ridgeline above, and there he spied, silhouetted against the sky, the form of several Giants lumbering along, toting heavy clubs over their shoulders.

Arendilas at once gave the command to take cover, so all of his party dropped into the grass of the hillside, hoping to remain hidden. But looking in the direction in which the Giants were headed, the smoke of their homestead's hearth fires could be seen rising into the sky. "Can it be these Giants are making for our grange?" they whispered.

At this they became fearful, for their families were at home, and defenseless; so Arendilas said, "Come! We must protect our homes and our folk!" So he stood up at once and called out, hoping to draw the attention of the monsters.

His companions saw what he was about, and joined him in this ploy. The Giants heard them. Three of the beastly figures stopped and peered down into the valley in their direction. Arendilas shivered, and the hair on his neck stood on end when the monsters had fixed their eyes on him and his party. Then Arendilas said to his companions, "Run now, in all directions! They cannot follow us all!"

So the party dispersed and ran into the hills.

The Giants seeing this split up to pursue them, laughing in glee as they charged headlong down the slope after their prey. Arendilas made for a grove near at hand, hoping to find refuge among the trees. Of that party, two escaped into the wilderness unmolested, and among these was Arendilas. But three of that number were marked and pursued by the Giants.

As Arendilas attained the wood a terrible cry reached his ears, and he realized that a Giant had caught up to one of his companions. So Arendilas steeled himself to return; coming out of the grove and round a hillside he watched in horror as the Giant snatched his companion by an arm, and tossed him into the air like a child's doll.

Arendilas shouted to steal the Giant's attention. But the brute was too busy with its sport to notice.

Arendilas' companion landed hard on the earth and lay still: Arendilas could not be sure whether he lived or was already dead. The Giant raised its enormous club and approached the still body, as if preparing to smash it into the earth.

A fury overtook Arendilas: In the fever of that moment he gave no thought to his own safety, but rushed into the fray, shouting, and throwing rocks at the brute to divert it. At last the Giant turned to face him, and a scowl of ire passed over its face.

Arendilas still carried his hunting spear, and this he leveled at the Giant's breast, but he dared not cast away his only weapon: The Giants often merely batted away the weapons of the Pleïstians, and shattered them, then turned upon their disarmed attackers in fiercer anger. Having no other recourse, Arendilas shouted at the Giant, and threatened it with his spear, hoping to draw it away from his companion.

So the Giant turned. Fixing its eyes on its new opponent, it abandoned its sport and tore after Arendilas in a fury.

Arendilas was a swift runner, but the Giant was hard on his heels. Giants lumber, and do not run: but they can cover ground swiftly with their long strides. So Arendilas sprinted again for the grove, only a breath ahead of his pursuer.

Perhaps had he gained the trees and underbrush he may have escaped unharmed, but the Giant saw his intent, and in a rage it threw its club at him. The great wooden bludgeon glanced off his shoulder and struck him to the earth. He rolled over in pain, his shoulder broken, and looked up expecting to see his own death looming over him.

The Giant, however, had stopped to retrieve its club, for Giants are stupid and dim of wit. Arendilas took his chance, and with his good arm he drove his spear into the thigh of the brute.

It is just as well he did not try for a mortal blow. The ribs of the Giants are heavy, thick and wide, and only with great luck or great skill might one strike through to the heart of such a beast, but such an attempt would have infuriated the creature beyond measure. As it was, his spear pierced the Giant's thigh, a wound deep enough to make it howl in pain and draw back from Arendilas in stunned surprise. It plucked away the spear and crushed it into splinters with its bare hand, then turned to face its attacker.

It hesitated for a moment, uncertain whether Arendilas might yet have another weapon with which to sting again. In that moment, a call came over the hills from the distance. The other Giants had tired of their sport by now, and they called to regather their troop. The Giant scowled at Arendilas, kicked dirt at him in disgust, grunted something incomprehensible, then turned and hurried to rejoin its companions.

Arendilas at last got to his feet, and clutching his broken arm to his side he stumbled back to the hollow where his companion had been left. He was by this time sitting up in a daze, his arm dislocated, his ribs battered and broken, and blood flowing freely from a wound on his head. By and by the rest of the company gathered to aid him, as well.

"I'm afraid we have failed," Arendilas said, when they had seen to their friend's wounds. "We have barely delayed the Giants, and they have gone on their way. If they are up to mischief I fear we have done little to hinder them."

His wounded companion struggled to his feet and said, "Then we had best get home as quickly as we can, and see what damage has been done."

So the company made their way homeward. Two columns of thick, black smoke rose ahead of them from the direction of their vale.

When at last they crested the hillside overlooking their homestead, they dropped to their knees in dismay. All lay in ruin: the Giants were gone, but every home and building of the grange had been smashed, crushed, broken, and plundered. The ruins of two of the structures burned, the beams of their broken roofs having caught fire from their own hearths: Giants of course do not carry fire and do not know how to use it.

Of the folk who dwelt with him in that grange, his wife and his two children had by good fortune been out in the fields gathering and foraging on their own, and so had been away at the time of the attack. But his father and mother were grievously injured, found in the wreckage of their house. One of his servants was found broken on the outskirts of the grange. Most of the others had fled when the Giants appeared.

But Ilurië was nowhere to be found. Arendilas looked all about the ruins, calling out her name. He dug desperately through the shattered buildings, and searched the hills and fields about the valley. No sign of her, nor any clue as to what may have become of her, ever appeared. Whether she had been taken away, or killed in the attack, or become lost in the countryside, no one ever learned. At last Arendilas sat down among the ruins of the grange, crying "Iluriё! O Iluriё!" and weeping without comfort.

So in that one afternoon Arendilas lost all that he possessed. But most of all his heart grieved ever after for his lost sister.

Arendilas and his folk settled in as best they could among the ruins of their grange, living in rude lean-tos and shacks while they began to rebuild. Their larders were empty, their tools and furnishings smashed or stolen, and they were hungry, haggard, and forever in fear that Giants would return.

As that summer drew to a close, it happened that messengers went through the land from all the distant villages of the Glyptians, calling for a council of clan elders to be held at the hill called Highgrove, or Wurroughloft in the Donish tongue, where that Tribe held their councils. (That place is still venerated to this day, where their weathered seats of stone still lie in a ring beneath ancient trees.) The situation with the Giants had become untenable, and the clans agreed to meet at Midfall,[3] before the final harvesting and gathering of the year.

When all had gathered, one of their number, one Myphoridas, who was the eldest and most influential of that Tribe, called them to order by saying, "We all know how beset we are by these continuing raids. The winter is coming upon us, and many of us are without homes, and our larders have been spoiled by these marauding Giants. Even those who have not yet been raided live in constant fear that they, too, shall be ruined at any moment."

This Myphoridas was the direct heir through long lineage of Glyptas, Cynodias' daughter: she who had received the gift of speech from Dôni. Myphoridas himself was thus well-respected by all the Glyptians, and revered as the patriarch of that Tribe. He continued his speech thus: "We are a generous clan, sharing with those in need, and harboring the unfortunate. But while we may make many plans to see our folk through this winter, we must decide here what to do regarding these Giants. Another such summer as this shall ruin us all."

A clamor arose among the assembled elders: Many there were who proposed that all their homes and villages should be abandoned, and the whole of that Tribe remove themselves to a new country. Myphoridas himself then said, "Such a move would be a hardship on all our folk. There are few places

---

3 That is, the Autumn equinox.

to flee, for there is ice to the south of us and ice to the west of us, which cannot be crossed. While the Giants move freely over the countryside from Batack as far as the borders of Niyarc."

Many of that council said, "Then let us go to Niyarc, to the far side of the C'heta, to the lands in the east beyond the marches of the Giants. Or join with the exiles in the Mountains of Division in the north!"

So a debate was taken up: while many were loth to leave the homesteads and villages of their homeland, many there were who thought well of this plan. For life with the Giants could not be borne.

But when this prospect had been debated for some time, Arendilas stood forth among the assembled elders. Many who had known him in better days did not recognize him, for he who had once been noble and lordly, of cheerful mien, now carried himself dark and grim, hunched and disheveled. This Arendilas arose and bitterly spoke his mind.

"To the east, you say? To the land of Niyarc? Do you forget, that our Tribe came to this country from the east in generations past, to escape to open lands? For the realms of Niyarc had become too strait to support our clan! There the Donites dwell: the Sorites who remain here in the north. Many Theresians and Menothians fill that country as well, and perhaps other Tribes and clans we have forgotten. There will be no room there to receive a Tribe as great as ours.

"As for the north, perhaps it is true the Giants fear that country: but for good cause! Do you fear the winter here in our homeland will be cold and difficult? The mountains of the north are yet more frigid and dismal! The earth there is rock and produces little fruit. It will not support a Tribe such as ours. And who is to say whether the Giants will not follow us there, as well?

"Why shall we flee like cowards before these unreasoning beasts? We have built our homes and gardens in this country, and it is good country."

Then Myphoridas said to Arendilas, "Your words cannot be denied. But what then do you propose? Shall we continue another summer as ever, in the hopes that the Giants have grown weary of their sport?"

Arendilas seethed in private anguish, and glowering at them all he said, "Indeed not! We have idled here too long in inactivity, merely hoping that our own homes will be overlooked by these ravening brutes. I myself have been guilty of this indiscretion, and you see now what has become of me. No. We must take matters into hand and fight for what is ours, and avenge the blood of those we have lost."

An outcry arose at these words, and the elders spoke incredulously: "Would you have us go out to battle with these Giants? What can we do to prevail against such monsters? It is easier to bring down a mammoth! Even were we to raise an army, where would we go to meet them in battle? We have no power to defy Giants!"

Myphoridas agreed, saying, "We cannot approach them but what they crush us with a single blow. Our very houses they crumple like kindling."

Arendilas said, "Alone we can do little. But that does not mean we need to suffer here in paralysis! Are there no Terumani in the land?" He waved a hand to the east. "The Hall of Phreïs is here at hand.[4] Or let us go to Liaibíri and seek the aid of the whole council of the Ádolthi!"

So began another debate among the assembled elders. The words of Arendilas gave hope to many, while others scoffed, saying, "What have the Terumani to do with our struggles? They eat and drink in their halls, and are not assaulted. Even Sorios our advocate seems to have forgotten us, and cares nothing for our plight."

Arendilas answered. "The very duty and purpose of the terumani is to care for and nurture all of Soria. The land suffers on account of these Giants. Surely they will hear our pleas and come to our aid, when once they learn how hard-pressed we have become."

Myphoridas then took the side of Arendilas in this matter, saying, "Whether the Ádolthi shall come to our aid or not we cannot predict, but unless we go and implore them, we shall certainly never know. It is a true saying that he who will not seek a path, will not find a way."

So at last the word of Arendilas held sway, and the leaders of the Glyptians were convinced. Then they said, "Who among us shall go before the seat of the Terumani and make our case?" And all looked to Myphoridas their elder for guidance.

But Myphoridas waved them off, saying, "I am aged and cannot make such a journey. Let Arendilas lead you on this venture. His is the zeal for this course."

Arendilas bowed to Myphoridas in deference. Then he turned again to the assembly and said, "If any will follow me, then let us go about the lands of Niyarc and Vordót, and gather leaders from all the Tribes of the Pleïstians, our Kindred: for the misery caused by these Giants spreads well beyond our own borders. Then we shall all go before the Ádolthi at Liaibíri and make our case."

So the clan elders agreed, and each went back to his or her place, and selected emissaries to go out and seek advocates for their cause. They journeyed throughout the northern realms even as autumn proceeded into winter, for the need was pressing. Though some had been less oppressed than others, yet in all places that they went the inhabitants complained of the Giants. They met many along the way who had suffered loss at their hands. Even the Donites on the far side of the River C'heta were nervous, for they had seen the fearsome omen of the monsters gathering on their borders, and with their river being frozen solid in the cold of winter, it provided no barrier should Giants reappear.

---

4 This seems an odd comment, as Timotéa, the Hall of Phreïs, was some hundreds of miles to the east, but it was perhaps the nearest of the great Halls of the Terumani, and more accessible than those in Rhotiéstir.

All therefore agreed to meet in the time of the spring thaw at the foot of the dark spire of stone which in those days was known as Dimmeltor, which rose high above the borderlands of Vordót by the River C'heta. When all had gathered, they would go as one body to Liaibíri.

So it came to pass. A great body it turned out to be, for the turmoil of the Giants had spread far and wide: several hundreds from the Kindreds of the Pleïstians, and a dozen emissaries from the Donites. When all had gathered and agreed together on their course, Arendilas raised his staff and said, "Follow me now! We go with one purpose before the Ádolthi, and shall make our case. Let none of us return to our place until the Ádolthi have been made to hear us." So that company raised their voice in a shout, and followed Arendilas eastward, taking the trails to Liaibíri.

Now Bël the Messenger of the Terumani had been observing the company as it formed at Dimmeltor, and when she saw them on the move she rushed to Phactorias. "A delegation is on the road from the mortal folk of this country," she said. "It would appear they have gathered to plead for relief from the plague of the Erescali." Bël hears many things that others cannot, and she knew the murmurings of that crowd.

Teruman Phactorias himself had not failed to observe the events of the day. The Heroes of the Sorians in Ritéol had already complained to him of the disaster, and he had worried in his heart over what might be done. "I fear we must at last deal with this problem," he sighed. "We must call the Ádolthi and the Ídolthi once again to come together at Liaibíri and hold council together. I shall go at once to Liaibíri to warn Ologéo, the master of that Hall."

Bël then went forth throughout the land to give the word to the Ádolthi. As for Phactorias, he hurried to Liaibíri and said to Ologéo, "A delegation from among the Kindreds of Toë has assembled: A great body several hundred strong is on the road even now to meet with us here."

Ologéo arose from his work and grumbled, "You have said before that these Kindreds would be your responsibility. Why do they bother us here?"

Phactorias replied, "They have assembled to complain of the matter of the Erescali. Giants have left the confines of Batack, and now wander freely over the countryside. They have done much harm, and cannot be controlled. These folk have a right to complain and seek our aid."

"Do they not have recourse to their own council at Ritéol?" Ologéo protested.

"The Heroes of that folk have no powers to aid them against the Erescali," Phactorias said. "They must appeal to us."

Ologéo said, "They cannot enter this Hall. If as you say they must be heard, you must go out to meet them in the field."

"The matter of the Erescali concerns us all. I have called for a council of the Ádolthi to meet us here."

"Well enough, but the host of the lesser Kindreds shall not enter this portal."

So Phactorias went out from his chamber, and exited the portal of Liaibíri, and waited on the portico.

The Ádolthi and the Ídolthi soon began to arrive at Liaibíri, and each went within to take chambers in that great Hall. But Phactorias himself would not go in. He remained frowning at the portal, seated on a bench outside the doors. All who saw him wondered at his mood.

At last Bël returned from her commission and sat with him, and said, "All have been informed, and soon all will have arrived. Will you not go in to join them in council?"

But Phactorias said, "My place is out here, to await the arrival of the representatives of the Toëites. If they may not enter the Hall of Ologéo, then we shall meet them here, on the lawn before his gates. All who would judge justly in this matter should meet with them here, as well."

So that word spread. Then the Terumani began to come out of Liaibíri, one at a time, and joined with Phactorias on the steps before the portal of that Hall. There they sat down to wait.

When some days had passed, the delegation of the Pleïstians and Donites were found on the paths to Liaibíri. In those days, the Terumani still lived openly among the Kindreds of Toë in Vordót. Nevertheless, the folk of those Kindreds seldom ventured into Rhotiéstir where the Hall Liaibíri lay. As the delegation of the Kindreds approached that district, word went out quickly among the terumani[5] who dwelt thereabouts, saying, "An army of the Toëites is marching into Rhotiéstir, and we do not know what their purpose might be!" Many doors were barred, and the terumani became afraid.

Arendilas and his company passed by them without paying heed, taking the straight road to the gates of Liaibíri itself. None of that company had ever been within that Hall, nor passed beyond the gates of its compound: but all knew the way. The fame of that Hall was great, among both terumani and the Kindreds: When they approached the hill upon which the Hall was built, none doubted that they had arrived at their destination.

Liaibíri itself commanded a hilltop, overlooking a large estate surrounded by a hedge. A grand stair descended from the portico of that Hall down to the border of the compound, and there a gateway lay open to the paths without. Phactorias came down from the portico to meet them at the gateway,

5 In this case the word appears to refer to the lesser terumani, i.e. the dræads and possibly næads who dwelt in the vicinity of Liaibíri. A community of these lesser terumani appears to have settled openly in the region, probably employed by or associated with the Ádolthi.

and said, "Who leads this company? And what is your business among the habitations of the Terumani?"

Arendilas stood forth, and spoke. His visage was grim, and his voice was gruff, as he said "I, Arendilas of the Glyptians, have brought this throng. We come seeking deliverance from the cruel trials which have beset us. It seems to us that we face our troubles alone, and the Terumani have forgotten their purpose in the land."

Phactorias waved to the company of the Ádolthi that awaited them on the steps before the portal of Liaibíri. That company formed a numerous throng itself, for many had come from throughout Soria. He said, "We have not forgotten, but await the word of your company." Then he ushered them through the gateway and into the grounds, and said, "You and your folk may camp here, on the lawn before the Hall."

So Arendilas and all his company set up camp, and they filled the sward which swept down from the Hall.

At last Ologéo came out and scowled at the great congregation before his Hall, and he said, "Why has this ungoverned mob filled my lawn?"

Phactorias smiled and said, "Because you will not receive them within your Hall. Yet their cause is just and we must hear them."

Ologéo said, "It was not so long ago by our reckoning that these were mere unreasoning beasts. And now they are said to have a 'cause'?"

"Is it still so hard for you to accept?" said Phactorias. "If you will not see them within your walls, then come out to them, and hear them. We must all judge this matter together."

"As you say," said Ologéo. "Yet they will not pass within my walls."

Arendilas was then given the opportunity to state his case. He described the many and ever increasing trials which had been caused by the Giants in recent years. Many tales had he heard of destruction and ruin, devastation and violence. "In all this," he said, "we hold that we are without blame. We have done nothing to provoke such violence. Not one among us has given offense to that foul folk, neither taking land, nor property, nor in any way disturbing their peace. Yet the Giants roam about wantonly and attack our folk for pleasure. They steal for themselves what we have gathered by the sweat of our own brows and crafted by the skill of our hands, and they leave us destitute.

"You may ask, why do we not defend ourselves and our property? I ask, how? We have no strength or means to defend ourselves. When we go out against Giants they easily overpower even the strongest of our folk. Our weapons they scoff at, and snap them like twigs. Our homes and our goods lie open to them, which they destroy for sport and plunder without hindrance.

"And not a few of our folk have perished at their hands: bright folk who once brought joy into the world, and are no more. They have left only a black emptiness behind, silently crying out to us for vengeance." And with that word his voiced choked and he could say no more.

The whole company of the Ádolthi listened to this complaint. Then Marcet the consort of Phactorias spoke at last, and said, "Have the children of Erescal no opportunity to present their own case? We have heard many accusations. But perhaps we have not heard the whole of the matter?"

Arendilas answered, "That you would not think this complaint to be the specious grievance of a single malcontent, we have assembled together to unite our voices in this cause. Each one among this body you see before you has a story to tell of the violence and harm that has been done to their folk. Each will attest to the truth of what I have said."

Then Teruman Reinodas arose to speak, shaking his head sadly. All knew Reinodas, for he was the father of that Erescal who had by his ill-considered actions ruined his companions and brought forth the progenitors of the Giants.[6] "We all know the fierce and untamed nature of the Erescali. They cannot be trusted in our midst. Moreover they are brutish and dull, and could not articulate a defense were they even here."

Phactorias said, "Many of us here assembled have witnessed these acts ourselves. I fear there is little question as to its veracity."

Ologéo said to Phactorias, "Nor do I doubt the truth of this matter. But what would you have us to do? It seems to me this is a matter for these little ones to settle among themselves. It is no concern of ours."

Arendilas then dared to raise his voice to Ologéo, saying, "You may do nothing, if you so choose. But if so, just wait and watch, for the tribulation shall come to you also. The Giants grow ever more brazen in their raids, and their range spreads, ever more broadly. It will not be much longer before they will venture to cross the C'heta, and shall even dare to assault the halls of the Terumani."

When they had heard the case and listened to the tales of many of the complainants, Teruman Phactorias said to Arendilas and his delegation, "Let us now consider this matter among ourselves. This is a weighty case and we must consider it deeply. You and your company may camp here until we return." So they excused themselves from the company of Arendilas, and they went in private into the council hall of Liaibíri to debate the matter.

Phactorias called them to order and said, "I fear the words of Arendilas are true. The Erescali are growing ever more impudent and rash. It was only with great difficulty and struggle that we restrained their forebears at Lucré, the mighty Hall of Vélopar. It may well be that they will presently assail us in our own Halls."

---

6 On this matter see The Tragedy of Erescal, page 40 above.

Teruman Catos rose up to speak. In those days Catos was still welcome among the councils of the Ádolthi, before the events of the Year of Sorrows, but even then he was the most combative of all the Ádolthi, and he said, "I have no fear of these Erescali. Let them come at us: We shall defend our own Halls against them! But is it our place to defend the abodes and property of these mortal Kindreds? I am not afraid of a fight, but this struggle belongs to them. It is not ours to fight." Now this he said in ancient days, long before he became the Guardian and ally of the Carnochites.

Teruman Phreïs said, "I suppose we should just abandon all our duties to care for the land of Soria, then. Or is there still some doubt the land suffers because of the Erescali?"

Ologéo intervened, "It would truly be the height of folly to intervene in this affair. We shall be embroiled in every quarrel of these contentious creatures, and we shall be forever fighting and striving along with them."

In this all agreed, even Storeia and her daughters not denying the truth of it. Storeia admitted, "In this matter the aggressor is clear, but what of Menoth and the Sorites? What of the Raccosites?[7] There shall surely be countless struggles among these folk, and how shall we ever choose which side to defend?"

Phactorias said, "Nevertheless, the Erescali are our responsibility, for it is we who let them loose upon the land of Soria. It is we who have brought about the Ice which has forced them out of Batack. It is because of us that the Kindreds now suffer this calamity."

Teruman Phreïs said, "Yes... Perhaps allowing them freedom was not our wisest decision."

"That choice is past," Phactorias said, "and cannot be emended. But perhaps we might see fit now at least to constrain them?"

Teruman Catos replied, "If we go out to face these opponents, it may be necessary to fight and do violence. I do not think you are prepared to do so."

At this challenge Teruman Parintës arose to speak. Parintës was known to all, for his own daughter Sestrel had been among the ruined youth of Erescal's party. He had mourned her loss for many years, and looked on the Erescali with sadness more than with ire. Yet he had always been a friend of Storeia, and fawned upon both Wenda and Dôni as if they were his own kin: he had defended the speaking Kindreds always in every debate. Now he took his turn to speak, saying, "It is clear to us all that the Pleïstians must defend themselves. No one here is likely to deny that. But it would be base of us to send them away without aid! We cannot fight their battles for them, but we can go with them and stand by their side."

---

7 The Raccosites, a clan of the Cerites, had been embroiled for years in a struggle to free themselves of the rule of Ceras, the Matriarch of that Tribe. On Menoth and the Sorites see The Lost Colony of Mahoto, page 138 above.

Deïni was astounded at this saying, and she objected, "Surely you're not suggesting we all abandon our Halls and join the Pleïstians in the field, as if in camps of war?"

Cosimë the wife of Ologéo said, "Even were we to spread ourselves throughout the land, and confront these Erescali wherever they might appear, it would accomplish nothing. Our presence alone will do nothing to cow them."

Parintës replied, "Our presence may not dishearten the Giants, but we can embolden the Pleïstians! One is enough. Send me, with the blessing of the council of the Ádolthi. I shall build a Hall on the very border of Batack, at the heart of the conflict, in the midst of the Glyptians who now stand there alone. I shall be both ally and advisor. But above all, they shall know that the Terumani stand with them."

This counsel was now taken up by the assembly, and few there were that disagreed with the plan. Ologéo alone, with a few of his closest followers, raised objection: for he still felt it was beyond the calling of the Terumani to ally themselves with the lesser Kindreds.

So when they had agreed on this course, Ologéo said, "Once again my own wisdom and advice is overruled, and we choose a path of absurdity. But let me at least mitigate our folly, if you will hear me on this one thing." Then gazing upon Parintës he said, "Let none of us join them in a fight, or we shall all come to regret it one day."

Parintës said, "It is my hope that all fighting may be avoided. But come what may, I myself shall not raise a hand against them. The Erescali, wicked as they are, are still descendants of my own lost daughter."

The Terumani went out at last to the camp of the Pleïstians and told them their plan. But the host that had gathered in the court of Liaibíri were dissatisfied, and many there shouted out, "Will you then do nothing for us? When will the assaults of the Giants cease?"

Parintës replied on behalf of the Terumani, "The Erescali are sovereign souls. It is not in the nature of the Terumani to overrule the will of any. But we shall do what we can to end this conflict. I myself shall build my Hall beside your own: Your struggles shall be my struggles, and even the Giants shall know that the Terumani stand with you."

Arendilas laughed at this, and he shook his head warily. "Come then," he said. "Come and see what we face."

The company of the Pleïstians at last broke up and returned to their own countries. Many of that company grumbled as they went. Arendilas also returned to his own place, and Parintës accompanied him.

Arendilas, however, did not take the straight route home, but without announcement or explanation his path took many detours. Here he would pass by the ruins of a settlement, smashed into the turf, with its inhabitants surviving in rude huts; there he would stop by the bleak caves and holes where certain folk now lived, afraid to rebuild for fear of raids. In another place they would come across an abandoned village, half in ruin and altogether empty, for its folk had fled to far countries in the hopes of escaping the onslaught. In yet another he did oblation at the graves of those who had been broken and lost in the violence of the day.

Parintës grew ever more somber along the way.

At last they reached the grange of Arendilas himself, and Parintës beheld the ruin of the vale. While many new shelters had been built, the comfortable homes of former times lay still in muddy ruin, for no one dared to rebuild while Giants ranged about. Then he said, "I came into this country to build a Hall, to be your neighbor, and establish a presence of the Terumani in your company. But I cannot now build a single room for myself until we have rebuilt your own homes."

But Arendilas said, "It would be wrong of me to accept such a favor while so many of my Tribe yet live in hardship and want. Build your Hall. Soon enough you shall see with your own eyes what we all have to bear."

So Arendilas returned to the labor of rebuilding the homes and storehouses of his grange, while Parintës chose a slope on the far side the hill, and began work on a Hall for himself. In such works the Terumani often had the assistance of the Ádolthi, or even of the sprights and dræads, the lesser terumani: but Parintës would accept no aid in this endeavor, insisting on laying each stone himself. Nor could he stomach making it grand and glorious, or filling it with comforts as was the manner of the Mansions of the Ádolthi. Rather he built it austere and spartan.

When Arendilas saw the work progressing, he spoke sourly to Parintës, saying, "Why do you build so humble a home? This is no home for Teruman. Build it grand, as is the wont of your folk! So it shall be a greater temptation to the Giants, and perhaps they shall leave our own dwellings alone."

Spring had come, and rumors had already begun to arrive that Giants were again to be seen loping about the country. Soon word came to Arendilas that a nearby homestead had been wasted by the brutes, and its folk had been forced to flee, or perhaps were dead: they could not be found.

Arendilas bitterly reported this to Parintës, saying, "It seems your presence among us has not changed the minds of the Giants. It would appear almost as if they care nothing at all that the Ádolthi stand with us."

This taunt stung Parintës in his spirit, so he went out at once to seek that troop of the Erescali. He spent several days on the trails of that country, following the rumors, until at last he came across five of the monsters at camp in a woody copse, dividing the spoils of yet another house they had recently ruined.

Revealing his full radiance,[8] he approached the group and demanded their attention. He said to them, "Offspring of Erescal, give account of yourselves! Why do you torment the folk of this country?"

The Giants, however, were but little daunted by his appearance, for they had grown defiant, and their aspect was yet more fierce than his radiance. "We go about our own business," they growled. "Get gone, and mind your own!"

Parintës replied, "You are causing great suffering in all places that you appear. Give back the goods you have stolen from the helpless, and return to the dark places whence you came. Leave be the folk that dwell in this country."

At this they laughed coarsely. "What do we care for the little folk that squirm beneath us? It is only fit that the strong take what they need from the weak." With that they hefted their clubs and maces, and they rose up as if to assail Parintës.

Even Parintës, Ádoleth though he was, became fearful, for the terumani, though they do not die in this world as do the creatures of Soria, can be gravely injured, such that their souls shall flee for a spell, and their bodies might take long to heal. So Parintës put forth all the strength of his aura, penetrating the spirits of the Giants and inspiring fear. At this the Giants hesitated. Slowly they lowered their weapons and dropped their hands to their sides. For a long moment they glared at Parintës, with hatred swelling up within their breasts: at last the will of Parintës prevailed, and they broke off from their assault. They turned way, and hustled off in the direction of Batack, glaring over their shoulders at Parintës as they went.

When they were gone from sight Parintës at last let down his defense, and dropped to a knee in exhaustion. There he remained for a long hour, recovering his strength. His head cleared, and he returned to his Hall to ponder his course.

It had taken much effort simply to repel a single attack by this single troop of the Erescali, and no one knew how many such troops or individuals came out from Batack to raid the countries of Niyarc. But he found reassurance in that he had succeeded this once, and he hoped that this troop, at least, would not return.

But the next day the same Giants came again, and went by secret paths avoiding him. It was not long before they had laid waste to another homestead.

Arendilas was busy laying sod for his roof when messengers came to him, bearing news of this raid. He threw down his spade and strode at once to report the matter to Parintës.

"What indeed have you come for?" he demanded. "The Giants still lay waste to our folk and our homes, and nothing has changed."

---

8 The natural state of the Terumani was said by some to be one of imposing size and stature. They were thought to normally wear a more approachable appearance among the Kindreds and creatures of Soria.

"What more can I do?" Parintës bemoaned. "I sent them in haste back to Batack, and will do so again if I can find them, though it costs me great pain."

"And they will return again. As long as these Giants live they shall continue to assault the clans and Kindreds of Vordót. They must be destroyed."

"What you ask I cannot do! I cannot take up arms against Giants. They are descended from Erescal and his company: The blood of Terumani is in their veins."

"But the blood of my own kin is on their hands," said Arendilas darkly. "For this they must pay a price."

Parintës, however, still held out hope that bloodshed might be avoided, so he gave counsel to Arendilas, saying, "Look about you! Your homes and villages lie open and without protection of any sort. All that you have lies waiting like an invitation to the raids of these Giants. Though it be a great labor, before you build your houses and barns, we should build keeps, more mighty than the Giants themselves. There you may safeguard all your stores of food and other necessities, where the Giants cannot enter. You yourselves may also flee there in times of peril, and escape their devilries."

Then Parintës took Arendilas to a hilltop overlooking the grange, and waving his arm he said, "You see all about you mighty stones and boulders. Gather these up, and build a tower atop this hill, overlooking your homestead and the fields where you forage. Follow the plan that I shall show you, and you and your folk shall be safe. In this I can offer you my aid, for the arms of the terumani are strong."

Then he gave Arendilas a vision of his design: Arendilas acknowledged that it was good, and he said, "This work we shall surely do, and we shall see it done throughout our country. Nevertheless we shall require blood for blood, or the debt is not paid."

So with the help of Parintës (for the Terumani are mightier far than the Kindreds of Toë) Arendilas and the Glyptians of that country began to build their towers. Others of the terumani Parintës was also able to enlist, for the dræads of that region despised the Giants, and were sympathetic to that cause. So throughout the region of the Glyptians this work was undertaken.

These keeps were made of the natural rock of the countryside, skillfully fitted and joined together. They were round in form, with heavy walls a mecath[9] thick or thicker, entered by a door too small for a giant to penetrate. Within the walls were storerooms and chambers where the inhabitants could take refuge. At the top, above the heads of the tallest Giant, a parapet capped each tower, from which defenders might cast fire and spears at their adversaries below.

When Arendilas had finished his tower, he convinced the folk of his

9 That is, approximately six and a half feet, or two meters.

grange to store their reserves of food, provisions and necessities in its storerooms, leaving nothing of use to a Giant in their own houses.

The tower of Arendilas had been the first of these keeps to be completed in the country of the Glyptians, and it was not long before Giants discovered it. A troop of the brutes came forth from Batack, and traveling across the country nearby they spotted it commanding its hilltop. Recognizing it as a work of the Pleïstians, they said among themselves, "Let us go across and plunder these runts, and we shall eat well tonight."

So laughing at their own lark they hurried across to assail it.

But the watchman of the tower had already spotted them from afar, and a horn blared from its parapet: all the folk of the grange fled into its walls and barred the entrance.

The Giants when they arrived were astonished at its height. But they raised their clubs and struck it mightily, expecting to crush it into rubble. The walls of the tower, however, did not so much as tremble, so staunchly was it constructed: as strong as if a feature of earth and hill itself. The Giants shattered their clubs against it, and they ceased their mirth.

Then Arendilas gave a command, saying, "These Giants have come knocking at our door. Let us see what these foul brutes think of our reply."

So the warriors who manned the parapet began to cast spears down from the height onto the heads of the Giants: stones also, and rags soaked in oil and set aflame. Not one of the monsters failed to receive a wound that day. At this attack the Giants were dismayed, and they ran from that place howling in pain and confusion.

After this, throughout all that country, the great keeps and towers of the Glyptians arose on the hilltops: taller than Giants they once were, built of great stones locked together, immoveable, stronger than the bludgeons of the Giants.

Many of that folk also removed themselves to the hilltops and ridges, where entire villages were walled within strong keeps that the Giants could not assail. In all this work they had the aid of Parintës and the terumani for many days.

Parintës counseled yet further: "We must build watchtowers along the fringes of Batack, from the Sea to the Surmont, that the borders of that forest might be always under scrutiny. No Giant should leave that forest openly. In the high places throughout your country watchmen shall keep vigil. Then the Giants may not pass unseen. Warnings you may send to your own folk by fire, smoke, or horn, so none shall be taken unawares. Then should the Giants come to your homes and villages, they can neither assault your folk nor plunder your wares."

This work continued for a long space of time: years would pass before all was completed. But as it proceeded, the Giants were ever more confounded, and could not drive out nor starve the folk of Vordót.

Nevertheless that brutal race could not be pacified. Spite arose in their dim and gloomy hearts, and they began to say among themselves, "We cannot easily plunder their homes and storehouses, but we can still squash the nasty bugs." So even though there was little to be gained in plunder, yet out of blind malice they would roam the country of Niyarc, seeking homes or villages to stomp out, and beat, and crush into the earth. This has indeed always been the way of those foul brutes, who find joy in the destruction of what they cannot build themselves. They are a jealous race, that hate with burning passion all those trappings of culture of which they themselves are denied.[10]

It came to pass, moreover, that if a Giant found any of the Pleïstians far from the safety of their towers, whether on road or trail, or alone in the fields or foraging, they would assault them for no cause beyond their own bitterness and the stupidity of their hearts. So the land still had no rest from violence and fear.

Parintës spent many days wandering about the country of the Glyptians, lending his arm to the rebuilding of homes and villages; healing the broken and wounded when possible; and listening to the stories of hurt, fear, and woe which one and all were eager to share. His heart grew ever darker and more morose, until he became nearly as grim of visage as Arendilas.

At last it happened that he returned to his Hall one day from one of these forays: his mood was bleak, and he thought to cross the hill over to the grange of Arendilas, to break bread with his host and share in his bitterness. But as he crested the hill, and looked into the valley, his heart stopped: all below him was in ruin. The houses which had been painstakingly rebuilt were broken and scattered; the green turf of the roofs was stomped into mud; their furnishings and clothing lay scattered about, torn, crushed, and covered in mud and slime. The folk of Arendilas' grange wandered about picking up what remains they could gather.

Parintës groaned dolefully.

He went down into the valley and found Arendilas, and said "What has happened, my friend?" This was the first time that Parintës had called him friend.

Arendilas complained, saying "Our towers have preserved us from utter destruction, but two of my folk were afield, and did not make it to the tower when the horn was sounded. They are missing, and we know not whether they live. Even should we find them alive, our homes are once again destroyed, and all our labor is once again brought to nothing."

Parintës said, "I shall go out with you to seek your folk. And I shall certainly help you rebuild."

"It is not enough," said Arendilas. "I receive reports every day, that the Giants attack our homes and assault our folk. If as you say you stand with us,

10 The Homadalan scribe which recorded this version of the tale had an axe to grind on this matter, as the city of Homadal had been the target of such a ruthless and meaningless attack near the climax of its Golden Age.

and name me as your friend, you cannot allow this to continue. We must do battle with these monsters, and drive them from our lands."

Parintës gazed upon the ruins of the grange and the misery of that clan. His heart gave in at last, and he said, "Though fallen Erescal himself yet lived, or even Sestrel my own defiled daughter was seen walking in company with these foul creatures, yet could I not deny you your right to defend your lives and homes."

At this statement Arendilas flinched, for Parintës had never before mentioned his daughter, and he perceived pain in Parintës' voice. "What tragedy has befallen your daughter?" he asked.

So Parintës said, "I have never yet mentioned this matter to you, as I feared you would believe it might taint my resolve in dealing with the Erescali. And indeed perhaps you would have been correct. But this is perhaps why the Ádolthi have considered me fit for this task, for they knew that I would not lightly raise my hands against that fallen race." So he explained to Arendilas how his own daughter had been among the company of Erescal, and how her mind and soul had been destroyed by that one's ill-conceived and jealous experiment, and she had been lost to him forever. Therefore his own daughter had become a progenitor of the Erescali, and his own blood ran in their veins.

"I cannot go out with you to fight and kill," Parintës said, "but if you and your folk are of a mind to do battle, we must do what we can to even your odds in combat."

Arendilas' visage relaxed. He grasped Parintës by the arm, and he said, "Now at last I understand. My own heart knows the pain you have felt for all these years." Then he related to Parintës the loss of his sister Ilurië.

Thus those two came finally to an accord in their sympathies for one another. So Parintës brought Arendilas over the hill to his own Hall, and there they sat down together and pondered their strategies and plans.

Arendilas complained, "Our bludgeons are smaller than those of the Giants, and the strength of our arms cannot match their sinew. How shall we face them in combat and survive?"

The Terumani, of course, have crafts that far exceed those of our own folk, but it had been forbidden that their own craft and skills be given to the younger Kindreds, lest their development be corrupted. But Parintës was resourceful, and he was not forbidden to advise and guide.

"Then we must strengthen your arms and your defenses. We cannot make you invulnerable to the blows of their clubs or the grip of their hands, but we can deflect their strength. Let us improve your weapons, and devise armor. Then I myself shall aid you in training your folk to do battle. Perhaps if we might teach you how to sting these Giants, those degenerates might learn to avoid putting their hand into the hive."

When they had discussed their plans at some length, they went out into the woods and countryside thereabouts, seeking materials and supplies to accomplish the designs which Parintës and Arendilas had devised.

For weapons they studded their clubs and staffs with sharpened spikes of horn, so that any blow would cause a Giant pain and injury. These maces were light to carry but stout enough that they would not snap in the grip of a Giant. The handle itself was short, but they attached thongs by which the weapon could be swung over the head, that the speed and force of their blows would be doubled.

Then Parintës showed them how to cut, glue and join together strips of cane to make shafts for their weapons: lighter than wood, stronger and more flexible. With these they made pikes and lances to replace their hunting spears: tipped with heads of sharpest obsidian, but without barbs, that they might easily be withdrawn and used repeatedly in battle.

They made for themselves armor from the shells of the great *dhaghatin* of the north:[11] light to carry, but stronger than wood or bone. These they reinforced within with a lattice of bent cane, and lined them with a padding of wool; they fitted them with straps so they could be born on their backs, as a turtle wears its shell. They were large and round, such a size and shape that the hand of a Giant would be unable to clutch it or crush it. So strong was this armor that only a direct blow might crack or crush it: all others would bounce away.

Finally, this armor they painted bright red, as red as blood, as a warning to their enemies.

Parintës then took the warriors of the Glyptians into the field, to train them how to use these things in battle. Male and female both: all the Glyptians joined together to defend themselves against the Giants.[12]

The armor of the Glyptians was large enough that if a Giant swung a club or limb at a warrior, that warrior could drop to the earth and huddle below its dome. The strategy that Parintës designed, therefore, was to have several warriors attack from the front, then drop to the ground as the Giants swung their weapons. Other warriors would attack from behind with their maces and pikes, then withdraw or take cover within their armor when the Giants turned to confront them. When hiding beneath the dome an aperture in the shell allowed the warrior to see what their opponent was doing, so whenever a Giant would turn away for any moment, a warrior would rise to attack with mace or pike, and whenever a Giant swung to attack, that warrior could take cover.

Not even the hand of a Giant was large enough to grasp the shells, but

11 This creature was a large animal with a flexible bony carapace, most likely a relative of the armadillo or pangolin.

12 A number of Tribes of the Sorians were accustomed to this practice, and even among the Sorians of Homadal in later ages the standing army consisted of both male and female soldiery.

should a Giant manage to overturn one of the warriors, the rest of the troop would attack at once, until that warrior regained the safety of his armor.

Parintës and Arendilas drilled the Glyptians in these techniques zealously, Parintës often taking the role of the Giants in these exercises, for he could match the strength of their blows. Though it pained him to do so, Parintës even revealed to them how and where to strike mortal blows to a Giant, for at times their lives would depend on it. So they learned the use of their weapons and their armor, until all had become adept at these new techniques.

In this way the risk of injury to the Glyptians was greatly reduced, and the strength of their own attacks greatly increased.

It was not long before the warriors of Arendilas came to confront a band of Giants. From one of the watchtowers of Glyptia a horn was sounded while the warriors were out in the field training. Arendilas looked to the tower, and the watchman on the parapet waved a flag in the direction of the troop, according to the signals that had been devised, revealing the distance of the troop and the number of Giants in the party.

The warriors at once headed for their keep, but Arendilas called them back, saying, "It is for such an opportunity that we have been training! There are but five of the miserable brutes, and a whole company of our best warriors here. Let us not retreat, but go forth and do battle. We shall teach them not to lay hand on our folk lightly! And if fortune is with us, we shall get a measure of revenge for those of our own who are no more!"

So the warriors of his company rallied, and shouted in defiance. Hefting their armor and their weapons, they hastened to meet their enemy in the field.

The Giants, when they saw them approaching, were astonished. Never had they seen such strange gear, and never had enemy or prey approached them so boldly. Growing nervous, they raised their clubs and clustered together. The Glyptians fanned out in the formation they had learned, and quickly surrounded the troop.

At a signal from Arendilas, they began their attack. The Giants growled and lumbered forward, swinging their clubs, but they could neither damage their attackers nor impede their progress. The warriors of Arendilas took advantage of this mistake to isolate their opponents, and pressed their attack on each one with mace and pike. Giants are always selfish, and will do nothing to defend their companions, nor do they have sense enough to defend their company from the rear when an attack is coming from before.

Every time a Giant turned to face one opponent, a pike would jab at it from behind. But the worst of the damage was caused by the swinging maces of the Glyptians. With these weapons the Giants were sorely punished.

In short order the battle ended. The Giants howled their dismay. First one, then another, then the whole company ran bawling from the field, back towards Batack where the forest would protect them.

Arendilas shouted to his troops, "We have pricked them, but they shall escape to practice future evil. Let us pursue them and put an end to them!"

But the warriors of Arendilas said, "It is enough. We have escaped with our lives, and none of us has so much as obtained a bruise. We shall not always be so fortunate. These Giants shall not be so brazen in the future. Perhaps they will even spread a word of caution to others."

So Arendilas gave in to their advice, but insisted they tail the Giants all the way to the fringes of Batack, that it would be certain the brutes would not turn and attack again at once.

With this success, the warriors of Arendilas grew in confidence. They began to go about the country of the Glyptians, encouraging and training the folk of all the villages and granges of the region, helping them to design and build weapons and armor, until all the folk and clans of that Tribe were armed and trained. Whenever a Giant or a troop of Giants was found, the warriors of Arendilas would surround them and press their attacks.

Parintës would often sojourn with Arendilas on these treks, for his strong arm was useful both in training the warriors, and in rebuilding the damaged settlements, or erecting keeps and watchtowers.

It happened one day on one of these excursions that the company he traveled with spied a troop of Giants in the distance, on their way into Niyarc. Arendilas said, "Assuredly these brutes intend mischief in our country. Let us drive them into hiding, or better yet slay them here in the field."

Parintës hesitated, saying, "I cannot raise my hand against these foes: you know why. But I will not remain behind as if in cowardice. I shall come with you, and help to strengthen in you in whatever way I can."

So the whole of that company went out to meet the Giants, Parintës walking boldly in their midst.

The Giants could not fail to spot the company of Arendilas on their approach, for their crimson armor was a warning to all: so those brutes stood their ground, and growled their defiance. "Do you come seeking to frighten us, as if we were sparrows? We shall not run, but fight and slay you and all your troop."

So they laid into the company of Arendilas. Parintës stood by, using the craft of the Terumani to inspire courage in the troops of Arendilas. Though the Giants took many blows the battle was neither quick nor easy. Two at last went running for the nearest grove, hoping to escape at least with their lives, but the largest of them stood and fought on.

The leader of that troop, a vast monster as tall and as sturdy as a yew, forced its way into the heart of Arendilas' company. In spite of the blows it received, it swung its club at Arendilas, and striking his armor low on the side, it was tipped over and spilled Arendilas onto the earth. At that single blow Arendilas was knocked out of breath, and both his pike and his mace flew from his grasp.

The Giant took its advantage at once, and grasped Arendilas in its massive hand. It shook Arendilas' armor from off his back, but Arendilas managed to draw a knife from his belt. He struck at the hand of the Giant, but it would not loose its grip. Instead, howling in pain and fury, it raised Arendilas high into the air, and would have dashed him to death upon the rocks at its feet.

Parintës stood near at hand, however, and his heart was torn, for he could not bear to watch his friend and companion killed before his eyes. Before he could consider his action, he picked up the pike of Arendilas from where it had been cast upon the earth. With a groan of desperation he aimed it and drove it home. The pike struck its mark, and the Giant fell. Thus was Arendilas spared, and lived to thank his friend.

Parintës however was dismayed, and bewailed what he had done. He dropped the weapon to the earth and cried, "A great wrong has been done by my own hand, that Teruman should strike one of these creatures in violence and anger, fallen and corrupt though they might be! Who knows what future harm shall come thereby!"

So indeed this act of Parintës was to be remembered in later days, when the Kindreds of Toë invoked it to demand the alliance of the Terumani in their own conflicts. Measureless discord and distrust would it bring about between the Terumani and the Kindreds of Toë in those days, and perhaps if that single act had never been done, the worst calamities of the Year of Sorrows may have been averted. So it was that the word of Ologéo would be fulfilled, that all of Soria would regret such bloodshed.

But it would be many years before the turmoils of those evil days. In that day Arendilas thanked Parintës, saying, "You have done only what is necessary in the heat of battle, and none here shall judge you."

"I am glad that you live, my friend," said Parintës. "And perhaps I would not hesitate to act again to save another life. But I have failed to keep my promise to the council of the Ádolthi."

Arendilas grasped his hand in camaraderie. "You have done enough. You may return to Niyarc, if you must, that no such need may arise again. For you have fully aided and armed our folk, and we are no longer helpless."

So Arendilas and his folk returned home to their grange, and Parintës returned in gloom to his Hall in Niyarc. There he brooded for many days, but received with joy each recount of victory which arrived from the lands of Glyptas. For in those happier days of Arendilas the Glyptians prevailed. Many a clash was fought by the Glyptians against the Giants, until those foul creatures learned once again to fear the open country, and they retreated at last to their former haunts in the shadows of Batack: to hidden valleys on the fringes of the Ice, where the remnant of the forest remained.

But most of all they learned to fear the Glyptians and their crimson armor, so that the mere sight of them would cause the Giants to retreat. Thus the Tribe of the Glyptians came to be revered throughout the north as the Defenders of Niyarc.

The struggle of those days became known as the First War of the Giants. In those days towers and keeps came to fill the country of Vordót, from the fringes of Batack whence the Giants would come, all the way to the borders of Niyarc. These keeps were stronger than the mightiest Giant, and though they have been abandoned for many a long age, their ruins may still be found today on the lonely hills of Vordót. From thence watchmen once surveyed the country, and if Giants were spotted horns were sounded to call the folk to flee into tower or keep, and to call warriors to battle.

Though most were the work of the Glyptians, others came to copy their form as well, wherever folk had learned to fear the Giants. Indeed, the greatest of the towers of that age was built by the Terumani themselves, atop Dimmeltor, on the far side of the River C'heta, on the border of Niyarc. Dúran the Watchman of the Terumani oversaw its construction himself. A stair was carven around it, spiraling to the top, and paved with alabaster steps: From its heights the land of Niyarc could be surveyed for many miles around.

Here Dúran the Watchman of the Terumani built the first of the portals of the Terumani, and here he kept vigil: A light was always kept kindled as a warning to the enemies of the Kindreds. Hence the spire of Dimmeltor became known as the Lamp. Though that portal has long been abandoned by Dúran and the Terumani, who have retreated to their hidden Mansions, this site has been revered through all the ages of Soria. It was revered in the days when Chrono the Mariner spotted its beacon from the seas of Vordót. It was revered in the days when Teruman Phreïs united the Sorians of Cyriosóti's clan.[13] And if rumors are true, it is said that it still stands today and fires are still kept lit on its peak, and it is revered by the Sorian folk who remain in Vordót.

As for Arendilas himself, it is said that he lived long, and became the chief of that Tribe. When the time came at last for his days in Soria to come to an end, the Glyptians tell that he was received into the Hall of the Guardians of the Kindreds at Ritéol in Vordót. Thus he obtained his rest, and he became a Hero of the Glyptians, to whom they look for aid in times of trouble and turmoil. But he remains forever grim, and hopes for an end of times, when the Terumani themselves might depart to their final purpose, that he might leave the circles of Soria forever and find again Ilurië his lost sister.

---

13 As is told in later tales, it was actually Teruman Phreïs' sons Jeïnaric and Marec who united the tribe of Cyriosóti, although Phreïs was responsible for obtaining the Guardianship of that clan on their behalf.

THE TALE OF GAULI AND THE GNOMES

1. Gauli and Erathôn

In the days of the Sundering, when Vélopar had isolated the Pleïstians from the Sorites by the great blanket of the Ice which walled off Batack, the Gnathosians had come to dwell under the fringes of Batack in the north. They became a furtive folk, hiding in the shadows of tree and root, ever careful of the dangers of that wood.

Now it came to pass in those days that a certain clan was dwelling in their camp near the highlands of the west, having occupied a redoubt among the massive roots of trees which gnarled around a jumble of great rocks and boulders. Here they had excavated dens, safe from Giant and drake, and even the wolves of the wood would be hard-pressed to assault them. Thus they felt secure in their stronghold.

Among that clan were two children, best of friends, who had been raised together since they were infants: Gauli, a daughter of the Gnathosians, and Erathôn her companion, a male-child.

These two were unruly and careless. Their parents continually warned them, "Do not go into the woods alone. There are many dangers in the forests of Batack, and all the more so in these bitter days when the great Ice has sealed us off from the south. The Giants, the drakes, and all evil creatures crowd the north, and are always seeking to do us ill."

The children, however, would not hearken to the warnings of their elders, but would often wander the woods together. For they had known no other playground, and they had always been secure in their forest redoubt. They could not believe in the evil things their parents spoke of. "We have seen no evil befall any of our folk in all our days," they said. "Surely these are mere stories told to frighten us into obedience."

It came to pass one day that the children were in the woods, far from the safety of their redoubt, when Erathôn found a broach of bright lapis lazuli lying in the mould of the forest floor: a glorious thing, polished and in a setting of silver, which metal was unknown to the Gnathosians. Showing it proudly to Gauli he said, "Look what beauty I've discovered! Such a thing could not have been made by our own folk, for never have I seen any Gnathosian wear a jewel of such craft and luster!"

Gauli said, "But who could have made it? Surely not a Giant, for that folk, if we have been taught true, is incapable of such workmanship, and utterly ignorant of beauty. Perhaps a nymph or spright of the woods has lost it."

Then Erathôn said, "Let us hunt and see what we might find, for more treasures may be lying about undiscovered."

So Erathôn pinned the broach to the cloak of Gauli, saying,"Such a beautiful gift should belong to you!" Then the two children began to search through all the growth and mould of that tract. Doing so they kept their eyes to the ground, and were inattentive. They were children, it is true, but they had been trained in the ways of the forest, and should have known better: all who dwelt in the forest were taught from the cradle to be always on guard.

It came to pass that when they had searched thus for some length of time, the day began to darken, and they at last thought to look about them: then they became afraid, for they did not know the country into which they had come, nor could they discover the path back to their familiar haunts. They called out for their families and their clan, but there was none to hear them in that lonely place. The night birds began their wailing, and beasts of the dark could soon be heard caterwauling and rumbling unseen in the black shadows of the deep wood.

So Gauli and Erathôn found a thicket, and hid among the branches: they huddled together in fear of the dark, and whimpered.

It so happened that a troop of gnomes, the oræads that dwelt in the burrows of Batack, were out of their warren at that hour: the master of their company, whose name was Lorumack, had lost a precious broach along the trail, and they themselves were hunting by torchlight for the very jewel which Erathôn had found.

The gnomes, of course, do not need torches in the woods at night: they care nothing for darkness, and even prefer it to the light of day. They live in warrens beneath the earth, and their eyes see better in the gloom and dark of moonlight than under the bright sun. But though they love the dark, they will carry torches when they leave their warrens by night, not merely for light, but to fend off the beasts of the night.

So it was that these gnomes were hunting in the dark, and they wandered near to the hiding place of Gauli and Erathôn. The two children heard the sound of their roving, and looking up from their thicket they saw the light of the torches wavering beyond them among the trees. Then Erathôn brightened and said to Gauli, "Surely these are the folk of our own clan, come to find us! For they will know by now that we are lost in the forest."

So they rose to their feet, and made their way toward the wavering torchlight, calling for their own parents and families.

But the gnomes for their part were startled when the children appeared, and shouted in alarm. Waving their torches at them, they made to frighten them away.

But Lorumack spotted the sparkle of the jewel on Gauli's cloak, and he let out a cry. "Halt! These children of the Gnathosians have stolen my broach! My precious broach! Take them!"

So the gnomes drew weapons and surrounded the children, and took them by force. Lorumack approached Gauli in wrath, and plucking his broach from the breast of her garment he said, "Thieves! Thieves! Who gives you the right to take treasures that do not belong to you!"

Erathôn grew angry, and would have contended with Lorumack, but Gauli constrained him and spoke softly, saying, "Pardon us! For we had no knowledge that the jewel belonged to you, but we came upon it by accident in the mould of the forest floor."

The gnomes are not evil, but they have no accord with the Kindreds of Toë, nor with any other kindred beyond their own. As for Lorumack himself, he was more selfish than most, and was embarrassed before his party, that mere children of this strange folk had stood up to him. So he said, "The workmanship of the gnomes is manifest to all: you surely knew it was not your own! No, not your own. Take these two back to the warren, where we shall pass judgment on their crime."

So the gnomes clutched them by the arms, and dragged them unwillingly through the dark paths of night, and brought them to their hidden warren among the boulders of a hillock.

From there they were brought down far into the deep tunnels of the gnomes, and placed into a dim and cold chamber. A door was shut and barred behind them, and a guard placed at the entrance.

There they languished for days in utter darkness. The gnomes seemed to have forgotten them, bringing them neither food nor water. They soon grew fearful and despondent, calling for help and banging on the door. But there was no response. They lost all measure of how long they had been kept there as prisoners in the dark: hungry, thirsty, and cold. They feared that they would perish there as if buried alive in a tomb below the earth, alone and unheard.

But at last the door was unbarred, and certain of the gnomes grabbed them roughly by the arms, and dragged them forth into the presence of Lorumack.

Lorumack sat on a seat of stone in a hall dimly lit by firebrands. Frowning down on them from his seat, with red light flickering on the ceiling about his head, he said, "What have you to say for yourselves? You were found with the jewel on your very persons, and your crime is manifest."

"We beg only mercy," cried Gauli, who was by now desperately hungry and parched, and thoroughly terrified and frantic. "We meant no harm to you or to your clan! Only please give us now water to drink and food to eat!" Erathôn agreed, crying and throwing himself on the ground at the feet of their captor.

Lorumack merely snorted his disapproval. Now one cannot say whether he was actually moved by the pleas of the girl, nor even that his heart held any mercy to show these children. But he decided in that moment not to have them killed, a fate which he had in fact been considering mere moments earlier. Which would have been an unusually cruel judgement, even for a gnome.

Instead he grumbled, “Take them back to their chamber, then, and we shall see what we can do with them.”

It is another fact about gnomes, that they are the most slovenly of the terumani. They will dig and mine their warrens tirelessly, and they are brilliant at crafting beautiful things of stone, and metal, and ivory or mother-of-pearl when they can get it: but when it comes to cleaning after themselves, they are lazy and indolent. Their warrens are often dirty and unkempt, and though this angers them, they will do little to amend the situation.

Now it came into the head of Lorumack that these two Gnathosian children were at his mercy, and would do anything demanded of them for a little bread. After all, he reasoned, they had committed a serious offense against the gnomes by taking for themselves a valuable jewel that clearly belonged to him and his own folk.

So he sent word to the guards which were in charge of the children, saying, “Give them no bread, and nothing to drink, unless they agree to clean and straighten my chambers.”

The judgement was handed down to the children, and they agreed, for of course they had no choice. They were brought to the chamber of Lorumack, and set to work in cleaning the space. Beside themselves with hunger and thirst, the children worked as hard as their condition allowed, and made the chamber as clean as a chamber of earth can be made. They scrubbed and polished the furnishings, they swept and sponged the flagstone floor, and they polished his trinkets and treasures (under the watchful eye of the guards, of course).

When they had at last finished, they were near to exhaustion and collapse. But Lorumack looked on their work approvingly, for his chamber had never been so clean in many months. So he said, “Feed them now, and return them to their own chamber.”

Then Lorumack thought to himself, “These children can be made useful, and will work hard at little cost to us.” And they were guilty, he said, of stealing his jeweled broach. He decided therefore to keep them, and put them back to work in the warrens when they had rested.

So it was that the children were brought forth from their chamber again the following day. Lorumack brought them before his judgement seat once more, and said, “If you will eat and drink, you will clean the kitchens of our warren this day. If you work hard and well, you shall eat, yes, you shall eat and you shall have a place to rest.”

So Gauli and Erathôn worked that day, also, for long hours, until their very bones ached, and they were faint with hunger and thirst. But when they had finished, Lorumack was pleased again, and decided to keep them yet another day.

When the rest of the gnomes of that warren began to see for themselves the work which the children had done, and how the chambers in which they labored became clean and uncluttered, they too demanded of Lorumack that they might borrow the children for themselves. So the next day also they were put to labor, and the day after that, and the day after that.

The days passed into weeks, and the weeks into months. Each day when they awoke—or perhaps each night: the children had no way of knowing, for all was darkness, always—they were given tasks: clean this chamber, or scrub that floor, or prepare meals for the warren. They were taught to mend and to make the garments which the gnomes would wear, and to clean their boots and hone their tools. They were even put to work at times in delving and mining with the rest of the warren. At the end of each day's labor they were given a little food and water, and returned to their little chamber, with a single small cot to lie on, and little comfort, and no light. Then the door would be barred behind them.

So months turned into years. There were always guards attending them: their door was barred each night, and a guard continually stood in the corridor without. Once or twice in early days Erathôn had tried to fight the way to freedom, but when caught both he and Gauli were punished severely: food and drink would be withheld for days, and for weeks afterward they performed their tasks in fetters.

At last the gnomes of that warren could not think of living without the children to labor for them. Gauli and Erathôn finally lost all hope, and could hardly remember the sunlight, or the trees and fresh air of the forest, or the blue sky above all.

2. Gauli and Thrittin

Years went on in this way, and the young children grew into youths. So long had they lived in the warren of the gnomes that they performed their duties and tasks without complaint, and had little thought of escape.

Now as the children grew, Gauli became comely, though her own folk would have seen her as ragged and crude. The Gauphrin, however—the gnomes—of all the terumani are in appearance most like unto the Kindreds of Toë, and might even be mistaken for Pleïstians. Gauli, likewise, in her disheveled state, might have been taken for a gnome. So it was that some of the gnomes of that warren began to covet her.

Erathôn was not oblivious to the looks they gave Gauli as she worked about the warren, and he watched them with growing suspicion and jealousy. For as they had grown up together, Erathôn had come to love Gauli himself.

So he said to Gauli one day after they had been locked alone into their chamber, "I must now rise up against these gnomes, our masters, and fight them for our freedom. If we do not, you shall soon be in danger."

Gauli however said, "Do not attempt such a thing! For if you fail they shall surely do you more harm than ever. I would not have you killed or tortured for my sake."

"What then?" said Erathôn. "I know what is in the hearts of these gnomes, and I will not allow such a dishonor to come to pass."

"Let me first talk to Lorumack our chief, and see if perhaps he might have mercy in his heart at last, after all these years of service."

Erathôn was doubtful of this course, for he had no love in his heart for the gnomes, and for Lorumack least of all: He trusted him no more than any of the others. But Gauli was insistent, so at last he gave in.

The following day when they were taken out to be assigned their tasks, Gauli asked to be taken to Lorumack himself. For, she said, Lorumack had privately requested her service that day.

The guard who attended them knew nothing of such an order, but he feared to anger Lorumack their master (and Lorumack was known for such unexpressed whims); so she was brought to Lorumack's chamber. When she had entered, the guard shut the door behind her. And Erathôn seethed.

But Gauli when she entered into Lorumack's presence bowed low before him, and pleaded, saying, "These many years we have served you and your warren, and have done all that you have required of us. Surely our debt is paid, and it would be fair and just to let us go free at last."

Lorumack no longer even remembered what offense had caused him to imprison the children in the first place. But he had come to think of their service as his due, and could not think of letting them go free. By now he not only had grown accustomed to their labor, but he feared that if he were to free them they would flee to their own folk, the Gnathosians, and in their bitterness they would raise a mob against him and his clan. Then the Gnathosians would fall upon them, and drive them from their warrens, and he and all his folk would be in danger of their lives.

So he said, "Such a thing is impossible. Impossible! You belong to this warren, and your lives are here among us. We are all you know, and you would be unable to survive in the world above."

Gauli replied, "Then let us perish in that world, and at least we shall no longer be in fear each day."

Lorumack grumbled, "You have food, and tasks to occupy your time, and a room in which to safely rest, far from the dangers of the world. We clothe you and give you what you need to live. What have you to fear?"

Then Gauli said, "Have you not seen how I am forever watched by the males of this clan? I cannot go about my business but what they cast doubtful eyes upon me."

At this Lorumack merely laughed and said, "What is that to me? I see no harm in such behavior."

But Gauli said, "Their thoughts are not innocent. If it does not come to pass that one of these shall do me some harm, then surely their females will grow jealous and wish to harm me themselves. Should anyone in your warren, male or female, bring me to ruin, then Erathôn also shall be rash, and you shall be forced to do him in as well. Thus you would lose the benefit of both our labor. In any event, the end shall be strife and discord within your warren, and all shall secretly blame you for having brought such trouble into their midst."

This argument disturbed Lorumack, and he frowned in contemplation. Above all things Lorumack feared the ill opinion of his clan. Looking darkly at Gauli he said, "You cannot be turned out of the warren. What would you have me do?"

"Only then offer us protection, that these evils not come to pass." To Gauli it was enough if Erathôn had no cause to risk himself, for she had come to love him as well. They had comfort in one another's presence both day and night, and she could not think of living without him.

Lorumack grumbled then, "Very well, very well. I shall assign a guardian to accompany you on your rounds: a trustworthy gnome who shall see to it that none shall treat you ill. Then you may do your labor in security and safety."

So Gauli bowed again and thanked him. She went out and reported to Erathôn all that Lorumack had said. So Erathôn was quieted for a time, although he still hated the gnomes among whom they lived, and the life of labor to which he and Gauli were consigned.

That very day, therefore, before they had finished their daily tasks, Lorumack sent to them a gnome by the name of Thrittin. Now Thrittin was a fatherly figure among the Gauphrin of that warren, known by all to be gentle of heart, and just and faithful. His whiskers were gray, but he was stout and hale, and held in respect both by young and old. He had often looked with pity on Gauli and Erathôn, and had never taken advantage or abused their service. Indeed, he at times had requested their labor for his own chambers, but had allowed them to rest while he went about his business, that they might have a spell of ease and relief from their burdens.

So it was with joy that both Gauli and Erathôn received him. Thrittin said to them, "Lorumack has given me a new responsibility, which I shall take on with pleasure. I am to attend to you on your daily rounds, and keep watch, that none may harm you or give you cause to fear."

So they both thanked him, and were grateful for his company.

From that time onward Thrittin went with the foundlings each day, accompanying them as they performed their tasks in the warren. When Gauli and Erathôn were separated for differing duties, he remained always with

Gauli to assure her safety. If any of that clan looked upon her with unwholesome glance, a mere disapproving glare from Thrittin would cause them to turn away in shame. So none in that clan dared to bother her any longer.

As the days went on, Thrittin became ever more sympathetic to the plight of his charges. His duty was to keep them busy about the warren, digging, cleaning, preparing food and raiment, and so on; yet he saw the extent of their endless labor, and he felt compassion.

So it came about that whenever they were out of sight of the other gnomes of that clan, out of kindness he at times would help them with their tasks. The two soon came to trust and depend on him as their only ally in that dark place.

But Gauli, especially, Thrittin came to care for as a father cares for an only daughter. He came to love her, and could not bear to see her suffer. He would give her special aid when needed, and made her burdens lighter whenever he could. Gauli also was warmed by his kindness toward her, and she looked forward each morning to his arrival at their door, in spite of the toil that the day would surely bring.

Some months went by in this manner. One day it came to pass that Erathôn was busy in the storerooms of the warren, stacking and packing barrels and crates, while Gauli was assigned to be cleaning the corridor floors and trimming the torches in the wall sconces: Thrittin also accompanied her in this task.

As they went about their rounds, they entered into seldom-used tunnels deep in the warren, and passed by an opening to an unlit corridor which stretched away upward into darkness. Gauli could not recall seeing this path before, and peering into it in wonder she said to Thrittin, "Here is a novelty I have never observed! What is this passage, and where does it lead?"

Thrittin then shook his head sadly, and said, "It is no wonder to me that you do not know it. This passage leads to the surface, the world of sunlight and air, which has been forbidden you and Erathôn. It is a covert route, for emergencies or secrecy, and it is seldom used."

At this word a thrill ran through Gauli's heart, and in a whisper she said, "How far is it to the surface, then, from here?"

Thrittin was cautious, for he was afraid to hurt her or break her spirit, but he said at last, "From this point it is not far. The corridor rises steeply upward, and opens onto a remote hilltop, hidden among roots and boulders."

Gauli had come to trust Thrittin more than any other in the warren outside of Erathôn alone, so she struck up her courage and said, "It is many years since I have seen the sunlight, and I have nearly forgotten the scent of fresh air. How I would love just to feel the warmth of sun on my face and the breath of moving air!"

"To be caught above, out on the surface, would surely bring swift punishment, on myself as well as on you and Erathôn."

"If as you say the passage is seldom used, what danger would there be of discovery?"

"The danger is slim, I cannot deny. The hill upon which the tunnel emanates is remote, and none goes there. Only the birds of the air would be likely to see you. But I cannot let you go!"

"I ask only to see, and then return again to my duties. If only I could behold once more the world outside I will be content, and return with you in peace: for I vow that I would risk no harm to come to either you or to Erathôn!"

Thrittin tried to dissuade her, but Gauli's spirit would not rest. Her pleadings at last turned his heart, and he said, "Come then: we must be quick. You will not have long to see what you wish, for we must return swiftly lest we be missed." Then he took one of the cloths they used to wrap the torches, and placed it over her eyes as a veil. "The sun, I fear, will hurt your eyes and burn your skin. You must wear this until the pain eases."

Then taking her by the hand he led her up the ascending passage.

At the end of the passage was a door of wood, hidden from the outside, masked so as to have the appearance of root and earth. When it opened, it was necessary to scramble up and out between the roots of a massive fir tree which commanded the hilltop. Thrittin went first, then taking Gauli by the hands he drew her up, and together they went out onto the crest of the hill.

For long minutes Gauli hid her eyes, unable to bear the light even through the veil which covered her eyes. Her head ached at the brightness of it. But at last, squinting and blinking, she was able to open her eyes.

Then Gauli gasped and gazed about breathlessly. From the crown of the hill she could look down upon the treetops of Batack, which rolled over the hills below and beside them in all directions. The sky that morning was the deepest azure, more clean and pure than the lapis lazuli gem which had brought about their misfortune. A few dazzling clouds floated overhead lazily, and the sound of birdsong reached her ears. It was springtime, and a cool breeze kissed her cheeks and fluttered through the folds of her garments.

Gauli tried to absorb all the experiences together, but it was too much for her to apprehend. Her mind reeled with the wonder of it all. She sank to her knees, and ran her fingers through the cool grass, and marveled in the clean moisture of the dew. She breathed deeply of air cleaner and more pure than any she could remember.

Then she quietly sobbed.

At last, too soon it seemed, Thrittin said plaintively, "We must return. If we are discovered it will go poorly for us both. You would be sorely mistreated, and I risk being expelled from my warren. You must tell no one of what we have done today! Not even Erathôn should know."

That evening, however, when she returned to her chamber and sat alone with Erathôn in the darkness, she told him in wonder of all that she had seen.

Erathôn grew wistful at her words, and closing his eyes he asked her to describe everything over and over, clinging to every word.

At last he said, "Could you find again this hidden passage on your own?"

"Perhaps," she said, but her heart feared what he was contemplating. "But I am never on my own."

"If we could only break free from our guards for just a little while, perhaps we could find it, and be gone from this accursed burrow before they knew of it!"

"Please do not try anything so rash, for these gnomes care nothing for us: should you fail they would rain anguish and suffering upon us. And we would surely lose Thrittin as our aid and ally."

"Then ask Thrittin if he might lead you to escape alone. He cares for you, and I think there is nothing he would not do for you."

"Even were that true, I could not leave you in the hands of these gnomes while I went free! Where should I go, and what should I do without you?"

"Do not fret for me. I would be happy just knowing that you have escaped."

"But Thrittin is bound by the law of Lorumack: They would expel him from the warren. I do not think he could venture such an act, not for any fondness or for any compassion. Nor would I wish that punishment upon him."

"Then at least implore him that I might also be granted a mere glimpse of the world above, as well. I think he would do this much for your sake. The words you bring of that world have broken my heart, and I would prize it now more than life."

Gauli did not admit to Thrittin that she had revealed her adventure to Erathôn, but when next she was alone with Thrittin she begged for him to bring Erathôn to the surface. But Thrittin was wary of Erathôn: he knew the lad was rash, and he would not permit it. Nevertheless, whenever she found herself alone with Thrittin thereafter, Gauli would repeat her request, pleading for his compassion. "For," she said, "the knowledge of such beauty is now a burden to me, and I would share it with my companion."

Thrittin soon grew worried, and feared that he had caused harm by allowing Gauli to see the lands above. So he refused to be moved for many days.

When weeks had passed in this manner, Erathôn at last grew weary of waiting. So one day when he and Gauli were alone in their chamber he whispered to Gauli, "Our task today is in a quiet place of the warren, and none shall be there to guard us this day but Thrittin. Let us make an excuse, and break from his presence. Then you can guide us to the hidden passage that leads to freedom."

Then Gauli trembled and said, "Please do not do this thing! I'm unsure of the way, and if we are caught it will go very hard on us, and on Thrittin as well."

But Erathôn said, "For months we have waited just for a glimpse of the open sky, and all in vain. We must take matters into our own hands, or it is clear we will never become free of this thralldom into which we have been bound."

At last Gauli gave in to his complaints. When the guards of the gnomes unbolted the door to their chamber they were given into the hand of Thrittin, and he led them to a quiet section of the warren, as had been planned, where they were to scrub the flagstone of the corridors and re-plaster the walls.

When they had labored at this task for some while, Erathôn whispered, "Thrittin is weary of watching us. Let us sneak quietly away, around the bend there beyond us: then we shall break away and run."

When Thrittin at last chanced to look away, Erathôn snatched Gauli by the hand, and dragged her quickly around a corner. He whispered to her, "Now lead us, if you can, to the passage which will bring us to the surface."

On they ran into dim and unused corridors. At first Gauli felt confident of her bearings, but soon the way became dark: No torches were lit, and light failed them utterly. They felt their way along as best they could. But at last Gauli whimpered, "It is no use. I am lost, and cannot find the passage again."

Just then a light flickered a short way beyond them, and they heard the murmur of approaching voices; soon the slap of footsteps on flagstone sounded hollowly through the corridor. "Quickly!" Erathôn whispered. "Back the way we came! Let us find a darkened hall or chamber in which to hide! When danger has passed we shall resume our search."

They turned to go back; but alas! A light seemed to be approaching from that direction as well. They staggered about in a panic, feeling the walls all around for any opening or hollow in which they might hide themselves. But they found nothing.

The flutter of a torch rounded the corner, and a party of three Gauphrin appeared. One of them spotted the companions and let out a shout. The gnomes rushed upon them, grabbed them roughly by the arms, and shoved them cowering against a wall. One of them waved a torch in their faces and said, "What are you doing here, alone in this hall? With none to guard you and keep you at your tasks!" Another said, "To your feet! We shall take you at once to the master of the warren to decide your sentence."

It may have gone very ill with the two at this point, but just then Thrittin appeared, coming from the other direction bearing a torch of his own: his was the opposite light they had seen in the corridor.

When Thrittin saw what was happening he spoke at once, saying, "Thank goodness, you have found them! We were busy about our work when our torch went out for lack of fuel, and the corridor we worked in was remote and unlit. They must have become disoriented in the dark, for they have not our sense of direction, you know. We called out, but we lost each other in the winding halls. We have been trying to find one another since!"

The gnomes who had found them looked at Thrittin doubtfully. "You must be more careful with these drudges," one of them grumbled. "For we are not far from forbidden corridors they must not take."

Thrittin said, "Lorumack himself tasked us to be in these remote parts today. But it was I who was remiss in allowing our torch to sputter. Restore the foundlings to me and we shall return to our task."

The gnomes roughly shoved Gauli and Erathôn into Thrittin's care.

When they had been brought back to the hall where their work awaited them, Gauli lowered her voice and sobbed her thanks, saying, "Forgive us for betraying you. We have repaid your kindness with mischief." But she dared not admit that they had hoped to escape the warren. Not even Thrittin would she trust with such a secret.

But in his heart Thrittin was indignant at the way in which his charges were treated, and he saw now that the children of the Gnathosians had set their hearts on escaping. Thrittin merely looked at them sadly and said, "You must not attempt such a thing again. Next time it may not go so well with us. The guards shall be doubly alert now, and all the exits shall be watched. You will not escape this way. Give me your promise. And trust in me."

From that moment he began to watch for a way to help to them, for he could no longer justify to himself the harshness of their treatment.

After this incident the watch on Gauli and Erathôn was doubled, just as Thrittin had predicted. They were henceforth always under the eyes of another guard as they went about their business. But Thrittin was always alert, watching and waiting for an opportunity.

3. The Sacrifice of Thrittin

One day it happened that Lorumack returned from a foray while Gauli and Erathôn were busy cleaning his chamber, and Thrittin was with them. Ignoring the foundlings he said to Thrittin, "Beware if you go out of the warren this night! Beware, for a Giant has passed through the area. We must caution the warren, for it may still be nearby. We must not let it discover our presence here!"

Thrittin knew the dangers of a Giant, for the Giants hate the gnomes, and persecute them madly when they find them.

Now it is well known that the Giants hate all living creatures, but the gnomes they seem to persecute most of all: at least so it has always seemed to the gnomes! For the gnomes are terumani, but they have none of the majesty or power of the Ádolthi, to daunt the Giants; nor have they the cleverness or craft of the dræads and næads to deceive them and conceal themselves. So if a Giant discovers a warren of the Gauphrin, it will dig at the tunnels madly, and do all in its power to drive them out. Whenever a Giant so much as sees a gnome, it will attack without fail, laughing at the sport of it all the while.

So Thrittin asked, "Are you quite certain it was a Giant?"

"Quite!" said Lorumack, and quite proudly, too, for he enjoyed having important news. "We came upon its trail in the forest, and could smell its stench. We followed along the trail in secret to see where it might have come from, or where it might be going, but we could not find it."

As he spoke Lorumack was inattentively removing his traveling garments: first his gloves, then his hat, and his cloak. Now as he removed the cloak, he set down on a table, quite absentmindedly, the lapis lazuli broach which he always wore when he went out. At the sight of it, Thrittin had an impetuous idea.

It was clear that Lorumack was distracted with his news, and unaware that he had removed the broach at all. It was also a fact that more than once Lorumack had lost that broach in the woods, and only found it again after much trouble and more searching. It was, in fact, the very broach which Erathôn had picked up himself, many years ago.

For a moment Lorumack turned his back as he went on talking about the Giant, and the foundlings meanwhile were busy with their cleaning. Thrittin impulsively slipped the broach from the table and into the pocket of his vest. Now had he had more time to give any thought to this plan he probably would not have dared it. If Lorumack had found him out it would have been difficult to devise an excuse on the spot, and he would certainly have been suspected of mischief. But before any of these considerations had entered his mind, the deed was done.

Thrittin had no doubt what would happen next, for he knew the habits of Lorumack. Before the following day was long spent, Lorumack discovered that his broach was once again missing, and he at once organized a party to search for it. But of course they found nothing.

Later in that day, when the foundlings were once again barred into their chamber and the search parties had all returned to the warren, Thrittin returned to his own quarters, and withdrew the gem of Lorumack from his vest. He stared at it for a moment, shaking his head and wondering at his own audacity. "Thrittin, you fool," he muttered to himself, "You're in it now, for better or worse." He sighed and said, "Let us see whether we can make use of this opportunity."

He spent several long hours working out a plan in his mind. At last he said quietly to himself, "Well, it's the best I can do. I shall be up half the night working at this. But if Lorumack is as heartless and conniving as I measure him, I may be so lucky as to turn this thing to a great good. Only I must be cautious and cover my own tracks well. Or all shall be for nothing."

Then Thrittin came out of his chamber at last, and went about the warren preparing what he would need. When all was ready, he slipped stealthily out of the warren into the dark.

...

The following day Thrittin said to himself. "Now I must see if I can turn the screws as I desire." So he shook off his doubts, and went to the chamber of Lorumack.

When Lorumack had ushered him in, Thrittin nodded his head respectfully, and said, "I want you to know that I searched the chamber of the Gnathosian foundlings, to see whether your broach might have been stolen. For we were in your chamber cleaning the day it went missing."

"Of course!" Lorumack declared, for now a dim memory returned of many years past, when once the broach had been lost in the woods. "And what did you find?" he demanded.

"I found nothing," Thrittin said. "As I expected. Indeed, the poor wretches have no place to hide such a thing, even such a small thing as that, in their barren quarters."

"Hmph! Then why have you bothered me?"

"Because I wanted you to know that they were innocent. And because there is another whom we have not yet considered."

Lorumack squinted at him. "And who might that be?"

"A Giant, you say, passed through our range that very day, as well?"

Then Lorumack's attention was piqued and he said, "True. But a Giant cannot do magic. It could not have taken a broach from me before I was even on the trail following it!"

Thrittin however replied, "Not beforehand, no. But what if the broach had dropped by ill chance along the trail? The beastly thing may have come back and found it, and taken it for itself."

Lorumack whined, "If that is true, I will never see it again!"

"Giants are not known for wearing jewelry," Thrittin said. "If the Giant has a nest nearby it might be hidden there with its other trinkets."

Giants will normally erect crude homes for themselves, or may inhabit the ruined homes of the terumani; but when they rove about the woods, which they often do, they will find a small hollow or glade among the trees in which to build for themselves nests where they camp. Here they will stomp about and flatten the grass and brush, sometimes filling the hollow with leaves, and surrounding themselves with a screen of branches.

Lorumack considered what Thrittin had suggested, and stroking his chin he muttered, "This is true, this is true. So perhaps if we could find a nest, one might search through its offal and discover the precious thing among its refuse."

"But no!" Thrittin objected, "If you must search the nest of a Giant, we should wait and see if the Giant abandons it when it leaves the area!"

"Nonsense. If it carries off the broach when it leaves, it will be gone forever!"

"But it would be foolish beyond measure to risk sending any of our folk into the nest of a Giant on such a doubtful errand!" No gnome had ever dared enter the very nest of a Giant, at least not that Thrittin had ever heard of. "If a Giant should return and come upon one of our own folk, it will know that a warren is near at hand. Then it will not rest until it has destroyed our tunnels."

Lorumack, however, chuckled to himself, and he said, "I did not say I would send our own folk. Not our own folk, no."

"But who else is there, who might be willing to search on our behalf?"

Lorumack rubbed his hands together in glee at his own cleverness. "If we were to send the children of the Gnathosians into the nest, instead of our own folk, we would be safe from discovery. Should the Giant discover them or the signs of their probing, it would not guess that they were from a warren of gnomes! No, not by a longshot! Our warren would be safe."

This, of course, was exactly the scheme Thrittin had expected Lorumack would devise, and he had his own plot in mind. Nevertheless he dissembled as if shocked, saying, "You can't mean to send Gauli and Erathôn, the charges you put under my care and protection!"

"And why not?" Lorumack grumbled. "Why not? What else are they good for, if not to do the tasks we ourselves detest?"

"But to put them in danger of their lives?"

Lorumack waved it off. "What danger? The nest will be empty."

Thrittin wished to discover what precautions and constraints the foundlings would be under, so pursuing the matter he said, "But we have spent years barring them from the world above. What if, being out under the open skies, they should think to flee?"

"Why should they flee the tunnels in which they have been raised? Why indeed? They have all they need to live here in the warren, and they are safe from the dangers of the wood. Nevertheless, who knows what may be in the mind of these strange folk. We shall certainly hobble them that they may not run. I shall send along a party of our best guards to watch them, that they might have no opportunity for mischief."

Thrittin complained, "Then the guards will have to take them alone: I cannot be part of this endeavor. The foundlings are my charges, and I cannot bear to see them in such danger. I will not suffer it."

"Well enough, well enough," Lorumack condescended. "You may cower here in the warren if you so desire. But do tell the little wastrels this shall soon be their duty. I shall send for them the moment we have prepared a party to seek out the Giant's nest."

When Thrittin was sure he had learned all he could of Lorumack's designs and schemes, he returned to Gauli and Erathôn to attend them on their daily chores.

"You will soon have a chance to be out of the tunnels and in the daylight," he said. "But do not rejoice too much, for there is danger involved. And you will be under the watch of Lorumack himself the whole time."

Then he informed them of what Lorumack was planning.

When they learned of the Giant Gauli cried, "A Giant? Isn't it enough they beset us with endless labor? How can they send us alone to face a Giant?"

"There's little chance the Giant will be nearby. It would do Lorumack no good to send you in at all if you failed to return."

"But how can they be sure?" Erathôn asked. "They don't even know where the Giant is!"

"Don't let them do this!" Gauli begged. "It's too much!"

"Will you be with us?" Erathôn said. "Only say that you will be with us!"

"I cannot," Thrittin said. "Lorumack would consider it a risk to the whole warren if I, or any Gauphrin, were in your company in a Giant's nest. You must go in alone."

Thrittin could see the black terror which crept into their eyes, and heard the quaver in their voices. He glanced at the guard standing by the entry to the chamber. Ever since the incident of the escape tunnel they were attended by a guard of Lorumack's choosing: one who would report any suspicious word. So Thrittin was unable to reveal to them his own preparations.

All he could do was to speak gravely to them, saying, "Do not be afraid! The nest shall certainly be empty when you arrive. As for the rest, you must do as I say. Should you hear the clamor of a Giant approaching, do not run, and do not fear. Trust my word! Lie low, and stay quiet. Do as I say, and all shall go well." Then he gave them a conspiratorial look and lowered his voice. "Trust me!" he emphasized.

It was not long afterward that messengers came from Lorumack, demanding the foundlings follow. Thrittin took Gauli by the shoulders and looked her in the eye. "Remember what I told you," he said. Then he let them both go, and he returned in haste to his own chamber.

So they were brought at last into the open air, beneath the shady green eaves of the forest. The sun could be glimpsed above glinting through the leafy canopy, and a cool, crisp breeze freshened the air. But neither Gauli nor Erathôn had any heart or spirit to revel in any of this.

They were compelled into the search party of Lorumack, and all trudged out together from the warren, heading for the trail where the Giant had walked. From there Lorumack sent his best scouts round about to probe the area.

Before the sun had passed noon above the crowns of the trees, certain of the scouts returned from their forays. "We have found the nest of a Giant," they said. "There were many foul sacks strewn about, in which the monster may have stashed your jewel. But we heard scuffling in the forest nearby, and dared not stay to see if the Giant slept there or not."

"Good enough, good enough," Lorumack said, rubbing his hands together. "We shall send in our Gnathosians and see what is there."

They followed the trail they had discovered, until one of the guards pointed ahead to a break in the underbrush ahead of them, entering into a dark hollow. "There, straight before us, it lies," he whispered. Lorumack himself would go no further. But he gave orders to his guards to take the Gnathosians to the brink of the nest.

"You must stay: Stay and watch the Gnathosian children," he commanded, "to see whether they search thoroughly, and to watch that they do not attempt to flee. But above all, the Giant must not know there is a warren of our folk nearby! If the monster returns, retreat at once, and flee the place unseen. So it will blame the Gnathosians and not our folk! Don't worry about our Gnathosians: they will be hobbled and cannot get far. When the Giant has left we may return in secret and recover them. Or bring back what remains of them, if the Giant has found them first."

At Lorumack's command they fettered Gauli and Thrittin, hand and foot, with hobbles of bars and leather, so they could neither run, nor could they even bring their hands together to undo the knots which bound them.

Then the guards took them by the arms, and crept on their knees to the very edge of the hollow. There the gnomes lost their nerve and began to tremble, and would go no further.

"You are in luck!" the head of the guards whispered, peering into the hollow. "It would appear the Giant is not at home."

Then turning to Gauli and Erathôn he said, "You know what to do. Go down into its nest, and take your time: search thoroughly for the broach of Lorumack. But make no attempt to flee. We shall be watching from the fringes, and you shall not get far!"

Then prodding them with the butt end of their spears, they drove them into the nest itself.

The nest was dim, and dark, and it stank of rotting meat, or worse. All about were signs of the Giant: broken bones scattered among the leaves; bits of refuse and offal; scraps of cloth or leather, a large limb which might have been a club; and a number of crude and filthy sacks filled with no-one-dared-guess what. The children stumbled forward, trembling, and stood staring in disgust and horror at the sight.

One of the guards hissed, and motioned from the edges of the hollow to be about their business.

Erathôn dropped to his knees and groaned. "We may as well get this over with," he whispered. He picked up the nearest of the bags and began to rummage through it.

It stank, and seemed to be filled with little besides garbage of the foulest sort. One old terra cotta bowl, cracked on the rim, and a filthy wooden spoon, were the most valuable items he had come across, when a muffled sound like the snap of a tree branch brought the whole company to attention.

He and Gauli froze. The guards of the gnomes pressed themselves to the earth, eyes wide. Another crack snapped, closer than the last, then more sounds of shuffling and stirring. A loud thumping reached their ears, like the sound of heavy feet: then they heard approaching the harrumphs and grunts of snorting breath.

From somewhere in the woods a warning call cried out, "Giant!"

A panic set in among the gnomes. None questioned which of them may have called out the warning: The clamor and snorting had already convinced them that a Giant was returning to the nest from its roving in the woods. According to the instructions of Lorumack they fled, far from the scene, and as quickly as they could run, that the Giant would not discover them or their warren.

But the foundlings they left alone in the nest.

Gauli and Erathôn scrambled to get out of the hollow, but their fetters would not let them run. They stumbled as best they could toward the fringe of the nest, tripping and tangling in the clutter. The snorts and thrashing of the Giant came nearer.

But then Gauli stopped suddenly, and she whispered to Erathôn, "Remember the words of Thrittin! He said if we heard the sound of the Giant returning we were to lie low and quiet, and be still."

"But if the Giant finds us here it will kill us!" Erathôn objected.

"What choice do we have? We are hobbled and cannot escape. Thrittin begged us to trust his word. So let us trust, and hope all ends well." Trembling and afraid, Gauli lay down in the matted grass of the clearing, made herself as inconspicuous as possible among the leaves, and closed her eyes.

Seeing he could do nothing else, Erathôn also gave in, and lay down beside her. "If we perish, we shall perish together," he said. He, too, shut his eyes against the approaching terror.

The crashing and crunching stopped suddenly, seemingly at the very edge of the hollow. There was one final call: a long, reverberating grunt almost like a roar, then all was quiet.

Gauli tried not to cry as she heard soft and quiet footsteps enter the hollow and approach. She dared not hope that Giants might be less violent than all the stories had told.

Then she felt a gentle hand on her shoulder, and a soft and familiar voice whispered "Don't be afraid!"

She and Erathôn looked up at once, and there was Thrittin kneeling over them, with a bludgeon in one hand and large sack at his side.

She would have cried out for relief and joy, but Thrittin said, "Do not greet me! We must be gone from here at once, before the guards regain what little courage they possess and return."

First he drew an obsidian knife from his belt, a very sharp tool, and working quickly he severed the fetters which prevented the foundlings from running. The rods he broke into pieces, and tossed them aside where they might be seen. He then scattered a few bits of torn fabric, and an old shoe or two that had belonged to Erathôn; at last he withdrew a flask from his sack, and from it he sprinkled the scene with blood from the butcher's.

Then he signaled for the foundlings to follow him.

He led them through winding and hidden paths to a quiet place in the woods where they would be well hidden. Two large packs awaited them there. He sat down at last and removed the fetters from their wrists.

"We must listen and be cautious, but I deem we are far from Lorumack and his scouts in this place. We can talk here."

At last Gauli broke down. "Never have I been so glad to see you! I thought for sure the Giant would crush us like snails at any moment."

"It has always been my job to keep you safe from harm," Thrittin said. "I would not fail you now."

Then Gauli stammered, "But... the Giant? How..."

Thrittin smiled. "I am the Giant," he said wryly.

Then he explained.

"There never was a Giant's nest. The hollow in which I found you was the abandoned nest of a *baghamôt*—one of the giant ground sloths that wander Batack. I myself made a few modifications to it overnight, with a good deal of garbage I collected from the kitchens, in the hopes that it would fool Lorumack and his scouts. It served its purpose."

"But what of the Giant which Lorumack followed in the woods not two days ago?" Gauli asked.

"That much was real. As far as I can discover it was merely passing through. I too followed the trail after Lorumack mentioned it. The trail was cold, and there was no sign the creature had turned aside to rest at all. It is long gone and far away."

"But we all heard the Giant in the woods!" Erathôn declared.

Thrittin reddened. "I'm afraid that was me as well."

"Then tell us all! What have you done?"

"As soon as you had been called to join the search party I slipped out the back exit. I came straight to this point while you were searching for a nest with Lorumack's party, and I waited.

"At last I heard the sound of Lorumack's scouts when they stumbled onto the 'Giant's nest' I'd fabricated. I made just enough noise to scare them off, then waited for them to bring you in to rummage. Then I'm afraid I had to overdo things a bit. I walked as noisily as could, breaking branches along the way, pounding the earth with a club, and snorting quite unpleasantly. For good measure, I shouted out the warning that a Giant was approaching, as I wasn't confident my acting would be enough to fool them all. Well, it would appear to have done the trick, I'm happy to say. I would not have liked to explain myself if things had not gone as I'd hoped!"

Elated as they were to have escaped the Giant, they now looked about apprehensively. For the first time they were able to enjoy the sight of the world above the warren, and they despised the thought of returning to that dark and tiresome place. "So what now?" Erathôn sighed. "Must we soon return to our duties?"

Thrittin gave a deep sigh and looked sadly at the foundlings. "I would not have taken such great risks for a mere jaunt to see the sunlight. The choice now is yours."

Gauli gasped. "You can't mean—?"

"It was my impression that you wished to escape your thralldom to Lorumack? There would be no softening his stoney heart to allow you to leave freely. Never. I'm afraid this was the best I could do for you."

The foundlings looked about the forest wide-eyed. Gauli then said, "Where should we go? What should we do?"

"Now you must flee, if you desire your freedom. I ask only that you bring no trouble upon our warren. For so would I rue that I had ever done you so great a mercy."

Gauli grew downcast. "Then shall we not see you again?" she said.

"I fear we must part, and our paths will not cross again. And I shall miss you both dearly. You are both young, and the world is full of danger and toil; my heart is torn within me to send you alone and unprepared into such trials."

Gauli threw her arms around him and said, "Then come with us, and we shall go together to make a warren of our own, far from this place."

Thrittin shook his head sadly. "I cannot. This is the warren I have always known: I am familiar and respected among this clan, and I have family and relations among them. Though with you they have been harsh for many years, yet among their own kind they are gracious enough. They are my own kindred, and I cannot abandon them."

So Gauli and Erathôn promised that they would flee far from the warren, and far from this country, never to return, so that no trouble would come to him on their account.

Then Thrittin gave them each a pack containing warm clothing, a knife and a trowel,[1] and rations to last them for several weeks. "You must learn quickly to live from the land: digging your own food from the earth, harvesting what you can from tree and shrub, and hunting for yourselves. You must prepare a den for yourselves before winter, laying up nuts and dried fruit; for the country is cold and inhospitable here in the lands above, for many months."

At last he pulled from his vest the stolen broach of Lorumack: the beauti-

1 A small shovel, which was an indispensable tool among the Gauphrin.

ful gem of lapis lazuli which had caused so much trouble. Thrittin smiled wryly. He handed it to Erathôn and said, "Lorumack will believe a Giant has taken it. If he discovers it again, perhaps he may suspect a ruse has been played upon him. Take it as a parting gift. It is only fitting that you shall have the very gem which has been the cause of so much suffering on your part, as reward for your years of labor. May the covetousness of Lorumack be damned for the injustice. I wish only that I could give you more.

"Take it now, as a reminder of Thrittin and the kindness he has shown you. Remember me fondly, as I will you."

So Gauli embraced Thrittin, and wept. "We shall never forget you, our only true friend in a lifetime of hardship."

Then many tears were shed, but at last they parted.

Gauli and Erathôn fled far from that warren, and dug a small burrow in which to pass the winter. They did not prosper that year, but they did not starve. When the spring arrived, they migrated to the north to be far from the gnomes of Lorumack's warren, and they settled in the mountains of the Surmont, where they delved warrens into the earth in the manner of the Gauphrin. For the life of the Gauphrin is all that they had known.

It cannot be said they lived always happy and at ease, for there were many trials in their new home; more than once they feared for their very lives, and for all they held dear. Nevertheless they were forever thankful for escaping their thralldom, and grateful for the freedom they had gained. For the rest of their days they remembered fondly the friendship of Thrittin, who had risked so much to win their escape, though indeed they never saw him again.

As for Thrittin, none in the warren ever discovered what he had done. When Lorumack's party returned and shared the report, Thrittin mourned for the foundlings as if they were dead: and little sorrow did he need to feign, for he missed Gauli sorely. He had no way of knowing whether they survived that winter in the wild or not, and he feared for their safety for many days. In fact, it was not until many years later that word reached him that a folk like the Gnathosians had been discovered living in the foothills of the Surmont, in burrows like the warrens of the Gauphrin: and their clan called themselves the Gaulians. So at last he discerned that the foundlings had made a home of their own far from Batack: and his heart rested.

Gauli and Erathôn had seven children in their new home, and their children eventually found mates for themselves, and flourished. Their clan quickly became large and prosperous.

Some hold to this day that the clan of Gauli found mates both among the Gnathosians and the Gauphrin, and so their blood is mingled.

The Gaulians that descended from those two are so like unto the Gauphrin that many cannot tell the one from the other. In feature and physique they are as children from the same mother. The Tribe of the Gaulians is short in stature, like the Gauphrin. The Gauphrin are more hairy than the other terumani, like to the Gaulians. The skills, tools and trappings of the Gauphrin are simple, like those of the Pleïstians. Their language is the same, for the Gaulians do not speak Donish as do the other Pleïstians, but Sorian.[2] Their customs as well are similar: for both of these folk spend their lives in tunnels and warrens delved from earth and rock.

It is said that the natures of the terumani and of the Sorian Kindreds are so divergent that they cannot be blended. Yet despite this, it is true that the Giants have in them the blood not only of Erescal the Teruman, but of the deïnings as well, and the deïnings are in nature nothing more nor less than the Sorites, yet without the gift of speech. Besides this, the gnomes are the lowest of the terumani, and are already most like unto the children of Cynodias: the Pleïstians.

Whether such things might be is beyond the ken of our kind: perhaps it is true, and perhaps it is not. Nevertheless, so like are the children of Gauli to the kindred of the gnomes, in form and in habit as well, that this rumor is hard to deny.

Years passed, and Gauli gained much in stature and eminence, and became recognized as the matriarch of the Gaulian Tribe. The Gaulians hold that she became a Hero, and waits in the Mansions of the Terumani until such time as her Tribe will need her.

2 The dialect was more ancient than that spoken in later ages by the Sorites, and diverged from it. In both accent and idiom it sounded most like the dialect of the Cerites, and for many years the Gaulians were thought to be related to that Tribe.

PART III

THE CYCLE OF CHRONO AND AHTEN

Introduction

The extended section which follows comprises a collection of tales which together form the Legend of Chrono and Ahten. The stories revolve around Chrono, a Plateosite of the Southrealm, and the sea-maiden Ahten. Many of the tales of the first half of the collection report loosely-related adventures regarding Chrono and his companion Duono. Each "chapter" was thus originally told as a separate story. Other tales of Chrono circulated throughout Soria. The selections found in this volume were likely considered by the Homadalan scribes to be the most reliable or the most popular of these stories.

The second half of the collection, while also divided into short tales, taken together form a continuous narrative describing the reunion of Chrono and Ahten, and their attempt to gain the blessing of the Terumani for their affair.

The stories were first written down in a form probably very close to the versions which appear here by an unknown scribe or scribes from the region of Plateos, most likely around the year 200 S.C.[1]

These tales were extremely popular throughout the Sorian cultural sphere. They were probably first popularized in the Southrealm of Soria during the days of Mizan dominance, when Chronositic Mizan traders spread them throughout their own sphere of influence. As Chrono had traveled throughout the Southrealm in the course of these stories, many local cultures were touched. Local landmarks associated with Chrono were found in many regions of the Southrealm, and local inhabitants took particular pride in repeating the stories connected with them.

Some of the stories were known elsewhere in Soria in slightly different forms, sometimes with popular local heroes taking the place of Chrono. The Allosites are reported to have told a story very similar to "Chrono and the Giant" with an Allosite hero. Among the Menothians the primary hero in many of the stories was Duono—who in those versions has become a Menothian—while Chrono plays a secondary role. The "Chrono-centric" versions of the stories had already been popularized in most areas of the Empire before the Menothians arrived, so the Menothian revisions never reached the same level of popularity. In some regions the original stories came to represent a more innocent era of days before the Empire, and these versions were likely retained as a form of subtle defiance to the new Menothian overlords.

Although popular among the Chronosites and Mizans as a sort of national origin story heroizing their founder, the tales were nearly as popular in other cultures simply as tales of clever exploits; as a story of unattainable

1 That is, Sorian Calendar, the reckoning in common use in the Sorian Interior.

love; and as an object lesson on the whims of the Terumani—and the manners in which they might (or might not) be moved to intervene on behalf of the Children of Toë.

It should be noted that many of these tales contain poems or songs as sung by Chrono or Ahten. Most of these verses also exist in a collection circulated as the *Songs of Chrono and Ahten*, selections of which are appended to the end of this work. The forms as recorded in the *Cycle* often differ from the versions in that work, typically following a more primitive, alliterative poetic style.

1. CHRONO AND THE SEA-MAIDEN[2]

This tale is told from the days of the Sundering, the Age of Ice, when the kindreds of the south, the Tribes of the Sorites, were separated from their kindred of the north by the great plains of ice which oppressed Batack.

Chrono, the father of the Chronosites, was a Sorite, a descendant of Plateos. Chrono dwelt with his brethren and his sisters in the household of his father Marcanto, in the Valley of Canto.[3]

One summer when Chrono was yet young and still in his father's care, Marcanto called Chrono to him, and said, "Your uncle Trachio, my brother, has no sons. He is building a new storehouse for his household, and he could use the aid of a strong arm such as your own. You may help him with building, and hunting, and such chores as you excel at. Gather what you need, and go over to sojourn with him for the summer."

Chrono agreed, for he loved to travel and see the country. So Marcanto sent him along with Duono, his trail-master and servant, and Duono guided him to the household of Trachio. Trachio lived a day's journey to the west, over the rounded highlands of the Trachian Range.

Trachio the uncle of Chrono welcomed his brother's son, and Chrono worked hard for him. So in the afternoons when the sun was warmest, Trachio would dismiss him from his labor and allow him to rest.

One day when Chrono's work was done he said to his uncle, "What lands lie over the ridge to the west, beyond the hill on which this house is built?"

"On the other side of that great hill lies the edge of the land, and the shores of the great Sea," said Trachio. "There the winds blow cold, and the mist obscures the sunlight, and the terrible raging waters of the deep pound forever on the shore. In the months of autumn the storms of Boros at times escape from their bonds, and they drive ashore with fearsome winds and terrifying rain that blasts like a flood upon the land. At all times evil creatures lurk in those waters. We do not go near it."

Then Chrono was curious, and he said, "I would see this great wonder! Take me to it."

In those days many of the Plateosites were superstitious, and they feared and hated the Sea. So his uncle forbade him, saying bitterly, "Beware of the Sea and its strange folk! They have no love for our kind! The Sea is no place for a child of Sorios."

2 In the Sorian mythos the sea-nymphs and Sea-folk are never described as "mermaids" in the familiar sense. They were in form much like the other terumani, and certainly did not have the tails of fish: the misleading word is therefore avoided in this translation.

3 This later became known as the Valley of Dôn when the Donites migrated to the region at the end of the Age of Ice.

Chrono's curiosity and unrest grew ever stronger as the days passed, however. The strange scent of salt air drifted over the hill and beckoned to him day and night. So it came to pass, as it was destined to, that one day he could no longer defy the impulse. When he had ended his chores for the day, and he was given his afternoon liberty, he secretly set off for the ridge of the hill, and entered the deep wood which capped it to the west.

The house of Trachio was built on the eastward side of the great hill Mizgad:[4] from that same hill on the westward side a path led through a deep and shadowy weald, and opened onto a steep slope where the wind-rippled grass swept down straight to the Sea. When Chrono came out of the woods he stopped in his tracks for wonder, and could not breathe. At his feet lay the vastness of the great Sea, stretching far away to the horizon as if it had no end at all, as endless and staggeringly vast as the sky overhead. In that season it sparkled blue, in ceaseless motion like the quiet breathing of a great and powerful beast. It was terrible in its immensity and power, yet Chrono thought in that moment that never had he beheld anything more breathtaking or more beautiful.

Chrono crept down alone to the foot of the hill, where a black rock bathed, on the skirts of which the waves were breaking thunderously. Unable to approach further, he stood upon the rock for a long while in uncertainty, afraid of the pounding and surging waters. White fountains of foam exploded into the air before him; invincible mounds of water pulsed and poured over the shelves and surged through the troughs below.

At last he surrendered to the call of the Sea, and he sat down to watch. For the rest of the afternoon he sat there in the spray of the crashing waves. The lights of heaven played upon the distant rollers and whitecaps like a sparkle of jewels; the roar of the breakers became a song and a harmony; the mist and the sea-spray which drifted ashore were cool upon his cheek as the touch of a maiden's fingertips. The afternoon drew on to evening, the sun lowered into the deeps of the west, and the surging waters turned to molten gold.

Chrono started as if awakened from a dream. The sun was sinking, and it would soon be dark, and it was a long walk, over hill and through a deep wood, to his uncle's house. Never had he been so late in heading homeward. "I must make haste, or my uncle will worry!" he said to himself. "Then he might keep me at home, and I might not escape to this place again!"

So he picked himself up at once and hurried back over the hill of Mizgad. The stars and the Night Veil[5] shone in full before he arrived at the house, and dinner had long since been cleaned up and put away. Nevertheless his mis-

---

4 The Mizgad referred to throughout this text was the cape of that name which faced the Strait of Endrev, and not the much later town of Mizgad situated on the Chronas Inlet some 20 miles from the open sea.

5 I.e., the Milky Way.

take was merely laughed at, and no one was the wiser, or guessed where he had been.

From that day, Chrono seldom failed to spend his afternoons on the westward slopes of Mizgad. He told no one where he went. If any asked, he said merely that he was exploring the countryside, which none questioned, for all knew him as a curious and venturesome sort.

He rambled over the pools at low tide, watching the red crabs which scuttled into the rocks, and investigating the spiky urchins and the blooming, turquoise anemones. He found sandy beaches where he cooled his ankles in the surf, and the rushing of the waves seemed as if playful hands were clutching at his ankles to draw him in.

At last a day came when the sun blazed hot, and the waters were cool, and the call of the surf could not be resisted. So he waded deep into the swells, and he dared to enter the sea: a thing unheard of among his folk. The water rose to his chest, then the surging waves lifted his feet from the sands, and for a moment he panicked, but struggling and paddling against the current he found he could stay afloat. When the wave washed out and his feet bounced upon the sand once more he rushed to the safety of the shore.

For a long while he sat on the sand watching the swells and breakers fearfully, but at length his courage returned, and with it a captivating curiosity that he could not set aside. He at last got to his feet, and cautiously returned to the waters. Many things could have gone wrong that day, for he had no lore to guide him, and no one to teach him. But either fortune was with him, or some instinct preserved him, and he learned the ways of the Sea.

So Chrono taught himself to swim. Many times he returned to that beach during the hottest days of summer, and entered the waters, and his strokes grew strong. As his courage grew, he began to dive among the crashing waves. Before long he had begun to swim even beyond the fearsome breakers. None before Chrono had dared such a thing: or if any had, no tale tells of it. The Sea was a terror to the Kindreds of Toë, and there was no boat in all of Soria.[6] Not even the Terumani had dared the seas.

But above all this, Chrono's favorite pastime was to sit in the warm sun on the black rock at the foot of Mizgad, and revere the restless waters. This he did, without fail, every day that he could escape his duties throughout that season.

The summer drew to a close at last, and Marcanto's servant Duono returned to fetch Chrono. "The days of summer grow short," he said, "and your

6 The word in the Sorian refers specifically to seaworthy vessels. As is made clear in other tales, small canoes, rowboats and dugouts were in use in inland waters, and among some clans even on enclosed ocean bays and coves.

father will be needing us soon to help bring in the stores for the winter. Pack up your gear, and let us return."

So regretfully Chrono sighed for his loss, and he repaired to his father's compound on the far side of the Trachian Range, far from the Sea. There he stayed, and went about his business at his father's house, performing his duties and chores, and behaved as ever before. But his mind and his heart were elsewhere, beyond the mountains, and try as he might he could not forget the awe he had felt when he sat at the shore each day. All through that autumn and the following winter Chrono pined for the sea.

Of course he dared tell no one of his longing. But whenever the winds blew from the west, carrying with them the salty air of the sea, Chrono's heart surged within his breast. And on gray and misty days when the sea-birds appeared from over the mountains and shrilled their plaintive cries, the yearning in his heart cried along with them.

When the snows of winter melted, and the duties of planting and tilling were done, and the warm breezes of spring began to burn into the first hints of summer, Chrono said to Marcanto his father, "Trachio my uncle has no sons in his household, and I was of much use to him in the summer past. Would I not do well to go across again this summer as well?"

This seemed good to Marcanto, so he gave him his blessing. He sent him across the Trachian Range once more, together with his trail-master Duono as guide and servant. So it was that Chrono came to dwell with his father's brother Trachio once again on the eastward slopes of Mizgad. In the afternoons, Chrono returned to his secret hikes over the crest and down the westward slope, to his black rock on the seashore.

Now at this same place, across the waters from the black rock of Chrono, another rock rose from the waves, like that upon which Chrono would sit, but separated from it by a wide stretch of open sea and strong currents. When the tide was high the breakers would crash and spray over its westward face like fountains of shining mist. When the tide was low, the sea-lions—the sea-hounds of the Tritynoi[7] — would bask on its sleek shelf. Chrono would often watch the sea-hounds from afar, and listen to their cheerful baying, and envy them their unattainable redoubt among the waves. For not even Chrono dared to venture so far from the safety of the shore.

It came to pass on an afternoon in the early days of summer that Chrono sat on the rock at Mizgad listening to the sea-hounds, when another sound reached his ears along with it: a high, sweet melody like the song of a flute, or the voice of the wind in the crowns of the forest. It piped and fluted clearly above the rhythm of the surf upon the rocks.

---

7 The Trityns, or Tritynoi, are the sea-folk: the næads of the sea. This is the proper name by which they call themselves.

Chrono rose to his feet to listen, for it was strange and beautiful, and never had his ears heard its like. Even the sea-hounds ceased their baying to give ear to its lilt. The song seemed to call to his soul: a thing of indescribable beauty as palpable as the sea itself. Now Chrono loved the Sea more than any of his folk, and the song which floated to him now seemed a very element of the Sea. His soul surged at the beauty of it, and the longing for the Sea overwhelmed him.

As he stood and listened he discerned in it the pattern of speech. But the voice he heard came from afar, seemingly from the sea itself; and if speech it was, it was a dialect strange and hard to understand, as if the waves had found a voice.

He trained his eyes upon the rock beyond the breakers, where the sea-hounds basked, and there among them he thought he descried the form of a maiden. She was tall and lithe, unlike the Plateosites of his own Tribe, but though he beheld her only in the distance through the mists, he thought her beautiful like one of the terumani, with long hair of shimmering silver, like the sunlight surging on waves. She was slender, and her complexion was silvery-white like sea foam. The lilt of her song filled his breast with joy as if everything of beauty in all the Sea had been distilled into her voice. The sea-hounds themselves looked up at her in silent devotion.

Chrono held his breath and sat down upon his rock, for he feared if the maiden saw him she would somehow vanish, and the magic of the song would end. For hours he sat unmoving, listening to her song in rapture, until the sun was low in the sky. Only then did it cross his mind to wonder who the maiden might be, or how she may have come to find herself on the rock in the midst of the sea. He pondered whether he should call out to her at last, or whether there might be some way to rescue her from her islet.

But when the disk of the sun reached down at last to touch the horizon, he saw her silhouette rise, and the maiden stepped down into the waters, and slid beneath the waves, and returned not up again. Chrono gasped in disbelief, for he realized all at once that she was of the Tritynoi, the Seafolk: a nymph of the Sea, of whom folk spoke in tales, but seldom with the conviction of belief.

He picked himself up and rushed homeward under darkening skies. Black night had fallen before he arrived. He apologized for his tardiness, ate a hurried dinner, and was soon in bed. But his spinning mind would not allow sleep. He had seen a Trityn of the seas with his own eyes! He had been blessed to hear the song of the sea-folk. And for all this, he could tell no one of the miracle.

The next day Chrono finished his duties hurriedly, and said to his uncle, “If I may, might I take my leave early this morning? I have found a new pathway to explore, and want to follow it to its end.”

Trachio smiled and consented. "Only try this time to return before nightfall," he laughed. So Chrono gathered his pack for the day, and he returned quickly over the hill and down to his rock. There he sat down, and fixed his gaze on the rock of the maiden expectantly, hoping again for the maiden to return, and longing to hear again the wonder of her song. Early in the afternoon, when the tide was low, she arose again from the waves, took her seat among the sea-hounds, and began to sing as before.

She sang in strange words, but Chrono soon found he could understand much of the maiden's song (for the tongue of the Tritynoi is not so far removed from that of the Sorites): she sang songs of the Sea, of the beauties of that domain, and the wonders of its creatures. She sang songs of the lore of the Tritynoi, and sagas of the heroes of her kind. At other times he discerned nothing more than a melody harmonizing with the waves.

Chrono was enchanted. After this he came every day he could break away from his duties, always coming down to the seashore, and waiting for the song of the maiden to begin. As for the maiden herself, he could see her only dimly, through the mists of the sea and from a distance, yet he thought her more lovely than any of the daughters of his own Tribe. Though it filled his heart merely to sit and listen, he soon found himself longing to approach. "But no!" he said to himself, repeatedly. "She is a Trityn of the sea, and that folk will have nothing to do with me or my folk. Be content that you have heard the song of her kind."

Yet his mind wandered as he sat and listened, and hopeless daydreams consumed him. Hopeless indeed, for she gazed ever out to sea, and never so much as looked his way, nor saw him on his rock at the shore. Twice he even dared to call out to her, but the crashing of the waves overwhelmed the sound of his voice from across the waters. To meet her was impossible, but he could not leave off thinking of anything else day or night.

Things had gone on in this way for some length of days. The longing within him took root and grew, and in the end he could bear it no more. It overwhelmed his heart, and he lifted up his own voice to sing. Thus Chrono returned verse to the maiden of the rock, saying:[8]

"Siren-singer, sea-mist sister,
Daughter of wave, of waters wide,
What soul receives your serenade?
What helpless hostage hears your hymn?

---

8 As with many of the songs in the following tales, a much-altered version appears in *The Songs of Chrono and Ahten*, in rhymed tetrameter. This version in alliterative couplets follows a more primitive, and possibly more original, form.

Your stirring song, soul-enslaving,
Lovely lilt, alluring lay,
Claims a consecrated captive.
Steers me seaward, shorn from shore-life.

Done are days of dalliance,
Of gazing glad on green of earth,
My soul is summoned to the Searealm,
Drawn to Dreiton's doubtful depths.

So sing secure, on stoney shelf
While trapped, I tread the tiresome turf,
Divided from a docile doom,
By breakers and the bitter brine."

Now perhaps such things are fated to be, but it so happened that Chrono's voice was pure and sonorous, a sweet timbre when he sang which mingled with the surf and rose above it, so that it could be heard from far off even over the crying of the sea. When Chrono had finished his song the Sea-maiden lifted her eyes and gazed shoreward from her rock in wonder. There she spotted Chrono standing upon the rock of Mizgad by the seashore.

Chrono was unlike her own kind, but he was fair among the sons of Sorios, noble and lordly of visage and form. He wore a tunic of blue like the dome of the sky, and his arms and his legs were ruddy. Moreover, the maiden herself had been enchanted by his song. But she dared not leave her rock in the sea, for the Tritynoi are terumani of the Sea. They have no communion with the children of Sorios, and little commerce even with the terumani of the dry land: so she was afraid. Nevertheless the rock upon which she sat was unreachable from the shore, and in that place she was secure; so she lifted up her voice again, and continued to sing. Only now she directed her song to Chrono.

For the waning of the afternoon they both sang across the waters. She lifted up her voice and sang to him in her own strange tongue, and he returned his voice in reply. They spent many hours thus in song, until at last, when the sun was low in the sky, the maiden smiled across the distance at Chrono. Then she slipped from her perch and entered the Sea, and she disappeared from sight.

Chrono returned to his rock every day as soon as his chores and duties were complete, and every day the maiden appeared likewise upon the rock of the sea-hounds. Now every day they sang to each other; sometimes in joy, sometimes in longing; sometimes in aching, and sometimes in despair. At any event, a bond formed between them across the waves, irrevocably divided as they were.

Many hours he simply gazed across the waters, longing hopelessly to approach. His heart swelled and his head swam when he saw that the sea-maiden gazed his way just the same.

Things continued thus for several months, so that Trachio, Chrono's uncle, began to worry about his nephew. Chrono had not told his uncle of the maiden, but he disappeared every afternoon and would not return until after sunset.

Autumn came, and Duono, the servant and trail-master of his father Marcanto, came from across the hills. Then Trachio tried to send Chrono home. "The time of gathering is upon us," he said, "and your father's house has need of you."

But Chrono was elusive, and kept finding excuses to remain. The storehouse roof required repair, or tools refurbished, or traders had arrived with a stock of goods that needed to be tended to. So he stayed day after day, making himself indispensable. And every day he passed over the hill in secret to the seashore, and nothing that Trachio could do could turn him from this habit.

At last Trachio called for Duono, and said to him, "I must know where my brother's son goes in the afternoons, and what it is he is doing, or whom he is meeting. His behavior is furtive, and the young fellow is deceptive with me. Go now and find him out by stealth, and report back to me all that he does."

So Duono waited until Chrono left the house, and crept after him quietly. But Chrono turned, and saw him, and said aloud, "Where are you going, Duono, and why are you following me?"

Duono answered, "I am merely going to Trachio's fountain to fetch water for the house, for the cisterns are becoming stale." And he broke off from following him, and fetched a pitcher from the garden, and went down to the springhead of Trachio on the hillside. Chrono went his way and departed from him.

The following day Duono again set out to follow him when he left the house, but again Chrono turned and saw him following, and called out, "Where are you going, Duono, and why are you following me?"

Duono answered, "I am merely going down to the river to cast about for fish for supper tonight." And he again broke off from following him, and gathered his fishing javelin and his net from the storehouse, and went down to the riverbank. Chrono departed from him and went his own way.

The third day again Duono set out to follow him, and again Chrono turned and saw him following behind, and called out, "Where are you going, Duono, and why are you following me?"

Duono answered, "I am going to the grove on the hillside to gather wood, for the evening will be cool, and we will have need of fire tonight." And he broke off from following him, and Chrono departed from him and went his own way.

Finally after four days Duono grew crafty, and he came to Chrono in the morning, and gave him the keys of Trachio's household.[9] "Please carry the keys of the household with you today," he said, "for Trachio entrusted them to me, but I must trade in Solanaris this afternoon, and must not chance to lose them in the market there. They will be safer here with you." Chrono agreed, and fastened the keys to his belt. Then Duono hid himself in the house, and feigned to have left for the day.

In the afternoon Chrono departed the house as was his wont, suspecting nothing; but Duono had fastened chimes among the keys. Now the keys of those ancient days were simple: round pegs of bone or wood, carved and notched to fit into a round keyhole. So Chrono did not notice the chimes hidden among them. But the keys rang as he walked, and Duono's hearing was acute, so he listened for Chrono as he left.[10] Then Duono followed from a distance, out of sight, for he could hear the keys of Chrono jangling as he went his way.

Thus Duono followed him over the hill and through the wood, and onward to his rock at the edge of the sea. There Chrono sat, while Duono watched him in secret from the woods at the top of the hill; and Chrono lifted up his voice and sang across the waters. Presently the sea-maiden rose from the Sea, and ascended her rock, and began to sing back to Chrono.

Duono watched in astonishment for a long while, but as nothing further seemed to be transpiring, he crept back to Trachio's house and reported all that he had seen. Trachio was dismayed.

When Chrono returned to the house at evening, Trachio was wroth. Clutching Chrono by the arm he demanded, "What is this that you are doing? To whom do you sing in the waters of the Sea?"

Chrono dissembled and replied, "It is true, I have gone down to the seashore in defiance of your will, for the sea is not what you fear. I sing to the sea because I love the sea, and all that is in the sea."

"Yet you will not deny that upon a rock in the sea there is a Sea-maiden; a Trityn," said Trachio, "and to her you were singing when Duono came upon you at Mizgad."

Chrono saw that he had been discovered, so he answered, "There is indeed a maiden of the Sea who sits at whiles upon a rock among the waves: at times I sing to her, and she to me. What harm is done thereby?"

Trachio shook his head and said, "This must end at once. I have forbidden you to go down to the seashore. The Tritynoi have no love for the sons of Sorios, and we must not anger them. They are a hard folk, and their hearts are cold as the waters in which they live: it is said that they come up from the Sea in the mist at night, and suck the life out of infants and children." Such was

9 These would not have been door keys, but most likely would have unlocked various chests or cabinets within the habitation.

10 It is possible the chimes would have been made of copper, which although rare and valuable in those times, would not have been unheard of. Simple round tubes of copper would have been about the same size and shape as the keys used for the locks of those times.

the rumor among the shore-folk in that day, for the Tritynoi had always been a secretive folk, more secretive than any others of the terumani. The Plateosites did not know them, and feared them.

Chrono denied the slander, saying, "This is not true: It is a tale of ignorant grandmothers and mischievous children. This maiden is altogether lovely. You do not know her! She is kind of heart, and sings only of love for all creatures beneath the sun and beneath the waves: creatures of the sea, and creatures of the air, and creatures of the dry land. There is no evil in her, and I love her."

Trachio drew back, greatly troubled by this news, and he feared the wrath of his brother, Chrono's father. "You are mortal," he declared, "and among mortals you are free to marry whomever you choose. Why lose your heart to this Trityn, from whom you are sundered by a gap greater than the Ice which sunders us from the Ádolthi? No less strange would it be to love a Giant than a Trityn."

Chrono answered with the all passion of youth, "And yet I do love her, knowing that we can never be united. It seems to me that she loves me also."

"Then what would you do? Will you waste your days singing to the empty sea? Will you grow old and die alone on this rock?"

Chrono's shoulders sank. "I suppose if I cannot be with her, I must die alone. No other will ever command my heart and my will."

Trachio shook his head decisively. "This must not be," he insisted. "You are the heir of Canto, and will be a lord among the Sorites. I will send you back at once to your father's house, and there you will forget this Trityn. You may not return to my house until you have married one of our own tribe."

So Trachio packed up Chrono's gear, and barred the door of his chamber against him, and compelled him to go with Duono. So he was forced from the house of Trachio, and from the Sea. He returned then to the house of Marcanto his father: Duono told Marcanto all that had transpired, and Marcanto also worried over his son.

For many days Chrono dwelt in his father's house in the Vale of Canto. Marcanto his father fretted for him endlessly, for he was listless there, and ever of a mournful spirit: he ate little, and drank no wine, and his father and his brothers never saw him laugh in all those days. But often he would stare into the west when the sun was low in the sky, and if any stood by him at such times they saw in his eyes the longing for the distant sea, and heard under his breath the humming of strange melodies unknown to them.

At last Marcanto lost patience with his son's idleness. He went to the house of his kinsman Carthrëan, the cousin of Canto, and he arranged with Carthrëan for the marriage of his daughter Mourelë with Chrono. Chrono had known Mourelë since childhood, and they had always been fond of one another. She knew Chrono as comely and honorable, and she agreed to the union. So Marcanto brought Mourelë back with him to his own house.

To Chrono he said when he had returned, "Come Chrono, and meet your bride. You are the eldest of my sons, and you shall be a lord among the Plateosites. It will not do for you to remain alone and childless all your days."

When Chrono saw Mourelë he groaned and said, "No, but this was wrong! I cannot marry Mourelë, however fair and noble, nor any other who is not my soul's mate. You may keep me here away from the Sea, but my heart remains bound to the mist-clouds and the foam upon the waves."

Marcanto grew angry. "Has this siren so enchanted you with her witcheries? You must shake off this spell, for a lord of the Plateosites must be able to judge with a clear mind. If you pursue this foolishness honor shall depart from our house. And you yourself will waste your days away in vain dreams. But whether you shake off this spell or not, you shall not insult our kinsman or Mourelë his daughter, but you shall marry her in the morning."

Chrono could not sleep that night, but sat staring at the ceiling. As fate had it, a breeze blew in from the west, and the mist of the sea with it: It sifted in through the windows and portals, so that the whole house of Marcanto was filled with the scent of salt air. The trees in the compound rustled in the breeze, and the sound as it passed bore with it the timbre of distant, unheard songs.

Chrono sat up suddenly. He arose from his bed in the dark of night, dressed himself silently, and slipped away secretly from the house where his father and his brothers slept. He looked uncertainly into the starry darkness. Never before had he made this journey alone, but always before he had been in the company of Duono the trail-master, and their goal had been the house of Trachio. Now there was no clear trail to his destination, so he set his steps hopefully to the west, traveling across open country by the light of stars and moon.

By the first gleam of dawn he had reached the highlands of the Trachian Range. From those heights he could see the glistening Sea below, a scattering of distant rocks and islands rising out of the azure mists. Far off on the horizon to the south, as if through a veil, he discerned the blue ridge of the Hill of Mizgad. He drew in the scent of the sea, and was very weary, and he laid down in the grass and slept.

When he awoke he turned to the south, setting his course for Mizgad. For the rest of that day and all through the night he followed the ridge of the mountains, eating the wild oats that were ripening on the hills, and whatever he could glean from the land, for in his haste and his stealth he had brought no provisions. At last, late in the day, he came to Mizgad, and the westward slope which swept down to the shore. His own rock waited there below, wet and black from the mists of the sea, and beyond it across the open waters the rock of the Trityn.

Then he rushed perilously down the steep slope. He arrived at last with the red disk of the sun low in the sky, and he was weary. He sat down upon his rock, gazing out to sea, not certain what to do, or why he had come at all. He began to sing as had been his wont: the sad and lonely song of one with little hope. But the rock of the Trityn was abandoned, and there was no answer. All was quiet but for the rhythmic breaking of the waves. Not even the sea-hounds rested there now.

As the sun was setting Chrono despaired, and he thought to himself, "I have lost my heart, and I have lost my honor. All is lost to me, I have nothing remaining among my own folk. It is better for me to die, if that is my fate."

So Chrono slipped from the rock and into the sea. The waters were cold and bracing, for winter would soon be coming on, and they shocked him out of his weariness. Without any plan in mind he struck out beyond the breakers for the rock of the maiden.

For hours he was in the sea, making little progress, for the current was very strong. The sun set, the sky above grew dark, and the waters became an inky terror: the embodiment of forsaken abandonment and death. But ahead of him, always out of reach, the blue luminescence of the coursing foam on the rock of the maiden beckoned him. Though he became exceedingly weary he never faltered in his stroke. Although it was night the gulls and the mews wheeled and piped overhead, as if marveling over a child of the land among the waves of Potomis.[11] Then the sea-hounds appeared and swam about him, and they seemed to be cheering him on with their baying.

Chrono lost track of how long he had been in the cold waters of the sea, but at last he reached the rock of the maiden, and he drew himself, chilled and bone-weary, from the waves. There was a hollow on the south side of the rock, out of the sea-breeze and the spray: There he curled up, and shivered, and lost consciousness, and knew nothing more.

He slept on through the night, and into the next day, and dreamed feverish dreams. When at last he awoke he was hungry, thirsty, cold, and weak. He did not know where he was, or how he had come to be there.

When he opened his eyes his vision was at first dim. He discerned a veil of shimmering silver above his head, and he thought, "I am sunk beneath the waves of the sea, and am surely drowned." But he blinked, and when he opened his eyes again and his vision came clear, he realized that he was seeing the tresses of the Sea-maiden.

For the first time he gazed full into her face. Now the form of the terumani is beautiful to the Kindreds, and Ahten was beautiful even among that

11 Potomis is a name often used for the whole of the sea-realm: all which fell under the dominion of Dreiton.

folk. Chrono found her lovelier than the maids of his own Tribe, for his heart had been enthralled by her voice and her song. She was lovelier even than he had dreamt. Her eyes were sea green, round, and as deep and pure as pools of clear water. Her lips were as pink as coral, and as soft and moist as sea-moss. Her skin was flawless and silver-white, as smooth and unblemished as evening fog. After the manner of her Kindred her gown was as of gossamer sea-mist; her form and her motions stirred his soul. She gazed at him now with love and concern. In his confusion Chrono thought he was sleeping yet, and seeing the vision of a dream.

Then she spoke, in the Sorian tongue in the manner of her own folk.[12] "Art awake, or dost swoon once more?" Her voice was lilting and soft, like the lapping of ripples against the rocks of a bay. His heart thrilled at the sound of it, for she spoke to him face to face for the first time, and affection was in her eyes.

At the sound of her voice Chrono came to his senses. "I know not if I am truly awake, or am yet in a dream. If dreaming, I pray that I might never wake."

The maiden became downcast. "Thou shouldest not have hither fared. For now art thou too spent to gain again the far shore where thou dost belong. Surely wilt thou perish shouldest thou remain here, lacking food and fresh water after the needs of thy kind."

"If die I must, then I shall die: The Sea has claimed me. I have lost honor in my father's house, and there remains nothing for me upon the hard land, where my own kind dwell."

"For thee to die I cannot allow," the maiden said. "For through thee and thy songs of green earth, and wind, and sky, I have been fated to love a son of earth. How then can I ever abandon him alone upon a rock in the sea, where he would be unable to survive?"

Chrono raised himself up, and spoke sternly. "Then do not leave. Here we are neither on the earth nor in the Sea. Perhaps the division that parts our Kindred can be forgotten here, if only for a season."

The maiden nodded resolutely. "For a time it shall be so. I shall provide for thee as I am able, until thou art perhaps strengthened to return to thine own shore, under thine own sinew. What will then become of us I know not. But until then, let us speak heart to heart: I shall tell thee of the Sea thou lovest, and thou shalt tell me of the bright air and the unmoving earth."

The maiden told Chrono her name, which was Ahten, and she was the daughter of Teruman Merten and Teruman Aviah, the lord and lady of the Tritynoi: They were of the Ádolthi of the Sea, and not mere næads as were most of the Seafolk. Chrono told her that he was Chrono an heir of Canto, descendant of a judge and a lord among the Sorites.

12 In the Sorian text the speech of the Seafolk, when conversing with the mortal kindreds, is often presented as archaic and formal.

Eight days they spent upon the rock while Chrono recovered his strength. The maiden would bring fish to Chrono, and shellfish, and such things as the Tritynoi prepare for their meals, which he would eat without cooking, since the Tritynoi do not have the use of fire. She contrived also to bring him fresh water, which she gathered from the mouth of a flowing stream on the far shore, in a vessel made from the shell of a nautilus.

But even when he had recovered Chrono could not bring himself to depart, nor did Ahten press him to do so. Another day he remained, then yet another after that, until eight days further had passed, while the two refused to part from one another. They spoke and sang of many things. Chrono taught Ahten of life on the dry earth, and the merits and gifts of his own kind, and of all the beautiful things of his world. Ahten for her part filled his soul with the love of the sea he could not behold, and taught him the lore of the terumani, of the history and virtues of all her kind.

Although they had already come to love one another through months of song, now they found that the more days they spent together on the rock in the midst of the sea, the greater their bond grew. Their hearts were alike, and fit for one another as a key is fit for a lock. They bonded in heart and soul as no two children of land or sea had ever bonded.

Ahten kept Chrono warm as best she could, but the frigid winds of autumn from seaward had begun to blow, and the rock was damp. At last it became clear that Chrono would need to return to the shore, where she could not follow.

"What are we to do?" Chrono said. "For union between your Kindred and mine is against nature, as surely as fire can have no union with water."

"I know not," the maiden mourned. "I am made for the Sea, and yet now I long to walk the solid green-earth with thee. Thou art made for the earth, yet thou desirest the coursing sea. I see, and fear, that we can never share a world."

Chrono said, "If I leave this rock, and leave the sea, my soul shall die within me. But if I remain here, my flesh shall perish."

"That cannot be. Wouldst thou then destroy that which I love? For if thou shouldst die, my own soul would die within me. Yet were I to go with thee to the dry land, without the protection of the deep and the sea-mists, my flesh would shrivel and burn away, and my lungs would be seared, and I would enter the long sleep."

"And that I could never allow."

The maiden lowered her eyes and sighed, and she said, "What then must we do? Thou art destined to be a lord among thy folk, and the lives of thy kind are but short in this land. Wouldst thou spend it all in hopeless waiting for that which we know will never be?"

Chrono took a deep breath and closed his eyes. He stood up and looked the Sea-maiden in the eyes. "We both know that to continue in this manner will bring us both to ruin. There can be no bond between the folk of the dry land and the folk of the Sea-realms. So I must go, and you must depart to the deep Sea. I shall return to the hard earth. But I swear I shall live unsouled among my kind." He looked away to east, to the dry land across the waters, and a tear like a drop of seawater wet his cheek.

The maiden bowed her own head and wept. "Unsouled thou shalt not be, for my soul wilt thou carry with thee always." She took a necklace of magnificent pearls from around her own neck, and placed it on his neck as a token. "These pearls are made in the sea, distilled of the very waters of the sea itself. It is a token of love from the deeps of Potomis. I give it thee on my oath, and the oaths of the terumani are unbreakable."

Chrono took a light chain of gold[13] which he wore, and placed it around the neck of the maiden. "This gold is dug from the earth and wrought in fire," he said, "a trinket from the world of the dry land and air, and a pledge of my faithfulness: so may you ever bear with you the soul of the son of the dry land who loved you."

"Whither then, Chrono son of Marcanto?"

Chrono shrugged. "I have lost honor in the house of my father. So I shall wander in the lands of Soria, and see what honor and reputation I can wrest from among strangers. Perhaps in so doing the forgetfulness of time may take away the torment of my parting from Ahten the daughter of Merten. Yet my heart shall never belong to another."

"And I shall mourn in Potomis, in the house of my father and mother," said Ahten. "Merten my father shall surely contemn me for this choice, but though the days of my sojourning endure long, never shall the memory of thee diminish, nor shall I give the soul of Ahten to any son of the Sea. This I swear, and will not regret it. Thou must never have doubt: The oaths of the terumani are certain. Even the Giants in their corruption must keep an oath."

So with great weeping and sadness they fell upon one another, until at last Chrono slipped into the waters, and swam for the shore. At length he reached the dry land, and he clutched at the pearls on his breast, and turned for one final gaze at the Sea-maiden. Then he set his face inland, and took the trail which would lead to his father's house, until the rock was out of sight behind him. As for the maiden, she watched Chrono the son of Marcanto until his form could no longer be descried upon the mountainside, then she slipped under the waves, and was gone.

Thus did Chrono and Ahten part ways, and the days of the wanderings of Chrono began.

When Chrono had parted from the Sea and turned his back on the maiden of the Tritynoi, he went eastward, far from the shorelands, and far from his

13 Gold would have been exceedingly rare and valuable, and this may be an anachronism.

father's house, where his name was in dishonor on account of his rejection of Mourelë the daughter of Carthrëan. But before he departed, he returned home to gather those things he might need for his wayfaring. He came in secret by cover of night, for he dared not face his father.

It so happened, however, that as he stole into the house, he was spied by Duono, the servant and trail-master of the household. Duono had known Chrono since that one's childhood, and had great respect for him: for Chrono was adventurous and curious, and more of his own mind than was his lord, Marcanto the son of Canto. When Chrono had left his father's house, Duono went out stealthily, and accosted him on the highway, saying, "Where are you going, Chrono my lord's son? You have been gone for many days, and no one knows where you have hidden yourself. We have gone even to that rock from which you used to view the Sea, but could not find you even there. And now you steal into your father's house as a thief, and leave again without a word."

"I do not wonder that you could not find me. I was not on the rock, nor on the land of Soria at all, but have been lost in the midst of the Sea itself."

Duono looked at him curiously, but he accepted the statement. "Then you have done a greater wonder than any of us had imagined. Come now, return to your father's house and be reconciled."

"That cannot be, for I've shamed my father, and my own name, in the spurning Mourelë. I can never marry her, nor any other of the daughters of my own Kindred."

"Then you shall have no home of your own, and walk the land as one exiled," said Duono.

"If that is my fate, so be it," said Chrono. "Or perhaps I shall win honor of my own, and a name of honor, far from my own country, and far from the Sea that has ensnared my heart." He turned again to continue on his way alone.

But Duono coming alongside him said, "Then do not go alone. You shall have need of a trail-master if you journey far from your accustomed place. We have grown up as brothers in the house of Marcanto. I shall walk gladly with you, hoping to share in the honors you win for yourself."

Chrono attempted to dissuade Duono, but Duono's mind would not be changed. So together Chrono and his trail-master set off into the east from the lands of his father, and the two sought for honor among distant folk.

2. CHRONO AND THE GIANT OF BATACK

In the days of the wanderings of Chrono, when he was estranged from his father Marcanto, he directed his steps eastward, far from the settlements of his own tribe, and taking the trails through the hill country of Lodbarria he headed for the country of the Cylosites. With Chrono also went Duono his traveling companion, who was a skilled trail-master.

For many days they walked on wide trails, and they passed many villages and settlements of the Plateosites, Chrono's own Tribe, but Chrono would not stop. "We are not yet far enough from the country of my dishonor," he said. "Let us go further, until we have left my infamy behind in the dust of the horizon." But in his heart, he simply wished to travel far from the Sea, for its nearness pained his memory.

At last they turned north, away from the settled regions of Plateos, and came at length to the Fords of Dunar on the River Næus. The Næus here spread wide over shallow, gravelly bars, and the waters were low at that time of year, and easy to traverse. But Duono stopped when they came to the fords and peered across to the far side thoughtfully.

"We have reached the end of settled country" he said. "If we proceed across the river here, we shall enter nothing but dark forest and the shadow of Batack." In those days the remnant of Batack had spread southward until it reached even beyond the River Næus and Lake Egano, for the snows and ice of Vélopar had taken all the highlands. The pleasant hills and groves which the Cylosites had settled in ancient times were now overgrown with wood: deep, and dark, and wild. It was autumn, but many of the trees of Batack do not drop their foliage, and many of those that do still clung to their cloaks as if huddling against the cooling weather. The forest before them glowered balefully.

Chrono said, "Then let us go into the shadows. What do I care if my deeds are done in dark or light?"

"But what do you seek in that dark country?" asked Duono. "Any folk who remain are few and furtive, and if you seek fame and honor, you will not find it there."

Chrono merely shrugged. "I know not what I seek, nor whom. But if danger lurks in the dark, there also awaits a chance for gallantry."

Duono then smiled, and said, "Danger you shall certainly find! So then, let us proceed."

So they hoisted their packs, and crossed the fords, and entered into the deeps of Batack.

There were no roads in the country in those days, only narrow paths that threaded over rock and root, and snaked through mounds of moss and fern, and wound under the heavy boughs that reached down to the dank and mould-strewn earth. Chrono and Duono kept their spears at hand, for the forest was the haunt of wolves and drakes, and Giants which had fled the Ice.

They traveled westward for some days, meeting with no one along the way, camping in the open under the leaves each night. They came a far distance into the forest, until the settled country they had left seemed a distant memory. Chrono began to despair of finding any folk at all, let alone any adventure worth pursuing.

But one afternoon as they began to seek a spot for their camp, Duono suddenly halted and whispered to Chrono, "Stop and listen! From among the trees I hear the whisperings of stealth."

Chrono trusted the ears of Duono, and he halted. Holding very still they listened to the sounds of the forest. All that Chrono could hear, and indeed all that most would have heard, were the sighing of the autumn breeze in the canopy overhead; the drone of bee, beetle and fly among the leaves; and the chatter of birds in the branches: but Duono heard above all this the rustling of footsteps on leaf and fallen branch.

"I hear nothing," Chrono whispered. "But what do you hear? Is this the sound of enemy, of beast, or of friend?"

Duono closed his eyes and held his breath, and after some moments he said, "These are signs of a single traveler, alone. The going is cautious and secretive. But I do not read the stealth of treachery in these movements. They seem not to be trailing us: in fact they seem not to have discerned our presence at all."

"Then let us announce ourselves, and see whether we can find an ally in this dark country."

So Chrono and Duono left the path they had been following, and went forward a space into the wild wood. Following the guidance of Duono, they soon spotted a Cylosite making his way though the undergrowth, off the beaten trail. He was thin and nearly gaunt, yet a placid smile glinted in his eyes. In one hand he carried a meager game bird which he had caught in a net. In the other he held a small hunting spear: a knife was at his side, and slung across his back was a stolid club. But he seemed to be no threat or danger, so Chrono appeared out of the woods to hail him, and Duono followed.

The Cylosite was greatly startled by their sudden appearance, and reached for his club. But Chrono extended his hand in greeting and said, "Hold! We are travelers from beyond the River Næus, from the country of Plateos; we come into this country seeking friendship and goodwill. We have come many miles and are weary, and we are looking for a place to rest. It would be good to break bread with friends. Shall we find hospitality among the folk of Cylos?"

The Cylosite examined them for a moment with his hand on his weapon, then smiled and took their hands. "Friends are always welcome in the country of Cylos. But I fear you will disappointed in our hospitality!" C'læod was his name, and when he had introduced himself, he added, "I am surprised to find strangers in this pitiable land! What ill occasion betrays you to this country?"

Chrono replied, "I come to this land seeking labors, to forget troubles I leave behind, that perhaps the name of Chrono will be spoken of in honor among folk I do not yet know. And this my companion is Duono, who has come willingly to join my quest."

C'læod bowed to them both. "Labor we have in plentiful supply!" he said. "The reputation you must find for yourself. But come if you will." He held up the small bird which he had caught, and shrugged at it. "Perhaps we will have enough for soup to share with strangers."

"We have provender enough," Chrono said. "But a roof over our heads and a warm fire for the night would be welcome. We shall repay your hospitality double, if fate is in any way kind to us."

"Then by all means join me. You and your provender shall be welcome in my house!"

As he turned to continue on the trail towards his village C'læod warned them, saying, "We must go stealthily on our way, for there is a Giant in this neighborhood. But I hardly have need to warn you, who appear as if by magic from out of the dark! Your own skills in stealth appear to be greater even than my own. Not that I boast, but I am yet alive, which is more than could be said for many in this country."

So Chrono and Duono followed after C'læod the Cylosite, who led them to his village.

This village was called Këuca,[14] but even in good times it would have impressed few: in those days most of the Cylosites of Batack lived in small settlements of round houses, drafty things built of vertical posts and roofed with conical domes of thatch which they gleaned from the leaves of the forest. The settlements of Chrono's homeland would have seemed a luxury in comparison. Nevertheless they had always lived comfortably, for the forest in that country was rich with all the things which that folk needed. What little the forest could not provide, they gained in barter with their neighbors, for the forest provided fruit and stock enough to trade. The Cylosites were skilled in leathercraft, in beadwork, in works of bone and ivory, and in medicaments, such things as were in demand among their neighbors.

But C'læod brought them to a village in disarray, and many of its houses lay in flattened ruin. Even at that late hour many were busy with raising fallen

14 The name means "a pleasant place."

timbers or thatching roofs. C'læod stopped at the entrance to the clearing and said, "I must apologize for the appearance of our village, for the Giant has done some remodeling of late. If we are fortunate, I shall still have a roof this evening under which you may find rest."

Seeing the destruction, Duono at last said, "I fear we have been brash in asking for your hospitality!"

C'læod merely smiled and said, "It is an honor to welcome guests, and all the more so when those guests bring their own provisions! Come to my house, and let us see if it stands this evening."

As they passed through the open space of the precincts the neighbors and kinsmen of C'læod looked up in surprise at the two visitors who followed him: visitors were rare in that remote country in the dark of the woods. The village was small, and soon all had been introduced to Chrono and Duono.

As the sky grew dark overhead, a small party was busy building a bonfire in a firepit at the center of the clearing, and they said to Chrono, "When you have rested and eaten, come out to join us at the fire this evening! We would relish any news you might bring from beyond our borders, and we shall sing for you whatever songs are left in our hearts."

So Chrono and Duono entered the house of C'læod, and they shared from their own provender with C'læod and his family. Though they carried nothing but travel rations, yet C'læod's mate Gretë gratefully accepted their gift as if it were sumptuous fare, and prepared a warm meal for all. When all had eaten she brought out a heap of plush blankets from a great chest, to prepare bedding for their guests. "We are lucky," she said, "For as yet our house has not been plundered. Many there are in this village who have no blankets of their own, but must borrow from friends and neighbors. Such are the trials of these days."

Duono said, "The troubles caused by this Giant seem beyond bearing. Do all your folk suffer such oppression?"

C'læod replied. "Not all, but many settlements and villages of this region. But come to the fire, and you shall have answers to all your questions."

When the children had been put to bed, C'læod and Gretë went out to the fire, followed by Chrono and Duono. There all the villagers sat in a circle warming themselves (for the air was chill in the lateness of autumn), while in the trees round about the village sentinels kept watch for any sign of the Giant. Among that group were the respected elders of the village, along with their chief, whom all called simply "the Counselor."

After all had satisfied themselves with questioning the strangers concerning the world beyond their forest, Chrono at last said, "We are grateful for your hospitality, but it is clear your village and your folk have suffered a ruinous attack. I shall gladly add my arm to the labor of rebuilding what has been ruined. For the accomplishment of such honorable deeds is the whole purpose of my sojourning."

C'læod the host of Chrono then spoke, saying, "For such an offer we thank you. Though none will turn you down, yet I fear your labor shall be to little effect. Whatever you build, the Giant will likely restore to ruin before the tracks of your feet have grown cold on the earth."

The Counselor then said to Chrono and Duono, "C'læod speaks wryly, but his words do not lie far from the truth. This Giant has struck our folk and our village repeatedly, and without compunction. If we rebuild, it strikes again. If we gather food, it steals again. If we walk openly in the forest to hunt, it attacks again. Our situation here has become dire, for winter approaches, and we have few stores to see us through."

Then Chrono said, "Even Giants have yet an ember of reason glowing deep within, for they are the children of Terumani yet, though corrupted and mingled with the blood of mortal creature. Perhaps by threat of arms you might compel it to leave this place, for even Giants are known to keep their oaths. When once they have been taught to fear, they do not easily forget."[15]

C'læod laughed at this statement and said, "Likewise we might simply compel the coming snows to pass us by, that we might have no fear of winter!"

The elders wagged their heads and said, "Seven times have our warriors appealed to this Giant, standing it off with boldness of arms, and seven times has it merely scoffed at our demands, and rampaged among us, so that good folk have been broken: and some have not returned to house and kin."

The Counselor said, "But we cannot hold out forever, keeping a watch on this Giant, and hiding ourselves in the forest whenever it comes out to pillage. Our kin in the west, by the shores of the Pindus, have counseled us that we should abandon our houses in the forest and join them in their country: but the forest is all we know. We would not survive without it. The wood and its riches have been our living for generations, and we will wither away if we cannot forage as is our wont."

At this another of the company spoke, saying, "Our neighbors in the village of Marrenech have even asked us to join them in cutting and burning a swath around our country, to clear an open space around our villages, that they may stand as islands in the center: so at least the Giant must face us in the open should it attack. Perhaps without the forest to hide in, it will leave us and our storehouses alone."

The wife of C'læod agreed with this plan, saying, "It is better than fleeing to the Pindus, for at least we would yet be near to our forest."

Now Chrono had always honored the terumani, and the more so since he had come to love the sea-nymph Ahten, so he was astonished at this suggestion. Therefore he said, "Such a plan seems extreme and rash! Do you not

---

15 The Homadalan compiler of these tales knew this well, for the Giants of Batack which had once laid waste to Homadal had kept their oath never to return, for generations after their defeat at the Battle of Adelanto.

know the nymphs or sprights that guard your wood? Before such destruction you would do well to seek their counsel. It would be unwise to betray the very protectors of the forest you love!"

The Counselor said, "Seek counsel of sprights? The sprights we fear, for they haunt our dreams and bring terror to us!" Such was the belief of that clan, for many in those times feared the næads and dræads just as Chrono's clan feared the Seafolk.

C'læod however answered, "Nevertheless we would accept aid from any quarter. If even the wolves and drakes might ally themselves with us, we would not turn them away. But the sprights have also fled, I do not doubt. The Giant is wanton, and attacks all that it sees. Many fair groves has it ruined already with its vileness."

Duono then said, "I know a little of Giants, for I have traveled the woods of Batack often, and have learned whatever lore there is on that foul folk. Giants love the dark of the forest, but they will come out into the sun to pillage. To burn your woods would be foolish. You would need to burn a swath from here to the horizon to deter it from its ravenings."

Chrono said, "You must not destroy the woods you depend on. You would be worse off than if the Giant had merely robbed you of your labor."

C'læod said, "So we will starve if we do aught, and we will starve if we do naught. Why, it seems all our options lead to starvation."

Then Chrono said, "If the Giant cannot be daunted by threats, then it must be driven from this country altogether."

At this even the strong and stalwart of the village laughed, and said, "How might this be? None among us has ever so much as bruised the skin of this monster. We cannot even draw near it. Not a few have been brought to a sorrowful end by its ravings: it can crush our kind with the flick of a finger."

Chrono said, "The Giants are large and powerful, but they are stupid." Now Chrono had left his home to perform acts of valor, and this adversity seemed to him an opportunity. "I shall go out against it myself, and I shall contrive a means to drive it off," he declared. "This venture I choose willingly, trusting to fate; for life is not sweet to me, and I shall lose nothing by the risk."

But Duono said, "And I, who value your life more than you do yourself, shall go with you! There must be someone included in this endeavor who has an interest in your safety."

At this the strong among the folk of the village were ashamed, and they said, "We cannot allow a stranger, and a son of Plateos at that, to go against a Giant on our behalf, alone, to his own undoing. We shall choose from among us those who are willing to go, taking our own lives into our hands, if you will lead us."

Chrono replied, "No! I dare not risk leading any to their demise! We are guests among you. I cannot ask any other to join me. Give me time alone to consider a plan, and we shall choose a course of discretion."

The warriors of the village, however, were abashed by the courage of Chrono and Duono, and were impatient to prove their own valor. So early the following morning they gathered in secret before the village rose up from sleep, and said among themselves, "Shall we let these strangers in our midst, and honored guests at that, face danger while we cower at home, and flee whenever this Giant appears? Let us take up arms at once, and go out against it ourselves. It is our own duty to save our village. And we shall preserve our own honor in the bargain."

This seemed good to them all, so when they had gathered up their weapons and armor, they slipped stealthily into the forest to seek out the Giant.

C'læod, however, had also arisen early to fetch water for his house, and he chanced upon the party as they were departing into the forest. They had excluded C'læod from their council, knowing that Chrono and Duono were guests in his house, so C'læod asked what deed they were about. But they evaded him and hurried away without answering.

C'læod rushed back at once to his place, and roused Chrono, and reported to him what he had seen. Then he said, "While your promise was given with good intentions, I fear it has provoked our warriors to foolishness. They are rushing into battle without a plan."

So Chrono roused Duono, and said, "We must hurry if we hope to prevent disaster. If harm should befall any of their party, the blame will rest on my own head."

So gathering up their arms, and taking C'læod with them, they rushed out and into the woods, following the trail which the warriors had taken.

Duono was a skilled trail-master, more skilled than many of his day (and in those days there were many skilled trail-masters). So he was able to follow the signs of their passing, despite the earliness of the hour and the dimness of the light. Nevertheless, the warriors of Këuca had a sizable lead, and they had rushed with purpose deep into the forest. It was only with great difficulty that Chrono's party kept up with them at all, and it proved impossible to head them off.

The warriors for their part traveled briskly with their goal before their minds' eyes. There was a certain cave a two hour's trek into the forest: a great hollow beneath the arched overhang of a sandstone cliff, overlooking a steep, wooded glen. The rim of the arch dripped constantly with water from a seam in the cliffside, which formed a musical curtain before the cave, drizzling onto a slippery stone shelf that descended from the hollow, down to a stream in the valley. This hollow they called Ash Cave, for in better days folk had often camped in that spot, for many generations, until the ash and cinders of their fires had grown into a great mound at the back of the hollow.

But in recent months the spot reeked, and had been befouled; and the footprints of the Giant had been found all about the place. It was clear that the Giant used it as a redoubt.

Straight to this scene went the warriors of Këuca, swollen with anger and eager to prove their mettle.

So it was that they came to the place still early in the day, before the Giant had fully roused, and their scouts found it slumbering in the hollow behind the veil of the waters.

The leader of that company divided them into three parties, and whispered, "The Giant can only attack one of us at a time. We shall have the advantage if we assault the nest from three sides. Each of you shall carry firebrands, and we shall corral the brute with fire: for Giants have no mastery of fire, and they fear it."

With this plan they split up and quietly took their places before the face of the cliff. Then after lighting their firebrands, at a sign from their commander they rushed the cave together.

The Giant was awakened by the smell of smoke. Rising from its resting place and spotting its pursuers it laughed a throaty laugh, and said, "Are the little folk of Cylos come to wake me? Come nearer, then, that we might have breakfast together!"

Then it unleashed a roar which made even the limbs of the trees to tremble, and it hefted its bludgeon from the floor of the cave, where it had been using it as a pillow. In a furor, it charged the first company to pass beyond the dripping waters, howling lustily. The warriors raised their firebrands to defend themselves, but the Giant merely batted at them with its club, knocking the torches to the ground, where they sputtered out on the wet stone.

The company raised their spears, and did not withdraw. The two remaining parties appeared, rushing at the Giant from three sides at once, hoping to wound it mortally in a sudden assault.

For a moment the Giant wavered, and the warriors of Këuca took courage. But when it saw that it was surrounded, it backed to the wall of the cave and swung its club about wildly, driving its attackers into huddles at the edges of the hollow. Then it waded into the throng, heedless of the points of their spears or the sputtering flames of their wet firebrands.

It was at this moment that Chrono and his companions at last caught up to the warriors. "We are too late!" Duono cried, when they heard the sounds of battle before them.

"Too late to prevent the battle, perhaps," said Chrono, "But not too late to lend aid, hopeless though it might be."

So he rushed to join the warriors, followed by Duono and C'læod.

But the assault went poorly. The Giant rampaged, and the club of the Giant swung among them like a scythe among the standing grain. Many of that company fell before it, and fled or were pulled from the fray by their mates. Chrono stood his ground, caring nothing for his own safety, and strove to injure the brute, dodging the blows of the club as deftly as he could.

But in the end the leader of the warriors cried out for retreat. Then Duono restrained Chrono and pulled him from the battle.

The Giant guffawed at their impotence and sat down beneath the arch of the cave deriding them. The leader of the company gathered his folk on the trail, at some distance from the cave, and sat dejected as they assessed their condition.

To Chrono he said, "We are honored by your valor and your effort, but we have failed, and our state is no better than had we remained at home. Let us return and nurse our wounds." But Chrono's mind was black with despair, knowing that but for his words the battle would never have taken place.

The company of Këuca bound up what wounds they could, and in a dark frame of mind they set their sights on the pathways back to Këuca, trudging and limping solemnly. The Giant had fought terribly, and many were wounded. Two of that company had been thrown and crushed, and were broken, and borne back to Këuca on biers.

When they had returned to their village, Chrono sat down wretchedly and mourned the fallen, saying,

"Woe, for friends   who followed to fight,
Whom I have ushered   to endings ill.
Better to balk,   abiding behind,
And live to look   for the light of morn,
Than follow a fool   to foul fortune
Now blameless blood   shall be my boon
To harmless hosts   who honored me.
So rather than reaping   recompense,
They suffer sorrows   I have sown,
And now by blood-bonds   am I bound."

The elders of Këuca, however, said, "Do not blame yourself, for these combatants have left this world honorably in defense of our village and our lives. Though we mourn them, we honor them also. And honor as well our guest who has joined us in this battle to no self-advantage."

But Chrono continued to brood over this turn of events. He sat all day within the house of C'læod and allowed none to approach him but Duono his companion.

Duono said to him at last, "You cannot hold yourself responsible for this disaster. These folk have taken on the challenge of their own volition, under the guidance of none but themselves."

"Nevertheless," Chrono replied, "I came here seeking to redeem my honor, and I have done nothing but bring further shame on my own head."

"Then let us win honor by helping these folk to rebuild their homes and survive the winter. I deem that this task shall be monumental enough."

"Such a deed is worthy of praise, but it does not repay the debt I now owe this folk."

Duono shook his head sadly. "You owe no debt. None shall seek to exact any dues from you for what has happened."

Chrono swore, however, "I promised that I myself would drive this Giant from their land. That burden is mine, for I have shouldered it."

"You cannot do what is impossible," Duono said.

"Then I shall do what I can, for I have sworn it," he said. He fingered the pearl necklace which Ahten had given him as the token of her own oath. "An oath is sacred."

He fell silent suddenly, for at this expression an idea had struck him. "I may have a shadow of a plan," he said to Duono tentatively. "Leave me in peace for a spell while I consider it."

The following morning Chrono arose early, and when he had roused Duono he said, "Can you find again the lair of this Giant? I need to have words with the brute."

Duono said, "I can. But can you assure me you will do nothing rash nor foolish?"

Chrono replied. "I am not rash. Time will tell whether or not I have been foolish."

So Duono rose also, and together they followed the pathways back to Ash Cave, where the Giant slept. When they had arrived at the shelf before the archway, Chrono told Duono to remain hidden in the woods. "I shall go forward and confront the creature alone, that it might hold me alone responsible for what I shall say."

Duono cautioned him once more, then Chrono stepped into the sunlight before the dripping water and hailed the Giant in a loud voice.

In a moment the brute appeared before them, a disparaging scowl darkening its face. At the sight of Chrono the Giant was startled, and it said with a sneer, "Hah! What's this? A child of Plateos in league with the puny Cylosites? Have your stubby friends[16] called you to protect them? But your bones shall break as easily as theirs!"

Chrono remained at a distance from the cave and said, "To break my bones you shall need to catch me, and I am not so easily caught. But either way, I've come to deliver you a warning and to make you a bargain."

The Giant laughed, and said, "A warning? Such big words from such a small runt."

---

16 The Cylosites were *stymphoi,* that is, one of the short Tribes of Soria, averaging about 4-5 feet in height. The Plateosites were generally at least a foot or more taller. It's not entirely certain, however, that at this earlier era the difference between the Tribes was so pronounced.

"You will like my offer! For I'm a reasonable sort, and I have respect for your ancient patrimony. It would not give me any pleasure to kill you if I can avoid such an end."

At this the Giant laughed him to derision. "Can I be frightened by the buzzing of a gnat? Consider again, for I shall have no displeasure over crushing you, little one."

"Fair enough! Then my bargain should be no gamble to you."

"I do not bargain with vermin of Sorios' line."

"The bargain is between you and me, and no other. If you can catch me and crush me, you have lost nothing. But if you see me again, perhaps it will be too late to bargain. So humor me first with your oath, then you may destroy me as you are able."

The Giant scowled. "Speak then, runt."

"My offer is simple. Only promise me this one thing. When I have you at my mercy, on your back and disarmed, will you then swear oath to depart from this place, and leave this folk, and never to bother them again?"

The Giant looked down on his opponent and whooped in laughter. Cursing Chrono it wheezed, "At the mercy of a stinking runt of Sorios?" Then jeering at him it said, "Of course! When that day comes I may as well depart this sorry earth completely!"

"There will be no need for that!" Chrono said. "Only swear that when that day comes you will leave this country for far and desolate places, far from the settlements of the Kindreds you despise, and leave be the folk of Cylos forever."

"I swear to that!" the Giant laughed. "But first I swear that I will crush your sorry body beneath my thumb!"

But Chrono was able to slip away and evade the attack. Before he disappeared, however, he called out from the woods, "Remember your oath. For I will return to exact it from you!"

He returned to Duono, and together they hastened on the paths back to Këuca. When they were a safe distance from the hearing of the Giant, Duono said to Chrono, "Surely you cannot trust the word of a Giant?"

Chrono replied, "I can, and I will. It is said that Giants will honor an oath, is it not?"

Duono nodded doubtfully. "So I've heard it said. But none I know has ever had opportunity to test it!"

"Ahten herself assured me that this is true, and they have that one redeeming trait. Her word will I trust with my life."

Duono then said, "I understand your strategy, but I do not see a means to its completion!"

Chrono winked. "Nor do I, as yet."

Duono shook his head. "Then let us hope you can devise a scheme shortly. Before haste makes you heedless."

When they returned to the village of Këuca, Chrono and Duono went a short way into the woods to ponder and plot, but the two of them together could not decide on any contrivance to bring about Chrono's object. Many plots were devised and discussed, but all were rejected as impractical, or impossible.

At last Chrono said, "Let us not despair. We shall contrive something. But for now let us rest our minds and return to the village."

They found the folk of the village beginning to gather around the firepit at the center of the clearing. C'læod found Chrono and Duono, and greeting them he said, "Tonight we must have a celebration on behalf of the souls who have been lost in battle. If you would be of help, come now and aid me: there is a task we must perform in preparation."

So they followed him into the woods. There C'læod looked about the ground intently, until he found a short stub of waxy, brown rope jutting out of the earth, as if rooted and growing in place. Then he handed them each a shovel[17] and said, "This is the place. Dig here. But dig carefully and gently, for there is something of value below the surface which we must not break!"

Unsure what they were searching for, they began to scrape away the earth around the rope, while C'læod held it taught and tugged. This rope had been treated with a wax or latex, and though it had clearly been buried for a long while, it had neither rotted nor frayed, and held strong. When they had dug some ways down into the loose soil, the spade of Chrono met something hard that rang when he struck it. "That is it!" whispered C'læod. "Dig carefully now until you have uncovered it."

So they worked around the area, and revealed at last a large ceramic pot, nearly the size of a cistern, tightly lidded and sealed. The rope was fastened in a loop around its flared neck, and with the help of Chrono and Duono, C'læod succeeded in drawing it from the earth.

Duono asked, "What is this mystery that we've retrieved? Clearly this is something of great value to be hidden so!"

C'læod answered, "One might call it precious: It is important to our ceremonies and celebrations. But that is not the reason we bury it in the earth. These jugs contain a libation which is the gift of the earth. "

He took a sharp knife and broke the seals, then he took a small wooden ladle from his vest and scooped a sample from the jar. "Try it," he insisted, and handed the ladle to Chrono.

Chrono sipped the fluid, and found it sweet, but pungent. At once he began to feel warm and pleasant, and his head soon began to swim.

"What do you call this drink? And from where do you get it?" Chrono asked.

---

17 This was most likely a large, hand-held scraper, either of stone or bone.

C'læod said, "It is called *judo*, and we derive it from the juice of a berry that grows in abundance in the summertime. We fill jars with the juice of this berry, and bury it beneath the earth. Then when it has fully aged and ripened we retrieve our troves, and the earth has turned it to *judo* for our pleasure."

Duono sampled it as well, and said, "It is like our wine, but stronger!"

"Many in the village prepare their own stores of *judo* in their own jars, but this trove has been reserved for celebration. It has aged for over a year, and will be especially ripe!"

C'læod took a sample himself, then smacked his lips, and put away his ladle. He winked at his companions and said, "Yes, it is ripe indeed! We must be heedful of how we partake, for it will act quickly and powerfully."

The pot of *judo* they hoisted and carried to the firepit.

When the day had passed into evening, the folk of Këuca gathered again around the firepit, and Chrono and Duono joined them in their ceremony. There they sat and sang solemn songs of tribute, and told tales and remembrances to ease their hearts. All present took ladles or cups, and partook of the judo.

Chrono and Duono imbibed freely. It wasn't long before Chrono's head began to swim, and a feeling of contentment overwhelmed him. Soon he wanted nothing more than to lie down and rest: There by the fireside he fell into a deep and restful slumber.

He did not wake until the following morning. He found himself on the bed[18] in the house of C'læod, for C'læod had borne him and Duono back to his own place. When C'læod saw his guests stirring he laughed and said, "I see you have at last rejoined the living. Perhaps you have underestimated the powers of *judo*?"

Chrono held his forehead and forced his eyes open. Several others were in the house of C'læod that morning, including the Counselor. "We became concerned for you and your companion." He nodded at Duono, who also began to stir. "We worried that perhaps your folk could not partake of *judo* and live."

Duono attempted to smile and said, "The drinks we have in our country are similar, but not so powerful. We merely have not learned to drink it, so it overcame us quickly."

At this word a thought came suddenly to Chrono, and he revived at once. "How much of this drink do you have?" he asked.

"Who knows?" C'læod shrugged. "Undoubtedly there are many gallons hidden about, for the Giant does not discover the pits where we bury them. Our food it has plundered, and we have nearly nothing left to eat, but our *judo* we have in plenty!"

"If I can convince you to part with it, it may save you this winter."

---

18 Undoubtedly simply a pile of furs and woven blankets.

The village Counselor shook his head, "It does not nourish: It will not help to see us through the coming scarcities."

C'læod winked, "Perhaps not, but it may help us to forget the miseries of our starvation."

"It may yet do more than that," said Chrono. "But I shall need a great quantity of it. Let us go aside and discuss my plan, and you may tell me whether it can be done."

Chrono and the elders of the village spent the remaining hours of the morning in planning, then C'læod and the village chief went about making preparations, while Chrono made one more trek to the cave where the Giant hid out.

When he had assured himself the Giant was at rest in the shadows, he called out to hail the brute.

The Giant hefted its club and came out to the shelf before the arch. When it saw Chrono it scowled down on him and said, "You have come to bother me again? Do you think to overpower me today? Or to run away again?"

Chrono called across to it, "I think today I shall run. But before I do, I must have a word with you. The folk among whom I dwell are starving, and must trade all they have left, in the hope of purchasing supplies to get them through the winter. For this mean state you are responsible."

"What is that to me? I care nothing if these little vermin perish in the winter."

"I come to warn you to leave them be, for tomorrow our folk will be traveling on the path which passes close by this cave, on the way to the crossroads, to meet with the Stegganese when they come by. I know how you love to attack and plunder, and despoil them of their goods. But should you try to interfere this time, I will thwart you."

The Giant merely wagged its head at Chrono's naivety, and said, "I thank you for the warning. You have done me a service."

Chrono said, "You have been warned. Remember your oath." Then he disappeared once more into the woods.

The next day the folk of Këuca prepared a merchant caravan, to head into the woods eastward. A journey of several hours in that direction would bring them to a trade route which at times would be frequented by merchants from the Tribe of Steggan. Their porters loaded themselves with many great pots and jars of *judo*: all that they could spare, and more. They also loaded packs with other such goods as might be traded.

Then the leader of that caravan looked sadly on the stock they had gathered and said, "I regret the *judo*. We should have made good use of it."

The Counselor shrugged. "It is for a greater good, if we survive the winter by its loss. We still have a few small stocks to share, and we can make more next summer."

Chrono said, "Let us do as we have planned, and if fortune is with us, all shall end well."

When all was in order, the caravan set forth cautiously into the forest. With them went both Chrono and Duono. The trail wended eastward through dense forest, and for much of the route thickets and undergrowth made it impossible to watch for approaching danger. It would pass close by the side path to Ash Cave where the Giant sojourned, so all in that party were nervous, watching over their shoulders at all times. Duono led the way stealthily, a short distance ahead of the troop, his senses heightened for any hint of menace.

Due to the heaviness of their loads and the closeness of the woods the going was slow, so it was several hours before they came near to Ash Cave. All in the caravan were weary and flustered when Duono brought word at last, whispering, "The Giant is on its way. It will be here shortly. Do as we planned. And above all save your own lives."

Chrono and Duono then disappeared into the forest to watch for the Giant.

As Duono had predicted, scant minutes had passed before the sound of the monster crashing among the trees became clear to all. The caravan stopped in their tracks. In a moment the leader of that company shouted out, so all could hear, "The Giant! The Giant is among us! Save yourselves!"

So all dropped their loads, every one of them, and pelted into the depths of the forest to escape.

The Giant appeared on the trail, and laughed in derision. For it found a great load of plunder lying scattered about on the path, all of it within a pleasant jaunt of its hideout. "Foolish runts!" it grunted vauntingly. Then it began to gather up the goods of the caravan, everything they had carried with them to bring to the trading post. Every last jug, pot and bundle it ferried back to its cave and piled into a heap against the wall.

"I have done well, today, at no expense of labor! Let us see what these witless clods have brought for me."

The Giant began to rummage among the pots and bundles it had gathered, laughing at each acquisition as if it were a birthday gift. It was not long before it picked up one of the judo jars, and examined it curiously. Pursing its lips thoughtfully (if any expression of a Giant can be described as thoughtful) with one hulking finger it broke the seal to see what was within.

It scowled for a moment when it saw the juice, then sniffed to learn whether it might be good to drink. It perked up at the aroma of the *judo*, for it was piquant and appealing: so it raised the jar to its lips and took a sip.

At once its eyes lit up, and it said, "Where have the stinking runts been hiding this?" It quickly swallowed down the rest of the contents. Without hesitation it cast about for another jar, and broke it open as well. One after another, then, it picked up and opened each and every jar, and gulped down the contents of every one, for Giants have no restraint or forethought on such matters. They will heedlessly glut themselves at every opportunity.

It soon grew bleary-eyed, then it began stumbling about the precinct of the cave unsteadily, babbling and laughing incoherently, before its club dropped from its hand with a resounding thud. It sat down indecorously in the water running down the slick stone shelf before the cave, and held its wobbling head in its hand. At last it dropped to the ground and curled up: it passed out, the waters of the springs from the cliffside dribbling unceremoniously onto its head and neck.

Chrono and Duono had been hiding in the woods nearby, watching all this in secret. When they saw that the Giant had laid itself down to sleep, they approached it carefully. It made no motion at all, besides snoring and drooling into the stream of water which ran down from the cave. Chrono kicked the club of the brute out of reach, then he approached the creature's head, and squatted down to peer into its unseeing eye.

"It would appear the *judo* has done the trick that a host of warriors could not. Let us take care of our business, before this beast awakens."

Among the goods that the Giant had stolen from the caravan was a great length of stout rope. Duono retrieved it from the heap at the back of the cave, and said, "How handy is this? The beast has prepared its own undoing for us!"

So Chrono and Duono laid hold of the rope, and they bound the Giant strictly, hand and foot, and bound its arms to its sides. Then with great effort they succeeded in rolling the brute onto its back, away from the dripping waters. When they had wedged stakes solidly into the fissures and cracks of the rock, they tied it down so that it could not so much as lift a leg or move an arm.

All this while, the Giant lay slumbering peacefully, with a contented smile on its lips, for the effects of the *judo* had not worn off, and would not for several hours yet.

When all was in readiness, Chrono sent Duono away: then he took his own spear in his hand, and he sat down upon the chest of the monster to wait.

The wait was long, but at last the Giant stirred, and its eyes fluttered. Chrono leapt at once to his feet, and standing on the chest of the brute, he placed the point of his spear onto its neck, and said, "Wake from your slumber! As you see, I have upheld my half of our bargain!"

The Giant woke up at once in a rage, and though it squirmed and strained, it found it could not move a muscle in defense, while Chrono its enemy stood above it with death at its throat. "What have you done?" the creature roared.

Chrono smiled placidly and said, "I have done little. You have taken care of the details. I knew you would never resist plundering a party of traders on the trail, and so close to your hideout, at that! So my company came along as if to trade: but I warned my folk, and they were prepared to drop everything they carried as soon as you appeared. For you should know, the sound of a Giant in the forest cannot be hidden. Duono my traveling companion is a trail-master of great skill, and his ears are like those of the bat. Nothing escapes his notice: certainly not the blundering of a monster in the woods!

"I was also confident that you would neither know, nor care, that the caravans of the Stegganese would never come this far into Batack so late in the year. So you see, the whole task of our caravan was only to bring you these offerings—which you have so heartily relished—and then to escape with their lives. I do hope you have enjoyed the revelry we prepared for you! Although I suspect you were not quite prepared for the headiness of the drink, having never tasted the pleasures of *judo* before."

The Giant moaned and looked down at the ropes which bound it. "But what is the meaning of all this?"

"I have done as I swore to do. I have you at my mercy, on your back beneath my feet, and unarmed. There lies your club," He nodded to the side where the club lay out of reach. "Fetch it if you will, and defend yourself."

The Giant gritted its teeth and strained at its bindings, but to no avail. Chrono said, "Be careful now, for you are in my power. I have no desire to slay you, but I will do so without hesitation if you do not comply. Remember, you swore me an oath, and I swore to spare your life under those terms."

The Giant snarled a growl of despair, and said, "What is it you want, you filthy dog?"

"Only what we agreed upon. That when you found yourself at my mercy, you would swear to leave this place forever, and never to disturb the folk of Cylos again."

Then that great and boastful beast grumbled like a petulant child, and it sued for mercy, saying, "I have so sworn, and I cannot recant. Only let me go, and I shall flee far to the east, away from this place, never to return! By the body of Erescal sworn!"

Now whether it is because some shred of honor yet remains hidden in the darkness of their corrupted souls; or whether it is only that a secret dread of the Ádolthi constrains them, yet it is true that the Giants will abide by an oath. Whatever the cause, this one virtue the Giants retain. So Chrono exacted his oath from the creature.

He then withdrew his spear, and leapt down from the chest of the monster. "I did not bargain for my own safety," he said, "so I will be leaving now. But I will cut free one arm for your sake. I shall leave a knife within your reach that you might free yourself. Then go and do as you have sworn, and we shall have no further argument with you!"

So Chrono withdrew from that place, but he and Duono watched in secret, for Duono doubted the creature's faithfulness. But the Giant did not dissemble. It got up from the ground, and when it had cut itself free from its bindings, it growled in disappointment: but it gathered its belongings and fled as it had sworn. It did not turn back.

When Chrono and Duono had repaired to Këuca, the folk of the caravan had already returned, and they gathered eagerly to discover how the plot had ended.

Chrono spoke to them exultantly. "I have kept my promise to you! The Giant has gone, and I trust it will not return. You may go back to Ash Cave at your pleasure, and recover all the goods you had borne on the trail. With the exception of the *judo*, that is: I'm afraid the Giant has disposed of that in its own way, though I promise you it has repented that choice!"

So it was that Chrono saved the folk of Këuca from the persecutions of the Giant of Batack. That foul brute never returned, and the Cylosites had peace at last. The folk of that village spread the tale to their neighbors, and all rejoiced that their country had been liberated from oppression.

In his heart Chrono gave thanks and honor to Ahten for this deliverance, for her vow had afforded him the clue by which he banished the brute from that land.

As for Chrono, his fame went out from that place into all the countryside round about. Then the name of Chrono was held in honor among the Cylosites, far and wide.

3. CHRONO AND THE BITTER WINTER

In the days when Chrono was estranged from his father, he dwelt for some time among the Cylosites who lived in the forest of Batack. He and his trail-master Duono had done them a great service, in that they had defeated and driven off a foul Giant, which had been despoiling that folk for many months, as is told in another tale.

For several weeks further the folk of that country had looked far and wide for any sign of the Giant. But it was nowhere to be found. All its haunts lay abandoned and forsaken, and no sign of its passing could be discerned. Indeed, the snows of winter had begun to dust the earth, and not so much as a footprint could be discovered. It became clear to all that the Giant had left the country and would not return, just as it had sworn oath.

Chrono and Duono therefore made ready to depart the village of Këuca, where they had been staying in the house of C'læod, that they might seek honor untinged in another place.

Winter was now full upon that country. These were the years of the Ice, when the winters were more harsh in all the countries of Soria. Throughout the country of the Cylosites the earth would freeze, the streams and ponds turn to ice, and even the great river Næus at times would freeze over from bank to bank. Ice now wrapped the limbs of many leafless trees. Many of the creatures of the wood would sleep until spring, and even the birds had left for better climes.

When the chieftain of Këuca, who was called the Counselor, observed that Chrono intended to leave, he thought to himself, "These strangers have accomplished deeds we were unable even to conceive. Perhaps they may yet save us from greater evils yet to come."

So he came to call at C'læod's house, and said to Chrono, "We thank you for all you have done, for our bane has been banished as you swore to do, and now we may live in peace. Would you leave now, when winter is on us, and we have no resources to pay you for this great boon? Would you leave so soon, with nothing to show for your labor?"

Chrono said, "We have asked nothing for our pains, and ask nothing still. If anything remains to be paid, it is our debt to you. It is because of my rash words that your own folk have suffered loss." The warriors of Këuca had indeed been provoked by the words of Chrono to go to battle alone against the Giant, and had suffered a tragic defeat.

The Counselor however said, "The pride of those warriors was the cause of their own trouble. You meant only to do good among our folk, and so you have done."

C'læod their host added, "Many lives have been saved by your artifice. Although I fear perhaps they have been saved only for the ravages of winter." Saying this he looked over his shoulder at the doorway of the house, for the bitter winds of winter were blowing in at the seams. In those days the Cylosites had not even proper doors for their homes in the woods, but merely hung the hide of an animal over the opening to keep out the weather.

"C'læod speaks the truth," the Counselor sighed. "Because of the long months of the Giant's ravening and pillaging, we have no stores. All we had gathered and harvested during the autumn months has been plundered and spoiled by the Giant. Our larders are empty. Many of our folk still have no houses of their own in which to take shelter. But if you must leave, do not worry on our behalf: we shall forage as best we can, though doubtless those of us who survive until spring shall all be somewhat thinner."

"So much greater, then, the reason for us to depart now, lest we burden you yet further," said Chrono.

"Only those who will not work are a burden," the Counselor said. "But you have completed the work you promised, and I see that you have no reason to stay. We are delivered from the Giant. Most of us shall likely live long enough at least to enjoy our freedom for a while."

C'læod smiled at the guile of his chief, and he winked at Chrono. "On the other hand," he said, "there is no reason for you to leave. What do you gain by striking out again?"

"We seek further labors and other honors, to amend for honors lost at home."

C'læod then said, "Well, if it is labor you seek, why not stay and labor with us? Though it remains to be seen whether such labor will bring you honor, or whether the shame of our poverty will cling to your backs."

"There is no shame in poverty," Chrono said. "Poverty with hard work is a greater honor than wealth lived in indolence."

The Counselor pretended to consider the question. As if he had just at that moment come up with the thought he said, "Hmm. Your wit and your good fortune have proven to be uncommon. Perhaps a means might be devised to save us from starvation, as you saved us from the Giant? Would that not be a work worthy of great honor?"

Chrono then went aside with his trail-master and companion Duono, and said, "It would appear the folk of this village are expecting some great wonder from us. A Giant I can face, and have no fear of death, for life is not sweet to me. But how can I conjure bread from snow and ice? I have no idea how to save a village from starvation!"

Duono said, "Nevertheless you have proven resourceful and clever. Perhaps some opportunity shall present itself. Even if not, there is no shame in staying to aid hosts who have been kind and generous despite their poverty."

So Chrono conceded, and chose to remain at Këuca.

A month passed, and then another, while the snows of winter grew deeper on the frozen forest floor. Chrono and Duono went into the country round about along with the hunters and foragers of Këuca. Though they gathered all they could find, there was little to glean from the hard earth and the snow-mantled forest. The season of fruit and harvest was long past. The beechnut and hazelnut trees were bare, and even the pinecones were stripped and empty. The ground was a rock too hard for parsnip or turnip. The forest in the winter of those days was as barren as a desert.

From time to time the hunters were able to bring down a rabbit or net a small bird. But most of the forest's goods had been spoiled or eaten by the creatures of the woods.

The meals of the folk of Këuca grew sparser, and the folk of that village grew ever thinner; all began to fear that debility and death would haunt them long before spring came to relieve them.

Yet in all this time no idea came to Chrono, nor to Duono, that might bring deliverance from the famine.

At last an evening came when Chrono and Duono were sharing a meager meal of broth in the house of C'læod, and Gretë the wife of C'læod scrutinized them. Wagging her head she said, "When you arrived in this place you were both stronger and better fed than most of our folk. But now look at yourselves! You begin to grow as thin as we."

C'læod agreed. "Perhaps the time has come for you to flee this place, in spite of the expectations of our chief."

Chrono said, "We would lose all honor if we saved ourselves while leaving friends behind in dire distress. Why not come on the road yourselves, you and your village, and we shall all seek aid together in a richer land?"

Gretë shook her head. "Where would we go? Who would receive so many, coming upon them destitute, with no provisions of their own, in the midst of the barren winter?"

Duono said, "Would it not be better to go on the trail seeking aid than to remain here and starve?"

C'læod laughed. "Imagine that! A whole village together on the trails, with no provisions for an extended journey!"

Gretë added, "And do not forget that we had been starved by the Giant for months before the winter even set upon us. Our folk are weakened by months of deprivation. If you would have us camp in the open in the chill of winter without our homes for shelter, why, it is the same as wishing hardship and death upon us!"

C'læod said, "I fear this village has chosen to survive together, aiding one another as best we can. Although," he shrugged, "we are as likely to perish together as to survive together."

Duono said to Chrono, "I will go where you go. Shall we choose the path of safety, or of sacrifice?"

Chrono said, "I shall certainly not sneak away like some craven. I did not banish a Giant only to deliver its victims over to starvation."

"But what more can we do?" Duono asked.

"Let us take to the trails tomorrow. But not to find escape for ourselves. Let us go south, to the villages and settlements beyond this country, where the Giant did not prey. It may be we can find some folk with supplies to spare, who will be willing to send aid out of mercy."

As no better plan presented itself, early the next morning Chrono and Duono packed what they could spare for an excursion of several days, and they went out from Këuca on southward trails.

After a day's travel they at last had gotten free of the ruination of the Giant. Early the following morning they sought out a large and prosperous village of the Cylosites, and finding the chieftain, they explained their need.

"We ask nothing for ourselves," Chrono said. "But if the gathering and harvesting have been good to you this year, we ask on behalf of the folk of Këuca that you might take a collection, and send relief. We shall gladly lead your company to the place. They will work doubly hard to repay you in kind when times and fortunes have changed. For the Giant has been banished, and next summer's blessings will doubtless bring much fruit and much enterprise."

But the chief of that place took counsel with the elders, and replied, "There are still months of winter ahead of us, and we must be cautious with what we have laid up." Nevertheless they withdrew from their larders a small offering of dried meat and turnips, and presented them to Chrono. "We would not have you think us hard of heart against our neighbors. But this is truly all we can spare."

Chrono thanked them for their generosity, and departed that place.

Duono looked at the goods they had received and said, "While I do not wish to begrudge their kindness, this shall do nothing to alleviate the hunger of a village. We shall have to go to very many such places to gain enough to do us good."

Chrono, too, sighed. "If none will come with us to Këuca, we have failed. We two alone cannot carry enough to accomplish our end."

From that point on, at each village they entered, they sought out the elders or chieftain of that place, and told them their mission.

They found the situation much the same in the next village they came to, and the one after that. None would send out a relief party, for all that folk feared the long winters of those days. Chrono and Duono packed what they could, and built a sledge to haul it themselves back to Këuca.

Chrono shook his head. "It is meager, and our mission has failed."

Duono said, "But it is better than nothing at all. With this we shall eke out sustenance for a week, at least, while our own hunters continue to gather what they may."

"And what then? Shall we go out again, yet even further, in the hopes of more charity?"

"Perhaps that is all we can hope for. But it is still a measure of hope."

Chrono grew morose. "Let us at least bring what we have received back to Këuca at once. The folk await our return. But I fear they will be disappointed."

So they took again the trails to the north.

They had been on the trails for several days, and it would take days to return, burdened now with the hauling of a sledge. On the third day of the journey an impenetrable layer of clouds drifted overhead and darkened the sky. Soon a heavy snow began to fall, swirling about in the breezes beneath the trees. The ground, already layered with a crisp icing, began to pile over with a deepening blanket that obscured the path.

All that day the snow continued as they walked. Had Chrono been alone and not with his trail-master Duono, even he might have become lost along the way.

Now as luck would have it, when they were yet a distance from Këuca, an hour or so from that village, a set of great footprints appeared in the snow, crossing their path, trailing off among the trees to the northwest. Each print was a cubit in length, and churned the snow deeply.

Chrono stopped short and studied them. "What do you make of these?" he asked Duono. "What sort of creature has passed by?"

Duono did not hesitate. "These appear to be the marks of a *baghamôt*, the ground sloth of Batack. They are still fresh. It seems to have passed this spot less than an hour ago."

Chrono had never before encountered one of those beasts, but he knew of them by reputation, and knew them to be large and meaty monsters of the forest. "If we were to take one of these down in the hunt," he said, "we could provide enough meat to feed our folk for a month. Perhaps more if it were used prudently."

"A *baghamôt* is vast, and armed with great claws," Duono warned. It would take a team of hunters to bring one down, and yet more to dress the kill and carry the meat back to the village. We cannot do this without help."

Chrono looked up at the sky. "It would take hours to bring a party back to this place. The snow continues to fall. If we do not follow the trail now, it will soon be covered with new fallen snow, and we might lose it completely."

"What else can be done?"

Chrono said, "You might hurry on ahead to the village. Leave the sledge for now, that you might make all haste. I will trail the sloth, and if I can catch up with it I will attempt to stop it, or turn it back towards the village. Either way, when you have raised a party of hunters, return as quickly as you can and follow me. I will mark my trail as I go."

Duono agreed to this plan, but he said, "Do nothing rash before I return. It is too large for you to take on alone!" Then off he rushed on the path towards Këuca.

Chrono for his part hurriedly set off on the trail of the sloth. Although marking his trail slowed him down, he broke twigs and branches to point the way, so Duono would be able to follow even if the deepening snow covered his tracks. He knew he would certainly be alone for hours, and perhaps into the evening before help could arrive.

At first the going was easy: the trail of the sloth was fresh, the prints deep, and the creature had followed a straight course over easy country, stopping seldom to forage. But the longer he trailed the beast, the more difficult the going. The path of the creature began to wind about, so that Chrono soon lost all sense of how far he had come from his own path, nor in which direction it was likely to lie. When he thought the going could get no worse, the trail led into a mass of brambles; these had not slowed down his quarry one bit, but they caught and tore at Chrono's clothing and scratched his arms miserably. Chrono lost much time in fighting his way through, but there was no other way around.

Meanwhile the snow continued to drift down all that day, and the tracks became ever more difficult to read.

The light eventually began to give out, and the dim gray of daylight faded into the gloaming of evening. Chrono stopped to listen to the sounds of the forest, hoping to hear some sign of Duono and his party coming to aid him, for many hours had passed since they had parted ways. But there were no sounds to be heard but the caterwauling of some distant creature on the prowl. The snow smothered all other sounds. Not even the twitter of a bird could be discerned in that lonely place.

At last the trail of the sloth, faint as it was, led down a steep embankment, down to a frozen brook at the bottom of a cleft in the hills. The sloth appeared to have slid down into this cleft, and broken through the ice to drink from a pool. But where it had clambered back out Chrono could not discover. He could find no further trace of footprints. Whether it had come out at the same spot it went in, or had traveled on along the stream bed Chrono could not guess.

Whether it had climbed out on the far side of the cleft, or had returned to the same bank it had started from, he could not tell. He exhausted himself scrambling up and out of the cleft time and again, hoping to find any sign of its passing: first in one spot then in another; first on this bank, then on the other; first upstream, and then downstream.

The dark deepened into the gloom of night. Clouds still veiled the sky and hid the light of the moon, and only the blue glow of the fresh snow could be seen.

"It is no use," Chrono said. "I have lost the trail, and I myself am lost and alone in the forest. No aid will come to me tonight. I shall have to make the best of it."

Chrono had learned much from Duono, and he had soon built himself a shelter of packed snow against the night breezes, and had managed a small fire to warm his hands. He bundled himself as best he could, and fell into a fitful sleep sitting upright against the slope of the embankment.

As soon as the sky had brightened in the morning, Chrono arose, examined his situation, and said, "It is clear there is no longer a trail to follow. The new snow has covered all. I would do best to head back for the trail I departed yesterday. But in which direction does it lie?"

When he had pondered this question for some time, he chose at last to follow the course of the brook downhill. There was a large stream which ran close by Këuca, known to the folk of that village as Camp Creek, and he hoped this brook might converge into that larger stream. He might then follow Camp Creek uphill and return to Këuca.

Chrono followed the course of the little brook downhill for some ways, scrambling along its stoney and ice-slick bed. After some time it became clear that the brook was veering off sharply westward. Chrono stopped and pondered. "I may not know where I am," he said to himself, "but I do not see how Camp Creek could run westward of my course!"

He continued on a bit further, hoping the course of the brook would shift again, but it continued westward. Chrono was on the verge of turning around and returning upstream, when the cleft he followed came to sudden end, and the forest opened suddenly before his pathway.

Now it so happened that Këuca was not far from the great lake Egano.

There at his feet lay the waters of that vast lake. Now Egano is greatest of all the lakes in the land of Soria, so that the far shore may not be seen beyond its horizon.[19] So great was that water that it had not yet frozen over in the

---

19 The so-called Sea of Misapec to the west was considerably larger than Egano. On early maps, however, the body is shown much smaller, and it's possible the lake was indeed less extensive in earlier ages. Or it may have been disregarded in this context, as it was a landlocked saltwater sea.

chill of winter, and indeed in many years the ice never covered it from shore to shore, even in the cold winters of that cold age.

In those days the forest of Batack had come to encircle the whole of the lake, and bare-limbed trees crowded the shore, clutching the rocky banks with sprawling black claws and stretching scraggly arms over the lapping waters. The lake spread before Chrono like a vast, gray mirror: a smooth plain of peace in the heart of the wild, fringed with the hoary fleece of Batack stretching beyond vision to the far horizons.

Chrono knew of Egano, as did all in that country, but in those ancient days few trails passed by its shores. When he had departed his home in the country of Plateos he had taken the settled pathways through the open hill country of Lodbarria on his way to the Fords of Dunar, and thus he had never seen the lake. The great waters astonished him, and for a moment he stood wondering if he beheld the Sea itself: then all the pangs of the forsaken Sea, and the loss of the sea-maiden, flooded his heart. Finding an open bank, he sat down beside the waters of the lake, and his woes overcame him, and he wept.

Then he raised a song to the lake, as once he had raised his voice in song to the Sea by the Rock of Ahten, saying:

"Great Egano, garnering glories,
I sulk and study, secrets sensing.
Wide waters wending away
To one web, oneness weaving,
A knitted network connecting all:
Convey my call, cries carrying,
Along the length of liquid links
From soul to Sea, spiriting sighs
To Mizgad's blessed, beloved brinks,
The confidante of Chrono's cares,
And holder of his hidden heart.

I learned to love at the lap of the Sea.
But pangs of pain replace those pleasures.
If former friendship finally fails
And soothing swells, once soul-sating,
Now rip and rend this riven wretch,
Whence then can Chrono cull compassion?"

When he had sat there a while singing seaward, he looked across the waves, and beheld an eldritch form rising up from the waters: and he froze aghast. It was dark of visage, with long hair of gray-blue, and regarded him from beneath glowering brows from beyond the waves. Beside that visage another form arose, like unto it, but fair and statuesque.

Chrono's spine tingled at their appearance, for they had the look of terumani, and none but a Trityn could arise from the depths in such a manner. Since the day he had departed the seas at Mizgad, and since his eyes had last beheld Ahten his beloved, he had not seen the form of teruman.

They approached the shore as if to confront him, and he could not read their mood. He felt vulnerable and small in their presence, but his curiosity compelled him to remain.

When they were still some distance from the shore they stopped and stood as stones in the midst of the waters, the waves breaking about their shoulders. The nymph spoke first. Her voice carried across the waves like an echo.

"Who art thou, Child of Sorios, that singeth to the waters of our realm with such sorrow and longing?"

Chrono did not hesitate to answer, for they spoke with authority. "I am called Chrono, a son of Marcanto of Plateos. I have come from a far country to this place, and do not know the names of the Tritynoi of Egano to honor you as you are owed."

The spright then answered, and his voice had the timbre of a trumpet. "That is no wonder, for the children of the earth do not know us nor honor us. We are Cornæos, and my mate Annæ; all the waters of this great lake are our domain."

Chrono bowed low and said, "I honor all the folk of sea and wave, for my heart is bound to the waters of the great Sea."

Then Annæ the nymph spoke again. "From our courses below as we passed nearby we heard the music of thy voice, and our hearts were enkindled at thy words. Could it be that we hear the voice of Chrono, the very child of Mizgad who loveth Ahten the sea-nymph, the daughter of Merten and Aviah?"

Chrono was astonished, and was struck dumb. But the nymph drew nearer, and repeated her query. So at last Chrono said, "I am. What do you know of me, næads of Egano?"

Cornæos answered him and said, "Thy story is known among the Seafolk, and related even among the næads of river and stream. Word passeth swiftly among the folk of the Sea, and hath reached even upriver to our dominion.[20] For Ahten is as a princess among her folk, and Merten her father a lord among that Kindred. It has been told, and the rumor spread throughout the realm of the næads, that the princess Ahten pines for a mortal of the Kindred of the Sorites, of the house of Plateos: Chrono by name. It is said that she hath declared to the chagrin of both her mother and her father that she will wed no

20 The tales do not make clear if this is the first winter after Chrono left home in exile, or some other winter in later years. Minimally 3-4 months would have passed since he had departed from Ahten, which may have been enough time for his tale to spread.

other, and spurns the suitors of her own folk, out of devotion to his memory, though she can never join with him, nor he with her."

"All this is true!" Chrono declared. "But I am astonished to hear my tale told in such a distant place!"

"As we are astonished to find thee here in the flesh, as if plucked living from a tale of far-off waters."

Then said Annæ the nymph, "And what of thee, Chrono of Mizgad? Has thine own fate proven less forlorn than that of Ahten?"

"No, for I myself will not take a wife from among the daughters of the dry land, for love of the maid of the Sea, and I am estranged from my own father's house in shame. I wander the earth and cannot rest."

"Alas then for thee, and alas for Ahten. Your tale is a sad one."

Cornæos said, "If thou wilt, we shall put forth word for thee, and this word traveling through the kindreds of the waters shall reach her anon. Thus she shall know at least that thou livest, and pinest for her as she pineth after thee. Such tidings will do her heart good."

Then Chrono said, "For such kindness I thank you. But your word must be swift indeed, or it may reach the daughter of Merten too late. For whether I shall yet live by the coming of spring is far from certain."

"What can be the meaning of such dark words?!" said Annæ the nymph.

"I would not burden the lords of Egano with my own woes," Chrono said. "Whether I live or perish is of little note. I seek only a path back to the village of Këuca, where I may take comfort among friends during our trials."

"We might help you with that," said Cornæos "There is a trail a short distance from this spot, which leads back through the forest and winds to the village you name. We know it, for the folk of that village come betimes to cast for fish in these waters."

Annæ said, "Come and walk with us, and we shall take you to the trailhead. But you must tell us your story as we walk! It may surprise you to learn that there are many among my kindred who would be anxious to learn more of the fate of Chrono of Mizgad!"

Cornæos and Annæ then came ashore to accompany Chrono: had Chrono but known, this was a great honor. It is rare to find any of that folk more than a few steps from the waters in which they dwell, for they hold it to be undignified to walk on the dry earth, and the arid air soon hurts their lungs and parches their skin. The way of the Tritynoi is to glide smoothly below the waves, and like the dolphin or the sea-hounds their grace in the sea is without compare. Yet they also come ashore, for they love the warmth of the sunshine, and so they will walk on the dry land when they choose, to our eyes bearing themselves with great dignity.

So they walked along the shore, alongside Chrono, and Cornæos said, "Tell us then more of thy story. What peril loometh over Chrono of Mizgad?"

So Chrono explained how he had left the home of his father in the country of Plateos, rather than wed a daughter of the Sorites when his heart belonged to Ahten. And how he had come into the country of the Cylosites seeking opportunities to do noble deeds and earn honor among strangers. Then he said, "But the winter is now upon us, and the folk with whom I dwell have no sustenance to see us through these months of snow and frozen turf. A Giant has plundered them for many months, and haunted the forest hereabouts, so that they could not gather as they ought for the coming winter, nor could they preserve from its raids what little they had gathered."

At this word Cornæos glowered, and his brow darkened his visage, and he said, "This Giant we know. The foul brute hath muddied the pools and streams, and befouled many groves of this country. It hath caused much sorrow among our folk."

"It shall cause you trouble no more: for I myself have driven it into a far land, and it has sworn never to return."

"Can this be true?" Cornæos asked. "If so, thou hast done wonders."

"It is," Chrono declared. "I exacted its most solemn oath, and it will not recant." So he told the tale of how he had overcome the Giant by trickery and had wrested an oath from it. "And yet our woes are not ended," Chrono lamented. "These three months now has it been gone. But though it is banished, the stores of my folk are depleted, and we do not know whether we might gather enough even to preserve us alive through the season."

Then the nymph Annæ stopped, and turning to her mate Cornæos she pleaded with him, saying, "This child of the earth hath done a great service, and earned the aid of the terumani."

Cornæos said, "It is not fit for the Seafolk to intercede for the kindreds of the harsh air and dry earth. Such a thing has never been done! Havui himself divided the kindreds of the waters from the kindreds of the airs, so they could have no communion. Besides which, the folk of this country are cold and hard toward us, and speak evil things concerning our folk. Shall we give gifts to those who revile us?"

Annæ replied, "But Chrono of Mizgad is a friend of the Sea, and he is known to our folk. Moreover if it be true that the Giant is banished, then hath he granted a boon to the terumani that should be rewarded."

Cornæos turned to Chrono and said, "We might provide for Chrono out of the abundance of our domain. Wilt thou abide by us here, by the shores of Egano? We shall bring thee meat fit for thy Kindred, if thou canst not supply thyself."

Chrono deferred at once. "Shame would be on my head were I to save myself while friends who have supported me perish! It would be better for me to perish in honor alongside them."

Annæ said to Cornæos, "Seldom have we seen such virtue among the mortal Kindreds. It is no wonder this one hath won the heart of the princess Ahten."

"It is true. I shall consider the matter as we walk."

They had traveled along the shoreline for some time as they conversed, while Chrono had told his tale. At last they came to an open place: a broad shelf fringed by a semi-circle of forest. Beneath the winter snows a slope of solid rock tipped down into the lake. Slushy ice rimed the shoreline here where waves lapped over the rim.

"This is the place," Cornæos said. "We must depart here, for the breeze chills us and sucks us dry. But at the head of this clearing thou wilt find a pathway leading into the forest. In the winter it is hard to follow, so attend to it carefully: at every fork bear to the left. This will take thee to familiar haunts, I trow, and lead thee to the very fringes of Këuca."

Chrono bowed. "I thank you, both for your company, and for your aid. The lord and lady of Egano are gracious."

"We have not finished with thee," the nymph Annæ replied, "Shall Chrono perish in such ignominy, who holdeth the soul of a princess of the Seafolk?"

"Canst thou find this place again?" asked Cornæos.

"I trust so."

"Thou shalt not starve this winter. Come to this place tomorrow about the middle of the day: thou and all thy folk, carrying with you nets, and baskets, and even blankets: all that you can carry."

"I shall talk to our folk and see what they might do."

"If they would be delivered from their plight, they must comply, for but one opportunity shall they be granted. Thou shalt not see us again, but shalt know when we have gone by."

Then Annæ took Chrono by the hand, and gazing into his eyes she said, "As for thee, Chrono of Mizgad: this word I offer to thy benefit. Do not lose heart. Seek council of the wise and powerful: Perhaps when the time is full there may be more paths before thee than thou canst know or hope."

Then the næads said no more, but disappeared beneath the waters and were gone. Chrono saw them not again, though long he remained behind on the shore and watched.

Following the guidance of Cornæos Chrono quickly found his way back to Këuca. When the folk of that place saw him returned they rejoiced for his safety, and a party went out to bring back Duono and his companions, who had been searching for him in the forest.

Chrono then called together the folk of the village, and told them what they must do to be delivered from their famine. But he did not tell them of the promise of Cornæos and Annæ, for he knew the Cylosites to be superstitious and fearful of the næads.

"Let all who can be spared come," he said. "Empty the village if it be possible! I promise that deliverance is ours, if we have the prudence to lay hold of it."

Many of that folk took hope in his words, but others doubted. The elders grumbled to the Counselor, "What possible hope is there to be had by this course? What is in Egano? A fish or two will not save us all, if that is his plan." It must be recalled that in that age they did not fish with nets from boats, for there were no boats in Soria.[21]

But C'læod the host of Chrono replied, "If you would scoff at his plan, scoff when he has failed, and not before, or it may be you who shall look the fool in the end."

The Counselor declared, "This Chrono is he who by himself, alone, delivered us from the persecutions of the Giant. Let us do as he asks, and we shall see what will come of it."

So all agreed to accompany him to the lake, not knowing what to expect.

The sky brightened in the chill of morning to the clamor of activity, the whole of the settlement bustling with the gathering of supplies according to the instructions of Chrono. Each bore his own net, or basket, or pot, or tarpaulin: indeed everything they possessed which might carry a load. Every inhabitant fit for the trail gathered for the excursion. Even the children of the village took up sacks and followed.

When all was in readiness, Chrono conducted them to the lakeshore. Then all sat down to wait.

At the appointed time Duono stood up suddenly, and listened, and said, "I hear the sound of waters rushing, like a cataract. Yet it comes from the direction of the placid lake."

The folk of Këuca then rose to their feet and looked out across the waves. The waters of the lake a short distance beyond them were churning, as if a turbulent wind were blowing: yet there was no wind. A broad wave of white water could be seen approaching the shore where they stood, and all began to wonder what the strange apparition might mean. As it drew nearer, a single voice said, "They are fish!"

All that crowd gathered up their baskets and nets at once: a great shoal of fish came leaping from the waters, as if driven like sheep before wolves. This great mass of fish kept approaching to the very spot where they waited, and was driven right up to the rocky shelf where they stood. The waters swarmed

21 As is mentioned in other tales, in some locations nets and fish traps were used in rivers and streams, especially during spawning season, but the practice may have been unknown in the vicinity of Këuca. Fish were generally caught with darts and spears in shallow water.

with them and foamed with them, and some leapt even from the water onto the dry land in their rushing.

Chrono said, "Go in, gather all you can. It is a gift from the terumani."

All raised a shout of cheer, and rushed into the water, oblivious to wet or cold. They scooped up the fish in baskets, and dragged them in nets, and filled all the containers they had brought. They piled their catch into the snow on the shelf of stone, and entered the waters again, and took yet more.

When they had gathered all they could, they set to preserving the bounty. Some of the catch they froze in ice from the edges of the lake and stored in pots and vessels to bring home to their village. Others went into the forest and gathered wood, and built frames, and kindled fires. There on the shore of Egano they set to smoking the rest of the catch at once.

So many fish did they collect in that one hour that they had no more fear of the winter.

All the folk of Këuca, and Duono also, wondered at this marvel, and the word spread in secret whispers that Chrono had worked a miracle on their behalf. Duono said to Chrono when they were alone, "You have again worked unexpected wonders. It was a lucky hour when I chose to follow you on your quest!"

None knew that Chrono had spoken with the Tritynoi in the lake, nor did that folk know that the Tritynoi are herders of fish. Nevertheless Chrono said to all that wondered, "It is a gift of the terumani. Let none speak ill of the Tritynoi from this day on!"

So it was that Chrono saved the village of Këuca from starvation. So great was their surplus that, together with the fruit of their own hunting and foraging, Këuca became the richest village of that country, and they were able even to share with their neighbors.

The fame of this act and the fame of Chrono spread throughout that country. Meanwhile Cornæos and Annæ repeated the story of Chrono's bravery and wit, so that the tale spread among the terumani, as well; his reputation of goodwill towards the næads and Tritynoi grew in kind. Even so far did the story reach that it was told among the household of Merten, and Ahten heard it and was proud: so the love of Ahten for Chrono also continued to grow.

4. CHRONO AND THE SANCTUM OF PARAS

In the days of the wanderings of Chrono, when he was dwelling among the Cylosites of Këuca, the word spread throughout that region of how he had delivered that village from the Giant which had tormented them, and how by a marvelous harvest of fish from Egano he had preserved them from the privations of winter and sure starvation.

This tale spread until it came to be known even among the Tribe of the Lophusites who dwelt in Lodbarria, to the east of the Cylosites, and even to their chief Róbigan, the judge and elder of that tribe.

When the bitter winter had passed, Chrono and Duono remained for a season among the Cylosites, and helped them in the rebuilding of their village after the ruination of the Giant. The spring had passed, and the summer was well along, when emissaries came to the village of Këuca from the far-off country of the Lophusites, seeking Chrono.

The village of Këuca was small and obscure, even among the settlements of the Cylosites, and rarely did they receive visitors of any sort. Thus the inhabitants of the place began to gather and gawk at this unlikely curiosity. The Lophusites are a tall folk, who bear themselves loftily and serenely. They wore elegant robes of silver-blue, and adorned themselves with ivory and obsidian ornaments. Even after the long journey they appeared regal and quite important. Word of the peculiar strangers spread quickly through the village, and the Counselor, the chief who presided over that clan, came out to greet them.

"We have come many days into the wilderness of Batack seeking one Chrono, a Plateosite who is said to dwell among this folk," the emissaries said. "Rumors and tales have led us to this very village."

The Counselor replied, "Chrono does indeed dwell with us, along with his companion Duono. "Come, and you shall meet with him yourself." So they were brought to the house of Chrono.

Bowing at his doorway, the emissaries hailed him respectfully. Their chief speaker touched his forehead in the Lophusites' customary gesture of reverence. "Róbigan our chief requests you to come with us to our valley," he said. "The fame of your exploits has reached us in our own country, and we have hope that you may give us aid. We have brought gifts, and should you come with us, Róbigan has promised to reward you well for your service." The two attendants came forward and laid finely carved ivory casks at Chrono's feet, filled with exotic spices and incense from their country, and an array of polished gemstones from the mountains: a very valuable trove.

Chrono looked over the gifts hesitantly and said, "I would do whatever I am able, even at risk of life or limb, for an honorable and noble task, and without thought of riches or reward: but first tell me, what is this labor that you ask?"

"Have you heard of the Sanctum of Paras?"

Chrono shook his head, but Duono said, "I have heard tell of a revered precinct in the heart of the country of the Lophusites, girdled by a circle of great standing stones, in the center of which grows an ancient tree. It is the heart of the Lophusite clan."

The emissary brightened and said, "You have heard nothing but the truth. This ancient sanctuary has been at the center of our community since Paras[22] first led our folk into this country. It was erected to honor and protect the tree itself, which has grown there since ancient days." A shadow passed over his countenance, and he continued with a tone of bitterness in his voice. "In late years our settlement has been defiled by gnomes, who have trampled and degraded the country with their careless activity. Their tailings pollute our fields and our homes. They steal from the trees and gardens we tend. But worst of all, they have now defiled the Sanctum itself with their tramping and their digging. We have harassed them when we find them, but we have been unable to drive them out."

"The gnomes are oræads: the dwellers of the deep earth," Duono said. "What lasting harm could they have done to your Sanctum?"

"You do not understand our heritage or traditions. None may enter that precinct without purification, and in a state of reverence. This custom is strictly adhered to and honored by all. But the gnomes care nothing for us and our ways. They dishonorably trample the whole of the precinct with their coming and going, and worse, they continually use it for the tailings of their diggings. They have desecrated the place!"

Chrono still wondered what need they might have of him. "Have you no ceremony of your own to consecrate the place once again?" he asked.

"That we do," the emissary assured him, "but it does little good when the same defilement is repeated at the thoughtless whim of these wretches. And there is more..." he lowered his voice and growled. "The sacred tree at the center of the sanctum has begun to show signs of distress. For two springtimes now she has failed to blossom, and the leaves on her branches have now begun to wither and grow sparse. And a month past, her canopy began to shrivel and brown."

Chrono frowned uncertainly. "I sympathize with your plight. But I do not understand how this involves me. Am I Ologéo, to restore life to a blighted tree?"[23]

---

22 Paras was the chief of the folk which became the Tribe of the Lophusites, who had led the migration from Niyarc in the age before the coming of the Ice.

23 Probably a reference to the tale told in "Ologéo and Dynis," above.

The delegate looked about nervously and spoke quietly in Chrono's ear. "We know that these Cylosites among whom you dwell are, well... fearful of the terumani, and do not honor them as do we. They are, I am afraid, small-minded and superstitious. But we have heard otherwise of you: how else could you have banished a Giant, or worked the wonder of the fish of Egano? We of the Lophusites regard the terumani as our companions and guardians in Soria.

"Now you must know that this tree is said to be the abode of a dræad whom we revere, whose name is Garadenië: she is the Guardian of our Tribe. So we have always believed, though none of us can claim to have seen her. The Sanctum of Paras is dedicated to her. We fear that she has abandoned her abode, for how else would her tree now be ailing?" He lowered his voice to a whisper. "Though few have dared to speak it aloud, there are those who fear that perhaps she will abandon our Tribe itself. If that is so, and we have no Guardian to stand before the Ádolthi,[24] we may cease to be a Tribe at all. Our folk may scatter, and fade, and be forgotten."

Chrono frowned. "But how can I hope to aid you in this?"

"We have heard rumor of you, that you are a friend of terumani. It is the hope of Róbigan that you who drives Giants from the forest, and has the favor of the næads, might succeed where we have failed in evicting these gnomes, and might even recall the dræad to her sacred precinct."

Chrono sent them away that he might consider their request in private, and he conferred with Duono. "What are your thoughts?" he asked guardedly. "Are these folk merely superstitious and delirious?"

Duono shrugged. "It is their tradition. It holds great meaning for them."

"All the more reason I should be afraid to meddle in the matter. Should things go awry, I might be blamed for the ruination of their Tribe."

"But should things go well, you would be credited with their salvation."

"But what use am I? I have had no dealings with gnomes. They would have no more respect for me than for any other mortal. And if this dræad exists at all, how would I even find her? Or if she has abandoned the place as they fear, how might I convince her to return? I stand only to disappoint them in this affair."

Duono counseled him, saying, "You have left your own country seeking honor and a name. If you go with these Lophusites, promising nothing, and you find no solution to their plight, you are no less than you are now. But if you chance upon deliverance in this matter, as you did with the matter of the Giant of Batack, or the fish of Egano, then how much greater shall your name be! And it seems to me you do indeed have the favor of the terumani."

Chrono grumbled, "If I had the favor of the terumani would I be an out-

24 While not utterly without precedent, it was rare for any nymph or spright to stand in the council of the Ádolthi. This may be a misconception on the part of the Lophusites.

cast in the wilds of Batack? Nevertheless," he sighed, "your counsel is good." So Chrono consented.

Duono and Chrono therefore packed what they would need for the excursion, and having bidden farewell to their compatriots in Këuca, they accompanied the messengers of Róbigan on the long journey to their village.

Róbigan dwelt with his household and attendants in the Vale of Garadenthi, which was the most ancient of the settlements of the Lophusites in the Southrealm. This vale was a wide hollow which rose in a crescent around a small circular lake at its lowest point—somewhat like a scoop of water in a shallow bowl tipped edgewise—nestled into the slopes of the green mountains of Octévo. Its woods were abundant with game, and the Lophusites who dwelt there cultivated their own groves of fruit and shade trees.

A trail entered the valley from a spillway out of the lake, and looked across the water to the Sanctum of Paras on the opposite shore. This was the most prominent hallmark of the vale, and was indeed the wonder of the whole region: an expansive circle of roughly cut standing stones, each more than two mecaths in height[25] and capped along the top with lintels in the form of great dolmens. It had been raised by the forebears of the current inhabitants, in a time so distant that none could say who had built it, or when, or even how, but it was rumored that the Lophusites had had the aid of the Terumani in those days.

In the center of the Sanctum rose a small knoll, and crowning that was a very large, and very ancient tree with a dome-like crown that dwarfed even the great dolmen hedge surrounding the precinct.

The emissaries led Chrono and Duono around the shores of the lake and past the precinct of the Sanctum to the village known as Garadenthi. Here in this fruitful vale, all about the Sanctum, the Lophusites had made homes for themselves. Though they called it a village, it was, like the settlements of the Cylosites, a loose community of windowless round houses standing apart from one another. The Lophusites were a tidy folk, and the village was a trim place, with grassy lawns and meandering pathways between the houses. Most were constructed of wattle and clay and thatched with straw. A few of the more important inhabitants had homes with heavy walls of mortarless rock and stone. The lintels of their doors were carved totems of wood or stone, many of them painted in bright colors, and many of the houses had wooden doors like those of Chrono's own folk.

From one of these stone houses Róbigan himself came forth to greet them. He wore a bright blue robe decorated with fineries and trims. On his fingers he wore rings of ivory studded with green and amber jewels, and he

25 That is, probably 13-14 feet high, or more than four meters.

carried one hand aloft self-consciously, as if required to show them off as a symbol of rank. Róbigan was a descendant of Paras, and he judged his Tribe as honestly as he was able, though he was of a simple and ingenuous nature. He lived in a large house of stone with several connected rooms which overlooked a cobble-paved plaza.

"Come," he said affably. "We have readied a house for you. Make yourselves comfortable, then come back to me, and I shall purify you to enter the Sanctum, so you might see what it is we must deal with."

The ceremony was neither long nor demanding, but very formal and meticulous. Chrono and Duono knelt at the paved way which entered the arena beneath a towering dolmen gate. An attendant of Róbigan's who appeared to act as priest anointed them with a scented balm as he uttered the words of their ritual, and they were instructed on the correct responses. When the priest had judged them to be in the proper state of reverence they were allowed to stand and enter the precinct freely.

"You see our troubles plainly, do you not?" Róbigan said dismally, gesturing across the sward within the stone circle. It had once been a magnificent place, with a lawn of bright green grass surrounding the knoll at the center. The tree which commanded the knoll was massive, its trunk larger than a house, smooth as satin, and silvery gray. It was deeply corrugated, as if formed of molten wax, and its monumental roots draped outward and down the slope of the knoll like an outspreading array of silver, serpentine walls, each one taller than Róbigan. The dome of the canopy reached out of sight, obscured by the lower limbs and a pavilion of hanging roots which had reached the ground to form a grove of silver columns, embellishing the space like the pillars of a temple.[26]

Yet now the whole of the precinct was in disarray. The grass was trampled and yellowed, a condition wholly out of keeping with the tidiness of the Lophusites. From the side of the knoll a mound of loose dirt and rock spread like the vomit from a mineshaft, and though much of it had since been cleared away, the remaining debris was a filthy blotch defiling the lawn. One of the standing stones of the circle leaned precipitously askew, as if its foundation had been undermined. As for the tree, it was plainly distressed, its leaves yellow and brown; the earth round about was littered with its fallen foliage. Many branches, dry and dusty gray, straggled among the mass, bare of leaf or bud.

"This is clearly no home of nymph or spright," Chrono declared sadly.

"Indeed," Róbigan agreed. "See how she withers!"

"Can you not merely restore and reconsecrate your Sanctum?" Duono asked. "Perhaps if the nymph would return on her own she might save the tree."

---

26 The exact identity of this tree is unknown, but from its description it is likely some relative of the fig.

"We have tried, of course," Róbigan said. "But we cannot be rid of the gnomes." His voice suddenly became harsh and fully of vitriol. "The greensward they pollute at a whim. And as you can see they expel their tailings from the very root of the tree. No sooner do we get the place clean swept but another deposit is cast from the shaft again. We have tried to dig our way in and block the tunnel from the inside, but the gnomes are too good at their delving. They plug the tunnel themselves so our tools can hardly penetrate the morass, and quickly re-excavate it whenever they need to use it for their tailings again."

"And yet I am surprised the nymph has abandoned her ancient abode," Chrono said, peering deep into the canopy for any sign of her presence. "The næads and dræads are said to be longsuffering, and will defend their homes when they are able. Are you certain there was a nymph of the tree at all?"

Róbigan looked shocked. "Do you mean to say she may have abandoned the tree even before the gnomes arrived? Why, that would explain much! We have been looking at this wrong from the start! Garadenië did not abandon the Sanctum because of the gnomes. The gnomes have moved in because she has abandoned the Sanctum! But what could we have done to have driven her off?"

"I did not mean to suggest that at all," Chrono interjected. "But we were told before we left Këuca that no one alive had ever seen this nymph."

"But the tree was healthy until two years ago," Róbigan argued, as if this fact alone verified the presence of the nymph. "What if some offense had been done in secret, or by accident?!" he fretted. "She must be appeased!"

Chrono and Duono exchanged a doubtful glance, but Róbigan continued as if unaware of their presence.

"We will leave gifts and offerings here, at the foot of her tree!" he said. He bent to Chrono's ear and added defensively, "Of course, this has already been done, but that was only a simple ritual offering, performed by myself and the elders. And we are surely not the ones who have offended her. "

"I have not said you or anyone has offended Garadenië, or any nymph at all," Chrono objected.

Róbigan ignored him. He clapped his hands together decisively. "I shall decree this, that all the folk of this settlement must bring a gift to the Sanctum! Then we shall again perform the cleansing ceremony. If you are correct, Garadenië will return and help us to drive off these gnomes for good." He grasped Chrono by the hands heartily. "Thank you! Thank you! You may have saved not only the Sanctum, but our Tribe itself with your wisdom."

Chrono tried to object that this was not his scheme at all. "I still have not confronted the gnomes, who are the visible cause of your plight. It seems it would be more to the point to deal first with that trouble."

Róbigan looked at him blankly, as if he did not even understand the gist. "I suppose you may try," he said, "But they are hard to find. The location of the entrance to their warren is a great secret. We have not discovered it. But come what may, you must be with us when we perform the ceremony. You have the ears of the terumani, I have been told. Garadenië may listen to your call above all others."

Chrono thought to tell him not to put too keen a hope on that, but it was clear it would be wasted breath.

The priests of Róbigan determined the most auspicious day for the ceremony, and for five days Róbigan gathered all that the folk of the region could bring: Many baskets and vessels full of their offerings they collected and brought into a storehouse in the village. No one of that Vale failed to bring an offering, and many even from further abroad joined in the invocation. The most humble of that clan brought simple gifts of flowers or sweet bread, while the wealthier among them brought baskets of valuables: carved ivory, incense, precious stones, and even gold.

Chrono and Duono, in the meantime, made extensive explorations of all the country around the village. There were many wild woods yet in that valley where a tunnel might be concealed, and the tunnels of the gnomes could be very long indeed. Chrono felt certain the entrance would be found among the gnarled roots of some ancient tree or grove, or among the jumbled boulders which here and there dotted the valley. It would not be unheard of even for it to be hidden away in the dark of some abandoned house or barn. But all their searching turned up nothing, and Chrono grew discouraged with the task.

When all was in readiness for the ceremony, Róbigan called upon Chrono to attend. All the gifts had by that time been brought into the Sanctum, and arranged around the foot of the tree.

As they walked to the precinct to be shriven he whispered to Duono, "I am afraid they have attached my name to this thing without my consent. Whether it fails and I am blamed, or succeeds and I am credited falsely, there is little honor in this."

"Nevertheless," Duono winked, "I am curious to see this thing through. If it fails, you will still have your own chance to work a wonder. And if it succeeds, we shall at least have witnessed a marvel."

Chrono and Duono were led to a place of prominence in the company of Róbigan and his priests. The folk of Lophos began to arrive from all the surrounding country and fill the precinct within the circle, each of them performing the oblation ritual, and entering with heads bowed and fingers pressed upon foreheads in a state of reverence. They kneeled on the grass in a great throng around the base of the knoll.

Róbigan himself performed the cleansing ceremony. He and the elders of the village did obeisance at the foot of the tree, uttering ancient words and pouring out an oblation of fine wine and perfumed oil, and imploring Garadenië to return to them and defend her abode. They petitioned the folk who had come to add their voices to the plea.

Róbigan stood up before the whole of the company and in a commanding voice said, "By the wisdom of the friend of the terumani, we call now upon Garadenië to return to her abode, and to cast out the gnomes who defile our Sanctum, and restore it to its former estate." He closed his eyes, and raised his arms into the air, and began to gesticulate.

Chrono squirmed at the attention brought on him by the declaration, but soon he was all but forgotten.

A great wailing hum, like a strange song, rose from the crowd, and circled the tree in waves, while a thousand arms and more were raised into the air, waving in motion like the wind in the standing grain. There was a palpable expectation that Garadenië herself was about to appear in their midst.

Chrono whispered to Duono, "Are we expected to join them in this extravagance?"

Duono shrugged and whispered back. "It would seem proper to honor their customs in their own sacred place. But I would feel fraudulent doing so."

"We have been given no instructions, so perhaps we may do as our conscience bids us." Chrono said. But he looked around the precinct, and as every other individual in the place was participating, he half-heartedly raised his arms and attempted to mimic their actions.

Long into the night the ceremonies and pleadings continued. Torches were lit, which burned all about the clearing, while the pitch of the pleas, and a growing sense of desperation, seemed to rise with the deepening darkness beyond the stone circle. Yet neither Róbigan nor his priests gave any indication of when, or whether, the ritual might come to an end. On the contrary, when the enthusiasm of the assembly seemed to be waning, Róbigan raised his voice again and shouted over the humming crowd, "I feel in my soul that Garadenië has promised to appear before us this night! Let none of us depart until she has blessed us with her return!"

But for all this Garadenië never did appear, and no word or sign of a nymph was to be seen.

The night deepened. The torches went out one by one. At last some few of the attendees broke off from their humming, and began to sneak off to their own homes, disillusioned and disappointed. Many of those who had come from afar faded back to their camps and accommodations. Those who remained of the thinning crowd began to hope and wish only that Róbigan would simply dismiss them all, and let them go in peace. Even the priests who attended Róbigan began to glance at him hopefully, wishing he would relent.

Arms grew weary beyond endurance, and the ritual waving lost its order and its vigor. The humming slowly faded. It was well past the middle of the night when the priests of the Lophusites at last said to Róbigan, "We have done what we can. Let the folk return to their own places, and leave the offerings for the nymph here. We shall rest, and see what the morrow shall bring."

Róbigan let out a dolorous moan, but he gave in. So all dispersed at last, and went wearily to their homes, leaving their gifts beneath the boughs of the tree. Chrono and Duono thankfully accepted this decision, and went to their house, exhausted, and expecting little or nothing. There were those, however, who gave sharp looks to Chrono as they departed, believing he had deceived them in calling for this ceremony.

The following morning found no good news, and no change to the Sanctum. Róbigan and the village of Garadenthi were disheartened. The rumor spread that Garadenië had been displeased with the offerings, and continued to reject the Tribe. Some also grumbled at Chrono, feeling his perfunctory participation in the ceremony had offended the nymph.

Chrono and Duono went to the Sanctum to investigate the scene themselves. The gifts remained unclaimed at the foot of the tree, as they had been left the night before. Chrono observed the tree on the knoll, but he could see no sign of recovery, and no sign of the dræad. The Sanctum itself remained as degraded and defiled as ever, and certainly showed no sign of improvement.

As they made their investigations the folk of the village began to arrive a few at a time to see the scene for themselves. Some of them began to dejectedly remove the gifts they had offered the prior evening.

"Their ceremony would seem to have failed," Duono said after a while.

"And we have failed as well," Chrono added. "We have failed to find these gnomes, we have failed to find this rumored dræad, and I am left looking the fool as a result. We must locate the warren of the gnomes if we have any hope of helping these folk and redeeming our honor."

"I have been contemplating that problem," Duono said, "but I have come up with no solution. The direction of the tailings they have expelled implies their tunnel approaches from the north, but the lake is in that direction," he said, waving a hand towards the blue waters lapping the shores some distance beyond the circle of the Sanctum. "So clearly it is a deception, and the tunnels of the gnomes must lie in the opposite direction." He waved his arm shoreward. "But which direction precisely, or how far their tunnels extend, I cannot guess."

"Even if we found the entrance to the warren today, we have no plan to deal with them."

Duono spoke the obvious. "With the aid of the Lophusites we might route their clan by force."

"To what end?" Chrono said. "Though we drive them off today, what is to stop them from returning tomorrow?"

"I have considered that," said Duono. "We might dig to the bedrock and sink a dike of stone into the earth surrounding the whole of the Sanctum, which might prevent them from entering the precinct."

"Such a work might take years to complete. We know not how deep the bedrock lies, nor can we be certain the gnomes will not simply dig through it. They are masters at excavation."

"Then what is left?" Duono said. "Are you imagining that perhaps these gnomes can be made to listen to reason?"

Chrono sneered. "It has never been said that the gnomes are a reasonable folk." He shook his head. "One way or another we must soon confront them, whether with reason or with threat of force. Let us consider our options carefully."

They were interrupted by a breathless curse, and a spew of muttered complaints. They turned to find one of the Lophusites on hands and knees near the base of the knoll, peevishly scrounging about to find something in the sandy earth where the gnomes had deposited their tailings. Chrono approached to inquire whether he might be of aid.

The Lophusite was busy scrambling in the dust, picking up a scattering of bright blue stones out of the rubble and dropping them into a basket beside him. "It is my own fault, perhaps," he muttered. "I should have packed my offering better, or wrapped it securely in cloth. Some careless oaf has spilled them all over the ground here."

Chrono and Duono both got down onto their knees to help. Finding one of the stones, Chrono examined it carefully, holding it up to the light. Although little more than a piece of dusty gravel at a glance, it was a deep, translucent blue which seemed to glow from within when held in a sunbeam. "They are quite beautiful," Chrono declared. "What are they?"

"They are sapphires from the mountains of Lodbarria to the south. I and my clan are miners there, and we dig them from the gravel in the foothills."

"That seems a worthy offering for the nymph," Duono said approvingly.

"Alas, but they are uncut and unpolished," the Lophusite lamented. "Not worthy enough, I surmise, and she has rejected them along with the other gifts. But I must retrieve them, every one, for you can be certain the gnomes will steal them all should they discover them."

"Indeed they would," Chrono said thoughtfully. He looked at the pebble in his hand, then glanced behind him to the shores of the lake beyond the stone circle of the Sanctum, and a breath of an idea came to him. "Is it possible to purchase these from you? I will trade you stone for stone from my own supply." He withdrew from a pocket in his sash one of the finely cut and polished gemstones which he had received from Róbigan in Këuca, before the adventure had begun.

"The stones will be worth more when they have been cut and polished."

"But they will be worth less for my purpose in that state!" Chrono said. "I would need them in their current rough and natural form." Duono looked at him curiously, but kept silent.

The Lophusite took the gem from Chrono and inspected it. "Are you a fool?" he said. "These cut and polished gems are worth far more than my own rough stones. You will be swindling yourself!"

Chrono smiled. "If the scheme I have in mind succeeds, it will be a trade well worth the loss."

The trader shrugged. "As you wish, then. But I'd advise you not to let it be known how you got these stones, or you will be taken as an ignorant rube. Every unscrupulous trader in the Vale will flock to your door."

When they had finished regathering all the stones from the dust, they left the precinct together and walked to the house where Chrono and Duono were residing. Chrono brought out his own cache of polished gems and traded for a quantity of the rough stones, which he put into a small bag and tied to his belt.

When the trader had gone Duono smiled knowingly. "Clearly you have a plan in mind. Would you care to explain?"

"I have a thought, though I would call it nothing more than a ghost of a plan." He fingered one of the rough stones. "I have a certain deception in mind, which we might work to our advantage. But first we must discover where the entrance to their warren lies. This is still our greatest challenge."

"Agreed," said Duono. "Shall we then resume our fruitless search of the countryside?"

Chrono sighed. "Go on your own, if you wish. But I think I will go off alone and give thought to this matter."

Chrono left the house, and he looked beyond the village for a solitary place to ponder the problem.

To the south of the village, on the slopes of the vale which rose toward the higher peaks of Octévo, a deep wood grew: a remnant of the forests which had once covered the vale. From these woods ran a clear brook into and through the village. It flowed down from the hillside and filled the lake at the bottom of the valley. Chrono by chance or foresight followed this stream upslope and entered the wood, for the sound of its babbling soothed him.

When he had hiked for no little while, the stream came to its head at a pool of clear water, in a wooded glen near the rim of the bowl, lushly encompassed by fern and white bellflowers. A wall of rock rose up behind the pool, and the water which filled the pool plashed into it merrily from a spring out of the very rock face which overlooked it.

It seemed a most peaceful and restful place, and it pleased Chrono. He stood for a long moment admiring the scene, watching the play of the sunlight on the surface of the pool, and listening to the babbling waters and the singing birds. Then he sighed, and sat down on a smooth rock by the side of the pool. For a long while he stared into the waters in silence, until at last a song rose up in his breast, and he sang,

"The weary wanderer,   woe-begotten,
Far afield   from friend and fief,
Seeking from strangers   stature restored,
Ever is aching   for honors earned
From far-off folk,   in foreign lands.
Craving acclaim   from curious clans.

But shambles instead   to shining pool,
Lustrous this gem,   this limpid jewel,
Like liquid light   Soul-uplifting.
A wondrous shrine,   wood enshrouded:
Gracious the giver   freely granting
Rest unasked-for,   ease decanting.

An honored name   I asked to earn:
But 'Chrono the Cast-off'   am I called.
So laugh should you learn   my luckless lot!
The Sea — who has stolen   my heedless soul
From lands above,   and love belayed —
My fervors she foiled,   fate-betrayed.

But gazing glad   on grotto fair
Renown here is nothing,   nor a name.
No need to posture   nor to compare.
The pool does not brood,   no envy bears,
She does not repine   for parities.
In Ahten's aura   she is at ease.

An honored name   I asked to earn:
No name do I own,   nor here nor home.
But garnering gall   and ill regard
Of service-seeking supplicants.
I sink now to scorn,   I slip away.
No honor's been earned   in this assay.

But whispering words,   the waters' voice,
No fault do they find,   none defaming.
Her glinting glance   does not disgrace,
Nor does she reproach,   nor disapprove.
Her kindness is quick,   her conduct cool,
They sate my sighs,   restoring soul.

...

Having sung these words, he stared down into the waters, and as he gazed a flickering light appeared, as of two shining jewels, or a pair of azure eyes gazing out at him. Many indeed would have thought it to be nothing more than a trick of the sunlight, flickering through the branches into the sweet depths of the pool, but Chrono saw it at once for what it truly was. In a voice of wonder he said, "Can these be the eyes of the nymph of this pool? Only a pair of eyes so lovely could do justice to a pool of such beauty."

At these words a nymph rose up shyly from the waters, with hair of turquoise and silver shoulders. She peered at Chrono curiously. In a timid voice she said, "Thy words are gracious, child of Toë. The tale hidden in thy song seemeth me that of that very Chrono of Mizgad, whose story we ken. Be that so? Else courteous as thou art, I durst not approach."

Chrono was astounded. "So Annæ of Egano spoke truly, that my sad tale has spread even to the pools and rivulets of the land!" he said wryly. "You have guessed correctly: I am indeed that Chrono, whose sorrows merely increase as his days are prolonged."

The nymph took courage and rose from the pool, and the water dripping as she did so tinkled like bells. She was robed in a veil of droplets sparkling like bright diamonds. She stole up onto the rock where Chrono sat, crossed her legs, and sat before him, peering at him curiously.

"Be not sorrowful," she said, "for we have heard the report of Ahten, and indeed thou art truly loved. Such devotion few can attain, be they requited or nay. So say all who know thy tale, and ken the lot of Ahten as well."

Chrono smiled sadly. "Though your words are perhaps true, yet they dim the pain but little. So tell me: How shall I name you, and how shall I name this pool of beauty?"

The nymph warmed to these sentiments, and spoke demurely: "We are Esperiénië, both myself and my waters, for my waters delight the children of the Lophusites who dwell nearby."[27] Smiling she added, "It pleaseth me that Chrono of Mizgad, whom the princess Ahten loveth, is also delighted therewith."

Chrono bowed and said, "You are both gracious and kind. Perhaps you may aid me in my fruitless task."

"I am but a minor nymph in a small domain. There is little I can do for the folk of your kind."

"Clearly rumors and tales pass quickly among your folk, however. Have you tidings of the nymph whom the Lophusites claim dwells among them, in the village below?"

"Garadenië?" the nymph asked, wide-eyed. "Surely thou knowest that Gauphrin[28] from the Batack entered into the Southrealm when their own lands

27 Esperiénië means delight in the Sorian tongue.

28 "Gauphrin," of course, is the proper name by which the gnomes were known among the terumani.

were frozen beneath the great Ice. It was long ago by the accounting of your folk." Chrono nodded. Esperiénië furrowed her brow. "This insolent folk hath reached us even here. They do much harm, for they are selfish. Finding the tree of the nymph to their liking, they have undermined it, and sickened it, and have driven her forth with all their diggings and turmoil."

"If the tree of Garadenthi was truly her abode, it has long been abandoned. I had doubted whether any nymph or spright might ever have dwelt there."

"Thou speakest sooth," the nymph complained. "She is gone. Now she wanders the woods unhoused. No one knoweth where she may have betaken herself, but her sighs and the songs of her lament haunt the evening airs."

"Then is there none to help her?"

"The Gauphrin are many. None but the greater of the Terumani, the Ádolthi themselves, might prevail against such mischief." Then she looked away to the north sadly and said, "And the Ádolthi are far from this place, beyond the Ice, and seldom turn their eyes to the troubles of the Southrealm. Not even Grënas[29] hath heard her plea, it would seem."

"Then we must help her ourselves!" Chrono said. He rattled the pouch of rough sapphires at his belt. "I have been considering a plan of my own which might encourage their departure. But I and my companion have been unable even to find the wretches, despite days of searching."

Esperiénië laughed. "But that is easy. The entry to their warren is no secret. At least it is no secret among the terumani who dwell hereabouts. I could lead thee thither myself."

Chrono brightened. "If that is so, we might yet find a way to evict them."

"Such a victory would be welcome indeed! The gnomes are bad neighbors. I for one would not grieve at their departure." She lowered her voice. "But I would fear to bring the wrath of that folk upon myself and upon my grotto!"

"The gnomes are capricious, but they are not a vengeful folk," Chrono reminded her. "Their works may exasperate their neighbors, but never have I heard that any clan of their kind has risen up to do harm by intent. Nevertheless, you needn't guide us: simply tell me where we must look, and what signs we must seek, and we shall do the rest. Your hand in the matter will never be revealed."

"Thou art as honorable and wise as the tales of thee have spoken. I shall help thee, then, if such tidings will be of aid." She then sat with him and explained in great depth how to find the entry to the warren. "Do not be fooled, for they have disguised it well with a door cloaked and concealed cleverly with root, leaf, and litter. Yet they do not lock their entries, trusting instead to their artifice."

"Once again I find I am indebted to the kindness of the terumani. But if I

29 Grënas was the lord of the dræads

dare ask, there is yet one thing more I would request, if it be in your power. I believe I have a plan which will rid us of them for good. The help of a næad, a nymph with power to control the waters, would be of great aid."

She pouted. "I have promised nothing. The gnomes are capable of great mischief, and I would not risk the pollution of my pool or my grotto."

"The plan I am contemplating is such that your aid would be done entirely in secret. Not even the wisest of the gnomes would suspect the hand of any outsider in the matter, least of all a nymph they do not even know exists."

She pursed her lips thoughtfully. "If that be so, perhaps would I dare aid thee."

"They shall suspect nothing but their own ill fortune. Let me describe my plan, and the aid I need from you. You may then decide whether it is safe to help." So he sat with Esperiénië, and explained to the nymph the whole of his plan.

At last she said, "Such power I can certainly exert, though it is far from my pool. If you can do as you say, I shall do my part. The gnomes will know nothing."

Chrono thanked her humbly. "Your aid in the matter will be unmentioned and unknown. I will report back to you when I have further news, if it pleases you?"

"I shall be glad of it. Come again when thou hast tidings." With that she slipped from the stone upon which she sat, and disappeared into a sparkling circle of ripples on the pool.

When Chrono had himself verified the location of the gnomes' entry passage in the woods, he returned to Garadenthi to seek out Duono. He found him within the confines of the Sanctum, studying the layout of the precinct and the tailings of the gnomes.

Duono hailed him, and reported sullenly. "I spent the morning, and much of the afternoon, in searching for the gnomes. They remain in hiding, and I am no better off than when we parted."

"Then I may have good news," Chrono smiled. "I have today discovered where the entrance to the warren lies," he said, "so now we have only to consider our plans."

Duono brightened at once. "We should go to Róbigan and let him know this news!" he said. Duono did not question how the discovery was made, and Chrono did not bring up the chance meeting with Esperiénië.

"I think not," Chrono said. "That one has misused my every word, and to be honest, I have begun to question his wisdom on these matters."

"You do not overstate the case!" Duono laughed. "But what then shall we do?

"I think I shall require your own unerring sense of direction. I myself would be utterly lost in the dark tunnels of the gnomes."

"I cannot guarantee I could find my way in or out of their twisting passages, but I always know north from south in any light."

"That, I think, will do," Chrono said. "Then we must examine the tunnels of these gnomes from the inside. Will you dare go down with me and confront them?"

Duono smiled. "You know I will not shrink from any challenge. Lead the way to their entry and we shall proceed."

"Good. I will explain my plan to you along the way."

The entrance to the warren was in a wooded area outside the village, not particularly remote, but well hidden in a thicket of branches, brush and roots. The door itself was, as Esperiénië had described, well concealed by a mantle of forest debris so that it could hardly be discerned from the forest floor itself. It opened at an angle into a slope below the exposed roots of an ancient sycamore.

Duono examined it as they approached. "I am surprised you have found it at all," he exclaimed.

"I stumbled onto it by pure chance," Chrono said, half-truthfully. "Perhaps some subtle motion or sound caused me to inspect it."

"In any event, how shall we proceed? I understand your plan, but how are we to explore the place without being seen?"

"It is daylight now," Chrono mused, "so most of the Gauphrin will likely be asleep. With luck we should have ample opportunity to wander the halls before we are discovered. But part of my plan depends on our discovery. If no one comes upon us, we will need to find them and confront them."

"Good enough for me," Duono said. He hefted his spear assertively. "In we go." Chrono carefully and quietly prized open the entry door of the warren, and they stooped to enter into the shadowy tunnel.

They had carried with them their weapons for security, and a small and dim lamp for light. Even a dim lamp would seem a bright light to the Gauphrin, however, so they hid its flame behind a basket as they drew shut the door behind them.

"I hear and see no sign of the gnomes," Duono whispered.

The tunnel headed sharply downward from the entry, into the deeps of the earth, before leveling off and winding away out of sight. The gnomes are a short Kindred, so Chrono and Duono were forced to hunch slightly as they proceeded. The place smelled earthy and the air felt moist and heavy in their lungs. Scents of burning lamp oil and cooking food wafted in from some of the halls, and the faint sounds of conversation behind doors could be discerned in the darkness, but they met with no one along their way.

They examined the corridors in silence, tapping each other on the arm, tugging on sleeves, and gesturing to communicate. Duono made mental notes each time they came to a fork or an off-shoot from the main corridor, and in several places placed marks on the wall with a charcoal stylus. There were many doors along the way, all of them shut, which they took to be the private chambers of individuals.

Most of the walls were plastered and the floors either paved or planked. The ceiling was arched, and plastered or vaulted with rough stone. Here and there along the way, however, they came upon sections of the tunnels which were unfinished, or newly excavated, with the raw earth or the gravelly strata of the valley's deep floor forming the walls. These were the areas which most interested Chrono. At last Duono nodded confidently and signed that he was satisfied.

Chrono withdrew from his pocket a small digging awl and gouged a deep hole into the gravel wall at the spot Duono indicated. He then took one of the raw sapphires from his pouch, stuffed it far to the back, and repacked the hole tightly so it was all but undetectable.

"Now let us announce ourselves," Chrono said aloud.

They followed the sounds of conversation, until the voices led them to a large domed room which seemed to serve as a dining hall. A number of long tables filled the space, and sconces in the plastered walls held strange copper lamps which dimly—to Chrono's and Duono's eyes—brightened the space. A few Gauphrin could be seen sitting and gambling together at one of these tables.

This space, as it happened, was directly below the Sanctum, having been cleared beneath the outspreading root stock of Garadenië's tree. Overhead a great network of roots held the roof in place—the roots of the tree. But many of them were mangled, severed, or hacked away, so that the tree was bereft of nourishment.

Chrono politely and firmly announced himself. "I would have word with the leader of this clan, if I might."

The gnomes at the table shouted and leaped to their feet in a sudden panic. Most of them had no weapons at hand, so they cowered behind the table or ran from the room. One of the number, however, drew a metal blade which he carried and stepped forward from the group. In a loud and angry tone he demanded, "I am Neborrick Tur, and I am the captain of the Day-guard. Who are you, and what is the meaning of this intrusion?"

"I am Chrono the Plateosite: myself and my companion Duono have been hired by the Lophusites to find you and speak with you. The first half of our job we have now done. If you will be so kind as to bring us to your leader we shall fulfill our duty and go."

"There is no need to disturb the leader from his repose. Anything you have to say you may say to me."

This plan seemed well enough to Chrono, and indeed Neborrick Tur's blusterous demeanor played nicely into his plan, so he proceeded without argument. "Well enough," he said straightforwardly. He spoke as if reciting from a prepared script. "The place in which you dwell is sacred, and you have polluted it. Worse still, you have driven the rightful mistress out against her will, so her abode now withers in disregard. We ask only that you allow the nymph to return to her own abode. You may find another place for your warren, far from this knoll, and we shall not pursue you nor concern ourselves with you any further. "

Neborrick Tur laughed outright. "What nymph? We know nothing of any nymph. The place is ours: By the labor of our own hands we have delved and shaped it, and made it our home. The earth here is deep and firm. There is ample forage in the woods and fields about the place," He waved at the sturdy roof above and added, "Such staunch and stable places are not easy to find!"

"Garadenië's claim to this site goes back uncounted years, to the Age before the coming of the Ice."

"And we have every right to delve wherever we please, for the earth below has been given to our folk from the very beginnings of time!"

"The Lophusites, I am certain, will gladly pay you for your trouble."

"We have no need of payment from the sunlight-dwellers. We have invested a great deal of labor and care into our warren here. We will stay."

Chrono nodded as if satisfied. "If that is your response, that is what I shall report, and our job here is done. So we shall be on our way." He bowed out of the room, but Neborrick Tur, of course, could not allow them to wander the warren unattended, so after first scraping his winnings from the table into a pocket, he brandished his blade, and escorted them toward the exit.

As they made their way past the wall where Chrono had hidden the sapphire, however, Chrono stopped suddenly and stooped to pick something from the loose gravel at the foot of the wall. He quietly slipped into his hand another of the rough stones he had taken from his pouch.

Neborrick Tur looked at the floor suspiciously. "What are you doing there?" he demanded.

Chrono demurred, clasping his hand behind his back as if hiding something in his fist. "It is nothing," he insisted. He looked the wall over purposefully, however, as if seeking something in the surface.

Neborrick Tur stepped close and thrust his blade at him threateningly. "Show me what you have in your hand," he insisted.

"It is probably nothing," Chrono said evasively. "Only a pretty stone." He quickly revealed the stone, and tried to snap it away again, but Neborrick Tur grabbed at him abruptly. He snatched the stone from Chrono's hand and his eyes momentarily lit up.

"You are correct, nothing but a pretty piece of gravel," he said. He put it into the pocket of his own vest.

"If it is worthless, then you will let me have it back," Chrono said firmly.

"No sunlight-dwellers may take anything from our mines, worthless or not. I shall keep it."

Chrono feigned guile. He lowered his voice and spoke into Neborrick Tur's ear, as if hiding his words even from Duono. "No one knows of this finding but you and I. I will gladly share with you if you'll allow me to come back and dig into this wall. Perhaps more such ... 'worthless gravel' can be found. It will be our secret."

"I tell you, it's worthless. But you and your companion are intruders. Get gone, before I call all my troops upon you." So he pressed them to continue toward the surface, while Chrono looked back longingly at the gravel wall.

When the door had been shut behind them Chrono said, "Now we must be patient, and trust to luck, and the greed of these gnomes."

"You're certain he will find the hidden stone?" Duono asked.

"I have no doubt. They love gemstones above all else, and blue above all gemstones. He will excavate until he discovers it, then he will keep on excavating hoping to find more. It is a weakness of gnomes. And I doubt he will alert his clan to its presence. The wall will be unguarded and forsaken except when Neborrick Tur himself is digging."

"Then let us also hope the gnomes are more greedy than they are careful, or your plan may yet fail."

Chrono winked cryptically. "I have already taken care of that. I believe Neborrick Tur will soon be in for an unpleasant surprise."

The following day Chrono and Duono returned to the warren of the gnomes. As they approached the door Duono said, "After yesterday's intrusion, can we expect the place to be unguarded?"

"I am hopeful. I quite expect Neborrick Tur is going to keep his discovery to himself. I suspect he has mentioned the incident to no one. If we run into him, or any other gnome, we will claim we have returned in secret to excavate the spot ourselves. He will certainly believe that."

But as Chrono had expected, they found the entrance unwatched and unguarded: Clearly Neborrick Tur was keeping the prior day's invasion a secret. They made their way carefully and quietly to the wall in which Chrono had hidden the gem.

An opening had been delved into the substrata, several feet into the gravelly wall off from the main tunnel.

Chrono smiled. "It's clear our friend Neborrick Tur has been excavating here," he whispered to Duono. "Where shall we place our next bait?"

Duono paused and closed his eyes (perhaps a bit superfluously in the dark of the mine) and concentrated on his sense of direction to choose a new spot at the deep side of Neborrick Tur's excavation. Chrono loosened the wall so that a small pile of dirt and gravel spilled to the floor, and dropped one of the raw gems on top of it. He then embedded two more gems deeply into the wall at the spot Duono indicated. When they had completed this task they made a silent and hasty retreat.

Each day after that they stole in and made their way to Neborrick Tur's excavation. Sometimes Chrono would cause a part of the gravelly face of the wall to collapse to the floor, and he would place a pebble of sapphire into the rubble. At other times he might embed one or two of the gems into the wall. Duono guided him in the path, adjusting the placement of Chrono's lures as necessary, so that each day Neborrick Tur would dig a little further in the direction they had planned for him. The tunnel deepened. It was not long before Neborrick Tur had excavated a long and deep shaft diverging from the main corridor, always veering northward according to Chrono's plan.

In the meantime Chrono implored Róbigan to wait patiently, saying only that he and Duono had a plan in the works. No details would he reveal to him, for he feared Róbigan's misunderstanding or intrusions might spoil their efforts, or further alienate him from the Lophusites of the village.

During all this time, Neborrick Tur had been coming to the wall each day at the end of his shift with his own digging instruments. The Gauphrin are experts at such excavations, and he was able on his own to continue mining into the gravel day by day, deepening his tunnel and disposing of the tailings quietly and quickly, without revealing his actions to anyone else in the warren, so that he might keep any findings to himself. Such diggings were not uncommon in a warren of gnomes, and no one thought much of the deepening tunnel.

Nearly every day he would find a stone or two, which he hid away in his own chamber. The walls of his tunnel remained firm and dry, and his tunnel was sturdy as only the gnomes can make them, so he paid little heed to how far he had been delving, nor to the direction his mine had taken.

But one day at last as he continued his secret excavation he struck into the wall with his pick, and a seep of water appeared, wetting the stones and dribbling to the floor of the tunnel. Neborrick Tur drew back suddenly in surprise. He cursed, for the gnomes do not like damp and watery tunnels. "Surely there are more gems to be found," he moaned, staring in disgust at the seeping water. "Perhaps I can dare dig just a little further?"

He put his pick to the wall once more, but carefully. He pried loose a few large stones, and scraped the wet and sandy gravel beyond. Now a little rivulet appeared in the wall, running to the floor and beginning to puddle.

Neborrick Tur cursed again. "This will never do. If the ground is so sotted in this spot we will need to seal off this tunnel completely."

Suddenly the gravel in the wall began to bleed with water. A great wet spot appeared where he had been digging, and the gravel itself began to slough from the wall. Neborrick Tur took a nervous step backwards to observe it, and with a shock of revelation he realized where he had been digging, and what must certainly lay above him. A sound of groaning and cracking came from the walls and ceiling of the tunnel, and the surfaces seemed to be moving of their own volition. Water was soon seeping from every crack and rough place.

Neborrick Tur backed away, and only just in time. A gush of water spurted from the wall of his excavation, which became a rivulet, then a stream, then a torrent. The walls began to collapse at the weight of the wet stone and gravel, and the water above that, and the ceiling began to collapse above him.

Neborrick Tur ran from the place squealing. "Flood!" he called out, hoping to bring his clan to his aid. Soon others began to swarm into the tunnel, wondering what could possibly have happened. "I have struck a flood!" Neborrick Tur said, but would not admit what he had been mining for.

Water was now pouring into the mine, and was soon sloshing about their ankles. "What have you been about? You have dug into the lake itself, you fool!" the others cried out.

They began desperately trying to seal off the tunnel he had made, digging gravel from the walls around them and packing it to block the corridor, but it was impossible now to halt the flow. The waters of the lake were far too inexorable to be stopped by mere piles of sand and gravel. It gushed into the tunnel, it poured over and through their barriers. It had soon filled all of Neborrick Tur's mine, and the waters continued to rise.

Nearly all of the tunnels and chambers of that clan were below the level of the lake, and it did not take long for them to realize that their entire warren was doomed to be drowned. A cry went up, and all the gnomes began to flee in a panic, salvaging whatever goods and treasures they might before the rising waters inundated the whole of the place. With one voice they all cursed Neborrick Tur, although none of them ever learned for what he had been mining in his tunnel.

As it so happened, Esperiénië had been holding back the waters of the lake from the strata in which Neborrick Tur had been digging, so the earth and gravel would remain dry as he dug, thus he never suspected his error until it was too late. When Chrono and Duono returned the next day to continue their subterfuge they found the tunnels of the warren entirely submerged, and all the gnomes gone.

The gnomes were driven out of the place, and could dig no longer in that valley. They departed into distant parts, blaming nothing but misfortune, and no one but Neborrick Tur.

Chrono laughed when he saw it. "It appears Neborrick Tur has taken care of our problem for us. You may go and inform Róbigan. I have one more task to see to, to complete our labor here."

Duono returned to the village, while Chrono went privately into the woods, upstream once more to the Pool of Esperiénië, and there he called forth the nymph of that pool.

Esperiénië greeted him, smiling, and said, "Hail, O friend of teruman and devotee of Trityn. What news hast thou?"

Chrono said, "Our tidings are good, for we have routed the gnomes from the root of Garadenië's abode as we planned. But I would ask one favor of you, if it pleases you. We have no way to inform the nymph Garadenië of what we have done, or that her abode has been restored to her. Can you send out word, that she might learn of these tidings, and return to her home within the Sanctum?"

"She wanders alone, and none knoweth where she layeth her head. Notwithstanding, the word shall go out among all the sprights and nymphs. Surely she shall hear by and by."

Chrono bowed and thanked her. "The folk of Garadenthi would revere and honor you for what you've done, if you would let it be known. But it shall be our secret," he winked.

The townsfolk of Garadenthi soon set to work restoring the Sanctum. The debris of the gnomes was cleared from the precinct, the lawn restored, the leaning stones set upright once again. The chamber the gnomes had excavated below the tree was opened up, and re-packed with sand, gravel, and good tilth, pressing out the flood which had filled the space.

It was not many days hence before the tree in the Sanctum had put out new buds on every branch, so that even the dried and brittle tendrils found life once again. The hanging boughs lifted themselves up, and raised themselves heavenward as if in rejoicing. So swift and unnatural was its recovery that it was clear that Garadenië had returned to quicken her abode.

When Róbigan observed it he declared, "Garadenië has returned, and our ancient home is blessed once more!" So the Vale of Garadenthi, and the Tribe of the Lophusites, was restored to its former prosperity.

The folk of that town perceived that Chrono had done a wonder for them like as he had done for the folk of Këuca. Many gifts did they leave, so that Chrono and Duono both became wealthy in that country.

That very night as Chrono lay in his house asleep, a sound came into his dreams like the tune of a flute or pipe: a gentle and musical whistle as lovely as the murmur of the breeze in the woods. Chrono awoke, and he rose up quietly and went out to the Sanctum. When he had put on the proper attitude of reverence for the space he entered.

Moving within the canopy of the tree was a figure lithe and lovely, whose skin shone silver like the moonlight, and her tresses were coral, as bright as the blossoms of the tree. Few eyes but those of Chrono could have spotted her motion among the leaves, for the dræads go secretly among the mortal folk, but Chrono had no doubt that he beheld the figure of Garadenië, whom none in the village had ever seen. He hailed her, and bowed to her in respect, and said, "The folk of Garadenthi are grateful for your return. May it cheer your heart to dwell once more in their midst."

The nymph was startled, and turned to face him. She leaped lightly to the earth as gracefully as a falling leaf and said, "If I guess correctly, thou art Chrono of Mizgad, who is rumored to be the friend of the terumani?" Chrono confirmed her guess, and she said, "I have suffered many days at the buffeting of these gnomes, who have no respect nor decency in their hearts, and I have languished in my exile so that I thought my heart should break. It is said I have thee to thank for this aid, and well-rewarded shouldst thou be. What gift wouldst thou have, Chrono of Mizgad?"

"That which I treasure most you cannot give. So I seek only a name of honor in this country, to restore the honor lost in my own household, since my heart's dearest treasure is forever parted from me."

"Thou hast honor already among the næads of the waters, both great and small. Now also shalt thou have the respect of the dræads of wood and wold as well, so withersoever thou goest thou mayest seek aid in thine endeavors. This word shall I spread for thee, and call thee friend also."

So Chrono bowed to her, and thanked her for her pledge.

Then Chrono returned to his place, and he and Duono had great honor from this time on among all the Lophusites. Chrono and Duono remained many days among them in their house in the Vale of Garadenthi at the behest of the elder Róbigan, and his reputation ever increased.

5. CHRONO AND THE CIRCLET OF THIOMOS

In the days of the wanderings of Chrono, when he was dwelling among the Lophusites of the east, Chrono and Duono took their leave from the house at Garadenthi. Chrono said to Duono, "We have done what we can at this place, and restored the hopes of these folk. We have earned honor in this deed, but our task here has been completed. It is time we move on from here, and seek labor in another country, lest our reputation grow stale."

Duono agreed with Chrono, so they gathered what belongings they could carry with them for their sojourn, and asking pardon and grace of their hosts, they left Garadenthi.

So they journeyed to the west, and skirting Egano on the north shore, they went through the country of the Cylosites down towards the Plain of Cylos. But Chrono would not go down to the Pindus, for that Sea is an arm of the Great Sea where Ahten's folk dwelt, and he feared his heart would betray him, and he might forget his pledge, and waste his days in dishonor and pining.

There were many small villages and communities of the Cylosites in that plain, even in that ancient time, and wherever Chrono and Duono sojourned they would stay among the folk of that place, doing whatever good and noble act they might find to do. The rumor of the acts of Chrono had traveled even to that region, so all the folk among whom they came were honored to host them as their guests.

Chrono and Duono would aid them in their building, their gathering, their trade, and the harvest of their plots.[30] But they found no mighty act to accomplish in this place, and Chrono grew restless.

At a certain time Chrono and Duono were sojourning for a spell at the village of Masson, where they had made a house of their own. In that vicinity was a waterfall that was known as the Fall of Sonoros, which surged into a rocky grotto from a wooded tableland above; and Chrono would go there at times with his javelin to fish for provender for himself and the folk of the village.

It so happened one day that Chrono crouched upon the bank near the foot of the falls, his javelin poised as he watched the waters for the silver flash of trout or perch, and he thought he beheld in the spray of the fall the form of a Trityn watching back at him from the mists. Now the sprights and nymphs of the terumani can hide themselves by their own craft from the eyes of the Kindreds of Toë, and they appear to be naught but mist or foliage, or the

30 Possibly this refers to the harvest of wild plots of food crops such as roots, vegetables, or berries, which may have been cultivated by the inhabitants of the country. It is likely that only very small efforts at horticulture were being practiced at this early age.

shadows beneath the foliage. But Chrono the devotee of Ahten the Sea-nymph had often encountered that folk, and had spoken with them openly. His eyes were more attuned to the vision of that Kindred than were the eyes of others of the Kindreds of Toë, and he was quick to see clearly what others saw only as shadow and mist.

Then Chrono called out, "Do I perceive Sonoros himself, the guardian of this waterfall? Why do you watch from the shadows? Why not come forth that I may see you plainly, and we might talk?"

Sonoros took shape out of the mists, and emerged from the waterfall. Peering intently at Chrono he said, "Thine eyes are sharper than any of thy Kindred, if thou didst perceive me in my seclusion! Who is this child of Toë who discerns the terumani as if charmed?"

"I am called Chrono, and name myself the Dishonored, who wanders in the lands of Soria without a home. Have you any word for me, or do you merely watch out of curiosity?"

So the Trityn Sonoros said, "Do I speak with Chrono of Mizgad, the friend of terumani?"

"So I have been called," Chrono shrugged. "But today I am merely Chrono the fisherman."

"It is little wonder, I suppose, if Chrono of Mizgad perceives the terumani even when they hide from mortal eyes."

"Then let us sit together a spell and talk. It has been long since I have enjoyed the company of teruman. I have been wasting away in this dull country, and I would relish any news from your realm."

Sonoros came up out of the waters and sat down on the rock near to Chrono. He paused for a long moment as if in deep consideration. Finally he said, "Rumor hath reached my ears which may be of weight to thee, but I fear to speak of it."

"There is no cause to fear," Chrono replied. "There is little that could be said which might darken my own dark humors."

"Then perhaps you already know," said Sonoros, "that Ahten the daughter of Merten doth languish in her home at Mizgad, and her kin fear for her. So it is said, or so have I heard told."

"What illness could have overcome her?" Chrono asked worriedly, "for she is teruman!"

"It is no illness, but that of a heart forlorn. Merten her father keepeth her at home as if captive, so little hath she to do but to ponder her misfortunes. Very many long days have passed since she hath heard word of thee, and she doth despair over thee, that mayhaps thou hast perished, or what is worse, hast forgotten her. Thus she withdraws from the company of her folk, and speaks but little, and eats less. So say the rumors, in any event, but how can I know if they be true?"

Chrono leaped to his feet in ire. "This must not be! We chose to part, in spite of our pain and sorrow, so that neither of us might waste ourselves away waiting in vain for that which can never be. She must live fully, and not fade on my behalf."

"Shall I then send word in the name of Chrono of Mizgad, to strengthen her heart?"

"If you can send word so far, you must do so at once! You must say that I live, and am yet faithful to her memory. No other has stolen my heart, nor ever shall!"

"What token shall I send, that she might know this word is not mere rumor and fancy. And that Merten perhaps might soften his heart toward thee?"

Chrono was dispirited at this request, and he bemoaned, "Alas, that I have no gift worthy of one so wondrous. Nor even a trinket able to be sent beneath the waves."

"Thy word shall I surely put forth among my kindred, and without delay. Perchance it shall soon reach even unto the Great Sea and the household of Merten. As for a token, I should be proud to send such a gift along, when thou hast opportunity. Thou mayest approach me here again, and I shall receive thee."

So Chrono went away from that place disheartened.

When he came back to his place at Masson he spoke his heart to Duono his friend, and lamented, saying, "Much good have we received for our labors, but among all the kind gifts and offerings of the Cylosites and the Lophusites, none might be sent beneath the waves, nor have I any object of beauty that is fit for such as Ahten the daughter of the Sea."

Duono shrugged. "I know little of maidens, and less of the Seafolk, but I should imagine that a jewel or gemstone of great beauty might please even a princess of that Kindred. Might we not trade out of our possessions to purchase such an item?"

"Only a gem of the greatest splendor would be worthy of such as Ahten, and all our earnings together could not purchase it."

Duono considered this, and he said to Chrono, "In this country, along the Road[31] to the west, on the journey to Shim, I know of a certain Mimminite by the name of Thiomos, who makes his living by challenging travelers to a footrace along the trail. He entices all who pass by, and all who flock to him, with the offer of a beauteous gem, of luster beyond compare, if they might best him in the race. Perhaps you might take your chance and challenge him for this gem, for you have always been a strong runner." Indeed in his youth, in his father's house, Chrono had earned respect for his swiftness afoot: Though his

31 In this age the "road" would have been a well-trodden trail at best. No paved roads existed in that ancient era.

father had at times bemoaned that Chrono showed no other talent in the athletic arts and sports of his folk, yet in a footrace he was unexcelled.

Chrono said, "If this is true, and the gem is as they say, I shall certainly undertake to win it."

But Duono warned him, saying, "All who accept the challenge of Thiomos must offer a treasure of their own as their stake in his game. And he has never yet lost: it is said that he is unbeatable. In this manner he has grown exceedingly wealthy. But it seems to me that luck is on your side."

"If luck were with me would my heart be bound to one so beyond reach? Yet I have little to lose. Let us go and see this gem, whether it is worthy for one such as Ahten daughter of Merten."

Chrono packed whatever trappings he could bear with him, which he might use as wager against the gem of the Mimminite, and they set off on the road westward. When they had traveled for some days the word came to them along the highway of the Challenge of Thiomos, for Thiomos was the name of that Mimminite. All said that he could not be bested, and none who knew him dared the race: but many travelers and merchants there were who happened upon him along their way and had lost their gamble against him. Venturers from afar also came to challenge him, for the fame of Thiomos had spread throughout the countries of the Southrealm. So all warned Chrono to be wary.

The camp of Thiomos was not difficult to discover. His tents and enclosures were magnificent, filled with all manner of wealth. His canopies were brightly dyed, and radiant with embroidery. All good things that might be desired were at his disposal, and good meat and drink were brought to him daily at great expense. He had servants as well, which tended to his affairs, and others who cared for the flocks and beasts which filled his paddocks and pastures.

When they approached the tents of Thiomos, one of the servants ran out to greet them: for they had the appearance of wealthy strangers, who might be game for his challenge. "Come, weary merchants!" he declared. "All who have business on this highway are welcome in the camp of Thiomos, who shall give you both comfort and rest until you proceed upon your way."

They were admitted into the camp, and given meat for their repast, and good wine, and a place to lay their heads: they were treated with all honor and courtesy as merchant travelers.

Chrono said to the servant of Thiomos, "I have come seeking to best Thiomos in his contest, for I have heard from far away that he is a great runner, and sets himself against all the world."

"You have heard only the truth," said the servant. "Nevertheless Thiomos will not race for nothing. But I see you are well-laden with goods among your baggage. Are you willing to stake a prize upon your challenge? For only so will Thiomos consent to the contest."

"Let us meet Thiomos himself, and see what he has to wager. Then we shall decide whether his challenge is worthy of our efforts."

So Thiomos came before them to greet them. He was not imposing in face or stature, but was tall and thin, and clearly in the best of health. His feathery hair was red and his skin was ruddy. Chrono was himself a strong and enduring runner, but though he knew at once that Thiomos would be a formidable opponent, he saw nothing about him that made him appear unmatchable.

When Thiomos had greeted them he said to Chrono, "I am told that you have come wishing to challenge me in my footrace. But I must warn you, many have come before you, hoping to defeat me, but none yet has done so."

"Yet even the Terumani themselves are not unbeatable. Should I challenge you to win this race, what have you to pledge as your stake in the game?"

One of Thiomos' servants stood by bearing a wooden casket. Thiomos snapped a finger, and it was brought to him. He opened it proudly and revealed the gem to Chrono.

Chrono gasped at the glory of it. The gem of Thiomos was a great opal as deeply lucent as the Sea itself, sparked by all the colors of wave and land. It was set in a glowing circlet of polished mother-of-pearl, like a diadem or crown, intricately carved by skilled craft from a single shell. None who beheld it could help but covet that circlet.

Now of all the gemstones to be found in sea or land, Chrono and Ahten held the opal in renown above all, for that stone symbolized to them all that was beautiful and pure beneath the sky. So Chrono felt at once that the Circlet of Thiomos was indeed the one gift fit for Ahten, and a fitting token of his devotion. He decided that he must acquire it.

So he said to Thiomos, "This treasure indeed is remarkable, and for this alone will I challenge you. What will you accept in wager against this gem?"

He opened up to him the trappings he had brought, and presented to Thiomos each of his goods one after another—much good stoneware of the highest quality; and a coat of exquisite beadwork; and boots of the most supple leather—all of the best of the things which he had acquired as dispensation by the kindness of the folk among whom he had dwelt.

But Thiomos was crafty, and he perceived the greatness of Chrono's desire. "None of these goods are worthy to be staked against the circlet," he said. "For should I fail to win, how great would be my loss in comparison to your gain. What else have you to wager?"

Chrono said, "The best of all I own you see before you, and a good price would you receive for any one of these items by any fair and honest merchant. Moreover you have set your circlet as stake in your game for years, and I perceive that you have already won the value of the circlet many times over, for your wealth and comfort is clear to all. Yet if no one of my treasures is worthy of the race, then I shall set all together against your circlet."

But Thiomos said again, "All that I see here is not worth the tenth of the price of this gem, which I acquired at great cost of labor. Another like it cannot be found. What can you offer of such great value?"

Chrono considered his answer, and he trusted himself to his fate, and he said, "I have nothing further to offer in wager but myself alone, and labor as great as that which earned you this gem."

"Five years labor would I demand of you should I win this race," said Thiomos, "for no less would my own labor be worth to gain such a prize. But if you win, this precious gem and its setting shall be yours to do with as you would, even were you to send it to the bottom of the Sea."

Now he said this not knowing Chrono's intent, for none had given him any hint of Chrono's desire and need. But Chrono took this as a sign of favor upon his fortunes, and he said, "So let it be. I shall wager five years of labor against the gem of Thiomos, and leave it for fortune to decide. I have little else in this world to hope for, and no more odious would this labor be than the wanderings I have taken on myself. Yet should I win, you shall surely grant this gem without fail."

So it was agreed, and so they swore oath one to another. It was arranged that they would race in one week's time, that Chrono might have time to prepare himself and become familiar with the course.

When Chrono and Duono had retired to their tent, Duono bemoaned to Chrono, "What have you done? For we know the skills of this Mimminite, whom none has bested in this race. Five years' labor is a weighty stake to gamble on such a risk. Should you fail, your days shall truly be dark and toilsome, and utterly without honor."

Chrono replied, "Little worse would it be than in the house of my father. Yet I think I shall not lose."

"How so? None has bested this Mimminite in all the days he has held this contest."

Chrono lowered his voice that he might not be overheard, and he said privately to Duono, "What do you think of that? He may be a formidable opponent, yet I see nothing about this Mimminite that should make him unbeatable in a fair contest."

"So have I thought myself," said Duono. "I surmise that some deceit is afoot, whereby our host, gracious though he may be, takes advantage of his opponents."

"If we can discover his secret, perhaps we may be able to counter it. Then I might hope to win this contest."

"You should train yourself on the course while we wait, and I shall listen and watch to see what I might learn. But think hard before you carry through your purpose. For in my estimation, no gem is worth the price you have gambled."

"We have sworn oath, and I will not forswear myself. I shall run the race."

The following morning Thiomos arrived early with several of his own servants, that they might show Chrono the course. "Let it not be said that I win by chance or unfair advantage," Thiomos boasted. "Learn the course, and run your best, that my victory will be undisputed."

He brought him well outside the camp to where a trailhead diverged off the main highway. "We do not race upon the highway itself," Thiomos explained. "That course might be obstructed by other travelers, with heavy loads, or beasts, or wagons[32] to block the way."

Walking briskly but tirelessly they guided him on the course of the race: This course was difficult and lengthy, and even treading at a vigorous pace it took two hours to complete. Coming down out of the camp of Thiomos the trail left the highway and broke off downhill, then for a long spell it traversed a rocky open plain, before crossing a log bridge at the little river Dereon. From thence it entered wooded country, and began a steady uphill climb over the hill of Pírata. Coming down from that difficult height it went through brushy and brambly country, then winding through rough and twisting land it came again to a level area at the bottom of the highlands, where the course ran among a field of tall reeds and bamboo thickets. Coming at last out of the bracken the final leg was a long and level stretch to the finish. Here it was that many a competitor had despaired, for by this time Thiomos could be seen far ahead of his challengers, so that none could hope to catch him.

This was the course upon which Chrono began practicing: he ran this course, or parts thereof, each day. Walking the course also time and again, he learned each intricacy and pitfall as well as he might; he strengthened his body for the run; and he planned his strategies that he might most judiciously exert his strength where it should be of greatest worth to better his chances at gaining ground. Yet in all this preparation, his suspicions grew, for he felt certain that something was lacking in his knowledge. Nothing about the course seemed so difficult as to defeat so many challengers.

Duono meanwhile ingratiated himself with the servants of Thiomos, fraternizing with them, chatting amiably, and sounding them out as best he might on the reasons for their master's success. Yet none offered any hint of a ploy or stratagem which might give Thiomos his advantage. Duono also found means to listen in secret to many private talks, but he could learn nothing for all his efforts.

32 Probably a sledge drawn by pack animals, as it's unlikely that the wheel was in use at this early age.

So Chrono and Duono were confounded, and the day of the race approached quickly.

Now Thiomos was a Mimminite, of a Tribe who are light upon their feet, and long of leg: many a skilled runner has come from that tribe.[33] As for Thiomos himself, he was skilled above the level of his own tribe.

But Thiomos had devised cunning means to thwart his challengers. He had indeed once been honest, but avarice and doubts had overtaken him, so that he no longer trusted to his skill alone.

Therefore on the day of a race he would send servants ahead along the trail, so that going upward into the woods from Dereon the course could be diverted by skillful ploy, so that rather than following the well-trodden and practiced course of the main path, the race traversed an alternate route: similar in all appearances, but riddled with clever pitfalls.

Going up into the woods, instead of traversing a firm path, the course became a hollow of deep sand, which dragged upon the feet of all runners: but Thiomos had set flagstones hidden beneath the sand, and had memorized each step through that course, that his own feet might never miss a stride. Then coming down from the hilltop into a brake of brambles, the trail could once again be diverted. Here the roots and creepers of the brush grew across the trail, threatening to trip up any runner and forcing him to pick his way cautiously. But Thiomos kept his course carefully pruned, so that he knew each step and ran the course with ease. Then yet a third time, in the lowland at the bottom of the hill, the course could be diverted once again from the known path, so that it passed through a low and miry slough, which sucked at the feet of all challengers. But Thiomos had built bars of hard earth out of sight beneath the mire, and he knew well the skillful placement of each stride, that he might never falter.

So he contrived that none could fully know the course beforehand: for though a challenger tried the course daily, yet on the day of the race itself he would find the conditions unfamiliar and toilsome, while Thiomos himself, through practice and skill, would navigate each challenge with ease. So it was that none could best Thiomos in the race, no matter how fleet. Yet Thiomos secretly congratulated himself on his honesty, for in truth he always ran the same course as his challengers.

The day before the footrace was to be held, Duono said to Chrono, "We have tried for this whole week, and have discovered nothing to our advantage. Come, show me the course you are to run. It may be that I might discover some secret which your eyes have failed to see."

Chrono assented to this plan, and the two set off to walk the course which

33 The line of the royal messengers of Homadal were all of the Tribe of Mimmin.

Thiomos had described. Now it must be said that Duono was a great trail-master, able to find a path where others might fail, and he possessed great skill at following all the signs of a trail, whether a marked highway or a covert passage through wild country. Many years had he worked as trail-master both for Chrono's father, and for Chrono's uncle, and now for Chrono himself, and his skills seldom failed him.

When they had passed over the little river Dereon and were entering the wooded patch, Duono became suspicious, and he said to Chrono, "Look here, how the trail is worn. Though the trail you have been shown is well-worn and clear, there is another trail to the left, less used, which disappears into the brush, and has been swept clean to cover its signs. Let us see what may be beyond this point to the left."

Pushing forward, they discovered that the plantings at the side of the trail were potted in such a manner that they might be moved, and the root and stock were meticulously concealed and camouflaged so they would not observed by a runner. Pressing beyond this they found the hidden trail of Thiomos, so nearly like to the true trail that Chrono himself thought they had followed the true course. But coming to the sandy hollow, Chrono exclaimed, "Such a tract cannot be found on the trail I have practiced, which Thiomos has shown to me. Such a pit of sand would slow a runner tremendously! But if this is deceit, how would Thiomos benefit by such a deception?"

But Duono observing carefully declared, "See how the sands are smoother and less disturbed at these spots? Like stepping stones they appear, and as a safe course through the trap. I would guess that Thiomos himself has placed them there to aid him in his run, but they remain hidden from his challengers." So examining further, they discovered the very stones beneath the sand which Thiomos used for his own sprint.

When the byway had merged again with the true trail, they pressed further, until again Duono said, "Look here, once again the trail diverges on the left side. Let us see what lies beyond."

So pressing on, they again found the deceptive shrubbery concealed to the runner, and a path beyond, like the true course, but passing through a tangle of brambles and roots. Chrono again exclaimed, "See now, how roots and runners enmesh this path. A contestant would need to pick his way cautiously indeed to avoid tripping up and spoiling his race!"

Duono however said, "But look, how the brambles are pruned, and the path is cleared of obstruction along these spaces. A skillful and well-timed stride might miss each snare. It seems to me that Thiomos has planned and practiced this alternate course to his own great advantage!"

When they had reached the end of this bypass and entered the true course once more, and had passed on further along the trail, Duono again spotted the deceptive diversion to the left, and when they had pressed through to the third byway, they came down into the sump of mire. Chrono said, "Surely this slough would suck at the feet of any runner. How might this deception be to the advantage of Thiomos?"

Walking carefully alongside the trail so as not to leave their own footprints in the mire, Duono prodded the muck with his staff, and he said, "There are firm places beneath the mire, such that a well-practiced and sure-footed runner might stride quickly across this leg without trammeling himself. So yet again the course is altered from the sure and practiced route to one in which Thiomos is certain to prevail.

"I am confident that tomorrow the plantings will be moved," Duono protested indignantly, "and the course you have practiced all week will be hidden! Tomorrow the deceitful course will appear as the only true route. It appears that this Mimminite has been deceiving and cheating his competitors for years."

Chrono said, "Shall we confront Thiomos with his deceit, and force an honest race?"

Duono considered this, and shook his head. "If Thiomos chooses to run a deceitful course, let him run it. But I shall put markers along the trail, so you will know the true course, the course which Thiomos himself surveyed with you: and you shall run honestly. Should you lose the race, then we might have recourse to complain of his deception and be free of this deceitful bargain. But should you win, you have run fairly, and he can have no complaint against any but himself."

This plan seemed good to Chrono, so he agreed to Duono's advice.

Rising early on the day of the race, Duono waited and watched for the servants of Thiomos. As he suspected, they also arose with the sunrise and they soon went forth to their work on the course. Duono stealthily followed after them, carrying with him a shovel and adze. Now Duono was as crafty as a gnome, and easily trailed them, being neither seen nor heard by any.

At each of the hidden forks in the course, he observed as they rearranged the shrubbery, the plantings, and rocks along the trail, to guide the race into the deceitful paths. They worked swiftly, and so skillful was their work that none might perceive that the trail had been redirected at all.

As they moved onward to each of the following forks, Duono came out of hiding, and rearranged the deceptive shrubbery that Chrono might quickly and easily press through. He then fastened a single red feather at eye level, at the spot where the trail diverged, according to the sign that he and Chrono had agreed upon, that Chrono would know where he might discover the easier course on the right. After these arrangements he hurried to catch up to the servants of Thiomos at the next fork; and so he marked all three of the sham trailheads.

Now as he headed back towards the camp of Thiomos where Chrono awaited, Duono said privately to himself, "It seems to me that this Thiomos has plundered many by this deception, and must be brought to task for it. It is only fit that we turn his deception back upon him."

So turning aside into each of the side courses, he took his spade and his adze, and he altered the course which Thiomos had prepared. He dug down the firm banks beneath the mire, that Thiomos might find no footing there. He re-routed the roots and runners of the bramble, that Thiomos' carefully planned steps would avail him nothing, and he might be tripped up on them instead. Finally he moved and shuffled the stepping stones beneath the sands, that Thiomos might find no purchase for his stride, and would be dragged to a halt.

Then covering his work and his steps with skill as great as Thiomos' servants, none could tell what he had done. When all was finished to his satisfaction, he hid his spade and his adze, and he proceeded to the finish line of the race course, as had been planned by Thiomos himself, that he might be judge and witness of the race's outcome on his companion's behalf.

When the hour for the race arrived, Thiomos and Chrono met at the starting point, and after greeting each other respectfully, a sign was given, and the race was begun.

Thiomos ran the course with ease and never lagged nor showed sign of weariness. For the first leg of the race Chrono ran closely alongside. But as they crossed the bridge over the little river Dereon and began the climb to the wooded zone, Chrono began to feign exhaustion, as if he had spent his energy too soon, and he began to lag behind Thiomos. So that by the time they entered the wood, he was lost to Thiomos' view. Thiomos then, coming to the diversion in the wood, took the lefthand trail, but Chrono, coming up behind him, found the mark which Duono had left for him, and pressed through to the righthand course.

Thiomos then found to his dismay that when he reached the hollow of sand, his practiced course availed him not at all: but his feet sank with each stride, and he plodded slowly through the patch with growing confusion. Nevertheless, as Chrono neither caught him nor passed him, he felt confident that his competitor would likewise be bogged down in the sands behind him, and coming out of the hollow he pressed on with renewed effort to gain more ground.

When the paths had converged again, Thiomos soon heard the stride of Chrono close behind him, and Chrono called out to taunt him, "I hale from the seashore, so running through the sand is but little difficulty for me. Your course should provide greater challenges for your competitors!"

Chrono remained behind a little way once again, so that when Thiomos had taken the lefthand path into the bracken, he would not observe Chrono pressing through to the true course. So Chrono picked up his pace to gain ground, while Thiomos headed for the tangle of roots and tendrils. Thiomos then reached the entangling ground and at once tripped over a root he had not expected, for once again he was dismayed to learn that the course had been changed from his practiced run. With his ire and frustration increasing, he worked his way through the remaining brambles, and lost much time in the process. Nevertheless, Chrono neither caught up with him nor passed him in all this bypass, so he again took comfort that his lead held sure.

But as he came again into the main path, he was astonished to find Chrono draw up immediately alongside him. Chrono taunted him again, saying, "I have spent years wandering among the trees of Batack and finding paths in trackless country. A challenge of roots and runners is of no concern to me."

Thiomos had struggled to fight his way through the sand and the brambles, and was winded: Chrono however still seemed fresh and sprightly. So as the path headed once more downhill, Chrono put on a sprint to take the lead, reaching the diversion around the bend ahead, that Thiomos might not observe his detour. Chrono then pressed through to the right, while Thiomos himself took his wonted course towards the slough, where he expected to take a quick and final lead. But reaching the slough, he could find no sign of his challenger ahead; striking the mire his feet found no footing, and he slipped at once and fell headlong into the muck. By now his consternation and confusion were great indeed, but he pressed on with growing fear, picking his way carefully and slowly through the sucking mire.

Coming at last back to the main pathway, Thiomos regained his pace as he exited the reed-lands. But in utter dismay, he saw Chrono now far ahead on the final stretch, unmuddied and untiring. Then Chrono called back to him to taunt him once more, "I am a friend of næad and Trityn: challenges of water and mud will not slow me down." So putting on a final burst of speed, he rushed toward the finish line. Thiomos put forth all his strength, groaning with the greatness of his effort, but his schemes had failed him at last, and for the first time he was beaten in his own race.

Both runners panted to regain their breath, but Thiomos moreover was covered with muck, his legs and ankles were cut and bruised, and his pride was wounded above all else. Yet he could not ask how Chrono had succeeded so easily in beating him, nor how his own course had been altered without his knowing of it, for doing so would force him to admit to his deceptions.

Duono then challenged him: "See now, you have been beaten in a fair race. Shall you indeed honor the oath that you have made?"

In spite of all, Thiomos was not without pride, and his honor would not allow him to go back on a solemn pledge. "Truly you have defeated me," he said, "and only Havui knows how you have bested me in a course at which I have never failed." So he had the circlet brought out by his bearer, and presenting it to Chrono he bowed low. "This gem which has been the coveted desire of many is now yours; and it shall now be my lot to find a new treasure to serve as my stake."

The word of this victory went out from that place into all the country round about, so all knew that Thiomos had been defeated in his race at last: and the honor of Chrono's name grew in the telling. Thus did Chrono and Duono take their leave of the camp of Thiomos, and they returned to their house at Masson.

When they had settled among their hosts once again, Chrono took the circlet and locked it into a box of delicately carven alabaster. When all was ready to his satisfaction he went out alone to the Fall of Sonoros, and he called for the Trityn of the waterfall.

Sonoros appeared from out of the mist, and greeted him courteously.

Chrono said, "Have you news for Chrono of Mizgad, the thrall of Ahten?"

Sonoros answered, "Thy word hath been sent on its way, yet no answer have I heard, nor do I yet know if it hath been received."

"Then if you will, send this treasure among thy folk to the maiden, that she might know that my love holds true for her alone. And that perhaps Marten her father might soften his heart." So he brought out the alabaster box, and revealed to the Trityn Sonoros the circlet which he had won from Thiomos.

At the sight of it Sonoros caught his breath and wondered at its beauty. "Thou hast well chosen!" he said. "Indeed this is a princely gift, and worthy a great princess of our folk: Such a gift as will reveal its beauty both in sunlight and beneath the waves. Truly thou art a mortal who doth fathom the hearts of the Seafolk! Go thou in peace, Chrono of Mizgad: Of a surety this gift shall be in the hands of thy beloved within a fortnight, even if I must bear it thither myself."

"As for me," said Chrono, "I shall await here in Masson until word returns from you, and I shall be comforted just to learn that Ahten is at peace. If she is happy while I live, I shall not have wasted my purpose in this world, even though we may never unite."

But Sonoros said, "Despair not utterly, my friend. Thou knowest not what wonders might yet befall thee under sun and sea."

So Chrono took comfort for a spell, and returning to Masson he awaited the word of the Trityn. So it was that at last word arrived from the channels of Sea and river and lake, that Ahten had wept for joy at the gift of Chrono, and her spirit took courage, vowing never again to doubt his devotion to her. Even Merten was compelled to hold this son of the earth in honor.

6. CHRONO AND THE PERILOUS CHASM

In the days when Chrono was estranged from his father he thought to go for spell into the country of the Stegganese. As a youth he had at times traveled as a merchant with his father, and with Duono as trail-master, and they had befriended a certain trader of that Tribe, Pheidros by name. It entered Chrono's heart to find him and visit with him, to learn how he fared. So with Duono he left the country of the Cylosites and took southward trails beyond the country of Lodbarria, to the valleys and hills where the Stegganese dwell.

When Chrono and Duono arrived at the gate of Pheidros' compound, they found the place shuttered and dark, with coverings over all the windows. Duono grimaced uneasily. "What bad tidings does this portend?" he asked. "We seem to arrived at a time of mourning!"

"Let us proceed," Chrono sighed. "Perhaps at least we might be of some comfort in hard times."

So Duono went on ahead to call for the master of the house. Pheidros himself shortly came out to greet them. "It is good to meet with friends of the past who many considered lost from this world. It had been rumored that Chrono the son of Marcanto, and Duono his servant, had fled from the house of Marcanto, and no one knew where they had gone. But strange tales of your deeds have reached us from afar, and we wondered whether they might be true. Come, and tell us the truth of these curiosities!"

Chrono gestured to the darkened windows and said, "Is it not true that we have arrived at time of mourning?"

Pheidros looked back at the house. "Ah, not mourning, but succor," he explained. "Calea my wife is stricken sore with her affliction, and can find no rest or comfort, so that she all but despairs of living and cannot bear the light of day. So we darken the house to ease her pains."

Calea had suffered from childhood with an ailment, which afflicted her at certain spells with blinding of the eyes and sore burnings in her head, so that she would be in misery for days at a time. For years this affliction had been treated with a remedy which relieved her, and in the days when Chrono and his father had traded with Pheidros, she had lived comfortably without complaint.

"What can have gone wrong?" Chrono asked. "Does the remedy no longer serve to relieve her?"

Pheidros shook his head sadly. "The tincture which once eased her symptoms can no longer be found, anywhere in the land. But come in, and you may speak with the apothecaries themselves."

So they followed Pheidros into the house. Calea was resting in a darkened room, attended by her physician. The air was heavy with sweet-smelling herbs, and they applied cooling poultices to her forehead and arms, but little good did it do. She greeted Chrono weakly.

When Chrono had properly saluted his hosts, Pheidros took him aside to speak with the apothecaries. Their chieftess was a Cylosite, for that Tribe was expert in all the medicaments of the Southrealm, and with her was a Steggarnese attendant. "How is it," Duono asked, "that the remedy for Calea's ailment can no longer be found?"

"Do not blame us!" the Cylosite protested. "We must distill this tincture ourselves, from the bark of the gray myrtle tree. But this source grows only in the Mountains of Lodbarria, in a gorge known as the Ravine of Pirin. Some years ago Giants invaded that cleft, and have made their nest in that place. These Giants fiercely assault all who approach, casting their refuse down upon them from the heights and shouting out horrible threats. No one can be compelled to go into that valley and gather the bark we need."

"Is it not the calling of your vocation to provide for the ailing?" Chrono asked. "Good folk are suffering without this remedy! Is there no one willing to brave this peril for their sake?"

"We are healers, not adventurers. The Giants have claimed the ravine. There is nought that we can do."

Chrono was provoked. He turned to Duono and said, "Is there anything to stop us from going up to Pirin, and retrieving this bark?"

Duono smiled and said, "You know I am always eager for new exploits. Let us go at once."

The apothecaries said, "You do not understand! The ravine is narrow, and there are many Giants dwelling there: You cannot avoid their attention. Then even should you get past them all, and live, and bring back as much of this bark as two can carry, we can distill tincture enough to last for a year, perhaps less. After that we shall again be at a loss and must face the same perils once more. Who would risk their life for so little?"

Chrono answered, "I have vanquished Giants in the past, and will find a way. But even should I fail, and perish, I shall at least perish in a deed of virtue, and heap honors to my name."

Pheidros intervened. "If the tales we hear of Chrono's deeds are true, we might yet dare to hope. What is this bark you must have?"

The chieftess scowled at Chrono and shook her head. "Pah! You go at peril of your own life!" But Chrono was insistent, so she shrugged and said, "Whether you are courageous or foolish, I cannot tell. But should you make it so far, this is the tree you seek." Then she described the tree from leaf to bark to root.

"The tree can be found in the deepness of Pirin," she said, "on the south-facing slopes where the sun shines full. This hollow in this single valley is the only place we have found it to grow in all the lands of Soria south of the Ice."

Chrono said, "Guide us to this ravine, and we shall see what we might accomplish."

The chieftess said, "One of our company may go as a guide. But do not expect them to go up into the ravine with you!"

So Chrono and Duono took their rest as guests in the house of Pheidros that night, but the next morning they rose early and took up their weapons and their packs, and they set their faces towards Pirin.

They were several days on the trail, for in those days the Mountains of Lodbarria were as yet remote and lonely places. Only a narrow and long-unused footpath led to the ravine off the main trail, heading southward into wild unsettled country. A guide from among the apothecaries led the way through a rocky land of scattered pines and willow groves, as the gray dolomite ridges of the Lodbarrian Range drew closer.

At last they came to a steep incline going up into the mountains themselves. Their guide halted and directed them to a trail, now much overgrown.

"I will go no further," he said. "But as you go up into the hills beyond, the trail will soon come to a sheer wall, which must be ascended by a steep and narrow path, with much toil. You shall know it by the stench, for the Giants which now abide in the valley above dump their refuse from the heights onto the trail below. This is the habit of those foul creatures.[34]

"Should you succeed in ascending the cliff without being discovered and obliterated by the Giants, you will enter a steep-walled ravine. You must then work your way through a thickly wooded valley into the deeps of the gorge. Even then your work is not finished, for you must find the sunny hollow deep within the mountains where the gray myrtle thrives. From thence you must take strips of bark from as many living trees as you might find, being careful not to strip the tree such that it will die. If after all this you gather enough to fill your sacks and return alive, without being struck down by the Giants, the luck of the terumani is with you indeed! If it is true that Sorios watches over his children in their need, then may Sorios watch over you!"[35]

So Chrono said, "We shall proceed. If you see us not within a fortnight, we shall not return."

"I shall set camp and wait for word from you here. But do not seek your own deaths on our behalf! It would be better for you to fail and return alive, than to become the prey of Giants in that pitiful place."

Thus they parted, and Chrono and Duono went forward on the upward path into the valley, and found all things just as had been described. They looked ac-

34 The Homadalans had several times in their history been the subject of this uncivil behavior of the Giants, who had repeatedly dumped stinking refuse onto their first Village.

35 In some traditions it was believed that Sorios, after being made a Guardian and Hero of the Sorian races, at times walked in the Land, watching over and aiding those who might be found pursuing a righteous and honorable cause on behalf of others.

ross a broad, trackless vale at a steep cliff on the far side. A narrow pathway followed a series of natural ledges, and in places was cut into the naked rock, snaking up the very face of the escarpment. Even from that distance piles of refuse and offal could be seen besliming the cliffside and the pathway itself.

"That is our pathway," Chrono declared sullenly.

Duono studied the layout of their course. "When we have made it so far as the cliff we would be difficult to see from above. I think the climb shall be safe enough, though unpleasant, if we make it so far undetected. But first let us disguise ourselves against discovery."

So they donned darkened clothing the color of a mottled forest floor, and they smeared their garments with slime from a nearby stream bed to disguise their scent. They made their way furtively across the open land, and when they had assured themselves they had not been spotted, they began the ascent of the wall. Chrono breathed a sigh of relief, for things seemed to be going well.

When they had ascended barely half the height of the ridge, however, Duono called Chrono to a halt and whispered, "I hear voices approaching on the ridge above!"

Chrono pressed himself against the wall of the cliff and peered upward. So sheer was the wall that little could be spotted above but the leafy limbs of the trees which jutted out over the drop. "It is unlikely the Giants will look down at the trail," he whispered. "It is probable they have come merely to dump their refuse." He shrugged and added, "We have nowhere to retreat, in any event. Let us be still and trust to our luck."

Duono of course agreed, as there was no other option, and they both waited anxiously, hoping they were safely out of sight. After what seemed several long minutes, the Giants could be heard directly overhead. Looking up once more, Chrono spotted the burly arms of six individuals extending outward over the cliff's edge, bearing heavy, and very dirty, bags. These they turned out all at once, so that all the stinking refuse and rotting matter in all six of the bags poured down in a revolting hail.

Chrono and Duono held their nose at the stench of it, but by good fortune they were not directly below the barrage, and the bulk of it passed by them harmlessly, though much of it bounced or splattered on the cliffside as it fell. The giants above guffawed at their game, then about turned and left.

Chrono and Duono relaxed at last, and continued their climb in silence. From thence the going was laborious and slow, but they encountered no difficulty from the Giants, and they entered the wood unseen and undiscovered.

Duono was a trail-master of uncommon skill, able to read the sounds and signs of the forest. The Giants are always large, clumsy and noisy, having no reason to fear any other creature of the woods; and their odor is rank and easy to detect. If any Giant was stirring about, Duono would know it long before they crossed paths.

As they went, Duono noted that the trail into the ravine was well worn, and surmised that the Giants themselves continued to use it for their own purposes. So they left the trail and made their way through the rough of the woods: but as the ravine was not wide, it was not long before the sound of Giants approaching caused them to take cover. From their hideaway beneath the brush they could see several of the great creatures stomping along the pathway.

In a whisper Chrono said, "These creatures, debased as they are, have yet a spark of reason within them. We have already had one narrow encounter. Our task will be greatly eased should we be at peace with them as we work. Allow me to approach and offer amity, if only for a season."

Duono did not approve. "All our dealings with Giants have been only of strife and violence," he said, "and I think the creatures know of no other manner of living."

"Yet they are descended of the terumani, however debased and ill-formed they have become. And these are not the Giants of Batack.[36] Perhaps the reason of the terumani lingers with them yet, and can be fanned to life."

So against the counsel of Duono, Chrono stepped forward from the shadows. "Hail, Erescali of the Ravine of Pirin!" he greeted them. "We have heard of your might and authority in these parts from far away, and have come to seek your aid in our mission!"

The Giants halted their march in surprise. The one nearest to Chrono stepped forward, a glowering scowl in its dark eyes, and it said, "What have we to do with the stinking brood of Deïni?"

Chrono said, "The blood of the deïnings runs in your veins as well, so we are kin. If you would not aid us in your might, bear with us for just a little while in your mercy, for we want nothing more than a short season of peace to pursue our labor."

But the Giant scoffed and said, "You shall have no aid nor peace, and your mission is in vain."

Chrono said, "We want only one thing, which in your benevolence you may grant. We would gather strips of bark from the trees in this ravine, which our folk desire for medicine. If the Giants of Pirin are as great as we have heard, such a trifling thing will mean nothing to them."

But the Giant said, "We know of your desire for this bark, for the little vermin of Deïni used to scuttle about in our woods to gather it. But we drove them out before, and so shall we drive you out as well." Then hefting his club the Giant heaved it at Chrono, who scarcely escaped being pummeled thereby. Then the whole company of Giants rushed at him, brandishing clubs and smashing through the woods, hoping to beat their enemy to a pulp. But Chrono and Duono were too quick for them, and vanished among the trees.

36 The Giants of Batack had a reputation for being particularly ill-humored.

When they had reached safety, Duono merely smiled and said to Chrono, "So I predicted! We shall have no help from these brutes, and they shall merely thwart us at every opportunity."

Chrono and Duono therefore made their way cautiously through the ravine thereafter. Duono's skills, however, kept them safe, and they traversed the way without being discovered.

When the day was spent and the hour was late, they came upon the hollow which had been spoken of by the apothecaries, and scrambling down into the place they found the gray myrtle in abundance. But in the center of the copse was a clearing where the foliage was trampled and much ruined, and it stank. There they found a great heap of the refuse of Giants, noisy with flies, much of it in fetid open piles, or gathered up into such crude sacks as the Giants were known to use. In the midst of it all, scratching themselves and snarling loathsomely, sat two Giants with their backs turned to them.

Chrono was dispirited. "The hollow we've sought, the one place we need to work freely, appears to be the very nest of these Giants," he whispered. "Who knows but what they all may return at any moment."

"We will do as we're able," Duono said. "If we can find a quiet spot away from the eyes and ears of the brutes, you may work to find the material we need, and I shall keep watch. At the first sign of the Giants I shall give you a signal, and we shall go at once into hiding. But for now, we should find a safe place away from this clearing where we might camp for the night."

So they departed into the woods. There in a well guarded thicket growing hard by the wall of the ravine, Duono found a secure and hidden spot for their camp, where they might hope to remain undiscovered by the Giants, and they took their rest.

The next morning, however, they awoke to find the whole troop of the Giants inhabiting the hollow. Chrono and Duono snooped about furtively, hunting for a source of the bark near the edge of the grove, out of sight of the Giants: finding a tree far from the Giants' nest, they began the work of taking strips from the stock. But before a few minutes had passed, the sound of a Giant was heard lumbering toward them, growling, "What vermin do I hear invading our camp?" And it thrashed about in the brush with its club, so that Chrono and Duono both feared for their lives, and fled that site.

Although they waited the whole day, the Giants did not abandon that place: eating, and drowsing, and doing whatever crude industry the creatures are capable of. At times they would come or go, sometimes bringing in bags of foul forage; sometimes carting off bags of their refuse. Some would stay behind, while others would return. There was a constant bustle of their activity throughout the day, insomuch that Chrono seldom had more than a few moments to move in among the groves to extract bark as the apothecaries had shown him, before the Giants would return and force him to flee. These few gleanings they dejectedly bundled, and they set them in the clearing before their camp at the end of the day.

The next day also was like the first, so that before they had worked more than a few minutes, a Giant crashed through the woods toward them, snarling, "I hear and smell the vermin children of Deïni,[37] whose presence we defy!" And smashing about with its club would easily have killed them were it not for the skills of Duono to aid their escape.

All that day, also, the Giants spent coming and going, wandering about and returning, and loafing about the better part of the day. Duono complained to Chrono, saying, "We have provisions only for a few more days before we must return from this ravine, unless we find forage from the land. If what we have learned from the apothecaries is correct, we have gathered scarcely enough material to make a week's worth of elixir. The Giants are too many for us two to drive out from this place, and too stupid to be baited away. And our very lives are in constant peril at their hands."

Chrono considered the matter darkly. "Tomorrow," he conceded, "if the Giants have returned again, let us scout the ravine further for another source, or we shall fail in our task completely."

This plan seemed good to Duono. On the third morning, no sooner had they begun their work, than once again the sound of storm approached, and a Giant flailed through the grove towards them, growling, "The vermin sons of Deïni come as before to pester us. You shall carry nothing from our grove. But your bones shall leave this valley in a sack of garbage!" And smashing about he sought to kill them, and Chrono and Duono once again scarcely escaped with their lives.

As they had purposed earlier they resolved to seek another grove of the myrtle trees. Each took a different path, agreeing to return to their camp before the sun set over the lip of the ravine in the afternoon.

Chrono searched intently throughout the day. Though he sought long, no tree could be found such as those in the groves of the sunny hollow where the Giants camped. As the day waned Chrono grew bitter, and he sat down on a rock far from the camp of the Giants to complain, saying,

"Feckless the fate   that found me here.
With tantalizing triumph   taunting near,
Ungraspable   while all but gained,
A profitless prize   impossible to claim.

37 The Giants of Pirin repeatedly refer to all Sorites by such curious terms as the "children of Deïni." This is probably no more than a reference to Deïni's relationship to the Sorites' ancestors as their discoverer and guardian. It is unlikely even the Giants were so stupid as to assume they were the actual progeny of Deïni.

This secret glen, salvation's source,
Assuaging anguish of ailing friends
Rewards our work with wages of grief,
Affords but failure, futile our pains.

The name of Chrono, acclaimed afar,
Feted by folk from far-off lands,
Would be unknown if not for aid,
Upheld and helped by covert hands.

Dare I hope for hidden heroes?
Secret saviors to succor me?
I boasted boons in boldness rash,
By brags I cannot bring to pass."

Then giving up the day's labor at last, he returned stealthily to the secret camp and met with Duono. But Duono also had failed in his search, and had found nothing for his pains but a few pieces of dried fruit remaining on the branches of a withered fig tree, and some of the late season's nuts, which he had gathered to extend their provisions if possible. They assessed the result of the day's labor, and laid it all in a pile before their camp. Chrono sighed and said, "One more day can we risk in this place, then we must admit our failure, and return in humiliation to the house of Pheidros."

So they agreed, and set their watch for the night.

Now it happened that deep in the night as Duono slept, Chrono was on watch. Giants do not go about at night, so there was little to fear; and a great weariness overcame Chrono. So he closed his eyes against his own will, and fell into a deep and unnatural sleep, as if enchanted. Not until the light of morning crept to the floor of the ravine did he awaken with a start.

He rose quickly and scrambled to the edge of the thicket, hoping their trove had remained undiscovered by the Giants in his neglect. At a glance into the clearing his heart leapt, and but for the fear of alerting the Giants he would have shouted out. For in the clearing, where their few scraps of food and bundles of bark had been the night before, he found a great heap of bark of the myrtle tree, neatly stripped, freshly gathered and tied into bundles. Beside that, on a mat of fresh leaves, was spread an array of wholesome dried fruits and nuts, enough provision to last them the whole day.

Then he awoke Duono and said, "What is this? Have you been gathering in secret by night?"

Duono rubbed his eyes sleepily and crawled forward to see the trove. He shook his head, as perplexed as Chrono. "How could I gather by night in silence, in the deep dark of this ravine, without so much as daring a light for fear of the Giants?"

"What then? Could this be a stash of the Giants that we missed in the gloaming when we made camp last night?"

"Certainly not!" said Duono. "What purpose would the Giants have for gathering bark in the manner of the apothecaries? These ignorant brutes surely haven't the skill to distill it into an elixir, if they even knew of its healing property! And the food of the Giants is always foul and unclean, and unlike this repast spread before us here!"

"Could it then be that someone else has followed us into this hollow who knows of our task?"

"Or perhaps in our discouragement, and by virtue of the dimness of light in this ravine, both of us have failed to discern the fulness of our gathering," Duono suggested doubtfully. "If not, we perhaps have witnessed a marvel. In any event, let us revel in our good fortune, and see what more we can accomplish this day."

Once again they set about for the day's work, attempting to gather whatever they might when the Giants were gone from the hollow, or were busy in the woods at the far side of the hollow. But still the Giants would not abandon the place, but loafed about throughout the day. Chrono and Duono had little peace; and once more their gleanings were few. Once again they returned to their secret camp in discouragement, and laying their gleanings before the thicket they said, "Our good fortune overnight has bought us one day further. Let us see what the morrow brings, and then we must decide."

So they again settled in to sleep for the night.

Now just as had happened the night before, Chrono was lulled into a deep and unnatural sleep while on watch. As on the prior morning, when he awoke, the stash at the entrance to their camp was doubled or tripled, so that the stockpile which lay before them was greater than they could remember or imagine.

Then were they indeed confounded. "Surely we cannot have so completely undercounted our gleanings from this task!" Duono said, "And again we have more than enough provisions for another day. Let us labor once more, and see what another day shall bring!"

So it happened for three more nights. Each day their gatherings were paltry, and achieved only with the greatest of difficulty, yet each morning when they awoke their stockpile had increased yet further.

At last Duono looked about them in the morning, and said, "Already we have here far more than we can hope to carry back with us to the apothecaries. Indeed, this stash is grown so great that we now risk the attention of the Giants, who, should they stumble upon it here, will be alerted to our camp."

But Chrono said, "Yet one thing we lack, which I should dearly like to acquire. If we could find a sapling of the tree, we might bring it back with us to the house of Pheidros, where it might be planted and nurtured, that they might grow a supply of their own, and never lack healing for Calea his wife."

Duono frowned however, and said, "While this is a worthy desire, it would take much effort and time to uproot even a small sapling with the tools we have carried with us. Such labor would surely draw the attention of the Giants upon us."

"Let me search, however, but one day further, and see what I might find. It may be that a healthy sapling grows in loose soil at the edges of the copse, where the Giants seldom stumble. With such good fortune as we have had this past week, perhaps we may yet find what we need."

But though they searched long and diligently, they found no opportunity to uproot any such sapling, and Chrono lamented in discouragement, "So be it. We have bark enough to distill a supply of elixir, so we must make do with this alone. We can only hope that the Giants will soon abandon this ravine, and the apothecaries may return on their own to the Grove of Pirin."

It happened that night as on the previous nights, that Chrono was lulled into a deep sleep during his watch; when he awoke, looking before their camp, he was hardly surprised to find ten hale saplings of the gray myrtle, their roots neatly wrapped in burlap and moist scraps of moss and mulch.

Then Duono said, "There can be no doubt that we have been aided by secret hands, though I know not by whom, nor how they have succeeded where we have failed so miserably. Let us at any rate thank our good fortune, and see to the business of transporting what we can from this ravine."

But Chrono answered, "Let us remain one more night behind, and leave a gift of thanks for our benefactor. Then let us both remain awake if we are able. I for one should like to discover who has been our savior in this thankless task, and to thank them myself for their aid."

Duono said, "Well might you wait one more night, and many more besides, if you should hope to bring out even the tenth of this trove we have acquired here. Though the richness of this stockpile would do much good for Calea for years to come, and many others beside her, we cannot possibly hope to carry such a load safely through the valley and down the wall without many days' labor and much peril."

Nevertheless Duono agreed to this plan, and they put together a gift of their blankets and blades, and such other few valuables as they had ported into the ravine with them, as well as an offering of flowers and blossoms which they had gathered. Then as the daylight turned to dusk, they settled in to rest and watch.

Deep into the night they watched, each one trying to keep the other from falling into slumber. But at last the spell became too much for them, and Duono drifted off to sleep, and Chrono's eyes began to sink.

Just when his mind began to drift into dreams a stirring was heard in the clearing before their thicket, and Chrono managed to crawl forward to peer into the dimness. There at last he saw the form of a spright of the woods, a dræad robed in darkness.

The spright had found the offering left for him, and winking, he sat down opposite Chrono, and said, "Awaken, friend of teruman, of nymph and spright. You may keep the gift you offer. The name of Chrono hath gone before thee, and thou art welcome here. Both water-nymph and wood-spright have spread the word of thy friendship, and of the great love thou hast for the maiden of the Sea."

The heaviness lifted from his lids, and Chrono said, "I am at a disadvantage. You know my name, but I do not know you."

"I am called Piriën, the spright of this hollow of the myrtle trees that you seek. I have long welcomed those who come for the healing bark: but it is long since any have dared set foot in this vale, for fear of the foul Giants that now infest my country."

"It appears we are in your debt. We would never have succeeded alone in our labor, for reason of the Giants. If we had the strength to go against them, I would drive them forth from this valley altogether, for they are a pestilence on the land."

Piriën laughed. "And a welcome change would that be. Alas, that I have no such power myself. But," he shrugged almost cheerfully, "I have my trees and my foliage, and they are well. Notwithstanding, I have been glad to aid the friend of the terumani in his quest. The song of your lament reached my ears at the fringes of my grove, and it hath pleased me to secretly defy the Erescali on your behalf."

Chrono replied, "Then I shall be so bold as to ask you one further favor: the trove we have laid up with your aid is great, and would do much good. But how shall we transport so great a load, in this land plagued with Giants? We will have to make many returns to transport it all, in every traverse remaining unseen in a narrow ravine while passing the Giants. We have now a great abundance of the bark, such that it will take days of constant danger to haul it out of the valley one pack at a time."

Piriën shook his head regretfully and said, "In this matter I fear I have no power to aid you. I cannot make the trees your porters." He smiled wryly. "Perhaps I have done ill in leaving you with such a burden!"

"You have aided us more than we can repay, many times over. If you would, though, sit with me awhile, that we might discuss this matter together. You have brought us a precious trove. I need only a means to convey it to those who need it."

So Chrono and Piriën sat up together holding counsel, and debating many schemes. Hours passed in this manner, but at last Piriën said, "You must rest, and I must depart. Much have we considered, but each design always ends on these two hurdles: that you cannot traverse the ravine with such a burden in anything less than a week; and that in so doing you cannot avoid the Giants."

"You speak nothing but the truth," Chrono said. Then suddenly a smile passed over his lips and he said, "So perhaps the only solution is to do neither."

"I'm afraid I do not see your meaning," Piriën said, raising an eyebrow.

So Chrono sat with Piriën and explained his plan.

"I shall do what I can," Piriën finally said, standing to go. "Though I must say, I find thee audacious!" he added with a wink. "I must away, but look for me again on the morrow, if I can fetch what you have requested."

So Piriën departed, and faded into the leafy shadows, and Chrono at last took rest.

When he awoke in the morning he told Duono his intent. He sent Duono out of the ravine, that he might contact the guide of the apothecaries, who waited for them below. "Instruct him to go to the nearest village or homestead," Chrono said, "and find folk willing to labor: and have them bring all the sledges and barrels they can find, to bear a bulky load to the household of Pheidros, who shall pay them well for their work."

"Have you a plan? The porters will certainly not scale the cliff, nor enter this cursed ravine to claim the prize!"

"They may wait below. I will see to the delivery."

"I cannot see how," Duono shrugged. "But you have managed stranger wonders."

While Duono was gone from the camp, Piriën returned, bringing with him six very large but crude and dirty sacks which he had stolen from the camp of the Giants, and a quantity of clean and wholesome leaves. Chrono examined it and smiled. "These supplies shall do nicely," he said.

"Then I wish thee luck, for you will have need of it," Piriën declared. And once more he faded into the forest.

Chrono spent the remainder of the day in wrapping bundles of the bark in the leaves, then stuffing them into the sacks, until all the trove that Piriën had brought had been neatly packed away. The saplings also he padded carefully and hid them away in one large sack.

When Duono returned at nightfall from his errand, he found the entire trove wrapped and packed away. "I see you have been busy. But I fail to see how this helps us. The quantity of packs has been lessened, but now each sack is more than we can carry! The two of us together could not drag even one such burden to the valley's edge, even if we work all night, stumbling through the dark while the Giants sleep."

Chrono said, "You are correct. But I do not intend to drag them nearly so far!" Then he explained to Duono his plan.

Duono sighed. "Let us work late, then take what little rest we can, for we must arise early to be out of the valley before the Giants awaken. If they discover our work we shall find it so much the harder to make our escape past them and down the wall."

It came to pass just as Duono had said. He and Chrono hurried from their camp as soon as dawn broke, taking not a single bag with them, for their hope was to reach the edge of the ravine before the Giants arose and got about their business. But in their haste they were less cautious, and they stumbled onto one of the Giants along the trail.

The Giant, seeing them, raised its club to threaten them, and growled, "You vermin pests of the brood of Deïni still dare to sneak about in our ravine?" Then it gloated, "Yet I see you empty-handed. So we have at least thwarted your useless mission."

But Chrono said, "Do not count us as thwarted before the day has ended. Sometimes success comes from the most unexpected of sources!"

At this the Giant rushed at them, swinging its bludgeon, and saying, "Should I smash you first, you shall have no cause to crow."

But once again Chrono and Duono were too quick for the brute, and they escaped in the tangle of the wooded valley floor, as the sound of the Giant thrashing about and roaring faded behind them.

They hurried on their way, and before the morning was far spent they had managed to reach the wall and descend to the plain below. There they found waiting for them the guide from the company of the apothecaries, who received them joyfully, along with a large company from the nearby countryside who had come with conveyances and packs.

Then the apothecary said to them, "It is well to see you, and to see you both alive. But what of the trove of bark you had promised? Were you then waylaid at the last by these Giants, and forced to flee with nothing for your labor?"

Chrono said, "Do not so quickly lose hope! Let us approach the wall and wait a spell, and see what transpires."

So they all sat and watched, keeping an eye on the ridgeline above. It came to pass, not long after this, that Giants appeared at the lip of the wall. Chrono rose to his feet and shouted up at them, to be certain he claimed their attention. "Ho, Giants of Pirin! Once again I ask, will you cooperate and leave us in peace? For I have brought today a great crowd to lay claim to our quarry."

The Giants spotted the company of folk below, and began to laugh and guffaw at Chrono's impertinence, deriding him and mocking his companions. They called down from the clifftop, "Look! The stinking children of Deïni gather below! But they dare not come up to get the treasures they seek, or we shall crush them and knock them from the wall like ninepins! Ho! For your affront take our offal upon your heads!"

Then as one they began to shake out the contents of their sacks from the edge of the cliff.

But rather than the stink and refuse they had expected, they showered the company below with a hail of neatly wrapped bundles. These fell lightly down the precipice, bouncing and settling in the grass at the foot of the cliff. At a command from Chrono a cheer went up from the folk in the plain before the wall, and all rushed in together, eagerly gathering all they could of the bounty, and carting it out of range as quickly as they might.

The Giants were confounded at this turn, and they looked at each other in blank confusion.

Duono laughed and said, "So the Giants who have thwarted us all this time have been our own accomplices after all!"

For while the Giants had slept, Chrono and Duono had spent the night in dragging the heavy sacks of their gatherings down into the heart of the hollow. There they found the refuse heap of the Giants, and as the brutes slumbered they replaced the sacks of the Giants with their own. Then they had stuffed refuse into the openings of their own sacks (being careful never to contaminate the bark which was wrapped securely within). So when they were done, they could scarcely tell their own trove from the refuse of the Giants.

This very trove the Giants themselves had borne on their own backs to the edge of the ravine, and dumped it in mockery onto their adversaries.

Then Chrono called up the wall to the Giants above, taunting them. "You refused us aid and refused us peace, and threatened to toss us from the wall as refuse: but instead you yourselves have become our porters, and have delivered our bounty to us! I'm sorry I can offer you no payment for your labor, but many of the children of Deïni shall find relief thanks to you, and shall praise the strong arms of the Giants of Pirin!"

At this the Giants flew into a rage, and began tossing boulders and limbs from the trees down from the shelf of the wall above. But the folk of the village had already gathered all the trove, and were safely beyond danger.

So it was that Chrono tricked the Giants of Pirin into delivering a great load of healing bark for the apothecaries of Steggan. And to this day when one finds aid from an unlikely source, it is said that "the Giants of Pirin have aided us."

The apothecaries were overjoyed to receive such a bounty, and with it they were able to produce a great quantity of elixir. So Calea found relief from her affliction at last.

Moreover Pheidros took the saplings that Chrono had brought back from the Ravine of Pirin, and planted a grove on his own lands: these Calea cared for herself, and they thrived. When they had matured, never again did Calea lack aid for her affliction.

The names of Chrono and Duono, meanwhile, went out through all that region, so that Chrono became more celebrated than ever.

7. CHRONO AND THE SPECTERS OF THE DEAD

This tale is told of Chrono and Duono, in the days when Chrono was estranged from his household and parted from the sea-maiden he loved. Together Chrono and Duono wandered the lands of the Southrealm together seeking deeds of honor; while Ahten remained in the house of her father and mother in the depths of Potomis, coveting any word from the realms of the dry land.

Chrono was abiding for a time among the Cylosites, in a certain village on the Plain of Cylos by the name of Derideth. There he and Duono dwelt with a tradesman of their acquaintance, who dealt in woven goods and pottery. They were welcome in that place, for they had made themselves useful to the folk of the village, helping in any task which was asked of them: for both Duono and Chrono were skilled at many crafts. All who knew them honored them as friends: moreover the miracle of how Chrono had rescued the Cylosites of Këuca from the Giant and from winter's peril was spoken of throughout that realm.

Now it came about one day that certain warriors of that village gathered together, banging their war hammers on their shields and raising a war-cry. At the sound of it Chrono and Duono came out of their place to investigate.

The commander of the party was named Repellen. He was the strongest and most skilled with his weapons, so all the warriors of Derideth accepted him as their captain and obeyed his orders. He brought his company to Chrono and said, "Come out with us to do battle! It will be good sport, and you will do us a favor besides. Our scouts have spotted a band of gnomes which has invaded our country. We mean to drive them back whence they came."

Chrono shared a suspicious glance with Duono, then turning to the Repellen he said, "You know that I will not shrink from danger, and do not fear combat, for I place little value on this life. I will gladly aid a struggle of honor and good repute. What is your grievance with these Gauphrin?"

The captain laughed. "They are gnomes. Does one need any grievance beyond that? The gnomes are a pestilence wherever they appear. They destroy gardens, groves and houses with their digging, and are thieves besides."

Duono said, "I have seen no sign of gnomes in this village. Nor have I heard any complaint of theft or loss."

"They have done no harm because we have kept them at bay. If we did not drive them off they would certainly settle in our land and do mischief, for that is their way."

Chrono tried to wave them off, saying, "I will not partake of vengeance for crimes that have yet to be committed. If they have done you no harm, what is the source of your anger against them?"

The troops of the Cylosites clamored at this, saying, "All know the harm that this folk will do if left unchecked! They are selfish and unprincipled, and will happily ruin whatever good thing they come across."

While Chrono knew this complaint to be valid, yet he had never known the Gauphrin to be malicious, or act out of rank belligerence. "You may go without me," he said. "I will gladly defend lives and property. But I will not partake in an unprovoked attack."

The captain of the troop said, "Unprovoked? Their very presence provokes us! Five times have they invaded our borders from the south, and five times have we driven them forth. Yet as many times as we drive them out, they return again."

This seemed odd to Chrono, so he turned to Duono and said, "What do you think of this? Have you ever heard of Gauphrin on the offensive, attempting to lay claim to land by violence?"

"The gnomes are opportunists. While they care little for others, I have never heard of so determined an invasion."

Chrono said to the captain of the troop, "I do not wish to partake in battle without cause, but I will go out with you and see this thing. My heart tells me that there is a mystery to solve here."

"Come then," the commander said. "But bring your weapons, for there may be a fight."

So it was that Chrono and Duono took up their spears, and the Cylosites took up their hammers and clubs. The commander of the Cylosites brought the party southward out of Derideth. They were led by the scout who had brought word of the company of gnomes, who guided them fleetly across the plain towards the site of their camp.

The Plain of Cylos is flat and open for many miles, and even in those days when the Ice had pushed Batack to the south, that forest was far to the east, and only scattered trees and copses broke the open grasslands. The Cylosites plowed through oceans of tall grass as high as their shoulders, and in places stands of wild mustard towered, even over the heads of Chrono and Duono. There were no tall hills to be seen, but here and there a homestead or village of the Cylosites could be found, often surrounded by gardens or groves of fruit and nut trees. While the Cylosites of Batack lived by the produce of the forest, those who had settled on the plain lived by the work of their own hands.

For several hours the company crossed this plain, until at last the scout brought them to a halt. In a quiet voice he said, "There is a gentle rise straight ahead. We will see the camp of the gnomes before us as we cross it. But go cautiously! If they have sentries on duty, they may spot us as well."

So the warriors held their weapons at the ready and proceeded stealthily up the slope.

As they reached the crest of the rise Chrono parted the grass, and saw in the distance a camp of gray tents. Only a few of these were visible, and they were difficult to discern, for they lay low in a hollow of the grass as if for cover. No smoke went up, no pennants fluttered above the field, and no troops of armed warriors could be seen.

Repellen the commander of the Cylosites summoned his troops and took counsel with them. "We have driven these gnomes out of this country enough times," he said quietly. "Yet they continue to invade. Let us take a new strategy."

So he divided his company into three parts. Two of these he sent southward to flank the camp of the Gauphrin, staying out of sight as they passed to either side of them. His own company remained hidden behind the crest of the slope. When his compatriots had established their positions they kindled watchfires of dry brush, sending up signals of smoke. When Repellen saw both signals, he quickly kindled his own fire, then raised a pennant on a tall pole, and with a loud shout he gave the command to charge.

The folk of his own party raised their weapons and lifted their voices, and ran furiously towards the camp.

The camp of the gnomes was roused at once. The tents disappeared in an instant, pulled down and whipped hurriedly into bundles. Any belongings they may have carried were clearly already packed as if in preparation for a sudden retreat. The hooded figures of a group of the Gauphrin appeared in the tall grass, hastening to depart. A line of warriors, if warriors they could be called, took a position between the charging Cylosites of Repellen's company and the rest of their folk, as if to protect them and enable them to make their escape.

But from the slopes beyond the camp of the gnomes the other two divisions made their own appearance. They had fanned out in a line to the south. Shouting and clashing their shields, they made a fearsome wall, cutting off the gnomes from any hope of an easy retreat.

A brief skirmish followed, the Cylosites assailing their foes harshly. The line of Gauphrin stood their ground briefly, dodging blows and fending off the Cylosites. But the wall of their foes drew in toward the fray methodically, enveloping them like a garrote. Cylosites are doughty fighters: though they are short, they are stocky and heavy-boned. The gnomes, however, though a bit taller than the Cylosites, are not used to battle, for they spend their days skulking in their tunnels and warrens beneath the earth. They are not a courageous folk. So the Gauphrin were soon outmatched. When it became clear there was no escape in any direction, they threw down their weapons and kneeled before their attackers in defeat. If any slipped away through the tall grass none ever knew of it. The captives scowled and snarled, but not one of them spoke a word.

The warriors of Repellen hooted and whooped at their easy victory. They rounded up the whole company of gnomes, male and female, children and all, and bound them hand and foot that they might not escape. Then they made then them sit down together in a circle in the middle of the broken camp, and discussed what should be done next. The Gauphrin sat silently, squinting bitterly and silently at their captors.

Chrono shook his head sadly, "It is good that you have failed to kill any of them. For they did not fight as invaders, but as defenders."

Repellen spat. "They fight like cowards, dodging and defending, and running when they have the chance, before we are able to strike them down."

"Either way, such a victory would bring no honor."

Repellen sneered down at them. "Nevertheless it remains to be seen what is to become of them. It would be better had they all died in battle. We certainly cannot simply expel them into their own country yet again. They have returned these five times. They will return again."

So a debate arose among the party of the Cylosites, whether all the prisoners should be kept in bonds, or put into stone dungeons, or put to death. All agreed they could not be set free or returned to their own country.

Chrono was aghast. "Surely you cannot think it just to put to death prisoners taken in battle?"

Repellen answered. "How else shall we be rid of them? We cannot keep watch on them forever. If we let down our guard they will tunnel their way to freedom and we shall be worse off than if we had never overcome them at all."

Chrono cast his eyes about the ruined camp. It revealed little, but it was clear they had lit no fires, possessed little baggage, and carried few weapons. There were clear signs of only a dozen tents, and no more than a score of individuals had they captured alive. "Is any such punishment meet for such a party as this?" he pleaded. "I think that we would have little to fear from this company. They are few, and poorly equipped."

Repellen shrugged indifferently. "It does not take a large group to start a colony of gnomes. If they make their home near any village of our folk they will bring it to ruin."

Duono concurred with Chrono. He looked pityingly at the group of captives. "These folk are destitute. They have more an appearance of refugees than of invaders."

"They will be rich enough on the spoils of our own folk if we allow them to go free. Do not be deceived."

Chrono grew indignant. "They have traveled far into your country already.

They have surely passed more than one village along the way, and several groves where good earth and roots for a warren might be found. Why have they left such places unmolested? It may be they have no interest in you or your villages at all! Let us question them and learn of their plans. "

"They will not speak," Repellen grumbled. "Whenever we encounter them they are as silent as stones. Even could we wrest or cajole a word from their surly throats, they would lie and deceive. Do you know nothing of gnomes?"

"I know that, nettlesome as they may be, they are terumani, after all. Would it not invite judgement to take the lives of terumani without justification?"

Repellen smirked. "As I understand it, the gnomes are as nettlesome to the Terumani as they are to our own folk.[38] I do not think they will care to defend or avenge them."

"Do nothing rashly! Let me see if I can convince them to speak with me."

Repellen sighed impatiently, but out of respect for Chrono he acceded to this request.

For several days, then, Chrono continued to make appeals to the gnomes, but they continued in their stubborn silence. They treated him with the same coldness with which they treated the Cylosites. Chrono could not even hazard a guess as to which of them might be their leader.

Repellen at last grew impatient. "We are wasting time, here," he said. "My warriors wish to return home. We cannot stay here forever watching these prisoners. Something must be done to end this stalemate at once."

So Chrono went a last time to the gnomes and pleaded with them. "Do you not understand that I am trying to save you? These Cylosites are thinking to do you violence! If you do not speak I cannot help you."

The gnomes, however, ignored him as if deaf.

Then Chrono went off into a quiet place away from the camp and sang a lament, saying,

"Who can hope to halt a senseless tragedy—
Presume to soften dull, insensate stone—
When facing down a seething mob, alone,
With neither status nor authority?

I can but watch, while powerless to save:
Am neither spoken to, nor am I heard.
One side as deaf and indurate as wood,
The other camp as voiceless as a grave.

38 In this instance Repellen is distinguishing the high Terumani from the common terumani, which of course would include the Gauphrin.

The harmless neck lies bare beneath the blade;
A spider's-thread of patience stays its stroke,
And feebly reins the bitter, bloody joke
Whose vengeful jape is waiting to be played.

So anguish black as midnight clouds my eye,
To look upon a pup condemned to die!"

When he had sung this song, Chrono sat for a spell in deep thought and quiet despair, but at last he got up to return to his tent. Now Chrono's song had been heard further than he had thought, so it was that as he passed by the huddle of the Gauphrin, one of them looked up in the moonlight, and caught his eye, and gave him a suggestive nod. Chrono glanced at the guard who stood watch over the prisoners, then approached the one who had signaled.

The gnome scowled as ever, but he whispered without looking up, "You are unlike the others. I would confide in you, but not within earshot of these Cylosite dogs." He gestured to the guard.

Chrono nodded. "Let me see what I might arrange."

He went at once to the tent of Repellen, and begged for one last opportunity to interview the Gauphrin. "But," he insisted, "It must be in a quiet place away from the camp, or I am certain they will not speak. Allow me to take one, just one, separated from their group. I give you my word that he shall return with me: and my word of honor is all I possess in this world."

So Repellen agreed, but he said, "You may take one and one alone, but it must remain fettered in your presence."

Chrono returned to the huddle of prisoners, and sought out the one who had signaled him earlier. At an order from Repellen the guard released him into Chrono's custody. Together they walked out of the camp, into the darkness and tall grass of the fields round them, until they were far from the camp of the Cylosites.

At last Chrono said, "You must make a case, if you wish to save the lives of yourself and your families. The Cylosites can barely be persuaded to show patience. It will not be long before they decree their judgement, and I can neither influence them nor stop them."

"We have no case to make to these wretches. They will do what they choose and bear the guilt of it. But I would that the truth be known by one with an honest heart."

So the gnome explained his story to Chrono.

The gnome went by the name of Agrar Denn, and he had been the leader of a warren from the woods beyond the Plain of Cylos, several days march to the south. Their warren had formerly been prosperous and comfortable, but had fallen on hard times. A certain Giant[39] had made its home in their country, and discovering their tunnels, it had pursued them ruthlessly. It dug up their tunnels whenever it found the entrances, and attacked their folk when it discovered them in the open. It had even gone so far as to poison their passages so they could not return. They had tried several times to remove themselves to new quarters, salvaging what they could of their belongings and provisions, but the Giant was unrelenting and implacable. It always found them out again, and attacked again, as cruelly as before.

"We are fugitives of this Giant and its persecutions. Fugitives, I say! Our folk have scattered, and not a few have perished. We are all who remain of that clan."

Chrono pondered. "Surely there is some remote spot in the forest nearby where you might settle without disturbing this creature?"

"The Giant spreads wide its claims, and seeks us out with a vengeance. And who knows but what more of its companions may soon arrive to follow its example? For this reason it was our purpose to flee far from that place, very far indeed, to the sanctuary of the Gauphrin where we may be safe and free from fear."

"It is clear, however, that you cannot live here among the Cylosites. They are little better than the Giants in regard to your folk!"

Agrar Denn spat. "Pah! We would not live in your nasty, open-sky country! No, not at all. We must pass through your lands to seek sanctuary."

"Must you cross the open plain, where you are easily spotted? Would it not be better to make your way through the forests to the east?"

A shudder passed over Agrar Denn. "That forest is the haunt of Giants. You forget we would have no warren to which we might retreat while we travel. The Giants are worse than the Cylosites. If we were caught above ground by Giants it would be the end of us."

Chrono shook his head. "You may fare no better among these Cylosites. Their judgement may be harsh. Many of them are pushing to have your whole party destroyed!"

"If they choose to strike us down, we shall fight to escape, come what may. We may not succeed, but the Cylosites shall feel our bite. Fewer of them shall return to their village than left it."

"I fear it may yet come to that," Chrono sighed. "I have no sway among these warriors. With luck I might yet convince them to stay their hand for a spell, but they will keep you prisoners, and treat you harshly even so. But at least prisoners have a hope of escape. If I but knew where your secret sanctuary was hidden I might find some way to get you there."

Agrar Denn looked at him doubtfully. "Secret? It is no secret. The Valley

39 Curiously, the word used for "Giant" in this passage might also refer to one of the Terumani. While the Terumani might at times have expelled troublesome colonies of gnomes, the degree of cruelty as described by Agrar Denn seems out of character.

of Chiccir is the sanctuary of the gnomes. All of our kind are welcome there, and dwell there in peace and safety from our enemies."

At the name of Chiccir Chrono started. "I know of this place!" he said. "The Cylosites speak of it with fear. It is a strange and eldritch country: the Cylosites say it is the haunt of wraiths and specters. None will go there."

The Valley of Chiccir was well-known among the Cylosites of Derideth. It lay little more than a day's march north of that village, and all the Cylosites of the Plain of Cylos spoke of it with dread. At the night of the full moon all the Cylosites of that country would remain indoors, hiding their heads beneath dark covers, for only so could they escape the hauntings of that night. The specters of the dead were said to come out of Chiccir and walk the earth on those nights, seeking the souls of the living. Any they caught outside would be dragged bodily into the realm of the dead, and what might become of them after that none knew or dared to consider.

This rumor was firmly believed by all that folk. Many of the Cylosites who lived in that region claimed to have seen the dogs of the dead running wildly through the land by moonlight, howling, and glowing with a corpse-like gleam. Still others claimed even to have seen the specters themselves by night, aglow with the pale light of death. Even the valley itself was said to glow in the light of the moon like the putrescent dead.

"The Cylosites are ignorant and superstitious," said Agrar Denn dismissively. "Ignorant and superstitious! If that is their belief, so much the better for us. As we have heard the tales, there is nothing in Chiccir but hillocks of good stone, softer than sandstone and easy to excavate, but hard as basalt once exposed to the air. The tunnels there are said to be dry and comfortable. Mines they have, also, of many useful elements. Most of all, the place is well defended from all our enemies."[40]

"Are you quite certain of this? The Cylosites clearly know nothing of it," said Chrono. "To them it is merely a place of fear and dread, that glows by night with a shimmer of corruption. "

At this Agrar Denn laughed. "It glows with the light of the moon, not the light of death! That valley is said by us to shine in glory by night!"

Chrono grew thoughtful. "If what you say is true, you have been fortunate to have said nothing of this to the Cylosites!" he said. "I now have a plan. Let us discuss this, and see if you might dare to follow it through!"

Chrono returned Agrar Denn to the custody of the guards as he had

---

40 The Valley of Chiccir was a large region of heavily eroded volcanic tuff, with many gullies, hillocks, and cone-shaped towers. Over many centuries of occupation by the gnomes it would eventually take the form of a walled city, the natural features of the landscape carved into homes and towers of fantastic shape and extravagant decoration. It would one day become the only city of the gnomes in Soria.

promised, and repaired to his own tent where he confided to Duono in whispered secrecy. "I believe I have a plan which may save the Gauphrin, and quell the fears of the Cylosites, in a single stroke. But I shall need your aid."

"You know that I am always at your service in performing a deed of honor. Tell me what it is you require."

"I do not think you will relish your role in this adventure!" Chrono quipped. "In some cases, doing what is honorable may earn us dishonor in the eyes of others."

"Try me and see," said Duono.

"If what I ask is too much, you may back out at any time," Chrono said, then he explained his plan in full to Duono.

The next morning, therefore, Chrono rose early and went to the tent of Repellen. When he had been admitted Repellen asked him how his interview had gone with the gnome.

"I learned only that they claim they are passing through your country, and have no desire to settle here. Is it too much to grant them passage and be done with this matter?"

"It is a lie," Repellen grumbled. "Do you not know this folk? They have deceived you for their own purposes. Do not have dealings with gnomes, for they are altogether corrupt and deceitful."

"Then what will you do? Killing them would be shameful, and I am not the only one who would judge you so. But you cannot keep them prisoners forever."

"It is a hard choice, but we must do what is best for our own folk. I shall decide their fate before nightfall."

"Then let me make just one more plea," said Chrono. "I have spoken with their leader. In a few days time the moon will be full, and the evil valley of Chiccir lies not far from here. They have asked only that if you keep them in bonds, you would hide them out of sight at that time. For they fear the specters of the dead which walk the earth on those nights, lest they be taken bodily into the infernal realm."

"Chiccir?" Repellen queried. "That haunted valley? What do they know of that place?"

"Nothing more than you yourselves: that on the night of each full moon the specters of the dead come out of that valley, seeking the bodies of the living. If you cannot let them go, they beg to be taken far from this place, or hidden in holes in the ground, to escape that fate."

Repellen then rubbed his chin thoughtfully as an idea came to him. "Chiccir is indeed not far from this place, maybe three day's hard march if we travel swiftly. Indeed, if we were to leave today, we can make it to the very gates of Chiccir before the rising of the next full moon."

Chrono drew back as if shocked. "What are you thinking to do?" he demanded.

"We might go to the gates of that valley, and set the prisoners out in the open before it." He shrugged. "If it should so happen that the specters of the dead indeed appear, as they say, it shall work to our good. Should they take these gnomes off our hands, it will save us the trouble of choosing their fate."

Chrono pleaded. "Is that not too terrible a judgement even for these gnomes whom you detest?"

"Would it be better for us to strike them down? We would be free of them at last, yet we would be clear of guilt. We ourselves will not lay a hand on them."

Chrono continued to object, but Repellen dismissed him. He then called his captains to him and gave orders to prepare to break camp at once. "And loose the bonds of the prisoners' feet, for they shall march with us."

Repellen did not announce their destination, but word of his intent soon spread among the members of his company. Though some of that troop laughed and made light of this plan, others there were who murmured against it, for many of the Cylosites feared that place and the specters said to dwell there. "It would be better," they said, "for us all to kill the gnomes now and bear the guilt of it, than to go near to that valley."

When Duono was told of the plan he recoiled in dismay. "I know of this place," he said with a gasp. "You would all be fools to go there on the night of the full moon!"

Those who knew Duono knew him to be both sensible and fearless. Such a word even from Duono the Plateosite was enough to shake them.

But Repellen would not be deterred.

For three days he made them all march, from early after dawn until the stars of evening forced them to halt. Few breaks did he allow, for his design required him to arrive in time for the night of the full moon. His troops became surly and exhausted.

But more than anything, the nearer they came to Chiccir, the greater grew the sense of foreboding that overcame them. Though the skies were clear, their hearts were dark. The nights were worse still. The members of that camp slept little, and when they slept, their dreams were restless and fearful, and full of hauntings and terrors. Soon enough no one continued to laugh or joke about their destination.

In spite of the hard march, it was evening before the company finally reached the vicinity of Chiccir. They had passed the edges of the Plain of Cylos earlier that afternoon, and the land had been rising before them in a landscape of weathered ridges and hills. The sun had now set below the western ridges, and in the hills before them a gap could be seen in the distance: from beyond this gap emanated a ghastly glow. Repellen himself then slowed their approach. The nearer they came to that gap the more timorous the warriors became, and the gnomes resisted their captors all the more.

As they continued to proceed, the eldritch cones and spires within the valley itself became ever more clear. They rose tall and spectral from the valley floor, pale and ashen in color; some straight and upright like vast hooded figures, others strangely bent or hunched as if diseased or crippled. In many of these strange spires black hollows could be discerned, like the empty eye sockets of long-dead skulls. All of these forms gave off a sickly glow in the darkening gloom. The Cylosites at last halted their progress, chilled to the spine. The Gauphrin sat down in the grass and refused to cast their eyes in the direction of that gleam.

"It is far enough" Repellen announced. Though he stood tall, the temerity in his demeanor was obvious. "There is a hollow here where we can remain safely out of view. I shall establish lookouts to keep an eye on our prisoners."

Duono stood staring into the gap beyond them, a dark cloud overshadowing his features. He gave a glance to Chrono, as if seeking guidance. Chrono nodded sympathetically.

"I cannot remain here," Duono said. "It is the night of the full moon. I will not risk being taken by the specters!"

Chrono said, "You are under no further obligation. You may retreat as far from our camp as you wish. We shall rejoin you in the morning."

"If any of you survive the night, that is," Duono grumbled. He hefted his pack and returned in the direction they had come, until he had disappeared from view.

Repellen scowled. "So much for the courage of the Plateosites," he complained. Nevertheless many of the warriors who followed him gazed enviously after Duono, wishing Repellen would give them leave to make their own choice.

"The night is quickly darkening," Repellen said. "Let us be about our business and have done with this matter. If the rumors are true we might be on our way home by the morning, and free of these pests."

The guards in charge of the prisoners forced them to their feet. "Come!" Repellen commanded. "You cannot stay here with us."

The whole company of the gnomes was marched forward, nearly to the gap which formed the gateway into that valley. There the guards bound them securely hand and foot, and bound them together in a circle such that none could undo the bonds of any other. They left them standing in the grass, and warned them not to try to move or escape, for they would be watching from their camp a short distance away.

They returned hurriedly to their company, for the sky was growing ever darker and the winds from the valley's mouth began to whistle. In the mean time Repellen had ordered the camp to be set up, well hidden in the tall grass. Their tents were kept low to the ground, below the height of the standing blades. Many of the troops dared not even hide in a tent, but chose to cower singly in still more covert hidden places in the ground. Repellen chose guards to take turns watching the prisoners, and ordered them to keep low, but to watch over the crest of the rise to assure the prisoners did not escape by night.

The moon rose. The first watch of Repellen's guards observed the prisoners in the distance for several hours. Nothing fearsome seemed to be happening. Some of the guards even began to grow more cheerful, and watched the prisoners with little caution.

But shortly after midnight a terrifying howl was heard coming from the direction of the valley. The guards at once dropped to the earth and hid in the grass, staring wide-eyed into the gap. The rest of the camp awoke—that is, any who had managed to fall asleep—but none dared to peek out from under their tents or out of their hiding places. The howl was soon followed by others, and before long a ghostly figure like that of a wolf or large dog was seen charging from the valley toward the camp. It was immediately joined by another, both glowing eerily in the moonlight.

The guards trembled and hid their eyes in the earth. Silent minutes seemed like hours as they waited to find out what would happen next. More howling cries resounded from the valley, and now from the hills around them as well. For a long while none dared to look up. The baying of the ghastly wolves seemed to be coming from everywhere now. Occasionally the padding of running feet and the rush of large figures coursing through the grass nearby told them that one of the creatures had passed them by. Even the panting breath of the monsters could be heard at times as they trotted through.

It was a long while before these omens ceased, and even longer before anyone dared to open their eyes and look up again.

The first of the guards to do so gagged and mouthed a voiceless scream as he shook his companion and jabbed a finger in the direction of Chiccir. They saw a distant line of glowing figures, garbed in tattered robes, staggering slowly and mechanically towards the circle of their prisoners. They saw no more. In a panic they scrambled down to the nearest tent and pulled the cover down over their heads, hoping to hide themselves from the eyes of the specters. Not a word or a sound was said.

From the distance, in the direction of the prisoners, a distant wailing like the despair of lost souls echoed from the valley walls. A few terrified moans and cries were heard, but then all sound was obscured by a renewed chorus of howls from the spectral wolves.

Few of Repellen's troops slept that night. Chrono alone of that company managed to get any rest.

In the morning all was silent.

Not until the sun was shining full upon the grassy hills around them did any dare to raise their eyes and emerge from hiding. Chrono was up already, and staring dejectedly in the direction of the Valley of Chiccir. Repellen himself rose at last, and cautiously joined him.

"It appears as if you have gotten your wish," Chrono complained bitterly. "The gnomes are gone. Unless they have all somehow escaped your bonds, they have been taken by the specters into that haunted valley. They will not bother you again."

Repellen insisted on investigating the scene. With weak knees he led his troops to the site of the camp where the gnomes had been bound. There was certainly no sign of any of them. Instead the ground about that place was marked with footprints of the dogs of the dead, and signs of an apparent struggle. Strange booted footprints mingled with those of the prisoners, and it appeared they had been taken in the direction of the valley. At some distance the tracks seemed to disappear onto rocky ground, but none of Repellen's company dared follow them further to see what had become of them.

The Cylosites looked at one another gloomily. More than one felt sickened by what they had done. But none ventured to speak their mind. Repellen at last grunted disgustedly and said, "Well, what's done is done. Let us return to Derideth."

As they returned on the trail toward their village, they came upon Duono camped alongside the path. He seemed disheveled and weary, as if he had had little rest overnight. The Cylosites greeted him coldly. Some of the warriors shook their heads at him, although secretly many were envious that he had escaped the dread of that night.

"How fared it with you?" Chrono asked.

"I had but little rest!" Duono said. "Let us go aside from this carping crowd, and I shall tell you in detail of my night."

When they were out of earshot of Repellen's company Chrono said, "From what I could see, things have gone according to plan."

"I did as you instructed, though I have been busy through most of the night in doing so. After removing myself from the sight of the company of the Cylosites I made my way as quickly as I could into the Valley of Chiccir, and not without trepidation! Nevertheless I found it as you described. It is indeed inhabited by Gauphrin, but they were hidden from sight within their warrens in the cones and hillocks of that queer place. Not a few hours had passed before I managed to convince any to come out of hiding to speak with me, and I feared our plan would be in vain."

"We first heard and saw the dogs of the dead, as they are called. Was that of your doing?"

"No!" Duono laughed. "When at last the Gauphrin of Chiccir came out to hear me the wolves had already begun to spill from the valley. They come out as they are wont on the nights of the full moon, to seek high places from which they might howl at her, and to roam about the country."

"The wolves we saw glowed like specters. Do all things from that valley then glow with the hue of the moon?"

"Not all, but much, it would seem. The folk of Chiccir mine a substance from the walls of the valley, a phosphor which glows by night, and especially by moonlight. They use it to paint their homes: the cones and pillars of stone in which they carve their tunnels. The Gauphrin, as you know, are fond of soft and dim light, and to them this phosphor is glorious. But all the creatures of that valley rummage through the tailings of those mines for the scraps of the Gauphrin, and take on the same glow themselves as the towers of the valley."

"Then Agrar Denn was right, and the rumors of his folk proved true."

"When I at last managed to explain my mission, the leaders of that folk chose to join in the deception. They brushed their robes with the substance, and set up their own howling and wailing as they proceeded, to give the appearance of specters. But within they were laughing at the Cylosites."

"So the Gauphrin of Agrar Denn's tribe are safe?"

"I could not stay and watch the end of the matter. But I was assured they would not return without them."

"The folk with me reported what they had seen: the specters of the dead coming from the valley in glowing robes, to retrieve the prisoners. This morning the gnomes were gone. I believe we have saved them, and Repellen shall certainly not seek them further!"

"Nor shall the Cylosites be troubled by that company, for the gnomes have gone to the refuge they sought, and will not come out from there to bother Repellen, or anyone else."

So it was that Chrono and Duono by clever deception preserved the Gauphrin of Agrar Denn from the hand of the Cylosites.

Many in Cylos believe in the Specters of the Dead to this very day, and will hide themselves if they see the omens of the dead at the time of the full moon. Few of that folk will approach the city of Chiccir, for such is it now called: it is the City of the Gnomes, and it is the only city in Soria which the Gauphrin have made for themselves. Many of the Cylosites of that region believe that the gnomes and the specters of the dead are in alliance.

Among the gnomes, however, the word of this deed of Chrono and Duono went out from there and spread throughout the Southrealm. So it was that even the Gauphrin came to honor Chrono. The name of Duono, especially, they hold in high esteem: for he it was who went privately to the leaders of Chiccir, and he it was who willingly took upon himself the greatest shame in the eyes of the Cylosites.

Now although the gnomes have few friends among the other terumani, yet the rumor of this deed made its way through the circles of the sprights and nymphs of tree and water, and even to the depths of the Sea. There after many days word came even to Aviah the mother of Ahten of the mercy and cunning of Chrono the Plateosite. Though she would not tell Merten of these tidings, yet she pondered the character of this child of the land who had given aid even to the Gauphrin. Then going aside to Ahten in private she said, "This Sorite for whom you pine is a child of honor. You will not find his like even among the sons of the Sea."

8. CHRONO AND THE ORACLE

In the days of the wanderings of Chrono, when Chrono was estranged from his father and parted from Ahten and the Sea, he traveled in the Southrealm with Duono his trail-master. Now it came into the mind of Chrono to visit the western settlements of the Plateosites on the far side of the Pindus.[41] Among those settlements were relatives of Chrono. So Chrono and his companion went westward: but they took the inland trails, for Chrono dared not go near to the Sea, for the sight and sound of those waters inflamed the pain of his loss.

There he found his own kin, and he dwelt with them for many days: He became the guest of Tharho the son of Martelos, the son of Telos who had been the brother of Canto Chrono's grandfather. He welcomed Chrono and Duono into his household.

While they were in that country, Chrono joined Tharho his cousin in his trade. Tharho was an itinerant trader, as were Canto and Marcanto, and Chrono was familiar with this enterprise, so he agreed to aid Tharho in his ventures. Duono also attended them as trail-master.

Now as they traveled from market to market about the country of the Inviant, it came to pass one day that Tharho grew wistful, and he gazed up with yearning at the mist-shrouded heights of the great peaks piling to the west. Then he said to Chrono, "What do you think? It is said that high in this mountain of Toreth Gandauin[42] there is a Hall of the Terumani. Tryma the Seer is thought to sojourn there at times, and may tell fortunes or grant boons to such supplicants as find him. Such is the lore in this country, at any rate. But I have yet to try my fortune on this venture. Shall we go aside to the mountain and see if the rumors are true?"

Chrono's curiosity was piqued, and he said, "Can this be he that is called Tryma the Wise; he who taught wisdom and reason to the Tribes of the Sorites when Ologéo would not do so for pride? He is of the Ídolthi, among the most noble of the Terumani!"

Tharho exclaimed, "The very one! He it is whom the folk of these parts call Tryma the Seer. It is said that he can see the solutions to many riddles, and knows much that is unknown, and can even foresee that which has not yet happened."

41 Most of the inhabitants of the Southrealm in those days were Plateosites. It wasn't until much later that their descendants came to be divided into a number of additional Tribes.

42 "Toreth Gandauin" is a Donish name. As the Diatrian Donites had not yet migrated to the area, the name as given here is an anachronism. The original Sorian name of the mountain and this precinct remains unknown.

Duono was skeptical, and said, "Can this be true? Have you met anyone who has been to the seer?"

"In my travels I've met those in this country who say they have found him at residence, and he has granted them audience, at times even revealing secrets and opening eyes to the future. But I myself cannot say yes or no."

"How can this be," Duono queried, "when it is said that the Ádolthi dwell in Vordót, beyond the Ice? There are many, in fact, who believe the Ádolthi have departed Soria altogether, and there is nothing north of us but Ice, to the very ends of the world."

Chrono replied, "The Terumani have secret ways by which they travel throughout the land, and the Ice does not much hinder them. Tryma could travel to his other Halls, if he so desired. For the Terumani do have other Halls besides those in Vordót. But I have heard nothing of this oracle from my father's house on the far side of the Pindus."

"The home of your father is far indeed from this country," Tharho said. "Here in the shadow of the Inviant it has long been said that Tryma has a Hall in the high mountains at Toreth Gandauin, and it is among his favorites."

Chrono said, "I for one have no desire to augur the future, but it would be worth a journey aside to see whether this thing is true. Let us then go and see what we shall see!"

So Tharho turned aside from his course, taking with him Chrono and Duono, together with their companions and porters. They went up into the mountains, and set their course for the lowering peak of Toreth Gandauin.

This mountain reared up steeply in the west, a tower so tall it was ever visible in the distance, always peaking over the top of the nearer foothills. A mighty spire of rock it was, wearing a venerable cap of white, which breathed a snowy breath in the eternal winds about its head. This peak they kept always before their eyes as they marched over trackless green hills and deep groves of fir and pine, ever steeper, and ever higher, into the lofty heart of the Inviant.

When they had traveled arduously for two days the green grass gave way at last to barren rock. A gravelly path was discovered here winding up into a deep cleft in a precipitous slope of rock, rising towards the very foot of the mountain. A pair of carven gray menhirs stood ominously tall, like ragged columns, at the entrance to this pass. Above it in the distance the sheer face of Toreth Gandauin rose into gray mists overhead.

Tharho looked up at the mountain peak and said, "This must be the gateway to the Hall of Tryma: at least, thus have they described the road who have been here. But what lies beyond the cleft none will say."

The pathway as it entered the cleft was paved with smooth stones, and seemed to be swept and manicured. But the valley itself was infested with an impenetrable expanse of thorn and thistle, and the path wound through the thorns upward in a narrow gap, like a hedge on either side, so constrained that no more than one at a time could press through; and even then that one's clothing would be continually snagged and pricked by the briers. The pathway continued thus steeply up into the cleft, twisting away into the distance until it curved out of sight.

"It is none too welcoming a sight," Chrono declared when they had explored the opening. "It will be slow going, and nigh impossible to port our camp or our goods into this breach."

So Tharho decided to set up camp at this point, where his porters could rest; but Chrono, Duono and Tharho chose to press onward, up the ascent on their own, though the afternoon was already drawing late.

Tharho took the lead, then Chrono, and Duono the rear, for it was impossible to walk even two abreast on that way. The going was as slow as they feared, or slower. The trail continued upward steeply without relief, winding continually between the walls of thorn and thistle. When they had traveled for some hours more in this manner it became clear that the day was growing short: The sun had long since hidden behind the mountain to the west, and the gap through which they climbed was deep and shadowy. They stopped to consider their way.

Chrono said, "We have come far, but we do not know how much further we have to climb."

"These thorns are relentless as the Storm," Tharho said. "It is unnatural, as if planted as a hedge along the trail. Should darkness fall upon us along this dreary path it will be impossible to find any spot to camp or take rest. It would be wise to return to our camp below, now, before it is too late."

But Duono was scanning the view up the hillside, and he said, "Look! There ahead glimmers a ray of light through the misty shadows: a warm and homey glow as from lamplight."

Chrono looked as well, but his eyes could see nothing ahead. "The way appears dark to me, but I trust your vision better than mine. What do you think?"

"It is but a short way off," Duono said. "If I could pass to the front on this accursed trail I would run ahead and see whether we have reached our goal."

Tharho sighed and said to Chrono. "If you trust your trail-master, I will not dissent. Let us then proceed."

So they pressed on, but the going was harder than they had foreseen. The valley grew dark, and although the glow from above became clear to all it seemed to grow no nearer for all their exertions. Their hopes soon turned to anxiety.

In spite of their efforts the stars had begun to glitter overhead before they came at last to a level area nestled in a stoney glade at the foot of the vast, glowering wall of Toreth Gandauin. There amid a grove of ancient fir trees rose a domed building of smooth gray stone. From the arched portal and the embrasures in the walls of this building poured a warm and welcoming light, brightening their hearts.

Tharho said, "Surely this is the Hall of Toreth Gandauin, the mountain home of Teruman Tryma the Seer, for its construction is beyond the skills of our Kindred."

Chrono said, "Whatever house it may be, let us seek rest and repose here for the night, if the lord of the place will allow it. Even if none are lodging in the building, surely it is lit now for the salutation of strangers."

But Tharho remarked, "See how the plaza all about the entry is bestrewn with wicked burs, gravel, and shards of obsidian like drake's teeth. What sort of welcome is this, then?" It was true, that the way to the Hall was paved with such obstacles, so that none might approach without enduring this courtyard.

Duono shrugged. "We cannot camp on the trail. And clearly it would be impossible to camp on the plaza of shards! I fear we have no choice but to seek the grace of the lord of the Hall."

So they advanced cautiously, stepping gingerly and lightly upon the gravel; the footpath crunched beneath their soles, and pained them as they walked, even through the leather of their shoes. Arriving at the archway they stepped thankfully onto smooth stone, and paused to look in wonder about the room which they had entered.

The chamber was in the form of a circle, with a floor of smooth alabaster or marble. A single door exited opposite the archway they had entered. The door itself was gleaming bronze, a metal which none of them knew, and was decorated with fanciful figures in panels. The dome overhead was painted in bright interwoven patterns which to their tired eyes appeared almost to move of their own accord. The whole was lit by curious lamps in sconces on the walls, which seemed to burn without heat or flame. The furnishings were sparse, consisting only of a few curved stone benches along the walls, but even these were carved with elaborate scrollwork like twisting vines.

There was no one to greet them. When they had waited in quiet for some little while, Tharho at last called out in a loud voice, "Greetings to the master of the house! We are travelers from below the mountain, seeking rest from our journey. If this indeed is the Hall of Teruman Tryma the Seer, shall we expect salutation, or must we return whence we came in the dark of night?"

It so happened that Tryma was set to arrive in his Hall in the Inviant for a season, and had sent before him several attendants and companions to prepare the Hall for his arrival: lesser terumani, the sprights and nymphs of the grove in which his Hall was built. The bronze door swung smoothly open, and one of these attendants came forth to the entry and greeted them, saying, "This is indeed the Hall of Tryma, but who are you to enter this house uninvited at night?"

Both Tharho and Duono were astonished, for although the terumani did not yet conceal themselves in their hidden Mansions, as they do today, yet it was rare for them to speak openly with the Kindreds of Toë; they wondered if indeed this was Tryma himself who spoke with them. Chrono however had spoken with the terumani on many occasions, and knew this to be a lesser spright, so he bowed respectfully and said, "If you'll pardon us, we have come miles out of our way seeking the house of Tryma, hoping for an audience with the lord of this place, and have been caught by nightfall on the trail below. We hope now merely for a kind reception, to know we have not labored this far in vain."

The spright smiled and answered him, saying, "I can guarantee no audience, but those who seek wisdom are always welcome at the table of Tryma. However I fear the lord of the house has not yet arrived for the season." He spread his hands and said, "You are welcome to remain here in the vestibule for shelter from the night, for I know the trail is difficult, and even more so in the blackness of night. Perhaps on the morrow Tryma himself may arrive, perhaps the day after, or yet another day. You may remain here and await his arrival if you will. But none may enter the inner Hall before the lord of the house returns."

The spright then returned into the Hall, leaving Chrono, Duono and Tharho alone in the vestibule. There they found nothing but the stone benches upon which to spread their scant bedding, and the floor was cold and hard. Tharho shrugged and said, "I had hoped for better hospitality, but this is more favorable than the courtyard, or the trail of thorns. We may as well make the best of the situation." So they made pillows of their packs, and wrapped themselves in their garments, and slept as well as they could.

In the morning they rose early, and were glad to rise from their stoney beds. There was none to greet them, and the bronze door remained shut. Although they called out for assistance, there was no sign of the spright who had spoken to them on the previous night, nor any sign of anyone at all living in the Hall. As they made a meager breakfast of pack rations, Tharho lowered his voice and said, "What do you think? It is a hard thing to wait in this cold and inhospitable place, with no assurance of a word from the Oracle. We have much business to attend to, and profits to be made. We would be shamed should we return to our homes at the end of the season with nothing to show for our journey. Furthermore our whole company is waiting for us below and will be wondering what has become of us. Should we remain here with no pledge that our host will even see us? Or return at once to camp and be on our way?"

Duono said, "We have detoured far from our course, and spent not a few days, in order to hear a word from Tryma. It would seem prudent to wait another day or two, rather than waste all the hours and labor we have already committed to this diversion."

Chrono agreed, saying, "I have no mind to see the future, yet even I would consider it a failure to leave now, when there is yet a chance we might speak with one of the Ádolthi."

So Tharho assented.

For three more days Tharho and his companions waited about the precincts of Tryma's Hall. They saw no more of the spright which had greeted them at first, and heard nothing further of Tryma or his arrival. At last Tharho grew impatient, and made up his mind to return to the camp below, for their supplies were gone, and their porters and aids would be questioning their long absence.

Even Chrono and Duono had become discouraged, for the time weighed heavily on them, and there were no comforts in the vestibule of Tryma's Hall. Thus all agreed to return to camp, and there to debate what their next step might be: whether to return to the Hall after replenishing their packs, or to abandon their quest for a later journey.

In a foul mood, they packed their gear, and departed from the vestibule of Tryma's Hall, then began the hike down the pathway toward the camp where their porters and companions waited.

They had been on their way for over an hour, and had come a long way down the mountainside, when another traveler appeared on the pathway below them, ascending in their direction, dressed in a heavy traveling cloak which was weathered as if he had come from a long journey. He trudged up the trail in a hunched manner, like the folk of Steggan, although he appeared to be as tall as a Plateosite.

Tharho stopped the company and grumbled, "Storm of Boros! What shall we do now? Clearly there is no room to pass one another on this accursed pathway."

Although the hood of his cloak obscured the stranger's features, he appeared to be of venerable age, for Chrono thought he detected a shock of white hair in the shadows. "We should treat the traveler with honor," he said. "Either we must force ourselves into the thorns, or we must return the way we came."

The figure at last reached their position, and all stopped. Tharho then said, "We beg your pardon, but the way is narrow, and try as we might, passing one another on this pathway will be accomplished only with pain and discomfort for all. We have come already a long way downhill and do not relish returning up this difficult ascent: but if you prefer we shall do so on your account."

The figure smiled pleasantly and said to them, "Whence have you come, friends? For I know of nothing on the pathway above but for the Hall of Tryma, and it would be surprising to find him at home."

"Indeed," said Tharho, "It is from Tryma's Hall that we have come. We have waited there three days for his arrival, but have heard or seen nothing of him in all that time. Now we go back to our camp to debate our further course. If you go seeking Tryma I would counsel you to do likewise, for he is not there."

"I do not seek the master of the house, but I have pressing business above at that Hall, and should get there as soon as may be. If you will walk with me a ways back uphill, perhaps we might find a spot to pass one another without inconvenience and pain."

Tharho sighed, "We have been on this trail both uphill and down, and have yet to discover any such spot. But let us make the attempt for the sake of your mission."

So Tharho and his companions turned and began the climb back towards Tryma's Hall, with the sojourner taking up the rear. The sojourner began to question them as they went along, asking, "What is it that you were seeking from Tryma?"

Tharho said, "We had heard that the Oracle has much of interest to say, and we wished to hear whatever he might expound for us."

The sojourner laughed. "It is true that Tryma has much to say! Whether or not it is of any interest is another matter. Although I suppose the truth of that may depend on the listener, not the speaker."

"Have you seen Tryma yourself, then?" asked Chrono.

"I have been to the Hall of Tryma many times! I am no stranger there."

"Then can you tell us what to expect?" Chrono asked. "Does he give words of hope, or words of gloom?"

"He will only give words of truth. Some have gone away despairing, I suppose, but that is never his intent! He will only give audience to those who are willing to learn the truth."

With that he began to expound as they went along, telling tales of others who had come to see the Oracle, and of how the words of Tryma had aided them and enlightened them. His conversation was cheerful and engaging, so they were encouraged along the way. Even Chrono, who feared the word of the seer, felt lighter in his heart after that discourse. Thus in spite of the hardship of the path, the way went quickly, so that before they knew it they found themselves once again on the Court of the Shards, standing before the portal of Tryma's Hall.

Then Chrono said, "Look, friend, we have returned the whole way so soon! And now I'm disinclined to return to our company below. Your companionship on the trail has been a pleasure. Shall we now await the return of Tryma together?"

To this the sojourner replied, "Tryma has already returned to this Hall. As a matter of fact, he has found your company on the trail a pleasure as well."

He then removed his cloak and hood, and they saw that the sojourner was himself teruman.

At this they recoiled, for now they understood that they had been speaking with Tryma himself. Then Tharho kneeled, and motioned for the others to do so, but Tryma waved a hand and said, "Pshaw! Stop that. Do not kneel or show deference. Even the greatest of the Ádolthi are not lords to accept obeisance. Besides which, the truth cannot be altered by formalities!"

So Tharho said, "We have heard that Tryma knows much, and can even give words which portend the future. It had been my wish to see our future, to know what paths will cause us to us prosper. Yet now this request seems rash and unworthy."

Tryma however was polite, smiling and saying, "You may ask what you will. Perhaps I may have a message for you, and perhaps not. I shall give you whatever answer is meet for your need. But be forewarned that in some cases the best answer is no answer at all."

Duono replied, "We will hearken to anything that the Oracle proclaims."

"Easily said. But I have found that often a listening ear might not hear, and he that hears might not listen."

Duono replied, "Is it not better to hear without listening, than not to hear at all?"

Tryma smiled at this reply and said, "Well-spoken! Nevertheless I must know your stories before I say yes or no to an interview. Sit now, and tell me: For what reasons have each of you come to seek my audience?" Then he turned first to Tharho, and said. "Tell me of yourself. Why have you come? And what do you wish to learn?"

Tharho said, "I am Tharho, son of Martelos, and I make my living in merchant trade. I have heard rumors of Tryma in my travels, and it is said by many that Tryma can see things that are yet to come to pass. So I came to see. If that is so, I had hoped to learn if there are dangers or pitfalls that lie before me, that perhaps I might avoid them, or at least amend their consequences. Or if there are opportunities yet to come, how shall I best pursue them?"

Tryma nodded and considered this statement thoughtfully: but he neither replied nor offered any word. Then he turned to Duono and said, "And what of you? What would you wish to learn?"

Then said Duono, "I am Duono, of no great house of the Tribe of Plateos: I, too, am a wanderer in the lands of Soria, but not for trade. I wander out of the bonds of friendship, hoping to be a comfort and aid to a worthy companion and leader, and above all to share in deeds of honor and fame. Yet I wonder if any in all the lands have noted our labor and our striving, or whether we have wasted our days away in vanity. If this be so, perhaps Tryma might guide us to opportunities unforeseen, where our work will not go unheeded."

Tryma nodded at this remark as well, but gave no answer, nor offered any word. But he turned to Chrono and said, "And you, last of all: Who are you, and what is it you seek from me?"

Chrono then said, "I am Chrono, a son of Marcanto, but am estranged from that house. I seek no word of prophecy. For the future which I cannot see may be bleaker than my blindness, and a word of foretelling might bring nothing but despair. I have left all that I knew for the sake of one whom I can never join, and pine for a joy which is beyond my grasp. Yet if Tryma shall speak, I ask only for the strength to bear his word."

When Chrono spoke his name Tryma raised an eyebrow. But he listened to Chrono's words as he had the others, nodded, and gave no answer.

When he had considered their requests silently for a space, Tryma said at last, "I should need to learn more of yourselves before such auguries can be cast. For augury is learning, not vision. But come! You may enter my Hall this day and dine with me. We shall talk, and I might learn much of what I need to guide your paths. Even if not, perhaps you will gain something from the conversation, for I am not without wit; or so I have been told!"

Thus Chrono, Duono and Tharho entered into the Hall of Tryma at Toreth Gandauin, and joined him at his table. There was a spring in the dining hall from which he filled goblets with sparkling, clear water which seemed to dance on their tongues. He set before them warm bread from his kitchens, together with rich butter and cheese, and offered them a variety of succulent fruits from a large bowl in the center of the table. Thus feasted, they spent the day in conversation with that Teruman.

But as the afternoon drew on, Tryma dismissed them, saying, "The time has come for us to part, I think. The afternoon is growing late, and you must have time to descend to your camp before it grows dark. It does grow dark indeed in the shadow of Toreth Gandauin!"

Tharho then said, "We thank you for your hospitality! But if I might dare to ask, have you learned enough to give us a word of augury before we depart?"

Tryma smiled and said, "If you'll bear with me, I have one further request: When you depart, search your hearts, and decide upon a gift of value, one you feel is worthy of the word you hope to gain from me. Consider it well! Then go about your business, and should you desire, you may return here in three weeks. At that time the worth of your gifts shall be judged. The value of the gift shall inform me of all I need to learn of your hearts. This is an old custom, which we have kept for many years."

So they bowed out, and left the Hall and its grove beneath the wall of the mountain. When they had crossed once more the Court of the Shards, they began at last to descend the trail towards their camp.

Along that narrow path they debated as they went what manner of gift they should bring to the Oracle.

Tharho was vexed, and said, "Have we come so far and waited so long for nothing? Can it be that even the Terumani are not above bribes and exploitation?"

Chrono said to him, "You are yourself a trader. Does this not seem both just and proper? You would not give away merchandise of value at a mere request from strangers. It seems fitting to me that a message of great value should be compensated by something of equal worth."

Duono agreed. "We should consider how much we value the word of Tryma. If we desire a valuable prophecy we should be willing to sacrifice in kind."

So Tharho was assuaged.

They returned then to their camp, and their company was relieved to see them. Then Tharho and his whole company departed from the feet of Toreth Gandauin to continue their business in the Inviant, and for three weeks they traded profitably throughout the region.

During this time Tharho, Chrono and Duono privately evaluated their profits and merchandize, wondering what to acquire as a suitable offering for Tryma. Each of them examined their own hearts, and chose from among their acquisitions that which they deemed the most valuable of their treasures.

When the appointed time had arrived Tharho once again led his company to Mount Gandauin, where they camped before the gate, at the foot of the Trail of Thorns. Then he and his two companions once more ascended to the grove of the Teruman, and crossing gingerly the Court of the Shards before the portal, they announced themselves at the arch before the vestibule.

Tryma himself came out to greet them. Looking mildly surprised he said, "So you have returned seeking a prophecy after all? Well, then. Come once more into the Hall and sit. When you have rested and been refreshed, you may present your offerings for my consideration. I will ponder their value and give you a word of truth in accord with their worth." Thus they entered the Hall of Tryma once again. As before, Tryma poured them fresh water and gave them repast that they might be at ease.

When some time had passed, Tharho grew restless and said, "My lord, we have come a long journey, yet again this second time, and we greatly desire to receive a word of prophecy from your lips. Our bellies are sated, but still we hunger. Shall we present to you our offerings and receive your word?"

Tryma nodded and assented. "As you wish. Come within, then, before my seat, and let us consider your offerings." He led them into an inner chamber of the Hall: an unprepossessing space, round and domed like the vestibule at the entrance. There were no decorations here, and no furnishings save a stone chair which was the seat of Tryma himself. The walls were bare stone, smooth and polished but without ornament. A small brazier burned sweet incense on a bronze stand beside the seat, and on the floor was a finely woven rug of wool. Tryma took his seat at the head of the salon, and gestured to the rug at his feet. "Let us begin."

Tharho stepped forward first, and knelt before the Oracle, on one knee in the manner of his folk, and bowed his head. Then he drew a cask from his tunic, and opened it, and presented from it a vessel of gold, weighty and pure, studded at the rim with fine gemstones. This he laid upon the rug at Tryma's feet and said, "I bring gold, purchased with much labor.[43] The value of this vessel exceeds that of many entire households, all that they might earn in this world. Thus do I give honor to the wisdom of Tryma, seeking a word from his lips. What can you tell me of my future and my fortunes?"

Tryma took up the vessel in his hand, and examined it closely, turning it over and judging its heft. After a moment he said to Tharho, "You came seeking wisdom in your trade, and have brought a suitable gift to that end. But whether there be dangers or pitfalls ahead, I cannot say. You may overcome them by your own strength and savvy, as you always have: and in so doing you gain honor and satisfaction I cannot bestow! As to opportunities: There is little wisdom I can offer you there, beyond what you already know to be true: deal honestly with all, neither cheating nor deceiving in any trade, and opportunity shall flock to you, and you shall flourish."

Then he placed the golden vessel of Tharho back onto the rug before him, and beside it he placed a single gold bar which he drew from a pocket in his robe, and he said, "We are provided for, of all the necessities of life, and we have no need of treasures. You have brought a gift which means much to you, it is true: but little to the recipient. Therefore I give you back what you value: gold I return to you. I could teach you much more concerning the value of true and lasting treasures, although it would take many days, and great commitment on your part. But I fear that I have no word of foretelling to give."

So Tharho withdrew, but he was discontented with this reply.

Duono's turn came next, and kneeling before Tryma he opened his pack, and withdrew from it a bundle of furs and fine fabrics: silks from the Hirna, and the finest sable from Batack, all wrought into elegant clothing of the most exquisite craftsmanship. These he laid at the feet of Tryma.

He said, "I offer raiment, to adorn and comfort you and your servants: Furs to keep you warm in the winter, and silks and linens to bring you pleasure in the summer. No finer apparel is made anywhere in the lands of Soria. For it seems to me that no greater grace can one grant a neighbor than to clothe him, for without clothing we are as the beasts. Food and drink may fill the belly, but raiment confers dignity and stature. Thus do I honor the wisdom of Tryma, and seek his word. What guidance can you offer to keep me in paths of honor?"

Tryma took up the raiment given by Duono, and examined the items, and smiled. Then he said to Duono, "You came seeking wisdom in your pursuit of honor, yet I must tell you that the very pursuit is the honor itself! The recognition of strangers is of little value, for fame is fickle and ever false. No honorable deed is wasted, whether seen or unseen. This your heart already knows. As to opportunities unforeseen, what would be the adventure if you knew what lay ahead? Your satisfaction and reward will be the greater by the

43 Gold would have been exceedingly rare in that age, and of immense value.

discovery! If you but had the time, there is much I could teach you of honor and glory, but your duties, I see, lie with your friend."

When he had finished this word, he folded the garments and set them on the rug before Duono, and added an embroidered vest of his own. Then he said, "Even the beasts have their own pelts to clothe them and keep them warm: it is the gift of Wenda—the gift of speech—which brings honor exceeding theirs to the Kindreds of Toë. We ourselves have raiment enough, and fire as well, to keep us warm. Such finery, I'm afraid, is of no value in my Halls. Your garments you may take with you. I have no further word of prophecy to give in return."

So Duono withdrew, but he also was disheartened by this reply.

A long moment of silence passed. At last Tryma addressed Chrono and said, "And what of you, Chrono son of Marcanto? Have you brought a gift as well?"

Chrono looked at his two friends, both of whom were staring at the floor dejectedly. Then he frowned and came forward, and he took a seat on the carpet before the seat of Tryma. "I had not thought to bring an offering, for I desire no news of the future. But on behalf of my friends I bring you this."

He carefully removed the shoes from his feet, and laid them before the feet of Tryma. "Before your portal we have crossed a court of vicious stone and glass, such as we have been cautious even to step across well shod. I give you as a gift the shoes from my feet, for without them I cannot leave this place. And I would not go hence without a word from you for my friends." Then he bowed his head and said, "As for myself, I am willing to hear what you have to say, whether good or ill."

Then Tryma laughed outright, and said, "Truly, you have given a gift of great worth. The value to yourself is beyond measure, and the value to me is insight into your heart and soul. We have learned more from your gift than from the most extravagant of treasures. Therefore you shall receive a word of equal import."

Turning then to Tharho and Duono he said, "The value of the gift of Chrono has opened windows of insight, and in honor of his request I shall have one word of prophecy for each of you. But you must come into my chamber in private: you may do with this knowledge what you wish, but you must share what you learn with no one, for the knowledge of things to come is not a thing to be trifled with!

"As for you, Chrono of Mizgad: my word for you I give openly that all may hear and know. You have not told all that you are, but the name of Chrono is not unknown among the Terumani! So listen now and hold these words in your heart."

Then the insight of Tryma followed the paths of wisdom and foresight which pervade the world, which string together order out of storm, and he spoke to Chrono a word of prophecy, saying,

"Chrono of Mizgad, Canto's curious heir,
Tales are told of you; tidings have reached me,.
Much have I heard of you, more have I learned,
But foresight is missing, much unimagined,
Lampless your pathways, lost beyond learning.
What end to your ardor? What outcome is earned?
It cannot be compassed; clouded the vision!
I see no mysteries; merely the manifest:
no Sea-nymph residing in sun-burnt lands,
Nor earth-child existing in undersea realms.
But Others there are, and alternate gifts.
Powerful friends may pity your plight—
Regard your request; revealing a remedy.
This matter is murky. No more can I say.

Modest your manner, demanding nothing:
Asking no oracle, augury spurning,
Yet foresight I give, informing the future.
Fame shall find you; yet feckless your fate
Lands may rebuff you; lonely your lot.
Exiled is Chrono; outcast his heirs,
But lasting your laurels, losing no luster.
A kindred your crown: for Chrono a Tribe.
Unseen in earth; unlike any other.
Soria's ranks swelling with sea-folk.
Many obey them, bowing to destiny.
Honor eternal, enduring inviolate.

Unerring this edict. This end is assured."

Then Tharho, and Duono, and Chrono accepted the speech of Tryma. He called each of them into his private chamber, and spoke words which no other might hear, as he had promised. Many guessed, but none ever knew what they had heard.

When he had finished with Tharho and Duono he called Chrono to him also in private, saying, "I have yet one more word for you."

Chrono followed him apprehensively into his chamber and said, "The oracle you pronounced spoke of a Tribe. Can you then say whether I shall indeed have descendants, and if so, are they the children of the Sea-maiden as well?"

"I cannot see so clearly. Such an outcome seems unlikely, as we both would imagine. I only foresee clearly a Tribe which carries on your name and your honor. If there is aid for you in this matter, you cannot find it here, for I have no such authority over nature."

"What then, have you yet to advise?"

Tryma shook his head. "The word I have for you is neither prophecy, nor advice. Only information."

Chrono bowed his head and said, "Speak, but speak mercifully. My heart is burdened with old despairs and loss."

Tryma said, "I can neither ease your burden nor heal your despair. But you should know that aid for your case will never come to you. This is no oracle or prophecy, simply a fact. I know the High Ones of the Ádolthi. Those with the power to aid you are far away and hard of heart, and have little respect for your Kindred. If any aid is to be found, you yourself must earn it, and you must go after it."

"Is there then aid somewhere to be found?"

Tryma shrugged and smiled. "If I knew, I suppose I could not tell you. Such matters are best left to unravel themselves. To know too much could prevent the very actions which might bring about the ends."

So Chrono accepted this word also, and pondered it.

When Tryma had dismissed them all with his blessing, they departed from that Hall at last, and returned to their camp. They were received with rejoicing and many questions, but none would speak aloud of what Tryma had said to them in private.

Only the oracle concerning Chrono was told and retold, for that had been given openly.

So before long the caravan continued on its way and Tharho and his folk went about their business. Thus they finished at last their trading, and returned to the home of Tharho with much profit. Then the word of this foretelling went out from Tharho's household, and the name of Chrono became known throughout that country; even the journeying merchants carried the tale abroad.

None could fully fathom the meaning of this word from Tryma, Chrono least of all, but he gained hope by Tryma's saying: he marked well the prophecy, treasuring it in his heart and his memory, though he had yet to see and understand its portent.[44]

This saying also spread among the terumani, and reached the house of Merten the father of Ahten. So Ahten heard, and wondered at its meaning. Even Merten himself brooded over it in his heart.

44 The Mizans, of course, saw its fulfillment in their own history, which they traced back to Chrono their founder. In a later age, the seafaring Mizans were to become for many years the dominant culture of the Southrealm, ruling other Tribes and controlling much of the commerce and wealth of that era.

9. CHRONO AND THE RETURN TO MIZGAD

In the days when Chrono dwelt among his own kindred in the house of Tharho, Chrono and Duono went about that region seeking good and noble acts to accomplish. Now many years had passed since Chrono had left his father's house in shame, and his name had spread abroad throughout the regions of the Southrealm, so the name of Chrono was spoken in honor from Steggan to Brontos,[45] from Lodbarria to the Inviant. But Chrono himself knew little of his own fame, and ever held himself an outcast and ashamed.

Now it happened at that time that Tharho the Merchant had begun to prepare a caravan to trade in the Eastlands around the far side of the Gulf of Pindus. Working together with Chrono and Duono who sojourned in his household, he purposed to purchase a good quantity of the twine of the Inviant for trade and barter.

The best twine in Soria, and strongest by far, was twisted from the web of a breed of spider which dwelt in the mountains of the Inviant to the west. This twine was highly prized by all who carried the bow among the Plateosites,[46] and could be sold for great profit throughout the Circumpintus, but in the Eastlands it was most prized of all: for the silk could only be harvested far off in the Inviant, and only certain craftsmen of the Plateosites knew the method of harvesting it and working it into twine.

But try as he might, Tharho could find no supply to purchase. So it entered Tharho's heart to go into the mountains to gather web that he might twine it himself, he and his workmen: for Tharho knew this craft.

So he said to Duono and Chrono, "Will you come with me into the mountains? I know where these spiders make their webs abundantly, and we three can gather much and make good profit thereby. But be warned: it is hard and perilous work. There are few who dare this industry. For the spiders are as large as plates, and are very venomous. We must avoid being bitten at all costs."

This plan seemed good to Chrono, for he sought always to fill his days with honorable endeavors, that he might not pine away in uselessness, dreaming of the Sea-maiden Ahten in futility. To this end he had often helped his relative Tharho in his trade. So he at once agreed. Duono his companion agreed also, for he had never balked at any adventurous task regardless of peril.

45 In those days there would not as yet have been a separate Tribe of the Brontosites, who were an offshoot of the Plateosites. This may be an anachronism, or possibly merely a geographical reference to the region which would later be the homeland of the Brontosites.

46 The bow has not been previously mentioned as a weapon in use among the Plateosites. It is possible its use was limited to certain clans or specific applications; hence the phrase "all who carried the bow."

After gathering their supplies, Tharho led them to the mountain country where they might find the silk. It was a week's hard trek into the mountains, for the Inviant is wild country even today, and so much the more so in those ancient days, when there were no roads or trails. There they established their base camp in the footlands below a range of fierce and massive dolomite peaks.

Tharho spent another day showing them the method for gathering and treating the web, saying, "You must follow this method precisely, treating the web with ash and lime, and winding the web carefully into cords and spools as I have shown you. When you have filled a spool you must wrap it and pack it carefully, and store it gently in the sacks we carry. For if you handle it poorly, it shall arrive at home as a mass which none might ever unravel, and it shall be of no value to us."

The spiders which spun these webs were terrible black creatures as large as a pheasant, with markings on their undersides as red as spilt blood, and with long and evil legs. They strung their cord haphazardly in the caves of that country, capturing and devouring whatever sorry creature might become entangled in their traps. The cords of their web were exceedingly strong, each strand as thick as a hair but stronger than a strap of the best leather.

A full day they hiked this valley, with walls of mountain boxing them in to either side. Copses of towering pine and shady maple speckled the valley floor, with thicker stands of wood along the southward-facing fringes, climbing up the lower slopes of the mountains.

At last Tharho pointed to a gaping, dark mouth in the mountain wall beyond them, and he said, "There lies our path, if you would dare. The spiders live only in such dark and silent places, where the web will not be disturbed by wind and weather, and where bats and skulking creatures lurk as prey."

The evening was approaching, and the valley was shady and dim. "Let us set camp here, and tomorrow we shall enter the cave."

So they found a safe clearing, and they set their way-camp for the night's rest.

Now it happened as they slept that night that Duono had a fearful dream, in which the sun was rushing from the sky like a falling star, while he and his companions were left standing on a lonely pinnacle, and though they knew they must hasten from that place before darkness fell, their legs were frozen, and they were unable to move in any direction. He awoke with a deep foreboding, which would not depart even with the coming of daylight.

When they had all arisen for the day, therefore, he said, "How many days will be spent in gathering this web? I have had a dream, an omen of ill. I believe our time here is short, and we should be hurrying home to our folk, not delaying here in the mountains for any profit."

But Tharho laughed, and said, "If you would return in a hurry, friend

Duono, then follow me into the cave. We shall find a great quantity of web in the depths of that cave yonder. It is as nasty as a Giant's nest, but with good fortune, we might fill our sacks with the purest silk in a single afternoon, and so lade our sledge that we might return in the morning, and be done. And still gain much profit from our journey!"

So Duono conceded, for he had never yet declined a task out of any foreboding, yet his heart warned him against this course.

So Tharho led them through a stand of pine woods and out again to a broad talus slope descending from the yawning mouth. There he stopped and gave them instructions. Each of them was given a lamp and a quantity of oil. Then each took up a lance tipped with a blade of obsidian, which could both stab and slice: this would be both their weapon against the spiders, and their tool for cutting the web. Then donning leather gloves and boots, and packing their spools, their sacks, and bags of powder, they followed him up to the cave, and entered into its maw.

"You must always be on guard in this place, lest you stumble upon one of the spiders unawares," Tharho said as the darkness began to close in around them. "Though they will not come out to attack without cause, should you disturb one it will bite. Or should you trip on a cord of their web they will come out of hiding to strike. Their bite is deadly, and not to be trifled with."

Duono halted and looked about cautiously. Strands of web hung from the ceiling overhead, and several spiders could be seen lurking in shadowy spots above. But the ground on which they tread was clear of them. "How are we to collect web from the heights?" he asked.

"We must go further in," Tharho explained. "There are certain creatures which prey on the spiders in the brighter areas near the threshold, which are immune to the venom: weasels and serpents and whatnot. We must go into the darkest deeps where they do not hunt."

"Serpents?" Chrono asked.

Tharho laughed. "Their venom is as nothing compared to that of the spiders. Nevertheless I suppose you might wish to watch your steps until we are further in."

The cave grew darker and blacker as they proceeded, until Tharho said, "For safety we shall light a lamp and go cautiously from here, for the spiders will be all about us now. But the most abundant sources will be further in."

So they proceeded by the wavering yellow glow of Tharho's lamp. They had clambered into the depths of the cave for an hour or longer, mostly heading downslope over slippery dripstone, scrambling through several gaps and down a long, twisting corridor, always watchful for web or spider. At last the passageway they followed opened up into a great hall in the blackness, so vast that the light of their lamp could not penetrate to the ceiling, nor to the far wall. All about them it reflected back the undulating forms of great webs, strung madly across the cavern in all directions. The floor of the cave was littered with the bones of bats, and night-birds, and rodents of all types. In many places bundles still hung among the tangles of the webs: creatures which had been bound and poisoned and were waiting to be devoured, some of them still twitching in their throes: the air was heavy with their stench. Here and there the great spiders could be discerned, hiding in the shadows and waiting for a disturbance in their cords, slowly twitching their long and menacing legs.

Then Tharho said. "This is the place! Let us set to, and work assiduously, and by tomorrow afternoon we shall be on the road home!"

Now Tharho was very skilled at the work, and never disturbed the creatures with his cutting and bundling, so he took very much thread to add to his pack. Chrono and Duono copied his work as well as they were able: but now and again they would disturb one of the creatures, which would come scuttling from its lair: then they would be forced to flee or to kill it with a stab of their lances. Then the horrible thing would lie twitching its terrible legs, an effect more dreadful than that of the living spiders.

Together they worked in this way for the rest of that day, cutting and spooling the thread, until they had filled all of their sacks and loaded their sledge.

At last Duono said, "Surely by now the day is waning, and we do not want to be stuck in this miserable place through the night. Let us return to our camp before the evening catches us."

But it so happened that as they had worked, several of the spiders had spun webs thickly across the shaft of the cave behind them, so that it was now impossible to exit without disturbing them.

Tharho was taken aback. "Storm of Boros!" he cursed. "We have been remiss, and should have watched the cave behind us as we worked. Now we have much work ahead of us to return from this abyss."

So Chrono said, "Let me lead the way. I shall slice through the web, and kill any of the creatures which come out. Then you may come behind quickly, drawing the sledge."

But Tharho warned, "The webs do not cut so easily, even with an obsidian blade. Hacking at them thusly might bring out more spiders than we could deal with handily, and we cannot even see in the dimness of our lamps what lies beyond. Clearly the spiders have been as busy as Vélopar in his labors! We might easily run headlong into a throng of the monsters and be overwhelmed. No. We must go cautiously and slowly, cutting as carefully as if each thread were a trip line. Our very lives here depend on caution."

"But," said Duono, "this will delay our escape, and we surely cannot spend a night among these creatures. Is there no other path out of this cavern?"

"I know of none, and it would be dangerous to hunt for one: we would still be surrounded by the spiders, and we might in the process become hopelessly lost in the tunnels, and perish here."

"Then," said Duono, "Let us leave behind our sledges and hasten as best we can. This place is evil and full of danger on all sides. Besides which, my dream yet warns that we should be on our way homeward as quickly as possible."

Chrono agreed, saying, "Better to leave the bags and get out quickly. It would be more expedient to come again tomorrow to retrieve our haul."

Tharho replied however, "Tomorrow or today, we will be delayed and the going will be slow. Better to do it once and have done with the chore. The peril is not great if we proceed slowly and watch carefully, but it will take longer."

In this manner they debated. Now Chrono had high respect for Duono, and the words of Duono had given him misgivings as well. But Tharho at last won out, and Chrono resolved to submit to the delay for Tharho's sake, saying, "Then let us stall no longer, and have at this labor as promptly as we may."

So they took up the sledge and they set to, and began the trek back to camp. Tharho cut the most skillfully, so he led the way, divesting the tunnel before them of web, while Duono and Chrono watched for lurking spiders, fending them off with their lances when any appeared to attack, or dropped by chance onto their sledge. Thus they strained at this labor for several hours, but still no sign of the cave entrance appeared before them.

At last they entered a large chamber where the floor opened up before them, and water dripped continuously from the ceiling. Great formations of dripstone cluttered the space. Webs of the spiders could be seen stretching among the formations, from floor to vaulted ceiling.

Duono stopped and looked about frowning. "Surely we have not been in this tunnel? Such a room as this I'm certain we would recall!"

Tharho agreed. "We have taken a wrong turn in the chambers behind and become lost. But there may still be an exit before us, as our direction seems not to have deviated from the straight way towards the mountainside. Shall we press on or go back?"

Chrono said, "We are weary, and have spent many hours in this cave. Even if an exit lies before us, I fear perhaps the sun has set and there is no light without the cave to mark the way. We should rest here for a night's watch, and hope to see a trace of distant light when the sun rises beyond us."

"If we must rest, we must rest together. All must agree," Duono said.

Tharho said, "But we shall need light to stay on watch. We have oil enough to last for days if we use it wisely, but we cannot rest for long. We must set watches, and keep no more than a single lantern burning with a single wick. If at any time one of us on watch spots the light of the entrance, let him awaken us that we might proceed at once to our escape."

It was a fearful camp which they set up amidst the spiders in the depth of the cave. Though each of them took their turn on watch as the others slept, none of them could spot even the dimmest light of day throughout the night, if night it was.

At last when all had rested, Tharho resigned himself, and said, "We have clearly taken a wrong tunnel in the dark. It would be wisest to return in the direction from whence we came, and go back to the great chamber. We can start upward again from thence. We must watch more carefully this time to be sure we do not go into a false tunnel."

The others agreed to this plan, so they headed back down into the deeps of the cavern. But the spiders had been busy once again, and the way was thick with web. It took more hours of disheartening labor before they once again gained the great chamber where they had gathered their load.

Here they stopped to carefully choose their route, for now they noted that several tunnels led upward out of that place in the direction from which they had first entered. But they could discern no clue to guide them: no glimmer of light, no breath of air, no tracks in the hard rock of the floor gave them any hint of their route. So they scratched a mark on the wall by the entrance into the tunnel they had already tried, and chose another tunnel which seemed familiar to them all. Finding this one also thick with spiders and web, they proceeded slowly and with caution.

A great portion of a day they spent, marking their way carefully as they went, for fear of another wrong turn. After a day's hard work, the tunnel began to open up, and the webs were few and feeble: but the way began to pitch downward steeply as if into the gullet of the mountain: a slope which none of them could recall from their journey in. So they again recouped, and Tharho said, "Clearly this path is also false, for none of us recalls this steep slope. But I feel confident we are headed in the true direction. Shall we continue on in hope of finding an exit ahead?"

Duono shook his head. "The direction may be true, but the slope is not. I fear this path will lead us yet more deeply into the bowels of the earth."

"And if there is no exit," added Chrono, "the climb back up this slope will be toilsome indeed!"

"Then let us return again," Tharho sighed. "There are only so many false routes from which to choose!"

Duono then lamented, and said, "There are yet more tunnels to try, and who knows how many diversions in each. Had we but marked our way more carefully as we entered we would have saved much worry and weary labor. Now who can guess the delays we face before us, if we even find our way out of this place alive."

Tharho merely smiled and said, "Do not lose heart. I swear by the hoary head of Sorios, the rewards will be great when we get to the markets of the Eastlands, and this ordeal will be forgotten and behind us. An open path and the mouth of the cave lies somewhere before us, and we shall surely find it shortly."

So their work continued. But the fears of Chrono and Duono were realized, for they tried each tunnel, and each tunnel's diversions, fighting cautiously through the web for every step they gained, and taking little rest. But one tunnel ended in a pool of water; another in a deep pit they could not cross; yet another constricted into a crack they could not traverse. In the end they had lost all track of time, nor did they know how many days they had already spent in the bowels of the earth with the loathsome spiders. Water abounded in pools and rivulets, but their food had all but run out, and all were weary of constant labor.

At last even Tharho began to grow concerned. When Duono suggested they must take another period of rest he hefted his jug of oil and said, "Our supply of oil for our lamps is growing thin, and I fear we have barely enough left for another day's search. I would counsel that when next we rest, we find a spot clear of web, and put out the lamp. The spiders do not prowl about like drakes in search of prey: they lie in wait and move but little. As long as we do not disturb a web we will be safe."

But Duono said, "What if as we sleep one of the spiders should choose to lay a web across us? Then even some motion in our sleep might bring it upon us."

"That may be a chance we must risk for the sake of our oil," said Tharho. "The danger of the darkness is now more dire than the danger of the spiders: If we run out of oil we shall be as lost and forgotten as the bygone lands of Niyarc. If we choose our resting place well the risk is slight. Let us work until we are worn, and then we must decide."

So they continued, spying about for a safe spot to rest as they went, until they came into a small chamber where but one spider had built its web in a corner. From this chamber three further routes diverged, and Tharho said, "Shall we make a choice now, or rest here and decide our course when we have rested?"

Chrono said, "If we can rest safely here, I would say to rest now. For I can barely lift my own lance, and my mind has grown so foggy that I do not trust my own judgement. I for one cannot think clearly or watch heedfully. Let Duono find a safe place to rest in this chamber, for I trust his instincts above all to find a safe path through any morass."

So Duono chose a small ledge, raised from the floor of the chamber, on the far side of the space from the spider's nest: here they chose to make their bivouac, and when they had taken a meager bite to eat from their supplies, they at last put out their lamp.

Duono took the first watch, and Tharho after him, so Chrono had rested for two watches when his turn came. He sat against the wall and stared into the darkness bleakly, rueing he had ever taken on this venture. Without the light of their lamps to reveal the walls of the chamber, all was utter blackness before him, though his eyes had had many hours to grow accustomed to the darkness.

In the midst of his watch, as he gazed into the empty blackness, the feeble glimmer of a thread of web wafted slowly at the far side of the chamber, so faint that he did not at first even realize he had seen anything all. Then thinking perhaps it was a trick of his eyes in the dark, he fixed his attention on it, until he was certain it was no phantom. Only then did he begin to discern the slightest hint of gray: an oval of darkness behind the thread, only slightly less black than the blackness of the chamber in which they rested.

So he woke his companions, and pointing to the wall, he said, "Is it my own madness speaking, or is there a hint of light from the far tunnel, glimmering on the web of the spider?"

Duono spotted it as well, and said, "Does the web of these spiders glow on its own, or do the spiders themselves put out an emanation?"

Tharho said, "I have never heard any such lore. I trust this is the distant glimmer of the sunlight of Havui, working its way through the chambers below the earth until it has reached us here in the deeps. It is well that we have put out our lamps in this place, for I think we might not otherwise have spotted this sign. At last I think we can see our way hence!"

They lit a lamp that they might safely cut their way past the spider, and with cautious hope they crept into the tunnel Chrono had spotted in the dark.

This path proceeded steadily upward, and the light grew, until they were able to put out their lamps at last. Then glaring before them the entrance of the cave finally appeared, as bright to their unaccustomed eyes as if they stared straight into the sun itself.

Rejoicing in their deliverance from their trial, they made their way out of the cavern as quickly as they could safely travel among the remaining spiders, and came into the sunlight and the fresh and moving air. When they had taken a brief rest, they made the final trek down to their camp. Here they were overcome at length by weariness from the restless, unmarked days they had spent in their struggle, and after a meal they bedded down and slept long.

They broke camp the next morning, and began the final journey down out of the Inviant, and on to Tharho's household. Now this road was also difficult, for now the sledge was loaded and heavy, and difficult to drag.

Thus when they arrived finally at the house of Tharho, they were received with great relief, for much time had this enterprise cost them, and days they had not counted: the journey to the mountains, the gathering of the web, the delay within the caves, and the journey home: all told this venture took near to a month.

Thus it was that when they arrived, the servants and family of Tharho came out to greet them anxiously. They sought Chrono at once, and said to him, "Alas! For a messenger arrived for you from a far country these three weeks past, and awaits you yet within the house. Very urgent is the message, but we were near to sending him on his way: for we had begun to doubt whether you would even return from this dangerous endeavor."

Chrono was alarmed at this word, and he rushed into the house of Tharho. There he halted in his tracks at the door, for before him in the house of Tharho stood Cardon, his own father's chief servant, whom Chrono had not seen for many years.

Cardon bowed to him respectfully, and said, "Have I indeed found Chrono son of Marcanto at last? Word had reached the house of Marcanto that Chrono dwelt with his cousin Tharho, but I had feared that I had come so far for nought."

Chrono bowed in return, and hailed Cardon. Then he apologized, saying, "Alas, but we have been gone this past month on a venture for profit, and have faced many and woeful delays upon our way. I must beg pardon, for your time has been wasted in waiting on me. You could have left your tidings with another to deliver, and been sent on your way."

But Cardon became downcast, and said, "The tidings I bring should best be told in person."

Then Chrono's face turned dark with shame, and he said, "Have you then news from my father, who cast me from his house in disgrace?"

Cardon set his face gravely, and he said, "I have no cheerful message to bring to Chrono, for in fact, Marcanto the father of Chrono has been stricken down by age, and lies perhaps on his deathbed, and he has asked once more for his son to return before he departs."

Chrono was dismayed. "Has Marcanto my father sent no soft word to his son, even on his deathbed?"

"I have no message but that which I have brought. Marcanto my lord has not revealed to me his whole mind on such things. Yet I know that he very much desired to see his son Chrono again in his own house, to point of tears."

Chrono sighed. "Then I must go again to see my father, if he still lives, though the journey to my father's house is long." But Chrono thought to himself, "Tears of sorrow and longing? Or tears of the shame and disgrace that I have brought upon him?"

Chrono went out from the house to Duono and Tharho, and told them the tidings he had learned. "So the warning of Duono's dream has come to pass!" he said. "The time is short. I must return at once to make peace if I may, hoping that the honor I have gained in my labors may assuage my father's years of disappointment. Surely it is not proper that a father should reach the end of his days ashamed by the actions of his son."

Tharho said, "I had purposed to go trading into the Eastlands and to visit with our relatives in that country, but I must first have our web twisted into twine. It will otherwise be ruined on the spool, and become worthless. Will you then proceed on this long journey alone?"

Chrono lamented, "Already this message had been several weeks in the journey from Mizgad, and yet more time has been lost awaiting our return.

Nearly two months have passed since my father was stricken. I must lose no time. It may perhaps be already too late."

Duono his trail-master said, "I will not abandon you now of all times. But if you would make this journey quickly, we must go by the shoreland routes, down to the Sea itself. For it might add a week or more to our journey should we take the inland roads as you have been wont to do up until now."

Chrono furrowed his brow at this, and he said, "Give me time to consider our options, but I must decide swiftly. We must leave no later than tomorrow at dawn. I shall choose my path before then."

Duono assented and said, "Then let us prepare our packs for the journey. We must travel swiftly with no sledge to hinder us."

Chrono lay awake that night worrying over this question: He still feared to go to the Sea, for his heart and his soul could not abide being so near to the realm of Ahten, yet to be ever parted from her. But his need now was great, and the need for haste overwhelmed all else.

Now in those days long past there was as yet no map, and none had ever yet attempted to fully describe the lay of those lands. Yet Chrono, and many who traveled that country for trade, knew that the lands around the Pindus make a great arc from Mizgad on the eastern shores around to the country of the Plateosites on the west. In his youth, when he had dwelt long in the house of his uncle Trachio, sitting atop the highest hill of Mizgad and gazing far across the Sea to the west, he had at times on the clearest of days descried the fringe of hills and mountains rising beyond the horizon. Chrono pondered all this deep into the night.

When the morning arrived, he joined his companions, and Duono said to him, "I am ready to hoist my packs and depart at once, whether we go by shore or inland. Have you made up your mind, and chosen your route?"

"I have indeed, but you will think me mad," Chrono replied.

"Mad or not, we must not delay."

"Indeed not. I feel great need of haste, for the days of my father, if he lingers yet among us, may be short, and I greatly lament that we have delayed our departure far too long in tending to our own business."

"Shall we then take the shoreline routes and hasten our journey?"

"No, but I shall do better than that," said Chrono. "For the shores of Mizgad are near indeed, nearer than we have dared to consider. I tell you, Mizgad lies just beyond the horizon to the east, and if luck be with us, we might be there in but three days."

Then Tharho and Duono were indeed astonished. "You cannot mean to cross the Sea itself!" Tharho said. "Do you intend to sprout wings like a wyvern, and fly to Mizgad? Or swim across the waters like the sea-hounds?"

Chrono replied, "I shall do both, if Duono will dare to go with me. For I intend to swim atop the waters in a boat, and cause the wind itself to fly us across the Sea."

Duono said, "Never has such a thing been done or dreamt of! The waves of the Sea are mighty, and the tides of the Endrev[47] are swift and unstoppable. No boat would survive in the great waters. Even if by some miracle one could reach the far shores of Mizgad, the breakers on the shoreline would shatter any vessel and he would perish."

But Chrono said, "I think not. If none has attempted this journey, it is only out of fear of the great waters. But I have myself swum beyond the breakers at Mizgad, and I know they can be navigated. As for the currents, the flow of the wind shall counter the currents of the strait, for the winds blow ever through that strait to southward, and they are strong. I have caught the winds of Endrev in my cloak and coat many times on the sward of Mizgad, and so strong is it that one can scarce stand in place when it catches and swells the fabric. To guide our course straight, we shall use a paddle as a rudder as the boatmen on the rivers do when they float downstream. As for the greatness of the waves, we might fit a covering of fabric or leather across the open spaces of any boat, and delay it from being swamped."

Tharho said, "You would stake your very life on such an endeavor, which has never been dared? For in the midst of the Great Sea, there shall be none to rescue you should your designs be wrong!"

But Duono said, "In all the days of our travels together, I have never known a plan of yours not to be blessed with good fortune. Never to this very day have I abandoned your side, even at risk of death. I shall go with you willingly, and we shall see what we might accomplish!"

With little further delay, then, they hoisted their packs and set out from the house of Tharho. The road from thence down to the Sea wound through hilly country for miles, so they traveled all that day southward, and camped late in the evening; rising early the next morning before the dawn, Chrono and Duono set out hoping to reach the sea by daybreak.

Coming around a bend of the trail on a hillside, the Sea came suddenly into full view as the sun was rising before them, stretching away blue and gold into the morning haze, and sparkling more deeply than the brightest of jewels.

It had been many years since Chrono had beheld the Sea with his own eyes. The sea air filled his nostrils, and all the memories and longing of it overwhelmed him. At the deepness and the beauty of it his heart failed him, and he could not take a step.

So he stood still, and sang this song.

---

47 The Endrev was the name of the strait which connected the Pindus to the Great Sea.

"O long-abandoned mistress of my soul,
Whose fatal bounds my wary feet have shunned—
As endless, empty, winter-tides unroll,
And years and steps, uncountable, compound—
With cold discretion keeping us apart,
While willfully I fled your fleeting call,
I've always known your mien would check my heart,
And my preemptive palisades would fall.
But now, with all your radiance revealed
In all your splendor, bursting into sight,
My long-accepted exile is repealed,
And I renege the season of my flight.

So now the dulcet lance I sought to flee
Has marked my breast, and it transfixes me.

The Sea! And nothing but the Sea at last!
Had I forgot how florid your array?
An azure raiment trembling on your breast;
Your sparkling splendor strips my breath away.
The dizzy raptures of my youth return
I feel the swimming passions I felt then
To wait and watch your winking currents churn,
And gaze upon your visage once again.
Refulgent face, diffusing heaven's light!
Your rippling steppes across horizons sweep
To foaming fringes far beyond my sight.
They veil the unseen mysteries you keep.

Your radiance I charily exalt,
But joys are lost within that liquid vault.

For what of her, enfolded in your press,
Whose straitened fetters still constrain my heart?
That hidden spark, a mite within your breadth,
Does she yet count the days we've been apart?
Were she to call, how would I hear the plea?
For should she pine, her whispers would be drowned.
Could any aching echo reach to me?
Should I but stop and seek, could she be found?
A tantalizing risk to contemplate!
Were I to halt, to stay upon your shore,

What desperate dreams might we rejuvenate!
What hopes redeem, what harmonies restore.

But I'm constrained to pass you on my way;
To touch your face, and sigh, but not to stay.

Then hefting his pack upon his shoulders, he took a breath, and led the way onward.

The Plateosites on the western shores of the Pindus were not so superstitious concerning the Sea as Chrono's own folk, and they had many settlements along the coasts. There they fished in the surf, and took crabs and shellfish from the rock pools. So it was that early in the day the trail to the Sea brought them to a village on the coast, Eisoros by name, which was built on the shores of a quiet bay. This bay was protected by a rocky peninsula from the crashing of the surf, and the folk of that village would even ply small boats into the bay to spear fish, or to scoop them up in little nets. It was for this very reason that Chrono set this village as his goal.

Chrono and Duono went down at once to the shore, where the fishers were returning with their morning catch, and when they had sought out the sturdiest and largest of the boats, large enough for the two of them and their packs, they at once arranged to purchase it.

Now as the folk of that town were skilled at building these crafts, they quickly found a craftsman of the village who was able to help them with their alterations. Then working together throughout the day and into the evening they refashioned the vessel to Chrono's design. They raised the gunwales, and fitted a notch into the stern for their rudder. As the boat seemed top-heavy and too shallow upon the water, Chrono thought to strengthen and deepen the keel to keep the boat from rolling in the open waves. Lastly, they found a stout pole, and mounted it securely forward of the thwart, and to this Chrono attached a great sheet of fabric. When all had been accomplished to his satisfaction, they found quarters in the village for the night.

The folk of that town had gathered to watch these workings throughout that day, wondering what the purpose of these strangers might be in such curious activity. When the morning dawned, Chrono and Duono took their boat down to the sea, and having stowed their packs into the vessel, they fastened sheets of fabric across the open hull, yet allowing themselves space to manage the craft, and pushed off into the bay.

Then the folk of Eisoros were astonished, for it was clear they brought with them neither net nor javelin, but were headed for the open sea beyond the bay. They began to call out to their townsfolk, saying, "Come and watch! These strangers are surely mad, for they are heading into the Sea itself!"

While others called out to them, begging them to return for their lives' sake, taking them for ignorant landsfolk who knew nothing of the waters. Still others got hastily into their own boats, and attempted to row out to them to shepherd them back to safety.

But as the boat reached the further side of the bay the exhalations of Endrev began to assail them. Then Chrono arose, and let down the boom to spread his sail: the wind caught it and filled it, and the boat pitched forward with a burst of speed that left their followers trailing behind.

Then all the folk of Eisoros who had turned out to watch were amazed, and wondered at their audacity; while many said, "Surely these fools dare the wrath of Dreiton[48] himself, and will quickly perish."

But Chrono wavered not one bit in his intent, and manning the sail as best he could, he stood forward on the thwart to gain his bearings, and gave instructions to Duono at the tiller to keep them on a true course across the strait.

Upon leaving the safety of the bay, the waves at once grew furious, and the current pressed at them, so that the boat rocked wildly, plunging from wave to wave, and pitching madly from side to side. The wind in the sail pressed the boat far aslant to starboard, so that Chrono was thankful for the keel they had contrived. He dropped to his knees for safety, and clutching at the mast he leaned with all his weight to port, dragging at the mast to keep the boat from capsizing.

Then Duono called out, "In all dangers have I followed you, and never before have I doubted your luck and wisdom: but at last even I have learned to fear for my life!"

But Chrono merely laughed, and said, "But look! Even the sea-hounds of Dreiton have come to welcome us into their domain!" And it was true, for the boat was soon surrounded by the baying of the sleek companions of Dreiton, who leapt from the waves to greet them.

Then Chrono said, "Do not give in to fears, but hold fast to the tiller, that we may not go adrift and be cast into the wide reaches of the empty Sea. I shall hold fast the sail, which like a great wing shall carry us in haste across the waters."

He took his place on the thwart, and manned the boom, and keeping an eye upon the heaving sea about them he gave instructions to Duono, that they might direct their course true, bearing into the face of the waves that they might not be capsized, and holding fast the wind which gave them speed.

Chrono's heart became filled with a new exhilaration he had never before felt, and it swelled in him like the tingling of wine, into every fiber and vessel of his soul. He sensed the waves surging beneath his feet, and the wind cooling his brow, and the spray of the sea upon his cheek. The salt of the sea air spiced his

48 Dreiton, of course, is the lord of Potomis, the Ídoleth master and shaper of the sea-realms as Vélopar was the master of the land.

nostrils, and he tasted it on his tongue. As if by instinct he knew the Sea like an old and familiar companion, and his boat like a well-trained beast. So it is that some say to this day that Dreiton himself in that hour breathed the very spirit of the Sea into Chrono, so he became at once both its master and its slave.

Thus in good stead they soon found themselves bearing upon the far shore, and the hills and mountains of Mizgad began to rise before them across the horizon, so that even Duono, taking his eyes from the rudder for a moment, recognized the approach of their ancient home, and marveled.[49] And he said, "Yet once again the wisdom of Chrono holds true, and the path you have chosen brings us swiftly homeward! If now your luck shall also hold out, and we be not dashed to pieces by the surf, we shall indeed be home in Mizgad itself in short order!"

The shore approached swiftly by the force of the wind, and soon the Rock of Ahten could be seen before them, still familiar to Chrono's eyes even after many years absence. Yet now the rock, which had been the haunt of Ahten whom he had loved in his youth, sat dark and empty. A pang pierced the heart of Chrono, and a tear from his eye blended with the salt spray of the Sea. But he did not flinch, and the thrill of the Sea in his heart renewed his strength.

Duono then spoke with alarm, saying, "The shores of Mizgad approach now too swiftly, and the waves breaking on the rocks ahead are more than enough to destroy our vessel, and drown us both into the bargain! What is your plan to preserve our lives?"

Chrono watched the shore carefully however, and was undisturbed. "Steer as I tell you, and we shall come ashore in safety. Only stay with the boat until the moment you feel the sand of the sea-bottom scrape the keel: then leap free and make your way ashore as quickly as you can."

Then Chrono bore off from windward and began to reef his sail, so the boat ceased its violent rushing. Passing the Rock of Ahten on the side downstream from the current, he directed the boat to the leeward side of the hill of Mizgad, where the breakers were not so high and perilous. Then at last he stood down from the thwart and took the tiller from the hand of Duono, and with skill as if the boat were his own life and limb he drifted broadside to shore behind the line of the breakers. When they reached the point of the breaking surf he turned swiftly to face the beach where a strip of white sand glared before them, and he let the breaking wave carry the boat rushing ashore. Pitching again parallel to shore the boat at last scraped bottom and began to keel over. Then Chrono and Duono leapt free into the surf, and Chrono taking the end of a line made his way swiftly ashore. With Duono's aid they drew their vessel from the waves.

Then Duono laughed, and said, "Truly you have the fortune of the Terumani

---

49 It is highly unlikely their course across the Endrev by coincidence brought them directly to their goal. It is possible the narrative simply omits the coastal journey which brought them to that point.

on your side, for never would I have believed such a journey could be made: and we are delivered up from the Sea as if rising from the halls of Death itself."

But Chrono was looking out to sea, his eyes fixed on the Rock of Ahten. There had the sea-hounds gathered, baying from its crags as if rejoicing for Chrono's victory. One by one they slipped into the waters, and were gone.

At last Chrono turned his back to the Sea, and said, "Alas, but we have no time to rejoice in our deliverance, nor have I leisure to pine for that which was lost in the days of youth long past. We must hurry to my father's house as quickly as our feet may carry us. If we are diligent we may perhaps yet reach his doors before the next rising of the sun."

So they took up their packs and set their path at once towards the house of Chrono's youth.

They marched inland, skirting the lands of his uncle Trachio, and across the hills of Trachia,[50] taking little rest, until the sun had set and the dark sky was filled with stars. They pressed on late into the night, and rested little, and when the early dawn had just begun to blush the edges of the starry sky, they at last reached the portal of that house.

There they were met at the door by Trachio himself, who fell down on his knees before them in joy at their reunion. He cried out, "Can this be Chrono, returned from his years of wandering at last to his father's house? And can this really be Duono himself? The sight of my dear ones returned brings joy to my heart I have not known for years!"

So Chrono greeted his uncle heartily, "Our parting in former days was harsh, but perhaps the passing years have softened both of our memories. It truly warms my heart to find you yet hale and well." Then his face darkened, and he said, "But what of my father? Does he yet live?"

Trachio said, "Yes, my brother lives. But he is weak, and does not always know what is happening around him, nor recognize all who come to pay regard. He is sorely stricken with the pangs of age and worry. Do not be dismayed if he seems not to know you. Allow me to go in before you, and prepare him to receive you if I might."

So Chrono waited, and Trachio ushered him at last into the room of his father, and left them alone.

The room was dark, and Marcanto lay unmoving upon his bed by a small window, staring out into the darkness in silence. Chrono approached softly, and he said, "My father! Do you know your son Chrono? He who shamed you in years long past has returned to ask your grace and pardon."

For a long while Marcanto made no motion at all, nor showed any sign

50 There are two locales named Trachia in these Tales: one in Vordót, south of Niyarc, and one in the Southrealm on the eastern shores of the Pindus. It is probable that the Trachia of the Southrealm was so-named by the Donites who migrated there after the end of the Ice, possibly in honor of Trachio who had once lived in that region.

that he had heard Chrono's voice, but he stared out the window as if unseeing and unhearing. Chrono feared that he had arrived too late after all, and that his father's mind had fled before its time. But at last Marcanto turned, and his eyes beheld his son. Then the flush of recognition lit his countenance, and a tear welled up into his eye. Stretching forth a spotted and trembling hand he spoke, "Chrono, my son!"

Chrono cried out, "My father!" Then Chrono fell to his knees at his father's bedside, and put his arms around his neck, and the two of them wept.

At last Chrono said, "My father, can you bear the presence of your son, who shamed you in the matter of Mourelë the daughter of Carthréan, and has these many years defied your will in the matter of the sea-maiden?"

Marcanto said, "Chrono, my son, my son! Indeed for many years I harbored my resentment and nurtured it, so that it grew deep-rooted like a weed in my heart, and choked out all love. But the stories of your labors have come back to me again and again, as if winging on the winds of the heavens; and all have spoken well of you! At last in my age it became clear to me that you chose the more honorable path. Since then I have longed these many days to see you again before I pass from this realm, and to tell you face to face that I was wrong to force my will against the leanings of your heart. And now here you are, and Havui be honored for bringing you to my side before the end."

"Then are you not ashamed of the son who defied you?"

"How can a father be ashamed of such a son? Each story of your deeds has filled me with secret pride, until at last my heart has swelled to overflowing and my shame was swept clean from every dark corner. I have wept, but only that you might not return, and I might never live to tell you so!

"The word of your exploits has gone through all of Soria, and in all places the name of Chrono the son of Marcanto is spoken with honor. Even the terumani, it is said, receive you with acclaim! Never has a father been more proud of the name his son has earned."

So it was that Chrono was reconciled to his father before the end. After some days Marcanto at last passed from the land of Soria, and went the way of his own father, and of all those who had come before him. Whither such as these go none can say.

But Chrono remained in his father's house, and being the eldest of his brethren, and honored by his father, he inherited responsibility over all that his father had left. He set all things in order for those left behind, distributing to his brothers, his sisters, and his servants the gifts, privileges and responsibilities of everything in that inheritance as he saw fit. All that he did was met with approval by his brethren, as well as his father's associates and relatives, for Chrono did nothing without fair judgement and honor.

10. CHRONO AND THE SEA MONSTER

Now after Chrono's father had passed on, Chrono remained in the compound of his father for a time, to set his father's estate in order. But his heart was now crying out to visit once again the rock in the Sea where he had met the Trityn years before. Each night as he lay upon his bed, the visions returned to him, as if not a day had passed since last he had left his father's house, and had left the Trityn-maiden behind in his despair. The fever grew in him with each passing day, until he could bear the torment no longer. He purposed at last to do that which he had for many years avoided, and to risk the heartbreak of seeing Ahten once again.

He said to Duono one evening, "Tomorrow it is my intent to cross over the hill of Mizgad and go down at last to the Sea. Do not follow me, and do not hope for my return. For I do not know what fate awaits me on that shore."

But Duono was abashed, and he said to him, "If you would have my counsel, I would warn you not to do this thing. For years you have held your resolve steadfastly, and much good has come to many because of it."

Chrono's uncle, Trachio, also overheard this discourse, and he at once agreed with Duono, saying, "Who knows but this Trityn will once again weave her nets of enchantment over you, and you shall in the end perish in disgrace and shame. This must not be!"

But Chrono would not be dissuaded, and he said, "You blaspheme that of which you are ignorant. The Seafolk are terumani, and as pure of honor as the dræads and nymphs of wood and pool. Ahten has cast no enchantment upon me, save that holy charm which every maiden casts upon the one she loves."

Duono said to him, "But what, if you are once again entrapped by longings and hopeless desire to waste your days in wallowing, what will become of you and of the name you have earned for yourself in all the lands of Soria?"

"Perhaps I risk all that I've gained," Chrono replied, "but nevertheless I must try to see the maiden Ahten once more, or my soul shall die within me here."

So Duono at last gave in, and he said to Chrono, "If it must be so, then let it be. Only allow this: that in ten days' time, if you have not returned, I shall go out and seek you, to see whether you might yet be saved."

To this Chrono conceded. So the next morning he assumed his pack, and took up his staff; then he left the house of Marcanto his father, and set his sights to the westward Sea.

Even after many years away, the trail was fresh in his memory. He crossed the Trachian Range, and by the following morning found himself gazing down the sward of the hill of Mizgad, sweeping down to the breaking waves of the Sea. Across the waters rose the old Rock, where the Trityn had first appeared and her song has first caught his ear. On that Rock they had first gazed into one another's eyes, and on that Rock they first embraced.

But now the Rock stood empty, bleak, and black with the wetness of the waves. Even the sea-hounds and the gulls had abandoned it, and it was utterly forlorn. So Chrono sat down upon the rocks at the shore of Mizgad, and sighed, and for a long while watched and listened to the driving waves crashing white upon its flanks. Until at last he lifted his voice and sang.

"The rock, forsaken and forlorn
Which once was swept by shimmering tress
And bore a maiden's sweet caress —
How fair the absent form that once was borne! —
Now sadly stands amid the surf,
And waiting, weeps wet tears of spray
To honor her who could not stay,
Who graces now a distant, deeper berth.

And I stand, gazing out to sea.
And wonder what's become of me.

"And so I now regret the course
That took my feet from hallowed shore.
For could I watch forevermore
I would not count one hour as a loss.
Or could return each treasured prize,
And all my laboring years have won,
I'd fain to have it swiftly done
For just another glimpse of Ahten's eyes.

Lost years of honor and acclaim
Are to my heart a hollow gain."

Then ending his song, he lowered his head, and wept silently.

But as he wept, a lilting sound wafted to him from over the waves, and he perceived it to be the sound of singing. A voice came across to him, saying,

"Long years have passed in silent vigil here,
Where once I heard my Chrono's hearty tone.
Long I waited, watching here alone,
No sound of singing wafting to my ear.

Ever wishing memory was false,
And we had never chosen to depart,
Nor made that choice which rent my fervent heart,
Trading joy for pain with every pulse.

But knowing what we chose, we chose for good,
To save us both from wasting, if we could.

So have I borne the sorrows of the years:
This rock a stony wall to guard my soul;
A fortress to defend a hollow hole;
A tomb interring loneliness and fears.
All my faith had parted long ago—
No hope I might regain such rapture pure!
This rock, forever empty, would endure,
A symbol of our chosen path of woe.

And so I left it, just as he left me:
By will, and yet unwillingly.

But now my heartbeat quickens at a song!
I clutch a trembling hand upon my breast,
And catch a flurried quiver in my breath,
And dare to dream my resolution wrong!
Is now, beyond all hope, a song returning?
Echoes of a long-lost rhapsody
Restore those moments to my memory:
Those faded fancies; my forgotten yearning.

I lift my anxious eyes above the Sea,
And lo! My Chrono has returned to me!"

So Chrono lifted his head, and gazed again at the rock beyond the breakers: there he saw the figure of Ahten, standing alone and gazing to the shore through the mists, and beckoning with outstretched arm. Then the love which had overwhelmed him those many years ago welled up in his heart, and renewed his spirit with all its youthful strength.

Now it so happened that the boat which he and Duono had sailed across the Strait of Endrev still awaited him there on the shore of Mizgad, tied to a stock high upon the sands. Chrono at once rushed to it, and untying it, dragged it down to the sea. There with great effort he towed it into the waters, past the breakers, and unfurled the sail; the strength of the wind dragged the keel from the bottom into the deep waters. Chrono took hold of the tiller, and guided the craft skillfully across the open waters to the rock of Ahten.

There he leapt heedless into the cold sea, and swam to the rock. When he had moored the vessel he climbed from the sea, and there he stood motionless and frozen in wonder, for he found himself gazing at last at Ahten, whom his eyes had not beheld since days of his youth. Though many years had passed, she appeared unfaded, just as his memories recalled: for she was teruman, and does not age as do the children of his own Kindred. Only her eyes revealed the trials of the years.

Ahten also beheld Chrono in wonder, for he had appeared as a figure from her dreams, and though he had matured, he was still beautiful in her eyes as he had been in his youth.

Then they fell into each other's arms, and for a long while those two sundered souls wept upon each other's neck, weeping tears of longing and joy.

Chrono it was who spoke first, saying, "How is it that you came to this forgotten rock, this empty monument, that you might hear my voice this day? For long ago we both swore to abandon hope and forsake this place."

Ahten said, "Many days ago word came to us that the sea-hounds had followed a small craft across the very Sea, braving the deep from the distant Cove of Eisoros beyond the Endrev. The course it set was straight to the rock of Mizgad, passing by our own lonely Rock as it went. Those that watched its strange course upon the waters said that one stood upon the thwart gazing upon that Rock with tears in his eyes as he passed. So we knew that none could that mariner be but Chrono the Plateosite, who alone among the Children of Toë had braved the waters of the deep, to reach this same rock in years long past.

"Thus the sea-hounds themselves signaled that Chrono had ridden upon the Sea, and had come ashore at Mizgad his old home. Since then have I come again to this Rock where first we met, and have listened every day for the lilt of thy song, setting hope against despair that I might see thee but once again."

Then Chrono said, "I regret that I had many concerns which kept me from this shore, or I would many days ago have returned to seek your face and hear your song. For my father was stricken with age, and has passed from the circles of this world, and I had many duties to constrain me in my father's house."

"Then hast thou done the right and honorable thing, and have no need of pardon."

"And yet I rue each day which I have spent away from your presence."

"Say not so! For the word of thy deeds and thine honor hath gone throughout the world, so that even here beneath the waves thy praise is spoken. Thou hast been ever brave, faithful to thy friends, merciful to thy foes, and honorable in all thy doings. Thou art well spoken of amongst all the terumani, both næad and dræad, and that is no little thing to have earned."

"For all this kindness from your Kindred I give thanks, and little would I have accomplished without their aid. Yet gazing once more into the beauty of your eyes, it seems a very little thing indeed!"

"And I again know rapture I had thought forever fled. But what shall we do? We've no more hope today than we had upon this same Rock those many years past."

"For now, I need no hope. I have no more need of honor, nor fear of shame. Though we can never truly be one, to waste away my remaining years, hopeless, but in your presence, is all I dare to strive for."

"Then let us spend together whatever hours we might steal, and we shall face our fate tomorrow or the next day."

So they sat upon the Rock as they had in days of old, and they spoke long and of many things; and were there any to hear it, the sound of their songs would have been heard from far across the sea.

Thus they conversed for days, and shared much of what had transpired since those days when they had first met. All their age-old devotion was renewed and strengthened. There they sat peaceably together on the Rock, and did not worry for the future. But each evening Chrono got into his boat, and returned to shore to camp on dry land and restore himself.

At last the time came for them to speak of their plans; and Chrono said, "I shall build my house here on the shores of Mizgad, that I might come here to this Rock every day. Though we cannot be united, is it not allowed that we might yet see each other when we wish?"

But Ahten said, "Alas, but I myself may need to abandon this Rock. For my folk are sore beset by trials in our ancient Hall, and Merten my father thinks to remove us from this place, and to find a new home. Should that time come, I would needs go with my folk, or remaining here alone would face daily dangers."

Then Chrono was astonished, and said, "I shall follow if I may, wherever you might go, even were it to the midst of the Great Sea. But what danger could be so dreadful that Merten your father, the prince, would think to abandon his ancient home and to displace all his folk?"

So Ahten explained, "A monstrous creature hath made this place its haunt, against which we have little power. A creature of slime like the sea jellies, but greater far in size and deadliness. A hundred tentacles it has, or more, each as long as the tendrils of the kelp trees: and each is armed with a fell venom. It hunts whatever it can find in the sea, whether of fish, or the sea-hounds, or my own folk. Already have several of us been stung, and lie in the age-long rest that our folk require to heal of deadly wounds, and they shall sleep beyond the lifespan of your own folk."

"Then can Dreiton himself not defeat this beast? Surely Dreiton has authority over all the beasts of the deep Sea?"

"Nay," said Ahten, "But Dreiton is far from the realm of Merten, and hath many concerns of his own. Might he even be reached in a timely way, there is no surety that he would come to us, simply to save the Hall of Merten from a natural beast of Potomis. Would Vélopar come to rescue you from a lion? Or Ologéo come to heal you of your sniffles? We cannot count on the aid of the high ones, for the monster is also the natural creature of Potomis, and the Ádolthi are not wont to interfere with the proceedings of nature. As with all trials, it is given to us to find our own solutions and salvations fit for each trial."

Chrono then became stern and said, "I have faced many dangers and trials, and have vanquished powerful foes. I shall face this also, and overcome this creature."

But Ahten feared for him, and said, "Ah, but thou knowest not! So great and dreadful a monster hast thou never seen! Better it would be to flee than to perish in the fight. Even Merten my father and all our folk know not how to defeat it."

Chrono however already had thought of a course, and he said, "You and your folk are bound in the confines of the Sea, but I have on my side the powers of the dry air, and the heat of the naked sun, and the weightiness of the land. Moreover I shall not fight alone. Trust me, and I shall bring aid to you and to Merten your father, as I have aided others."

Now it happened that on the following day Duono the companion of Chrono arrived, as he had planned, to see whether he might bring Chrono back to the house of his father in the Valley of Canto. Chrono was in his place on the Rock of Ahten when Duono arrived, and seeing him upon the shore Chrono turned to Ahten and said, "There is my aid, who has been with me through many trials. This one is brave and faithful beyond measure. And he is my friend. I wish, if you dared, that you night come with me into the boat, that we might sail to the shore together to meet him. Seeing you he will not fail to give us his aid."

Ahten trembled at this, for she was shy of the Kindred of Sorios. But with Chrono's persuasion she conceded, only insisting that she must not leave the boat, and her feet must not touch the dry land. With the grace of a swan she slid into the vessel. So Chrono sailed across the strait which separated them from the shore of Mizgad, with the Trityn upon the thwart, her gleaming hair flowing like the sea breeze itself.

Then Duono saw them at sea, and he knew it must be Chrono and the sea-maiden whom he loved. He shook his head in sorrow, knowing that Chrono was once again bound to her, and would not willingly return with him.

But as the boat reached the shore, he came forward to greet them: and his eyes fell upon the maiden of the sea. Then was Duono himself smitten with her beauty. He kneeled, and he said, "Chrono, in all the years we have sojourned together, I have borne with you in your hopeless devotion to a maiden of the sea, and I have ignorantly tried to help you to forget and to bear yourself bravely. But I have not understood before now. For now I see with my own eyes, and now I believe that the treasure you have guarded in your heart is worthy of every pain you have spent."

Ahten blushed, and she said in reply, "And thou, Duono friend of Chrono, art as all the tales have described. For thou art kind, and gracious, and one to be trusted."

Chrono said, "Now perhaps you will understand if I do not happily return to live among my own. But more than this, I hope I might convince you to join with me in yet another labor, for the folk of Ahten's house are in peril."

Duono said, "I have joined with you always in every danger, and have not failed you. Yet should I ever have thought to abandon you, having seen this maiden of the sea whom you love, for this cause alone I would not fail you now."

So Chrono and Ahten told Duono of the sea-monster which had beset her folk. Chrono said, "I have a plan which might destroy this creature, though the folk of the Sea have failed. If you would listen to me, let us see if we can accomplish this work together."

Chrono then explained his plan to Duono, and Duono shook his head. "Only one with the luck of the Terumani could conceive such a plan! Yet I shall gladly see it through with you, for we two together have accomplished many wonders."

So the two began to assemble and fabricate their arms for the struggle to come. Returning to the house of Marcanto, Chrono's inheritance, they brought back to Mizgad a supply of the strong, silken cord of the Inviant; and bladders and wineskins to make floats, such as the fishers of the rivers used to string their nets and float their catch; and spears and javelins which they refashioned into barbed harpoons. They also brought leather, which Chrono's craftsmen made into armor to deflect the stinging tentacles of the sea-creature: breastplates and vambraces, greaves and gloves.

While all their supplies were being assembled, Chrono set to work on strengthening their boat. When they had crossed the Strait of Endrev, Chrono had noted many shortcomings of their vessel, and he had laid awake at night, at times, dreaming up contrivances to improve it. He added sturdy pontoons that it might not capsize in the struggle or the waves. He raised the boom of the sail that it might not obstruct their movements. The rudder he fixed to the stern that it might not be lost. Then he fastened cleats to the gunwale, to stay the lines of the harpoons.

As they were still testing and proving their equipment, Ahten appeared to Chrono, and said, "If we mean to defeat this monster, we must needs be swift. For it hath stricken again, and we were hard-pressed to escape its maw.

Another of our folk hath been stung and must enter the long sleep. My father Merten is now determined to find a new home far away from its haunts."

Chrono counseled with Duono, and when they had finished their parley he said to Ahten, "Tell your father to give us yet two more days, if he dares. If we have not taken the beast by then, we shall have failed. Tomorrow if the wind is strong we shall seek it out. But we shall need the help of your folk to bring it from its lair and draw it to the surface where we might strike."

So Ahten went down to Merten with this message.

The next day Ahten returned, and with her came a throng of her folk, and the sea-hounds attended them. None but the sea-hounds dared to raise their head above the waves, but the Seafolk could be seen below, teeming dim and ghostly in the gray waters. Ahten alone approached Chrono on the shore, and from the waves she called out, "If you would take this monster from the sea, then get into your boat, and follow us to the open sea. The monster is active even now, and we hope to draw it forth into your hands. Come!"

So Chrono called out to Duono, "Come at once. The hunt awaits us!" They fetched their boat hurriedly, and pushed into the waves; the wind caught the sail, and carried them swiftly into the pitching swells beyond the breakers. The waters surged and foamed before them from the seething throng below, while the sea-hounds leapt from the waves and bayed their throaty calls. The vessel of Chrono sped in their wake, trailing a great cluster of floats, whisking across the surface as if on ice, the great breath of Endrev driving them forth to their mark.

When they had gone some distance, far from shore, the waters grew suddenly still, and the sea-hounds and the whole throng of the Seafolk slid suddenly away. At this the hairs of Chrono's neck stood on end.

"This sudden emptiness chills my heart!" said Duono. "I feel death below us."

Then the head of Ahten appeared at the side of the boat, but terror filled her eyes. She gasped, "This is the place. If you will wait here, I think you shall find your quarry awaits you. Only take caution, and do nothing foolish! For I would not lose you now, when we have found one another again after so long a parting!" Then as she looked about, the waters below began to surge slowly and queerly, and she said, "Return to me, Chrono!" Then she slipped beneath the waters, and Chrono saw her form speed away more swiftly than he had imagined her kind could go, as swiftly as the dolphins. Then he and Duono were utterly alone.

Chrono furled the sail and dropped a drag line to slow their progress. Duono taking the tiller drew the boat about, circling over the strange waters. As they watched, the sea below them grew gray, then pale, then they could discern the outline of a vast form rising up below them, monstrous and horrifying in its shape and dimensions. Like a monstrous platter it appeared, its skin a sickening ashen hue, its undulating surface glistening like slime. So great was it that it seemed to them as if an island were rising from the deeps to assault them.

Chrono shouted, "The beast rises directly below us! We must be off or we shall be swamped!" At once he began to trim the sail to catch the wind and escape, but he was too late. The waters of the sea poured off the canopy of the great beast like a cascade over a mountainside, and their boat was a toy in its flow. They tilted wildly in the rush of the waters, and but for the pontoons fastened to the sides would surely have capsized.

But Duono seeing the opportunity raised his harpoon, and thrust it mightily into the back of the beast, and it stuck.

The monster's canopy, though it appeared as filmy as a sea-jelly, was a strong as a tanned hide: so the harpoon of Duono stuck fast and would not come free. As for the monster, it did not perceive the harpoon, until Chrono and Duono began to draw in their line, and it sensed that it was being tugged toward the surface. It could not swim strongly like the great whales of the deep, but pulsing hideously in the waters, it attempted to descend, and the boat rocked violently at its strength. The pontoons held, and the boat did not tip nor capsize.

Chrono and Duono began to attach their floats as the battle continued: using all their strength they would draw the creature in a little and attach another float. Whenever the creature would rise up from the depths within their reach they would send another harpoon into its canopy, and attach yet more floats. The battle was long and tiresome, but at last the floats prevented the creature from descending into the depths, and Chrono and Duono began to draw in their lines. So it became trapped on the surface of the sea, where the sun began to crack and bake its slimy back.

Yet it did not seem to tire, and the struggle continued.

Then Chrono said, "The battle will not end until we drag the monster from the sea." But they were now far from the haven at Mizgad, and the shoreline itself was a distant ridge to the east. The monster continued to fight fiercely, so Chrono could scarcely control the boat even with the full strength of the wind in the sail to aid him.

Grappling with the tiller, Duono said, "We are growing weary. We must act quickly, lest we lose the creature at sea and our struggles are wasted."

Chrono inspected the pontoons and the rigging, and he added, "Or before our vessel is ruined by the fight and we are swamped here in the deep: for the battle is fierce."

Duono surveyed the now distant shoreline, and said, "If the winds hold strong, I believe we can tow the monster to the shore. But alas, all the shore, as far as my eyes can see, is little but rock and breakers, which will surely smash our vessel to splinters."

Now Ahten had been watching the contest from a distance, safely beyond the range of the tentacles of the sea-monster. Seeing their distress, she called out to Chrono across the waters, "I shall find you a beach of sand, where the waves do not crash upon the rocks! Watch for the sea-hounds! They shall guide you to the haven you require!" Then she slipped beneath the waves.

So they fought. The sea-monster would try to descend, and could not, then it would try to rise and swamp their boat: but the pontoons held, and the boat would not tip.

But inevitably, after many such attacks the boat began to groan, and the seams to split, so that the waters of the sea were seeping into the vessel. Chrono and Duono fought to bail out what they could, but they began to fear the vessel would not hold out to the end. At last Chrono said, "If we must cut the creature loose, so be it. For the sake of the plea of Ahten alone would I withdraw, for I care not for my own life."

Duono also said, "Nor would I be deemed a coward in the end. But for your sake, and the sake of the sea-maiden, I will abort if I must."

"Then by all means we must save the boat, for we have no other hope of surviving."

All this time Chrono held the sail full to the wind, and Duono guided the boat shoreward as best he could against the struggles of the beast, while the winds of Endrev pressed them ever further from Mizgad.

The sea creature rose from the waters again, and lifted the boat upon its back, then sank once more. At this attack one of the cleats broke free, and the line with its floats drifted from their grasp. So Chrono said, "Now is the time. We must surrender, or we shall soon lose control of the beast. Should it attack us at sea, we are doomed."

He got out his knife, and began to cut one of the tethers: but at that moment, the sound of baying came to him from across the waves. Then his heart lifted up, and looking out to sea, he saw the sea-hounds leaping in the waters: a great concourse of them, bounding through the waves far ahead of the boat to port. Chrono shouted out with joy, "Ahead! The Hounds of Dreiton have arrived to guide us!"

At this he stayed the sail with a line, and took hold of the tiller, and fought fiercely to guide the boat against the struggles of the beast below them. Duono meanwhile did his best to fend the creature off, jabbing at it with his lance, and tightening the bonds to the floats. Following the course of the sea-hounds, they at last beheld an opening in the rocky shore, and a glistening beach where the surf crashed upon sand far from the jagged reefs.

The wind was faithful, and its strength drew them shoreward under Chrono's guidance, towing the monster with them as they went. When they had begun to approach the shallows, Chrono said, "Now we must loosen our lines, for when the boat strikes the sands, we must leap ashore and drag this creature from the sea by sheer strength. We shall need length enough to escape the tentacles of the beast, and to wade ashore until we gain our footing. Swimming in the waters the beast would have us at its mercy."

So they began to unwind their cords from the cleats, and the boat drew away from the sea-beast. The floats, however, kept the monster from slipping away into the deep. The winds of Endrev pulled it along, and soon the waves rushing ashore began to push upon it as well. Its canopy began to swell above the surface, pulsing with a sickly glimmer: and even its evil tentacles began to whip through the air.

Chrono guided his vessel into the path of a breaker, and pointed the bow ashore: so the boat rushed landward, until the keel struck the sands. He leapt into the surf without a further word, and Duono followed: laying hold of whatever lines they could, they hurried from the helpless boat, and gained the shore as quickly as the strife allowed.

Then began the toil of dragging the beast from the waters. By now the monster had been washed into the shallows, and could not swim: but its very weight was beyond their reckoning. As each wave pushed it shoreward, they gained a bit of ground, but when the waves washed back to the sea it was all they could do to dig in and hope to stand their ground. They had upon this beach no purchase to stay them and aid them, and their strength in the struggle was waning.

Then Chrono glanced about, and spotted within reach, just beyond the sand, a stout tree with a sturdy trunk. "Let us pull our lines about the tree!" he shouted. "It shall keep us from being drawn into the sea with this beast!" So they slackened their hold on their lines, and taking the loose ends they ran about the far side of the tree, and returned to the beach. From there they renewed the struggle, and using the tree to keep the line taut, by slow degrees they brought the sea-monster shoreward to its doom.

But as the creature was dragged up from the waters and onto the shore, in its throes it lashed about in fury. One of its horrible tentacles swung back to where Chrono dragged upon his line. He had come too close, and it struck him in the wrist, between vambrace and glove, where his skin was exposed and unprotected; and Chrono cried out for the great pain and agony of its sting.

He stumbled and fell to the earth as if dead. Duono let out a cry of dismay, and rushed to the side of his friend. But Chrono, as he swooned, ordered him, "Leave me! You must finish drawing the creature from the depths and secure the lines, that it might perish at last in the sun and not escape."

So Duono did as Chrono had commanded. He returned to his own line, and with all the strength he had left he dragged upon the line. The creature was drawn from the Sea, and all the water in its canopy leaked out in a flood. It writhed its final throes, and the heat of the sun baked it, and it was no more.

Then at last Duono returned to aid Chrono.

Now Ahten had for some time been watching from the waves, far a-sea for safety: When she saw Chrono fall she had cried out in distress. Now at last she appeared in the surf. Then for the first time she set foot upon the shores of the dry land. There she rushed to the side of Chrono, and falling down beside him she wept for fear.

But Duono had reached him first. Finding no life in his friend, he moaned, "Alas! But he has fled this realm to join his father!"

Then Ahten wailed, "Woe, that such a one should perish in the end on such a task! Had he never sworn to aid me and my folk, he would yet live!" And she fell upon the body of Chrono, and wept.

Duono stood over her, helpless to comfort her. For a long while they stood thus: Chrono prone on the sand, and the sea-maiden weeping on his neck, and Duono his companion silently standing over them both.

At last Duono noted that Ahten's skin was dry and beginning to fissure, and he knew that every moment on the dry land was an agony to her; so he said softly, "You must arise, and return to the sea, lest you also meet a fate such as that of the sea-monster. For Chrono would not have it so." Then taking her by the arm, he lifted her to her feet, and would have brought her safely back to the waves.

But at that moment, looking as it were for the last time upon her beloved, Ahten beheld a flutter of Chrono's eyes. Gasping, she fell upon him once again, and placed her cheek to his lips. Then she cried out, "He is not dead, but swoons! But life is tenuous in him, and may flee yet. We must get aid, and swiftly!"

Duono said, "I know of no apothecary or physician who could arrive here in under a week's time, and I have no confidence they would have any balm or elixir to help."

So Ahten looked at him, pleading, and said, "Then I must go and fetch my father. For though he is not a healer, his powers over life are great, and his wisdom is the wisdom of many ages of your folk. Stay thou here and comfort him, and keep his body warm until I return."

So she ran to the surf, and plunged into the waters, and was gone.

Duono looked down upon his stricken friend, and could think of little he might do to aid him. But as Chrono's arm where he had been stung was growing swollen and red, Duono tied it off with his belt, that no more venom might make it to Chrono's heart. Then he pressed on his chest to help him to breath. But for all this Chrono made no response. For an hour or more Duono worked, until at last Ahten reappeared. With her strode Merten her father, doughty and with a flowing beard the gray of the winter Sea. Never had Merten entered the shorelands of his own volition since the day he had received the Halls of the deep, but at his daughter's pleading, and in his respect for what Chrono had done, he conceded.

Duono drew back at the sight in awe, for Merten was mighty among the Seafolk. Merten strode quickly to the side of Chrono, and said, "Such courage should not be so ill rewarded, for these folk do not heal as do the terumani: when his soul has fled, he will be gone."

Seeing the place where Chrono had been wounded, Merten said, "It is well that you have tied off the wound, for it may save his life. But it will go ill for the arm." Then he cut the wound with a blade and applied a poultice he had brought with him to draw out the poison. Taking Chrono's head in his hands, he strove long and hard, peering into the depths of his mind and spirit, calling him back from the brink of death. Until at last Chrono gasped, and he began to breath easily. Nevertheless he did not return to consciousness.

Merten stood up, and bowing his head he said, "I have done all that I can. Life is in him yet, but I cannot bring him back further. Such work is beyond me."

Then weeping in her despair, Ahten said, "Then we must go to one who can. We must call for great Dreiton himself."

At this Merten hesitated, and said, "Dreiton is not at my beck and call. Who am I among the multitude of the Seafolk to call upon him?"

Then Duono dared to speak, saying, "Is Dreiton then so distant? And are you not a lord among the Seafolk?"

To this Ahten agreed. "If he will hear the call of any, he will hear you, my father. What this son of Sorios has done on behalf of the Seafolk this day, and indeed all his dealings with all the terumani in all his life, have earned him the right to this request."

So Merten at last conceded, and said, "Then I must return to my haven in the deep. I will call for Bël, and send her to Dreiton: and if he will come, we will see what we will see." Then he turned and departed into the waves, and was gone.

Duono made a shelter for them on the beach, and placed Chrono upon a pallet, and brought him into the shelter. There he remained by his side, bringing him water and sustenance day by day. Ahten came each day to sit beside him when she could, but the dry land and air sapped her strength, and she could not remain long for reason of the pain. When the day was spent she would return to the deep, to the house of her father and her mother, to await word from Dreiton.

Now it happened that all the folk of Merten's household and his whole company rejoiced in the deed of Chrono and Duono, who had freed them of so great a peril. So without fail, all of them upheld the two sons of the dry land before Dreiton to seek his aid. In the end even the heart of Dreiton was turned, and he came forth from his Hall in the great Deeps of Potomis.

Then to Chrono's beach came Dreiton forth from the surf, the waves themselves parting before him, his untamed hair and his beard hoary as the salt of the sea. There he stopped and beheld the now shriveled and brown remains of the beast that had terrorized Merten and his folk for so many days, and had placed many good Seafolk into the long sleep of the terumani. He nodded in respect, and strode to the shelter Duono had built. Behind him followed Ahten together with her parents, Merten and Aviah her mother.

Duono stood trembling in the presence of Dreiton, for Dreiton is of the Ádolthi, among the greatest of the Terumani, who seldom comes forth from his realm.

Dreiton saw Chrono upon his pallet, and his face was sorrowful. But he spoke, and his voice was as deep as the thunder; and he said, "This one is brave and mighty among the children of the Land, and it saddens me to see his fate has brought him to this. Leave me alone with him for one hour, and I shall do what I can."

So Duono, Merten and Ahten left the shelter which Duono had built, and waited anxiously on the sands of the seashore. Murmurings were heard from within the shack, and at the rumbling voice of Dreiton the sand below their feet trembled.

At last the rumblings from within went quiet. Then Dreiton came out from the shelter, his head bowed. "You may go in to him," he said. "He has returned from the brink, and he shall live. But he needs time to regain his full strength: time and the care of his friends. His arm, I fear, will not heal." Then Dreiton departed at once into the sea without another word.

So rushing through the entrance Duono and Ahten fell upon Chrono and wept for joy. Chrono raised himself from his pallet and sat up to greet them. Looking at his withered hand, he smiled wryly and said, "A small price it is, I suppose, if we have succeeded in destroying the monster of the deep."

Duono said, "But so much greater would that cost have been, my friend, had Dreiton not brought you back from the fringes of this world."

Chrono shook his head. "You do not understand," he said. "Not for Dreiton himself could I have been recalled from that journey upon which my soul had fled. But Dreiton pleaded for the sake of Ahten the daughter of Merten." He took Ahten by the hands and peered into her eyes. "Only by this reward could the strength for such a return be bought."

So it was that Chrono and Duono earned themselves great glory and honor in the eyes of Merten and the Seafolk. The word of this act spread throughout the Sea, and all the Seafolk spoke the name of Chrono with pride. Duono and Ahten tended to Chrono and restored him to health; but ever after was Chrono lame in his left arm.

11. CHRONO AND THE BATTLE OF AHTEN

This tale is told of Chrono and Ahten, of the days after he had returned to his father's house and made peace, and dwelt again in the country of Mizgad. Chrono had earned glory in defeating the Sea Monster of Mizgad.

When Chrono had defeated the creature, he spent many days on the beach where the creature had perished. There Duono built a shelter of stone and turf to keep him from the weather, for the days were turning cool and the mist from the sea was damp. A fire was kept burning by night, and Duono had brought blankets and warm clothes. Chrono was as yet weak and unable to travel because of the strength of the venom and the gravity of the wound he had gained in the fight.

In all that time, Chrono could not sail to the Rock of Ahten. So Ahten came each day to attend him, though the dry air choked her, and the weight of bearing herself out of the waters wore upon her. Duono had given her a cloak of fine cotton, which he would dampen in the seawater to keep her comfortable. Nevertheless Chrono knew that she suffered on his behalf, so he strove all the harder to regain his strength.

Now it happened that in those days when Chrono was recovering, Merten the father of Ahten came often to see him as well. He had grown to honor Chrono above all the land-folk, and to consider him a friend of his own Kindred. He rejoiced to see him gaining strength each day.

When Chrono had recovered enough that he could get up from his pallet and walk, Ahten arrived one day, and Merten her father followed behind her. Then Merten spoke gravely to Chrono, saying, "Chrono son of Marcanto, thou who hast helped to rescue the Seafolk from the menace of the sea-monster, thou hast earned the trust and honor of our Kindred. Thy sacrifice hath been great on our behalf, and the price paid was nearly thine own life. If there is aught I might offer thee as reward, I will surely grant it for that sake."

Chrono did not hesitate, but said, "There is but one reward which I would seek, and that I fear you cannot give. For I would ask only the hand of Ahten in marriage. Having that, no other treasure could my heart or soul desire."

Then said Merten, "For many years hast thou remained true to thy love for my daughter. There is no other, neither from among the sons of Land, nor from the sons of the Sea, who hath so much right to take Ahten as bride. A blessing I might give. But alas! Neither canst thou live beneath the waves, nor can Ahten survive a life ashore, and our very natures are incompatible with yours."

Then Ahten spoke, saying, "Then we ask boon of Dreiton himself, who hath seen with his own eyes the great honor of this child of the land. Is it not in the power of the great ones of the Terumani to change the nature of the creatures in their domain? Is it not true that the daughters of Storeia gave the gift of speech to the Kindreds of Toë, and have changed their course in Soria forever? And did not even haughty Teruman Ologéo give wings to the Pyterrians?"

But Merten said, "Not even Dreiton himself hath such things within his power. Though he might rule whatever lives and speaks beneath the waves, yet he hath no power to change the form or spirit of any. Such a power, if any might have it, lies not with Dreiton, but with those greater even than he."

Merten, however, felt compassion for his daughter and for Chrono, and he said to him, "If this truly is your wish, then I would commend you to the highest of the Ádolthi. Perhaps Ologéo or Phactorias may have a solution that even great Dreiton himself, the prince of us all, is unable to bestow."

The Ádolthi have means by which they can call one another across great distances, and they alone had the means to travel beyond the Ice which divided Soria in those days. So Ahten said to Merten her father, "Let us then beseech the Terumani to come to us here, that we might implore them for this gift."

But Merten shook his head, and said, "Alas, but the Halls of the Ádolthi are in the north, beyond the great Ice that divideth the Kindreds of the land. Phactorias is reclusive and pragmatic, and never leaves his Hall but for his own purposes. And Ologéo is proud and bitter, having no love for the speaking Children of Toë. He will be hard to persuade, and will not make such a journey for this request: for he sits in his Hall of Liaibíri and broods, and does not venture to these southern regions in these days of Sundering."

"Then I shall journey to the Great Ones," said Chrono. "For the days of my life shall be nothing without Ahten."

"But," warned Merten, "only the fishes of the sea or the birds of the air can make such a journey. No mortal is able to cross the Ice and live."

"Then when I have regained all my strength, we shall take our boat, and sail around the Ice to the lost lands of the north."

But Duono said, "Alas, but our boat, I fear, is beyond repair. It was damaged in our battle with the sea-monster, and what the battle did not do, the surf has finished. For as we spent our strength in dragging the creature from the deep, the waves and breakers had their way with it, and it is in ruin."

"This is hard news. But there are other boats in the land, then."

Then Merten said to Chrono, "You do not know the trials which would beset you on such a journey. The passage would take very many days at sea. The Ice which covers Batack comes down to the shore, and caps the Sea itself. There it breaketh upon the waters across the whole of Batack and Vinteren: mountains of ice calving from its face into the sea. There is no landing in all that way, hence there is nowhere to come ashore, and no means of provisioning yourselves along the way. No boat which exists will be suitable."

Chrono considered this, and he said, "Then we ourselves must build a vessel suitable for the venture. We must make a house to go upon the sea."

Ahten ventured, "If thou indeed wilt make this journey, then I must go with thee. Thy kind must appeal to the Council of the Mortals it Ritéol, to Sorios the father of your race, and the Heroes that live there. And they have not the power we seek. We must come before the Great Ones of the Ádolthi. I am no great one in the realm of Soria, but the word of teruman, however insignificant, may hold more sway with that folk than that of thine own Kindred."

"Such a journey will be long and full of unknown perils. How can I allow this?"

"How can you deny it? For I will not be separated from you again."

"And I also shall attend you, as I always have," said Duono. "For this adventure would be the greatest of all we have done together."

Merten sighed upon hearing their resolve. "Seeing you are so determined in this matter," he conceded, "I shall beseech the aid of Dreiton once again. For having seen thy sacrifice, he, too, doth honor thee among the children of the land. So perhaps he might bless your passage, and safeguard you along the way."

When Chrono therefore had regained his strength, he sent to his household in the Valley of Plateo, where he had retained the servants of his father Marcanto, having employed them in his own service. Among those were carpenters and craftsmen, skilled workers with wood and stone, with leather and cord. These he called to come to him at Mizgad, on the far side of the hill from the house of Trachio his uncle. On that hillside Duono and Chrono had built a house across from the Rock of Ahten, by the very shore of the sea.

Chrono also sent to the villages of the hilltops and Mountains of Plateo[51] for lumber, for many large and fine oak trees grew in that range, and the folk of that region profited by harvesting their forests. From the merchants of Protos he purchased a quantity of pitch, for in those days none yet had mastered the art of planking a great boat so it would not leak.

Then Chrono worked diligently at drawing up his plans for the vessel, for no such craft had been dreamt of since the days when the Kindreds of Toë had received the gift of speech. Even the Terumani themselves—the Ádolthi and the Ídolthi—did not build such crafts nor go upon the Sea. He consulted his craftsmen and carpenters, for although none of them had built even a small boat, their skills and trade had taught them much about the working of wood, and how to craft it, and join it, and give it strength.

Even Merten counseled him in his design, for he warned him, "The waves of the Great Sea, which you must traverse, are greater even than the waves of

51 In historical times this range of low mountains on the eastern side of the Pintus became known as the Trachian Range.

Endrev and the Pindus. Moreover you may be beset by storms, and the waves of those tempests are as tall as the hills. Your vessel must be strong enough to survive their pummeling, and with length enough to bestride the troughs. Do not allow your vessel to ride high in the water, for it might then be easily overturned by the ferocity of those waves. Or if it rides too low you may be swamped. And you must bear with you whatever you might need to repair your vessel at sea, for there are no havens along the way, and you shall find none to aid you on that journey."

Duono also cautioned him, saying, "The craft you mean to build is too great to beach as we did in our boat. We shall need to tow along with us a small craft, to carry us ashore and back when we need to leave our vessel. You will need anchors[52] to hold the vessel offshore, as well, so it will neither drift to sea, nor run aground."

So Chrono set to work. He and his craftsmen constructed his vessel with a sturdy frame: a strong and deep keel carved from a single oak tree, and ribs to shape the hull, with four stout thwarts to give it strength. As large as a house it was, nearly four mecaths in length, and nearly a mecath and a half wide.[53] He paneled it all about with oaken planks, and sealed all the joints with pitch where it would settle below the waves. He added pontoons to stabilize it. Then he built a deck of wooden planks to keep out the waters from above, and a rail that he might not be washed from the deck. Below the deck he divided the space into storerooms for their supplies. Upon the top of the deck he built a cabin where he and Duono might live.

Never had any boat in all the Land of Soria been so constructed.

He fixed a mast to the second thwart, made of a single tall pine, that he might catch the winds above the sea; and a yard to carry the sail. He added cleats to the gunwale to stay the rigging. Two large oars he fixed through the stern as rudders, which he contrived by joint and crossbeam to turn together, and made notches to hold the tillers in position, that a single pilot might guide the vessel. For he and Duono would be the only crew: no other of his servants would he ask to make this perilous passage, and none would dare to volunteer.

For Ahten he built a small berth at the stern of the vessel, below the waterline and between the rudders, where she could rest in the waters of the sea as they traveled. For even Ahten of the Seafolk could not be asked to swim so far without rest.

As for Chrono himself, he had felt the living sea beneath his feet and had

52 Anchors in this period would have been little more than heavy stones firmly attached to a cord or rope. Such anchors would have been used in river fishing to prevent nets from drifting. It is evident that Duono envisions the use of a similar network of anchors and lines to tether the boat in place off shore.

53 That is, roughly 25 feet long by perhaps 8-10 feet wide.

breathed the spirit of the sea: the knowledge of sea-lore was within him as if by nature, as in no other of the children of Sorios.

When all was in readiness, he gathered all his servants and craftsmen, and they drew the craft into the shallows when the tide was low, where they propped it upright on beams; then Chrono and Duono climbed aboard and waited. The tide rose, the breakers were soon crashing upon the bow, and the boat was lifted from the bottom. Chrono unfurled his sail and put to sea.

Then Duono was discomfited, for never before had anyone stood and walked on a vessel at sea. Feeling the surging of the waves beneath his feet, he clung to the rail with white knuckles and was afraid to move. But Chrono laughed and sang out his pride, saying,

"I stand, and walk upon the flood,
Unresting waves beneath my feet,
And cross the waters like a god!
No mortal ever matched this deed.

No hero ever stood so bold
To stride away from solid earth
To stroll where only waves have rolled,
And over tides go marching forth.

This is a triumph to applaud,
With boasting for the vict'ry won!
So bow before us, whelmed and awed.
A miracle is all we've done!"

Merten then gave strong warning, saying to him, "It is now the midst of winter. Though the weather is mild in these southern regions, the winters will be fierce as you proceed northward. You should wait for warmer days before you strike forth on your journey."

So Chrono replied, "It is well. We shall wait, and get to know our vessel."

Taking their craft into the Pindus, Chrono and Duono together spent the winter learning to sail, and tack, and navigate the vessel. Chrono had his craftsmen and carpenters build a dock at Mizgad, that he might safely moor the vessel when they returned at the end of each day. There they refined and made improvements to the craft as their experience with it grew.

At last the short days of winter began to lengthen, and the warmer breezes of spring brought gaiety to the lands, greening the grass and trees. Then Chrono said to Duono and to Ahten, "Now the time is come. Let us go to the north, and find the Halls of the Ádolthi, and see what we might accomplish in their presence."

Merten came forth once more to bid them farewell, and with him came

Aviah the mother of Ahten. To Chrono he said, "Take care, for no child of the land has ever attempted such a venture, and neither I, nor great Dreiton himself, can predict its outcome. Yet we shall ask of Dreiton, that he might seek you out when he may, and give you aid if possible."

"But be aware," said Aviah, "that Dreiton hath no power over the wind or the waves; Havui alone hath such authority, and he wields it most sparingly, and for his own ends, which we do not know."

Merten then spoke once more. "I will not tell you which course to take, but this counsel will I give. You may find the countries of the north by sea in one of two ways. You might stay within sight of the shore at all times, and follow the coastlands until you have passed the Ice, where the coastlands curve away to eastward. Or when you have rounded the eastern shores of the Hirna, you may strike forth across the deep sea to northward, and so go directly to your goal. But know this: there are perils by either choice!

"If you choose the coastal route, you shall surely find your way: but the journey will be long and frigid. There will be icebergs like mountains calving from the face of the great Ice, which will wreck your vessel as easily as one crushes a snail beneath the boot. And should a storm blow in from seaward, it may drive you into the rocks or the ice, and your vessel will be broken, and you would surely perish in the frigid surf.

"But if you choose the route of the deep sea, you will have little to guide you. Far from shore to eastward, after days at sea, you might find the warm current which flows toward Niyarc and Vordót, and so would it speedily bring you towards your goal. But it is fickle. Should you miss it, or read its signs incorrectly, you might miss the lands of your desire entirely, and perish from hunger and thirst in the midst of the Great Sea, or land astray in distant, unknown countries from which you might never find means of return. Moreover, far a-sea the storms are fierce and the waves a terror for a craft such as yours. Ahten may be safe below, but you will face the fullness of its ferocity in your vessel."

Then Ahten said, "However we reach the countries of the north, how shall we know where to seek the Halls of the Ádolthi?"

Merten replied, "There are few harbors along that rocky coast. You should seek the outlet of the river C'heta. There you may make landfall and seek those Halls. There are paths from thence, and there you will find the country well settled by the children of Sorios; and a strange folk you have not known dwell in that country as well. They may guide you on your way."

"Surely there are many rivers flowing into the sea of the north?" Ahten said.

"True, but they are swift and shallow. Only the C'heta shall offer harborage. A great tower of rock overlooks that country, known as Dimmeltor, where it is said a beacon is kept burning by Dúran the Watchman of the

Terumani. I have never seen it, nor any of my kin. But if you find that lamp you will know C'heta is close by. You will know the river for it flows from a deep cleft in the rocky bluffs within sight of the Lamp of Dúran, and its waters stain the sea far from shore. Even then your task is not complete. I know nothing of the country beyond the shores. Whether there be any waters whereby Ahten may approach those Halls is beyond my ken."

Then Aviah the mother of Ahten spoke, saying, "But know this: We have sent word that you seek the audience of the great ones, and Dreiton himself has assented: so you will be looked for. If possible, you should go to the Hall Liaibíri, the Hall of Ologéo; or if that is not possible to the Hall Timotéa of Phreïs. These are the chief halls of that country, where all the terumani, great and small, are wont to sojourn at times."

Then Merten, Aviah, and Ahten embraced one another and wept, for they could not know if they would see each other again. At last Merten said to Chrono, "Now go, and take all care, for the life of my beloved daughter is now in thy hands."

Trachio also, the uncle of Chrono, had come to the dock at Mizgad to bid them farewell, and said, "Parting again is hard. It seems we have only just now rejoiced in your return after so many years absence. Who knows now whether we shall ever set eyes upon one another again? For even should you live and see the Ádolthi themselves, yet the journey will be long, and the answer of the Ádolthi is unsure. Should you even return, whether in joy or in heartbreak, it will be many days hence. And I am aged."

So Chrono embraced him and said to him, "You have never understood the call of the Sea to my heart, yet you have desired for me only what you held to be best. I leave my house here by the shores of Mizgad in your hands. You may hold it in trust until I return, as if it were your own. Should the day of my return never come, it shall belong to you and your heirs."

Duono also bid farewell to his friends and kinsmen. Then the two of them boarded their vessel, and released their moorings, and with Ahten in the sea before them, they put off from shore.

Then Chrono stood upon the deck, and gazed outward to the south where the Endrev opened to the great Sea, and he said,

"Upon the deck I set my feet,
And feel the surging sea below—
The rhythm of its pulsing flow,
Its rise and fall, its steady beat.
How like the breathing of a beast!
A vast and lusty living thing;
So meekly to her mane I cling,
A mote upon that heaving chest.

And now, the sweeping Sea bestride,
The canvas swelling in the gale,
On into endless spans I sail,
When from my home I turn aside.
A boundless compass we explore:
No tracks are scribed on that expanse,
No path is drawn to distant lands.
We cannot know what lies before.

Behind me the familiar shore
Holds everything I have achieved.
But it must wait, for I must leave,
Perhaps to leave forevermore.
And what? If I should not return,
Why should I miss my land of birth?
Homeless I have stalked the earth,
A guest wherever I sojourn.

So why this flutter in my breast?
Why this foment in my heart,
Which roils now when I embark,
And now endeavors to protest?
The blustering winds behind me blow:
'You only leave your name behind.
Whatever fortune you may find,
The sea has called, and you must go.'"

So Chrono and Duono set their sail and manned the tiller, and the winds took them. Then they left the familiar lands which Chrono had known; and Ahten, traveling alongside, left the familiar waters and comforts of her home.

For many days their journey took them always along the coastlands, within sight of the shore: first to the south out of Endrev, then eastward as they rounded the cape of Theresia.[54] They dared not put forth into the deeps of the Sea where they could not sight the land, and where their anchors would find no purchase. Therefore their vessel followed every curve and inlet of the long shoreline of the east. Each night they would put down their anchors, for they would not travel in the dark when they could see neither the shore nor the rocks, bars and islets which imperiled them along the way. Thus the journey was long and arduous.

---

54 The Cape of Theresia was so-named in much later days when Theresian Pleïstians had settled the region. At this time it would likely have been uninhabited and unnamed.

Such a sojourn was too great for Ahten to travel without rest, but only scant hours could she endure aboard the boat. Therefore she took her repose in the berth which had been prepared for her at the stern of the vessel. It offered no comfort, being little more than a bench below the waterline with a net to enclose it. She had no such luxury as her booth in the Hall of Merten at Mizgad. But she bore the hardship cheerfully.

In this manner with much labor they rounded the coast of Soria. In those days much of the country was uninhabited and remote, so they were able to land the ship's boat ashore to refill their barrels with fresh water, and at times they would find fresh fruit or game ashore to replenish their stock. Ahten also was able to procure seafood such as she was accustomed to, although she had little opportunity to prepare it in the manner of her kindred. When they came to the coastlands of the Stegganese they were able to find villages from which to purchase such supplies as they were wanting. The villagers and inhabitants of the coast who beheld their ship were astonished, for no boat nor ship had ever been seen nor dreamt of, with mast and sail to power it; nor had any traveler ever come to them from the Sea. All who met them were amazed, and the name of Chrono continued to be spread abroad.

It came to pass that after many days of such progress one of their water cisterns was becoming depleted, and Duono said, "See there ahead, a stream of fresh water flows into the sea. Let us put our ship's boat to shore, that we might refill the cistern: for we do not know the country ahead, whether we might find another such stream."

Chrono observing the countryside said, however, "We should use caution if we land here. It appears this country is inhabited, and I see the signs of a village near the outlet. We have left the country of the Stegganese behind us, and I fear we may have reached the country of the Cerites."

Now for a long age the Cerites had dwelt in the Hirna as a kindred apart, not communing with any others of the Sorites; that Tribe was utterly estranged from all their kindred. Archea the mate of Sorios, and Ceras the daughter of Archea, had long abided there as guardians of their Tribe: for Deïni had made them Guardians at Hiren's request, that they might have the lifespan of the terumani, and watch over their kindred. These two had for a long age ruled that folk, nurturing their quiet hostility toward Sorios and the Sorites, and vaunting themselves in their seclusion and independence.[55]

Putting down their anchors, they left Ahten to guard the ship, and they rowed the ship's boat toward the shoreline. But by the time they had drawn up upon the beach, a band of Cerites was already gathering in the hills, readying themselves to go down and meet them, brandishing weapons.

Ahten had been watching Chrono from the pontoon beside the ship,

55 See "The Estrangement of Archea" page 60 above.

where she rested at times in the waters of the sea. Seeing the Cerites gathering with arms, she was alarmed. She dove into the waters and swam swiftly towards the shore, calling out to Chrono, and warning him to return at once; but neither he nor Duono could hear her voice over the crash of the surf.

So they got out of their boat, carrying jugs to the riverside. No sooner had they drawn water from the river, than the Cerites arrived at the beach and confronted them. One among them, who appeared to act as their captain, came forward and shouted over the voice of the waves, "What child of Sorios dares to enter the country of Ceras? What business have you in our country?"

Now in these days the speech of the Hirnans is incomprehensible to the Sorites, nor do any of the Kindreds of Soria share their tongue. But in those days long ago, the tongue of the Hirnans was not so far removed from the tongue of the Sorites, so Chrono was able to comprehend their speech. He answered back in his own speech, "We come only seeking water for our ship, and we shall be on our way."

But the Hirnans, seeing the large boat at sea, were suspicious and fearful, and they replied, "The water of Ceras belongs to Ceras, and it is not for the children of Sorios. Get gone from our country and return to the dog-countries of the west, where you belong! When the wing[56] of your vessel has passed out of sight, beyond the horizons to the west, we shall rest and pursue you no more."

"But we are on a journey, far beyond your country, and will not be returning to the west for many days."

Then said the captain of the Cerites, "You lie. There is no land beyond our country. Only Ice."

Chrono said, "But beyond the Ice lie the lands of Niyarc and Vordót. Thither is our goal, and we have no issue with Ceras nor the folk of the Hirna at all."

"Then you are worse than spies from the west: for you may seek to bring Sorios and all the Sorites down upon us out of the north to oppress our country."

Chrono and Duono began to fear, for they were greatly outnumbered. So Chrono said, "If Ceras wishes no dealings with her brethren, her wishes shall certainly be respected. Only let us depart to our ship, and we shall leave you in peace, with no ill will between us."

But the captain of the Cerites said, "Nay, but you shall come with us, and appear before Ceras our Matriarch. She shall judge what is to be done with you and your vessel."

So at the point of their spears and their javelins they took Chrono and

56 "Wing" here refers to the boat's sail: in the Sorian tongue, and probably the Hirnan tongue as well, the sails of a ship were often referred to as its wings.

Duono, and bound their hands, and led them away from the beach. But Chrono turned to face the Sea as they led him away, and he called out to Ahten, in the hopes that she might hear, "Go, and preserve the boat! We shall have need of it when we return!"

Seeing this, Ahten was dismayed, and she cried out and said, "Let not Chrono be taken from me, when we have found one another at last after so much pain—and when he hath done so much for my kindred!" But there was none to hear her, and she was left alone.

At once she returned to the ship, determined to aid them, but uncertain what she might do. Going after them was out of the question; for she was bound to the Sea, and could not remain long ashore. So she ascended into the ship, where she climbed the mast pole as high as she could, that she might see further ashore; from there she beheld the eastward road upon which the Cerites traveled with their captives. She noted the path and their direction as well as she could from her distance, but could not imagine what she might do with this information.

It was not long before she observed more of the Cerites coming down from the surrounding country, gathering a flotilla of small fishing boats and canoes along the banks of the river. It seemed clear that they intended to cross the ocean over to Chrono's vessel, but there was considerable argument ashore concerning this plan. The Cerites, just as the other Sorites of the Southrealm, had never dared to go into the deep ocean beyond the breakers.

Seeing this party assemble, Ahten said to herself, "Now I am in trouble indeed. If these Cerites seek to take the boat away, I have little strength to stop them, and cannot overpower them in a fight. Then the ship will be gone, and we will be trapped in this evil country!" So she pondered what she might accomplish.

Then she thought, "Surely these Cerites do not know how to use the sail, for Chrono alone of all the children of the land has mastered the art, and even he took months to perfect its use. Should they try to take the ship, they must row it hence. So I might steal away their oars from below. But first I must make the ship fast, that they cannot steal it away by any art."

At this resolve she fetched ropes and cords from the ship's supplies, and she dove into the sea once again.

Now the berth which Chrono and Duono had built for her at the stern of the boat had been constructed firmly to the frame of the vessel, with its beams extending below the hull: and none could see its frame from above. Working quickly, Ahten fastened ropes securely to this framework. She then dove to the deeps. The sea-bottom here was not smooth and sandy, but rugged with rocks, rills, and great stones. To these she fastened her ropes, as firmly and tautly as she could: and it should be said that the skill of Ahten with ropework was great, for the Seafolk make much use of nets and cords in their dwellings in the deep. Then she removed the anchor lines as well, and likewise she fastened these to the berth, out of sight. Thus she affixed the boat of Chrono fast to the seafloor, so that it would not move though the Storm itself were to break upon it: but all her craft was out of sight below the waters, invisible to the eyes of the Cerites.

When she had finished her work she looked up and saw the canoes and skiffs of the Cerites had at last dared to pass beyond the breakers, approaching Chrono's vessel. So she rushed to the surface, and peering cautiously above the waves, she saw that they were armed: for they had heard Chrono call out to the ship, and they feared they might find armed resisters aboard. Then she said to herself, "Surely I alone shall not be able to thwart so many beweaponed attackers. But I will delay them as I am able."

On the deck of the ship was kept a long pole with a hook, which Chrono and Duono had used to draw the ship to the dock at Mizgad, and which they found useful for drawing things in from the water, or pulling the boat ashore at such times as deepwater shelter could be reached in any quiet cove or inlet. Ahten hastened onto the ship out of sight of the Cerites, and taking up this boat hook she plunged back into the waters, and dove beneath the vessel.

Above her, silhouetted against the sparkling sky, she beheld the canoes and skiffs of the Cerites, rowing toward the ship of Chrono. She fixed her gaze on the one which had come nearest to their vessel, and rising up suddenly beneath it, she extended the boat hook out of the water, staying hidden below the hull herself. With this hook she grabbed the gunwale of the boat, and pulling with the skill and dexterity of the Seafolk, she overturned it from below, spilling the attackers suddenly into the waters.

The Cerites were not skilled at swimming: Like all the Sorites of that age they feared the water, and feared most of all the open Sea: so they panicked and floundered in the waves, calling to their companions for help. The nearest of their comrades, seeing their predicament, came at once to help them; but the rowers in that boat scoffed at them, saying, "This is not the time for a bath!" For they presumed that they had overturned their own boat by lack of skill on the waters.

Ahten, however, reached her pole again out of the waves from below, and overturned this boat, also.

Now the rest of the flotilla began to grow nervous, for they sensed that something was amiss. Several more boats came to their aid, and these also were capsized or sunk. Soon a host of the attackers flailed in the water, clinging to the overturned canoes and skiffs, or attempting to swim to the shore, or to the boat of Chrono. These latter Ahten attacked from below, jabbing at them with the boat hook, so that they became afraid and turned back. A few of the Cerites, unable to swim, and weighted down by their clothing, sank beneath the waves: in spite of her ire, Ahten had mercy on these, and with her pole she pushed them to the safety of the overturned boats, where they might at least cling to the sides and not perish.

By this time the entire force was in disarray, and none knew from whence they were being stricken, nor how their boats were being overthrown. Moreover, the Cerites were not warriors, but such settlers and inhabitants of the hill country thereabouts as had answered the call to arms when the ship of Chrono had been spotted in the sea. So they were unprepared to do battle with an unseen foe: some of the boats turned back towards the shore in retreat. But a leader of that tribe, one who was judge over the Cerites of that country, took command, and ordered them to return to the fray.

So the battle endured at great length, with the Cerites becoming ever more shaken and fretful. Many of their weapons spilled into the waters and were lost, and Ahten stole what oars and paddles she could reach, and sent them gliding out of reach into the breakers. But in the end there were too many of them: and swimming or rowing at last to the side of Chrono's boat, they began to clamber aboard and overtake the vessel. So they occupied the craft, though as yet they feared to gain their feet upon the rocking deck. Then Ahten descended from the surface to consider what next she might do. Yet she remained near at hand, just below the hull, that she might hear what the Cerites aboard the vessel might say or do.

When the Cerites had crawled all about the ship and assured themselves that no attackers remained aboard, they gave a cheer, as if they had won a battle against a mighty foe. Then their commander said, "Let us take this vessel, whatever it might be, and bring it ashore. We shall take it for the use of the Matriarch, who will reward us greatly for this prize!"

So creeping unsteadily to the sides of the ship, they clutched at and dragged with them whatever oars and paddles they had managed to save from the onslaught of Ahten. At the orders of their commander they leaned out over the sides of the ship, and extended their oars from the gunwales, hoping to row the vessel shoreward toward the mouth of the river.

But they were unaware of the net of cords that Ahten had prepared out of view beneath the hull; and the vessel would not move. At this event the commander of the company grew angry at his rowers for their weakness. But row as they might, even with all their strength, the boat moved not an inch.

So the deputy of the party grew fearful, and said, "What witchery is this, that these Sorites of the west have brought to our shores? As if by some magic our boats were overturned in the sea, and by some unnatural force this vessel cannot be moved from its place. We should leave this place at once and preserve ourselves alive!"

The commander growled at this suggestion, and said, "There is no witchery, but doubtless our inexperience with the waves of the deep has caused our disaster in the approach, for none of us have ever set forth from shore." Then he peered over the rail, but he could see nothing below the waves: and none would dare, not even the bravest of them, to dive below the sea. He said, "Surely it is by some practical art that these Sorites have contrived to fix the craft in place, so that it may not be moved."

One of the Cerites of the troop then ventured to speak, saying, "When we beheld the craft moving along the coast, the wing was spread wide. Perhaps the vessel is so crafted that only the wing can cause it to move."

So the commander caused the sail to be unfurled. But they knew nothing of how to set the yard, or fix the lines to the cleats, that the sail might fill with wind, so it fluttered powerlessly: and the cords of Ahten yet bound the vessel fast to the seafloor. Nothing availed them to move the boat in any way, and the means by which the boat was secured remained a mystery to them.

Then the commander of the Cerites said, "If we cannot move the vessel, we must occupy it here at sea, and wait for word to return from Ceras. Surely she will know what to do with this craft: she shall force the Sorite spies from the west to teach us its secrets."

The deputy however objected, "Surely you cannot mean to leave us here overnight. Even now the sun is descending. It will be a dark night, for the moon will be narrow, and late to rise. Our folk are already terrified. Let us return to shore, for this ship is clearly unable to move from its spot until we get word from the spies."

The commander shook his head vehemently. "We do not know if these Sorites came alone, or are merely the forerunners of a fleet of that folk. There may be aid on its way from the west even now. We must occupy this vessel to prevent any from taking it from our grasp."

"How shall we fight?" the deputy grumbled. "Most of our weapons now lie at the bottom of the sea. Our party is not a troop of warriors ready to risk their lives, but they hope to quickly return to their families awaiting them on their own homesteads."

"Then we shall sharpen sticks and defend as we must. We are Cerites, and must do this for the safety of our country and the honor of the Matriarch."

So the commander ordered all to find whatever rods and poles they could gather up, and break them into pieces to fashion into crude weapons. As they proceeded with this task the sun at last set over the horizon to the west, and deep darkness fell over the sea. That party settled down to camp on the deck of Chrono's vessel for the night, though all of them were wet, cold, and full of doubts.

Then an idea came into the heart of Ahten, to cause the Cerites yet more mischief. In the daylight she had not dared to rise to the surface so near to the ship, but in the deep dark of that night she gained confidence. So with the stealth of the terumani to aid her, she silently and secretly arose from the waters to cut free each of the boats and canoes which the Cerites had moored to Chrono's vessel. She then drew them far from the ship, and cast them into the breakers, that they would be driven ashore. So quietly and stealthily did she work, and so dark was the night, that none noticed the activity at all, though the sentries kept their watch.

Then Ahten, observing the sentries standing guard by the gunwale and peering out to sea, fetched the boat hook she had taken from the deck. She reached secretly from the water with the pole, and hooking one of the sentries by the collar, she pulled him suddenly overboard and into the waves. As he floundered in the water she stole away the spear from his hand, for he had dropped it in the plunge. Dragging it to the bottom of the sea she fixed it there so that it would not rise to the surface.

His screams of panic brought the other sentries to his aid at once, and woke all aboard. As they drew him from the water he shouted, "There is witchery on this vessel, and the Sorites have surely cursed it! We should be gone from this place, before we are all drowned in the sea!"

Some of the Cerites considered that he had merely stumbled over the rail in the dark by his own blunder: but others now grew yet more uneasy. One or two secretly checked to see whether they might get into one of the skiffs and steal away on their own.

Only then was it discovered what Ahten had done. A cry went up, "Our boats have been taken! And we are trapped here on this cursed vessel!" So the commotion was great. For the ship was far from shore, moored to the seafloor and immovable: and not one of the Cerites could swim so far.

In the midst of this mayhem, Ahten again reached forth, and hooking another of the Cerites by the collar, she snatched him overboard as well. Then hurrying to the other side of the boat, she reached forth yet again, and snagged yet a third into the water. From each of them she stole away with whatever weapon they carried, whether spear, or javelin, or knife.

So all on deck was now confusion and frenzy. Some of the company boarded themselves into the ship's cabin or went below deck to hide in the hold, while all the rest began to huddle towards the center of the deck, fearing to go anywhere near the rail. Even their commander now recognized that their situation was dire, for there would be no easy escape to shore should they be forced to flee, and it was clear that they were being assailed by an unseen foe whom they were unable to fight; moreover it soon became clear that their very weapons were disappearing as well.

So Ahten stayed awake far into the night, watching the ship from her vantage in the waves. Whenever any of the Cerites dared to approach the rail, she hastened to the ship's side, and pulled him from the deck, and stole away his weapons. Before the night had passed, all that company was too terrified to move, and all cowered together amidships.

But at last Ahten said to herself, "I am weary, and I must rest. Still I must choose what next might be done to thwart these Cerites. For they have all our stores of food and water, and can hold out for many days. And above all I must find a way to send aid to Chrono and Duono."

When the morning sun arose at last, the Cerites aboard the vessel grew somewhat less anxious, but they began to consider their predicament in earnest. They were far from the shore, and they had no boats left to reach it. So the commander ordered that the pontoons be removed from the side of the vessel and drawn aboard the ship, that they might be used as floats should they need to return to land. "Nevertheless," he said, "We must remain aboard this craft until word comes from Ceras, and not abandon our advantage to our enemy."

So he set some of his company to the task of seeing how the pontoons might be removed without sinking the vessel: for they had few tools to work with besides the blades of their own spears, and whatever tools they might find below deck in the hold.

But by this time Ahten had awakened and returned to her watch; as soon as any of the company leaned over the rail to examine the pontoons, she immediately grabbed him with her hook and dragged him into the sea. Still more of their weapons were lost to Ahten's quickness and dexterity in this way; and once again all the company of the Cerites began to fear, refusing to go near to the ship's rail.

Then Ahten began to consider her options. She said to herself, "If I were willing to drown these Cerites as rats, I could pick them off slowly: but such a task could take weeks, for they will grow ever more cautious and wary, and they have our supplies. Moreover aid may come to them yet from the land. I must finish this task, and finish it quickly, that I might then find a way to send aid to Chrono."

The Sea in that region was as yet the domain of her own Kindred, though she knew not where their dwellings might be. So she made up her mind to leave the ship for a spell, that she might seek out a settlement of the Seafolk, and appeal to them for aid against the Cerites; although she could not be certain whether any might be willing to aid her, for the Seafolk avoid any dealings with the Kindreds of the land.

But before she departed, she lifted her voice above the waters, disguising her sweet tones with a terrible shriek, so that even Chrono would have trembled to hear it. She cried out to the company occupying Chrono's vessel, saying, "You have raised the ire of my folk, the Kindred of the Sea: so now consider yourselves, how you might choose to perish at our hands!"

The Cerites aboard the deck all heard the strident tones of her voice, but none spotted whence the cries came. It seemed a voice disembodied, carried to them from the wind and waters. A chill came over one and all, and the words of her saying struck terror into all aboard the ship.

Ahten submerged then, to seek out the aid of her own Kindred.

The voice of the Seafolk, when they call one to another beneath the waves, travels far, so they can hear a cry of distress for many miles in the waters. Calling out in the voice of the Seafolk, Ahten went about from the place where Chrono's ship was moored to the bottom, in a widening arc ever further from the vessel. But for many hours no sound of reply returned to her. At last the moving beams of the sun beneath the waves began to angle eastward as the sun sank lower in the skies beyond the roof of the sea: and she decided to return to the vessel. For she feared that the Cerites aboard might discover her absence and gain confidence to do harm to the boat.

But as she prepared to turn back and head shoreward, a returning call came to her from across the miles of the deep: she knew it without a doubt to be the voice of her own Kindred, answering her plea. So she determined to head out at once and find the place. Moving swiftly through the waters she followed the returning calls, until at last she met up with a small party of her own folk, hastening for their own part to reach her.

The eldest of that party named himself as Ériven Son of Éemyn, and he greeted her warmly, anxiously asking what distress beset her.

Then said Ahten, "I am in straits: for I have been traveling with a company who have been beset by Cerites from the land. My company has been taken captive, I know not whither: and I am left alone. Though I have done my part to harass the Cerites as I am able, I am unable on my own to drive them from our boat."

Then Ériven frowned, and said, "What child of the Sea has need of a boat?"

Ahten then admitted, saying, "I travel not with a company of Tritynoi, but with Sorites from the west: friends of our Kindred who have done us much good."

"Nevertheless," said Ériven, "our Kindred have no commerce with any children of Sorios. They have their own affairs, and we would not meddle in them."

Then Ahten said, "I would not dare to ask, but this Sorite is dear to me. We go to the north countries, to seek the aid of the High Ones of the Terumani. For we wish to be united, and so the business of Chrono the Sorite is indeed the business of the Seafolk: for Dreiton himself has approved this course."

Then were Ériven and his company amazed, and Ériven said, "Is this that same Chrono who defeated the monster of the deep on behalf of Lord Merten, the prince of our Kindred?"

"It is indeed. And I myself am the daughter of Merten, and together we watched as Chrono with his valiant companion overthrew the monster: and he nearly lost his life in so doing."

At this the Seafolk became indignant on Chrono's behalf, and their ire was raised against the folk of Ceras. Ériven said, "Then you shall have our aid, come what may. You are high-born among the folk of the Sea, and Chrono is a friend of the Seafolk like no other. Return now to your vigil, and we shall go back to our dwelling, and raise a host of our folk. On the morrow you shall find us here. Then you shall lead us, and together we shall put these froward Cerites to shame!"

Ahten returned to the ship, and found it yet sound: The clashes of the prior day, and the warning she had shouted in the morning, had terrorized the Cerites so that even their commander could compel no one to crawl out to the pontoons. Arriving shortly before nightfall, Ahten kept vigil for hours, making certain that none of the Cerites dared even to approach the ship's rail. When she had at last rested from her labor, and the next morning had dawned, she prepared herself to seek out the party of Ériven.

It had now been over a day since any of the Cerites had received any signal of her vigil, and she had been absent for most of that time, not knowing what they had been about. She feared lest they begin to ease their minds regarding their dire situation, and dare some mischief while she was away on her errand. So rising above the waters, she cried out in a harsh voice once again, saying:

"One final mercy we afford,
One fatal opportunity.
So dare the sea, and grope for shore
If you forthwith might hope to flee.
For they who rashly choose to stay
Shall face their fate by end of day!"

Then she listened from below the hull. When she had satisfied herself of the murmur this new saying now caused among the Cerites, she went below, and set her course to meet the company of Ériven.

When she had found them, her heart leapt for joy: for Ériven had assembled a great company of her folk, some sixty strong: each armed with a stout hunting javelin. Ériven said, "Lead us now, Lady of Mizgad. We shall do as you bid."

Ahten said, "Never has it been the desire of my Chrono to kill when lesser force can gain the day. He has extended grace even to Giants. So I beseech you now, spare the lives, even of these base and stubborn Cerites, if you may. For by my efforts they are cowering and their arms are grown weak; and many are disarmed. Albeit they may put forth a fight yet, so look to yourselves. We must drive them all from the boat of Chrono, and retake our vessel: deck, and hold and cabin."

So Ahten leading them, the whole company of Ériven followed to the site where Chrono's ship was moored to the bottom. There Ériven beheld the handiwork of Ahten, and he smiled and said, "I see you have been busy, Lady of Mizgad! I wonder whether you need our aid at all!"

Ahten said, "Nevertheless one maiden alone cannot force these invaders from the ship. Now is the hour come when they must fight or flee."

So she advised them to assail the ship of a sudden, all boarding at once from all sides, and so to catch the Cerites unawares. "We must enter the cabin and the hold at once, before they are able to take up their arms, and so to avoid a fight in the passages if we may. All whom we take should be cast to the waves. As for those who might flee, I would have you aid them on their way past the breakers if it be possible in the fracas, and so to display to them the mercy of Chrono and the patience of the Seafolk. But if any stand and fight, and try to strike mortal blows, you shall do as you must."

To this Ériven agreed. He divided his company into three bands, and assigned to each their task. Then Ahten fetched a weapon from the stash she had stolen from the Cerites, that she might join them in the conflict. But Ériven said, "Nay, Lady! You have a mission to complete by the will of Dreiton, if your Chrono can yet be rescued. You must not risk your life: Though you would recover of any wound these Cerites might strike, yet it might not be for a lifetime of these Sorites, and your recovery would arrive too late for Chrono. Let us take the brunt of the risk to ourselves, that we might preserve you for Chrono's return!"

So she conceded. "I shall remove myself from the fray," she said. "But I will surely board the ship with you, that I might help to guide you. I alone know this craft from my own experience."

Ahten led them below the ship of Chrono, and they made their way silently to the vessel, as yet remaining out of sight beneath the hull. Ahten and Ériven gave their instructions, and when all had taken their positions, and each had prepared for his own charge, Ériven gave a signal.

The strength of the Seafolk in swimming is without parallel, and they are able to leap like dolphins from the water, so at once all of the leading force leapt from the sea. Landing aboard the deck as one, twenty Seafolk from the deep, wild and hoary with the swirling mists of the sea to shield them, surrounded the company of the Cerites like a terror from their darkest dreams. All that company shrieked in sudden shock and horror, and knew not where to turn or how to fight. Many of their weapons lay useless at their feet as the Seafolk rushed in.

The skirmish on deck was loud and disorderly, but soon the terror of battle overcame the Cerites, and they began to leap over the rail, hoping to escape in the water. Among these was the deputy of that force, who himself was first to leap into the sea. Those who did not leap were forced overboard by their assailants, and soon all of them floundered in the waters, without exception. Even there their troubles did not end, for Seafolk remained in the waters below, forcing them from the sides of the vessel towards the shore.

Ahten also had landed aboard the vessel at the stern, and lifted up her voice to give orders and guide her folk. While the battle took place on the deck, other warriors threw open the hatch to the hold, and rushed the door to the cabin, before any resistance could be raised. Her Seafolk swarmed into those strongholds, as the second wave of Ériven's company thronged aboard to support them.

The commander of the Cerites had taken refuge in Chrono's cabin with his strongest warriors, and he heard the cries of terror and the commotion without. One of his defenders at the entrance to the cabin shouted out in a panic, "We are boarded!"

"Take up your arms and hold the door!" the commander ordered. There was in fact no solid door to shut, but only a heavy woolen cloth which battened the entry against the elements. All the defenders within the cabin rose with spear in hand to prevent their attackers from entering. But the Seafolk had reached the entry before they could so much as rise to their feet. The Seafolk swarmed into the room, javelins raised. Loud and fierce was that clash, and Ahten feared for her own folk, for she could not see what happened within the cabin.

Most of the defenders of the commander had little skill in battle. They were soon disarmed, and their spears clattered to the deck. Only two of that company had any training, and these fought with skill and courage, but the Seafolk were quick and strong, and outnumbered them: Two or three of Ériven's party fell upon each of the Cerites, and they had no chance against such odds. In the end they too were overpowered.

The battle for the hold may have gone ill, for the Seafolk could not swarm through the hatch in force. Fortunately those who had taken refuge in the hold had even less will to fight than those above. Most of these had lost their weapons to Ahten in the first melee. It was dark below deck; they had no one to lead them; and in fact these were already the most unnerved of that company, for these were they who had been hiding in the hold since the attacks of Ahten had terrified them all. They were taken entirely unawares when the Seafolk suddenly began to stream in through the hatch. They took up their makeshift arms to defend themselves, for they feared for their own lives.

"Lay down your weapons, and you shall not be harmed!" Ériven commanded, for he it was who led that charge. Many at once capitulated, but others feared to submit. A skirmish was fought here below, as well. But the Seafolk continued to drop in from above, until there was no hope of victory, and all that party pleaded for mercy. They too were forced into the sea, but the Seafolk below nudged and helped them past the breakers.

Now this was the only battle to take place between the Kindreds of the Land

and the folk of the Sea.[57] In the end the force of the Seafolk was too great. The Cerites were poorly armed, outnumbered, and outclassed. Furious was that battle, and in spite of the mercy of Ahten and the Seafolk, not all of the Cerites returned to shore that day.

Most of those who had by the aid of their attackers made it to shore dispersed into the hills, fleeing to their own homes and villages as quickly as their legs would carry them. But a small party regrouped around their commander on the beach, waiting for further instructions. Not even the commander stood tall. All that party were exhausted from the struggle and the desperate swim through the breakers: bedraggled, wet, and dispirited by their sudden rout. Many had received blows and injuries which they now nursed and bound.

As they regrouped and considered their next steps, one of that company shrieked suddenly and pointed to the breaking surf, for Ériven had arisen from the waves. Head and chest rose eerily above the waters, his arms raised in warning, his coal-black hair radiating like a tangle of tentacles. A mist swirled around him. The Cerites cowered and drew back, expecting a new assault from the Sea.

Ériven lifted his voice in a terrifying pitch and called out to them: "Do not attempt again to take what does not belong to you. Now go! And deliver now this message to your Matriarch: we demand only he who is ours, Chrono of the Plateosites, be returned to us, unharmed and at once: he and his companion, both. Do this and no further consequence shall beset you." Now Ahten had chosen Ériven to speak on her behalf, for his appearance was frightful to the Cerites, and the timbre of his voice a terror. One last word Ahten commanded. "Chrono has the favor of Dreiton," Ériven declared, "and Dreiton's folk shall defend him!" Even the Matriarch Ceras herself, great though she was, would waver at the name of Dreiton: for he was mighty among the Terumani.

As the Cerites huddled on the beach, Ériven and Ahten returned to the ship of Chrono, to consider their course. Ériven said, "We have succeeded in our goals thus far, but there is still the question of Chrono. How might we aid him and his companion? I do not trust these Cerites to deliver your message to Ceras. Nor do I trust haughty Ceras to condescend. We must send to Chrono whatever aid we can."

Ahten replied, "But he has been taken on landward roads to the east: I know not whither nor how far from the Sea. Neither I nor any of your company can follow them far on such a trail."

"This is true. But there are others who may yet be of aid to us. There are yet

57 The "folk of the Sea" in this case refers only to the Tritynoi themselves, and not to the later Mizans, who were also known as a "folk of the Sea." In future generations there were to be many battles between the Mizans and their land-bound cousins.

næads in the country of the Hirna, and dræads moreover. I do not think they will hold allegiance to Ceras or to Archea herself when honor is at stake. It is well known that Chrono has been a friend of the terumani for many years, and his name is held in honor among all."

"Then I shall make my way up the river into that country, and see what I might discover," said Ahten. "But if any of your company are willing, we should set a force to guard the ship from further assault until we return. I do not know what these Cerites might yet purpose to do."

"This we shall surely do, Lady of Mizgad. Further, I shall also send some of my own company to scout the country hereabout, that we might find sympathetic terumani of any degree. We shall spread the word of our straits, and see what help we might gain."

So it was that the Sea-maiden Ahten by her own wiles defeated the warriors of the Cerites, and saved the ship of Chrono. But Chrono and Duono were prisoners of the Cerites, and were lost to her, far from any hope of escape.

12. CHRONO AND THE MALICE OF CERAS

This tale is told of the struggle of Chrono and Duono in their captivity in the Hirna, when they had been taken from their ship on the shores of that country. Now when they had been taken by the guards of Ceras, Ahten had been left alone to defy their servants aboard the ship of Chrono. With the aid of her Kindred, the Seafolk, she had overthrown the Cerites and had been left in command of the vessel, and no one dared confront her further.

But of these matters Chrono knew nothing. For while such things were transpiring by the ship of Chrono, Chrono himself, and Duono has companion, were being led on the inland roads from the shore, eastward within the Hirna, and were brought after two days to the Hall of No'Cerës: the Hall which Ceras the daughter of Archea had built for herself in the Hirna. This Hall was built solidly of stone, like all the town of No'Cerës: a cold and unwelcoming place built on a hill, with many stone stairways and alleyways. The Hall itself spread across the highest level of the hill, with many chambers opening into a multitude of courtyards, where fountains flowed, and fruit trees were planted, and shady arbors protected the Matriarch and her retinue from the summer sun.

Ceras the daughter of Archea and Sorios had lived very many years in that country, an age or more by the measure of the Kindreds of Toë. Though gray and mature to appearance, she was yet hale and full of vigor, for she had been made a Hero and Guardian of her folk by the gift of Teruman Deïni at the request of her brother Hiren. But while most of the Heroes of Soria did their work in secret, subtly influencing the hearts of their folk unseen, or appearing among them in disguise, Ceras dwelt among the Hirnans openly, ruling that Tribe from her Hall No'Cerës as their Matriarch. All in that country knew her and bowed to her.

So it was that Chrono and Duono were brought before her, and Ceras herself came forth to examine them. Her judgement seat was in the largest chamber of that Hall, with tall windows opening to the sun, a vaulted roof like those of the Terumani, and a dais where the Matriarch would sit. She had a high seat there, like a throne of ivory, to place herself above all visitors: scowling down from that height upon Chrono and Duono she said, "Who are these prisoners, and what have I to do with them?"

The captain of the guard which had brought them said, "Lady, we bring before you for your judgment two spies from the lands of the Sorites to the west. They have admitted openly that they seek to reach countries beyond the Ice, where Sorios dwells. Moreover they were taken on our very shores, stealing water for themselves from our own River Aqali in the emirate of Deruqán. For all these reasons we have brought them before you for your inquest."

They then described the great boat of Chrono, larger than a house, which could hold many spies or warriors, and which had been spotted traveling along the coast by means of a white wing, proceeding without oar, or paddle, or punt: such a vessel as no one had ever seen.

Now Ceras was ever distrustful and brooding, suspicious of strangers, and the word which her guards had brought her disturbed her. So she put both Chrono and Duono to hard questioning, demanding to know their true purpose, and the secrets of their winged ship. But Chrono said, "My errand is my own, and shall redound upon none but myself and my companions. The boon that I seek none can provide but the High Ones at Liaibíri, so we have no choice but to pass your lands on our course." Beyond this he would say little more; for he feared for Ahten upon his vessel, lest they drag her also to No-'Cerës, compelling her to leave the safety of the Sea. Neither would Duono provide the Matriarch with any information.

"It is no matter," said Ceras at last. "What you will not give willingly we shall take by force; and by our rights within our own country."

Then she said to her captain, "As for these spies, they are fit for nothing. Put them into a gaol and hold them there while I debate their fate. I must consider how best to defend our land from the meddling of Sorios and the Sorites. Who knows what deeper plans are being hatched?"

There was gaol house in No'Ceres—a heavy stone structure with many cells—for the Matriarch kept order in her realm by strictly-enforced rules. So Chrono and Duono were taken to a windowless room of stone; a heavy wooden door was closed and barred behind them, and guards were placed without to keep watch. Thus they were kept, with little food and no comfort, to wait for further judgment from Ceras. No word had come to him of the Seafolk and his boat, so he worried still on Ahten's behalf.

After several days had passed, messengers arrived from the coast, breathless and shaken, demanding to speak to the Matriarch at once. So Ceras admitted them, and she was informed of the attack on Chrono's vessel, and how the vessel had been as immovable as an island: They then described the frightful attacks from the sea, against which there was no defense, and how at last the vessel had been lost to the Seafolk, who were in league with the Sorites.

"In addition to all this," their leader said, "their captain declared that they had the sanction of Dreiton himself, the lord of the Seafolk. So we were warned to let the prisoners go which had been taken from the boat. So now, Lady, I rue that we have done so wickedly, and hope that your highness in your magnanimity has allowed them their release: for I fear that harm will come to us and all our kindred should we continue to hold them captive."

But Ceras dismissed the messengers, saying, "If Dreiton wishes these spies to go free, let Dreiton himself come to me and declare his will. I will not accept the message of his pawns, delivered to me by my own vanquished servants."

But in secret she worried and brooded over this word. She determined therefore to send a strong force of warriors to the coast to watch the vessel, to guard against incursion; but she was afraid to take any further action against the boat if it proved to be guarded by a host of the Seafolk.

Chrono and Duono had now languished in their cell for a length of weary and sunless days. Each day when their provisions were delivered, they asked to be seen of the Matriarch, but no sign or signal was given that their demands were heard at all.

Chrono began to make note of the actions of their wardens, and to probe out weaknesses in their cell. At last he said to Duono, "We must make plans to force our way to freedom. How long shall we wait here for the judgement of Ceras?"

Duono warned, "If there is yet hope she might grant us freedom we should not inflame her with such an affront. Our safety is better assured should she release us of her own will than if we break free."

Chrono replied. "Have you seen any cause for such a hope? If clemency should arrive before we strike, so be it. But we must prepare ourselves for a fight, and watch for our opportunities. For I am anxious on behalf of Ahten. She is unable to sail the boat on her own, and the Cerites may be undertaking some mischief." Now the Matriarch had ordered that no word should reach the prisoners concerning the Seafolk and their victory over the Cerite guard.

Duono said, "We do not know what lies in wait for us beyond these doors. There may be many guards unseen, and the whole force of the household of Ceras and all this country may descend upon us at once. We do not know the countryside, nor the ways to return to the coast whence we came. Such an escape will be no small task!"

So Chrono said, "I do not take this path lightly. But necessity forces hard choices."

So they kept watch on their guards, and listened through the cracks of the door to learn their habits, and their comings and goings. They pried stones from the floor, and secretly fashioned slings[58] and garrotes of their sashes; they were able as well to knap stones from the wall into rough blades. Thus armed, they began to devise plots to overpower their captors by stratagem or surprise.

Some days passed in this manner, but no opportunity arose in all that time. The guards were cautious, and the door was unbarred only long enough

58 The "sling" referred to was most likely not a device for throwing stones, but a heavy stone bound into a sling and used as a cudgel in close combat.

to provide meager food and water for the day. At last Chrono said, "We can wait no longer. When next the door is unbarred in the morning, let us take our chances and attempt to overpower the guards, come what may."

Duono warned, "Should we fail, we risk a harsher sentence of bondage, or even death."

But Chrono said, "I have seen no sign that Ceras holds clemency in her heart. And death is better than the unending darkness and discomfort of this cell."

Now in the night, as Duono slept, Chrono lay awake brooding and mulling in his mind how the struggle might unfold. But as he stared at the ceiling in utter darkness, a faint light bloomed in the corner of the room. Looking down from the ceiling, he discerned the fair form of a dræad nymph sitting on the floor opposite him. She smiled on him, and whispered, "Chrono, child of Mizgad: the tale of thy plight hath been spoken abroad throughout this country. Ahten and the folk of the Sea have sought our aid. I am Sëluria, a dræad of the groves of the Hirna, and I am come to offer thee solace, and give what aid I am able."

But Chrono said, "I am humbled by your offer, but we shall not risk harm to any but ourselves. For tomorrow we plan to break free from this wretched place, or perish in the effort."

"Do not so foolishly," said the dræad. "For Ahten awaits thee, and values thy life! This aid we have chosen to offer thee and thy companion: I have in my charge the groves of this country, and the fruits thereof. At my command they may wither and drop, or grow to full ripeness. If thou shalt give the word, we shall withhold the fruits of the groves of Ceras, even of her own garden. She shall know that the word of Chrono hath commanded it, and fear. So she shall surely release thee and thy companion and send you peaceably on your way. But if not, the dræads of this country are prepared to spread this blight throughout her domain, until her heart is turned."

So Chrono bowed, and said, "As you wish, fair maiden of the groves. I am in your debt, and cannot repay your kindness."

"Kindness given is kindness earned," Sëluria replied. "And the wound of thy left hand is all the proof needed that kindness to thee and to thine is well-justified."

So she left, and Chrono's heart was filled with hope in the darkness.

In the morning therefore, when Duono awoke, Chrono revealed to him his new plan. Now Duono had neither seen nor heard the nymph as he slept: nevertheless he shrugged, and trusted Chrono, for with such plans had Chrono often succeeded in the past.

When the door was unbarred, and the guard placed their rations within the chamber, Chrono called out, "I have a message for the Matriarch! We have waited long enough for her judgment. So now I give this warning: unless she relent and send us on our way as we have patiently requested, the fruit of the groves of her household shall wither and drop. Let Ceras therefore take care to do what she knows to be just and right."

At this word the guard who had set the food before them merely laughed and scoffed, and went on his way shaking his head. He did not pass the message on to Ceras. The day passed as had the others before it: no word came to Chrono or Duono from the Matriarch, and no change was made to their sorry condition.

That night therefore, the nymph Sëluria appeared once again to Chrono, and said, "I have seen no sign that the Matriarch hath relented, for you and your companion both continue to languish here in this dreary cell. It is the desire of my folk to lay waste to the fruits of this country, beginning at the Hall of Ceras."

Then Chrono said, "Do as you have promised. We shall see if we can change the stubborn heart of the Matriarch."

The next day Chrono repeated his warning to the guard who brought them their food, and once again that warden shook his head and went away unbelieving.

Later that afternoon, however, when he went in to attend Ceras in her Hall, he overheard her complaining to her gardener, saying, "It's summer, when the fruit should be ripening on the trees. But look! All the fruit on my favorite apple tree has suddenly withered and dropped from the branches. What can have gone wrong?"

The gardener examined the tree, and said, "This is altogether strange. We noticed just this morning the fruits in all the groves of this precinct were shriveling from every branch, as if ruined by a sudden frost: and yet the nights have been mild and the weather warm. Much of it had already begun to drop to the earth. What curse or blight can have struck us so early in the season?"

Then the guard who had delivered rations to the prisoners recalled the word that Chrono had given him. He came timidly before the Matriarch, and dared to speak, saying, "Lady, this is indeed a strange thing. For yesterday morning when I delivered the rations to the prisoners from the Sea, one of them shouted aloud that he had a message for your highness. He claimed that he would cause this very blight to happen if he were not sent on his way."

Then Ceras grew ill-tempered and suspicious, and she called the guard before her to question him: so he repeated to her all that Chrono had said, adding only, "Yet I believed him not, and did not pass the message to you as I ought. So perhaps I am to blame for this loss. Yet truly it seemed the empty ravings of a desperate soul."

Ceras grumbled. "So it assuredly was. Or perhaps rumor had passed to him early of the beginnings of this blight, and he thought to lay claim to it himself. But if the Sorite gives another word, I charge you to bring it to me at once."

So she bided her time to wait and see, and she did not relent. That night therefore, the nymph Sëluria appeared again in the cell, and seeing Chrono still a prisoner she said, "Clearly Ceras hath not yet chosen to do as she ought. We have determined then to spread this blight further as we promised. Have patience, and do not yet despair. We have words of comfort for thee as well: tidings have come to us that Ahten is safe, and waits patiently for your safe return."

At this word Chrono sighed with relief, and asked for news of her. "How has she managed the ship? What mischiefs of Ceras has she faced?"

"I know only that she and the Seafolk have sent word asking for aid in obtaining your release. It was said that she is secure. I know little beyond this, but for rumors and guesses."

"Then there is still a chance for mischief to come. So let us proceed swiftly, for the sooner we may return to strengthen her, the safer she will be."

The nymph agreed, and she gave him a message from her own Kindred for him to deliver to the Matriarch of the Cerites.

The following morning, when the guards came to give rations to Chrono and to Duono, Chrono announced the words the nymph, saying, "The Matriarch, mighty and honored as she is, has still not seen it in her heart to do right by me and my companion, and to send us peaceably on our way. Therefore know this: the blight which has struck her and her own gardens shall expand into the countryside, and spread outwards into the lands of the Hirna. In an ever widening ripple, beginning here in the gardens of No'Cerës, the fruits of her groves and forests shall wither and drop, so there shall soon be no fruit for the season in any part of her domain. All shall see that the curse has spread outward from the grove of the Matriarch, and all shall know that what she has failed to do has caused this blight to spread. But if she relents and sends us on our way as she knows is just, the groves shall be healed, and the fruit shall return to the branch."

This time the guard hurried immediately to the Hall of Ceras: she admitted him at once, and he delivered the message. Then Ceras said, "Let us wait and see what comes to pass. But speak to no one else concerning this message, that whatever comes to pass, none might claim it was by the word of Chrono."

But others of the guards had overheard the words of Chrono as well, and the rumor was already going forth through the country of the Cerites. So the blight spread out from No'Cerës, and the summer fruits began dropping from the trees and the groves throughout that country. The rumor could not be stopped, and all that folk began to whisper that the blight was due to the stubbornness of the Lady of No'Cerës.

News of these whisperings returned to Ceras, and she was embarrassed and wroth: so she had Chrono dragged before her.

Now it had so happened that the night before, the nymph had visited Chrono again. She had given Chrono yet another message for the Matriarch, saying, "Behold: the Matriarch of the Hirna yet withholds the justice due to Chrono and his companion: and they are still held in confinement. Therefore know that the næads of the pools and streams and springs of the Hirna have also offered their aid, both nymph and spright alike: for as long as Chrono is held captive, so long shall the pleasant waters of the land be held in bonds, beginning again with the Hall of Ceras. So all shall know that Ceras herself is the source of the dearth. But the very day she relents and does what she knows to be just and right, the waters shall return to their place."

Ceras, however, not knowing of the visit of the nymph, demanded of Chrono, saying, "You must stop spreading the word that you have called for a blight on our land. The folk of the country are ignorant and believe your lies. So you have made me your enemy. If you will not relent and hold your tongue, we shall redouble the pains of your confinement."

Chrono answered, saying, "I am confined in a cell by your command, and have no power to spread rumor, either for or against the Matriarch. Whether the words go out to the country is of no concern to me. The word I have is for your ears, trusting that you would know to do what your heart tells you is just, and send us on our way. I speak for your benefit. So know, therefore, that the fruits of your groves are only a beginning of the warning we bring. For if you send us on our way now, the fruit shall return to the bough: but if not, even the springs, and pools, and rivulets that give you joy shall withhold their waters." So he delivered the message of the næads to Ceras.

So Ceras sent him back to his gaol, fuming in her heart and troubled in her mind. But she did not recant or relent.

The following day, however, the saying began to come to pass as Chrono had foretold. The pleasant waters of the Hirna began to dry up, beginning at the Hall of No'Ceras: the sparkling fount in the center of her court, from which Ceras drew her water, suddenly went dry, and bubbled forth no longer. But Ceras still did not relent, saying in her heart, "It is nothing but chance!"

From that day onward, however, the malady spread thence, so the folk of that country had to draw their water from muddy holes in the earth, and gather rainwater into pots and cisterns; and they began to curse the stubbornness of the Matriarch.

When this news came back to Ceras, she brought Chrono from his cell once again, and threatened him, saying, "If indeed these maladies are your doing, call them off at once. For I can make hard your confinement, so that you will curse your ever coming to this country."

But Chrono said, "The maladies you face are not by my doing, Lady, but by yours. For the day you send us peaceably on our way, the maladies will end. Until that day, however, it is not in my power either to call them off or to relieve them. I only warn you of them for your profit."

So Ceras grumbled, "A curse on you, and on all Sorites. So if you will not release the waters and the fruits of our land, I can neither give you water nor food. Stay in your cell and starve, and it shall be by your own curse that you perish."

With that she sent him back to the gaol. The guards were commanded to bring no more food or water to the prisoners until they begged for mercy and recanted of their curses.

But it came to pass that Sëluria the nymph visited Chrono by night again, and she said, "Do not fear, and have patience yet. Though the will of Ceras is strong and she is proud, yet she is a Guardian, and she hath been given a measure of the wisdom of the Terumani to guide her: she shall surely recant in the end. Until such time, thou and thy companion shall be provided for: behold, a spring shall trickle from the wall of this gaol to provide you water, and a fruit tree shall we cause to spring forth from the floor itself, and provide for your needs, until she relents."

So it happened just as the nymph had said. The following morning a trickle of fresh water, pure and delightful, trickled from the wall of the cell. Mushrooms sprouted from the damp rock of the walls, and a small tree, no larger than a boxwood, had grown up from the floor: already, even in the darkness of that cell, had it flowered and begun to bear pleasant fruit, like red plums.

At these signs even Duono was amazed, and he said to Chrono, "Many miracles have I seen since we have traveled together, but this is the strangest of all! Truly you have the favor of the terumani upon you!"

Ceras then waited for several days, hoping for word to arrive that the prisoners had recanted and begged for her mercy. But when no word came she began to fear that they had perished in silence, so she commanded the guards to open the cell. When they had done so, they discovered the spring and the fruit tree, and were astonished: it was not without a measure of fear that they brought word of this wonder to their Matriarch.

Ceras was troubled by this news, yet she would not relent, and she grew yet more bitter. Stomping her feet in defiance she said to the guards, "Bring the prisoners out of that place, and find a new hole to throw them into: a dry and utterly barren place, that they would repent of their curses. Seal it shut that none may go in or out. But I am not without mercy. Leave a hole in the wall, that they might call out for lenience, and call off the troubles they have brought onto our country. If they do, I shall lighten the burden of their captivity."

So it was done as she commanded. A dry cistern was found, cut from the solid rock, and the guards of the Cerites brought Chrono and Duono there and cast them in. They then sealed the top with a great stone, and delivered to them the word of the Matriarch, saying, "You shall not come out of this place until you repent of the curses you have brought onto the house of Ceras."

Then Duono said to Chrono, "It seems to me that in spite of the wonders done at your bidding, our situation merely gets worse with each turn. How might we take matters into our hands from this hole? We have hidden upon our persons as yet the weapons we fashioned in the prior gaol, which the guards have not discovered, but we are now sealed into this basin. Is it better to call off the curses on the land, that we might be returned to the gaol? There at least we might have hope of forcing our way to freedom when they give us our rations."

Chrono answered, saying, "Allow me another night to consider. I shall give you my judgment in the morning."

Duono said, "In the morning? How shall we even know morning from this dreary hole?"

Sëluria, however, discovered the new prison of Chrono, and visited once more in the nighttime. Then she said, "Do not lose patience. Thou and thy companion shall soon go on your way, freely and in safety, with the blessing of this Tribe. In all places the Cerites now grumble against the Matriarch. Not even Ceras can hold out forever against the will of her Tribe. We shall continue to provide food and water for your needs, even here. What is more, I shall cause a bed of moss to grow for your comfort, so you shall not suffer in this place until the time of your release."

So it happened as she had described. When Chrono and Duono awoke in the morning, the basin into which they had been sealed was profuse with a lush garden, which sparkled and glowed in the tiny beam of sunlight from the hole above. Small trees like boxwood shrubs had arisen from cracks in the stone, bearing pleasant fruit, just as before; and a bright spring of crystal water trickled from the wall into a gentle pool. Moreover a thick cushion of moss had grown upon the floor like a bed, softer than a pillow of down, and with a sweet aroma like fine cedar. Flowers also brightened the corners like little stars in the darkness, and ivy and ferns draped the walls.

Then Duono laughed, and said, "You have outdone yourself once again! Perhaps if wait a little longer, we shall soon be living in a palace!"

But Ceras continued to wait. The blight and the dearth continued to spread across the whole of the Hirna, and the folk of the countryside all around murmured now that the Sorites should be cast out, before they were all ruined. Their pleasant springs and pools had run dry, and their water was foul and bitter. Moreover as the springs ran dry, so the creeks and rivulets began to dry up in their beds, and even the rivers began to run lower in their banks. Every fruit and nut from their groves and woods had shriveled.

But no complaint nor cry for mercy came back to Ceras from the cistern. At last she grew impatient, and commanded that the stone be removed, that she might investigate.

When this had been done, the guards were astonished beyond words at what they beheld. They brought back tidings of this further wonder to the Matriarch.

Then Ceras raged, and cried out, "Who is this Sorite, that the springs and groves of our own country show favor to him? They have appealed to me time and again for my judgement on their case. So send them this judgement, that if they do not relent by the morning, I shall put them to death, and put an end to their curses."

At this her counselors and guards balked, saying to themselves, "Is this course wise? What if, perhaps, they alone can call off the curse: then shall the dræads and næads of the country abandon our land, and there shall be no end to the dearth. Then we shall forever have nought to drink but mud from the puddles, and nought to eat but root and grain." But they were afraid to defy the will of their Matriarch.

So some number of them conspired together in secret, and said, "Ceras is not the only authority in our land. Let us seek Another, before this danger comes to pass. For it would be irrevocable."

Now it so happened that Archea, the mate of Sorios and the mother of Ceras, still dwelt in that country, having a Hall of her own on a fertile tableland overlooking the Sea, which she had named Qorepheglán:[59] an unpretentious place of uncut stone with beams of hand-hewn wood for her ceiling. In this age Archea had not yet returned to the north, and remained estranged from Sorios.[60] So she dwelt on the mesa at Qorepheglán, at peace with those who dwelt in that country, tending her own orchards, and communing at times with her daughter Ceras, and with Hiren the Teruman of her folk.

The counselors and guards of Ceras therefore stole off by night, hastening to carry the word of the Matriarch's threat to Qorepheglán. Archea lived more simply than Ceras, with few servants: The messengers from No'Cerës were quickly admitted into her presence without formality. "What message do you bring from my daughter?" she asked, with some measure of concern, for the messengers were clearly agitated.

So they told all, how Ceras their Matriarch had continued to confine Chrono and Duono in prison, in spite of the many signs that they had the favor of the terumani on their side. Then they said, "And worst of all, she

59 According to an ancient tradition of the Cerites, centuries after this Hall of Archea was abandoned, it was to become the site of the city of Eglaceras: the ruling city of the Hirna.

60 On this matter, see "The Estrangement of Archea" above.

threatens to kill them in the morning. If she does so, we fear that all the curses which have fallen on our land shall remain unabated forever."

Tidings of Chrono and Duono had already reached her ears, and even her own groves and springs had been touched by the dearth. But Archea had softened as the years had passed, and was not so hard-hearted and proud as her daughter Ceras. She still hearkened to the word of the lesser terumani in her realm.

The messenger from No'Cerës continued. "We fear that Ceras your daughter oversteps her authority in this matter, so we come to you in secret asking your intervention. Only do not reveal our dissension to the Matriarch! For it may go hard with us, and we should certainly lose our positions and be turned out of her Hall."

Archea said, "You have done well to bring this matter to me. Go back at once and return to your place. I shall guard your secret."

Then Archea at last broke her silence, and that morning she called Ceras to come to her at once to her Hall. So Ceras came before her, for she had respect for her mother, and said, "For what cause have you called me from my own Hall so urgently? There are important matters I must attend, for our country is under siege, and a blight threatens us all!"

Archea said, "Rumor has reached my ears concerning the imprisonment of the Sorites on your orders. It is even rumored that you intend to do them violence. Such an act is not fitting a Guardian of our folk, and it must not happen."

Ceras raised her voice and complained, "These Sorites have invaded our realm, and stolen what belongs to us, and trammeled upon our dignity. They are defiant and curse our land, and have brought derision onto me and my house. Why should I not have done with them?"

But Archea asked her to relent. saying, "Nothing is gained by defying wisdom for the sake of pride. The terumani have chosen their side: word of this matter has reached me from the nymphs and sprights themselves. It seems these Sorites have sacrificed much to aid their kind. Moreover the mission of these two even now, so it is said, is to seek a union between Sorite and Trityn. The circumspect course is to send them on their way, and cease our interfering. Then you shall restore bounty to our land, and you shall be regarded as a hero once again."

Ceras protested, "How then shall we defend ourselves from the meddling of outsiders? What should we do if the Terumani themselves descend upon us from the north?"

"We are made Heroes to our Tribe by the will of the Terumani, and we are beholden to them. We gain more license by respect than by rebellion."

Ceras grumbled in her heart, but in the end she submitted to the will of

Archea. Back to her own Hall she went, and she ordered her guards to bring Chrono and Duono from their cistern, and to appear before her. When they had come she growled at them, saying, "I have had enough, and my duty is to my Tribe. Get gone from my country, and do not show your faces here again, or the consequence shall be on your own heads. Only call off the dearth you have placed upon my land, that we might have rest from your wickedness."

Chrono replied, saying, "We thank you for your grace, Lady Ceras. If it comes to pass as you have said, and we return safely to our boat, unharmed and in peace, the pleasant waters shall quickly return to their places, and the fruit shall return to your boughs: and if my word shall have any sway, your year shall end in abundance such as you have not known. Then your name shall be spoken of with honor."

So Ceras upheld her word. She assigned a cohort of her own guards and warriors to escort them along the road, and they guided them as quickly as feet could carry them to the mouth of the Aqali, where their ship's-boat was yet beached. Once they were absent from the presence of the Matriarch the guards became courteous and condescending to their charges, treating them now as guests: for the wonders they had seen had turned their hearts to the prisoners. They now spoke amicably and in good cheer, and provided for them good rations and lodging along the way.

When they arrived at the beach, they came upon the company of the Cerites who had been ordered to keep watch on Chrono's vessel, camped along the shoreline. The captain of Chrono's guard, however, displayed the token of the Matriarch, and said, "The prisoners have been freed, and your company is dismissed. It would be my advice that we do all in our power to speed them on their way."

So this company also set to the business of sending them off. They hurriedly recovered their boat and refitted it for the sea. Then they gathered jugs and cisterns, and filled them with water and wine for the ship's supplies, more even than the boat could carry: food and other supplies were also gathered, to replenish what had been wasted in their prior attack and the ongoing siege.

Their commander said, "We would bring you yet more for your journey, but not one of our warriors will dare cross the surf, or approach your vessel by any means. For they all fear the terrors of the deep, and the Seafolk. We ask only that you depart now in good grace, and do not punish us for the excesses of the Matriarch."

As Chrono and Duono boarded their boat to depart at last, Duono was surly and kept silence. But Chrono said to them, "We thank you for the civility you have shown us along the way. We send our gratitude to the Lady in No'Ceras for the grace she has shown. If I am not mistaken, the sweet waters shall quickly be released from their prison, and the fruit shall return to your trees in abundance."

At this word the guards said, "We in our turn thank you for your forbearance. But bear in mind the command of the Matriarch. We who have known your demeanor among us may be gracious, but those who have not been in your company will take you as enemies. For we have all been strictly ordered not to allow your vessel to land again upon our shores, nor allow the soles of your feet to touch the sands of the Hirna. This order has been sent to all the guardians throughout our lands."

Chrono acknowledged this warning. While Duono grumbled, "We would expect nothing else."

Thus Chrono and Duono returned at last to their vessel. There Chrono's heart leapt for joy, for Ahten stood at the prow of his ship waiting to greet him: tidings of their release had already spread through the company of the nymphs and sprights and had come to the Tritynoi.

As Chrono had promised, the næads and dræads of the Hirna released their hold on the fruits of that country, so a great abundance came upon the Cerites that year.

Although the agents of the Matriarch gave credit to Ceras for this release, the rumor of Chrono spread through that land. So it came to pass after some years that even in the Hirna, in the land of the froward Cerites, the name of Chrono was lifted up and honored. Although the Hirnans are opposed to all others, warring with them and troubling them, and even making slaves of all other Tribes, yet they do not trouble the Tribe of Chrono.[61] To this very day the folk of Chrono's Tribe alone, of all who dwell in Soria, have the respect of the Hirnans.

---

61 The Homadalan scribes who published this volume would have had a particular grievance against the Hirnans. The oppressive Hirnan Empire had eventually reached even as far as Homadal, forcing the Homadalans into a period of exile and hiding which lasted for over thirty years.

13. CHRONO AND THE TRIALS AT SEA

This tale is told of the days when Chrono and Duono, together with Ahten, undertook to journey by boat beyond the Ice, that they might request boon of the Terumani who were at home in that country.

It had so happened that, landing in the Hirna to replenish their water, Chrono and Duono had been taken captive by the Matriarch of that country for a length of days. But Ahten had been left to guard the boat whereby they traveled. By means of her own wisdom, skills, and courage she had thwarted the Cerites from usurping the vessel, and with the aid of the Tritynoi, her kindred, she had overthrown them completely.

Now of all these tidings Chrono had been kept in darkness during the days of his confinement. When at last the Matriarch had released him and he returned to the vessel, he found it inhabited by the Seafolk, with Ahten at their head. So he said, amazed, "I see things have unfolded here which must be told in full! What tale lies behind this strange sight?"

Ahten was modest and would not boast, but she told what she could of how she had secured the boat to the seafloor that it might not be moved by any force or craft, and how she had harassed the invaders day and night, and had at last gone to obtain the aid and support of her kindred in the depths of the Sea. What she would not tell, Ériven her kinsman told in full, so that Chrono and Duono received the full account of all her deeds.

Then Chrono was proud beyond measure, and loved the sea-maiden all the more. So he sang her praise, saying,

"The beauties of the sea-maid all behold.
No shroud has ever veiled her fulgent eyes,
And many praise her for her placid ways,
Acclaim her kindness, and her selfless soul.

But who discerned the deeper treasure there,
Unfathomed in the ocean's azure breast!
Within that modest cradle, who had guessed
There loomed a richer trove, beyond compare?

The Hall of Merten lurks beneath the blue,
So none can see the splendors of that manse.
And Dreiton's Halls are hid from mortal glance:
Magnificent, but ever out of view.

So those of us who only ever know
The sparkling surface of the sundry Seas,

Who only bless its beauteous boundaries,
Might never guess what glories gleam below.

So Ahten's unexpected merit lies
Behind the modest beauty of her eyes.

That gentle heart is also valiant,
Her secret wiles disguised by modesty.
Her graces cover cunning bravery;
Her patience fortified by adamant.

The tidings of her artful victory,
Her prudence leading the courageous rout,
Are drops of rain that end the arid drought
And usher in a day of revelry.

So even I, who thought I knew her well,
Whose virtues I did often celebrate,
Am shamed to learn I did not estimate
The fullness of her value after all!

Such steady and resourceful wiles
The humble suitor justly hails!"

Chrono and Duono then looked over the vessel, top to bottom, to take stock of their situation. "Thanks to the valor and prudence of Ahten, we have our ship and our supplies," he said at last. "But we have been delayed many days by the hostility of Ceras and these Cerites. The summer is now far gone. We do not know, for none has traveled that route in full, how many days remain to gain our goal. Shall we proceed, or turn back in failure?"

Duono replied, "There is no journey-staff of the Sea to guide our ways, but I should counsel to press forward. We may as yet have time in plenty to complete our journey. Or we may have been destined to meet the bitter days of winter even had there been no delay."

Then Ahten said, "I, too, would counsel to proceed. Each day that we delay, we postpone our hopes yet longer. We have overcome much at the hands of these Hirnans. Let us not waste that effort by abandoning our mission."

So Chrono said, "Then let us consider our way forward. Thanks to the generosity of the guards, we now have enough water for a length of days. But should we need to refill our cisterns we shall need to find lonely and uninhabited spots until we have passed the borders of the Hirna, for the edict of the

Matriarch stands against us. The Hirnans are more froward even than the tales have told."

Duono added, "Knowing not how long a journey lies before us, we cannot fully judge our rations. We shall need to go ashore to hunt and forage before we reach the Ice, I trust."

Chrono said, "It is my hope that we shall be beyond the borders of the Hirna before we have gone so far. But no one knows how far the dominion of the Matriarch may reach."

Then Ériven spoke and offered, "Much succor can be drawn from the sea itself, if you have net or line. Ahten and my clan may aid you in that endeavor. But you shall soon be beyond the help of the Seafolk. For we have little commerce with the cold seas of the north, and if any of our folk dwell there, we know them not. As for fresh water such as your Kindred require, we have no source."

"Then I judge that we should follow the coast towards our goal. If we must eventually put to shore to supply ourselves, we shall do our best to find remote and uninhabited country."

So they agreed.

Thus they proceeded on their way. For a number of days they watched the shoreline carefully, marking the settlements of the Hirnans where they found them. As they made progress to the northeast, the signs of settlements and homesteads became ever fewer, until the land became blanketed with impenetrable forest.

At last the coast curved due northward, and the shore became a palisade of cliffs rising to a high plateau. From thence a cold wind began to blow seaward from the highlands, so that the boat was forced to tack against its gusts continually. Then Ériven and his company took leave of them, saying, "The waters from this point are forever cold and miserable to us, and we do not bear it lightly. Be careful of Ahten, for she will face much discomfort on your way: the garments of the Seafolk do little to keep us warm in the waters."

Chrono and his companions thanked them for their aid. Chrono bowed his head said, "We shall ever be indebted to you and your clan for the aid you have given us, both in the struggle with the Cerites and in our journey onward."

"Consider it no debt, but a favor for the princess-daughter of Merten and Aviah. For the Seafolk have never yet required the aid of the folk of land and air, and your debt indeed could never be repaid!"

"So be it, then," laughed Chrono. "But let there ever be friendship between my folk and yours." Then to show his respect for Chrono, Ériven bowed in the manner of Chrono's own kindred (for the Seafolk have no such custom), and he took leave of the boat: so they saw him and his folk no more.

Now indeed the journey grew harsh, for with each day's travel the coast grew ever colder and more foreboding. Floes of ice appeared, as smooth and white as rich cream, nodding in the gray waters as they sailed northward. The forests on the ridge of the plateau thinned, and patches of snow and ice began to appear in the highlands, even though the long days of summer continued.

Duono scanned the waters worriedly. "At any time, I fear, we may reach the fringes of the Ice itself," he said. "Let us find a haven ashore, where we might hunt and gather such supplies as will carry us beyond its limits. I suspect we are far from the reaches of the Matriarch by now."

So they found a remote cove, where the woods came down to the shore, and made camp. There they filled their cisterns, and gathered meat and fish; berries and roots. They honed their tools, and mended their nets and cords, and made such repairs to the boat as were necessary. When all was in readiness, they put to sea once more.

At last one morning as the coastlands began to curve to the northwest, the keen eyes of Duono spotted a glow upon the horizon, and he said, "I see before us the eternal snows and ice of Batack."

Indeed, as the vessel drew onward, the cliffs, rocks and woods to which they had grown accustomed gave way to a vast field of white blazing in the sunlight. Ere the day's end they had reached the Ice itself: a terrible cliff of ghostly blue and white as tall as the sky, pressing its feet into the very waters of the sea. It stretched off before them further than the horizon, further than eye could see or mind could grasp. It spoke in roars deeper and mightier than thunder from the heavens, as bergs the size of mountains broke off from its ragged edge and launched into the waters of the deep amid great clouds of icy breath.

Then Chrono feared for the boat and for his companions. "We must put off further from the edge of the Ice, for our boat is as a beetle at the feet of a Giant in these waters."

They set sail, therefore, as far from the fringe of the ice shelf as they dared, though they feared also to leave the sight of it, lest they go too far adrift and founder in the endless waters of the north. Yet even here the floes and the bergs of ice surrounded them, so that they were afraid for the ship at every moment. Ahten would go before them, warning them when they approached too near to the unseen masses of the floating bergs below the waves. But the waters had grown ever more frigid, so that she could hardly bear the cold.

At last Duono said, "Ahten suffers indeed for our sake. We must give her relief from the chill of the sea."

Chrono agreed. Now they had aboard the vessel on their deck a brazier to cook their food and warm themselves: so Chrono heated a pot of seawater over their coals. With this he dampened a woolen blanket, and Ahten came aboard, and sat in the cabin wrapped in the warmth of the blanket whenever the chill of the seas became too much to bear. Chrono gave her a cot to sleep on, and he and Duono took turns during their night watches keeping her blanket moist with warm water, that she might rest. For it had become necessary to keep on watch at all times, day and night. The crushing shelf of the Ice pressed far from shore, forcing them in deeps where they could not anchor: and the continuous passage of bergs and floes required endless vigil.

Thus they proceeded to the north, hugging the fringes of the Ice as nearly as they dared: and their days and nights alike were fraught with unending peril, misery, and disquiet.

One morning the day dawned upon them cold and red, and scarlet-tinged ribs of cloud painted the sky from horizon to horizon. Chrono scowled at the skies. "What is your thought?" he said to Duono. "The look of the skies is that of the coming of a storm: and we are here in the midst of the sea, far from the safety of any cove or bay. Dare we move inward towards the Ice, and hope to find a haven where we might ride out a storm in safety?"

Duono frowned darkly. "I have seen no sign of land or shore for many days. I fear our peril would be greatest near the edge of this terrible palisade of moving ice."

"At least in the shadow of the Ice we might be sheltered from the wind and waves: for the winds are blowing from the northwest, off the table of the Ice and out to sea."

"Little good would that quiet do us, if a mountain of ice were to break upon our heads, or should we run upon a berg and destroy our hull. The floes are as thick as locusts at the foot of the shelf."

So they debated. At last Chrono said, "Let us then proceed on our way far from the fringe, and wait out the day. We shall make a run for the north. Perhaps if our luck remains with us the storm may not come as feared, or may pass us by."

But as the day progressed, the sky grew ever more lowering and black, and the winds which moaned off of the Ice grew ever stronger. Then at last the rain began to fall, a cold rain in driving drizzle as sharp and frigid as hail, then in great drops, then in howling sheets that pounded their deck and soaked them to the skin.

So powerful did the winds become that Chrono furled the sail, and even then the storm drove the boat before it, so that they continually manned the tiller to stay on course, and to avoid the boulders of ice which swirled about them. Many times a floe would strike the hull with a fearsome thud in spite of their efforts, yet the hull was strong and continued to hold.

Thus did the storm continue into the night. It was dark, and the white line of the Ice had long since vanished from view. So black and foul had the weather fallen upon them that they soon had no inkling of their direction at all, if not for the direction of the unrelenting wind itself, and had no notion of their own heading. All they could manage was to avoid striking the icy obstacles which swarmed past them, keeping the wind to starboard when possible. But the storm blew so fiercely that the boat spun about like a leaf on a swirling stream.

An endless night of drenching labor they spent without rest in the shrieking terrors of the dark. There was little opportunity to speak. The screaming winds drowned out the pitch of their voices, and all their attentions were focused continuously on saving their ship and their own lives. A morning at last dawned, but dark: so dark that it could barely be discerned from night. By this time it was clear that they were far at sea, distant from the shore, and the edge of the Ice lost beyond an unseeable horizon. Only the broken floes which spun by them told of its existence, and even these were more sparse than before.

Yet worse than all this, the further a-sea they were blown, the greater the waves which scourged them. Even Chrono felt weak at the very sight of them: Mighty ridges of storm-black water towering overhead, living and heaving mountains more terrifying than any monster of land or sea. These rushed upon them unstoppable, wave after dreadful wave, with no respite, and even Chrono doubted he would have dared the journey had he foreseen such terrors. By now the churning of the sea was so powerful it took the efforts of both Chrono and Duono together to force the rudders to their will, struggling to drive the prow of their vessel into the rising wall of each onrushing behemoth lest it tip them over broadside and spill them into the watery hell which engulfed them.

For now the waves which overwhelmed the boat were the greatest danger. In their desperation Chrono and Duono leashed themselves to the mast by tethers around their waists, for they no longer trusted their footing or the rails of the boat to preserve them from the waters coursing across their deck.

Ahten at least was safe. She had abandoned the boat altogether for the calm of the deep below the waves, despite the chill. But neither could she rest. She followed along from beneath the vessel, watching the surface continually, that she might chance to rescue Chrono or Duono should they be washed from the deck. From time to time she risked raising her head above the waves into the driving storm, to assure herself that both of her companions still held to the deck.

In this way the storm went on throughout the day, and yet another endless night as black as a cave. On they struggled, without rest and with scant nourishment, working mechanically with little room in their unresting minds for hope. Their exhaustion grew so great that they began to fail in their exertions. Then the waves would catch them broadside, and toss the boat like a twig, tipping them perilously aslant. The pontoons as yet still held, and they did not capsize.

But their luck and skills could not hold out forever. At last their efforts failed them, and a mighty wave caught them full in its fury: cresting and washing over them, higher and harder than any that had come before. With a terrific crack the mast of the vessel snapped in two, and was swept away.

Duono's tether was tied to the stump of the mast below the break, and he was preserved. But Chrono was not so fortunate: when the mast snapped his cord remained tethered to the reeling spar, and Chrono was dragged with it from the deck into the seething waters.

For a moment he knew not whether he was still aboard, in the wash of a wave, or in the deep itself. Yet as he struggled for his footing he could not find the boat beneath his feet: neither deck, nor cabin, nor rail. He floundered in the heaving sea, desperately looking about for any sign of the vessel, but all was lost in the darkness and the ever-pitching morass of the churning waves. Calling out to Duono for help was of no avail, as even had his voice been heard over the monstrous howl of the wind and roar of the waters, Duono would have been helpless to aid him.

The rope about his waist kept him tethered to the drifting mast, which the wind and the waves tossed about, and the frozen fingers of Chrono's one good arm could not untie the wet cords in the frigid waters. So he drew himself along the cord until he reached the floating mast, and clung to it for life, spending his energy trying merely to stay afloat, his mind blank of anything but the need to keep his head above the waves.

He soon lost all track of how long he had been afloat in the tossing sea. The cold, the exhaustion, and the hopeless toil drained him of all energy, and in the end his mind began to drift away.

But as he was about to lose his grasp on life and sink into the waters, a warm hand clasped his arm. Looking feebly towards this apparition, he beheld the face of Ahten, grim and resolute.

Taking a knife she kept at her side, she severed the cord which leashed him to the mast. Then she called into his ear, "Save thy breath, for we must go below!"

Then beneath the churning waves they went: and all was peace. Chrono opened his eyes in the waters, and though he could see little beyond darkness and a blur, he looked up and perceived the roiling surface of the sea above him, yet silent and unable to touch them in the depth.

The Seafolk swim strongly and swiftly, for both their hands and their feet spread into fins when they swim: so Ahten took Chrono by the shoulder and drew him along. When his breath was spent, she breathed of her own breath into his lungs to preserve him, for the Seafolk do hold air in their lungs as do we. At last the hull of the boat could be seen—a black shadow pitching in the dark seas above them—and she sped to the surface like an arrow.

When they broke from the waves Chrono gasped for air, once again tossed about in the seething waters. Ahten raised her call to the pitch of the Seafolk, which can pierce the skies, and hailed Duono. At that shout Duono looked beyond the rail, and spotting them in the waters he cried out for joy. He left the boat to drift, and after securing one end of a cord to a cleat he tossed the rope out to them: for the pitching of the vessel was so great in the storm that it was now dangerous for Ahten to approach. So Ahten bound the rope about Chrono's chest, and with her aid from below, Duono arduously drew him safely from the waters.

The waves continued to toss the ship, and with no one at the tiller they were helpless before the onrushing mountains. But Duono could not leave Chrono on the deck, for Chrono was too cold and weak to stand, and would surely be washed over the rail. So he trusted the boat to fate and luck, and he pulled his companion into the rough shelter of their cabin. He lashed him hurriedly to a bench, and rushed back out in the hopes of saving the boat before another wave capsized them completely.

There to his unlooked-for relief he found Ahten on deck, manning the tiller and guiding the craft through the waves. Taking his place at the tiller beside her he called out through the wind and rain, "Yet again we are in your debt, princess!"

Then Ahten said, "Rest if you can. I can hold the ship for a while!"

Now the strength of the Seafolk is great for their size, and Ahten, slight as she appeared, handled the rudders with skill. But Duono said, "Never should it be said I shirked my duty and forced a maiden and princess to do my labor!"

But Ahten replied, "You are exhausted beyond measure, and we know not how much longer we shall be trapped in this storm. Rest if you can, for we will need the full strength of your arms yet!" Then she looked about at the raging storm and laughed bitterly. "Have no fear for me. There is no chance the dry air will wither me on such a night!"

So Duono also retired to the cabin to rest his limbs and regain a measure of strength. The waves which rushed across the deck battered the cabin, and pulsed in and out of the door. Yet he and Chrono were safer there from the wind and the waves, and so great was his exhaustion that in spite of the violence of the seas Duono sank at once into a fitful sleep.

Being of the Sea herself, Ahten was better able than either Chrono or Duono to read the signs of the wind and the waves. So while she tried to guide the craft safely through the waves, she also began to work her way to the south and westward. For she perceived the full scope of the storm, and guessed the route toward its fringe and toward safety. When Chrono and Duono therefore were able at last to leave the shelter of the cabin, Ahten took command of the vessel.

Thus she ordered that they all take their turns at the tiller, two at a time, while the third took rest, and supped as best they could in the pitching vessel. They did not argue, but allowed her to guide the craft, for she made her way with a skill and confidence they did not yet understand.

So through another long night they labored, and long into the following day. Until at last by nightfall the winds began to lessen, and the driving rain had turned to a patter. Finally in the night, forgetful of all their dangers, they let the boat drift, and found the relief of sleep at last.

When the night was spent, the day dawned through the breaking clouds, and the sea itself rested. Then Ahten returned to the water to find rest in her berth, for now the airs were dry and the long labor without the support of the Sea had drained her strength.

But when they awoke, Ahten returned to their side, and they all examined the vessel. Most of their supplies were below deck, or had been lashed down before the storm, so little had been lost. But the damage was great. The hold was deeply awash, and boat rode low and heavy in the sea. Both of their rudders showed damage from the continuous strain, and a lengthwise split had ruined one of them. The ship listed hard to port and waves lapped at the port rail, for the pontoon on that side had filled with seawater and remained barely afloat, just below the surface. The starboard pontoon had splintered away so completely no trace of it could be found. Their small ship's boat remained tethered to the stern, but it had been swamped, and it dragged now below the surface. Ahten could find no great damage to the hull, but they felt certain that they would soon discover leaks between the planks.

When they had finished all their inspections, they sat down together on the slanting deck to confer.

"Our situation is not good," Duono began. "The damage from the storm is great, and we shall have much work before us if we hope to survive."

"You do not overstate the case," said Chrono. "It is good that we built the ship with a solid deck, else we surely would have been swamped long ago. As it is, our deck barely rides above the surface now, so full has our hold become with seawater. Before anything else, we must all begin the work of bailing out all we can.

"I fear moreover that when we have cleared away the seawater we shall find that the flood has spoiled most of our food, except what we had preserved in the cabin, above the flood."

"Food I can procure from the sea," Ahten said. "Though the waters are cold and the hunt is difficult, I shall find us enough to survive."

Duono said, "We must do what we can to keep you warm and well, even if that means we go without food. But water we must have. I have found only one cistern whole and uncontaminated by the seawater."

"We are far from land, I fear," said Chrono. "And where we might find fresh water is beyond my ken. What we have will last for a week, if we use it wisely, but we shall need to make for shore as soon as repairs can be made."

"Heading for shore may indeed be our largest concern," said Duono, "For our mast is gone, and though we have spare fabric for a sail, how shall we spread it to catch the wind?"

"We have spare oars, and spare rods and poles which have not been lost. We shall contrive what we can to catch the wind, though they shall not be as robust as what we had built." Then Chrono stood and scanned the horizon all about them, and he said, "My greater concern is that we have no idea where in the Sea we might be. For days we have been driven before this storm, with nothing on our minds but bare survival. How far we have been driven is beyond my reckoning. We have assuredly gone far southward to escape the storm, and the storm itself was driving southward, as well. Nor do we know how far to the east we have been driven. If we head to the west or to the north, it may be that we shall miss Soria altogether, and where in the Sea we might find ourselves is beyond our guess."

Now the Mizans in later ages became great navigators, and learned to discern their position by the height of the sun and the constellations, by the length of the days and nights, and even by the familiar currents and waves of the Sea itself. But Chrono knew nothing of these things.

Ahten said, "Alas, but my kindred seldom venture so far from the shallows into the dark and frigid deeps of the Sea. I may seek help below the waves, but I fear we shall find none in these remote waters."

Chrono sighed. "Then let us begin to bail and to make repairs. Unless we find help unlooked for, we shall head west and north as strictly as we can, and trust ourselves once again to our good fortune."

Duono looked about the vessel dolefully and said, "Our luck would appear to have failed us at last!"

But Chrono replied, "We have survived this storm. I deem our luck has held!"

Two full days they spent adrift in the sea, bailing water from their hold, and repairing what damage they could. The hull had been battered by the waves, and many leaks were found among the planks, but Chrono was able to patch them with pitch and cord, with Ahten aiding him from outside the hull. Chrono looked upon the boat with pride as it rode once again above the waves. A spare rudder they had brought, which took the place of its damaged brother, and the other was strengthened with a pole. They then repaired and re-floated their remaining pontoon, and bailed and repaired the ship's boat.

The mast spar, however, they found they could not replace. Although they contrived sails with the spare poles, they caught but little wind, for they sat low on the deck, below the steady winds. The boat was large and heavy, and required a tall and full mast. Moreover the strength of the winds had waned, so there was little force to press them on their way. The boat now moved slowly and ponderously when it moved at all. The wind prevailed from the east and the current of the waters from the north, thus they had need to tack continually to make their way to the northwest.

Two days they spent thus struggling, and making no progress at all. At last Chrono conceded, "We shall never make it back to land and to safety on this vessel without a mast. We may need to abandon her and make a mast of our remaining poles for the small boat, for the wind will drive the small craft swiftly. Thus we shall escape with our lives, but we will need to abandon our quest."

Ahten said, "Must we then relinquish our hope?"

Chrono replied, "Our time is growing short if we hope to reach safety, and live. And without life, there is no hope."

They struggled on, but it became clear that all their efforts accomplished nothing. At length even Ahten agreed to this plan.

They drew the small boat onto the deck of their vessel, and using the spare wood and poles they had aboard they fashioned a sturdy sail for it, and mounted it into the boat through the thwart, as Duono and Chrono had done with the vessel that had carried them across the Endrev. Then they strengthened the keel for a journey in the deep, attached cleats to the gunwale, and affixed an oar as a rudder at the stern. When they were finished Chrono looked upon it resolutely and said, "It is not even as seaworthy as our first vessel, but it may suit to save our lives."

Duono worried, saying, "Shall Ahten follow us in this craft, or go on ahead as quickly as she may? For we will have no means of keeping her warm in the frigid waters."

Ahten said, "I shall not abandon you, for it may be that my skills beneath the sea will be required. We have come to the south, and the waters are not so cold as formerly. But I shall bear the cold willingly for your sake."

"This is more than we dare ask of you," Chrono said. "Our safety is nothing to us if you risk yourself."

"But my safety is an empty reward if in the end I lose you. We shall travel together."

So they lowered the boat into the waters, and loaded their scant supplies into it: all that they could safely carry. When Chrono and Duono had boarded, Duono took a last look at the ship they had built with much labor, and which Ahten had preserved against great odds, and which they had repaired after the storm with still more hope. Shaking his head he said, "If we set forth now from this vessel, it shall be adrift forever, and we shall never behold her again."

Chrono said, "So let us send her off into the deep with our blessing and thanks. For she has served us faithfully, and has been the deserved object of much sacrifice to us all."

So with all their hopes dwindling in their hearts, Chrono unfurled the sail, set their stern to the ship, and they took flight to the northwest.

14. CHRONO AND THE JOURNEY TO VORDÓT

In the days after Chrono had returned to Mizgad, and had been reconciled to his father and his father's house, it came to pass that Chrono and Ahten determined to travel to the countries beyond the Ice. For he had gained the favor of Merten and Aviah, the father and mother of Ahten, and together they sought the boon of the Ádolthi, that they might circumvent the division which separated their Kindred, and be joined.

Many trials had beset them on this journey. But after overcoming much, they had been overtaken by a great storm from the west, from over the Ice: it had driven them far from their course, and had done much damage to their vessel and to their supplies. But worst of all, it had destroyed the mast which caught the wind, and they had been forced to abandon their ship in favor of the small boat they had towed along, one which could fly easily with a small sail.

So they had been compelled to abandon their quest, and they proceeded with heavy hearts and with sinking hope, sailing to the northwest that they might with luck reach safe haven in the lands of Soria once more.

For days they kept their heading to the northwest, as well as they could manage, but no sign of land yet appeared. They ate little, for much of their food had been spoiled in the storm, and they had been able to carry little with them in the small boat, besides. Ahten augmented their supplies with what she was able to catch from the sea, but as they were in the deeps of the Great Sea, far from the shallows, little could be gleaned from the seafloor itself.

The question of water, however, was more dire. Only one cistern had been spared through the storm, which they had divided into jugs for the small boat. Though they used it sparingly, Chrono and Duono watched their supply dwindle each day with mounting disquiet. And yet no sign of land appeared, nor seabird, nor sea-hound.

At last Chrono said to Ahten, "We can bear our hunger, but water we must have. While this small boat travels more swiftly than our broken ship, we must continually tack against the wind, and the winds are slight. We may not reach land in time to save us. Can you proceed ahead directly, as straight and swift as possible, to see if land lies ahead or not?"

So Ahten agreed. Swimming swiftly forward on their heading, she traveled all that day, but when she returned she had no good news. "The floor of the sea is as deep and featureless as that of the great Sea, and I see as yet no hope of land for four or more days of your travel. Nor can I discern whether our heading is true."

Chrono looked miserably at the dribble of water left in his jug, and he said, "Then perhaps can you travel in a circuit beyond the boat, to the north where the seas are colder, and see if you can spot a floe of ice in the midst of the sea? Melting it we shall have water enough to fill our jugs again."

So Ahten agreed. Swimming then swiftly to the north, she traveled all that day. Returning and finding them in the evening she said, "No ice have I found at sea, but this I discovered: The seafloor rises to the northeast. Perhaps it rises even to landfall, though I had no time to pursue it so far."

"Is it possible," Duono asked, "that we have been blown so far southward that Soria now lies to the north?"

So they debated whether they should alter their course in the hopes of finding some unexpected haven. For their water had reached an end, and their thirst beset them sorely.

Then Chrono said, "If we continue on our current bearing we have scant hope of reaching land before we perish from thirst."

"But a course to the northeast would lead us away from all that we know or hope to reach. The land of Soria surely lies somewhere to the west. We are ignorant of any lands to the east."

Chrono looked bitterly at his empty jug. "Our thirst compels us. I say to take our chances of straying, and commit ourselves to fate and fortune."

So they changed their heading, and turned their prow to the northeast.

It so happened that the winds which prevailed from the northwest aided them on this course, so they had little need to tack, and their boat went more swiftly among the waves. Ahten dove before them to scout their way, and returned shortly reporting, "The seafloor continues to rise ahead. Hold out yet one more day!" Then she dove before them once more.

So they suffered through that day. Ahten came back to them in the evening saying, "I see now many seamounts which rise steeply from the seafloor! None lifts its head above the waves, but my hope does not flag. Continue through the night, and let us see what the morning shall bring!"

She had brought fish, which they ate raw, giving some slight relief to their parched tongues. Chrono and Duono pressed on, guiding the boat in shifts by night. When the dawn at last began to break, Ahten dove before them again to scout their way. Returning shortly she exulted, "A seamount lieth ahead which bears its head above the waves! Follow me now, and let us hope against hope that water may be found there."

She led them onward, following the seafloor as it rose upward to the north. In the air above, seabirds were spotted, for the first time in many days at sea. Then at last on the horizon a hint of an island appeared: a small eyot, barely more than a rock jutting from the sea, but on its rugged crest a stand of pines reached tall, promising water.

Then Chrono and Duono would have cried out for joy but for the dryness of their throats.

With all their remaining strength they brought the boat ashore, and moored to the root of a fallen pine on the leeward side. Stumbling out of the vessel they climbed the crags, and found among the rocks pools of fresh water left from the rains, and trickles which smeared the boulders, dripping into the sea. They plunged their hands and faces into the icy drink, and took their fill: never had any wine which passed their lips pleased them better.

When they had refreshed themselves fully they explored the island to assess their situation. There was little to explore. A small grove of pines topped the rocky knoll. Many branches lay strewn about, fit for firewood, torn from the trees in the recent storm, and several entire trees had been toppled and lay prostrate upon the ground. For food they found an abundance of mussels and clams clinging to the edges of the eyot, and crabs scuttled among the rocks. There were no flowing streams, but rainwater still filled the hollows, and water seeped from the moist ground in many places.

Having satisfied themselves that they had seen all there was to discover, they built a fire on the shore near the rocks, that Chrono and Duono might dry themselves at last, and that all of them might warm themselves from the cold winds and the frigid waves. There they sat and conferred.

Chrono finally said, "We might remain here long and recover from our trial at sea, but soon we shall need to continue on our way. We still do not know in which direction to find Soria, nor how many days from hence land and water may yet lie. We have no more jugs to fill than when we left our ship. If we leave this island, we may soon find ourselves in the same straits once again."

Duono suggested, "If one of us were to take the boat alone with all the jugs filled, the water would last twice as long, and he might travel twice as far. But one other would need to remain here on this island, and hope for rescue."

Chrono frowned. "One might hope to dwell here for many days. There is certainly food enough from the sea, and water enough from the springs to keep one hale. But the hope of rescue would be secured by a mere thread."

Duono said sourly, "A miserable prison it would make if rescue never came!"

Chrono looked about the islet and mused, "Yet more is this irony. For here on this island are trees fair enough for a stout mast. If we but had our ship here with us now, it might be repaired. We could then fill all our cisterns, and might even hope to continue on our quest."

"Alas," said Duono, "But to have made the journey on that broken craft would have taken many days longer, and Ahten would now be seeking her homeland alone."

As they had spoken thus together Ahten had been sitting nearby upon a boulder overlooking the sea, that she might refresh herself in the mists of the crashing waves. There she sat gazing thoughtfully to the south. Speaking cautiously she said "The chance is small, but I believe I might lead us to our ship if we follow the winds. In any event, I am more confident of finding the boat than of finding a safe harbor in any direction from this remote and unknown speck!"

"Even were that possible, little good would it do us," said Duono. "We cannot bring the ship here without water. And we cannot bring water to the ship."

But Chrono frowned thoughtfully. "It may not be beyond hope: if the wind remains at our back as we go south we should travel swiftly. The winds would be more favorable for returning north than they were for sailing west. Using your plan the water might last long enough! With Ahten's help a lone traveler, carrying all the water, may be able to return here, even with a disabled ship, before the water runs dry."

Ahten said, "Should your water run short before we reach the island, I might fly on ahead and refill a jug for you; for now that I know the way I can swiftly find this island and return again to the ship, provided your course stays true."

"But our ship has been adrift for many days," Chrono bemoaned. "Finding it is all but beyond hope. It may even have strayed into a wayward current and be beyond our reach by now."

"Nevertheless there is little risk in this scheme," Duono shrugged. "If you cannot find the boat, you can return again to this island, and we are none the worse for the effort. I shall risk remaining behind, that you might venture on this errand with Ahten."

So it was decided. Chrono and Duono then spent their time recovering from their ordeal and regaining their strength, while they built for Duono a snug shelter among the boulders. When all was in readiness they put all the water jugs into the boat, and Chrono boarded the vessel.

"Be off!" said Duono at last. "Do not worry on my behalf, for I shall be more safe and warm than you until you return!"

"Indeed you shall!" Chrono laughed. "I fear that even with the eyes and the Sea-lore of the Seafolk to aid me, our ship shall be as lost as a lone pebble on a beach. We may be casting off on a fool's errand to nowhere."

So Chrono unfurled the sail and set his course to southward. Ahten dove into the deep to scout the way.

Reading the seafloor, the currents, and the winds as easily as the Kindreds of the air can follow a familiar landscape or a well trodden path, she led Chrono skillfully towards that place where they had left their vessel. On the fourth day out she halted. Then coming up from the seafloor she brought Chrono word, saying, "This is the spot! Remain here in the midst of the sea, and I shall go on ahead and find our vessel."

Chrono looked all about and smirked. "All the horizons are as one to my eyes," he said. "I'll have little knowledge of whether I move with the sea or remain at rest!"

So Ahten said laughing, "Then allow the boat to drift freely with the wind, and I shall find you. For the path of the wind is the course I shall follow in my search. Wait for me, and do not lose hope, for I may not return for days."

"I shall wait and I shall watch. But I have scant hope left to lose!"

Then Ahten bid him farewell, and she dove into the waves and departed.

The great vessel had been drifting unmanned for many days, but since the storm had abated the winds and currents had been slight, so Ahten hoped they would faithfully and swiftly lead her to the vessel. She trailed its likely course, diving deep to mark her bearings from the seafloor, rising to the shallows to read the currents, and lifting her head from the highest waves to scan the horizons. But days passed, and the further she went from Chrono's boat, the wider the arc of her search was forced to grow, and ever more vast and empty the ocean seemed to be.

As dawn broke on the fourth day she made for the surface, seeking the tallest of the cresting rollers. Rising with a wave she lifted her dispirited head to scout the troughs, and a lonely, dark speck appeared, foundering among the billows, not far off from her course. A thrill filled her heart, and she dove beneath the waves to rush to it. In moments the dark speck had become the bulging blackness of the hull overhead, and she sprang from the sea rejoicing. Thus she sang,

"Thou dame who erstwhile shouldered all our hope,
And bore upon thy back our breathless bourne:
Thy loss had left us grievous and forlorn
With little gain to grasp at, or to grope.
So foundering a-sea, we did protest,
But left thee, as we had to in our need.
Forced to follow fortunes fate decreed,
And so compelled, to then renounce our quest.
How low our spirits sank upon thy loss!
How dark our days when thou wast in our wake.
How drear and desolate that tack we'd take
Away from every aim which steered our course.
But sighting thee again my spirit soars!
How sweet to see thee set upon the Sea,
Alone and empty though thy chambers be.
For hope again thy faulted form restores!

And all the aspirations that surround thee
Live and rise again, for I have found thee!

So marking well the spot in the sea, and the condition of the currents and the winds, she made her way swiftly back to Chrono's boat, buoyant and proud.

"Come!" she hailed him. "Our vessel yet lives. She is empty and adrift, but she rides the Sea valiantly. But we must move as swiftly as the wind can carry you, for she has drifted far. A day and a night for your boat, I would guess."

"Lead then!" said Chrono, unfurling the sail once more. "We shall fly upon the wind if we can!" So Chrono followed, and at last they both returned in joy to the vessel they had built.

"I regret that the search has taken longer than I had hoped," Ahten said when they had boarded. "Moreover the eastward winds are not so strong. I fear the ship may falter, and you may once again expend your fresh water before we reach the islet. Shall I go on ahead to see if I might retrieve water for the vessel?"

Chrono gazed to the far-off northern horizon. "No," he mused, "I shall need your help to manage the craft. We cannot let down anchors here in the depths, and we shall need to continue on course both day and night if we hope to reach our goal. Though I might man the tiller for many hours, I shall certainly need to take rest."

"Then shall we plunge forward and trust again to chance?"

Chrono studied the vessel carefully. "We have come further from the islet than I had hoped, and spent more time in our search. We may still be able to bring our ship in, but speed is now our greatest need, or our labor is in vain. Let us cast free the remaining pontoon, for it drags on the vessel and slows our progress. The danger of depleting our water while still far a-sea outweighs the danger of capsizing in the breakers, as long as the fair weather holds."

"Good then," said Ahten. "Shall we also cast away the spoiled supplies which weigh us down, that we might float lighter upon the waves?"

When they had agreed on this plan, Chrono reset all their contrived sails, that they might catch the easterly winds; then Ahten took the rudder as he worked at removing the remaining pontoon. When this task had been accomplished, and the severed pontoon had limped away astern, Chrono took the tiller while Ahten brought up from the hold whatever ruined supplies and provisions could be spared, and cast them also into the sea.

At last Ahten studied the sea, and she said, "We have gained speed, yet I deem the ship could gain still more if we could eject yet more weight."

Chrono sighed and looked dismally at the cabin. It had taken a beating in the storm: it leaned sadly to the side, and many planks of its walls had been blown away. "Let us remove what we can of the cabin and see how she rides. Should I need shelter from the weather, I can take rest in the hold."

So he worked at dismantling the cabin, removing the planking and tossing over whatever could not be put to use. When nothing remained but the frame and a portion of the roof, Ahten at last declared, "I think we have lightened our draft all that we dare. We can go no more swiftly than we do now."

Then Chrono looked about the deck and laughed, and said, "Were we to lighten her yet more, we should soon be riding unhoused upon the sea!"

In this state they proceeded to the north. Ahten guided them unerringly on their course, and the winds held: though their progress was far from swift, it was straight and sure.

While Chrono and Ahten were searching for the lost vessel, Duono was not idle. He searched among the downed trees and selected a sturdy pine, straight and hale. He then took the blade of his knife and fixed it to a handle as an axe.[62] With this he trimmed the stock free of limb and branch, removed the bark, and scraped it smooth. He cut the required length of beam from the stock, and dragged it to the shore where he hoped their ship might moor.

As this project advanced he also spent his hours in catching and smoking such fish as he could spear in the surf, and foraging for edible seeds and roots to add to their reserves. An abundance of cones had blown from the trees in the storm, and the nuts within were still fresh and wholesome; so these he gathered and stockpiled as well. Mushrooms he found also, and a quantity of these he succeeded in drying for their stores.

Each evening he sat before the entrance to his shelter peering southward for any sign of a sail on the horizon, and making supplication to Havui for the safety of his friends: for in that lonely and desolate place that Silent One was the only company to be found.

Until at last one morning the makeshift sails of their vessel appeared before his eyes far a-sea, and his heart leapt with hope.

When they had moored the ship Duono rejoiced to see them, but he bemoaned the state of the vessel. "I see you have succeeded in bringing back our own ship. But the sea has been hard on her! She is but a husk of that which we had crafted!" he declared.

"Not the sea," said Chrono, "but necessity. I fear we had need of a few alterations!"

Duono scratched his head uncertainly. "Shall we set about restoring her once more?"

"We have neither the time nor the tools to craft proper lumber. As long as we can fit her with a new mast and spar we shall be satisfied. Her hull is yet sound, and with a new mast she shall go swiftly and surely on the sea once again."

"The mast I have seen to, said Duono, gesturing to the spar he had fashioned, lying upon the shore. "As to the pontoons, perhaps we can contrive a pair of simple rails to serve. The cabin can be mantled well enough with fabric."

"Whatever we do, let us do it swiftly. For I feel the time is pressing on us and our mission. Much time has been lost in this detour, and the days of summer are at an end."

There was no harbor on the islet, but on the leeward side the rocks dropped

62 This "knife" would have been a stone blade of versatile design which could have been fixed into any variety of mountings for different uses.

sheer into the sea, where the depth was such that the ship itself could be drawn close in, directly alongside the boulders. Duono in their absence had contrived to affix a cushion of boughs from the trees, so the rocks might do no damage to the vessel. Here they moored the vessel long enough to drag aboard the mast which Duono had prepared, while Ahten went about the business of filling all their cisterns with fresh water, and bringing aboard all the provisions which Duono had gathered in their absence. Then Chrono unmoored the ship and pulled free of the rocks, a short distance from shore, where he was able to set down anchors.

Duono meanwhile had noted the condition of Ahten as she toiled, and he said, "Lady, you are exhausted from the sunlight and the full weight of laboring ashore! You must rest!" So he took upon himself the task of heating water, and he prepared for her a warm pool among the boulders.

As she rested and recovered her strength, Duono and Chrono set to the task of mounting the new mast amid the thwart, and pursuing such other repairs as they could hope to accomplish in short order. One of the improvised sails was left at the rear of the ship as a stud sail, affixing the tallest of their poles through the deck, for Chrono found they gained more wind and more propulsion thereby. The rails of Duono also served as better than his pontoons, for they were light, and did not drag in the waters as the vessel went, yet they stabilized her in the surf nearly as well as his heavy pontoons had done. Thus their boat, though crude in appearance, had grown swifter and more sure by the effort.

So they all worked to prepare to journey once again, while the days grew shorter, and the winds more chill.

At last all was in readiness, and the ship was in order as well as they could fashion in the rudeness of their situation. "Our repairs have been accomplished, and our vessel is seaworthy once again," said Duono, "We may put to sea with the coming of dawn. But the time has come to choose our course."

Chrono considered this and replied, "When we left Mizgad, we had two options, and much time. Now we have little time, but three options. We are far a-sea. If we set a northward course straight across the deep, we may find the current Merten had spoken of, and quickly reach Vordót: but we still risk missing our goal utterly, and meeting instead a slow death in frigid seas. Or we might head to the west, where we may yet hope to find the coast of Soria. There we might pick up our former course, following the coast northward to find the lands we seek: but we are likely yet miles south of the fringes of the Ice, and we know not how many days this journey will take. Winter and its storms may be arriving soon.

"And now a third choice lies open to us: if we dare not either course, we may admit defeat and attempt to return to Mizgad."

"I do not relish any of these options!" Duono quipped. "Caution would choose the return to Mizgad. But when have we ever chosen the route of caution?"

"Indeed," said Ahten. "But who can say whether even the route of caution is sure? We are as yet utterly ignorant of our bearings! I cannot say with any confidence what course shall bring us to Soria's shores. Even should we strike the coasts of Soria, you might find yourselves ashore in the land of the Hirnans. You shall surely find no aid from that wayward Tribe!"

Duono at last said to his companions, "We have considered all hazards, I trust. I leave the decision to you. This quest has been yours from the beginning, and I have come only as your friend and aid."

Chrono said, "I would not lightly risk the life of so great a friend and aid as you have been to me. It would be my choice to head for the coast of Soria, and find our way north from there. The chance of being lost at sea, should we go northward from here, is too great."

So Ahten also agreed.

When morning dawned, Chrono unfurled the sails at last, and caught hold of the eastward wind, and set his tack to the northwest. In that direction they saw the greatest hope to return to the lands of Soria. Thus they left behind forever the islet that had been their salvation, and none knows its whereabouts to this day.[63]

For days they traveled, and yet no sign of land appeared. Ahten dove to the depths in search of any rise of the seafloor, but she could only confirm that they still sailed across the deepest of the Deep, barren but for the occasional skeleton of some vast sea creature. Both Chrono and Duono began to fear that they had been blown so far from their course by the storm that Soria was now beyond the horizon to the north, or that they had already passed it entirely. Their eyes found nothing but a circle of blue in all directions, day after worrisome day.

Only Ahten had any sense of their bearings, and even she could not be sure in which direction the coasts of Soria lay, whether to the west, or the north, or even behind them now to the northeast.

So she said one day to Chrono, "You can no longer depend on my skills to guide us. I fear that we are so far from the waters of my ken that I am of no use to us at all."

"If only we had the wisdom of the dolphins to direct us," Duono said. "They are never lost, even in the deepest of the Deep and the most remote of horizons." Saying this he gestured beyond them to the north, for his sharp eyes had spotted in the distance the glistening silver backs of a pod of dolphins leaping among the waves.

63 The island was clearly far at sea beyond the maps even of the Mizans, and it is possible that with rising sea levels after the melting of the ice sheets it later sank beneath the waves.

Ahten gasped for joy at the vision. "The steeds of Dreiton!" she exclaimed. "These are the very servants of great Dreiton himself! And hope unexpected hath come to us at last!"

Without another word she dove into the waters, leaving Chrono and Duono scratching their heads, and she swam to join the dolphins and hail them to the ship.

The dolphins are the most clever of the creatures of the sea, and are able to discern much and to perform many tasks: and the steeds of Dreiton are the cleverest of all. They followed her eagerly to the ship to await her instructions. She took the opal from the circlet that she wore, and wrapped it well in canvas, and contrived a pouch with a strap to hold it. This she gave to the leader of the pod. Then she ordered them to return to Dreiton their master, bringing him the token as an emblem of her need, and to lead him back to them if he could be so moved. To the wonder of Chrono and Duono, the dolphin took hold of the pouch in its jaws. The steeds of Dreiton piped their delight at their new task, leapt into the swells, and rushed away to fulfill their calling.

When they had disappeared into the distant waters, Duono asked of Ahten, "Shall we attempt to hold our position here in the midst of the sea, and wait to see if Dreiton arrives?"

"Nay," she answered, "We dare not lie still in the waters. Continue on your course. Fear not! The skill of the dolphins exceedeth that even of the Seafolk for finding their way in the empty seas. If they return at all, they shall track us and find us. If we have received grace of Dreiton, perhaps he shall arrive with them himself."

So they continued on their course, still hoping for signs of land.

Now it was no accident that the steeds of Dreiton had been found coursing the far reaches of the Great Sea. But neither Chrono nor Ahten knew their tale.

It so happened that Merten and Aviah had sent word to the Terumani concerning the quest of their daughter, and many among the terumani of the north had looked for their arrival for many a day. But the months of summer had passed, and even the autumn was well-advanced, and no sign of them had appeared. No word of them returned to Merten, and his heart had grown black with worry for his daughter, and for the honorable Son of the Air who had risked his life on behalf of his Seafolk.

So Merten called Bël the messenger of the terumani, and pleaded with her, saying, "The days have long passed in which the ship of Chrono should have safely reached haven in the north. Go to Dreiton, the lord of Potomis. He alone has power to search the vastness of the Great Sea."

Bël said, "You know that Dreiton reposes in his great Mansion beneath the waves. Never does he bother himself with the speaking Kindreds of earth and air! Even the burdens of your own kind, his own Kindred, are a small matter to him."

"If he shall have respect of any, it shall be of Chrono. This Chrono is a soul of honor. When he had obtained a mortal wound battling a sea monster on behalf of our Kindred, Dreiton came forth himself to call back his soul."

"As you wish!" Bël conceded. "But can I promise nothing." Then she flew upon her secret courses to the Mansion of Dreiton.

So it was that Dreiton had heard the plea of Merten, and he did as Merten had predicted. He shrugged off his repose, and followed Bël back to the Hall of Merten.

There he conferred with Merten, saying, "What is your hope, my friend? For you must know that their souls may have fled beyond the measures of this world."

"If that is so, only bring back to us here that which remains among us."

"The soul of Ahten may return after the healing sleep, but if Chrono has departed there is no return for his Kindred."

"Indeed, so it is. Nevertheless his form should be interred in honor among our folk."

"I shall do what I can, but Merten my friend, there is little hope in this. The seas are immeasurable, and we must search for them from the airs above to the nethermost fathoms of the Deep."

Merten said, "For me it would be beyond hope. You have greater vision than I or any of my folk. You may find what my eyes cannot see, and you command other eyes which may aid you. It is still the hope of a father and friend that they may yet live."

So Dreiton agreed, but his heart was heavy, for his hopes were dim, and even should he find them yet alive, there was little aid even the Ádolthi could offer beyond counsel and vision.

So at the behest of Merten, Dreiton had set out to search his realm. To aid him in the hunt he had sent forth also his dolphins, the steeds of Dreiton, to seek the ship of Chrono in the uttermost places of the sea. So those clever servants of Dreiton had been patrolling all the waters of the eastern seas.

Still two more days passed, and in spite of the hope brought by the coming of the dolphins, Chrono could not help but to grow morose about their struggle. But on the third day, about the middle of the day, the waters about the boat begin to stir, and the vessel was surrounded by the shining fins of the dolphins, piping merrily in greeting. Then the rumble of a deep voice as of thunder sounded from below, and lo! the locks of Dreiton appeared before them in the sea.[64] Then Ahten leapt aboard the vessel rejoicing, and said, "We have found favor with the Ádolthi indeed! For Dreiton has come!"

Then Dreiton rose from the waves before the prow, his robes of sea mist

64 Sea foam was often poetically referred to as "the locks of Dreiton."

roiling about him, and his hair of gleaming white flowing behind. He came forth from the sea onto the deck of their ship, and he looked about keenly upon their work. He frowned thoughtfully and nodded in approval.

Speaking in his voice of thunder he said, "I had not beheld the handiwork of Chrono and Duono, the sons of earth and air—your vessel for going upon my seas—though word of it had come to me from the children of the Seafolk. Now seeing with my own eyes, I shall acclaim the cleverness of your craft."

Chrono knelt on one knee in the custom of his own folk, and apologized, "Yet what you see is but a shadow of our work! For we have passed through storm and starvation, and our craft has suffered much."

"Through Storm and trouble much wisdom is gained. I foretell that your sea-lore will grow to fullness in days to come."

"But children of earth and air we are yet, and have not the wisdom of the seas to guide us. So we must now seek the unearned favor of Dreiton!"

"So have I guessed. But that must wait. I have come to return that which belongeth to another." Saying this he turned to Ahten. Then he withdrew from his shining robes the parcel Ahten had made, and opening it presented her with the opal she had sent forth as a token.

"All know the opal circlet of Ahten," he declared, "which she received as a gift from the Son of Earth and Air. So I knew that my steeds had found you, and that you yourself were in need. For no other reason would you part with a gift so precious. I now return the gift to its rightful possessor. And I ask: what great need has so pressed you to place such a treasure at risk?"

Then Ahten said, "We have come far, and overcome many obstacles. But by a fierce and terrible storm from Batack were we blown far from our way. We fear now we are lost at sea, and know not the way to go. All around us, for many days, have we seen naught but the circle of the edge of the world. While below, in our own realm, we find nothing but fathomless depths and endless fog. So we pray for your aid to return us to safety."

"To safety? Then have you forsaken your quest?"

"Nay, Lord Dreiton! When we have once again found safety upon the shores of Soria, we hope to continue on our way."

Then Chrono dared to speak, saying, "If indeed we have found favor with the lord of the Sea, dare we ask you to give us aid, that we might fulfill our quest, and seek boon of the Ádolthi in Vordót?"

"I have little to offer but counsel."

"The counsel of Dreiton is aid enough!" said Chrono. So Dreiton nodded, and Chrono proceeded. "We have set our course to the northwest, hoping to reach the shores of Soria once more. If we so continue, will we reach our goal?"

Dreiton frowned. "If you keep fast to this course, you will. But you are yet far to the east of the coasts of Soria, and far to the south of the Ice. There would be many days ahead to complete this journey. What then would be thine aim?"

"We shall renew our journey along the coasts. Thence we shall sail beyond the Ice to Vordót where the Ádolthi have their Mansions."

Dreiton pondered, and waving to the northward seas he said, "But the year is late. The season of snow and freezing storm is nigh upon you. It would be foolhardy beyond reason to attempt such a journey in the days ahead. Even I have no power to aid you against the forces of nature itself."

"We might then head to the north and cross the open sea, to seek the current which leads to that country. But if we go north, we may fail to find that current. To go astray in the polar seas would be certain death."

"Thou speakest the truth."

Then Ahten pleaded her case, saying, "Dost thou not know the way to Vordót, Lord Dreiton? Such a small thing would it be for thee to pilot us on the way!"

Dreiton smiled at this, and said, "This quest is thine own, Lady. To aid any individual so personally, even one of the clan of Merten, is beyond my calling. Such partiality would be a great affront to the thousands of thy folk. Or then I should needs lead home every dog[65] that goeth astray, and bind every finger that pricks the needle."

"Yet," said Chrono, "you have come so far from Potomis merely to find us. Would you then leave us again, in no better state than you found us?"

Dreiton heaved a great sigh, and said, "This much I may do without inequity. I shall send my steeds to the coastlands of Vordót. They shall follow the straight route across the open sea, and shall come swiftly to that country. If you might follow them on the way, your guidance shall be sure."

Though Dreiton said this resignedly, yet in truth he had grown fond of Chrono, for among all the children of earth and air, Chrono alone evinced the love of his Sea-realm. He had come to respect Duono, as well, for that companion of Chrono was faithful and courageous, and had made himself the friend of the Seafolk for Ahten's sake. And he was charmed by Ahten, for there was none to compare with her among the daughters of the Sea; and she had no fear. These three had proven themselves doughty and determined beyond scores of their fellows, heroes among their Kindreds. So he wished them success in their quest, and determined in his heart that he would do them some future good if it were in his power.

Chrono bowed his head in thanks. Ahten crossed her hands over her heart in the salutation of her folk. Dreiton smiled on them, and said, "Fare well, then, ye sojourners upon my Sea! Set your course to the north, and follow my steeds as swiftly as you may, for they shall take but scant rest upon the journey! As for me, I must return to Merten and Aviah with word of your safety!"

So saying he took his leave, and descended into the waters of the Deep. Then he departed swiftly to the west, to bear good tidings to Merten.

---

65 I.e., a "seahound," or sea lion.

At this the steeds of Dreiton began to circle the boat eagerly, leaping from the waves and piping their impatience. Chrono shouted, "Quickly now! Set the sails to follow to the north, or they shall be off without us!"

"I shall hold them, if it be possible!" Ahten shouted. "But make haste!" Then she leapt once more into the waters and began to circle the boat with the dolphins.

Chrono and Duono at once set their sails and fixed their rigging, and taking the tiller he bent the rudders to a northward course, and took flight with the winds. At a word from Ahten the steeds of Dreiton were off, pouncing through the swells ahead of the prow as if in exaltation.

The winds from the west were fair and brisk, and filled the sails. So the ship skipped lightly across the waves, and followed the course of the dolphins fleetly. The silver steeds of Dreiton leapt before them and all about them, their cheerful eyes keeping watch on the vessel, and Ahten herself swam with them, leaping through the waves. Straight and true was their course, speedily making their way northward.

Northward they went, and the further north they reached, the more frigid and icy did the west winds grow, for winter truly was setting in. The waters about the ship seemed more gray and joyless. Bergs and floes from the Ice far to the west began to chase after them once again.

Until one day the airs changed, and warm blew the winds from the southeast. "The current of Merten, which shall guide us to Vordót!" Chrono announced. "The steeds of Dreiton have led us true, and our way at last is sure!"

So they set their mainsail square and took in the stud, for the wind now blew full from their stern to the northwest. The dolphins themselves followed the current, and no longer rested at night, but made their way straight and true across the deep.

In scant days the current grew less distinct, and curved away eastward. The long-absent seabirds first appeared, shrilling their greeting. Then ridges of land came into view: the hills and bluffs of Vordót which no eyes of Chrono's folk had beheld for many a thousand years, blue and misty upon the horizon and rising from the waters as if from beyond the edges of the world.

So Chrono rejoiced, for the goal of their quest at last stood before them. The steeds of Dreiton departed into the depths. Then Ahten returned to the ship, to the arms of Chrono. There she rested a little, and said, "Through so many trials and troubles have we come! Much have we born to reach these shores."

"But without you, all would have failed," Chrono replied. "My love for you has been a touchstone to guide me through all the years of my wanderings, but my esteem for you now surpasses even the heights of my love! May the Ádolthi have mercy on our plight, and give ear to our request!"

So came the long voyage of Chrono and Ahten to an end, and they reached at last the shores of Vordót beyond the Ice.

15. CHRONO AND THE SEAFOLK OF THE NORTH

This tale is told of the days when Chrono and Ahten arrived in the north, and how they sought there the boon of the Ádolthi and the Ídolthi.

For months Chrono and Ahten had journeyed by sea, along with Duono the companion of Chrono, seeking audience with the High Ones of the Terumani in the lands beyond the Ice, that they might by some stratagem or craft of those great ones be united at last. That journey had been long and full of hardship, for none had ever tried the course by sea; and they had been beset with trials of imprisonment, and storm, and deprivation, and disorientation.

But in the face of all obstacles, they succeeded at last, and reached the coasts of Vordót. There the current they had followed curved away to east, and so they departed from its course. They entered the cold waters of the north country. The short and frigid days of winter had arrived. Already small rafts of ice drifted lazily about them, and packs of ice could be seen clustering along the shoreline.

The coastlands of Vordót are rocky and dangerous for a long stretch, with cliffs black and sheer rising directly from the surf. There the waves crash endlessly upon the ragged foot of the cliffs, both at high tide and low. Few harbors or coves can be found along that coast secure enough to land a craft, and at this season the gathering ice made even those small landings unapproachable. Chrono set his anchors off shore that they might pause to decide their further course.

"According to the word of Merten, we should seek landfall at the outlet of the river C'heta," said Chrono. "We shall know it by the stained waters from the river running into the sea from a cleft in the bluffs; and if we can put to shore there, we shall find the folk of this country and may seek their aid."

"We have followed the current of Merten to its end. But from here, shall we find the river to the east or to the west?" asked Duono.

"That I cannot say or guess. And Merten did not say."

"The currents of the sea are not fixed as are the rivers of the land," Ahten said, "but diverge from their course by season or weather. One cannot be exact in stating where a current may lead a traveler at any given day or hour."

"So how shall we choose our course?" asked Duono.

"The easiest course would be to follow the winds eastward," Chrono replied. "Yet my heart tells me the lands we seek lie to the west."

Ahten then said, "Beneath the waves I might travel swiftly westward, unassailed by the winds, and scout our way. Wait here. If I find the earth-stained waters of C'heta, I shall bring back word straightway."

So it was decided, and she parted from them.

Now on the very day she departed, the sunlight fled, the sky dimmed to soulless gray, and a ceiling of cloud lowered to the top of the bluffs: then a bitter chill gripped the sea breeze, and flurries of snow and sleet began to pelt the ship. It was not long before ice began to encrust the rail and the mast, and to stiffen the sail of their vessel, weighting it so heavily that they could only with difficulty tack to catch the wind. Little rafts of pack ice circled about past them, and though they tried their best to divert it with poles, from time to time one would strike their hull with a threatening thud.

Then Chrono gazed after Ahten's course to the west, and he was troubled.

Four such miserable days was she gone, and on the fifth day she returned to them with news. "The waters of a great river stain the seas to the west." she said. "But the winds blow strongly from that quarter, and are cold. I deem that it shall take more than a week's sailing to bring us to that point. And whether it be the C'heta, or some other flood, I cannot say with certainty."

Duono looked about the frozen deck of their vessel, and said, "Our boat is heavy laden with ice. Ice such as we have never seen in the winters of the south. I fear that a single week could become two weeks, or more."

Ahten had come aboard the vessel to report to them, and Chrono feared at the look of her: she was pale, and she shivered, and her visage was wan and weary. "We have been reckless," he moaned, "and heedless of the hazard of these northern seas! Winter is descending upon us, and the waters here are frigid beyond even those beneath the Ice in the summer; it is beyond Ahten's ability to bear!"

So they compelled her to come into the ship's cabin at once, and warmed her with damp blankets heated by their brazier, and gave her warm water to drink, seasoned with herbs. But she shivered for hours before the warmth revived her, and even then she seemed weak and feeble.

"What shall we do?" asked Duono. "We cannot allow her to return to the sea in these icy waters, yet she cannot long bear the dry air."

"We shall need to provide warm water for her berth as best as we can, but we shall soon need to find fuel in plenty for our brazier. How we might manage that, when the shores of this country are unapproachable, I know not."

"Or," said Duono, "we might return to the warmer waters of the current from the south."

"But we could not remain there long, for we will soon need water and food," Chrono lamented. "Let us quickly be underway to the river C'heta. If the word of Merten is true, we shall find there a landing fit for going ashore. Let us hope those whom we meet in this country shall be inclined to aid us and bring us the fuel we need."

So they set out at once. But indeed, so strong were the opposing gales, and so heavy with ice had their vessel become, that they could mark but little progress. Much of their time was spent watching for the floes of sea ice which now often came drifting from the west before the cruel winds. They watched the unending bluffs to starboard: only with great doubt could they guess whether they even moved from their place in a whole day, more than a few scant miles. Ahten, going into the depths, might fare better at navigating their course, but they dared not send her away from the ship again.

So Ahten would stay aboard in the cabin as long as she could bear. They warmed the air with their brazier, and set a pot of water into the fire to make steam, that she might bear it longer. But at last she would need to return to her berth below the surface. Using sheets of sailcloth they contrived to enclose the space, and poured heated water about her, which would warm her for a little while.

For four days they tacked to the west, making but little progress. The winds did not change, nor did the icy weather abate. It was not long before the fuel they had aboard began to grow dangerously scant, and they could find no landing ashore where they might stop to gather wood: so Duono and Chrono began to consider once again dismantling the vessel itself for firewood.

At last Duono studied the shoreline, and he said, "All the elements oppose us on this course. I cannot see that we have made any progress toward C'heta at all."

Chrono replied, "It is no good. We must turn around and sail with the wind at our back, and hope to find landfall to the east. Perhaps the current of Merten will keep those shores less frigid, but if not, we must seek to return at once to the south."

Ahten opined as well, saying, "To do so would be to fail at our mission! And to abandon our hopes, after we all have so valiantly labored, and overcome so many trials!"

"But the safety of Ahten is of more weight," Chrono said to her tenderly. "If you should enter the long sleep, before you awaken I shall doubtless have departed the lands of Soria for that unknown country to which all my Kindred must in the end go! Then indeed would all hope be lost."

So Ahten at last agreed to this course. Chrono and Duono brought the ship about; the wind caught the heavy sail, and filled it so that ice cracked and fell from it in clattering chunks, and it pressed them swiftly eastward.

But Chrono's mood was dark. He sat at the stern of the vessel, gazing forlornly into the lost west, and sang a lamentation.

"I own the wailing of the weary waves,
The ceaseless sighing of the surging swells.
They drone a dreary dirge, a dream which fades,
And thrum a dying echo of heartbeat-knells.

"My song, a sigh of sorrowful lament
For happy hopes now hove astern.
My voice, a groan of grievous discontent
Where once the love of Sea did burn.

"The Sea! Which was the cradle of my joy,
The dame of every dream which I have dreamt;
What once she freely gave, she sweeps away!
And spurns me now with cold contempt.

"How cruel the clinging curse that hounds our quest,
Assailing us in endless waves of trial,
Assaying us in each ensuing test.
And threatens now to end it all.

"We've come too far to simply turn away,
When now our journey's perils seemed complete.
And so we rue this drear and dread delay!
To see success, but only grasp defeat!"

When Chrono had finished his song, Ahten came to him from her berth, and taking his hand in hers she said to him, "Do not sing so sadly nor grievously of our fortune. Perhaps at winter's end the waters may grow tolerable, and in a distant month we may make the journey without fear. If not, I shall return to the waters of the south, and you shall go on alone to appeal to the Ádolthi. It may yet come about that they shall hear your voice, even you alone, and they may yet have favor on you and upon our cause."

Now the voice of Chrono was yet sweet and pure: as it had set aflame the heart of Ahten in years long past, so even now it had reached across the waves of the sea, and was heard below by unseen ears. Then came a sea-maiden of the north to the surface, to hear better the singer of this mournful lament, and to see what form of soul sang so purely.

She beheld the ship of Chrono, and Chrono himself sitting at the stern, and she was amazed. No such vessel had ever before been seen in all the waters of her realm, nor had any voice of the children of the land ever sung so poignantly of the Sea. Yet she was afraid to approach, for her folk had no dealings or commerce with the children of the land.

But watching from afar she saw Ahten approach the son of the land familiarly to comfort him. Then her curiosity overwhelmed her, never having seen such familiarity between the Kindreds. Setting aside her caution, she drew near to the ship, and spoke.

"Hail, maiden of the sea, and son of the land! From what strange countries come ye into these waters on so strange a craft, and with such strange habits: and what is the meaning of this lament you have sung?"

Chrono drew back, astonished at her sudden appearance. Even Ahten herself was amazed in her turn: for the Seafolk of her realm knew nothing of the Seafolk of the north, nor had even Merten her father knowledge of that clan. Calling out to the sea-maiden she said, "Hail to thee! We have come from distant waters, away far to the south, beyond the Ice! Come, if thou wouldst! Join us on our vessel. We would speak with thee, if it pleaseth thee."

"But I am of the water-folk, and cannot bear the dry air."

Ahten encouraged her. "The mists of the sea shall guard thee for a spell, as they do me also. For I too, am a daughter of the Sea, and must return thither anon."

So the sea-maiden of the north took courage, and she drew herself aboard the vessel of Chrono and Ahten. She curled her legs under her and sat down on the deck across from them, keeping a nervous eye on them, and ready to leap into the sea at any sign of trouble. Her appearance was strange to them all. She was clad head to foot in a garment of leather: silvery in sheen, beautifully wrought with embroidery and cord-work. It fit her slender form like a second skin. Even her head and her hair were bound in a hood of this make, so only her face was revealed; her cheeks were ruddy with the cold of the winter winds across the deck.

The sea-maiden, for her part, observed everything about her with wonder in her eyes. Most of all at the apparition of Ahten, and of how that Trityn was found familiar with the children of the earth. She bowed her head gracefully and said, "I beg pardon of thee and of thy company, for such a strange vision have my eyes never beheld, to see sons of the land walking upon the Sea, and a daughter of the Sea in the arms of mortal. Nor have my ears ever heard a song of the sea sung by a child of the earth. Many questions would I ask of you. I shall have a marvelous tale to tell when I return to my clan tonight!" She introduced herself as Miriën of the clan of Eledoriën.

Ahten crossed her hands over her heart and said, "These sons of the earth whom you see are Chrono, the friend of the Seafolk; and Duono his companion and guide who hath seen us through many troubles. And I am Ahten, daughter of Merten the king of the Seafolk."

At this the sea-maiden wrinkled her brow and tipped her chin, saying "King of the Seafolk? I do not know Merten, nor Ahten his daughter. We know only Ontariën our lord, and Seneca our lady." Ontariën and Seneca were the chieftains of the Seafolk of the north: that kin had been sundered from their brethren since ancient days, and none alive knew their story, save perhaps Dreiton himself. It is said that Havui sent them into the world apart from the Seafolk of the south at the beginning of the world.

Chrono, beholding the blush of her cheeks, said to her, "Come into our cabin, and sit with us for a spell, if you would: there we shall be out of the chill of this wintry blast. We keep the air within warm and moist for Ahten's sake. There we shall gladly answer all your questions. We also may have much to learn of you, for your presence here is a surprise to us beyond belief!"

The sea-maiden hesitated, peering timidly at the canvas-clad frame which now comprised the ship's cabin. Never had any of her folk entered a house of the earth-Kindred, and she knew nothing of these strangers. But Ahten reassured her, saying, "Have no fear. These mortals are honorable, more so than many of my own Kindred!" Then she offered her a hand.

Were it not for the presence of Ahten, no persuasion could have compelled her, but the steamy warmth leaking from the door-flap, and the kindness of Ahten, settled her. Duono took the tiller that they might retreat into the cabin.

The sea maiden entered and stared in wonder at the glowing brazier and the steam which rose from its edges: never had she, or any of her folk, known fire. She raised her hands and approached it cautiously, absorbing its warmth.

"There are many mysteries about you which I must learn!" she said.

"Then sit," said Chrono, "and we shall answer all."

There Chrono and Ahten spoke at length with Miriën the sea-maiden, and they related to her the tale of the long plight of their separation, and how Chrono had at last been forgiven by his father, and had earned the respect of Merten the father of Ahten; how they had chosen to seek the counsel and gift of the High Ones of the Terumani in the northern countries, that perhaps they might finally be united. They told also of the many trials they had overcome to reach the northern Sea.

Then Chrono said, "It is for this very reason that I sang the lament which you have heard. For we have come a long way through endless trials, but now the bitter cold of this sea forces us to turn about, and to fail our quest after all. For Ahten's race is unable to bear these cold waters as are your folk."

At this Miriën laughed and said, "My folk? Think ye, we are so different from you? Or know ye nothing of winter in your own country?"

"Our winters are cold," said Chrono, "but of such a bitter clime as this we have no knowledge!"

Miriën laughed. "Then blame not the froward Sea, as thy song hath dared: but blame your own ignorance! I do not wonder at your current plight, for you are gravely ill-prepared for this clime!"

"Then the words have been rash which I uttered against the Sea that I love. It is not by choice, but by ignorance and chance that we have arrived so ill-prepared. Indeed, we had hoped to arrive in these seas long before the chill of winter, but many delays and hardships beset us along the way. Help us, if you can!" said Chrono. "And we shall be in your debt! By what magic do your folk bear these frigid seas?"

Miriën then gawked at the diaphanous gown of sea-mist which swirled about Ahten, and she said in wonder, "What is this strange and filmy garment? It is nearly as if thou didst wear naught at all to protect thyself from the cold waters!"

Ahten looked down upon her garment of sea-mist, and felt ashamed. "These garments are such as all my folk wear," she apologized, "and we know nothing else. They serve us in all seasons, warm and cool alike."

Miriën replied, "But I say that it is a wonder you have not frozen blue, and gone into the long sleep. Have you no pelts to keep you warm?"

She removed her hood, that she might show them its make. Then they perceived that the garment she wore was lined within with fur: for the Seafolk of the north wear the plush pelts of the seals of that country, turned to the inside. "In these garments our warmth is preserved, and the skin without shieldeth us from the chill of the waters. This attire alone makes tolerable the frigid seas of winter. Even thus attired, we seldom venture to the shallows in this time of year except to hunt and forage: the waters of the deep are cold, but not so bitter as these winter waters of the surface."

Ahten examined the hood of Miriën and said, "We indeed have no such apparel, and the making of such a thing is unknown to us." She warmed it over the fire and handed it back to Miriën.

Then Miriën said, "If Ahten shall come with me, my folk shall fit her with a garment such as this. I promise as well that all who meet thee shall be delighted to discover a cousin from the distant seas."

"Shall we set anchor and wait here?" Chrono asked.

Mirien protested. "If you would hear my word, I would counsel you to hurriedly seek safe landfall! Ice shall soon be forming even on the ceiling of the sea itself. If you do not reach haven before the coming of the ice, your vessel shall be further encumbered, and may soon be overwhelmed." In the chill of the winters of that age ice would cap the entire Sea of Vinteren each year, locking in the whole of the northern countries. For though the merciful breath of Wéodar brought springtime and summer to Vordót and Niyarc, the winters of the north were more bitter then than in these times.

"The haven we seek lies to the west, and to hurry against the winds is impossible."

"I do not know the haven ye seek, but verily, though the way is difficult and slow, it shall become yet more difficult if ye delay, unless this vessel can fly upon solid ice as well!"

So this plan was discussed, and it was decided that Chrono and Duono would proceed alone towards C'heta, seeking the dark-stained current flowing from that river. As for Ahten, she departed with Miriën to meet the Seafolk of the north, to revive herself among that clan and learn their winterlore. Afterwards would she return to Chrono at C'heta, if she did not even overtake them along the way: for her travel beneath the waves would be swifter than their travel against the winds and ice.

So Ahten left, and Chrono and Duono turned the ship about. As they proceeded westward the prediction of Miriën began to transpire: Ice became everything. Pack ice grew ever thicker in the seas about them, and they were hard-pressed to avoid colliding with the floating debris. Ice weighed down their sail; ribbons of ice trailed from the mast; a heavy crust of ice began to build on the prow and the rails. The deck became slick and slippery with the stuff. The wind and the snowy blasts of the sea plagued them as well, so that they were always cold, damp, and miserable beyond bearing. The cabin, now a mere tent of canvas, offered little protection from the weather, so they were forced to take refuge in the dark of the hold.

Thus the days passed, slow and frigid, while little progress was made. The bitter air began to suck hope from the heart of Chrono. His fears grew that they would be frozen into the sea before ever they reached the haven at C'heta.

One day at last the clouds cleared, the bright sun shone on the glistening gray sea, and the freezing wind died to a whimper. The mast sagged on its spar. Chrono and Duono stood by the rail and stared across the flat sea before them. "My heart is gladdened by the sun," Chrono said, "but how shall we proceed, lacking wind to fill our sail?"

Almost at that moment he rejoiced to hear the voice of Ahten calling to him from the sea. Stumbling to the rail, he gazed across the waves, and saw that she had found them again along the way. Now she was clad as the northern seafolk, and a radiant smile brightened her eyes: the brightest he had beheld in many days of their hard journey.

"Hail, Chrono, my beloved!" she called. "Behold! I come bringing friends from the Northern Sea!"

Then he saw that Miriën had returned with her. Peering into the waters, he saw below the surface, too wary to show themselves above the waves, a company of the seafolk teeming about the ship.

Miriën alone raised her head and shoulders from the sea and called out to Chrono, "My folk indeed rejoiced to meet our lost relation from distant seas: as we gathered to hear her story, all were enchanted by the tale of Ahten and the Friend of the Terumani. If you will pardon our impudence, many folk of my clan wished to see this wonder with their own eyes!"

Chrono laughed heartily, and said, "The clan of Miriën, and all the seafolk of the north, are more than welcome to gawk at our folly!"

"But what of thy vessel?" called Miriën. "For I had told my folk that I saw it with my own eyes, running at great pace upon the sea, as swift as the seahounds. Yet here ye sit, stagnant upon the waters. You are yet a long journey from the river mouth: if ye make not haste, ye shall ne'er arrive there before the winter ice locks you in its grip!"

"Alas, but the going has been contrary," said Chrono. "We need the wind to sail, and when last we met, you saw us running with the wind at our backs. But turning about, the eastward winds have opposed us for all these days. And ice, as you see, has bogged us down yet further. Now to add further insult, the wind has died altogether, and we have no draft to fill our sail at all! We might wait for the winds to rise again, but the spreading ice alarms me."

"That will never do!" Miriën squeaked. "Ye must make progress, and quickly, before ye are trapped or crushed." Miriën then laughed in her turn, and said, "If the wind hath failed thee, let the friends of Ahten aid thee! Wait here, and I shall return apace."

Chrono looked up at his limp and ice-laden sail and said, "As to waiting, it seems we have little choice in that!"

Miriën replied merrily, saying, "If my folk have any sway, that shall soon change." Then she disappeared with a ripple below the glittering waves to confer with her clan.

Soon the seafolk disappeared from view, darting away to the east. Ahten came aboard, and passed on their instructions to Chrono and Duono, saying, "Take in the sails. Then take every length of rope you can find, and make them fast to the cleats: fasten them to the ship in any way you can. Then cast the ends into the sea. And I think we shall have another miracle to save us."

So they did as she said. When they had finished with this task, they waited, for there truly was nowhere to go. At length the seafolk of Miriën returned.

With them, however, came powerful sea-beasts: like dolphins in appearance, but larger and heavier, with round heads and small eyes. They were as white and brilliant as the floes of ice which floated lazily by. Each of these beasts wore around its girth a yoke of leather, studded with rings formed of a substance like pearl. They rose to the surface, puffing steam from their blowholes and waiting patiently as the folk of Miriën's clan took the ropes from Chrono's ship, and fastened them to the collars of their beasts.

"What are these creatures?" Duono asked in wonder.

"We have no name for them," Ahten replied, "but the folk of the North call them their *indriëthin*, and they use them to draw their burdens. They have never been tested towing a ship on the sea, but they are powerful!"

When all of the beasts of the Seafolk had been harnessed to the ship, a command was given below the waves, and the ropes of Chrono's vessel drew taut, groaning at the strain. Soon all the creatures pulled together, side by side: Chrono felt the deck move beneath his feet with a lurch, and the vessel began to glide to westward across the placid waters, the surging white bodies of the *indriëthin* cleaving the waves before them.

Chrono exulted. "If only we had had such servants at our beck from the day we left Mizgad! How much easier would our journey have been!"

Ahten replied, "We do not know them in the south. Even if we had such beasts, each one follows the lead of its own master, so we would needs have traveled with a whole company of my own folk. Moreover they take years of training to learn their tasks. But we can at least be thankful for their aid at our time of need."

So Chrono and Duono relaxed for a space, and spent the hours watching the coastline move past them, or gazing at the team of sea-beasts before them in wonder. Rafts of ice floated silently past them, and Duono quipped, "It would be a cruel irony if we were to be sunk now after surviving so much." But the Seafolk were watchful, and careful to avoid these hazards.

Throughout that day, and into the evening, the *indriëthin* plowed their way forward and westward through the icy waters of that coastline. The sun had set, the sky was a deep blue-black, and the stars had begun to glimmer in the cold skies above, when the sharp eyes of Duono spotted a gleam of golden light landward, from beyond the bluffs to the north. Pointing to it he called Chrono and said, "Can this be the Lamp of Dúran spoken of by Merten?"

Chrono strained his eyes to scrutinize it. Although far away to the north and difficult to discern, it appeared indeed to be beacon atop a distant pillar of rock on the horizon. "If so, we must be close to our goal. And not a moment too soon. Already the ice grows thicker around us, and we will soon be unable to make any progress at all."

The sea-beasts began to turn slowly to the north under the guidance of their handlers, bringing the ship around to face the shoreline. The twinkling of lamplight began to appear in places in the highlands above the rocky bluffs, and palely glowing wisps of smoke drifted skyward from hearth or fireside. As the ship entered the effluence of the C'heta Chrono felt the motion of the waves alter: a change in the pattern of the swells, and a smoothness like a pathway in the sea.

The air was chill, but still no wind blew. Except for the lapping of water on the hull, the creaking of the planks, and the occasional puffs of breath of the *indriëthin*, all was silence.

The sea-beasts slowed their pace, and came to a drifting halt. The tethers grew slack, and Chrono's vessel began to drift. Miriën and Ahten together rose from the waves and clambered aboard the vessel. "I can taste the muddy waters of C'heta on my breath," Ahten said. "The folk of Miriën's clan would ask leave to depart here. The Gate of C'heta lies before us. If we proceed to the north we shall see it as a great gap in the cliffs. Beyond it lies a wide bay. We may make landfall there, and our sea journey will be at an end."

Miriën added, "Ye shall be safe there. The waters of that bay are still, and though it will also ice over in winter's chill, the crushing floes of sea-ice do not enter that bay."

Chrono bowed to Miriën. "Already our debt to you and your clan is beyond measure. But we shall not be able to put in to shore until the winds begin to blow once more. We are helpless here amid the floating rafts of ice."

Miriën frowned. "We would gladly aid thee further, but our folk despise the muddy waters of C'heta. Nor do we wish to be seen of the strange children of the earth who wait beyond that cleft. Seldom do any of our folk enter that bay beyond the Gate."

Ahten turned to Miriën. "The night is falling swiftly, and the moon will be dark as well. Might ye bring us safely into the bay by night and leave us adrift?"

"I will speak with my clan," Miriën said. "Perhaps when the rising tide brings clear waters into the bay, and the last light goeth dark on the highlands above we might be so bold. But we shall needs go stealthily and in silence."

Chrono said, "I will gladly obey your every whim if we at last get to shore, safe from the ice at journey's end!"

The folk of Miriën agreed to this plan, so Chrono and his companions settled in to wait. The Seafolk kept watch on the expanding ice floes, preparing to divert them with the help of their *indriëthin* if the need arose, but in the still air and gentle current there was little movement of the ice. Nothing more than an ever-increasing chill to the air warned them that the seas were slowly freezing, while a rime of ice was gradually building on the hull at the waterline.

At last a dim crescent moon arose over the sea, and soon the last of the ridgetop lights twinkled out into blackness. Ahten reported to the seafolk below: the lines of Chrono's vessel groaned and went taut once again, the frame of the vessel groaned, and the ship began to move shoreward.

Cliffs loomed black before them, and the unnerving rumble of surf reached their ears. When it seemed they were bound for disaster on the rocks ahead, a great cleft was suddenly sighted in the blackness of the cliff-wall, splitting the bluffs as if riven by the blade of a vast ax. A spit of sandy shoals extended into the sea from the eastern bank, wearing a skirt of ice which glowed in the dim light. The boat was drawn cautiously to the west of this spit, making for the gap in the bluffs.

The Gate itself soon towered over them to the right and left, mighty pilasters of barren rock. The sea-beasts drew them in beyond the seawall, where the canyon opened into a bowl like a great, round lake surrounded by dark bluffs. Through its midst the current of the C'heta swept a clear path through thin crusts of broken ice: thousands of plates drifting about the quiet waters of the bay. The bay was round, as if punched into the highlands by a great hammer. Indeed in after years the legend of the Mizans claimed that that is nearly the truth: that Vélopar foresaw the need of Chrono, and was angered that no safe landfall was to be found all along that northern coast. In frustration he himself hammered the great bay at the mouth of C'heta into the rocks.

The sides of the bowl were broken into strata cascading like stair steps, glazed with layers of snow. Even in the dim light these glowed softly like frosting on a layered cake. No sign of home or house could be spotted within the bowl, but not even the eyes of Duono could hope to pierce the corners of the dark.

The *indriëthin* stopped their progress, and the vessel came to a drifting halt in the current of the river. The seafolk appeared at the side of their beasts, unhitching the creatures from Chrono's lines. All was done in silence.

Miriën and Ahten again rose before them and drew themselves aboard the deck. Miriën gazed nervously at the dark ridges surrounding them. "Thus far, and no further, may we draw you," she whispered. "Henceforth ye must depend upon the wind again, or anchor here in the midst of the bay where the waters are still."

One by one the ropes went slack, and Chrono and Duono began to draw them into the vessel. As the boat began to drift slowly with the current of the C'heta, Chrono took the tiller, and with a dull crunching against the prow he guided her out of the current into the ice of the eastern shore. The vessel came to a stop and stood perfectly still in the waters.

Ahten sighed deeply. "We have reached the shores of Niyarc at last, and our long journey by sea is at an end!"

Duono, too, was astonished. "Never would I have imagined such a journey was possible! What we have accomplished is a marvel."

Chrono and Ahten then turned to Miriën and embraced her warmly. "In the end we have once again depended on the kindness of others to see us through," Chrono said. "How can we repay you and your folk for this wondrous favor?"

"We wish nothing more than to be a part of your great tale when it is sung in ages yet to come!" she replied. Her eyes darted about at the dark walls of the surrounding crater. "We must away. Fare ye well, and may the good will of the Terumani find you at last!"

She then slipped into the waters. The sea-beasts of the clan descended swiftly out of sight, and the Seafolk of the North followed into the depths. Miriën appeared at the stern and waved cheerily, then she also dipped below the swells, and departed.

So it was that Chrono and Ahten, with their companion Duono, completed the first sea-voyage in the realm of Soria, in an age long before the Mizans came to rule the seas. For many years the Mizans passed this tale on to their children, naming Chrono the Seafarer as their founder.

As for Chrono and Ahten, their tale was not yet at an end. They had reached Niyarc at last beyond hope, but the trail to Liaibíri and the Ádolthi yet lay before them.

16. CHRONO AND THE TRAIL TO LIAIBÍRI

This tale is told of Chrono and Ahten, and Duono their companion, when their arduous sea-journey had at last been completed. They had arrived at the shores of Niyarc in the realm of Vordót, seeking to find the Halls of the Ádolthi to ask boon of the High Ones who dwelt there.

The sky brightened late in the bay at the mouth of the C'heta, after a long northern night, and Chrono and Duono awoke to find the ship settled firmly in place: no hint of motion disturbed the hull. Wondering at the strangeness of this circumstance they rose hurriedly and threw open the cabin.

The tide had gone out overnight, and a layer of white ice now reached out from the shore, enfolding them and holding them fast. Though the ice was not thick, it would be possible simply to walk to shore.

Ahten had taken her rest in the deeps beyond the bay, since the shallow waters of the bay were murky and cold. She returned with the sunlight, however, and punched through the ice to reach them—but she did so laughing and in good humor, and she joined them on deck. "We have reached the shores of Vordót at last," she said. "What is our next step?"

"We must make our way to the Halls of the Terumani, of which Liaibíri is the greatest." Chrono frowned. "But we know nothing of this country. I do not think it is near at hand. Our ship will be useless on the swift waters of C'heta. Can you yourself travel the rivers and streams, or take the land routes?"

Ahten considered the question thoughtfully. "The rivers are turbid and unpleasant. They leave a foul taste to my kind. And such coursing waters are difficult to navigate. Even the næads remain mostly by the quiet pools and backwaters of their domains. But what must be done I will attempt to do."

"Then should we get so far, how will we enter the Halls of the Terumani? Can you leave the waters of your realm?"

Ahten replied less confidently. "I can remain hours from the sea before there is any danger, as you know, if we might do as we have done on the ship: provide vapor and moist coverings in which to take refuge. It is not pleasant, but it will do. When we have reached the Halls of the Terumani I am confident they will provide what is necessary."

Chrono looked dismally at the ice-encrusted bay and the snowy heights around them. "It is unfortunate we have been so delayed as to arrive in the midst of winter," he lamented. "I fear there is nothing we can do to provide warmth and moisture for you. Anything moist will surely harden to ice within minutes. We must go speedily from the waters to the Halls."

"Then we must discover a water route which will bring us near to the Hall we seek," said Ahten. "Of that we are as yet ignorant."

"Good enough," said Chrono. "When we have refreshed ourselves we shall hike up to the highlands above the bay, to seek aid and guidance from the inhabitants of this country, as Merten your father advised us."

Duono had been keeping watch as they spoke, and he now pointed to the bluffs ascending from the beach before them and said, "Such a climb may be unnecessary, as it appears the folk of this country have already discovered our presence!"

The bluffs rose steeply to the highlands, and no houses or huts could be discerned within the bowl itself, but a party could be seen descending well-trodden paths which led down to the shore, pointing at the boat and its occupants, and conferring among themselves. The words of their speech could not be puzzled out. All were clad in peculiar, fur-lined jackets and leather breeches, unlike the long, flowing cloaks of wool worn by Chrono and Duono. More folk could be seen standing on the ridgeline peering down into the depression.

Duono spoke quietly to Chrono when he spotted them. "We should have arms at hand. We do not know whether they will be hostile, as were the Cerites of the Hirna. I for one would not choose to repeat our adventure there!"

"Nor I," said Chrono. "Nor do we know their superstitions concerning the Seafolk. I would entreat Ahten to conceal herself within the cabin, or to slip unseen into the waters, until we are assured of their intentions."

"I shall remain aboard with you," Ahten said. "But at your bidding I shall retreat from sight for now."

The folk of that country were Sorites, as were Chrono and Duono. But they were the Donites: the remnant of the Sorites who had remained in the north when their kinsmen had migrated to the warmer regions of the Southrealm.[66] Uncounted years had passed since the Ice had blanketed Batack and divided them from their kinsmen. In that long era the Donites had grown softer in feature and physique, and in many other ways had diverged from the Sorites of the south. The Plateosites, for their part, had grown ruddy and lanky in that time. So it was that Chrono and Duono appeared to the folk of that country to be strange and outlandish, and the Donites who came down to them seemed as if from another Kindred.

Chrono took his place on the deck near the bow of his ship, looking down upon the stony beach beyond the ice—to the Donites a tall and imposing figure. Their company gathered on the shore, remaining at a cautious distance. Some of this number ventured forward a few paces and addressed him in cautious voices.

Chrono could not understand a word of their speech. He looked dumbly to Duono for advice, but Duono shrugged. Chrono turned to the party on the

66 On this matter, see the tale "The Desertion of Steggan" page 68 above.

shoreline and nervously addressed them in his own tongue. "Hail to the folk of Niyarc! We come seeking the friendship of the folk of this country. Do you greet us in peace?"

In the long ages since the Sundering that folk had been encompassed by the Pleïstians, and all of them had at length come to speak the language of Dôni which had been given to that Kindred. They stared at one another blankly at the strange speech of Chrono.

There were those among them, however, who heard the words of Chrono and said, "They speak the language of the Terumani! Do we have here any of our sages who speaks the forgotten tongue of our forebears?" There were as yet some few who had passed down the ancient tongue for many generations: These were sometimes called upon to speak with the terumani who still dwelt thereabouts.

One of their elders was pushed forward from the crowd. His back was unbent, but his voice quavered as he spoke. "Whence came ye into our country, appearing as if risen from the Sea itself?" he queried. "What manner of folk are you? Are you Seafolk from the depths?"

The language of Chrono, and even Ahten's own dialect, had through many ages of separation diverged from the tongue of the elder, and his accent was strange and difficult. Yet Chrono discerned that the elder was speaking his own tongue, and he said, "No, we are descendants of Sorios, as you yourselves. We traveled here upon the waters of the Sea in the vessel you see before you." Chrono was afraid to announce the presence of Ahten until he knew the disposition of the crowd. "Do you then fear the Seafolk?" he asked.

The elder did not translate this question, nor wait to get an answer from his companions. "We know nought of that folk," he said, "and neither fear them nor love them."

"Then if you are a fair-minded and judicious folk, we welcome you to join us on our vessel. There we shall sit and talk. You shall learn our long and baleful tale, which has yet to find its end."

When this message had been passed on, the rabble conferred among themselves, and chose a small party to go aboard.

They entered into the cabin, and their amazement redoubled: never had any of that folk seen one of the Tritynoi, who were little more to them than a rumor and a fairy tale. The beauty of Ahten, moreover, flustered even the Donites, who are the comeliest of all the Tribes.

Ahten bowed her head graciously, and Chrono spoke, "This is Ahten, a princess of the Seafolk from far distant waters. I myself am Chrono, born a chief among my own folk in the lands of the Southrealm, beyond the Ice. We have come across the sea through many trials to reach this country, for we have been told that the Great Ones of the Terumani maintain their Halls in Vordót and Niyarc, and we seek a great favor from those lords."

Thus the story of Chrono and Ahten was related to the elders of the Sorites. All were amazed that such a curiosity should arrive in their land, and long did they sit together and converse, for they wished as well to know all that Chrono and Ahten, and their companion Duono, could tell them of the lands of the Southrealm, and of their long-sundered kin.

At last Chrono said to them, "Merten, the lord of the Seafolk of the south, advised us to seek the aid of the folk of this country. Are you able to guide us to the Halls of the Terumani? We have little hope to pay you for your trouble, for everything we may have bartered has been lost through our trials at sea."

The elders replied, "It is a custom among our Tribe to aid the traveler, all the more so when they have arrived among us bringing news of distant kin we had long ago forgotten. But few there be, if any could be found at all, who have traveled to the Halls of the Terumani. For the Terumani in these days are retiring and reclusive, and mind their own business among themselves. We seldom see sign of them and have little to do with them."

"We shall travel alone if need be, but we do not know the way."

"We can send you on the paths toward Niyarc. Perhaps ye may find others along the way to guide you further. But ye should know that when ye have gone beyond the marches of our own country ye shall find none but the Pleïstians: a strange and eldritch Kindred who have no knowledge of the ancient speech. We cannot promise their aid."

"If you can direct us as far as you are familiar, we shall somehow find our own way from there." So the Donites sat and described the directions and the paths which would lead northward to the Halls of the Terumani. As they spoke Duono busily scratched signs in the manner of the journey-staffs, hoping to make record to guide their way. But he soon began to frown, and at last he stopped and said, "If what you describe is true, our paths will bring us on a long trail, many days eastward and far inland. How shall Ahten attend us along the way? She is Trityn and cannot be so far from the water."

Chrono then spoke with the elders, saying, "Ahten has born many troubles and hardships to come with us thus far. Is there no sea route, or even a path of rivers or streams we might follow, by which she might accompany us to meet with the Ádolthi?"

The elders frowned and said, "The Hall of Liaibíri lies inland, near the mountains of the far north, far from the Sea, and far even from the great rivers of this country. The streams and rivulets will all be frozen this time of the year, many of them frozen solid. Even the rivers may freeze over. If you would go there, you must take roads and trails of dry land. We know no other way!"

Ahten then sighed and said to Chrono, "So I had feared before ever we left Mizgad, though I had not counted on the winter freeze. Yet I chose the risk and do not regret the hardships of the journey."

Duono said, "Had you not been with us, Lady, we would never have succeeded in our journey, and may not have survived at all. You have already proven your worth many times over!"

The elders of the Donites said, "Alas that we have neither craft nor magic to aid you in this matter. But whatever we can do, we shall. You shall not leave us empty-handed, but you shall be well-provisioned when you set forth."

Promising to return with more aid, they departed and went on their way.

Chrono and Duono spent several days in the Bay of the C'heta fretting over this matter as they prepared for their journey. The Donites in the mean time had quickly spread their tale throughout the region, and many came to see this curiosity and gawk at them. They were in awe of Ahten, and there was no want of visitors coming to do homage to her and bring her little gifts. But they brought gifts as well for both Chrono and Duono. Warm leather jackets were brought, with linings of fur like those of the Donites' make. Others provided a wealth of trail rations: packs with smoked meats and salted fish; dried fruits; hardtack, and other fare for the journey; and a sled to bear their provisions.

A journey-staff was made to aid them as well. In that age there were no maps among any of the Kindreds of Toë, and the written word was a dim vision of the far future. But the Kindreds of the north had preserved the art of making journey-staffs, to guide travelers on their way, and it had changed little from the craft which Duono also knew. So the Donites found a trail-master of their folk, and they prepared a journey-staff for him; for the destination they placed the sign of Liaibíri. This sign the Pleïstians also would know, that perhaps they might be made to understand, and be moved to help the sojourners on their way.

The day when they must choose their course could not be avoided. Chrono, Duono and Ahten sat together in the drafty cabin of their boat and conferred on the matter. "We must bring the Terumani here to Ahten," Chrono said. "I shall go alone. If Ahten must remain behind, Duono shall remain as well to ease her stay. Then he might also restore our ship as he waits."

"Nay, but Duono must go with you!" Ahten said. "Duono is your trail-master: only he knows how to read the journey-staff, and he has great skill in navigating unknown country. I shall remain behind by the sea, to watch over the ship and care for it. For we may yet need it again."

"Ahten is right," Duono said. "I have been your companion from the start. And I think the Donites of this country will not leave her lonely!"

Ahten smiled. "They shall help me rebuild our boat. And I shall wait patiently for word from you. Or for the coming of the Terumani."

So as there was nothing else to be done, it was decided that Chrono and Duono would depart together.

At last all was in readiness for the journey. Chrono and Duono hoisted their packs to prepare for the climb up from the bay, but Chrono halted and turned once more to bid Ahten farewell. They fell upon one another's neck, sorrowing bitterly to be parted after their long journey together.

Then Ahten sang a lament, saying,

"How hard to send thee off on thy campaign,
And see thee square the back to me again:
Thy footprints pointing from this hopeful shore,
To other realms I never may explore.

So far together we have made our way,
Through endless toil, trial and delay.
Side by side, and with one precious goal,
Striving jointly, as a single soul.

And now to part again! How cruel the joke!
Such damned absurdities we must invoke!
That gain can only come through poverty,
And severance be the path to unity.

And yet this lot I mustn't curse nor hate,
But I must set our hopes on thee, and wait."

Chrono said, "Do not lose heart. I shall bring the Terumani here to you, even if I must convince stubborn Ologéo himself. Fortune has met us repeatedly along the way. It may be that Havui himself has brought us to this brink, and will not abandon us." Then he turned stoically, and ascended the trail to where their sled awaited them.

For some days they traveled in the country of the Donites. This was a well-settled land of friendly and curious folk like themselves, though few could be found who spoke the Sorite tongue. It was a country of rocky hills, bright in its winter jacket of snow, patched with dark stands of wood and weald. Stockades and homesteads stitched the terrain together, rough rail fences enclosing yards and courts around mound-like, turf mantled houses. Wearing the leather jackets they had been given by their hosts they attracted but little attention as they went. They followed well-traveled roads, clear and smooth, though icy and hard.

The Lamp of Dúran on the Spire of Dimmeltor burned yellow in the distance, guiding them surely according to the marks of the journey-staff, glowing reassuringly both day and night. But this beacon they soon set behind them, as the staff directed them beyond it to less-distinct paths northward, then arcing eastward away from the ravine of the River C'heta.

The trail from there became ever more difficult to follow as they left the settled country of the Donites, even with the guidance of the journey-staff: in that season snow covered all the land, and many of the signs and markings of the way were obscured. The weather, as well, soon turned bitter once again, with blowing snow and freezing fog to veil their vision. The hours of daylight were short, and the nights very long: with each day's journey the hours of darkness grew longer and more frigid. The hours in which they could travel were few and troublesome.

They followed the guidance of the journey-staff for a count of days, while the undulating hills they had first encountered grew gradually more craggy, and the going more difficult. Few travelers were abroad, so the trails were untrodden and hidden in the snow. At last even Duono could only with difficulty read the signs of the country. He halted at last at a ridgeline, and gazed ahead through the murk across a landscape of indistinguishable rock, hills, and great boulders; all was concealed beneath a cloak of uniform white. Then he said to Chrono, "I cannot be sure of my way. If I read the signs incorrectly here, we may go far astray into rugged country ahead, and spend many days backtracking to find our way again. It would be prudent to seek aid from the folk who dwell hereabouts, if that is possible."

But by then their trail had taken them out of the country of the Donites, the Sorites of the north: along the way they had begun to encounter here and there a strange folk: tall and brawny; mangy with shaggy hair, and beards upon their faces and necks, who had stared at them from under heavy brows as they passed. Chrono said to Duono, "These must surely be the Pleïstians: the unknown folk of the north of whom we have been told. Shall we seek aid from among them?"

"I see no better option. Let us show ourselves friendly and mild, and perhaps they will see fit to accept us."

There were many small hamlets and villages in the region, and it wasn't long before they came upon one of these. The homes of the Pleïstians were different than those of the Donites: square buildings of lumber and clay, with steep, heavily-thatched roofs that descended nearly to the level of the alleys, swept clean of the recent snowfall. Many of them were built right up against their neighbors, clustering together in tight-knit community around an open, central market square.

Chrono and Duono entered the village nervously, and made their way along a narrow, muddy street to the market. Here they found several villagers warming themselves at an open fire: for the first time they could see clearly the measure of that Tribe. For a moment they hung back in the shadows of the alley observing them. As it happened, that district was home to the imposing Menothians. Even in those ancient days, the Menothians were taller than any Plateosite by a cubit or more, and mighty in limb and sinew, so that they appeared as daunting as Giants to Chrono and Duono. "Dare we disturb these titans?" Duono whispered, "I fear if things do not proceed peaceably we shall come out the worse for it!"

The Menothians had not yet spotted them, and seemed to be in the midst of lighthearted conversation, laughing and chatting among themselves. Chrono said, "They do not appear to be a threat. I shall do as you see best. If the danger of losing our way in the wildlands outweighs our fear of these Pleïstians, let us proceed."

So Duono hailed them. The speech of Duono was strange to the Menothians, and his form unfamiliar: for he had neither the language nor the appearance of the Donites the Menothians knew. They stopped their conversation in surprise: they arose as one and glared at the newcomers, suddenly menacing and suspicious.

Duono took courage and bent his knee before them, imploring them in his own tongue to receive them, hoping they might understand his manners if not his words. "We are travelers on a long road from distant lands, and we seek to find the Hall Liaibíri of the Ádolthi." He then presented the journey-staff and, pointing to the destination sign, he said, "Can you aid us on our way?"

The Menothians questioned him in a strange tongue, like that of the Donites but still harsher in ring and tone. But neither party could understand the other. Nevertheless at the word "Liaibíri" the Menothians were roused, and they began to converse intensely among themselves.

At last a decision was reached, and three members of that party stepped forward. One of them examined the journey-staff once more: stabbing at the sign with a hairy finger he repeated the word Liaibíri, and waved a massive hand beyond the village towards the east. Then he clapped them on the shoulders, nodded vigorously, and took hold of the harness of their sled. With another nod of his head he and his two companions headed out of the village to the open trails. With gestures and a spate of incomprehensible words he urged Chrono and Duono to follow. Chrono and Duono glanced at each other doubtfully, then shrugged and joined them.

Little could be said along the way, for the Menothians had no interpreter. On a hard path northward these Menothians led Chrono and Duono, stopping only late in the evening, when they found lodging in a rude village along the way. Here they were warmed at the hearth of their host, and were given a hot stew, warm bread, and spiced wine, all of which Chrono and Duono accepted gratefully. When all had consumed their fill the Menothians sat together by the fire in conversation, and Chrono and Duono were shown to a small room warmed against the winter chill by a brazier on a stone hearth, where a dry bed awaited them, piled high with furs and woolen blankets.

As they settled into the room Chrono said, "These Pleïstians have proved themselves hospitable beyond our expectations or hopes. Though surely they know we have little hope of repaying them, they have gone to great lengths to aid our journey, and have provided more comfort to weary strangers than if we had been their own familiar friends."

Duono cautioned, "But can we be sure of their aid? We do not share a language. How can we know they have even understood our objective?"

Chrono replied, "Our hosts have repeatedly assured us by word and gesture that they have understood that we seek Liaibíri."

"Nevertheless," said Duono, "if I read the marks of the journey-staff correctly, the path we are on appears to diverge from the signs and marks of the staff. I fear these Pleïstians may lead us astray."

Chrono said, "For what cause might they guide us falsely? If they wished to rob us, they have had ample chance before now, and certainly they would have had no reason to show us such hospitality as this night."

Duono shrugged. "Whether they lead us astray by design or by mischance, I cannot say. But we should surely be heading to the east by this time, while the paths we are being led on are taking us northward."

Chrono said, "There may assuredly be more than a single road to Liaibíri. Let us be on guard, and see what tomorrow will bring. But for now," he said, settling down into the pile of furs, "I shall enjoy the most comfortable night I have spent in many a long and tiresome day!"

The next morning they awoke before the sun, and when they had broken fast on a meal of warm bread thick with butter, the Menothians went out upon the trail once again, and taking up the sled, they gestured emphatically for them to follow northward into the hill country. Although Duono objected privately to Chrono, they had little choice but to follow. So their paths brought them into steep, snow-draped ridges, while the Menothians plodded tirelessly on, stopping only occasionally to cheerily encourage their retinue to follow.

Now it so happened that Verias, the Guardian of the Tribe of Menoth, had a Hall not far from that place, which he called Tryndom. It was carven from the granite dome of a round hill, in the middle of a flourishing wood called the Grove of Verias: in older times this grove had been the whole of his domain and interest. In those days Verias was not yet surnamed Teruman, for in truth Verias was neither Ádoleth nor Ídoleth, nor one of the High Ones of the Terumani at all, but a mere dræad of the grove which bore his name. But being ambitious and zealous, he had built his Hall Tryndom there among the Menothians, after the manner of the Ádolthi; and there he would confer at times with the elders of that Tribe: for he loved Menoth the patriarch of that Tribe, and his design was to make that Tribe great in the land of Soria. And if his own name might be augmented thereby, as well, so much the better.

This grove lay to the north, over rugged terrain through the wintry hills. It was to this Hall that the Menothians conveyed Chrono and Duono, for Verias was the only teruman they knew, and they trusted he would be able to help the travelers.

But none of this could they explain to Chrono and Duono. Another whole day they trekked, until some hours before nightfall they entered the Grove of Verias, and ascending the hill they pointed excitedly to the entry portal of Tryndom: this was a great arch of alabaster which Verias had built into the hillside near the top of the dome, carven skillfully with ornament of vines and scrollwork, and gated with a pair of imposing bronze doors embellished with sculpted panels and gilt with shining gold. The keystone was graven with the bust of a mammoth, the emblem of Menoth's Tribe.

On the porch before this portal the Menothians tethered the sled, and called out for Verias.

This place was clearly a Hall of Teruman, for no such structures could the Kindreds of Toë build in those days. "Can it be that we have so soon reached our destination," Chrono said, "and come to the Hall of Liaibíri?"

Duono frowned and stared at the journey-staff. "It cannot be! Unless the Donites who sent us on our way have deceived us, themselves. For the journey-staff they provided tells us that our paths should still be bringing us a count of days far to the east. And we have followed not a single mark of this staff since leaving the village of the Pleïstians!"

Shortly Verias appeared at his door and welcomed his guests.

Though Verias was not of the Terumani, yet he dressed and lived as do the High Ones of the Ádolthi: Unlike the wood-nymphs and sprights, who dress in simple garments of nature befitting their own settings, Verias wore a robe of white trimmed with blue, and over it a winter cloak of woven wool died a shimmering silvery gray. On his head was a filigree of ivory, and he wore ivory rings on his fingers. He ushered them into the room, standing tall and proudly, with one arm behind his back, nodding as each of his guests passed him.

The Menothians bowed to him as they entered, explaining to him that they had come upon these travelers in their village, and that they seemed to be seeking the Terumani in Liaibíri. At the name of Liaibíri Verias' attention was roused, for he was ever watchful for any pretext to insinuate himself among the High Ones in Liaibíri.

"Why then have you brought them to me?" he asked, though inwardly he was flattered.

"We cannot ourselves offer them aid, for we have no business in that far region," they said, "But we cannot explain this to the strangers, as we cannot comprehend their speech. Perhaps you will have knowledge of their tongue?"

Verias was puzzled by this remark. There were many dialects in Niyarc and Vordót, but it was rare to find any who could not use the Donish speech of the Pleïstians. Only one other possibility came to mind, unlikely as it might be: All the terumani speak Sorian, for the tongue of the terumani was the first speech given to the Kindreds of Toë by Wenda. So Verias turned his attention to Chrono and Duono, and in the Sorite tongue he asked, "Do you speak the language of the terumani?"

Chrono and Duono had stood by fidgeting uncomfortably as this conversation took place, but at Verias' question they roused at once. His accent was strange to them, but they were able at once to understand his speech. "We are Sorites from the Southrealm!" Chrono declared. "The tongue we speak is common among those Tribes, and the only one we have known."

Verias was incredulous. "The Southrealm?" he asked. "From the realm beyond the Ice of Vélopar? How is this possible?"

So Chrono explained concerning the vessel he had built, and the long journey they had carried out. Then he introduced himself and Duono. "And missing from our party is a third: Ahten the sea-maiden, who could not travel the paths of dry air with us."

When Verias heard the name of Chrono he became all the more attentive. He thanked the Menothians for their service, and he instructed a servant to show them hospitality and allow them to refresh themselves at his table, then to generously provide them with food and extra furs for their return journey.

Verias himself escorted Chrono and Duono into his own chambers and sat them down in private. When he had brought food and drink, and had made them comfortable, he sat back as if to converse casually with his guests. "So you are Chrono, the one called Friend of the Terumani? " he said. "The word of your journey has reached the terumani of the far north, and many eyes have been watching for you." Rumor had reached even Tryndom that Dreiton had sent word concerning this Chrono and his betrothed Ahten, that they sought audience with the High Ones, and should be given aid if they were found.

Chrono was taken aback. "It humbles me to learn our tale is known so far from my homeland," he said. "But I'm afraid we are left with many questions. We know nothing of who you might be, nor why we have been brought to..." He looked about the chamber, frowning, "... to this place. We seek the Hall of Liaibíri, where Ologéo holds court among the Ádolthi."

Verias chuckled: a flippant laugh that came off as if rehearsed. "Of course, of course! Forgive me my discourtesy! I had not considered that the Menothians who escorted you were unable to elucidate along the way." He bowed slightly and stiffly at the waist, but not too low, lest he taint the picture of regality he strove to maintain. "I am Verias." There was a silence, and he continued. "Known among the Terumani as the Guardian of the Menothians?" He waved a hand about the room proudly. "And this imposing Hall is of course great Tryndom." He waited for acknowledgment. Chrono looked to Duono for guidance, but Duono merely shrugged. "The court of the Menothians?" Verias added.

"I fear that our lack of familiarity might offend you," Chrono apologized. "We in the Southrealm have heard nothing of Tryndom, nor of the Menothian Tribe."

"Hmph," said Verias, his countenance falling. "A pity for you. But never mind. In due time all shall know the name of Verias, and revere my Menothians. Someday undoubtedly the Ice shall retreat, and we shall go abroad once more."

"Be that as it may," Duono interrupted, for it seemed this discussion was getting them no answers to their questions, "We have been brought here in ignorance. Why have we been waylaid to this remote place, if you know?"

"My friends only meant to do you good. They know that I am Teruman, and if there be any in this region who might guide you safely through this country, it is I."

Duono was out of humor. "Then can you help us?" he asked irritably. "For we wished only to ask clarity along our route. But now we have been led so far off our course, that it will be a daunting adventure merely to find our way back to the trail marked by our journey-staff."

Now it occurred to Verias that if he merely gave them directions and sent them on their way, there would be little credit for him, and none in Liaibíri might ever hear word that he had helped at all. So he said, "I shall do all in my power to see you safely on your way. But tell me, if you would, what is your mission? It is rare that any of the Kindreds of Toë might seek audience with the Ádolthi. I may be of more aid to you than you know."

"Our boon you surely cannot grant," said Chrono, "for not even Dreiton was able to grant us the boon we seek. So we hope to have word with the High Ones: Our desire is to bring the Ádolthi to meet with Ahten at the sea, for the Hall of Liaibíri lies too far from the sea for Ahten to reach. Then together we will make our appeal. But failing that, I myself shall make our appeal on my own, if I must. But I must address the Ádolthi themselves."

Verias was ambitious, but not entirely foolish, and he realized he would only look the fool if he offered to grant boons too high for his powers. So nodded thoughtfully. "Aha," he said, "Well, perhaps my presence alone may aid you. You are mere mortals, the lowest of the speaking Kindreds. My voice shall hold more weight with the Ádolthi, for I am teruman, and the Guardian of the Menothian Tribe. My word might sway them to grant your boon where the pleadings of your own mortal lips would fall flat. Or at least to come to the seashore to hear your case. Let me go to Liaibíri myself and make the case on your behalf. You may return safely to the shore to await the fulfillment of your quest."

Chrono was suspicious, for he could read plainly that Verias had private motives, though of what those motives might be he could not hazard a guess. So as courteously as he could he tipped his head and said, "Certainly not, your grace. My companions and I have traveled many weeks of days through great peril to come this far, and we cannot be turned back now. The quest is mine, and I will see it through to the end, hopeless though it may yet prove to be."

"But surely you will let me aid you along the way. I am not Dreiton, to send you off into peril without any promise of aid."

"Only place us on a sure trail which we can follow plainly," Duono grumbled, "and we shall have all the aid we need."

Verias frowned as he considered this, but he saw no advantage to be gained in such a course. "Nonsense," he said at last. "What would be thought of the hospitality of Verias were I to permit you to become lost in the frozen wilderness, far from aid? You shall rest here tonight and refresh yourselves for the journey ahead. In the morning I myself shall go out with you, to bring you to the Hall of Liaibíri."

In spite of their misgivings, Chrono and Duono consented to this plan. It seemed only a benefit to have a guide who knew the way to Liaibíri, and one withal who spoke the languages of the lands through which they traveled, whatever his own motives might be.

So it was they left the next morning, Chrono, Duono, and Verias, along with one of Verias' retainers. They returned southward from Tryndom along the same trails by which they had arrived, heading down from the rugged hills, only turning eastward when they had reached the easier trails of the more level plains of Niyarc. The party did not travel swiftly, but they at least traveled in some level of comfort. Verias saw to it that they had plenty of rest along the trail, and as he was familiar with the countryside and its many households, homesteads and establishments, he was able to procure at every stop the best of fare, so that Chrono and Duono had hardly any need to resort to their own provisions from the sled.

The nights were spent in warmth and comfort in the homes or lodges they found along the way: all the folk of that region knew Verias, and were eager to please him, as he was known for his largesse among the Menothians, and they knew they would do well out of the bargain.

The weather remained cold and the chill wind was ever at their backs, creeping under their collars. But the sun had begun to shine brightly, dazzling their eyes in the morning treks. The countryside itself posed no new challenges. They left the country of the Menothians and entered the lands of the Theresians: a Tribe nearly as large and daunting as the Menothians, but somewhat less regal in aspect, broader in girth and with jowly cheeks. Their settlement looked much the same as those of the Menothians, and the accents of their speech were altered. Chrono and Duono would scarcely have noted the differences, but Verias became somewhat more deferential, as these were not his own Tribe.

At last the trail turned northward once again, into the foothills of the

Division Range. The land began to rise, and beyond the ridges could be seen in the distance the towering peaks of that range, blue and white, with billowing mountains of cloud piled up behind them.

The trails they had followed became a wide causeway, wending up into the hills of Niyarc. The homes of the Theresians and other Pleïstians became few, and the Halls and the imposing homes of Terumani appeared along the way. For this was Rhotiéstir, and in this region the Terumani had long lived in the open, for a great age even before the days that the Sorites or the Pleïstians had received the gift of speech.

In those days the Mansions of the Terumani were not yet hidden from the eyes of the Kindreds of Toë, nor were any Halls or houses yet abandoned in the land of Soria. Any who dared might come to them and seek admittance, whether of the terumani or of the children of Toë. Nevertheless the Kindreds of Toë, both Sorite and Pleïstian, were daunted by the Ádolthi and by the sublimity of their manors. Rarely did any venture to approach.

Liaibíri was the greatest of the Halls of the Terumani in all of Soria, save perhaps for Lucré the great Mansion of Vélopar. It spread across a hilltop before an expansive sward which faced southward overlooking the plains and hills of Niyarc. In this season the trees which hedged the property were bare of leaves, and the sward covered with snow, but even so it glistened in icy magnificence. The Hall itself loomed tall, as if built for Giants. Its walls were of cut obsidian, unlike the rude constructions of the Sorians. Gleaming pilasters framed great windows of crystal: From within glowed the amber light of the Terumani, whose source is unknown to the Kindreds of Toë to this day.

Neither Chrono nor Duono had ever beheld any such building or hall in all their days, for in those ancient times the Kindreds of Toë had no art for the building of great halls or mansions: it would be many thousand years yet before the raising of the Grand Pavilion of the Menothians or the Emir's Palace of the Hirnans. There were of course Terumani in the Southrealm, even not a few of the Ádolthi, and many had built Halls and Mansions of their own, but they were rarely visited by the Sorian Tribes, and there was none to compare to the grandeur of Liaibíri in its zenith. Even the Hall of Tryma at Toreth Gandauin was but a hovel by comparison.

Chrono and Duono were halted in their tracks when first it appeared before them, as if their feet would not dare to complete the journey. Duono said, "We have come far and overcome many obstacles to reach this place, and have made our way against all odds. Yet now that I stand here with the place itself before me, I find it daunting to take these final steps!"

Chrono remained resolute, however, and he replied, "We had certainly never doubted the place would be a font of grandeur and awe. From the very start of our adventure we knew it would be so. Let us not delay in finishing what we have started."

Verias smiled down on them and said, "Come along then, children. You need not fear, for I shall go in before you to Ologéo, and smooth the way for your entry."

Beyond the sward a broad flight of marble steps rose up to the crest of the hill. It was swept clean of snow and ice, so they ascended the final approach, and stood at last on a wide threshold before the graven doors: the very porch of the congress of the Ádolthi. Even Verias seemed momentarily in doubt at that place, and when they had gazed at the closed portal for a long moment Duono said, "What now? Do we simply knock on the door and let the Ádolthi come out to us?"

Verias said, "Liaibíri is the Hall of the High Ones. The Kindreds of Toë may not enter without leave of the Ádolthi. But have confidence: I myself shall endorse you before Ologéo. Soon, I assure you, you shall have your audience."

So Verias entered into Liaibíri, and Chrono and Duono sat down on the porch together to await his return.

Liaibíri, of course, was the Hall which Ologéo had built as the congress for all the Ádolthi and the Ídolthi, and he was held to be the lord of the Hall. Many of the Ádolthi and the Ídolthi had their own chambers in Liaibíri, but those who did not would come first to Ologéo to seek admittance. So Verias boldly asked for Ologéo as he entered, confident that the news he brought would be received warmly and he would be praised for having escorted Chrono safely to Liaibíri in his own company.

But Ologéo was busy in his studies, and grumbled when Verias appeared before him.

Verias proudly said, "Teruman Ologéo, I come bearing good news! Chrono, the Friend of the Terumani, I have found wandering in the barrens of Niyarc. I myself have brought him safely through the wilderness and the weather here to greet you."

Ologéo, however, had little interest in small matters, and if any had bothered him before with such a tale, he had paid little heed, and had no recollection of it. "Who is this Chrono?" he said, frowning. "And who are you to barge into my chambers with so strange a message?"

Verias at once became afraid, but he said, "Have you then not heard the tale of Chrono and Ahten, which has been told and retold among the terumani, and has even come so far as to be heard among our folk here in the north? And I am Verias, the friend and Guardian of Menoth, the father of the Menothian tribe, whose Hall Tryndom lies in the Grove of Verias. I myself am the host and guide of Chrono!"

Ologéo scowled and squinted at him. "I know nothing of this matter. Nor do I know this Hall of Tryndom. Would I not know of you, were you of any importance?"

At this word Verias became defensive of his own honor, and he at once forgot the mission of Chrono. "The children of Menoth," he said, "are the most noble of the Tribes of the Pleïstians, whom I have taken under my care. They are destined to be rulers among the folk and Kindreds of Soria! To me and to my Hall Tryndom in the Grove of Verias they look and depend for guidance and aid. If you know them not, you have been asleep here in this Hall!"

Ologéo merely shrugged and waved him off. "You have bored me, and I have no interest in this thing. You may refresh yourself here in the Hall, and warm yourself from the winter airs; then return to your own place at your leisure. But please do not show your face before me again."

The blood rose to the cheeks of Verias at this humiliation, and his temper flared. So he stormed out of the presence of Ologéo, and stomped forth from the Hall of Liaibíri.

At his appearance Chrono and Duono both rose up at once, expectant of the news he would bring. But he merely waved them off in bitterness, and said, "Your petition is denied, and you have brought me nothing but shame and ridicule. A curse be on you and your folk!"

With that Verias called his attendant, and together they tramped away, heading at once for the trail back to his own Hall. There he left Chrono and Duono, standing alone and confused at the very threshold of Liaibíri.

Thus began the animosity of the folk of Verias against the folk of Chrono, and never did that bitterness die in a long age yet to come.[67]

67 This was held by the Mizans of future generations as the first cause of the many wars waged against their Tribe by the Menothian emperors.

17. CHRONO AND THE DECISION OF THE TERUMANI

This tale is told of the days when Chrono was once again separated from Ahten. For having come through great troubles to the country of Vordót to seek boon of the Terumani that dwelt there, hoping to find a cure for the separation that kept them from joining, they found at last that Liaibíri lay too far from the waters of sea or river for Ahten to complete the journey. So she remained behind with Chrono's great boat in the haven at the mouth of the C'heta, while Chrono and Duono together pushed on to find the Halls of the Terumani.

Along the way Verias, the Guardian of the Menothians, had learned of their quest, and promised them audience with Ologéo. But Verias was rejected and shamed by Ologéo; he abandoned them on the threshold of that Hall, and returned to his own place.

Chrono and Duono stared after him until he and his retainer had disappeared from sight, uncertain what to do next. They did not dare rap on the doors of that mighty Hall, as if it were nothing but a common lodge. There he and Duono remained in silence for a long while. There was no further sound nor sign from within the doors of Liaibíri. All was silence. Hours passed, as the sun slipped down the ramp of the sky.

At last Chrono sat down on the cold steps descending from the portal, looking down the sward and southward toward the distant Sea where Ahten waited in vain. At last bitterness overwhelmed him, and he sighed deeply.

Then Chrono complained, saying,

"Such a thing! For all we've done
Through endless miles, and countless trials
To reach at last the hallowed halls,
The purview of the Vaunted One,

And find there naught but fastened doors;
Rejection stern and taciturn,
A posture bent to scorn and spurn,
Rebuffing us with no recourse!

The Terumani, we've been told,
With joy embrace our humble race.
And gladly guide us in our ways
And oft our own affairs uphold.

Yet when we seek them in our need,
If we're possessed to make request
We find them silent and suppressed?
With no one there to intercede?

Ears which will not hear our pleas,
Their eyes shut tight against our plight,
To send us slinking from their sight,
Without a care for our unease.

To whom may Sorios' children turn,
When those with sway shoo them away,
And pay no heed to what they pray?
And Ádolthi their sorrows spurn?"

Now it happened that Wenda the daughter of Storeia was sojourning at that time at Liaibíri, in the chambers of her mother. Wenda it was who first brought the gift of language to the deïnings: to Sorios and his children. With her had come Shadow her cat, who had been Wenda's companion for a long age by the account of the mortal Kindreds, for by the help of Deïni she had been granted life at Wenda's pleading. The cat followed Wenda nearly everywhere she went, as it had been doing for a long age, and it had followed her to Liaibíri as well.

Wenda often allowed the cat to wander the gardens of Liaibíri, and she had done so on this day. But evening was now approaching, and Wenda went out to call the creature in for the night.

As she walked among the snow-dusted hedges the voice of Chrono reached her, and she paused to listen, her heart moved by the tones. When the song had ceased she went on her way and found Shadow. "You heard the sound of song also, I presume?" she said to the cat, picking her up. "Who can this be, for the song was a complaint of the mortal Kindreds against our kind! Yet they sang in the ancient tongue which I gave to their Kindred: Many long years has it been since I have heard any of that Kindred speak anything other than the strange tongue of the Pleïstians!"

Shadow demanded to be put down, in her sharp-clawed feline way of making demands. Wenda dropped her to the ground, and the cat stared away in the direction of the portal. Wenda scratched her head. "Well? What is it?" she asked. "Then you heard the singing as well?"

Shadow made a noise and began trotting towards the portal of the Hall. Wenda shrugged and gave pursuit. There she found Chrono sitting at the threshold of Liaibíri, and Duono his companion at his side. The cat plopped herself down at Chrono's feet.

The two Sorites looked up at Deïni expectantly, and a bit uneasily. It was rare for any of the children of Sorios to make their way to Liaibíri in those days, and Wenda could not recall when she had last seen such a sight, if ever. She stooped to pick up her cat once more, and turning to the strangers she said, "Who are you, and why do you complain so against the Terumani?"

Chrono did not know with whom he spoke, yet it was clear she was Teruman. He bowed his head politely and said, "I am Chrono, an abject petitioner, who has come from a far country with Ahten my beloved, to seek a boon from the High Ones. I apologize for my complaint, but though our cause is desperate and our hopes may be in vain, we had thought at least to speak in person with the Terumani, that we might make our case in their presence. But the door has been shut to us, and we have been rejected without a word."

Deïni looked at Shadow. "Can it be, then, that Chrono and Ahten have succeeded in their journey?" she said to the cat, as if it knew their story itself. Turning to Chrono she said, "We have heard word of your quest from Dreiton, and many have been watching for you throughout Niyarc! Who has dared to turn you away at the very threshold of your objective?"

"I cannot say for certain, but Verias our guide failed to gain access from Ologéo, and the portal to the Hall is shut, and Verias has now abandoned us here without recourse."

At this news Wenda was indignant. "Doubtless this is the mark of Ologéo himself. You may not have gained the favor of that High One, but you are certainly not forbidden from entering Liaibíri. I am Wenda, and what I do in my own chamber is my own business: Not even Ologéo will defy me. Come then, and join me within my chambers: you and your steadfast companion. I would dearly love to hear your suit."

The door was opened, and Chrono and Duono followed Wenda into the great Hall of Liaibíri.

There was little opulence to dazzle the eye, but the rooms and chambers were rich in stately grandeur. The vault of the ceilings soared overhead as if built for giants, while the floor beneath their feet was lushly carpeted. Everywhere they turned their glance, works of art decorated the walls, and a wealth of cabinetry displayed curious artifacts and intricate devices whose purposes they could only guess. Warm light spilled from every corridor and chamber.

"Truly, I have never felt smaller," said Duono as he gazed about.

Wenda merely smiled, "We do not lightly permit the Children of Toë to enter these chambers, as we would not willingly place a stumbling-block before your own emerging cultures. Few of your folk have been privileged to do so."

"Few of our folk would dare tread these halls," Chrono replied. "But my need is greater than my awe."

So she brought them to her own chamber: a room of her own, belonging to her mother Storeia. Wenda ushered them to plushly padded chairs, unlike anything his own folk had devised for comfort. Chrono found that joys and marvels unbidden crept into his consciousness, and he felt a reverie in this place he had not known since first he met Ahten in the lost years of his youth.

When Wenda had assured herself that her guests were comfortable, she said, "Tell me now the full story of your adventure, for we have heard rumor of your quest. And such tales are a delight to my heart."

Chrono and Duono then opened their hearts to Wenda as if enchanted, and time passed unmeasured as they told the whole of their story to her. So Chrono recounted how first he had discovered the Sea-maiden on the rock at Mizgad, and how the lilt of her song had enchanted him beyond recovery. How his father had forbidden him to visit her, and how at last he had defied the will of his father and brought shame upon himself by fleeing his home to join her on the rock in the midst of the sea. There their love for each other had crystallized and they became hopelessly bound to one another: hopeless, for no joy would they ever be able to share.

The many years of wandering he told, and how Duono had been his faithful companion in every adventure. He told how he had ever found friends among the terumani of the Southrealm. Finally he told how he had returned home to find his waywardness had been forgiven, and of how he and Ahten had found one another again at last. The full story of their voyage to Vordót they told, leaving nothing out of their trials and triumphs.

Above all he extolled the virtues of Ahten, who had remained true to their love for all the years of his wandering, and had proved herself courageous and resourceful beyond measure on their journey north.

When at last all had been revealed, Wenda sighed and said, "Much have we heard already of your story, and of your great love for Ahten, and your friendship with the terumani. Yet to hear your own words is a thrill to my soul, and the tale of your journey is new to us. So much the more do we honor this quest having heard it. It is clear that Ahten herself loves and honors thee as much as thou lovest her."

"There is none more worthy in all the lands of Soria. Surely if the High Ones could see her for themselves and hear the words from her own lips, they would hearken to our plea, and grant us the boon we have wished for through all our lives."

"Ah, but you do not know Ologéo! For he lives by cold reason alone, and the turning of his heart is a thing few, if any, have accomplished."

"Then cannot you give us the gift we seek? Surely you, who gave the gift of speech to our Kindred and changed our course in Soria forever, surely such a boon is not beyond your powers?"

Wenda shook her head. "I have great skills in the workings of the heart and imagination, but I have no craft to alter your very nature. It is doubtful such a thing might even be done by Vélopar, or," she glanced meaningfully at Shadow, "even by Deïni. Only Teruman Ologéo has been known to perform such an act. And no one understands his whims."

"Then is there no hope?"

"I cannot predict." She glanced at the darkness outside her window. "We have gone on very long, and it is late. Rest here in my chambers for the night. In the morning I myself will go to Ologéo to see what might be done."

So when morning had come and Liaibíri was once again busy with the sounds of activity, Wenda went to the chamber of Ologéo, and asked to speak with him.

Now Ologéo had never esteemed Wenda, ever since she had given the gift of speech to Sorios and his children. It was Ologéo's belief that speech should be the faculty of the terumani alone, and he had never forgiven either Wenda or her sister Dôni for spreading the gift to the Kindreds of Toë. Nevertheless she was held by the greater part of the Ádolthi and the Ídolthi as one of the High Ones, and greatly gifted among their number. So he looked up from his work and greeted her grudgingly.

She said, "Forgive me for intruding upon your studies, Ologéo, but you have recently dismissed a claimant with a cause worthy to be heard. I would have you sit a spell and listen to me, and judge if there is anything you might do to aid him."

Wenda told Ologéo of the quest of Chrono and Ahten, how they had dared the seas to reach Vordót from the lands beyond the Ice; and how they had come here now to seek his aid from among all the Terumani in Liaibíri.

When she had finished the tale Ologéo said, "If they wish a blessing, fine: if you have given them encouragement, I shall not stand in the way of such a union, outlandish though it may be."

"But Ahten is teruman: and more than that, a child of the sea. So neither can she join Chrono in his world, nor can he join her in her world."

At this Ologéo grew wary, and speaking coldly he said, "For what then do you come to me?"

"You alone of our order have the power and craft to work such a change in the flesh, that they might be united, and share a life together, either on the land or in the sea."

Then Ologéo laughed. "Such a little thing, then? Only to change the order of nature itself to suit the whim of a single child of Sorios? Shall I not also be asked to pull a star from the sky as a wedding gift? Or to raise up a mountain as a palace for their children?"

But Wenda was not discouraged nor turned aside from her purpose. "I know that Chrono is no one of note," she said, "to dare ask so much from one as great Ologéo. Yet know that he is favored by the terumani throughout the Southrealm. Merten himself has sent them here on this mission, and even Dreiton has approved their course."

"Where then is Merten? And where is Dreiton?"

"The mission of Chrono and Ahten is their own. Is it not enough that you have the word of Ahten the daughter of Merten? She is a princess among her folk."

"Where then is this maiden? A teruman I might hear, though nothing more than a nymph of the sea. But what is this son of Sorios to me?"

"Ahten waits in the sea, where her kind must dwell. But together they traveled long and overcame many trials to reach these shores. At the mouth of C'heta she waits, and no nearer to us may she come. For this very purpose she attended them all these many miles from the lands beyond the Ice, and suffered much, that she might speak with you in person. So we would implore you, hoping only that you might be persuaded to meet her at their ship. There you shall hear her case plainly, and that of Chrono as well. You may judge as you see fit when you have heard them out."

Ologéo waved her away. "You ask much. I have my own business, and I will not journey to the Sea for such a preposterous request. If they wish me to consider their suit, let them come to me themselves."

"But Ahten is a daughter of the Sea, and cannot make such a journey. Such a trial would undo her."

"Is that any concern of mine? They have contrived to bring a child of the earth and air across the sea. So perhaps also they can contrive to bring a child of the sea across the earth."

Wenda at last returned to her chamber and spoke to Chrono and Duono, saying, "Your request is denied. But do not give up hope yet: There may be other ways to turn the heart of Ologéo. Have patience and take courage. You may remain here in my chambers until I have exhausted my efforts."

So Chrono and Duono thanked her for her compassion, and she found lodging for them within her chamber.

Wenda then went out, and she sought out Bël, the messenger of the Terumani. Bël's vocation was to go to and fro throughout Soria, but she was sojourning by chance at Liaibíri at that hour. Then Wenda said to Bël, "Ologéo has affronted me, and denied even to hear the request of a worthy petitioner. Will you aid me in this matter?"

She then explained to Bël the mission of Chrono and Ahten, and how Ahten waited by the sea hoping yet to plead her case before Ologéo.

Bël said, "Of this Chrono I have heard report in my wanderings: he is the one whom they in the Southrealm call the Friend of the Terumani. The sea-princess Ahten as well is respected among the children of the Sea. Have you a message for me, and one to whom I might deliver it? I know not if any other besides Ologéo can do this thing they ask."

So Wenda told her to spread the word, if she was willing, among all the Terumani, both Ádolthi and Ídolthi: and to let it be known throughout Soria that Chrono and Ahten awaited the boon of the Terumani in Vordót.

So it happened that as Bël went about bearing these tidings, she sought out Teruman Dreiton: for Dreiton himself was aware of their quest, and had given them both advice and aid. Finding him at sea in his own wanderings, she hailed him, and he came to the surface that he might hear her word. There he rejoiced at the news that Ahten and Chrono had reached the northern countries safely, and that Chrono had even made it so far as the Hall of Liaibíri.

"But," said Bël, "Ologéo turns him away, and will not see him, nor hear his case, nor even go to the sea to meet with Ahten Mertensdaughter."

Then Dreiton seethed, and said, "From the start their chances were slim, but for Ologéo to turn them away without so much as a hearing is an outrage. That Teruman has puffed himself up beyond his sway."

"But what is to be done"? asked Bël. "Who else among us can accomplish what they ask? Phactorias or Vélopar perhaps might have the strength, but I fear the particulars of such craft is beyond them. Only Ologéo has done such a feat."

"Then we must see to it that Ologéo hears their case."

Now during all this time, Ahten had remained near the ship in the haven at the mouth of the C'heta. At times she would go out to sea to escape the muddy and churning waters of the river, at other times she would hover near the vessel to make certain it remained safe. At all times, however, the Donites of the region treated the vessel and the sea-maiden with respect; many came daily to see her and offer her whatever service they might, for her beauty and character had charmed them, one and all.

But days passed, and no word came to her of Chrono or his journey to Liaibíri. The Donites had heard nothing since he had left the borders of their own country. So she waited in suspense for any sign or tidings to arrive.

One day as she waited by the ship one of the villagers remarked to her, "We saw a thing this morning such as we have never before observed. For though the sea is in its winter coat, and nearly frozen over with a shelf of ice, yet we saw dolphins at play, leaping through the gaps and whistling to one another. Never have the dolphins shown themselves at this time of year!"

Then Ahten's heart quickened, and she said to herself, "Could these be the steeds of Dreiton, returned with a message from their lord?" So thanking the villager, she dove beneath the surface and swam swiftly out of the bay and into the wide sea.

There she at once heard the voices of the dolphins, which the tumult of the roiling river had obscured. Beyond that blared the sonorous horn of Dreiton. So Ahten rushed for the sound, and there beneath the waves and the gathering ice she found Dreiton, hastening northward to find her.

"Lord Dreiton!" she exclaimed. "How is it you come to this country from your wanderings in the Sea? Have you news of Chrono's quest?"

Dreiton's brow furrowed and his voice boomed. "I do. Chrono has reached the Hall of Liaibíri where the Ídolthi reign, but Ologéo the haughty will not see Chrono nor hear a word of his plea."

Ahten quavered at this word, and she said, "So have we failed, after all we have been through?"

Dreiton replied, "You cannot fail who have not been given a chance to strive. I cannot promise any outcome, but Ologéo shall be made to hear us, and you yourself shall make your case."

"But how can that be, seeing as I cannot leave the sea and venture to the Halls of the Terumani?"

"I once said it was not my place to aid thee in thy quest, for I would not show favoritism among the folk of thy Kindred. Yet to spite Ologéo in his pride I would do this, and much more than this." So he took Ahten by the hand and said, "Walk then with me. The mists of the Sea shall surround us upon the way, that you shall not grow weary and weak from the burden of the dry airs."

So Ahten followed Dreiton, and took the hand of the Teruman of the Sea; together they rose up from the waters, and ventured onto the dry land. A great cloud of mist swelled up from the waters and surrounded them, and Ahten found that she could breathe freely and easily in the presence of the sea-lord. So they climbed the pathways from the haven at C'heta up to the bluffs above.

The Donites of the region, those who had come daily to see the sea-maiden, beheld the swirling cloud of sea-mist passing through their midst. Within its depth the graceful form of Ahten was discerned walking among them, and with her went the mighty bulk of Dreiton, light flashing from his brow. Many there were who gasped in wonder at that sight; those who were fortunate to witness the marvel themselves told the tale for many years thereafter.

Dreiton took swift and easy trails to the causeway of the Terumani, and in his presence Ahten walked tirelessly day and night: so it was that the pair reached the Hall of Liaibíri in scant days. When they had ascended the stairs before the portal, Dreiton threw open the doors, and announced himself in a great voice, saying, "Dreiton has come! And Ologéo shall receive him, whether he wills it or no!"

With Ahten still in his presence, he strode boldly through the corridor straight to the chambers of Ologéo, and bursting into the room he said, "So,

Ologéo! You said you would not hear any but the Princess Ahten herself? Well here she is: I have brought her to you. So now you shall listen to her story, and hear her petition!"

The word had spread quickly through every corner of Liaibíri that Dreiton had brought Ahten to the chambers of Ologéo. So word came to Wenda in her chambers, and she at once went to the nook where Chrono was lodged, and taking him by the hand she said, "Now is the time come! Quickly. Ologéo cannot deny you now!" So she also hastened to bring Chrono to the private chambers of Ologéo.

There Chrono was astonished to see Ahten herself standing before Ologéo, with Dreiton at her side arguing his case. Though he was humbled and awed to be in the presence of those great ones, yet of all in that room, the nearness of Ahten stole his breath away. She turned and caught his eye, and though her face was stern, a glimmer of joy flashed in her eyes to see him.

Wenda then spoke boldly to Ologéo, saying, "Now here also is he who is called the Friend of the Terumani, whom you have refused to hear. Have you any further excuse to dismiss them?"

So was Ologéo confounded. But he quieted his pride, and he peevishly quipped, "It seems I am invaded, and I shall not escape." Then he sighed and took a seat, and gestured for his guests to do the same. "Speak then. Let it not be said that Ologéo has no sense of humor."

So at last the mission of Chrono and Ahten was fulfilled, after many long and dangerous toils, and a journey which would have defeated many others. There in the Hall of Liaibíri, in the very chamber of Ologéo himself, they sat down before Ologéo, together with Teruman Wenda and Teruman Dreiton: and there they made their case.

"So then," said Ologéo, turning to Ahten, "tell me your story and present your suit."

Ahten said, "Thou must hear both me and Chrono, for the tale belongeth to us both." Then she began, and Chrono and Ahten in the presence of Ologéo told once again the full account of their meeting, and their long devotion, and their many trials together. Then Dreiton and Wenda spoke as well, relating how Chrono had many times proven himself a friend to the terumani of the Southrealm, and had spent his life gaining an honorable reputation throughout that region, and so had earned the right to be heard.

When all had been said, Ahten bowed humbly before Ologéo after the fashion of the land folk, and she entreated him to have mercy on their case. "For," she said, "unless we are greatly mistaken, Lord Ologéo, you have both the might and the craft to breach the impenetrable barrier that divides our Kindreds, that we might truly share a life together, whether on land or in the sea."

Now even the cool heart of Ologéo could not help but be moved by the ardor of the sea-nymph. Nevertheless he remained obdurate, for never had he allowed that the Kindreds of Toë should be counted as peers of the terumani.

Attending then to Chrono he said, "Would you truly give up your life on the lands of your birth, to squirm like a fish beneath the waves of the sea?"

"I am prepared to do so. For the sea-maiden has filled my heart with the wonders of the worlds below: And even were there no wonder in the depths but Ahten herself, that would be cause enough to give up all else that I have known in this life."

Then turning to Ahten he said, "And as for you, would you willingly give up the comforts of the sea to trudge heavily about forever on the burning surface of the lands?"

"If that is the fate that awaits me, I shall stare boldly into the face of the bright sun for the sake of Chrono. That child of earth has already changed me to the depths of my soul, and the world that produced him must be filled with glories I cannot even conceive."

"Indeed?" Ologéo sneered, glancing at them both. "Such daring words from such innocent souls."

"They do not come to you in naivety, Ologéo," said Wenda. "They are well aware of the sacrifices one or the other must make. Each is more anxious to sacrifice their own comfort for the sake of the other. Does such devotion mean nothing to you?"

Then Dreiton turned to Chrono and Ahten and said, "You have done your part. Leave us now. We must confer alone with Ologéo on this matter, for it is of great weight, and its solution may bear upon the destinies of many in Soria. Soon you shall have your answer."

Chrono and Ahten bowed out of the room. Ahten was taken to the chamber of Dreiton, where she could rest comfortably in the mists and waters. Chrono returned to the chamber of Wenda.

Then Dreiton sent word throughout Liaibíri—and Bël also took the word quickly to the country round that Hall—that all of the Ádolthi and Ídolthi should meet at once in the council-chamber of Liaibíri.

Many of the Terumani then came swiftly to the Hall of Liaibíri to hold council with Ologéo: among them came Phreïs, and Phactorias, and Deïni the daughter of Phactorias; Storeia and Dôni also joined with Wenda; Teruman Tryma the wise also was there; Cosimë the spouse of Ologéo came along with her sister Wéodar; even Catos made his appearance. Such an assembly had not gathered in that place for many a long year. But Verias would not come for spite.

So this crowd of the High Ones assembled, and Ologéo scowled and said, "Have so many come to assail me and oppose me to my face?"

Dreiton said to Ologéo, "Indeed not. You may have allies among this crowd. For this very cause have I called so many, that you not be overwhelmed by one faction alone."

Then Tryma said, "You are truly the very wellspring of knowledge and reason among our Kindred, Ologéo. That fact will none of us here deny. But compassion has its place as well: the cause of Chrono and Ahten has touched many among the terumani, both great and small. We would not have you dismiss them outright without a show of compassion."

Then began a great discussion among the assembly, debating the wisdom of allowing such a union. Some took the cynical side of Ologéo, but many there were who made a case on Chrono's behalf.

In those days Phactorias was the protector of the speaking Kindreds, so he spoke to Ologéo, saying, "Truly I will admit, the request of Chrono is extravagant, and no such thing has ever been dreamt of: to join in union clumsy mortal with graceful teruman. But this case is singular: none like Chrono has ever arisen before, nor is another like him likely to arise."

Deïni herself spoke, saying, "Indeed Phactorias speaks truly. Never have I seen such devotion by any child of my Kindreds for any teruman. Chrono is without parallel, and his request is unique."

But Ologéo answered, "Many things are unique which are not right."

Then said Dreiton, "Maybe you would prefer to judge by merit? Surely this one deserves a gift, if any among the Children of Toë. Look at his hand. Chrono bears in his body the mark of his devotion to the terumani, for unless I'm mistaken, this hand is not healed from his battle with the Sea-Monster which beset the folk of Merten's household."

Ologéo answered, saying, "But is it wise to defy nature simply to repay a debt?"

"If you will not consider it for the sake of these small ones alone," Dreiton said, "consider it for the sake of me and my own Kindred, my Seafolk. Though you yourself do not value the gift, you terumani of the dry lands above have both the Sorites and the Pleïstians with whom to commune; yet we remain alone beneath the waves. We also would have companions with the gift of speech at home in our domain. This son of the Sorites has earned the right to become the father of such a race, both for his great love of the Sea, and for his enduring love of a princess of the Sea, as well as for those wounds he has earned in selfless service of my Kindred."

Ologéo replied, "The speaking Kindreds among us are not an unsullied blessing. You will face many strifes if they enter the seas as well."

"And we shall learn much thereby, and grow greater."

Then Storeia appealed to him also, saying, "Surely you—even you—know what it is to do a kindness for some deserving soul out of nothing more than compassion and fondness? We have seen that for the sake of a mere request you gave wings to the son of Dynis the nymph.[68] Surely this is no more difficult a request?"

At this Ologéo blenched and had no answer, for the Ádolthi did not know his motives in that matter, and he was ashamed to reveal them.[69] But his heart stirred within him at the mention of Dynis' name. And Cosimë the spouse of Ologéo glowered.

So Ologéo grumbled, "Why must they always come to me? It is not my duty to alter all the creatures of Soria into a state not theirs by nature."

"If not yours, then whose?" said Storeia. "For nature is your domain, and change is a part of nature, as surely as trees grow from tender saplings through many years into mighty pillars of life, and fall once again to fade into the soil. Even the mountains rise and crumble with the ages. The whole of your strength lies in the powers of change."

At last Ologéo lowered his head, and he said calmly, "Bring the children back to me. We shall see what can be done."

Ologéo then met with Chrono and Ahten in private, in his own chambers. When he had questioned them at length once more on their desire and their motives, he said at last, "It is unfitting that one of you should be forced to give up all for the sake of the other. Who should decide such a doom? And how shall one live, knowing what the other has sacrificed for their sake?"

Ahten lowered her eyes. "Then shall you do nothing for us?"

Ologéo looked softly on her, and said, "I did not say that. But what I must do, I must do to you both, that your natures would correspond. Both of you shall gain, but both of you shall suffer loss as well. That is the manner of any great gift. Are you willing to accept a gift that comes with a sting?" So he described to them his plan, and what gifts he could bestow, and what faculties he would need to excise.

Then turning once again to Ahten he said, "Moreover this one thing I myself am not at liberty to change: Chrono shall remain mortal, and your children shall be mortal. The life of the terumani is a gift beyond my capacities, and even to request such a thing is beyond the rights of his kind. Yet you yourself shall have the unnumbered days of the terumani. What sort of union can you enjoy for so short a spell?"

Ahten lowered her eyes and said, "I understand, and so have I always feared. I have craft enough to add some few years to his life, but I know the end of our walk together must some day come. Nevertheless the memory of such a love shall be with me and strengthen me to the end of my days, whenever the days of the terumani in Soria shall cease to be."

Ologéo shook his head sadly and incredulously. To Chrono he said,

68 See "The Gifts of Ologéo," page 178 above.

69 On this matter, see the tale Ologéo and Dynis, page 51 above.

"Think well upon your choice, for there is no return for you and your progeny. Having made this choice you shall hereafter be as the children of Pyterris, outcast from among the Kindreds of Toë, who I surmise will never fully accept your kindred."

"My choice was made for me a lifetime past. To this very end have all my hopes directed my every pathway. Together Ahten and I shall make a course of our own: those who will not accept us we shall at least cause to regard us."[70]

"So then, if this is truly your choice, let us begin the work."

When the work of Ologéo was finished, Chrono and Ahten remained for many days in the Hall of Liaibíri. At first they neither saw nor felt the changes which had been wrought in their natures, but as the days passed, they evolved slowly.

Chrono's form was changed that he might live and swim under the sea as do the Seafolk. His form became more sleek, and hands and his feet became as the hands and feet of the Seafolk, able to flatten and spread wide that he might swim powerfully and swiftly. He was given the vision of the Seafolk, able to see clearly and see far in the murk of the deep. He received also the lungs and breath of the Seafolk, that he could dive deep for days without breathing the open air. He also became able to consume seawater without peril.

Though he could live on the land and under the sun as formerly, he craved ever after to be near to the rejuvenating strength of water, whether of sea or of pool, and could not bear to be parted from it. The air felt harsh and dry on his skin and in his lungs. Forever afterward he bore a form strange to the folk of his own Tribe, and indeed to all the children of the land: for he carried the appearance more of Trityn than of his own Kindred. So it was that those who knew him not were afraid of him and shunned him, as Ologéo had predicted.

As for Ahten, her nature was also changed that she might breathe the dry air without harm, and live under the sun without desiccation. But her back became more rigid, and her form less lithe, that she might be able to stand and walk unhindered in the weight of the airy world without tiring. So her skills beneath the sea became less adroit. She bore this burden as well—that she could no longer bear the water indefinitely, but would need to refresh herself betimes in the open air, to savor the energy of undiminished sunlight.

When all had evolved according to the designs of Ologéo, he called them once more to his chambers. There he said, "Your transformation is now complete. You may return to your own realms, or remain here in the north, as you

70 In later centuries the Mizans took this as a prophecy of their rise to dominance in the countries of the Southrealm.

see fit. But now you must choose: whether to spend your days together upon the land, or within the sea. I have given you a choice, so that neither of you will have complaint against the other, and your life together will be peaceful. May you find together the contentment you have long dreamt of: if you shall be so fortunate, you shall have a greater gift even than many of the Terumani."

So saying he left them, and returned to Cosimë his spouse.

Chrono and Ahten then left the Hall of Liaibíri, walking together openly and freely. The winter had by this time turned to spring, when all the lands of Niyarc were robed in glorious green. The air was mild, so Ahten was clothed once again in her flowing, gossamer garments as of sea-mist.

Then Chrono said, "The gift of the Terumani is great. Now we may live our days together, for whatever years are given me to dwell in this world."

Ahten also was grateful, but she said, "Alas for the shortness of those days. Yet know that never shall my love for thee wane, though the years pass uncounted beyond thy departure. I and thy children after thee, through generations, shall always love thee and honor thee. And after all, the final fate of the terumani themselves is unknown: the day may come when we shall be united again."

So they went down together to the sea, to the boat they had left behind months earlier: Duono awaited them there. There they debated together, whether to dwell in the sea or on the land, as Ologéo had advised.

But at last Duono said, "Why must you choose either the land or the sea? Ologéo knew nothing of this vessel. Here you might both live peacefully all your days: forever in the sea, and forever in the sunlight. And upon this vessel I might always be near, to accompany and aid you, which is a treasure I would not lightly give up."

This plan seemed wise to them both, as the wisdom of Duono had always enlightened them. Then the three of them, together with assistance from the Donites who lived in that region, worked together to build an even greater vessel: three masts it bore, and a cabin divided into rooms as a house, with a hold below the deck that could contain all their comforts and needs. It was sturdy and swift, and as years passed they forever improved it and refined it.

On such ships and boats Chrono and Ahten lived all their days, forever remaining near the world of sunlight and air, and ever near the Sea.

Thus Chrono came at last to the end of his long quest, and united at last with Ahten they set forth on those journeys which would take them to the end of their days in Soria. In all the days of Chrono and Ahten, together with their companion Duono, they did only deeds of honor, ever respecting and esteeming the terumani among whom they dwelt.

18. EPILOGUE

For some years Chrono and Ahten remained in Vordót, near the seashore on the great vessel which was their home. Ahten bore a son and a daughter: Plesio and Moäsë. There in the north they built two harbors, for they needed to come ashore betimes to refurbish their ship, and to replenish their supplies. At the mouth of the C'heta River, in the country of the Donites, they built the harbor of Moäson, which they named for their daughter Moäsë. Further west, at the shores of the Carpet Plain, they built the harbor of Plesion: here they had found a pleasant haven at the foot of a grassy slope, for the forbidding bluffs of Vordót tapered off in that place.

There in those settlements, by the rhythm of the waves of the sea, they built houses, that they might have easy commerce with the inhabitants of those countries. Many of the Pleïstians and the Donites settled there as well, to trade with them and minister to them. But they stayed there seldom, for they loved the sea-life above all.

Their descendants would become the Chronosites, lovers of boats and ships, many of whom spend their entire lives at sea, and are at home as much beneath the waves as in the airs above.

Henceforth all the children of Ahten and Chrono would be counted among the Kindreds of Toë, but alone among the Kindreds they are friends of the Seafolk.

Chrono and Ahten had children in Niyarc, and they found spouses for their children both from among the Donites and the Tritynoi. Many grandchildren and further progeny were born to them, until at last the Chronosites became a Tribe of their own.

In a later age, in the days of the ascendancy of the Menothians, and in the days of Cyriosóti, the Chronosites of the north were more like the Seafolk than their cousins in the south, for the Mizans of the Southrealm have more of the line of the Plateosites in them. But in this age it is rare for any Chronosite to couple with either the Seafolk or the Sorites, for they are a Tribe of their own.

When their children were grown Chrono said, "I would return to the country of my youth, that I might see again whatever kin are left to me once more. And my eyes would rejoice at the sight of Mizgad where first we met."

Ahten agreed, saying, "I also would dearly love to see the Hall of Merten my father once again, and to bring our children to the arms of my mother Aviah, as well."

So they provisioned their ship, and they made the journey to the Southrealm. Little needs be said concerning that voyage, for they had learned much sea-lore, and their ship was seaworthy, and they both had the skills and crafts of the Seafolk as well.

Seven of their descendants returned with them, but two of their children remained in Niyarc. Thus the Niyarcian Chronosites—the Chronosites of Cyriosóti's[71] tribe—are descended from that first generation of Chronosites, and are not a splinter group of the Mizans as some have claimed.

Chrono and Ahten left the proximity of the Terumani, and returned at last to the shoreland of Mizgad in the vicinity of Ahten's Rock, where they founded the first settlements of Chronosites in the area later to become the Mizan homeland.

Now Jeïnaric the son of Phreïs was going about the Land, and coming one day to Mizgad, he observed Chrono and Ahten, who had long ago been forgotten by the Terumani of the north. Chrono had aged, and it was clear that he would not have many days left to dwell in the lands of Soria. It sorrowed Jeïnaric to think that Ahten would live on in loneliness after Chrono had departed from the Land. "Such a tragedy should not be," he lamented.

So he went to Ritéol, to the great Hall of the Heroes of Soria. There he found Sorios the father of the Kindreds, the Lord of that Hall. When he had awakened Sorios from his slumber he said to him, "Is it not in the power of the Ádolthi to make Heroes from among the Kindreds of Toë, as you have been made a Hero? Would such a one not gain the indeterminate life of the terumani, to guide their Tribe or Kindred through the ages?"

Sorios nodded, "It is true. But it is a gift not lightly given, and a burden not lightly received. One finds that the passing ages bring little more than a yearning for rest. I have watched over the folk of this land for many years. I have accomplished little, I fear, and have seen many things to bring sorrow as well as joy."

Jeïnaric replied, "You know the tale of Chrono and Ahten, whom Ologéo himself has gifted, that of all the Kindreds and Tribes of Soria, they alone live in both land and sea. Their children ever after shall have this trait as well. Of all the Children of Toë, is not Chrono fit to be the Hero of his Tribe? Surely his kin shall be a Tribe apart for all the days that the Land of Soria shall exist. They shall need a Hero from among their own folk to be their Guardian, that they might have one to speak on their behalf in the councils of the Guardians. Would you accept such a one into the Hall of Ritéol?"

"A hero such as Chrono would do great honor to this Hall, for he has lived nobly all his days. But is not for you or me to give such a gift, if gift it

71 Cyriosóti was the pivotal Hero of the Sorian tribe which founded the Homadalan nation, the scribes of which recorded these tales.

is. Few among the Terumani have the skill to do such a thing, which will be all the harder in the case of Chrono, whose nature had need of mortality to evolve the transformations of Ologéo."[72]

"Is it not evident that this need has passed? His change is accomplished, his children have received it as well, and he has no more need of mortality."

"Your desire in this matter is just," Sorios said. He smiled and added, "And I'm afraid you cannot hide the fact that you're moved by compassion for Ahten, as well. But it is far from certain that such an effort will succeed in one so altered. Let us go to Deïni with this petition, and with my own endorsement, for the power of life like that of the terumani lies with her alone. If she shall judge this matter as proper, then go, and do as you see fit."

Deïni was abiding at that time in her Hall on the Shelf, near the Hall of Ritéol. Sorios brought Jeïnaric to this Hall, and they told her his desire. Deïni is compassionate, and it was clear that Chrono's Tribe would require a Guardian of their own. There was little to debate on the matter. "I wish only that someone had come to me with this request sooner," she said. "He is very aged by the lifespans of his kind. I hope we still have time to grant this boon before he passes from this world. You do not understand the thin thread by which his kind hangs as they approach the end of their days!"

So Jeïnaric and Deïni made all haste to traverse the Land. As quickly as the Terumani are able to move, they came to Chrono and Ahten at their home in Mizgad. There Deïni was relieved to find Chrono, still hale, but aging after the manner of his Kindred. Ahten his wife waited upon him in his need, still bearing the ageless beauty of her own Kindred. Duono also dwelt with them in their household, though now greatly aged and wizened.

Chrono seeing them recognized Deïni at once, though many years had passed since he had appeared before the Terumani at Liaibíri. Welcoming them into his household, he said, "For what cause am I blessed to receive the company of the Great Ones of the Ádolthi? For my life has been but a little thing on the byways of this world. My time here will soon pass, and I shall be on my way."

But Deïni said, "In all your life you have proven to be a friend of the terumani, both great and small. All your works have been honorable. The Terumani have had compassion on you. If you desire, we shall strive together, and if we are successful, you might be endowed with the indeterminate life of the terumani. So you shall always be a Hero to your Tribe, and a Guardian on their behalf, that you might be an aid to the Terumani. The folk of your Tribe will hold you in honor, and seek your aid in times of turmoil, and your blessing in times of fullness."

72 The term translated here as "mortality" in Sorian carried with it connotations of "transmutability," i.e., creatures whose forms continually changed through the progression of their lives, unlike the terumani.

Then Chrono said, "This is a weighty decision. For though I mourn that I must leave this world, and most of all that I must be bereft of Ahten for all time, yet what is the story of a life if it has no conclusion? And how shall I continue my weary years if I can not go to rest from my labors as do all the Children of Toë?"

Deïni said, "It is true that there is always labor to be found for the Heroes of the Tribes and Kindreds. But you shall always have the help and fellowship of the terumani. As for an end to your life's story, even the terumani shall come to their own end at last, though none of us yet knows what lies beyond that journey."

So Chrono asked for time to weigh the matter, and he consulted in private with Ahten and with Duono. Then Ahten said, "It is selfish of me to wish this for my sake, but my heart has been full all the days I have known thee. I would not happily have that gift end."

Duono also said, "Of all the Children of Sorios whom I have known in this world, none has ever more deserved this gift than yourself. Go, and receive this gift of the Terumani, and be blessed to live with your bride."

So Chrono returned to his visitors, and said, "I will accept this labor, for the sake of Ahten, and for the sake of my children and my children's children. I have but one request, if you might be able to grant it."

"Speak," Jeïnaric said, "and we shall do what we can on your behalf."

Chrono said, "All the days of my life, from my youth until this very day, Duono has been my true friend in every labor and every trouble I have faced. He has never forsaken me nor failed me. It would be base of me to fail him now when we reach the end of our days. If you can give this gift to me, can you not also give it to Duono for my sake? For though he is not the father of a Tribe, he is yet a hero of my clan, and my children shall always honor him to the end of days."

So Jeïnaric and Deïni consented, and were glad of this request. "How can we deny such a prayer, for Duono has also proven himself to be the friend of Ahten many times over. He shall also be called Friend of the Terumani on her account."

Deïni entered her labor, and applied herself to the great gift she alone had power to give. Such a work is tiring, even to the High Ones of the Terumani, but when she had finished, Chrono was restored in sinew and limb, so he became hale and hearty as in former times, although the hand of Chrono forever suffers the wound of the Sea Monster of Mizgad. Then the story of Chrono's life and Duono's life were scribed into the Lifebook of the Terumani.[73]

---

73 The Lifebook of the Terumani is not to be taken as a literal book, but a metaphor of the collective knowledge of all the terumani, of everything within their realm.

Then Ahten rejoiced, and fell weeping upon her husband with all the joy of youthful love.

So that pair dwells forever together among the terumani. Duono also, the companion of Chrono, accompanies them, and is their aid and counsel in all things.

They lived among their kindred for many years, a long age of the Kindreds of Toë. Until that day came when the Ice retreated, and the Kindreds were reunited, and the Terumani retreated at last to their hidden Mansions to withdraw from commerce with the Land. Then Chrono and Ahten also retreated for a spell to the Mansion of Merten, and they are among the great chiefs of the Council of the Guardians of the Kindreds, who meet betimes at Ritéol in Vordót to defend the causes of the Kindreds.

To live below the waves forever was not their desire. So they built for themselves their own Mansion: a Ship of Sea-mist which still sails the Sea, veiled from the eyes of the Kindreds. From the deck of that ship they keep watch on their descendants, together with Duono their aid and companion.

But it is said that Chrono and Ahten are not lost from this world. For the seafarers of the Mizans to this day claim that at the moment of the rising of the sun, or its setting, at the very edge of the sea, their barge at times may be spotted by those who look carefully, an azure wing sailing before the disk of the sun. And the voice of their singing can still be heard at times, rising above the wash of the waves when far a-sea.

And not a few, from throughout the land of Soria, claim to have been visited by that trio. For ever and again some one will avow that Chrono has come to aid them in their trials, as he always has done for an honorable cause.

But whether this is true, none we know can say.

APPENDIX A

SELECTIONS FROM The Songs of Chrono and Ahten

The following collection of verses are not formally included in the *Tales From the Age of Legend* as published by the Homadalan scribes who collected the preceding work. I have appended it to the main body as it may be of interest to those familiar with the story of Chrono and Ahten related in the *Ancient Tales of Soria.*

The poems and verses in these selections were popular throughout Soria, particularly in the Southrealm where they originated. Several collections existed, separately referred to as the *Songs of Chrono and Ahten*, and containing much of the same material. Other songs not found in any published collection were also popularly held to be the product of that pair.

Many of the songs in the collection can be found in the *Tales*, but in somewhat varied renditions. In some cases the differences are minor, while in others the versions as recorded in the *Tales* follow more ancient conventions and poetic formulae. In very few cases a version in the *Tales* duplicates the version from the *Songs*, and would appear to have been lifted verbatim by the Homadalan redactors.

All of the songs here collected date from ancient times, and their author is unknown, although they were attributed, of course, to Chrono and Ahten. At any rate, it is clear that considerable revision and rewriting had been performed on them over the ages, as language, styles, and cultural references underwent evolution. The versions in this collection were decidedly "modern" by Sorian standards. One must assume they are largely the product of a much later writer or writers. However one cannot entirely rule out the possibility that Chrono and Ahten themselves acted as their own revisers, as according to legend they still at times would visit the Sorian world.

The selections in this appendix are not exhaustive. They were chosen to expand on the narrative related in the *Tales*, and to add an additional level of depth to, and understanding of, the characters and motives of the stories' primary protagonists. I have also included in this selection versions of the songs which appear in the *Tales*, that readers might be able to compare for themselves the differences from the (presumably) original versions.

Captivity

Chrono—
O siren-singer, sea-realm's daughter,
Darling of the oceans wide,
Dulcet songstress of the water,
Mistress of the whelming tide,

Is there a suitor of your songs,
A favored soul you serenade?
Some thief to whom your verse belongs,
Who hijacks all the hopes I've played?

Are you so heedless of your spells,
To cast enchantments unaware?
Such magic all resistance quells
With every captivating air.

Your lightest trill would lords subdue,
So there can be no hope for me!
My vanquished neck I bow to you:
From shore-life shorn, and bound to sea.

My dreams are summoned by the Deep
From callow days beneath the sun.
She calls a tryst which I must keep,
And days of dalliance are done.

But I am built for rock and earth,
For grass-robed hills and sweeping lands.
My feet are formed to tread the turf;
No step to brave beyond the strands.

Your rock is safe, I dare not come!
But I may gaze a-sea, and pine,
Divided from a gentle doom
By breakers and the bitter brine.

Seasons of the Air

Chrono—
If you could walk the earth with me,
Such marvels could I show you here
That you would wish to breathe the air
And leave the safety of the Sea!
You'd witness glories without peer,
Such wonders as you'll never know,
Confined to waters there below,
In inadvertent exile there.
You have not learned the love of earth,
The splendors of our sunlit lands

And wonders of our world's expanse:
Let me persuade you of their worth.

If you might walk beneath the skies,
Then I must be your ears and eyes.

Hemmed by borders of the strands,
Can anything in sea compare
To changing seasons of the air
That circle in their yearly dance?
We welcome them as faithful friends.
But in your airs forever blue,
What season can be known to you?
What changes mark the yearly rounds?

Spring
Are there scents in liquid deeps
To match the fragrance of the Spring?
When flowers are awakening,
And blossoms quicken from their sleeps.
Seductive perfumes grace the airs,
A panoply intent to tease
And captivate the roving bees,
To wing them to their wanton lairs.

Pure sunlight from the sky distills,
Apotheosing into green.
Divine transfiguration! Seen
In glory on the grassy hills.
The skeletons of branches grim
With coursing life are filled anew.
A budding cloak of verdant hue
Adorns each resurrecting limb.

The rapture of reviving life!
We live it with each vernal breath
When springtime conquers cold and death,
And brings us vigor, rich and rife.
The hopes-restored that season brings
Can have no ecstasy to match
Down in your misty habitats.
I'd have you envy us for Springs!

Summer
You may have marvels where you dwell,
But have you anything so grand
As summertime upon the Land?
A season with no parallel!
The fruits of summer must be sung,
When underfoot the berries swell.
And overhead is wealth as well,
Where fruits like golden orbs are hung.

The boughs grow heavy with their yield.
They drop their cache for all to share.
Their tender flesh they do not spare:
A feast of rapture in the field.
The bursting grape betrays the vine—
The fruit that sacred gladness brings,
The earth's own blessed offerings—
The lifeblood of the summertime.

The sun conveys her soft commands,
That we must from our toils rest,
Beneath the arbors, shadow-blessed,
Put off our chores and stay our hands.
Our summer is a time of ease
When all things to their fullness tend.
The sun's bright rays our worries mend,
To steep our dreams in fantasies.

Fall

Is autumn known in your domain?
When sweat and labor bring reward.
Then summer's yield is heaped and stored
And nature moils for our gain.
The grains put on their tawny robes
And bow their heads with golden crowns,
Regaling us with lavish mounds
To hoard into our treasure-troves.

The vines produce their jangling gourds,
Or rinds that shelter amber meat.
These are the days of melons sweet,
Such bounties as the earth affords.
A nut and acorn fusillade
Is launched upon the ground below.
We gather what the woods bestow:
Their delicacies armor-clad.

Into the streams our nets are laid,
For fish who leave the sheltering seas.
Now we may take them as we please,
A streaming harvest on parade.
We fill our larders with the wealth
Which autumn's copious bounties bring
In basket, barrel, sack and sling,
We stock a breath of nature's health

While all about the fields and farms
The trees put on their fiery cloak,
Until they've wearied of the joke,
Then coyly bare their slender arms.

Winter
And what of winter down below,
What in the sea competes with frost
That rimes like twinkling fairy-dust?
What magic matches drifting snow?

Confetti dancing on its way,
Which cannot fathom up from down.
At sport awhile, it swirls around,
To mock the gloom when skies are gray.

Then cloaks the ground in downy white.
It softens every angry edge,
And clouds the thorn and bristling sedge;
A flossy fleece of heaven's light.

The snow would surely earn your love.
If only you might watch it fly,
Or drifting down from Halls on high,
Then you would praise the airs above!

And what can Ahten know of ice?
Which drips and drapes like living jewel,
And shelves the surface of the pool:
A pavement fit for paradise.

The crack of ice, the crunch of snow:
The brush of snowflake on the skin,
The thrilling nip of icy wind...
Such things the Mer-folk never know!

A Song of the Sea

Ahten—
The world above you've touted wondrously.
You mustn't doubt that I could come to love
The virtues of those airy lands above.
But Chrono! Could you only come with me!

You must not think the sea that you survey
Is all there is to see, with nought behind.
From shores above you merely see the rind:
A formless flatland, featureless and gray.

You see the surging waves which are our sky.
They are for us a rippling canopy,
That veil a world your eyes can never see
And hide the marvels that below them lie.

But O! the wonders that would steal your breath!
If you might plunge with me into that depth.

There are no seasons in the deepest blue,
Forever cool and dim, as you surmise.
We find the seasons in our liquid skies,
And long for them as lovingly as you.

Remember that we do not walk, but fly!
You spend your whole life fettered to the ground,
While we below are not by anchors bound,
But in our liquid ether soar on high.

The waters of the seafloor may be chill,
But summer finds the shallows and the shore,
And to those balmy waters we can soar,
A pleasure jaunt that we can make at will.

In those shallows, luminous and bright
The summer shares her lustrous, silken light

Your summer sun is glaring, harsh, and cruel,
But ours a rippling, ever-changing show
That dazzles as it dapples all below,
And capers down, a lustrous, living jewel.

The sparkling sun which flashes in our sky;
Her glinting beams which from the heavens pour,
like restless dancers, flit across the floor,
And tiptoe on the sands as they go by.

No hall above could be so full and rich,
No painted hue could match the living gleam
Of colors such as you have never seen.
A blazing riot carpets every niche.

We have no fear for storms of wintertime,
Or deadly drafts that into houses blow;
For nothing freezes in our realm below.
We rest, serene and cool within our clime.

Your winter winds may cut you like a knife,
But winter is our time of providence.
The welling up of currents cool and dense
Provoking a paroxysm of life.

Our clouds are living, surging, swirling things:
The fish that shimmer silver in our skies,
Embodying abundance realized,
That comes regardless of our laborings.

Summer Night

Chrono —
Here upon this grassy hill
That rises from our favored beach,
Beneath the heavens' endless reach
I lie awake, and drink my fill.
Ah! To gaze through crystal airs
At undiminished, quavering stars!
At steady Venus, sanguine Mars
Who beam unblinking from their lairs.
All the planets ever run
Along their true, unswerving track;
Now gaining, and now falling back
Upon the highway of the Sun.
Their paths the mystics love to trace,
But none shall ever win that race.

To sit and gaze at end of day!
For in the night the summer air
Will brush the brow and tousle hair
And whisk the weary cares away.
Mere air can lift a leaden yoke.
The breath of breeze will sooth and calm
The daily burdens as a balm,
As welcome as a mother's stroke.
The star-bugs rise to greet me there,
To add their twinklings to the light
Which distant heavens cast at night,
So stars surround me everywhere.
Above this sward the portals clear,
Then into heaven's deeps I peer.

Nighttime in Potomis

Ahten—
When darkness falls upon the living roof,
The sun descending down to distant rest,
We also dive, returning to each nest,
Every soul retreating to his booth.
And there I lie, unweighted in my bed,
The waters folding me in sweet caress.
My crown is pillowed with their cool embrace,
No heavy airs to press upon my head.
Thence I gaze into a rippling sky—
A dazzling canopy of moving light.
Behold, a thousand silver windows bright!
A million moons to tease the eye!

The beauties there can overwhelm
In Potomis, in Dreiton's realm!

The Wanton Sea

Chrono—
The waters of the living Sea—
When Ahten dives beneath the waves—
They clasp her close in sweet embrace
With liberties forbidden me.

How envious my empty arms
Which cannot Ahten's form enfold,
Nor in their berth her graces hold,
And are deprived of Ahten's charms.

The Seas are not so timorous!
Her modesty they do not spare,
But run their fingers through her hair
And fiddle with her flowing dress.

Her very lips are not immune!
Her breath they mingle with their own.
A rapture yet to mine unknown
Who pine for that forbidden boon.

The seas their license lightly take
Which I would hold a treasure dear.
Ah! To press my Ahten near!
And quench what dreams can never slake.

Breathing

Ahten—
The naked air you breathe is but a whiff
Of all the seething life the sea bestows.
But I imbibe with every seasoned breath
the very life that in and through me flows.

Your parching atmosphere perhaps sustains —
In truth you cannot live without its aid —
But what we breathe runs in our very veins.
It is the substance out of which we're made.

Your insubstantial vapors are not seen;
Cannot be held; your weight they will not bear.
We live and move as one with our demesne,
Begotten of the living liquid air.

We occupy a sigh corporeal,
Awash within our own identity.
How wondrous, then, the unity we feel
In living, breathing, being of the sea!

My Ahten's Form is Not Like Mine

Chrono—
My Ahten's form is not like mine,
My dust desiring the divine.
How could she love a lump like me?
A beast that keeps her company?

My folk are thick in stock and trim,
With heaviness in every limb.
We are formed of grit and grime,
Not made to mix with the divine.

For I'm a creature of the earth,
But she by gods was given birth.
The form of terumani fair,
With matchless charms beyond compare.

Her lissome limbs are nought but grace;
Enchantments tingle from her face.
Her every motion is a song
Which sparkles as she flows along.

She cannot move but in a dance,
A playful frolic which enchants
A clumsy pauper such as I,
Who heavily goes tromping by.

Doubt

Ahten—
Where goes the tuneful son of earth and air
When flying from his wonted perch each night?
What mysteries await him, out of sight:
What apparitions, fanciful or queer?
If from my liquid prison I could fare,
And trace his dusty steps, what marvels might
My bleary eyes behold by harsh sunlight?
What odd, exotic marvels should appear!
He goes away; I cannot fathom where.
To mantled vales I cannot postulate.
An airy shroud I cannot penetrate
Hides forest, field, or house I cannot share.

The world beyond the hills I cannot see,
And so it roils curiosity.

Who seeks his camaraderie?
What hearth is his? Who greets him at the gate?
Who spreads his evening board, or fills his plate?
Has he a daily task to oversee?

What chores are his responsibility?
What curios does he accumulate?
A favored garden he might cultivate?
Does herd or flock exact his husbandry?
What folk are his? Who keeps him company?
With whom does he betimes associate?
'Tis folly, failing sight, to speculate;
But are there secrets that he keeps from me?

So every eve I sink down to my bed
With all these questions swirling in my head.

Beyond the hillside, where I cannot tread
Do unseen rivals wait to meet him there?
Waits there a maiden, genial and fair?
Perhaps another whom he loves instead.
I hear the songs he sings to me alone;
His voice is ever dulcimer and glad.
So what has ever given me to dread?
Or made me doubt the fervor he has shown?

Nay! I myself those seething ghosts invite
Who taunt, and tear, and teary qualms incite.

Ahten's Eyes

Chrono—
What, if I had never seen her eyes,
Vouchsaved my stainless soul unseared,
Or had I never gazed into those fires;
Had I my heart this hopeless searing spared?
Had not beheld the vessel there, which keeps,
As set within an alabaster crown,
The beauty of those opalescent deeps,
Did I never in those depths have drowned?

What then? What else might be my lot?
Thus ungoverned, would I better fare?
Such freedom would be dearly bought!
To give up glory to escape the snare!

Thou Must Depart, and I Must Stay

Ahten—
Thou must depart, and I must stay
When landward over hill you go.
And I shall only heartache know,
And pine that thou hast gone away.
Then muted will the beaches be
When over wave I lift my head.
Your song has fled, my ears are lead,
And nought but silence beckons me.
Then I must other hallows seek,
And to the liquid depth depart,
Where tears will not betray my heart,
For weeping cannot stain my cheek.
For me there shall be no reprieve
From mourning thee when thou hast gone.
And I must meekly carry on
Below in silence, where I grieve.

The Distant Sea

Chrono—
I gaze from fair Egano's shore,
And watch her wavering waters wending far,
Beyond horizons, into haze,
To follow countless currents, endless ways,
That carry finally to the boundless Sea,
And someone there who dreams of me.

No pond or puddle lies alone,
But shares a web which weaves them all as one,
Each drop and drizzle on the land
Connects it finally to the distant strand.
Unbroken fabric binding everything,
From surging deeps to sparkling spring.

O waters that connect us all,
If you could but convey my aching call,
From here to Sea, send forth my sighs,
To far-off shores where my devotion lies!
To cordial Mizgad's blessed, beloved brink,
Connected by a liquid link.

The Sea was once my dearest love,
In years before misfortune made me rove—
The confidante of Chrono's cares;
Diviner of my closest, silent prayers.
I learned to love at the lap of the seas,
Whose savor sours into lees.

Your soothing swells which used to please,
Which satisfied my soul, effecting ease,
Now seem a dream of long ago,
For now you measure out a pulse of woe.
If you no longer bring my heart relief
What song might mend this gloom and grief?

Sorrow on the Loss of Honor

Chrono—
Was I so bold, to seek to win a name?
Rather, laugh upon on my luckless lot!
"Lost and Luckless" is my epithet!
For all my strivings sputter into shame.

He whose heart would not find love on earth,
But sank instead to sorrows under Sea,
Fettered there by fates forbidden me,
And sweetness shrouded now behind the surf.

Was I so bold, to seek to win a name?
No name I have at home, nor here at hand;
In father's house nor in this distant land:
I garner ill regard instead of fame.

As for they who vainly sought my aid—
My hopes have only harmed them after all.
To help them is beyond my wherewithal!
Such honors earned in earth are mere charade.

How Many Days and Years

Chrono—
How many days and years have passed me by
Without a glimpse into my Ahten's soul,
Or into that deep font which is her eye,
The bright and sparkling essence of her whole.

But other toils impose upon my pride—
The cares and struggles of this barren vale—
At times it almost seems I set aside
The ever-present moments of our tale.

But every evening when I go to rest
The haunting of your image takes its spot;
Your shining songs my silent thoughts arrest,
And vaunt themselves above all other thought.

I lie awake and cannot but recall
Each moment and each flurrying emotion.
And as I sleep, into my dreams you fall,
Demanding, and deserving, my devotion.

You do not fade with any passing time;
The fog of distance does not dim your shape;
Nor can I lose the trilling of each rhyme.
Nor would I, if there even were escape!

The Well Within

Ahten—
A hollow like a deep and empty well
Lies somewhere hid within my sighing breast.
What was a niche his company would fill,
I find is now an acrid emptiness.

It broods there like a seldom-ventured room,
A vacancy as a barren as a prayer;
A cavity of hopelessness and gloom.
A hidden hole of darkness and despair.

Our brave farewells were never meant for this,
But meant to spare us years of hopeless grief.
This was the very purpose of our rift,
So I must choose to find my strength, and live.

And so I will endeavor to revive
By plunging in to treasured memories,
Where all our sweet-sad glories still survive;
The perfect, stainless raptures of those days.

For think! There are no hollows in the sea;
Unstoppable, she fills each empty hole.
The permeating press of memory
Is likewise fit to swell my sorrowing soul.

I Came to Pirin's Glen

Chrono—
I came to Pirin's glen to gain a cure,
To help restore a weary sufferer.
And bring a friend the elixir which heals:
The balm that only Pirin's valley yields.
But destiny denies me my success,
And all my pains have only brought distress.
Our toils are rewarded with travail,
Our labor has been vain if I should fail,

Feckless was the fate that found this place,
Elusive triumph laughing in my face,
And out of reach while all but in my grasp,
A mocking prize, impossible to clasp!
The name of Chrono is enlarged among
The folk who dwell in far and distant lands.
But everywhere my name would be unsung
Had I no help from undiscovered hands.

Where now to wait for covert charity?
What doughty hidden hand delivers me?
In pride I made a promise to my friend,
But find I cannot see it to its end.

To the Sea

Chrono—

O long-neglected mistress of my soul,
Whose skirts I shun like consecrated ground—
As endless, empty, winter-tides unroll,
And years and steps, uncountable, compound—

With cold discretion keeping us apart,
While willfully I fled your fetching call,
I've always known your face could stop my heart,
And my defending palisades would fall.

But now, with all your radiance revealed
In all your splendor, bursting into sight,
My long-accepted exile is repealed,
And I must end the season of my flight.

So now the dulcet lance I've tried to flee
Has gained my heart, and it transfixes me.

The Sea! And nothing but the Sea at last!
Had I forgot how florid your array?
An azure raiment trembling on your breast;
Your sparkling splendor strips my breath away.

The dizzy raptures of my youth return.
I feel the swimming passions I felt then.
I clutch my chest, and watch the currents churn,
And gaze upon your visage once again.

Refulgent face, diffusing heaven's light!
Your rippling steppes across horizons sweep
To foaming fringes far beyond my sight.
And unseen treasures hidden in your keep.

Your radiance I charily exalt,
But joys are lost within that liquid vault.

For what of her, enfolded in your press,
Whose straitened fetters still constrain my heart?
That hidden spark, a mite within your breadth,
Does she yet count the days we've been apart?

Were she to call, how would I hear the plea?
For should she pine, her whispers would be drowned.
Could any aching echo reach to me?
Should I but stop and seek, could she be found?

A tantalizing risk to contemplate!
Were I to halt, to stay upon your shore,
What desperate dreams might we rejuvenate!
What hopes redeem, what harmonies restore.

But I'm constrained to pass you on my way;
To touch your face, and sigh, but not to stay.

The Rock, Forsaken and Forlorn

Chrono—

The hallowed rock, forsaken and forlorn
Which once was swept by sacred, shimmering tress
And bore a holy maiden's sweet caress —
How fair the form that formerly was borne! —
Now sadly stands amidst the sighing surf,
And waiting, weeps wet tears of sorrowing spray
To honor her who was not meant to stay,
But hid herself in distant, deeper berth.

And so I stand, gazing out to sea.
And wonder what the fates have done with me.

The memory moves me to regret the course
That ever took my feet from hallowed shore.
For could I wait and watch forevermore
I would not count one hour as a loss.
Or could return each treasure and each prize,
And all I in my laboring years have won,
I would fain to have it swiftly done
For just another glance from Ahten's eyes.

Lost years of earning honor and acclaim
Are to my riven heart a hollow gain.

Song of Reunion

Ahten—
Long years have passed in silent vigil here,
Where once I heard my Chrono's hearty tone.
Long I waited, watching here alone,
No sound of singing wafting to my ear.
Ever wishing memory was false,
And we had never chosen to depart,
Nor made that choice which rent my fervent heart,
Trading joy for pain with every pulse.

But knowing what we chose, we chose for good,
To save us both from wasting, if we could.

So have I borne the sorrows of the years:
This rock a stony wall to guard my soul;
A fortress to defend a hollow hole;
A tomb interring loneliness and fears.
All my faith had parted long ago—
No hope I might regain such rapture pure!
This rock, forever empty, would endure,
A symbol of our chosen path of woe.

And so I left it, just as he left me:
By will, and yet unwillingly.

But now my heartbeat quickens at a song!
I clutch a trembling hand upon my breast,
And catch a flurried quiver in my breath,
And dare to dream my resolution wrong!
Is now, beyond all hope, a song returning?
Echoes of a long-lost rhapsody
Restore those moments to my memory:
Those faded fancies; my forgotten yearning.

I lift my anxious eyes above the sea,
And lo! My Chrono has returned to me!

Astride the Sea

Chrono—
I stand, and walk upon the flood,
Astride the waves beneath my feet,
and cross the waters like a god!
No mortal ever matched this deed.

No hero ever stood so bold
To march beyond the firmament
To stroll where only waves have rolled,
And pace across the tides unbent.

This is a triumph to applaud,
And boast about the vict'ry won!
So bow before us, whelmed and awed.
A miracle is all we've done!

Into Seas Unknown

Chrono—
Upon the deck I set my feet,
And feel the surging sea below—
The rhythm of its pulsing flow,
Its rise and fall, its steady beat.
How like the breathing of a beast!
A vast and lusty living thing;
So meekly to her mane I cling,
A mote upon that heaving chest.

And now, the sweeping Sea bestride,
The canvas swelling in the gale,
So into endless spans I sail,
When from my home I turn aside.
A boundless compass we explore:
No tracks are scribed on that expanse,
No path is drawn to distant lands.
We cannot know what lies before.

Behind me the familiar shore
Holds everything I have achieved.
But it must wait, for I must leave,
Perhaps to leave forevermore.
And what? If I should not return,
Why should I miss my land of birth?
Homeless I have stalked the earth,
A guest wherever I sojourn.

So why this flutter in my breast?
Why this foment in my heart,
Which roils now when I embark,
And now endeavors to protest?
The blustering winds behind me blow:
"You only leave your name behind."
Whatever fortune I might find,
The sea has called, and I must go.

Hidden Worth

Chrono—
The beauties of the sea-maid all behold.
No shroud has ever veiled her fulgent eyes,
And many praise her for her placid ways,
Acclaim her kindness, and her selfless soul.

But who discerned the deeper treasure there,
Unfathomed in the ocean's azure breast!
Within that modest cradle, who had guessed
There loomed a richer trove, beyond compare?

The Hall of Merten lurks beneath the blue,
So none can see the splendours of that manse.
And Dreiton's Halls are hid from mortal glance:
Magnificent, but ever out of view.

So those of us who only ever know
The sparkling surface of the sundry seas,
Who only bless its beauteous boundaries,
Might never guess what glories gleam below.

So Ahten's unexpected merit lies
Hid behind the beauty of her eyes.

The gentle heart is also valiant,
Her secret wiles disguised by modesty.
Her graces cover cunning bravery;
Her patience fortified by adamant.

The tidings of her artful victory,
Her prudence leading the courageous rout,
Are drops of rain that end the arid drought
And usher in the day of revelry.

So even I, who thought I knew her well,
Whose virtues I did often celebrate,
Am shamed to learn I did not estimate
The fullness of her value after all!

Such steady and resourceful wiles
The honest suitor humbly hails!

Upon Finding Again the Lost Sea-Vessel of Chrono

Ahten—
Thou dame who erstwhile shouldered all our hope,
And bore upon thy back our breathless bourne:
Thy loss had left us grievous and forlorn
With little gain to grasp at, or to grope.

So foundering a-sea, we did protest,
But left thee, as we had to in our need.
Forced to follow fortunes fate decreed,
And so compelled, to then renounce our quest.

How low our spirits sank upon thy loss!
How dark our days when thou wast in our wake.
How drear and desolate that tack we'd take
Away from every aim which set our course.

But sighting thee again my spirit soars!
How sweet to see thee set upon the sea,
Alone and empty though thy chambers be.
For hope again thy faulted form restores!

And all the aspirations that surround thee
Live and rise again, for I have found thee!

The Fickle Sea

Chrono—
I own the wailing of the weary wave,
The ceaseless sighing of the surging swells.
They drone a dreary dirge of dreams that fade,
A dying wisp of heartbeat-knells.

My song, a sigh of sorrowful lament
For happy hopes now hove astern.
My voice, a groan of grievous discontent
Where once the love of Sea did burn.

The Sea! Which was the cradle of my joy,
The dame of every dream which I have dreamt;
What once she freely gave, she sweeps away!
And spurns me now with icy breath.

How cruel the clinging curse that hounds our quest,
Assailing us in endless waves of trial,
Assaying us in each ensuing test.
And threatens now to end it all.

We've come too far to simply turn away,
When now our journey's perils seemed complete.
And so we rue this drear and dread delay!
To spy success, but only find defeat!

On Parting Again

Ahten—
How hard to see thee off on thy campaign,
Thy footfalls tripping from our hard-won shore
To other realms which I may not explore,
and have thee square thy back to me again.
So far together we have made our way,
Rejoicing to have had thee by my side.
Striving jointly, by our love allied
Through endless toil, trial and delay.
And now to part again! How cruel the joke!
That gain can only come through poverty,
And parting be the path to unity.
Such damned absurdities we must invoke!

And yet my lot I shall not curse nor hate,
But vigilantly hope on thee, and wait.

On Rejection

Chrono—
Such a thing! For all we've done
Through endless miles, and countless trials
To reach at last the hallowed halls,
The purview of the Vaunted One,

And find there naught but fastened doors;
Rejection stern and taciturn,
A posture bent to scorn and spurn,
Rebuffing us with no recourse!

The Terumani, we've been told,
With joy embrace our humble race.
And gladly guide us in our ways
And oft our own affairs uphold.

Yet when we seek them in our need,
If we're possessed to make request
We find them silent and suppressed,
With no one there to intercede.

Ears which will not hear our pleas,
Their eyes shut tight against our plight,
To send us slinking from their sight,
Without a care for our unease.

To whom may Sorios' children turn,
When those with sway shoo them away,
And will not hear a word they say?
And Ádolthi their sorrows spurn?

Age

Chrono—
The down upon my neck is silver-gray;
My vivid eye now sees as through a haze.
Oh, how the hasty years have run away!
And I attend the evening of my days.

Whose frame is this? It cannot be my own!
I see a shriveled hand which once was hale
Now furrowed, thin, and spotted brown,
And wonder that this thing is mine at all.

The joints which bore me boldly into fray
Now groan complaints, and griping insults hurl.
Their grinding plaints protesting every day
That I'm no longer useful to this world.

When did I start to count the days ahead?
Or waste my thoughts on passing from this realm?
In youth the days seemed boundlessly to spread!
A never-ending voyage at the helm.

Yet now each day and minute is oppressed
By fatal shades which haunt my weary mind.
Without relief I find myself possessed
Of wistful cares for what I leave behind.

But still my bride enjoys the flush of youth,
And nothing marks the passing of her years.
Her eye is bright. Her cheek is smooth.
Her lithe and lissome graces persevere.

Her essence shall not wane when I am gone,
She cannot aim to follow where I go.
Her vernal years uncounted carry on,
And she unfading shall for ages glow.

The Memory of You

Ahten—
The greatness of your heart has led me here.
Though knowing that you must depart someday
My love yet grows with every fleeting year,
And I have gladly followed on your way,

For though we knew this pass would lie ahead,
The coming day compelling us to part,
Yet never have I entertained regret
Nor suffered sorrows to betray my heart.

No flutter of the breaths that we have shared
Will ever be forgotten or bewailed.
I sanctify the ventures we have dared,
And every sea and inlet we have sailed.

The memory of my Kindred tarries long:
I'll not forget nor disregard your part.
It shall forever in my soul be strong,
And resolutely thrive within my heart

Our many days together have been sweet
They shall as one endure, forever real,
A sacred place of comfort and retreat,
A testament no future can repeal.

But could I follow on the path you take,
Go with you to that unadventured realm
From all I hold familiar, for your sake,
With nothing but our hopes to man the helm ...

To dare the paths into a world unguessed!
I'd leave behind the days of lingering here,
And take upon myself that final quest
Without a hesitation or a fear.

But I cannot.
                    And so I labor on...
And will, to unseen endings of my days,
Continue those devotions I took on,
That will not fade though ages pass away.

But no one knows the climax of my kind,
Our final currents hid beyond the mist.
Perchance we might some hidden passage find;
That you and I might be as one at last.

KINDREDS AND TRIBES OF SORIA

KINDREDS	TRIBES	CLANS*	LANGUAGE	TRADITIONAL HOMELANDS
SORITES	Carnochites	Allosites	Sorian	Eastern Footlands, Interior Deserts
		Ranochites	Sorian	Eastern Footlands, Interior Deserts
	Cerites	True Cerites	Ceritic[1]	The Hirna
		Protosites	Sorian	North of Gulf of Pindus
		Raccosites	Sorian	West of the Hirna
	Chronosites	Mizans[2]	Sorian	Eastern coast of Mizan Sea/the Sea
		Non-Mizans	Sorian	Scattered
	Stegganese		Sorian	Eastern Lodbarria/Lon Plata
	Cylosites		Sorian	Eastern Pindus and Cylos Plain
	Plateosites	Plateosites	Sorian	West of Gulf of Pindus
		Mimminites	Sorian	Northwest of Gulf of Pindus
		Barntosites	Sorian	South of Misapec/Tretew
		Camptosites	Sorian	Niyarc
	Donites[3]	True Donites (Trachians)	Donish	Niyarc/Don Valley, south of Egano
		Lophusites	Sorian[4]	Environs of Egano
		Diatrians[5]	Donish	The Division Range; The Inviant
PLEÏSTIANS	Menothians	True Menothians	Sorian[6]	Egano and western Lodbarria/east of Misapec
		Mastozians[7]	Donish	North of the Cliffs
	Theresians	True Theresians (Mecathians)	Donish	Theresian Peninsula
		Wenta-Theresians	Sorian	Interior Deserts
		Barnto-Theresians	Donish	South of Pindus and the Pateo
	Auchenians		Donish	Southeastern Inviant and coastlands
	Glyptians		Donish	Therana'eth Plain (south of Inviant, and coastlands)
	Predorians	Smills	Donish/Sorian[8]	Northern Footlands, Interior Deserts
		Dirii	Donish/Sorian	Northern Footlands, Interior Deserts
CYNODIANS[9]	Gnathosians	True Gnathosians	Donish	Batack and the upper Naeus River/east of the Cliffs
		Meterrians	Donish	Vinteren and Batack
		Gaulians[10]	Gauphric/Sorian	Batack, the Surmont, and Southern Table of the Cliffs/Interior
	Mas'chians	East Mas'chians	Sorian	Batack
		West Mas'chians	Sorian	The Inviant
Mixed Kindreds	Leáni[11]		Donish/Sorian	Interior Deserts
	Badites[12]		Ceritic	Eastern Hirna
Unrelated Races	Gauphrin (gnomes)[13]		Gauphric	Scattered, Batack, the Cliffs, the Inviant, etc.
	Dræads		Sorian	Forests, groves or grottos
	Næads	Tritynoi (Mer-Folk)[14]	Sorian	The Great Sea, the Pindus Gulf, and (reportedly) Egano
		Nymphs/Sprights	Sorian	Rivers, Lakes, Streams throughout Soria
	Giants[15]		corrupt Sorian	Batack/the Inviant
	Terumani/Ádolthi		Sorian	The Mansions (unseen dwellings throughout Soria)

* "Clan" is an ethnological term used by some Sorian scholars. In vernacular use these were also Tribes.

APPENDIX B

The table on the preceding page is included to aid the reader in deciphering the somewhat vast and confusing classifications of the Sorian populations. These groupings were partly cultural, and partly ethnological, but were well-known to all Sorians of historical times. While not essential to comprehending the stories included in this volume, it should be noted that many of the tales from the age of legend were in effect origin stories of the miscellaneous Tribes. Not all of the classifications mentioned in the Table appear in this volume.

Footnotes to the Table

1. Ceritic was a branch of the Sorian language group which through long separation had become virtually unrecognizable to most other Sorian speakers.
2. Most Mizans in later times spent their entire lives on boats and ships on the Great Sea. A few small islands remained of their former homeland, but few lived on land for more than a few months at a time. They lived by trade and by harvesting the sea, repairing their ships in their remaining ports and in a few secret harbors. After the Mizan Wars some Chronosites scattered into isolated communities throughout Soria. Another group of Chronosites had long dwelt in Niyarc, and some of them migrated in historical times to the Sorian Interior.
3. The designation of Donite Tribes is somewhat confused and has more to do with language than heredity. The Sorite tribes which had remained in the north before the Age of Ice became known as "Donites," mainly because they spoke the Donish language and shared the Donish culture of the Pleïstians who remained in Niyarc after glaciers had separated the northern Tribes from their southern brethren. The Pyterrians and the Meterrians were Cynodians, but were usually grouped with the Donites for linguistic reasons.
4. The Lophusites of the Southrealm were closely related to the Trachian Donites of Niyarc and are therefore classified as Donites. When the Donites migrated to the Southrealm the Tribes intermingled freely, although the true Donites proudly retained their Donish tongue.
5. The Diatrians were sometimes classified with the Pleïstians. They bore traits of both Sorite and Pleïstian lines, with the physique of Sorites but the “furry” appearance of the Pleïstians. One way or another, they had remained in the north country during the Age of the Sundering, and spoke Donish like the Pleïstians.
6. The Menothians, like all the Pleïstians, had originally spoken Donish in Niyarc. After the Migration to the Southrealm and their reunion with the Mahotians of the region, the Menothians shifted to Sorian. The Menothian dialect of Sorian became the lingua franca of the southern regions after the expansion of the Menothian Empire.
7. The Mastozians were an enigmatic pygmy Tribe, closely related to the Menothians but much smaller in stature.
8. The Smills and the Dirii spoke Donish among their own groups, but because of their proximity and intermingling with other Sorian-speaking Tribes, most all spoke Sorian as fluently as their own tongue.
9. The Cynodians—that is, Gnathosians and the Mas’chians—were difficult to classify. A splinter branch descended from Cynodias the Father of the Pleïstians, but probably not through Pleïstë, they were sometimes included in that Kindred. Some considered them a third Kindred. By descent the Pyterrians and the Meterrians were also Cynodians, having descended from the Gnathosians, but these were usually grouped with the Donites. The Drëconi also descended from Pyterris, but are not included in the table, as they arrived late in the historical era from their distant island homelands.
10. The Gaulians resembled the gnomes; according to legend they were the descendants of Gauli, a Gnathosian maiden who had been captured by gnomes. Though descended from the Gnathosians they were considered a separate Tribe. Some included them with the mixed Kindreds in the belief they had intermarried with the gnomes.

11. The Leáni were apparently related to the Smills. They were a shunned Tribe in much of the Interior, considered to be the result of interbreeding.
12. The Badites were a mixed-Kindred tribe of the descendants of escaped slaves. Unlike other nations of Soria, the Cerites of the Hirna made slaves of other Tribes and other Kindreds. On occasion these slaves were freed or escaped, and many of them found their way to an enclave in the far north of Hirna, where they developed their own culture, and intermarried out of necessity. In most cases the offspring of unions between Kindreds were infertile. In the case of the Badites, however, some of their children were able to bear young, and eventually a distinct Tribe resulted from the mix.
13. The Gauphrin, or gnomes, were an ancient folk which dwelt underground in tunnels or burrows. They were seldom seen, and rarely interacted with the other inhabitants of Soria. They were considered terumani, unrelated to the mortal Kindreds; but alone of the terumani they were thought to be mortal. They spoke their own language, apparently unrelated to the major linguistic groups of Soria, but were evidently able to communicate in Sorian when necessary.
14. The Tritynoi, or Mer-folk, were a legendary race of sea-folk. Unrelated to the Kindreds, they were considered terumani, akin to the dræads and næads. They had no ordinary dealings with the terrestrial dwellers of Soria, and were very rarely seen. The Chronosites, according to legend, were the descendants of the singular pairing of the Plateosite Chrono with the Sea-maiden Ahten.
15. The Giants were a coarse and violent race which infested the region of Batack, and in scattered groups in other remote regions throughout Soria. They were the corrupted descendants of terumani which had mingled with the unspeaking deïnings. Their adult height seemed to vary from 10 to 14 feet, although some accounts described them as reaching as much as 20 feet tall. Although they could speak a rudimentary language, and made primitive tools and clothing, they were considered brutes, only a little above the animals. Their dealings with the Kindreds of Soria were in all cases brutal, as the Giants took pleasure in wanton destruction.

APPENDIX C

ORIGINS: REDE II

The Works of Vélopar

Originally the work known as "Rede II" included all the tales from "Origins" through "Vélopar Divides the Kindreds," excluding "The Tragedy of Erescal" and "Ologéo and Dynis." The divisions are my own, and the "Tragedy" and "Dynis" tales have been inserted into their proper places in the chronological record. Another, much shorter version of origin tales, known as "Rede I," has been removed from this volume: Its style is abstruse, and contains numerous deviations from the narrative of Rede II.

I've separated this introductory passage and moved it from its original position, as the tone is decisively more formal than the rest of the tales, and the subject matter a bit esoteric. It has been included in the appendices, as the matter may aid in understanding the place of the terumani within Soria, and particularly the important role of Vélopar among that Order.

Out of the great storm Boros, Havui made all things. All was wind and smoke and tempest beyond measure, a horror of turmoil and confusion. Great was the din of it, unendurable and dismaying. The storm was in all places, and nothing yet existed but bedlam and confusion. But Havui stretched forth his will and his might, and he it was who tamed the winds, and gathered the smokes, and penned in the tempest and the gale. Havui stilled the great noise of it. He gathered the storms into his control, and gave them form and order and substance, and made Boros bow to his control. Thus it is that all things are made of the storm, and storm is in them yet, and shall be forever until the end of days.

Out of the substance of storm Havui made great lands beyond reckoning, stretching forth in all directions beyond knowledge, and he filled them all with good things and orderly of his own device. He made the land of Soria for the Sorian Kindreds.

Havui let in the waters of the Sea, into the midst of the land, and made the gentle waters of the [Gulf of] Pindus. There the waters are blue and warm: he made them a blessing for the Sorians. There he made the winds to blow warmly and steadily, and the sea was made good for navigation.

On the eastern shores of the land he raised up the great highlands of Batack, and planted there the Great Forest of Batack. For many leagues the forest spread, deep and dark, and was filled with hidden things. There he made homes for the dræads and sprights who inhabit the woods, the nymphs and the næads who inhabit the waters, and the oræads and the gnomes who delve the earth.

Havui lifted up mountains in the south: Lodbarria in the Southrealm, east of the Pindus: the steep summits and outstretched ridges, full of fertile valleys, ripe with rains of springtime. The Inviant he raised up west of the Pindus: mountains towering and domineering. He punched hidden valleys between the ranges and peaks, shadowlands where many secret things find safety and obscurity. These mountains hide their heads in the clouds, and wear their shimmering crowns of argent.

Havui went to the Interior, and broke the highlands, and the earth fell. On the east and the north of the Interior he raised up the Scarp, and below it he set the lowlands and the great deserts of the Interior, the rivers and pans which fade to dust and sand and gravel.[1] He set this as a barrier in the midst of his land, a place where few would dwell, and few would travel, yet rich in the good things of rock and rill: where gems, and crystal, and ore of many kinds are hidden and stashed.

In the midst of the Desert he made mountains to spew forth ash, and he built there mountains of rock and ash. There he made a place for the great smokes and clouds at times to escape from the storm within the earth.

Havui pressed down Misapec on the west of the Desert, the great sea of salt that none can drink.

Then Havui looked north of the Desert, and there he built the Türem and the Surmont, rows of ridges and highlands and mountains to pen in the Desert: a wall of mountains to compass the sand and dust. Beyond them he created many lands, the Gill of the north.

Havui looked to the west, and he laid down the plain of the Plata: grasslands from one horizon to the next, as far as eye can see.

Havui carved rivers into the land, bringing life to all corners. He made the great rivers: the Næus, and the Sartóq, and the Hogar.[2] The many smaller rivers and tributaries he carved as well, that all places might have their share of his waters. Even the Desert would have her share in season.

At the north of the land he made the great range of the Division Mountains. Beyond this lies no one knows what. North of the land is ice and cold and darkness, and great mountains blanketed in ice, where the cold winds ever blow; where the storm is not fully tamed. Havui made a wall of mountains to pen in the storm, so the land of Soria may be at peace. Fearsome are the mountains of the Division in the north.

But at the east of the range, as a sign of his favor, he placed the Gleaming

---

1 This is somewhat at variance with the statement a few pages later that in the earliest time the Interior was not yet a desert. It is possible the writer merely referred to this as the ultimate design of Havui.

2 This may be a later conflation, as the Hogar was unknown to earlier geographers.

Gateway, below the peak of Depharmen, the mightiest peak of that range, with his head in the heavens; ever golden in the slanting rays of the northern sun. Beside him lies the Stair of Depharmen, a pass from the fearsome north, but a pass great and trying; from thence would come the Sorites into the land, from the Storm beyond. We call that land Toë, but we know little of that country, for no one has returned over the mountains of Division into that country. Below the peak of Depharmen, in the land of Niyarc, the Sorites made their first home in the land

When Havui had finished his building, he brings Terumani into the world. The elder Terumani first, and after them come children born of them. Their number is unknown and perhaps unknowable, and the fullness of their purposes are hidden from the children of Sorios. It is certain that many come to do the will of Havui, but others do as they please. Many there are who watch over and inspire the kindreds and the creatures of the land of Soria. But many have other interests and they act indiscreetly, neither knowing nor regarding the effects of their actions.

Terumani are brought into Soria, both a help and a danger to the land of Soria and its inhabitants.

Terumani were sent first into the land through the Pass of Toë, the Gleaming Gateway[3] of Mount Depharmen and Mount Toë, sent by Havui to possess and improve the lands of Soria, and to care for its myriad creatures. That place from whence terumani come is unknown and beyond: Some call it by the name of Ohayoh, and say that the Terumani lived there long in peace and joy before the land of Soria was made, but then they crossed over the Caïm Bridge and do not return. Whatever may be the truth, at the Pass of Toë they entered the land, and there they became the masters of Soria.

The great of the Terumani are the Ádolthi, and the lesser are the dræads, the næads, and the oræads.

Mightiest among these is Teruman Vélopar. Teruman Vélopar beholds the open lands of Soria, the handiwork of Havui, and it is his thought to fashion the lands into homes for Terumani and those else to come. He comes into the land with a mighty hand, and is the arm of Havui: he moves earth and sea to form gardens for the lands of Soria. The terumani are content to wait and watch, anxious and keen to see his invention.

He pushes the mountains to their places, and makes broad and fertile plains fit for habitation. He excavates the lakes and the seas. He levels the plains of the north: the broad country of Niyarc. He plows the barren Rode

3 In the Sorian the word translated here as "gateway" carried the additional meaning of a signpost or titled entryway, a connotation which is impossible to bring out in translation. "Toë" literally means "origins" or sometimes "childhood," but in its use as a geographical term the meaning was lost.

and divides the rough countries thereby. He grades the Slope[4] as a barricade, and levels the plains below and the plains above. He raises the high rampart of Batack. He digs canyons and he channels rivers, to flow where he needs them. He sets the bounds of the Interior, dividing and taming the rock and clay. He goes south, and quarters the regions of Lodbarria and Theresia, the Don and Egano, into their tracts and plots, giving order and structure to all the country. To the west he goes, and apportions the lots thereof. Only the Inviant he leaves untouched for reason of awe, and he cannot improve it. The dust of his labor arose for an age, and great was the tumult of his work: ever moving back and forth upon the face of Soria. But great was the glory of his labor, and Terumani delighted to watch.

The terumani moved out into the country that Havui had made, and that Vélopar had cultivated: they made homes for themselves to be close to the land, and watch over the creatures and the countries they came to care for. The Halls of the Terumani they built, where they dwelt and from whence they watched their charges. Many of them moved out into the far reaches of the land of Soria, and made Halls for themselves in the lands they received from Vélopar.

Teruman Vélopar himself helped to build the Halls of the Terumani. These were the first dwellings of Terumani in the land of Soria, and they dwelt therein for a long age, openly and in the midst of the Kindreds whom they nurtured. But these dwellings can no longer be found among us, and the terumani left them sorrowfully: for many great works they did from those Halls. But they are no more, and none knows where they lie, unless they be the dolmen ruins which betimes are discovered in the lonely places of Soria.[5]

Then at last Vélopar rested from his labor. He retreated to the borders of Soria, in the foothills of the Division Range, and made for himself a Hall in which to take his ease, which he named Lucré; splendid was the bounty and luxury he accumulated in that Hall. Seldom now does he come forth to do his work, though his arm does not grow weak, nor his back lose its great strength.

When terumani moved out into the countries of Soria, choosing those lands which they most loved and desired, they made gardens of them. Some were lovers of grass, and flowers, and wide open skies: and these sowed the regions across the Interior down to the Plata, embellishing them with all the fruitful crops of the field. In springtime when the rains fell and the sun grew warm, the whole land became resplendent with the bright flowers of their lawns. (Now at this time there was no desert in the midst of the Interior.)

Others loved the tangled and aromatic scrub, and they filled the north-

---

4 Also called the Scarp.

5 In other tales it is stated that while many Halls were abandoned, Liaibíri, and many of the Halls of the Ádolthi, were simply hidden from the perception of the mortal Kindreds after the so-called Year of Sorrows.

ern plateaus and mountains with their scented gardens, as far as the Surmont and into the great plains of the Gill. The blossoms of spring brought delicate scents to all this country, but summer's heat brought the greatest pleasures, for then the very leaves of their workmanship exuded the spice of their balm. Betimes they would even burn the land with fires, and aromatic smokes as of incense would fill the airs: and the earth would be renewed and nourished thereby.

Some there were who loved the rich bog and willowy marsh, and they planted and nourished the river plain of Sartóq: many-kneed cypress straddling the waters, and leagues of reeds reaching to the limbs of the trees and waving their heads in the breath of the airs. There in the open pools and washes they brought forth floating gardens of green cress and water-clover, and they sprinkled their work with the star lilies, pastel-hued and ever looking to the heavens with wondering eyes.

To the far north went those who loved the dark fir and the spreading brush. They filled their country with the woolly branches of the conifers: tall stands and groves like scattered islands ruling over the scrub and heather of the ridges. In the autumn when the summer suns begin to wane does the country bloom, scented like perfume in the unmoving air, bringing rest to the souls who enter there. In the winter when the snows cover this country with their glistening blanket, the fir trees lose not their vitality, but stand straight and unbending with their arms cloaked proudly in sleeves of silver and white.

Some planted woods and forests: in the hill country of the Hirna, and mountains of Lodbarria, and the coastlands of Auchenia. Then Batack, the Great Forest, greatest of all, sprang up across all the eastern plateau which Vélopar had prepared, from the Sea all the way to the Slope, even filling all the hills and valleys thereof from the marches of Niyarc down to Egano. Many fruit-bearing orchards they made here. While over all, the mighty oak and shady sycamore, the whispering beech and the spotted birch, thrust their vaults skyward, upheld by columns of golden light: a vast unending hall of cool shade, with carpet of moss and grass and leafy mould, rich and loamy beneath the feet of the terumani. Here was room for many things to grow and hide and thrive.

The highest and mightiest of the Ádolthi made many Halls for themselves throughout the land of Soria, in all of these realms. Yet in the beginning of days their most sumptuous Halls they kept in Vordót of the north.

Then also did the lesser terumani go out into the lands, and made their secret homes in all those places where their hearts found joy. These did not build Halls for themselves as did the greater Terumani, but lived in the bosom of nature itself, for they are in substance of nature themselves: as fully as the tree, the lake, or the ancient hills. The dræads, tall and ligneous, inhabited wood, and forest, and tree. Many there were who inhabited oak, or willow, or fir, choosing for themselves the best and brightest situations, and embellishing and enshrouding their secret homes therein. The smooth-skinned næads, slim and beautiful, possessed the waters: permeating pond and lake, river and sea, cascade and pool, in all the secret places throughout the wide land. And the grim and furtive oræads, dwellers in cave and earthen tunnel, went out and delved homes for themselves wherever the earth was deep and wholesome.

These then are they which came into the land of Soria many generations before the beginning of legends. They found it empty, and they settled there, and made it their own. For long the terumani lived alone in the land, and there was no other voice in the country but their own. They cultivated the land, planting and propagating, and tending to their domains, that they would flourish. They saw also to the beasts and small creatures of the country, breeding them, and apportioning to them according to their needs, that such creatures might also thrive. The terumani labored at these works, and the land produced abundantly.

So the terumani prospered, and Soria prospered.

APPENDIX D

On the Transliteration of Names

A few notes may be in order on the method used for the transliteration of Sorian names into Latin characters. While many place names have been translated into English (e.g. "the Division Range" or "the Carpet Plain"), most others have been transliterated into their Latin-alphabet equivalents. I cannot refer to a concrete rule concerning this practice, except that in many cases the Sorian spelling was itself corrupted from its original spelling, or that at times its literal "meaning" had become archaic, or lost in casual use.

Names of individuals have invariably been transliterated, not translated, even where a translation is possible.

The Sorian alphabet as it had evolved by the era of Manoto, when this publication was produced in Homadal, followed a relatively simple phonetic scheme of some thirty characters. While individual writers spelled words phonetically without much regard to rules, the Homadalan Academy had adopted its own set of standards, and in fact had produced its own dictionary. The names of persons and places within this volume follow the spellings as dictated by the Academy, which had commissioned this volume under Manoto's edict.

There should be little confusion regarding the pronunciation of consonants. However the following specifics should be noted. The letter C is always hard, as in "cat." The sound of F was typically pronounced as a mild plosive, (somewhat like the German "Pferd,' but without closing the lips) so I have normally transliterated this as PH. The sound of an English J does not appear in the Sorian alphabet, and where I have used "j" it would have been pronounced as a fricative, closer to "zh," rather like the "si-" in "occasion." TH in Sorian is always soft, as in "thing," and never voiced as in "that." S is alway soft, as in "sound," never as "z" even at the end of words.

The Sorian alphabet had characters both for the "kh" sound (a voiceless velar fricative as in Scottish "loch" or German "ich,") and a plosive "ch" sound as in "children." I have used "ch" for both when transliterating from Sorian, as the "kh" combination has a peculiarly foreign appearance which does not seem in keeping with the general tone of the translation. In almost all names in this volume it represents the hard "kh," as in Chrono or Trachia, the most notable exception being the initial CH of Chiccir.

There were twelve characters used as vowels. These include characters for A, E, I, O, U, pronounced regularly as in father, tether, ravine, go, lunar. Additional vowels included a long E as in "they," and a full I is in "quite." A

Sorian character included as a single vowel was pronounced like the OU in "doubt," which has been transliterated either as ou or au in this volume. A few additional characters in Sorian could be used either as vowels or consonants: these were Y (when a vowel, pronounced somewhat like a German Ü); W (when a vowel transliterated as U or pronounced as a short or unvoiced W); R (pronounced and transcribed as ER, as in <u>ter</u>m); and an unvoiced stop, represented by the ' mark in this translation, which was used either as a consonant representing a glottal plosive (as in Hawai'i) or a vowel rather like a voiceless schwa (as the unvoiced middle syllable of appetite).

I have not distinguished between the short and long E or I in most names, except at times to use the diacritical mark or the acute accent to this end (e.g. Éthel should be pronounced more as "Ay-thel" than "Eh-thel"; Gretë would be "Greh-tay"). In a few cases I have used æ to represent this long E. The long I seldom occurs in this work, but most notably Ídolthi would have been "ī-dole-thie," not "ih-dole-thie."

Double vowels were frequent in Sorian, especially EI and IE. These were not treated as diphthongs, but in all cases, both vowels of a pair would be pronounced as a separate syllable. Thus Deïni would be pronounced "day-in-knee," and not "day-knee" or "die-knee" as might seem proper to an English reader. I have used diacritical marks in almost all instances to emphasize this distinction, although such marks would not have been in use, or necessary, in Sorian. Occasionally the acute accent has been used for this purpose where it also happens to fall on the accented syllable of the verb pair, as in "Rhotiéstir."

I have occasionally resorted to the use of a double consonant according to English rules to denote the short length of a preceding vowel, as in "Meterris" or "Steggan," although such doubling was rare in Sorian spelling.

Regarding the names of Tribes and Kindreds, I have in most cases anglicized these into palatable forms rather than relying on strict transliteration. In Sorian the most common means of designating a race or clan was the use of a final "-i" or "-in," which is in essence merely the plural form of the proper name of the family or line. Thus the race of Cylos would be "Cylosin," that of Mimmin would be "Mimmini." Such rather unpleasing words have been rejected in favor of "-ite" for the Sorite Tribes, and (usually) "-ian" for the Pleïstian Tribes.

In a similar manner I've frequently used a more familiar "-ia" suffix for place names, in substitution for the Sorian "-dal."

It should additionally be pointed out that when transliterating names from the speech of the gnomes, or words of Donish or Ceritic derivation, I have followed a different plan, to distinguish these as "foreign" spellings from what would have been familiar to Sorian readers.

INDEX

www.ingramcontent.com/pod-product-compliance
Lightning Source LLC
Chambersburg PA
CBHW060552310726
48982CB00008B/1100/J
* 9 7 9 8 9 9 1 9 2 3 2 0 0 *